Conspirators of Gor

Conspirators of Gor

John Norman

AN [e-*reads*] BOOK

New York, NY

Copyright © 2012 by John Norman
An E-Reads Edition
www.ereads.com

The Gor books available from E-Reads:

Table of Contents

Chapter One

I had not expected to be sold.

I suppose very few do.

And certainly not on another world.

The collar is not uncomfortable. Usually I am not aware it is on me. It is noticeable, of course, when I see my reflection, as, for example, when I wish to adjust it a bit, on my neck, that it may sit more attractively on me. He wishes the lock, for example, to be squarely at the back of my neck. He is clear on that point. It is perhaps the first thing one notes, when one looks upon me, or any girl, whether she is in a collar or not. I think he will keep me in a collar, as he likes me that way. I realize now that I belong in one. I did not always realize that, but I suspected it. Most girls are not collared, but some of us are, particularly those who have been brought here from other places. They expect that we will wear collars. Surely, whether or not a girl wears a collar is the most important thing about her. You see instantly what she is, and you understand how she is to be treated. Too, in the collar, you know what you are to do, and how you are to act. The collar makes things very simple.

The collar might be removed, but that would make little difference, as we are marked, tastefully but unmistakably, most commonly on the left thigh, high, just below the hip. That is done shortly after we are brought here.

By that sign, if by no other, we are identified as what we are.

Usually we are distinctively garbed.

We are not to be confused with free women.

The tunic conceals very little. Men will have it that way.

1

Here I am no longer ashamed of my body.

I do not feel self-conscious, as I am an animal.

Here I am a far less beautiful animal than many, but, I think, too, I am a not inferior animal, either, to many. I have seen the eyes of men upon me. It is an interesting feeling, knowing that one is an animal. If I had not been of interest to men I do not think I would have been brought here, an animal, for their markets.

It is an interesting feeling, knowing that one is an animal, and is desired as such.

Men decide how they will have us before them.

I do not mind.

Rather, it pleases me.

It pleases me to be so, before them, as they will have me be, unmistakably displayed as what I am, honestly, forthrightly, without subterfuge, or hypocrisy, so markedly and visibly different from themselves, an animal, which may be of interest to them.

I do not object.

Rather, I am pleased.

How the free women hate us for that!

Here I am well displayed or exhibited. Here I may not conceal my nature, and needs. The tunic, the collar, the mark, make that clear.

Here we are helpless. We are denied our finest weapons, pretense, prevarication, and deceit.

How free we are, then, animals, so different from their free women.

How the free women despise us, and how we fear them!

I have learned how to walk, and move, and turn, and hold my head, and speak, and many things.

We are expected to improve our value.

Men expect much from an animal of my sort.

We are trained, as other animals.

I think it pleases them to train us.

Too, they clearly enjoy owning us, as well as other sorts of animals.

At night we are usually chained, or kenneled.

I did not always wear a collar. I was not always subject to the chain, the kennel, the whip.

I come from far away.

It is a very different place from those with which you are likely to be familiar. It is called Earth.

Chapter Two

On your world you take so much for granted.

I wonder sometimes if you see things as they are. You value your lives, surely, and your Home Stones, and your fellows, but I wonder if you value your world, truly, or, perhaps better, value it enough. Perhaps you will value it more if you could see it, if only for a moment, through the eyes of another, one astonished, one from a quite different world, a world which was much like a charnel house, or a smoke house, a world with little pride, but much vanity, a world of crowding, scrambling about, cruelty, hating, treachery, hypocrisy, pollution, noise, corruption, foulness, a world muchly lacking in pride, and honor, a world without Home Stones.

I suppose you find that strange, a world without Home Stones.

Indeed, I wonder if you believe me, that there could be such a world, one without Home Stones.

It does exist.

I am not permitted to lie.

I am collared.

Conceive then, if you can, a world such as that from which I was obtained, a world without Home Stones, a world so meaningless, so forlorn, so petty, so empty. What are we worthy of, we, we without Home Stones? To such as those with Home Stones, of what value could such as we be? I touch my collar, and suspect. Of what else could we be good for? I look in the mirror, and understand.

I hope to please my master.

I am well aware of the penalties for failing to do so.

The men here are virile, and powerful, and are not patient. We learn to obey instantly, and unquestioningly.

It is very different here, from the world from which I was brought.

I do not object.

I think that I, even on my old world, longed for something like this, a world in which nature was recognized, and respected.

I wonder if that is hard to understand.

I do not think so.

Here is a world on which men take us, as it pleases them, and master us.

I do not object.

This is a world on which I kneel, and, head down, humbly lick and kiss the feet of my master.

He permits this.

I am grateful.

Do not despise me.

I am a female.

This is very different from being a male.

How long I longed to be taken and owned! How long I longed for a collar, and a master!

Now I am as I should be.

I am collared, and mastered.

Many of you, as I understand it, disbelieve in the existence of Earth, or, if you give some credit to the stories, you speculate that it lies to the east, beyond the Voltai, or far to the south, perhaps far beyond Bazi and Schendi, or west, like the Farther Islands. If you have attained, on the other hand, to the Second Knowledge, you understand it is alleged to be a different world, one of several orbiting Tor-tu-Gor, Light-upon-the-Home-Stone, but, even so, many of you, even with the Second Knowledge, remain skeptical, regarding it as no more than a myth or fable, and then, again, better credit the suppositions of the First Knowledge that it, if it exists, is here, on your world, but in a remote area, far from civilization.

But here I am to speak little of my old world.

In this narrative I am to deal, at least largely, with certain dark matters, political and military, matters which few here suspect, matters certainly unbeknownst to the vast majority of you, you who, in your scattered communities, in your villages, your towns, and walled cities, inhabit this fresh, wild, unspoiled, scarcely populated, beautiful place. You do not realize the danger which threatens you, what lurks in the brush, in the shadows, so to speak, so close, even at your elbow, and, too, far off, yet close enough, what crouches, watching, in the sky.

Know, good Masters and Mistresses, that others know of your world, sparkling in the darkness of the night, your morning world, so fresh, green, and sunlit, others who inhabit metal globes, who once owned such a world themselves, so beautiful, but destroyed it, and who now long for another.

I am to speak.

Many will disbelieve what I say.

And what could most do, even if they credited this narrative?

But I am to speak, nonetheless.

When in the presence of free persons, we commonly kneel. When we speak, when we are permitted to do so, we commonly speak softly, and with our heads lowered. But this is known to you. It is appropriate. We are collared.

So please forgive me for addressing you, for speaking first.

Do not think me bold.

I assure you I have learned my place.

My master has taught it to me well.

Many women on my old world do not know their place. At one time I did not know it, but I know it now.

My master has taught it to me well.

I am content in my place, for it is where I belong.

I have been commanded to speak.

I must obey.

I have no choice, I am collared.

But, too, I wish to speak.

Suppose then, if you wish, if it is easier for you, that I have been admitted to your presence, unworthy though I am, and am kneeling before you, head down, naked if you wish, a meaningless, purchasable barbarian who, with your permission, begins to speak.

She will speak of cities, and secret places, of a metal box, a Metal Worker, of beasts, large, hirsute, and dangerous, of an underground workshop, of pride, ambition, and devotion, of warriors and slaves, of gold and steel, of cords, and silk, of ships and worlds.

And so she begins.

Chapter Three

On my former world, Gorean, the Language, is spoken rarely, and then only secretly. That is another thing you may find difficult to understand. But even on your world there are places where Gorean is not spoken. Surely you know that. Too, on my former world we do not have the serums you take so much for granted, assuring youth and strength, youth and beauty, serums so readily available, so inexpensive and abundant, that you administer them thoughtlessly and routinely, even to such as I. On my old world, such things would buy cities and ransom Ubars. On the other hand, I have here seen disputes resolved with blades, fleet tabuk felled with arrows, men confronting larls with no more than spears. Time kept with sand and water. Your swiftest ships knifing the water, propelled by no more than wind and oars. How primitive this seems to me, this country of paradoxes, of marvels and anomalies. I have gathered that much of this has to do with the rulings of your gods, called Priest-Kings, reigning from the dark, palisaded Sardar. But we are told little of these things. They are not for such as we. Matters of such moment are not discussed with us, no more than with sleen or kaiila. We rage with curiosity, and learn that curiosity is not becoming to such as we. But perhaps, finally, you know as little of your gods, your sovereigns, or Priest-Kings, as we. But we do know they exist. I have seen melted stones, where their ships have landed.

I have spoken of those who lurk in the brush, so to speak, and who watch from the skies.

They have powers far beyond your keenest steel, your sharpest spears, your swiftest arrows.

And they desire your green, fresh, unspoiled world.

The least of them, the weakest and most defective, armed with engineering, technology, and weaponry, could destroy the finest bands and prides of your Scarlet Caste, could reduce the mightiest walls to rubble, burn your ships like kindling, demolish to dust the loftiest of your fortresses.

Your only protection against these Others, these Different Ones, the lurkers and watchers, are your gods, your Priest-Kings.

But what if they should tire of you, and desert you?

I was not brought here to be embroiled in intrigue. It was not my choice. I was brought here as most from my world, as animals for your markets, selected for qualities and attributes of interest to strong men, qualities and attributes for which strong men, historically, even on my old world, will bid and pay, those qualities and attributes so despised in us, and yet coveted, I think, by your free women, beauty, desirability, weakness, vulnerability, femininity, a readiness and longing for submission, an inevitability to become, in a man's hands, the helpless, begging prisoner of our own passion, a desire to love and serve, to give all, to belong unstintingly and wholly, to be a sort of woman, meaningless and worthless, a man's subdued, yielding, grateful, loving slave! And yet, put them in a collar, and see if they are different! Subject them to the suitable and uncompromising power of nature, to exposure on the platform, to cages and kennels, to thongs, to the chain and whip, to thorough, unqualified, absolute domination, and see if they do not hasten, quickly and gratefully, to press their lips to the sandals of masters!

Chapter Four

"Slave," she said. "Kneel!"

"You are not a free woman!" I said. "Are you so different from me? That bit of cloth you wear is as much a mockery of a garment as that which clings about me! Do I not see a metal circlet clasped close about your neck, which, I trust, is locked in place? If it is not, remove it, and I will kneel before you."

"Barbarian!" she said.

"We are no different," I said. "We are now the same, whether barbarian or Gorean!"

"No!" she said.

"I might sell for as much, or more than you!" I said.

She put her hands on her collar, her eyes flashing. "I was once free!" she said.

"So, too, once, on my world, was I!" I exclaimed.

"Liar!" she said. "See your upper left arm. You came here with that brand!"

"It is not a brand," I said. "It is a medical thing, a trace, a mark, the residue of a medical procedure, called a vaccination."

"It is a blemish," she said.

"It is very tiny!" I said.

"By such things, tiny, betraying brands, marking them as slaves," she said, "many barbarians are recognized."

"They are not brands," I said.

"Perhaps by such brands," she said, "the hunters recognize slaves."

"That is unlikely," I said, "for women on my world do not rush about, unclothed."

"What a liar, you are!" she said. "Many of your women are unveiled. Many times their arms are bared. I have seen slave garments exhibited which were concealed beneath the clothing of women on your world, obvious slave garments, garments so tiny, so soft, so smooth, so stimulating to the base, possessive instincts of men. And your hands and ankles might be noted on your world, or often so. And what of the beaches on your world, where slaves are exposed by their masters with little garmenture?"

"Few would be slaves," I said.

"Then proto-slaves," she said, "exhibiting themselves for prospective masters, displaying themselves brazenly, hoping that they might thereby come to the attention of masters."

"I assure you," I said, "my world is as complex as yours, perhaps more so."

"In the markets," she said, "I have seen chained barbarians exhibited in such garments."

I did not respond. I was unfamiliar with such markets, save from the inside.

"To be sure," she said, "only a fool would buy a clothed slave."

I had, of course, as doubtless she had as well, been sold naked. Few such experiences are as telling in making clear to one one's femaleness.

"Perhaps, on the other hand," she said, "it is by such brands that the hunters mark out their picks, their selections, their prey, for a later, convenient acquisition, a preliminary, provisional mark, scarcely noticeable, which will do, until a more appropriate marking, in the pens."

"No," I said. "Such marks often go back to childhood."

"They select them so young?" she said, interested.

"No," I said. "And men of my world are often similarly marked."

"Male silk slaves?" she said.

"Not at all," I said.

"I have seen such milky, frightened things in the markets," she said. "Some women like them. But they are men, of course, and there is always the danger that one of them, seeing here what men may be, may revert, and turn on one."

"Many men on my world are capable of being masters," I said, "and doubtless some are masters."

"It must be a fearful experience," she said, "when one's silk slave turns on one, perhaps binds one and disposes of one in a small market, taking the coins and departing the city."

"Perhaps few would have such courage," I said.

"Let us hope so," she said.

"I think that mark was a brand," she said, "by which the hunters recognized you as a slave."

"Not at all," I said. "It would not have been visible. It would have been concealed by the clothing I wore."

"How then did they recognize you as a slave?" she asked.

"I have no idea," I said, though, in truth, I had an idea of such matters. Who could not have seen the slave beneath my clothing? Could not a practiced eye have discerned saleable lineaments beneath that cloth? Who could not have looked upon my throat and not speculated on how fittingly it would have been encircled by a metal collar? Who could not have looked into my eyes, severely, and not seen the trembling, waiting slave?

"You must have been assessed," she said.

"Doubtless," I said.

"Where, when, how?" she asked.

"I do not know," I said. I did not know. It might have been anywhere, at any time, perhaps when I least suspected it, on a bus, in a subway, on the street, shopping, waiting for a light to change, stepping in or out of a taxi, in a corridor, in the aisle of a market, in a classroom, on the campus, anywhere, anytime.

But then I was sure I knew.

It had been at a party, in the house, if nowhere else.

"It is unusual that you would not have been assessed naked," she said.

"Perhaps," I said.

I did not tell her of a troubling dream I had had, weeks ago, after the party. I had dreamed I had been sedated, and stripped in my own bed, in the house, in my room, and, in the light of a flashlight, a sort of torch without fire, held by one man, had been turned about, and, roughly, in one way and another, handled as expertly and casually as might have been a slave, by two others, even measured. The men had then tied me, supine, my hands and ankles fastened well apart, to the posts at the head and foot of the bed. It seemed I was struggling, futilely, trying to regain consciousness, trying to awaken, unsuccessfully, while the men conversed nearby, with low voices. I sensed they had come to some sort of agreement. Notations were made, on some sort of device. I twisted, and squirmed, and bucked and thrashed, wildly, jerking against the cords, fastened several times about my wrists and ankles. Then I lay back, knowing that I could not free myself. I was helpless, absolutely helpless. The flashlight was turned on me. Two of the men laughed. I then fully lost consciousness. I awakened in the early morning, in the house, in what, in your reckoning, would have been something like the Fifth Ahn, whimpering, and then suddenly I screamed, before I realized, with unbounded relief, that I was safe, so safe, in my own room. But somehow, inexplicably, I was naked. Somehow, in the night, I had slipped from my night gown. I did not see how that could be. I shuddered. I felt small, and helpless, and frightened, and quietly, not moving, lay in the bed, my legs drawn up. It had been a most unusual, and frightening, dream. I was still uneasy. I still felt its terror. But in a few moments I had recovered myself sufficiently to regard the dream with amusement, but then, suddenly, a moment later, cried out with horror. Two of the other girls entered the room, Eve and Jane, and the house mother, Mrs. Rawlinson. I drew the covers about me. "A dream," I explained. "A dream!" My two friends, Eve and Jane, looked to one another, and then left. The house mother, Mrs. Rawlinson, however, dallied a bit, and regarded me, the covers drawn up about my neck, and smiled, and, as it seems to me now, knowingly. I and two others of my sisters in the house, my sorority sisters, for a sorority is a sort of club, my friends, Eve and Jane, had had, some days ago, a fearful contretemps with the house mother. Examining our rooms in our absence, while we were in class, certain books had been discovered, literature certainly inappropriate for our prestigious house, one of the most exclusive and inaccessible on campus, and inappropriate, as well, for our small, expensive, illustrious, private institution, one of the most selective in the northern hemisphere of my former world, save for certain reluctant concessions to political pressures, abetted by special grants and fellowships, and inappropriate, as well, for members of our class, that of my sisters and myself, our social station. I think there was no girl in our house who did not derive from a background of refinement and great wealth. Too, I think I should mention that our sorority was generally recognized as the richest and most desirable sorority on campus, amongst several others, of similar repute. We lived arrogant, tasteful, condescending lives, in keeping with our superiority. On the other hand, we underwent much supervision by our peers, and house mother, Mrs. Rawlinson, and much attention was devoted to our activities. Though we were undeniably privileged and special, we were not as much at liberty as might be supposed, for our freedoms were limited in certain ways, that as a natural function of our station and the reputation of the house. For example, our classes, interests, books, majors, and such, were to be such as were suitable for us; our charity work, if done, was to be restricted to suitable charities; our acquaintances were to be proper, of a suitable class, position, background, appearance, and such; and, in particular, one must be judicious in dating. We were not to date beneath our station, for, just as you have castes, we have social divisions which, in their way, are also strict. Certainly we were expected to behave in such a manner as to, at all times, maintain the dignity, prestige, and reputation of the house. Accordingly, our social activities, where the men, or boys, were concerned, were to be limited to a small set of men's clubs or fraternities, in their ranking comparable to ours. The girls of our sorority, or club, I might add, were not only rich, but, too, tended to be aloof, refined, aristocratic, spoiled, and vain. That is clearer to me now than it was at that time. Also, there seemed to be another criterion imposed on membership in our house, but, as obvious and generally recognized as it was, it was never mentioned explicitly. Each of our girls was extremely beautiful. We were the Ubaras of the campus, so to speak. To date one of us was a coup for the lucky fellow, and one of our common pleasures was to disdainfully refuse such dates, unless, of course, requested by young men whose wealth and social position was superior to ours. What is the point of beauty, if not to open doors, to bargain, and to enhance one's prospects?

Were we not prostitutes, in a way, ready to sell ourselves, high-priced merchandise, for power, position, station, and wealth?

You have probably guessed the nature of the "inappropriate literature" discovered by the house mother. But perhaps not.

Just as many of you doubt the existence of a world called Terra, or Earth, so, too, many on my world doubt the existence of your world. Indeed, I did so, as well, until I found myself here, naked in a slave pen, chains on my limbs. In any event, though the evidence for your world doubtless exists, in many ways, on my world, what evidence is recognized is, as far as I know, subjected to alternative explanations, ignored, or explained away, in one way or another. This is not to say, of course, that Goreans are not here and there on Earth. My presence here, for example, makes that clear, or, at least, that there are those on Earth who know of Gor, and are familiar with her. This is not to deny, of course, that better information might be housed in various intelligence communities on Earth, evidence which it would be wise to treat with circumspection. In any event, various manuscripts pertaining to your world have appeared, in a variety of languages, on my former world, despite efforts to suppress them, to deny them to the reading public. And even if such efforts should prove overtly successful it is not unlikely that some copies will elude the insecure and bigoted, and will continue to circulate, as an underground literature, if nothing else, hidden here and there, and passed secretly from hand to hand, a badge of understanding and brotherhood, in defiance of haters and tyrants concerned to engineer a pathology congenial to their political ambitions.

In any event, in my room, and apparently in those of Eve and Jane, Mrs. Rawlinson had discovered certain of these books, apparently, as I then thought, to her astonishment, embarrassment, dismay, and indignation. Certainly I had hidden the books, I had thought well, in a trunk, covered with clothing, had confessed to no one that I had read such things, and was terribly self-conscious at having done so. I was miserably embarrassed that this secret was discovered. What would Mrs. Rawlinson, my sisters, others, think of me?

Worse, I could be publicly humiliated, disdained, ostracized, and summarily expelled from the sorority, with all the devastating social consequences which that might entail.

A delicate and fragile world, carefully constructed and maintained with an eye to the future, might tumble about me.

I was frightened.

I was suddenly, for the first time in my life, vulnerable, at risk.

I would be on the outside, alone, ignored and despised, the gates shut against me.

How delighted would be Nora, and certain others of my sisters, at my downfall, my discomfiture!

How rapidly and eagerly would this welcome news of my exposure be broadcast about the campus!

I had come upon such books by accident, in a store dealing with old books. I was curious. I looked into one or more. I was startled. I could not believe, even from the first pages, the nature of what I read. I did not understand how the authors, Tarl Cabot, and others, might have dared to write what they did. Did they not know the formulas? Were they unaware of the political requirements imposed on contemporary literature? Were such so obscure, or difficult to discern? What an unexpected paradox, to put aside the rules, to deny orthodoxy, to speak so plainly, so simply and quietly, and naturally, of a culture so different from ours, and to speak of it not to denounce it, but to understand it, to speak of it from the inside, instead of disparaging it from the outside, from the alleged vantage point of some arrogant, unargued, unquestioned position or posture whose credentials were not only dubious but nonexistent. What of the simple test of life consequences? Is it obvious that an unnatural culture which produces vehemence, confusion, hysteria, sickness, treachery, hypocrisy, mass murder, and hatred is obviously superior to a culture compatible with nature, and her kinds and differences, a culture in which nature is recognized and celebrated, and enhanced by all the ennobling sophistications of civilization, rather than denied?

In any event, if only to my dismay, and fear, the books spoke to me.

Too, they spoke to me of secrets I had long concealed from myself. My life was boring and empty, and largely mapped out for me. I was on a road, cold, glittering, metallic, and arid, which I did not much care to follow. I did not know myself. Perhaps I was afraid to discover myself. What might I learn, what might I find? I did know that I was a scion of a series of species bred for thousands of generations for a world quite different from the one in which I found myself, a world less populated, greener, more open, more perilous perhaps, and certainly more beautiful. And I knew, too, that there were men and women, and that each had been bred beside the other, for countless generations, each in the light of the other, and I suspected, from my thoughts, my needs, and dreams, that they were not identical, but that each sex, so radically dimorphic, had its own wonderful nature, each nature complementary to the other. What of relationships, so pervasive amongst mammals? Had such things not been selected for? Was nature so hard to read? Did the consequences of denying her lead to happiness, or fulfillment? It did not seem so.

But, still, I had been caught.

Books had been found in my room.

Mrs. Rawlinson had sternly summoned me, and Eve and Jane, before her. We were then alone, frightened, in the room with her. The room was not well lit. Her straight, menacing figure was outlined against the wide window behind her. I soon realized, from the books on her desk, that Eve and Jane, too, were familiar with such books. I wondered how many other women, and men, knew of such things.

Could it be that I was not alone, that I was not an isolated, shameful exception to the pompous glories of political orthodoxy?

How rare is courage!

How mighty is the shuffling, drifting, dull, pressing herd!

Eve, Jane, and I exchanged frightened glances.

Oddly, I wondered which of us might be found most beautiful on a Gorean slave block. Do not women wonder about such things?

And what of Nora, and my enemies in the house?

Would they be so different, barefoot in the sawdust, turned, exhibited, in the torchlight, being bid upon?

"Shame! Shame!" said Mrs. Rawlinson, pointing to the books on the desk before her, the window behind her.

"What have you to say for yourselves?" she asked.

There seemed little for us to say. I felt tears of shame course my cheeks. Eve and Jane, too, sobbed.

"I thought so," she said. "Know that there is no place for such as you in this house. This is terrible, terrible! You are an insult to the house, to your sisters, to the national organization. You are finished here, disgraced. You will go to your rooms, pack your belongings, and leave the premises before nightfall."

"No," we wept. "Please, no!"

"Tomorrow morning I shall bring the matter to the attention of the house board, and your sisters, following which the evidence will be presented, and the vote taken, the outcome of which I do not doubt will be to publicly and officially expel you from the house, and, concomitantly, the national organization."

"Forgive us!" begged Eve.

"We are sorry!" said Jane.

"For offenses less meaningful, less heinous, expulsion is in order," she said.

"Is it truly so great a matter?" I wept.

"Quite," she said. "You may now leave the room," she said.

"Please, no!" we wept.

She pointed to the door and, shuddering, stumbling, numb, we turned about, unable to speak, unable to comprehend the dissolution of our reality, the sudden and catastrophic loss of our position and status, taken as given and unassailable but moments ago.

We had been everything, and now, in moments, we would be nothing, we would be despised and negligible, would be then no more than others, inferiors. The shame of this expulsion would be general knowledge, and certain of our sisters, I thought I knew which ones, Nora, and others, would see to it that the cause of our expulsion would be well publicized. Our continued presence at the school would be intolerable.

"What do you think you are," asked Mrs. Rawlinson, "reading such things?"

We turned back to face her.

Something had been different about her voice. She suddenly seemed other than she had been.

"We are sorry, very sorry!" said Eve, hopefully.

"You are silly little bitches," said the house mother. "I wonder what you are good for?"

This was not the tone of voice, nor the diction, to which we had become accustomed. Her carriage, oddly, now seemed slimily lithe, her voice younger.

She was new to the house, as of the beginning of the semester. I was suddenly less clear as to her age.

"Do you wish to be reported, and expelled?" she inquired.

"No," we said. "No!"

"Remove your shoes," she said.

We looked to one another, in consternation.

"I see you must vacate the premises," she said.

We removed our shoes.

"Now," she said, "kneel before me."

"It is acceptable," she said. "I am a free woman."

I did not understand this, nor, I suspect, did Eve or Jane. Surely we were all free, all of us. Who was not free?

She came about the desk, and pointed to the rug, at her feet.

"Here," she said.

Scarcely understanding what we were doing, almost numbly, we knelt before her.

It was the first time I had ever knelt before another person. I suddenly felt, overwhelmingly, the significance of this, placing oneself before another human being, in what was clearly a posture of submission. I was shaken. It was as though I had been struck a blow by nature. Was I in my place? Were Eve and Jane? I almost fainted, with understanding, and uncontrollable, suffusing emotion.

"So," she said, "you think you know of the Gorean world?"

We looked up at her.

"Get your heads down, to the carpet," she said, "and place the palms of your hands beside your head."

We were thus kneeling before her in what I would later learn was the first position of obeisance.

"Now you are as you should be," she said.

We trembled before her, but, too, it now seemed clear that

we would not be required to leave the house, that no motion for expulsion would be brought to the floor in the morning, before the board, before our assembled sisters.

"You think you know something of the Gorean world," she said, "but you know nothing."

I suddenly realized that she before whom we knelt was not incognizant of the world of which she spoke.

I suddenly suspected that she, too, was a reader of this unusual literature, in which one encountered a different world, a natural world, one so far removed from the negativities and artificialities of our own.

I was very much aware of my forehead pressed to the carpet.

"What little sluts you are," she said. "It is clear what you are good for, and the only thing you are good for."

How dared she call us "sluts"?

Then, to our astonishment, she laughed.

"Girls will be girls," she said.

A laugh escaped me, one of relief. It was a merry jest. But, somehow, we did not raise our heads.

"Look up," she said.

We did so, but did not rise to our feet. We had not received permission to do so.

"What naughty young women you are," she said, "to read such books," indicating those on her desk.

We struggled to smile.

"Remain on your knees," she snapped.

We did so.

"Surely you understand how inconsistent such things are with the certain dictates and dogmas of our culture," she said, "with, say, certain principles and notions which are to be taken as beyond question or review, principles and notions which are to be accepted uncritically, mindlessly, without inquiry or investigation, because they have somehow come to exist, and understand, as well, how they might frighten some individuals, individuals of certain sorts. At the least they are not clearly in accord with various prescribed political proprieties."

We nodded, but remained on our knees.

"Still," she said, "I am prepared to be lenient."

"Thank you, Mrs. Rawlinson," whispered Eve.

"Please," I said.

"Please," said Jane.

"Expulsion may not be necessary," she said.

"No!" I said.

"I am not unaware," she said, "of the stresses and pressures imposed upon young women, even proper young ladies, refined and well-bred, such as yourselves, by biology. Indeed, how could you escape them? What could you do other than pretend they do not exist? But such pretensions would be unavailing. They will have their way, in one way or another. They will frequent your thoughts; they will emerge in your dreams."

We dared not respond.

How could Mrs. Rawlinson, a house mother in a sorority such as ours, dare call attention to such things?

"Do you know what such things tell you?" asked Mrs. Rawlinson.

"No," said Eve, uncertainly.

"That you are females," said Mrs. Rawlinson. "And doubtless, in young men, stresses and pressures also exist, quite different from those which trouble you, which you strive to ignore or repudiate, but complementary to them. They, too, in this world, have their different whisperings, which they, too, are expected to strive to ignore or repudiate. But it is hard for them, as for you, to ignore the drums of nature, pounding in the blood."

It struck me as strange that she had used the expression 'in this world'? What other world could there be? Could there be another world, one in which one need not strive to ignore or repudiate what one truly was? Was it so wrong, to be true to one's nature, whatever it might be?

Was nature so terrible?

Had it not preserved extant species for countless generations?

"Too," she said, "you are young, intelligent, healthy, curious, and hormonally active. Too, perhaps you are not wholly happy, or at ease with yourselves. Perhaps you are miserable, bored, unsatisfied. Perhaps you are uneasy, and know not why. It is understandable, then, that you might wish to look into such things."

"Yes, Mrs. Rawlinson," said Eve.

Then she put her head down, quickly, frightened.

"Your interest in such matters," said Mrs. Rawlinson, "despite what you might think, is not unusual. Many thousands know of these things, here and abroad, in Europe and Asia, and elsewhere. To you, it seems it is a secret. But surely it is a strange "secret" which is unbeknownst shared by multitudes, each of its keepers perhaps unaware of the others. But, too, there are many places where the enemies of nature are less entrenched and powerful than here, places where it does not occur to men and women that obvious biotruths, such as the complementary nature of the sexes, are to be routinely suppressed."

"We thank you for your understanding," said Eve.

"Yes, thank you," said Jane.

"So much!" I said, fervently, gratefully.

"Still," said Mrs. Rawlinson, "you are guilty. You have had in your possession literature quite improper for this house and the school."

"Yes, Miss Rawlinson," said Eve.

"Moreover," she said, "you are not common, ordinary young women. You are very special young women, young women of high intelligence, education, refinement, wealth, taste, and breeding. Indeed, you are ladies, but not ladies in so exalted and powerful a sense that such as you would grovel and tremble in the very presence of such."

I did not understand this.

"Rather," she said, "you are ladies, here, young ladies, in a somewhat archaic sense of the term, a term associated with station, quality, and gentry."

"Yes, Mrs. Rawlinson!" said Eve.

"And, as such," she said, "in the possession of such literature, well aware of its political impropriety, you have behaved inexcusably."

"Mrs. Rawlinson!" protested Jane.

"Stay on your knees, sluts," she said.

"Sluts!" protested Jane.

She had called us this before.

"Who else would read such things?" she asked.

Eve burst into tears.

"Yes," said Mrs. Rawlinson, "'sluts,' all of you, and less than that, far less, if you but knew."

I did not understand her.

I was afraid.

"You must be punished," she said.

"No!" said Jane.

"No!" I said.

"I see," said she, "that expulsion from the house is in order."

"No!" we cried. "Please, no!"

It is difficult to convey my feelings, and, I suspect, the same might have been said for Eve and Jane. We were afraid, uncertain, and confused. In a moment we might be lost. In a sense, we were helpless. We were before the house mother, awaiting her pleasure and decision, on which our future might depend, and, as she would have it, unshod, and on our knees.

The thought came to me, unbidden, sudden, that I was where I belonged, on my knees.

"Be kind!" I begged.

"You will be punished," she said, "all of you, and exquisitely, in a way which will be wholly appropriate to your fault, in a way which will both conceal you and reveal you."

We understood nothing of this.

"I will see to it that you will pay for your indiscretion," she said. "I will see to it that you will suffer for it. I will see to it that you will be profoundly and exquisitely humiliated, that you, all of you, will be openly and publicly shamed, excruciatingly so, deliciously so, and yet in such a way that only we, you and I, understand fully what is occurring."

Eve, Jane, and I exchanged frightened glances.

"You are familiar to some extent with the Gorean world," she said. "That is clear from the books found in your rooms. Therefore, it is only fitting that such things be considered in your punishment."

"Mrs. Rawlinson?" stammered Eve.

"We shall arrange a party," she said. "To some, perhaps more than you suspect, it will be clear that it is a Gorean party; to others it will be no more than a delightful, exquisite entertainment, a costume affair, with a Roman or Greek flavor, hosted by the house, to which selected members of particular fraternities will be invited."

Such parties, and others, I knew, innocent and pleasant,

but subtly, implicitly, and unmistakably stimulating, were not unknown on prestigious, sophisticated campuses

Needless to say, we were much relieved.

"The highest fraternities!" said Eve.

"Of course," said Mrs. Rawlinson.

These would be the fellows from whom even we hoped for attention, and dates.

Such a party, eagerly arranged and planned by our sisters, would be the talk of the campus, and the envy of other sororities, our rivals, which, I suspected, would soon address themselves to similar affairs.

"It will take some days to prepare," said Mrs. Rawlinson. "There is the question of a proper decor, an apt menu, and such. It will not be difficult to arrange music. Dancers, too, may be obtained."

"Is this a punishment?" asked Eve.

"For you three, yes," said Mrs. Rawlinson.

"I do not understand," I said. "May I rise to my feet?"

"No," she said.

"There would be the matter of costumes?" said Jane.

"Quite right," said Mrs. Rawlinson.

"How could one come by a proper wardrobe?" asked Jane.

"It would have to be improvised," said Mrs. Rawlinson.

"Robes, and such," said Eve.

"Yes," said Mrs. Rawlinson.

"But the women would have to be veiled," said Jane.

Mrs. Rawlinson regarded her.

"It must be unpleasant to drink through a veil," said Jane.

"It shows crudeness, to be sure," said Mrs. Rawlinson, "but low-caste women, in public, commonly do so. But do not be concerned. Our party will be intimate, and private. In such circumstances high-caste women commonly dispense with veiling."

"But they might enter, veiled?" said Jane.

"Yes," said Mrs. Rawlinson, "and, if they wish, they may eat and drink behind the veil."

"I did not know that," said Jane.

I did not know it, either.

"Much may be done with a veil," said Mrs. Rawlinson, "at the

discretion of its owner, an adjustment, an inadvertence, a slight
laxity, a glimpsed cherry lip, a sparkling eye, and the knife is
turned about in the heart of some luckless fellow."

"Delightful," said Eve.

"How will we distribute the garments, the roles?" asked Jane.

"Would not everyone choose those of high caste, even those
of Ubaras?" I asked.

"We will select the roles, and distribute them by lot," said
Mrs. Rawlinson.

"Very well," said Jane. "That seems fair. It would not do to
have thirty Ubaras in the house."

"The lots, to some extent," said Mrs. Rawlinson, "will be
rigged."

"How is that?" asked Eve.

"I think that Nora will be our Ubara," she said, "and certain
of her friends the Ubara's confidantes, or attendants."

"Why is that?" asked Jane.

"My choice," said Mrs. Rawlinson.

"Oh," said Jane.

I was sure that Mrs. Rawlinson was very much aware of
certain interpersonal relationships obtaining in the house.
There was no secret about such things.

"I hope," said Eve, "I will be of the Merchants. Their robes
are yellow and white, or gold and white. I think I would look
stunning in such robes."

Eve had strikingly dark hair.

"I trust I will be of the Builders," said Jane. "Their robes are
yellow."

"Their official caste robes," said Mrs. Rawlinson. "Goreans
do not always wear their caste's colors."

"I did not know that," said Jane.

Mrs. Rawlinson looked at me. "And you?" she said. "Perhaps
you would care for the robes of the Scribes?"

"No," I said. "They are poor. I do not know why they are a
high caste."

"Perhaps then," said Mrs. Rawlinson, "the green of the
Physicians. They are a high caste."

"No," I said. "They, too, are not rich enough. I gather their
pleasure is in their healings, and not in their fees. They are too

devoted to their work, to their research, serums, and medicines, and distributing the benefits of their administrations and learnings indiscriminately, denying such to no one."

"That is in their caste codes," said Mrs. Rawlinson.

"They are fools," I said. "People sometimes need their skills and knowledge, even desperately. That is when they could make others pay, and well."

"Yet they seldom do so," said Mrs. Rawlinson.

"To neglect such opportunities seems to me unwise, and scarcely comprehensible."

"The caste has its traditions, and codes," she said.

"Such practices, and refrainings," I said, "seem an unlikely route to the prestige of a high caste."

"Perhaps," said Mrs. Rawlinson.

"Where is their wealth, their power?"

"The personal physicians of Ubars do well," said Mrs. Rawlinson.

"But the others?" I said.

"There are the traditions, the codes," said Mrs. Rawlinson.

"Wealth is power," I said.

"Only if it can purchase steel," she said.

"In any event," I said, "I would like, like Eve, to be of the Merchants. Surely there could be more than one."

"Of course," said Mrs. Rawlinson.

I, too, had dark hair. I thought it would look well against white and yellow, or white and gold.

I had little doubt that the Merchants was the wealthiest caste. It seemed to me, then, that it should be the highest caste. Of what value, for example, was the Scarlet Caste, the caste of Warriors, if not to protect the gold, the wealth, of the Merchants?

"None of you," said Mrs. Rawlinson, "will be of high caste."

"But," said Eve, "if we are of low caste, of the Metal Workers, the Cloth Workers, the Workers in Wood, the Leather Workers, the Bakers, the Tarnsters, or such, we would have to be placed lower at the tables."

"But," said Mrs. Rawlinson, "you will not be placed at the tables, at all. As mentioned, the lots will be arranged. It will seem that it was merely your fortune, a matter of chance, that the lots fell as they did."

"No!" said Eve.

"Never!" said Jane.

"Certainly not!" I said.

"Yes," said Mrs. Rawlinson. "It will be your role to serve the feast. You will serve attentively, efficiently, and humbly. You will be alert to the needs of the guests, an empty plate, a glass in need of refilling. You will be swift to respond to summoning, of any sort, for example, to bring a laver of scented water to a place, that the guest may rinse his hands, or to lend your body, clothing, or hair, if a guest wishes, to wipe grease from his fingers. You will not speak unless you are spoken to. If spoken to, you will respond softly, with deference. Your head is to be lowered, unless you are ordered to raise it; you are not to meet the eyes of a guest, unless commanded to do so. You are to be self-effacing. You are prohibited from participating in the feast, in any way, either by eating or drinking, unless commanded by a guest. One may wish to feed you by hand, or cast scraps to the floor, which you are to retrieve on all fours, without the use of your hands. If a pan of water is set on the floor for you, you are to approach it on all fours, bow your head, and drink from it, humbly, as an animal. Each guest will be furnished with a switch, which he may use on you, if he is in any way dissatisfied with your service, or, if he wishes, for no reason at all."

"Never!" said Eve.

"This is your punishment," said Mrs. Rawlinson. "There is still time for you to leave the house."

Jane began to sob.

"The guests, and your sisters, will think this all a matter of the lots," said Mrs. Rawlinson. "Thus, in a sense, your fault, your punishment, will be concealed, and yet, in a way, its consequences will be well revealed."

"You would have us be as kajirae?" said Jane, aghast.

"Slave girls—*Gorean* slave girls?" whispered Eve, scarcely daring to form the words.

"Precisely," said Mrs. Rawlinson.

"But the fellows would not stand for such a thing," said Eve. "They would object. They would rush to rescue us."

"Do not be too sure of that," said Mrs. Rawlinson. "I think they will see it as all in the spirit of good fun. Too, I suspect that most will be pleased to see you, or any number of other young women, so. Further, the young men will be informed that any attempt to interfere with matters will result in their immediate ejection. I think things will go splendidly."

"How will we be clothed?" I asked.

"I have decided that," she said.

"As I understand it," I said, "kajirae are commonly clothed sedately, in long gowns, if with bared arms, at such feasts, that is, if free women should be present?"

One scarcely dared conjecture how they might serve, if free women were not present.

"Not always," said Mrs. Rawlinson, "particularly if the kajirae would be recent captures from an enemy city, or, say, enslaved rivals of the free women attending the feast, or such."

"I gather," I said, "that we are not then to be allowed the dignity of lengthy, concealing gowns."

"No," she said.

"You would dare have us appear in public in less?" I asked.

"Yes," she said.

"No, no!" said Jane.

"It is all in good fun," she said.

"How then," asked Eve, "are we to be clothed?"

"Obviously then," I said, "in a garmenture appropriate to slaves."

"Tunics, then," said Jane, in misery, "tunics fit for slaves, slave tunics."

"I am sure," said Mrs. Rawlinson, "that you would all look quite fetching in such tunics, slave tunics, particularly of the sort designed by men, by means of which the beasts boast of the lineaments of their properties."

"I will never put such a thing on!" exclaimed Jane.

"Never!" said Eve.

"Never!" I said.

"We might perish of mortification!" said Jane.

"Scarcely so," said Mrs. Rawlinson.

"Still!" I exclaimed.

The thought of myself in such a garment was shocking, insupportable, so exhibited, so displayed! How unthinkable, would be such a thing!

It would be as though I were a slave!

"I gather, from men," she said, "that such things are extremely attractive."

"They demean a woman," said Jane.

"How can one demean a slave?" she asked.

"But you need have no fear," she said. "I have no intention of putting you in slave tunics."

We exchanged glances, of relief.

"You will not wear slave tunics," she said.

"Thank you, Mrs. Rawlinson," we said.

"No," she said, "you will not be allowed such dignity. You will serve in camisks, all of you, in the common camisk."

"Never!" we cried.

"Remain on your knees," she said.

The camisk is a narrow rectangle of cloth, with an opening in the center. It is slipped over the head, and belted snugly, commonly with a double loop of thong or binding fiber, this fastened with a slip knot at the left hip, that it may be convenient to a right-handed man. The double loop provides enough thong or binding fiber to bind the occupant, helplessly, hand and foot. The slip knot at the waist of the camisk is similar to the disrobing loop at the left shoulder of some slave tunics, by means of which the garment may be conveniently removed, a simple tug loosening it, permitting it to fall gracefully about the ankles of its occupant.

"We will never wear such things," said Eve.

"It seems expulsion is in order," said Mrs. Rawlinson.

"No!" we wept.

"Would you prefer to serve naked?" she inquired.

"No, no!" we said.

"It is not unusual for a Gorean feast to be so served by kajirae," she said.

I did not doubt that.

"Many men claim it improves the appetite," she said.

"No, no," whimpered Eve, tears coursing down her cheeks.

"I am told so," said Mrs. Rawlinson.

"Relent, be kind," pleaded Jane.

"But many," she said, "prefer the tunic, or camisk. It gives them something to remove."

"You would punish us so?" I wept.

"Your fault was grievous," she said. "You may beg to be permitted a camisk."

"I beg to be permitted a camisk," said Eve.

"I beg to be permitted a camisk," said Jane.

"I beg," I said, "to be permitted a camisk."

"It is all in good fun," she said.

Jane, Eve, and I exchanged glances, of dismay, and misery. We would be almost nude, exhibited, as might be slaves, and the others would be fully clothed, veiled, robed, and such.

Clearly she had conceived a suitable punishment for such as we, a punishment fully appropriate, given our fault, having dared to read of a natural world.

"Your left ankles," she said, "will be encircled several times with small, colored cords, on which bells will be threaded. Slaves are often belled. It stimulates the men."

We looked at one another, miserable.

"Collars, too, would be appropriate," she said. "One would not wish your necks to be naked. Common dog collars will do for you, particularly as you are bitches. But they will be locked on your neck. You will know yourself well in them. Small padlocks will do, to which I shall hold the key."

Eve began to cry.

"I assume you will all know enough to kneel in the presence of free persons, save when you are serving, fetching, and such."

I nodded, in misery.

And Nora, and her clique, and the others, would be such, free persons!

"You will all need a little coaching," she said, "in posture, grace, and such, which I shall supply, but the important thing is that you should know yourself as slaves, that you should understand that, fully, in the deepest roots of you. Given that understanding, much will come quite naturally. Most of your serving, I assure you, will be quite proper, quite innocent. For example, in serving wine to a male you need only do so on your knees, your head down, extending the goblet, held in both hands, between your extended arms. You need have little fear that you will be expected to serve wine in the typical Gorean fashion, which is so stimulating to a male, and, I might observe, in passing, too, so helplessly and erotically stimulating to the slave as well. One would not wish you to be dragged to the kitchen by the hair, and enjoyed on the linoleum, would we?"

"No," we whispered.

"But Mrs. Rawlinson," said Eve, "if the boys see us thusly, how will they see us?"

"As lusciously desirable," said Mrs. Rawlinson, "but only as slaves."

"What if we do not do well?" said Jane.

"I am sure you will do well, very well," said Mrs. Rawlinson. "And remember, the guests will be furnished with switches."

We recalled this.

"It is unpleasant to be switched," she said. "You will try to do your best, will you not?"

We looked to one another.

"Yes," we said.

"And remember," she said, "you are to address all free males as Master, and all free females as Mistress. Do you understand?"

"Yes," we said.

"Yes, Mrs. Rawlinson," she suggested.

"Yes, Mrs. Rawlinson," we said.

Several days later, the party took place, and Eve, Jane, and I, half-naked, belled, and collared, served as kajirae. Our punishment, as Mrs. Rawlinson had suggested, was exquisite. As she had anticipated, we were well shamed, excruciatingly so. We knew we were being punished; the guests did not. I supposed I should have been grateful.

I learned, for the first time in my life, at that party, something of what it might be to be looked upon as a slave. I could not remove the collar, of course, unless I had recourse to tools. Accordingly, it was well on me. It was the first time, of course, that I had ever been in a locked collar. Interestingly, though I would have told no one at the time, I was erotically charged, even in my shame. Could I be, I wondered, a slut, or less? The bells, too, with their subtle rustle, marked the least of my movements. It was a strange feeling, to be belled. In some strange way that, too, aroused me. Did they not say, so to speak, 'You are a slave, a belled slave'?

Eve, Jane, and I were, I suppose, quite popular at the party, at least with the young men. Many times, unnecessarily I was sure, we were summoned to serve one or another of them. I think this did not much please several of our sisters, also at the tables.

"Slave," called Nora, in her sumptuous robes, as our Ubara, "to me!"

I hurried to her, and knelt before her, head down.

How pleased, I thought, must she, my enemy, be to have me so before her!

"My hands are greasy from the meat," she said. "Come closer."

Then, while she chatted with the young man beside her, she pulled me by the hair closer, and held me, painfully, my face down, at the table, and wiped her hands, carefully and firmly, in my hair.

Then, turning to me, as though she had just then noticed me, she said, "Get out!"

I withdrew to the side, kneeling.

My eyes were hot with tears. I kept my head down.

"To me," she called again, later. "Stop!" she then said, when I was a few feet from her. I knew enough, from Mrs. Rawlinson, to kneel, immediately.

"You must be hungry," she laughed.

We were hungry, for we were not permitted to participate in the feast. Too, on Mrs. Rawlinson's instructions, we had been denied lunch, and, later, kept locked in a room behind the kitchen, until we had been brought forth, covered by a large sheet, and introduced into the common room, now arranged as a banquet hall. We had been knelt, and the sheet, swirling, lifted away, revealing us, camisked, collared, and belled. "Slaves!" had said Mrs. Rawlinson, in her own robes, with an expansive gesture, and there had been much laughter, and some gasps, for even our sisters had not been apprised of how we would appear, and, too, there was some hooting from the young men, and vulgar noises, and an appreciative, even enthusiastic, clapping of hands.

Then, at a sharp clapping of Mrs. Rawlinson's hands, we leapt up and hurried to the kitchen, to bring forth the fare, the sweets, the candies, the nuts, the bowls of fruit, the herbs, the bread, flat, circular loaves of bread, which would be divided into eight wedges, the many covered dishes of boiled vegetables and hot meat, the vessels of wine, and such, and placed these on the serving table, from which place we began to serve the guests.

"Are you hungry?" inquired Nora.

I did not know what to do.

"You may speak, slave," she said.

"Yes," I said, "—Mistress." I had been informed by Mrs. Rawlinson that those in collars must tell the truth. How vulnerable this makes them. They are not free women.

She then took some scraps from her plate and cast them about, on the floor.

"Feed," she said.

Burning with shame, but yet, too, eager for food, I crawled to the scraps and, head down, without my hands, fed. That was the first time I had fed thusly. Oddly, I was glad to feed, even grateful.

Could I be, I wondered, a slave?

And how significant this would have been, I thought, had the scraps been cast to the floor not by Nora, but by a man!

I was suddenly overcome, almost unable to move.

I was overwhelmed by a sudden, momentous sense of meaningfulness.

How meaningful suddenly seemed my posture, my garmenture, the bells on my ankle, the collar on my neck.

How small I seemed, how degraded and mocked, and how worthless, how helpless!

And my sense was not just one of meaningfulness, as profound as that sense might be, and as comprehensible as such a sense would be, given the circumstances, but, rather, startling me, and frightening me, one of fittingness, of propriety, of rightfulness!

Could it be that I, despite my antecedents and background, my upbringing, education, and indoctrination, was a slave?

Since puberty I had suspected that some women were slaves. Were not the blossoming subtleties of my body, and those of others, such that they had been carved out over countless generations by the lusts of men? Were we not delightful prizes, goods, like fruit and animals, to be seized and exploited? Had we not been selected to be delights to possessors? Had we not been selected to be roped and snared? Had we not been, in our way, bred for the auction block?

Yes, I thought, there must be rightful slaves, women who cannot be whole, cannot be fulfilled, who will never know true happiness except at the feet of men, owned, and mastered.

Could I be one such?

Never, never!

Surely not, surely not!

It went against everything I had been told, everything I had been taught.

Could it be that what I had been told was false, that what I had been taught was untrue?

Who was I?

What was I?

I sensed Nora walking about me, and was confident she had in her possession her switch.

In a moment I heard a pan placed on the floor near me.

I looked up, from all fours.

I felt the tip of her switch beneath my chin, and, responsive to its pressure, I lifted my head, and then, on all fours, my head up, guided by the switch, by its gentle pressure, first on one side of my face and then the other, I was moved about, faced to the left, and then to the right, and then, again, ahead, being exhibited to those at the low tables, the men cross-legged, the women kneeling, some guests lounging, bemused, on an elbow.

"She is a pretty thing, is she not?" said Nora.

There was a generous assent to this, particularly from the young men.

Our sorority was quite particular about such things. No one was accepted as a pledge, let alone initiated, who did not meet certain standards.

Our house was envied on campus, and, by some, held in contempt. Sometimes it was referred to as "the house of meaningless beauty," sometimes as "the harem," sometimes as "the slave market," which, I supposed, was a reference to a girl's judiciously selling herself, so to speak, to the highest bidder. One fellow had referred to it, jokingly, as "the pleasure garden." I had gathered, then, that I might not be the only one about who might be familiar with certain forms of forbidden literature. But the expression, of course, is familiar, and well-known. I did not inquire into the matter, for I would have been frightened to meet a male who might be familiar with such things. I wondered, though, what it might be like to be within the walls of such a place, waiting for the bell, sounding my particular notes, that I must hasten to the room of preparation, to be prepared for the slave ring of my master.

"I think she looks nice in a collar, don't you?" asked Nora. "I think she belongs in one, don't you?"

I could not remove it. It was locked on me.

I saw Mrs. Rawlinson, in the background. She was smiling. I recalled that I was being punished, well punished.

I suspected that the sight of a woman in a collar was stimulating to men. I wondered if they knew that being in a collar had a similar effect on its occupant.

I had little doubt that orgasms were easily obtained from an obedient, yielding, helpless slave.

What choice had she?

None!

But did the men know how eagerly the slave sought the embrace of her master's arms? One supposes so. Surely they must know the need, the passion, of the slave. How helpless is a woman once her slave fires have been ignited. Do the masters truly not understand the slave's uneasiness, her whimpering, her sidelong glances, the bondage knot in her hair, her kneeling before him, the pathetic way she presses her lips to his feet, hoping to call herself to his attention?

Surely the strongest chain on a slave is her nature and her needs.

And I wondered, suddenly, what it would be to encounter a man so virile and strong, so powerful and lustful, that he would be satisfied with nothing less than my absolute possession, with nothing less than owning me, with nothing less than having me as his slave.

And what would it be, to be at the feet of such a man?

Could there be such man? Could there be such a place, such a world?

Nora's questions were greeted with obvious agreement.

The switch drew my attention, and that of the guests, to the pan which had been placed near me.

It was a pan of water.

"Drink," said Nora.

"Please, no," I protested.

"Please no, what?" inquired Nora.

"Please, no, Mistress," I said.

"Drink," said Nora, sternly.

I put down my head, and, on all fours, not using my hands, drank.

I was drinking as a slave. How strange to be in such a posture, I, a free woman, performing such an act. What feelings coursed through my body, strange feelings, unaccountable feelings. I could not understand them. But of course I was being punished. I must remember that. That must be all it was, all it could be. But such feelings, so broadcast, weakening, and suffusive! Could it be, I wondered, that I was a slave.

I had had only a swallow or two when Nora's slipper swept across the floor and upset the pan.

"Clumsy slave!" she said.

Then, suddenly, I felt a stinging rain of leather cracking on my back, and then I was rolling on the floor, crying, turning about, trying to fend the blows which fell upon me, and then I struggled to my knees, and put my head down to the floor, covering it with my hands. She struck some more blows, lashing blows, on my arms, and calves, and back, and then, perhaps weary, returned to her place.

"What a careless, clumsy slave," she remarked.

I shook with sobs, and pain. I was not brave. Nora had conquered. She had defeated me, I was shattered, and subdued. She had won. I did not even think of myself as a free person. I felt myself to be something different, something helpless, meaningless, and unworthy. I was camisked, collared, and belled. I was only a punished slave. I knew then that I would strive to please her.

The leather had taught me my place.

She was mistress. I was slave.

I wondered if Eve and Jane, in their exposure, their humiliation, and degradation, in their punishment, had suffered as I had. I did not doubt it. How could it be otherwise? Neither had been switched as I had, but each, more than once, when deemed less than fully pleasing, had felt a sharp stroke, sometimes a merry stroke, across the back of her legs. Certainly, though excruciatingly sensitive to our exposure and shame, we all strove to play our roles well, for we were all constantly under the exacting scrutiny of Mrs. Rawlinson. She retained our confiscated books, and might, we knew, at any time, initiate the proceedings which we were desperate to avoid. But I wondered, too, if Eve and Jane, now and again, in their serving, in their awareness of how they were looked upon, doubtless as never before, in their sense of exposure, of vulnerability and helplessness, in their hope to be found pleasing, and their fear of failing to be found so, had had feelings analogous to mine, those unaccountable feelings which a woman might feel, if she sensed her legs within no more than a scrap of cloth, if she lightly touched her finger tips to her throat, and found a collar there, if she were to understand, in its full moment, that she did not belong to herself but to another, that she was a property, and no more, that she was owned, that she was slave. I wondered if Mrs. Rawlinson knew what she had done to us, what she had forced us to feel, what she had forced us to suspect about ourselves.

At last the party was over, and the guests departed, and our sisters, laughing and chatting, weary but excited, retired to their rooms. Eve, Jane, and I were permitted to remove our bells and were placed in maid's gingham uniforms, and set to clear the tables, tidy the room, and attend to the dishes. It was only when the work was complete that we were aligned, and Mrs. Rawlinson, behind us, one by one, removed our collars.

"You may thank me," she said.

"Thank you, Mrs. Rawlinson," we said, and then fled, sobbing, to our rooms.

It was some days after the party that I had had the troubling dream to which I earlier alluded, that in which it seemed that men were in my room, that in which I had sensed myself meticulously examined, and then, as I struggled to awaken, to escape the dream, bound helplessly, my wrists and ankles widely separated, while the men conferred. When I awakened, whimpering and frightened, I had screamed. Then I had realized, to my relief, that I was safe in my own room. Strangely I was naked, having apparently somehow slipped from my nightgown in the night. For some time, I remained in the bed, frightened and troubled, even though it was now clear to me that I was in my own room. After a bit, however, my alarm seemed foolish to me, and I regarded the dream, for all its seeming reality, with amusement. It was then, a moment later, that I had cried out with horror, this the outburst which had brought Eve and Jane, and Mrs. Rawlinson, to the room. I had drawn the covers up about me. "A dream," I said, "a dream!" Mrs. Rawlinson had been the last to leave the room, and she had smiled before leaving, smiled knowingly, as it seemed to me at a later time. The reason for my outburst was simple. There were cord marks on my wrists and ankles.

Chapter Five

"Slave," she had said. "Kneel!"

"You are not a free woman!" I had said. "Are you so different from me? That bit of cloth you wear is as much a mockery of a garment as that which clings about me! Do I not see a metal circlet clasped close about your neck, which, I trust, is locked in place? If it is not, remove it, and I will kneel before you."

"Barbarian!" she said.

"We are no different," I said. "We are now the same, whether barbarian or Gorean!"

"No!" she said.

"I might sell for as much, or more than you!" I said.

These remarks, and those which had followed, recounted earlier, were not unprecedented in exchanges between native Gorean slaves and imports, such as I, merchandise brought from Earth, particularly when they are unfamiliar to one another. I had, at this time, been better than three months and four passage hands on your world. You might note that I was not without my collar vanity. I had literally suggested that I might bring as much off the block as she, though she was Gorean. To be sure, this would depend on the bidders. It had not taken me long to realize that I, and others like me, were commonly despised by Gorean women, both free and slave. The men, on the other hand, I soon discovered, though commonly regarding us as inferior and worthless, were not immune to our charms. Certainly they bid nicely for us, and were not reluctant to put us in their collars. We needed the men and hoped to be purchased by them, for they would protect us from the women. We needed only serve them with eager and abject perfection, in all the diverse ways of the female slave. Something more was involved here, of course, than the simple animosity of women, particular and generalized, for rivals, or the usual suspicion of that which is other than oneself, or different. We imports brought high prices. This was doubtless, in part, a result of a different and exotic cast of merchandise, but, too, I think there was little doubt that the prices paid for us were not unrelated to the quality of the goods sold. When a city falls, or a caravan is taken, one will usually add to one's chain what is at hand. On the other hand, sometimes a woman is stripped and dismissed, whipped from a camp, or the smoking wagons. To her humiliation and rage, she has been rejected. She is insufficiently attractive to be a slave. She would not sell, or might sell for no more than a pot girl. Contrariwise, the girls taken from Earth are apparently selected with great care, for beauty, intelligence, and, I suspect, somehow, though I am unclear how it is assessed, for latent, and eventually uncontrollable, passion. I frankly see no reason to believe that the women of Earth, in general, are either better looking or not, when compared with their Gorean sisters, nor, of course, that they are better or worse than we. I would think them much the same. Clearly we are all female, and human. On the other hand, the Goreans have an expression, "slave beautiful," and that clearly means beautiful enough to be a slave. Accordingly, the women in collars, Goreans or not, tend to be females of a sort which is of interest to men. And, as you might recall, if you would forgive me, the imports from Earth are not acquired randomly, say, in virtue of the fortunes of war or raiding. They are selected with great care, apparently by men, or women, who are professionals in such matters. I have often wondered about Mrs. Rawlinson, whom I suspect is not unacquainted with my fate, and perhaps that of others. I wonder if she is amused, to think of us as we might now be. At different times it had seemed her voice was different, younger, and, at times, it seemed her posture and carriage was more that of a younger woman. I had come to suspect that she had been disguised, and somehow placed in the sorority for some purpose. I recalled she had once identified herself as "a free woman." I had been puzzled by that at the time, but now it seemed somehow meaningful. She had said this shortly before she had had us kneel before her. If Mrs. Rawlinson was Gorean, or in league with Goreans, she had certainly been well placed to examine and assess a number of supercilious, vain, intelligent, highly cultured, beautiful young women, women conveniently gathered together, women nicely located and accessible, self-selected women, beauties all, of a sort which, once collared, might be of interest to men. I wondered about Eve, and Jane, and the others. Too, I wondered about beautiful, arrogant Nora, who might now find herself on the other end of a switch. I have spoken of collar pride. I soon learned collar pride. I learned that I was "slave beautiful," and that the female slave is the most desirable and exciting of human females. What woman would be immune to such flattery, the flattery of chains, the tunic, the collar, the whip? What woman, in her vanity, would be insensible of the compliment paid to her, the compliment of thongs and bracelets? How could she be unaware of the tribute and honor paid to her, that she should be cast amongst the least and most worthless of animals, the most desirable of women, the female slave? So I came to be proud of my beauty, and its meaning. The collar may be viewed as a simple contrivance, a device prescribed by Merchant Law, identifying a slave and, if the collar is engraved, often her master. Free women may view it as a badge of inferiority and degradation, and perhaps appropriately, from the social point of view. But the collar, too, as I have suggested, may be seen as a badge of quality, a token that the woman has been found desirable enough, and beautiful enough, of sufficient interest to men, to be put in a collar. It is no wonder the free women, encumbered in their robes, uneasy within them, perhaps, for all I know, seething with need, suspecting the joys of the collar, hate us so.

We are as natural and real a part of your world as the unpolluted air you breathe. You think nothing of our presence. It is there, as that of your other domestic animals. You find us on your streets, and in your markets, shopping; you note us waiting for our masters, our necks or ankles chained to street rings; surely you have seen us on holidays, promenaded on our leashes? Are we not everywhere, hurrying about, intent on our errands? We are in your homes, and kitchens, and fields. Do we not serve in the paga taverns, sometimes nude and belled? Do we not, sedately tunicked, as serving slaves, assist free women with their complex ornaments, their perfumes, robes, and veils? Do we not gather gossip for them, and carry messages for them in their petty intrigues and assignations; do we not accompany their palanquins? Will you not find us in military camps, and stables? Do we not serve well in the baths? Is it not a great pleasure of your visitors, foreign ambassadors, and such, to see us in your towns and cities, doubtless comparing us to those in theirs? Do we not fit in well with your colorful architecture, your broad boulevards, the lovely statues and fountains, and, surely, with your extensive, shaded public gardens, with their secluded, winding paths? Surely your slaves are one of the delights, one of the pleasures and joys, of your world. It is easy to see why you would not give the least thought to letting us out of our collars. You want us in them, and we will be kept in them. Indeed, who but a fool would free a slave girl?

Deny this, if you wish, but I have discovered, on your world, that such as I are not only accepted, as your other animals, but are, in a way, prized. Surely you are aware of the jokes, the songs. Certainly we are muchly sought for? Is it not for us that citadels are stormed and caravans raided, that we may be coffled and led naked to your markets? Surely you cannot deny our importance, negligible though we may be? Are we not somehow special amongst your animals, though we commonly sell for less than a sleen, and dozens of times less than a tarn? I think so. And I do not think you would wish to do without us. No. Are we not well worked, and are we not beautiful? And you find many uses for us, to which we are put.

Sometimes I marvel at your world.

Here, as not on my former world, the slavery of such as I is not questioned. Its utility, value, naturalness, and appropriateness is accepted, and understood. In a natural order, a natural order refined and enhanced with the rituals, customs, and institutions of civilization, would there not be such as we? Is it not the natural right of a natural master, that he should have a slave, or slaves? And is it not the natural right of the natural, needful slave, that she should kneel to her master? What begins in the caves, with fastenings formed from the sinews of beasts, may flourish in the boulevards, where delicate, graceful bracelets may confine the small wrists of women behind their backs.

We are subject to your whips, and wear your chains.

Surely that is obvious.

But is our lot so miserable?

Men and women are different, very different.

Surely you know that.

Here women such as I find ourselves a very real part of a very real world.

Here we know who we are, and how we must be.

Here we have a role and an identity, to be sure one inescapable and imposed upon us, whether we will have it so or not, for we are only animals, only slaves. But consider us, if you will, and our natures, though one need not consider a slave. Do you think slaves do not have natures, even though their natures may be scarcely worth noticing, and despicable?

We do have our natures.

Do you think all gratification, or fulfillment, is on the side of the master? It is not. Why are we commonly so radiant, so content? Have you not wondered how that could be? Many of us, once embonded, once brought to the feet of a man, find ourselves. Enslaved, we learn we are of the slave sex. We then desire, with all our heart, to be slaves, worthy slaves of our masters. Can you, who are free, understand that? I suspect your free women can. Perhaps they awaken, sweating and screaming, in the night.

Your world is a natural world, on which exist dominance and submission, and I have learned that I am not dominant. To be sure, I knew this even on my world, a world in which such things are clearly recognized, in all their obviousness, but denied. They are not denied here, as I learned, on my knees, looking up, into the eyes of masters.

Some are slaves, and some masters.

Why should the slave not be a slave, and the master a master?

How long we waited for our masters! How we need our masters! How precious are our masters, and how we, trembling, hasten to serve them, to please them, and as a slave!

I, for one, am content. I belong in my collar. Keep me in it.

And yet, too, I am only a slave, and sometimes tremble in

terror. We cannot choose our masters. We may be bought and sold, exchanged and bestowed, wagered and stolen. We may be ignored, despised, and beaten. Who knows to whose whips we must press our lips obediently?

I was taken in the parlor of the house.

I was summoned downstairs by a man's voice. I descended the stairs, frightened. But surely these were workers, summoned by Mrs. Rawlinson. But where was she? I shook my head. It was in the late afternoon, in the fall. I remember how the light came through the windows. Somehow, unaccountably, I had fallen asleep after lunch. Where was Mrs. Rawlinson? Where were my sorority sisters? The house, a large house, seemed empty.

Then I was suddenly very afraid, for I was now sure it was empty. I could not run past the men, and one of them was behind me. Another blocked the stairs.

"Who are you?" I asked, pleasantly enough. "What are you doing here? May I help you?"

Three of the men arranged chairs before me, the backs of the chairs facing me. They sat on the chairs, their arms on the backs, regarding me.

I stepped back a pace or two.

Where were my sisters? Where was Mrs. Rawlinson?

On one side of the room, a lamp had been overturned. Here and there, oddly, some lengths of ribbon lay on the carpet, red ribbon, white ribbon.

"What do you want?" I asked. "Doubtless Mrs. Rawlinson, she is the house mother, summoned you, but for what purpose I do not know. I think the house is in order. It is in order, as far as I know. She is not here now. She will doubtless be back later. May I help you? You could come back later."

"Remove your clothing, completely," said a man, he in the center chair.

I looked at him, disbelievingly.

"Must a command be repeated?" he asked.

I looked about, wildly.

There was something familiar about this question. It seemed I had heard something like this before, or read something like this, at one time or another.

I put my hand before my mouth.

"No one will hear you," said a fellow.

I looked at the fellow in the center chair, he whom I took to be their leader.

"Now," he said.

I remembered then where I had come upon that question. It had occurred in one or more of the books I had read, those compromising books which Mrs. Rawlinson had confiscated. It was a Gorean question. And I knew the sort of person, a female person, to whom such a question was likely to be addressed. Such persons were expected to comply with commands instantly and unquestioningly. Failure to do so, I suspected, was unwise.

I reached to the top button on my blouse.

"Who are you?" I asked.

In a few moments I stood naked before them.

"Stand straighter, and turn about, slowly, and then face us, again," said their leader.

"What do you think?" asked the leader, of one of his confederates.

"Forty, perhaps sixty," said the fellow.

I understood nothing of this.

"Back toward us," said the leader, "your wrists crossed behind your back."

I did so, and, shortly, with two or three encirclements of cord, snugly knotted, my wrists were tied behind my back.

I remembered the words, 'forty, perhaps sixty,' and gasped. This must stand for forty, or sixty, thousand dollars. I suspected then that I was to be taken to the Middle East, and would be destined for some rich man's harem.

I struggled, futilely.

The leader came about, and stood before me. He held a generous length of ribbon, silken ribbon, in his hand, some feet in length. He wound this twice about my throat, and then knotted it, closely, under my chin. He jerked the knot tight. I felt the pull against the back of my neck. The ribbon was white.

"You are white-silk," he said.

In my reading I recalled the significance of white-silk, but how could they know that I had not been "opened for the pleasure of men," that I was a virgin? Then I remembered my strange dream, of several days ago, after the party. If it had been no dream, I supposed such a determination might have been easily made at that time, perhaps while I slept.

Then I stiffened, for one of the fellows was crouching beside me, on the left. I felt a metal anklet snapped about my ankle.

I had been ankleted.

"I know what you have in mind," I said, "but you will never get me to the Middle East! You will never be able to sell me in a secret market!"

"You are not going to the Middle East," said their leader. "And there will be nothing secret about the market in which you will be sold."

"You are going to sell me?" I said. "Truly?"

"Your lineaments are not without interest," said a fellow.

"That was clear from the film," said another.

"Film?" I said.

"Taken at the party," said a fellow.

"You look quite well in a camisk," said a man.

"You know that word?" I said.

The fellow laughed.

"To be sure," said another, "it was a rather generous camisk."

I had been mortified, for I had been half naked. And I was dismayed to learn that some record of my humiliation, of my punishment, and, I supposed, of that of Eve and Jane, too, had apparently been made. I suspected Mrs. Rawlinson would not have been unaware of the filming. Perhaps she had arranged it, for a record of the party, which might later have been of interest to the guests. But how could these men have known of this, how could they have managed to see the film? Had it been stolen? Had it been given to them? Had it been sold to them?

"It may be a long time," said another, "before you are again permitted a garment as concealing as a camisk."

"You will never get me to the Middle East!" I said.

"You are not going to the Middle East," said the leader. "You are going to Gor."

"There is no such place!" I said. "There is no such place!"

I struggled.

I was aware of the metal on my left ankle, snugly enclosing

it. I was aware of the ribbon twice encircling my throat, knotted there, a ribbon of white silk.

I was nude, and my hands were tied behind my back.

I was helpless.

"There is no such place!" I said. "There is no such place!"

I was then, from behind, gagged.

Two men then placed me on the rug, gently, and one crossed my ankles and another tied them together. I then lay on the rug, gagged, and bound, hand and foot.

"Put her in the van," said the leader.

I was lifted and carried through the backdoor of the house, where a van was waiting. I was placed in the van, on the metal floor. The floor had some broad grooves. Such a feature, I supposed, was in the interests of cargo, affording a run-off for possible spillages, a higher, drier surface to protect against dampness, perhaps a less frictionated surface to facilitate the loading or unloading of boxes, crates, and such. It would not, of course, be a pleasant surface to lie on, as I would soon learn. One man climbed into the back of the van with me, and the doors were closed. Shortly thereafter the van left the driveway.

We had driven for perhaps two hours when I began to whimper. My body was sore, particularly given the recent roughness of the road, my jarring and jostling, and the hardness of the floor. In places on my body there were temporary marks, from the grooved flooring.

The man said nothing, but he removed his jacket, folded it, and placed it under my head and shoulders.

I looked at him, tears in my eyes, gratefully.

Then I lay back.

Had he been waiting for me to whimper, I wondered. Had he been waiting for me to beg?

I knew I had begged.

I did not know if this had pleased him or not.

But I had begged.

It was an hour later, and night must have fallen. The man snapped on the dome light in the rear of the van.

I lay before him.

He turned away, and, from a box to his left, he drew forth a thermos, and a small sack. I watched him, as he unwrapped a sandwich, and began to eat.

After a bit, he looked at me.

"Are you hungry?" he said.

I struggled to sit up. I nodded, piteously. I was cold, thirsty, famished, and bound.

"We are in the country," he said. "It would do you no good to scream."

I nodded.

"On your knees," he said. "Approach me."

I managed to kneel, and make my way to him.

"Turn about," he said.

I struggled about, and he untied the gag, and drew it away.

"Face me," he said.

I did so.

He poured some fluid from the thermos into the cup of the thermos, and held it to my lips, and I drank.

It was warm tea.

"That is enough," he said, withdrawing the cup.

"Would you like to eat?" he asked.

Again I nodded, desperately.

He began to finish his sandwich, but before doing so, tore off a portion, and held it to me.

I extended my head to him, to take the bit of sandwich, but he drew it back, a little, so that I must reach farther forward to take it. Then, when I had done so, he permitted me to reach it, and take it.

He had well impressed on me that he was in control of my food.

He finished the sandwich, and I had finished the bit permitted to me.

"You may lick my hand," he said.

I licked his wrist, and the back of his hand.

In this way, I expressed my gratitude, that I had been given drink, and had been fed.

"May I speak?" I asked.

I had said this naturally, understandably enough, for I was afraid. Yet, almost as soon as I had said the words, I wondered why I had used those particular words, in that particular way. Surely they seemed appropriate; but they also seemed familiar. It was as though I had heard them before, or read them somewhere. Then it occurred to me that I had read them, or something rather like them, in those books which Mrs. Rawlinson had discovered in my room, which she had seized, to my consternation and shame.

"No," he said.

"Shall I replace the gag?" he asked.

I shook my head, negatively.

He had said we were in the country, and that it would do no good to scream. Certainly that seemed plausible, given the roughness of the road. And I hated the gag. How helpless a woman feels when speech is denied her! Too, he was a powerful man, and I did not doubt that even the suspicion that I might cry out might earn me a blow which might render me unconscious. Too, I saw those large hands, and did not doubt but what they might, if he wished, snap my neck.

I would not cry out.

"Lie on your stomach," he said.

I lay on my stomach across his jacket.

He checked the bonds on my wrists and ankles. Apparently all was in order. They needed no adjustment.

So I lay on my stomach, under the dome light, bound, as the van sped on through the night.

I became very much aware that he was looking at me, prone and bound, lying across his jacket, under the dome light.

I began to suspect, trembling, what it might be for a man to see a woman so. And I was well aware that I was not unattractive. I knew that I had been accepted as a pledge to the sorority at least in part because of my beauty, as had been the other girls. We were a house of beauties. Certainly we had teased, and taunted, and dismissed, many young men who had sought our company. We were angling for the best on campus, for whom we were willing to compete. So surely I must not simply lie there before him. He was a strong man, and I was helpless. Was I not like a tethered ewe, in the vicinit/ of a tiger? I feared the teeth, the claws, of such a beast, but, too, I wondered what it would be to feel them on my body. I became much aware of the anklet

49

fastened about my left ankle, the ribbon wound twice and knotted about my neck. I must attempt to distract him.

"I beg to speak!" I said.

Again, I had the sense that these words were somehow familiar. In any event, they expressed how desperately I wished to speak.

"You may speak," he said.

"Untie me," I said. "Let me go!"

"No," he said.

"I am naked," I said.

"Yes," he said.

"Where are you taking me?" I asked. "What are you going to do with me?"

"You are being taken to a collection point," he said, "from which point you will be shipped."

"Then there are others," I said.

"Several," he said.

"As I?" I asked, pulling a bit at the bonds.

"Yes," he said.

How helpless I was!

"Free me," I said. "I can give you money, much money! I can make it worth your while, very much so!" I recalled that a fellow in the house had said something like 'forty, perhaps sixty' in response to another's question. I could double or triple forty, or better, even sixty, thousand dollars for my freedom, simply from immediately available resources and accounts. "Whatever you, and your fellows, might get for me," I said, "I can give you more, much more! Let me go!"

"But what of the others?" he asked.

"Surely they are rich, as I!" I said.

"Not at all," he said. "We take some who have little to commend them but their extraordinary beauty, their high intelligence, and latent, exploitable needs."

"If they cannot pay," I said, "then let it be done with them as you will."

"It will be done with them as we will," he said.

"What of my sorority sisters?" I said, frightened.

"They are all in hand," he said.

I thought of Mrs. Rawlinson.

"All of them are rich," I said.

"No," he said, "all are penniless, destitute, as you are."

"I do not understand," I said.

"If you were to be freed this moment," he said, "you would soon discover that every economic resource you had has disappeared, vanished, save, I suppose, your body, which might bring you something from time to time on the streets."

"I do not understand," I said.

"There are ways, arrangements, documents, transfers," he said.

"You're joking," I said.

"No," he said.

"You already have everything I could give you?" I said.

"And something more," he said.

"What?" I said.

"You," he said.

"You will never get away with this!" I said.

"On your world," he said, "you guard your goods, your automobiles, yachts, jewels, gold, almost everything, but not your women. We do not make that mistake with our women. Your women are like public fruit, ripe, moist, fresh, and tempting, dangling within easy reach, harvested without difficulty at our pleasure."

I thought it odd, the expression "on your world."

"We harvest judiciously," he said, "with an eye to only the finest stock, wherever found, Japan, England, Germany, France, Denmark, wherever it may be found. We are particular."

"I am to be flattered?" I said.

"You and your so-called sisters," he said.

"I see," I said, bitterly. My body was sore, cold, and tired, even lying on his jacket.

"In your party," he said, "did you notice the eyes of the boys on you, and your camisked sisters?"

"Eve, and Jane," I said. "Yes, it was difficult not to be aware of that."

"Perhaps that was the first time you were ever looked upon that way," he said.

"Yes," I said, "but on the beach I was not unaware of the eyes of men on me."

"That white, one-piece bathing suit," he said, "was amusing, so putatively modest, and yet so subtly expressive."

He knew about the suit!

"You enjoyed taunting the fellows with that," he said.

I did not respond.

"And then," he said, "when they were lured in, when they were encouraged, when they thought themselves welcomed, turning the freezing blast of a cold stare upon them, feigning surprise, indignation, and innocence. How useful was that little suit in your trivial, pretentious girl games."

"Let me go," I said.

"Surely you are aware of what I might do with you now, if I pleased," he said.

"Yes," I said, frightened. I wondered what it might be, to be put to the purposes of such a man, no boy, but a man.

"There are examination positions," he said.

"I do not understand," I said.

"You will learn them," he said, "and assume them instantly upon command."

"I am afraid," I said. "Please free me. I will make no trouble. I will say nothing. I will not go to the police."

"Do you think we do not have arrangements with the police?" he said.

"On the street," he said, "it may be as simple as stopping and lowering your head, while being scrutinized, and assessed."

"Assessed?" I said.

"But at the party," he said, "the look of the men was quite different, was it not?"

"Yes," I said, shuddering. "But I was half-naked, and I had to behave in certain ways, I had to be obedient, subservient. I was being punished, and so, too, were Eve and Jane!"

"Did it not excite you to be so clad, to act so, to be so looked upon?" he asked.

"'Excite me'?" I asked.

"Sexually," he said.

"How dare you!" I said.

"I see it did," he said.

Bound, tears of shame welled in my eyes.

"How do you think you were looked upon?" he asked.

"I do not know," I said.

"You were half-naked and there were collars on your necks, locked collars," he said.

"So?" I said.

"How do you think you were looked upon?" he said.

"I do not know," I said.

"Speak," he said, not pleasantly.

"As slaves!" I said.

"You, and your sisters, are shallow, petty, vain, spoiled, mercenary, meaningless, little bitches," he said. "You are worthless."

"No," I said. "No!"

"What," he asked, "if you should meet not the men of your world, boys, half-men, subdued men, furtive glancers, guilty, shamed, crippled men, men trained to betray their nature, taught to suppress their manhood, but other men, natural men, quiet, unpretentious, powerful, confident, self-assured men, men who look upon women as delights, as delicious creations of nature to be fittingly brought within the ambit of one's power, to be owned and mastered."

"Could there be such men?" I asked. I was terrified because I, and my sisters, in our meaninglessness, were worthy to be to such men no more than slaves. But better I thought to be the abject slave of such a man than the pampered darling of a rich weakling, of the sort to which our background and the nature of our lives directed us. Owned by such a man one would strive to please him. One would hope, trembling, to be found pleasing

"There are such men," he said, "even on Earth."

"Surely not!" I said.

"There is nothing wrong with the men of Earth," he said. "They are the same as those of which I speak. It is a cultural matter. It is possible that in a thousand years the men of Earth will come to understand what has been done to them, and they will find themselves."

"Are my resources, my wealth, truly gone?" I asked.

"Yes," he said.

"Then I cannot use them to purchase my release, my freedom," I said.

"No," he said.

"Doubtless they are worth far more than I would sell for," I said.

"Certainly," he said.

"But my value," I said, "is not negligible."

"I gather," said he, "you are curious to know what you might sell for."

"Yes!" I said.

I turned my head to him, with difficulty. He was smiling. I did not realize, at the time, that I had acknowledged myself the sort of woman on whom a price might be set.

"It is hard to say," he said. "We speculated that you might go from somewhere in the neighborhood of forty to sixty."

"So that is what a beautiful woman, one as beautiful as I, would bring on the Arab slave market," I said, "forty to sixty thousand dollars."

"I do not understand," he said.

"You intend to sell me in the Middle East," I said, "to some sheik, some rich merchant."

"No," he said.

"To be held captive in some remote desert palace?"

"That seems unlikely," he said.

"He would buy me for a wife," I said.

"Scarcely," he said.

"Surely not for less," I said. "Surely not for a mere concubine!"

"No," he said.

"Then?" I whispered.

"Yes," he said.

"No, no!" I said.

He was silent for a bit. I sensed the van making a turn.

"I am a free woman!" I said.

"Free women," he said, "regard themselves as priceless. You did not."

"What then," I asked, "do you think I am?"

"That should be clear," he said.

I struggled in the bonds.

"You will not be sent to the Middle East," he said.

"Where then?" I said.

"Gor," he said.

"Do not tease me," I said. "Be kind! Be merciful! Do not sport with a stripped, helpless captive!"

"Gor," he said.

"That is fiction," I said. "It is only in books, only in stories, only in stories!"

"Gor," he said.

"I told you in the house," I wept. "There is no such place! There is no such place!"

Then the van had stopped, I had no idea where.

Then I was aware of a hand in my hair, which pulled my head up and back, and, from the side, from my left, a soft, folded bit of white cloth, some six inches square. This square of cloth was damp, with some chemical. It was placed over my nose and mouth, and held in place, closely. I struggled for a moment, and then lost consciousness.

* * * *

"You look well in chains," he said.

I was well illuminated in the light of the torch.

"Please give me clothing!" I begged.

"Clothing is not necessary," he said, "as you are a slave."

"I am not a slave!" I said.

He pointed to his feet.

I crawled to him, the chains on my wrists and ankles dragging on the large, flat stones, and, head down, frightened, pressed my lips to his feet.

"See?" he said.

"Yes," I whispered, "—Master."

He then exited, bending down, and the small iron gate closed behind him. A moment later I heard a key turning in the lock, and was in darkness.

I realized I was on Gor.

Chapter Six

In the small room, with the panel bolted on the outside, where we were commonly housed when not serving in the large outer room, the Gorean girl, well collared, had accosted me, demanding that I, a mere barbarian, should kneel before her. I had refused. She, with her beauty, her marked thigh, her encircled neck, was no more than I!

"How then did they recognize you as a slave?" she had asked.

"I have no idea," I had said, though, in truth, I had an idea of such matters.

"You must have been assessed," she had said.

"Doubtless," I had said.

Suddenly the door had been unbolted from the outside, and Tela, first girl, entered. All of us in the small room immediately went to our knees, and put our heads to the floor, the palms of our hands on the floor beside our heads.

"I am frightened," said Tela. "Something is wrong."

We dared not change position, as we had not received permission to do so.

"Be as you would," said Tela.

We looked up.

Usually Tela's switch dangled from her wrist.

It was not there now.

She was clearly frightened, and her alarm spread to the rest of us, not now serving. I was the only barbarian in the room. We feared Tela, for she was first girl, our switch mistress. I had never seen Tela frightened before, except before the masters.

There were two of us in the outer room, who would be, as far as I knew, serving.

"What is wrong, Mistress?" asked Midice.

"The guests have fled," she said.

I did not understand this, for the tables, the games, did not close until the early morning.

"I fear the masters are undone," she said. "They have departed."

"What is going on, Mistress?" asked Midice.

"Listen!" said Tela.

"Oh!" whispered Lucia.

"The drums of guardsmen," said Daphne.

"They are coming closer," said Cara.

"Closer!" wept Portia. I gathered she had had dealings with guardsmen before. She seemed very much afraid.

"What of the masters?" said Dina. She wore the tiny Dina brand, "the slave flower." The Dina is a familiar slave brand, but not nearly as common as the cursive Kef. The girls who wear that brand are often called "Dina," doubtless from the mark.

"I do not think they will escape the city," said Tela.

Our house was one of several on the Street of Chance in Ar.

Outside the drums had stopped, and we heard shouting, and pounding, from the sound of it, the pounding of spear butts, on the door.

"You know nothing!" said Tela.

I sensed that Faia and Tirza, in the outer room, must have hastened to the door, and, struggling, removed the long, heavy beam which secured it. I would later learn that the masters, as they departed, had instructed them to set the beam in place. In this, they may have been hoping to gain time.

The doors burst open and there were heavy footsteps, as of high, military sandals. I heard Faia and Tirza scream. There were shouts, and a crashing, and piling, of furniture.

In a moment I sensed fire, and, through the door, saw wild shadows cast on the walls, of armed men, breaking tables, hurling them to the center of the room. I smelled smoke.

"Run, run!" said Tela, hastening back, into the larger room.

We, in our serving tunics, crying out with fear, hurried out, into the larger room. Smoke was now billowing from the flaming heap in the center of the room, the tables, the wheels, the boards, the boxes of gaming pieces. We fled toward the welcome of the opened door, but our passage was blocked by a lowered spear.

"Where is your master?" said a voice.

"Masters!" said Tela. "But we do not know!"

Addressed by a man, we all knelt.

My eyes stung.

I began to cough.

"Who is first girl?" asked the man.

"I am," said Tela, "if it pleases Master." She was trembling.

"How many are there?" asked the man.

"Eleven, including myself," wept Tela.

The soldiers, or guardsmen, despite the fire, were pulling down hangings, and prying loose panels from the wall. Two inspected our holding room, and two others rushed to the kitchen, and storage rooms. Then they, and the others, their work done, the premises rummaged through, the decor torn, scratched, and ravaged, exited behind he before whom we knelt, who barred our way.

"We are slaves," wept Tela. "Have mercy on us! Let us out!"

An officer appeared behind the fellow who barred the door. "Close them inside, and block the door," said the officer. "They are not stupid. They know what was transpiring here."

"No, Masters!" cried Tela, from her knees. "We know nothing!"

"We are ignorant!" cried Faia.

"Who knows what transpires with masters?" cried Midice.

"We are only slaves!" cried Tirza.

"Slaves!" wept Lucia.

"We dared not inquire, Master," said Daphne. "Curiosity is not becoming in a slave!"

The heavy door was swung shut before us. We rose to our feet, coughing, and weeping, and screaming, struck at it, pulled at it, tried to open it.

"The back is chained shut," cried Cara.

We sank down, behind the door, scratching at it.

I was blinded with smoke, half strangled, with a lack of air. We could not help who had bought us.

I slipped to my belly before the door.

I put out my fingers, and touched the wood.

Then suddenly the doors swung back, and I saw light, and smoke billowed into the street.

My lungs drew in the bright, clean air of Gor.

A hand seized me by the hair and drew me forth on all fours, and then thrust me down to the street, on my belly.

"Fasten your hands in your hair," said a man.

We lay prone, in a line, side by side. Midice was to my left, and Luta, who had spoken to me so contemptuously in the holding room, was to my right. I thought to myself, "See, Luta, we are not so different."

I was aware of sandaled feet stepping about, amongst us.

We did not look up.

After a time, a voice said, "A silver tarsk, for the lot."

"Very well," said the officer, "but see that they are sold in the Tarsk Market."

"A stipulation?" said a voice.

"Yes," said the officer.

"Done," said the voice.

I heard a clink of coins, and, shortly thereafter, I felt a rope looped about my left ankle, snugly, and knotted, tightly, and then passed to Midice, on my left, and thence to those beyond her.

"A silver tarsk!" I thought. "We have been given away!"

"Keep your hands fastened in your hair," said a fellow.

Then another said, "Kajirae, up!"

We rose to our feet.

I stole a glance at he who seemed to have completed the purchase, in which I was an item. He was a small man, in a dirty white tunic, with a yellow sash.

I kept my hands in my hair, while the tunic was cut from me. We were then, in ankle coffle, herded through the lower streets of Ar, to the Tarsk Market.

The first step is made with the left foot.

Chapter Seven

The cages, of heavy, cable-like woven wire, are made for tarsks, not kajirae. One cannot stand in them. They are long, narrow, and low. Thus, more than one can be placed on a sideless, flat-bedded wagon, roped in place. Too, like the common slave cages designed for kajirae, they may be stacked.

I hooked my fingers in the wire, and looked out, frightened, from my knees. The Tarsk Market has its name, obviously enough, I suppose, because it is a general market for tarsks. Certainly the smell of tarsk was all about. And there was little doubt, from the condition of the cage, that the previous occupants of the cage had been tarsks.

Needless to say, it is only low slaves who are vended from such a market.

I lay down in the cage, on my right side, in the straw, facing the back wall of the warehouse.

How vulnerable we were, as slaves!

But, had we been free women I did not doubt but what we would have been abandoned, left in the house, to perish in the flames.

The marks on our thighs, our collars, had saved us. We had been saved, but only as animals.

It is often safer to be a slave than a free person. Who, for example, would bother slaying a tarsk, or a kaiila?

Instead, one would herd them, or rope them. One would appropriate them.

It is for such a reason that free women, trapped in a burning city, a fallen city, being sacked, will not unoften steal collars from their girls, and fasten them on their own necks, hoping to be taken for slaves, to be spared as slaves.

I had recognized two of the soldiers, and the officer. They had been patrons of the house.

They had lost heavily.

Of course we were guilty! Did we not know of the manipulation of the tables' spins, of the dishonest stones, the fraudulent dice, the ostraka which, to the informed eye, could be read?

Did we not invite in the patrons, at the door, with our smiles, the glances over our shoulders, our fingers lightly touching our brands beneath the cloth, not silk, but rep cloth, for ours was a shabby den for its purposes. We served as the slaves we were in the wide, low-ceilinged, ill-lit interior of the outer room. We would bring the gamesters paga and ka-la-na, and platters of meat and bread, and cakes and sweets, to keep them at the tables. We pretended zestful enthusiasm for their playing, as if it might be our own. How we rubbed against them, so inadvertently, laughed, joked, touched their arms, and hands, applauded their boldness, pretended dismay at a loss, pretended chagrin and sorrow when they made to leave the tables. Rather they should choose and again match ostraka, hazard another turn of the wheel, another placement of the stones, another roll of the dice! We must serve our paga and ka-la-na modestly, of course, for the men must be kept at the games. Indeed, we served it in the manner that Eve, Jane, and I had been instructed by Mrs. Rawlinson to serve beverages at the party, kneeling, our head down, extending the goblet, held in both hands, between our extended arms. I suspected that Mrs. Rawlinson, at the party, had been amused, seeing us so. This posture and attitude, I suspected, was not unknown to her. Perhaps she, watching, envisioned us so serving at another time, in another locale. But even so, would not anyone seeing us so have found the behavior interesting and not without meaning? Did it not seem clear, the sort of female who must serve so? But even so, our service must be modest. We must not so excite the men, that they might be distracted. We were not paga slaves who, if too frequently spurned, may expect their master's whip after closing. But more than once I had felt Tela's switch, and had been driven from the outer room, to the holding area, weeping and shamed, while the men laughed, to be chained, supperless, to the ring by my mat. I could not help myself. I was now other than I had been on Earth. Men had seen to that.

How the fellow who had accompanied me in the van would have been amused, to see his prisoner, the vain, aristocratic young lady, indeed, the debutant, afflicted by need, slave need!

As the reader, if reader there may be, may have gathered, I had been much troubled on Earth, not knowing who I might be, or what might be my nature. I had been alarmed by casual thoughts, sometimes stealing upon me when I was unprepared to resist them, certain frequently recurring daydreams, and surely the strange, wild, unaccountable realities revealed to me in the astonishments of my troubled slumber. It was at such times, that I found it difficult, despite my upbringing, my education, and background, to see myself, and feel myself, as I had learned I should see myself, and feel myself. Who were others, to tell me who I was? How was this a freedom, to be told how to be? How strangely false and unsatisfying seemed the culture to which I was expected to conform, and that which I was expected to perpetuate! Was I truly an artifact, a meaningless, unhappy puppet of a dismal world, responsive to strings I had neither designed nor requested? Perhaps humanity, in its flight from nature, into its thousands of ideologies, superstitions, and pretenses, had unknowingly betrayed itself, building up about itself, brick by subtle brick, its invisible prison, satisfying only those who might profit by its exploitation. But perhaps, too, there are no prisons, other than those we ourselves make, or will accept. It would be interesting if the walls we most fear, within which we feel ourselves the most constrained, within which we most lament, do not exist. In any event, I knew that I carried in my body, as other human beings, a history and a heritage extending back to the first blind, reproducing forms of life, ages prior to the complex marvels of the unicellular organism. To such an organism could biology be irrelevant? Surely templates must exist in the human organism, as in other forms of life, perhaps subtler and vaster, but just as real. Could my behavior, my promptings, what would satisfy me, what I would need, be wholly independent of my form of life, be unique amongst all living forms, merely accidents and oddities imposed upon me from the outside, beginning with the first flash of light, the first breath, the sobbing birth cry of a small, bloody animal? That did not seem likely. The cultures which denied men and women to themselves, for their own purposes, in their own interests, inertial, self-perpetuating structures, productive of misery and alienation, were inventions of recent date, the mere tick of a clock, marking a moment in millenniums. If there was a human nature, had it been fabricated, truly, so recently? Might it not have been formed in other times and other places, a consequence of other conditions, as an entailment of alternative realities? Might we have been formed for one world and precipitated into another, a quite different world, an alien world, one in which our form of life finds itself homeless, finds itself in exile?

I saw no need for civilization and nature to be incompatible, to be enemies.

Might not a civilization be possible in which nature was recognized, refined, enhanced, and celebrated? In such a civilization surely there would be a place not simply for seasons and tides, for surf and wind, but for men and women, as well.

I had not been long on Gor before I was brought naked and back-braceleted into a round chamber. Its diameter may have been ten feet, or so. It was a plain room. The ceiling was domed, perhaps fifteen feet above my head. The walls were bare, but penetrated by two small, barred windows, some feet over my head, through which light fell dimly. The flooring was of large flat stones, as in my cell. The guard then turned about and left me there. The door was closed behind him, and I heard the bolt put into place.

I saw no one, but I was sure I was seen.

I lifted my head. "I am a free woman!" I said. "Return me to Earth!"

My declaration received no response.

I do not know how long I remained in the room.

The guard eventually returned, and, holding me by the left upper arm, conducted me back to my cell.

We stood without.

The bracelets were removed.

"Do you speak English?" I asked.

I was bent down, his hand in my hair, and I was thrust within the cell, and the door was closed, and locked.

I no longer wore chains within the cell, but I was left, as before, in darkness.

I felt about in the darkness, hoping to find food. There was a depression in the floor, which contained some water. Obviously I could not lift it, and, after trying to cup water in my hands, with little success, given the shallowness of the depression, I bent down, and lapped at it. I felt about and located the food pan, which contained some porridge-like material, and a thick crust of bread.

How could they treat me in this fashion? Did they not know who I was? Did they think me some waitress, some clerk, or secretary?

I would soon learn they thought me a thousand times less.

I cried out, in anger.

"I am a free woman! Let me go! Release me! Free me! Give me clothing! Give me decent food! Return me to Earth!"

My voice rang against the stones, in the small space. But I received no response to my cries.

I determined that I would show them what a woman of Earth could be, and a woman of my background, of my class, of my position, of my intelligence, and education. I would resist them.

Though I had often sensed myself a slave, and a rightful slave, I must now permit no countenance to such thoughts, to such suspicions, to such secret fears. I am a free woman, I told myself, over and over again. I am a free woman. I am a free woman. I am not a slave. I am a free woman!

I must be a free woman, I sobbed. I must be a free woman!

But what, I wondered, if I were not? What if I were a slave? What if I should be, as I had often feared, a slave, a rightful slave?

From time to time, in the darkness, I felt the white ribbon which had been twice knotted about my neck in the sorority house. Now it seemed grimy, and damp, from the cell. But it was still there.

The rounded, steel anklet which had been snapped about my left ankle in the house was gone when I awakened on Gor. I gathered that it had served its purpose, whatever that purpose might be.

I held to the ribbon.

What if I should be a slave, I asked myself, a slave?

The next day I was introduced again into the rounded chamber, similarly unclothed, my wrists, as before, braceleted behind my back.

The guard told me to kneel in the center of the room, and put my head to the floor.

As he left, I remained standing.

What free woman, I asked myself, as I was, would do such a thing?

When he returned I shrugged my shoulders, and lifted my head, proudly. I would show them what a woman of Earth could be, particularly one of my refinement, intelligence, education, and class, and a member of my sorority. And thus I was returned to my cell.

The next morning I was routinely branded, and then returned to the cell. I could not believe the casualness with which I had been marked. I might have been any domestic animal! A moment after the iron had marked me, and I was screaming in disbelief and pain, a scarf was placed over my eyes, and I could not even see the mark, which now made me, I sensed, somehow, radically and irremediably different than I had been.

I would learn later that I wore in my thigh, small, but clear, imprinted there, the cursive kef. I would learn, too, it is a common brand, marking common slaves.

Following my marking, still blindfolded, my thigh burning, I was returned to my cell, but now, by means of a belly chain and bracelets, my wrists were fastened behind me, closely, at the small of my back. Thus, I could not reach the brand. Another chain, something like a yard in length, run from the belly chain, held me to the wall behind me. My feet were then joined, pulled forward, and chained to another ring. A consequence of this chaining was that I could not much move from my place. I could lift my knees, draw back a bit, and sit up. I could also lie on my left or right side.

As I could not reach the water, or feed myself, I was tended by a young, tunicked woman. In the light, small as it was, that came through the opened door, I caught the glint of light on metal. Something was on her neck. Then I realized the woman was collared!

"Have mercy on me," I whispered to her. "You must understand my plight. Be kind! You are a female, as I!"

She placed her fingers lightly across my mouth.

Then she held a pan with water to my lips, and I drank.

"Do you speak English?" I begged.

I hoped, of course, that anyone sent to tend me might be familiar with my language.

A thick wedge of dried bread was thrust to my lips, and then forced into my mouth. It gagged me as effectively as leather or cloth.

"You were displeasing," she whispered to me, frightened. "You did not kneel as requested. Fortunately this fault was committed before you were marked. I advise you not to be so foolish in the future. You have been marked."

I tried to speak, as I was desperate to do, but could not do so, for the bread. Then she was gone, and the door locked.

The next day I was again conducted to the round chamber, as before, stripped, back-braceleted.

How had they known I had not knelt as requested?

Clearly, as I had suspected, they must be able to see into the chamber.

Before the guard left me in the room, I was again instructed to kneel in the center of the room, my head the floor.

The heavy door closed. It was bolted.

As far as I could tell, I was alone, and yet, as before, I sensed I might somehow be under surveillance.

I was afraid. My knees felt weak. I was afraid I might fall. I pulled against the bracelets. I looked about, searching for tiny cracks, or openings. There might be any number of such, undetectable from where I stood. I might be seen, and as I was, stripped and braceleted, from a thousand places. I felt the stones beneath my bare feet, was conscious of a tiny movement of air on my body.

How alive, I thought, must be the body of a slave!

How alive to small things, a breath of air, a scent, subtle, scarcely noticed, the texture of a bit of cloth on her body, the feeling of a carpet or tiles beneath her bared feet, a rustle of chain in an outer room, are they coming for her, the weight of a manacle on her small wrist, the solid, cold feeling of bars clutched in fear.

And what, if she were bound and blindfolded, the touch of a master?

I wanted to throw myself to my knees and put my head down to the stones.

I felt a desperate desire to prostrate myself before the unseen others, if they were there.

It seemed every muscle and nerve in my body cried out to me to kneel, to place myself in a posture of submission.

It seemed to me that I belonged in such a posture.

"It is what you are," something seemed to say to me. "Be what you are! Do not fight what you are! Do you not know, Miss Allison Ashton-Baker, for all your pretensions, you are a slave. You belong on your knees!"

No, no, I thought.

"Do not be afraid," something seemed to say to me. "Acknowledge your reality! It is not wrong to be what you truly are. Only then will you know yourself whole, and, enslaved, most free."

No, I cried out, to myself.

"Do you really think you will be given a choice?" asked the small, insistent, internal voice.

I am a free woman, I said to myself.

"You know you belong on your knees before men," said the secret voice. "You have wanted to kneel before them, and submit yourself to them, as a slave, for years, since the first hopeful budding of your body."

Certainly not, I said to myself.

"Have you not dreamed of masters?" asked the voice.

Do not torment me, I said to myself.

"You wish the men, then, to see to it?" asked the voice.

I do not understand, I wept to myself.

"Perhaps they will help you," suggested the voice.

I do not understand, I said to myself.

"Apparently you wish for them to do so," said the voice.

I sensed myself on a threshold, tottering on a brink, between conditions and realities, between what I was and what, for years, I had been told I should be, what, for years, I had pretended to be.

Then I straightened my body, and threw back my head, proudly. "I am a free woman!" I cried. "I am a free woman!"

Almost at the same time, the voice which had so tormented me, that small, insistent, inward voice, somehow within me, again spoke. "Foolish slave," it said, "do you not know slaves are not permitted to lie?"

I remembered reading, in the confiscated books, that there were penalties for such failures and faults in a slave.

Then I looked about, in terror.

I remembered that I had been marked.

Had I been less than fully pleasing?

I feared so.

Hopefully no one had heard me, hopefully no one would know!

Scarcely had my cry ceased to ring within the stones when the bolt was thrown back, and the guard entered.

He put his hand tightly, painfully, in my hair, and forced my head down, to his hip. Then I was dragged, stumbling, from the chamber. I remembered, from the books, something of what was being done to me. I was being conducted somewhere, where I did not know, in the helpless, shameful, leading position commonly used with a female slave. "Forgive me," I cried. "Please do not hurt me, Master!" How easily those words escaped me. Might they not have escaped the lips of a frightened slave? And how naturally I had addressed a free man as "Master!" I recalled, from the party, that all free males were to be addressed as "Master," and all free females as "Mistress!"

I was taken to a side chamber. One of my hands was freed from the bracelets, and then both hands were fastened together again, but before me. I was placed before a dangling rope. I looked up. It was threaded through a heavy metal ring over my head. Most of the rope was on the other side of the ring. It ran to the opposite wall, where it was looped, loosely, about a large hook. The end of the rope near me was fastened about the chain of the bracelets.

"What are you going to do?" I asked.

A moment later I felt my braceleted wrists being pulled upward, toward the ring. The guard hauled on the rope until I was stretched, and I could just feel the stones of the flooring with the tips of my toes. He then secured the rope, fastening it about the hook on the opposite wall, holding me in position. I was well extended. What position could this be? He then tied together my ankles, and fastened them to a ring on the floor.

Why was I fastened in this way?

What could he intend?

I feared I knew.

"Please," I said. "Forgive me! I will try to be a good slave!"

Had I not been marked?

He was behind me. I sensed he had something in his hand, perhaps retrieved from a peg on the wall.

"Forgive me, Master," I wept. "Please, Master!"

I had never been struck in my life, until the party, when I had been subjected to the lashing of Nora's angry switch.

I would have done almost anything to escape that switching. I remembered, in the pain, blind with misery, acknowledging her Mistress, and myself slave.

She, my enemy, and rival, being acknowledged Mistress! And I no more than a groveling, frightened, beaten slave at her feet! What a triumph that must have been for her, to see her despised rival, in beauty, in popularity, cringing at her feet, belled, collared, half naked, weeping, a slave with no option but to endure the displeasure of her Mistress!

That beating had been unpleasant, to be sure. And I could well understand how a slave will dread the switch, and do much to escape it.

Surely I would do so!

I had no wish to feel it again!

I tried to turn, to look behind me. I could not well see what he had in his hand. "What are you going to do, Master?" I asked, frightened.

Then I was put under the slave whip of Gor.

I am sure the beating was light, and intended to be more informative than anything else, but, still, I had, for the first time in my life, felt the flexible, broad-bladed, five-stranded Gorean slave lash, designed specifically for the discipline of female slaves, a lash designed to punish but not to mark.

Released from the rope, and my ankles freed from the ring, I sank to the floor. I was scarcely aware that my hands were once more being fastened behind my back. I lay there, my body afire, a whipped chattel, a slave.

I could not believe the pain.

I now knew the penalties which might attach to a slave's lapses.

I would now strive to be a good slave, a pleasing slave.

I now knew I could be whipped, and would be whipped, if I were not pleasing.

I would do my best to be pleasing.

I could see the boot-like sandals of the guard, near me.

How small, vulnerable, dependent, and weak then seemed my sex. How different we were from men!

How obviously, if they chose, they were the masters!

And here, on this world, they had so chosen.

I struggled to my feet, sobbing, and hysterical, looked about, past the guard, and ran to the opened door of the small chamber, and, barefoot, ran down the hall. I was not striving to escape. I came to the opened door of the rounded room and stumbled through it, and knelt in the center of the room, trembling, my back aching, with my head down to the stones.

In a few minutes I was joined by the guard.

"Your training will begin in the morning," he said.

"Yes, Master," I whispered.

"You may thank me," he said.

"Thank you, Master," I said.

I now knew I was a slave. It had been well taught to me. My only hope, now, was not to permit myself to be mastered. To be sure, I would have masters, as I was a slave. But it is one thing to be a slave, and have masters, and it is another, I thought, to be mastered.

I must never permit myself to be mastered, I thought.

And yet, as I knelt there, I knew I wanted to be mastered.

Yes, Allison, I thought, you want a master.

Since puberty you have wanted a master.

And now I suspected, a slave, I might be easily mastered.

You know, Allison, I said to myself, you may have many masters, and be mastered by any or all of them, as they might please.

Yes, Allison, I thought, you will doubtless be mastered many times. Then I thought to myself, you are no longer "Allison," slave, for slaves have no names but at the pleasure of their masters. You are now nameless. It is masters who will name you, as any property, or beast, if they please, and as they please.

My training will not be detailed. Interestingly, it lasted only a few days. One learns the kisses and caresses, the kneelings, the manner of tying sandals, of dressing and bathing masters, and such, but most attention was devoted, interestingly, to the acquisition of Gorean, and a number of servile skills, such as cooking, sewing, cleaning, laundering, and such. The point of Gorean, I suppose, was to provide a barbarian slave with enough linguistic skill to make her survival more likely. It was not hard for me, and I suppose for other female barbarians, to adapt myself to Gorean. I do not think there was anything surprising or anomalous in this, for the linguistic skills of women, for whatever reason, tend to be considerable. Is not language the art, and joy, of women? To be sure, the intensity of the instruction, and the immersion in the speech world of Gor were doubtless relevant. Perhaps of importance, as well, was the natural way it was taught. I learned it much as a child learns his native language, in the beginning by ostension, and then by metaphor, correction, refinement, and intuition. Even throughout human history on Earth, women, I realized, as I now, must strive to learn the languages of conquerors and masters. It seems not unlikely then that the women who most swiftly and successfully learned the languages of their captors and masters, and were then most successful in pleasing and placating them, would be those most likely to survive and breed. Whatever may be the truth in such matters, my skills proceeded apace. To be sure, I was highly motivated. I wished to survive. Too, I did not care for the occasional impatient admonition of the switch when I badly misused a word, confusing similar sounds, or found myself guilty of some lapse in grammar. On the whole, I enjoyed the lessons in Gorean, but, initially, tended to resent the instruction in domestic felicities. I came from a class in which such things were for other sorts of women, low women, and such skills were, however important they might be, below me, and my kind. Certainly I knew nothing of cooking, and such things. Such things were the concern of servants, whom we hired, inferior women, of one sort or another. I tried to make this clear to my instructresses, who found my reluctance amusing. "For servants?" one said. "But you are less than a servant. You are a thousand times below a servant, for you are a slave!" And another said, "A master will expect you to do such things, and well, and I do not think it would be wise to disappoint him." Another said, "If your master is not satisfied with your meals you may expect to be whipped. You are a slave, not a free companion, lofty in her dignity, who may be as clumsy and inept as she wishes." "Do you understand?" asked another. "Yes, Mistress," I said. "Keep your stitches small and neat," said another, "and do not burn your food." "Yes, Mistress," I said, and then addressed myself diligently to those tasks to which I had hitherto regarded myself as superior.

I had now been fitted with a collar of the house, one which had been hammered about my neck. It was large, high, heavy, and uncomfortable. I could scarcely lower my chin. It was quite different from the light, lovely, comfortable, but quite secure, common collars which Gorean masters commonly lock about the throats of their kajirae, collars, for example, of the sort which I envied in my instructresses. Perhaps the point of such collars, the house collars, was to make their trainees eager to be brought to the block.

The grimy white ribbon which had identified me as "white-silk," had been cut from my throat, before my head and neck had been laid across the anvil, for the hammering shut of the house collar. But then, when the house collar was in place, a smaller ribbon, also white, had been looped and knotted about the house collar. It, at least, was clean.

"It is only of rep cloth," said one of the instructresses.

"Not of silk," said another.

"She is too plain," said one of them.

"No," I said, "I am beautiful!"

"She will do," said another.

I did not understand this. I knew myself to be extremely

beautiful. But then, at that time, I did not understand the general high quality of Gorean kajirae. What gifts they are for men!

"Do not despair, Allison," said one of the instructresses. "You will grow more sensuous, more beautiful, in your collar."

"In my collar?" I said.

"Of course," said one of the instructresses.

"The masters know what they are doing," said another.

I had been permitted the name, Allison, but it had been made clear to me that it was now only a slave name. Somehow this seemed very meaningful to me, that 'Allison' was now a slave name.

As my progress in Gorean continued, and I became more adept in servile skills, being permitted to launder for the guards, and do some simple cooking for their mess, I was granted a tunic. Doubtless it had been worn by others before me, but, to me, it was inordinately precious. Certainly I would do much to keep it.

One of the first things I had done, when introduced into a training room, one walled with mirrors, was to hurry to the side, and examine my thigh.

"Vain slave!" laughed an instructress.

In the mirror one achieves a certain distance from the brand, and sees it rather as another might look upon it. In the mirror I saw a branded slave girl, and, a moment later, with a frisson of recognition, I realized the branded slave girl was I.

"It is a nice mark, Allison," said one of the instructresses.

"Sometimes such things are bungled," said another.

"Not by our iron master," said another. I recalled that it was rumored that she was not unoften in his arms.

How frightful, I thought, to be badly branded. To be sure, such things seldom occurred. Most marking is done by members of the caste of Metal Workers. Most such shops will have a slaving iron, and it is often at hand, and, if not heated, ready to be thrust into the glowing coals of his forge. The Metal Workers, too, do most of the collar work, measuring, fitting, and such. Some free women are branded and collared within an Ahn of their taking.

I regarded the mark.

I recognized that it clearly enhanced my beauty, perhaps a thousandfold. The matter, however, was not purely aesthetic. I did not doubt that much more might have to do with its meaning, what it proclaimed about its bearer!

I examined the mark. It was small, fine, lovely, and tasteful, and telling in its meaning.

And it was on me.

"We have work to do, Allison," said one of the instructresses.

"By nightfall," said another, "you must learn to bathe a man, care for his leather, and kiss his feet."

Could there really be more than one way to kiss a man's feet, I wondered.

I would learn there was.

I looked into the mirror.

The slave, I knew, is the most seductive and desirable of women.

How can free women compete with her? The free man may find the free woman of interest, for example, in matters of family, position, power, and wealth, but is it not the despised, meaningless slave to whom he turns for pleasure?

Is it not the slave which his biological heritage demands?

I sensed the power of the slave.

Can we not drive men mad with pleasure?

I considered the brand. What jewel, what ring, what necklace, I wondered, has the free woman, to compete with that?

But consider the slave.

Consider her plight.

She is owned.

She well understands that she is property. The collar is hers, the whip is his. Is it any wonder she is concerned to be found pleasing?

Too, if she need not fear the competition of the free woman, she must fear that of other slaves. What if she is found lacking? Will she not be thrown into the market, and another purchased?

Are not animals such as she cheap?

"Keep me, Master!" she begs. But perhaps he is tired of her. Perhaps he now wants another. She has failed, failed to be such that he would never think of selling her. So back to the block with her!

She pleads, but she is slave, and he master.

I had wondered if it is not the slave which the male's

biological heritage demands. But, if this were so, I asked myself, it seems unlikely such a thing could exist in isolation, as some sort of biological anomaly. What then of the female, what then of the woman? Might there not be then, as well, something which is demanded there, or longed for there, by the woman, a consequence of her own biological heritage? If the male's heritage demands the slave, might not the heritage of the woman demand, or long for, the master?

Are there not genetic insistencies which whisper about our hearts?

At this point in my training I thought mostly of the male, learning how to be appealing to him, learning how to please him, and such.

This is surely comprehensible.

I had felt the Gorean slave whip.

I did not, at the time, understandably enough, sense what might be done to the slave, what might be done with me.

I had needs, of course, but little more was involved, at first, than curiosity and uneasiness. When I was a girl I did not even comprehend, nor was I informed, as to the nature of the changes in my body, changes which were preparing me for men. Much of this, in the beginning, was little more than an unfocused restlessness. I felt stirrings within me into which I was not to inquire. It was not appropriate for a woman to do so. If they existed, they were to be, at best, sources of dismay and regret. Did not I, and my acquaintances, laud our superiority to such things, in effect competing with one another in our alleged frigidities? To be sure, at least from high school on, I was alarmed at intrusive thoughts, thoughts so unlike me, so improper for me, which I tried to dismiss, and, too, by incomprehensible dreams for which there could be no possible explanation, dreams in which I found myself in chains, dreams in which I found myself in the arms of masters. Certainly I was taught to suspect and fear certain embarrassing suspicions and promptings. Such were not suitable for one of my sex and class. These suspicions and promptings, such thoughts, were not only incompatible with my dignity and self-respect, but incompatible with the conventions and proprieties in terms of which my life was to be managed. Indeed, for years I had been

taught to ignore my needs, to minimize them, to conceal them,
to suppress them, even deny them. I must pretend to others that
I was untroubled by such things, which were only to be found, if
at all, in the lowest and most despicable of women. I feared I, in
my discomforts and afflictions, might be unique amongst other
young women of my acquaintance. Surely they were superior to
such embarrassing weaknesses. Or were they lying to me, as I
was lying to them?

From whence, to one of my intelligence, education, refinement,
class, and breeding, could come such thoughts?

I thought of the history of a race.

Somewhere within me could there be a weeping slave,
yearning for her master?

In any event, in my early weeks on Gor I was startled at the
openness of my instructresses, eagerly discussing the attractions
of the guards, the pleasures derived from their attentions, their
joyful helplessness in the arms of one or another, their hopes,
sometimes pathetic, of being summoned to this slave ring or
that, their misery at being ignored, their plaintive agony if
denied, for more than a day or two, a man's touch.

Indeed, I saw one crawl on her belly to a guard, place his foot
on her head, and beg to be caressed.

I understood little of this, at least on a fully conscious level,
though I do not doubt but what I understood it well enough
on a deeper level, but I did not think it wise to question the
instructresses.

But at the same time I began to feel, in my own belly, ever
more insistent sensations.

This was internal to me, not merely a pretence or calculation,
designed to avoid the whip's fiery, encircling coils.

It was also very troubling to me.

It is hard, of course, to pretend to indifference in certain
matters when one is barefoot, collared, and clad in the brief rag
of a slave.

The slave's very condition is imbued with sensuality.

To merely look upon her is to see her as sensuous.

What is the very meaning of her collar, her condition, and
tunic? Does it not say, "Here Masters, behold, here is a female

slave. She exists for your pleasure. She is a property. She is
yours. Do with her as you will."

She is the most needful, the most helpless, the most sexual
of women.

"You will learn to obey, will you not, Allison?" inquired one
of my instructresses, early in my training.

"I have already learned, Mistress," I said. I had felt the slave
whip of Gor.

"Intelligent women," said another, "learn swiftly to obey."

"It takes stupid women a little longer," said another.

"But only a little longer," laughed another.

"And why do you obey, Allison?" asked the first instructress.

"Because I am a slave, Mistress," I said.

"You are terrified not to obey?" asked one.

"Yes, Mistress," I said.

"You do not wish to be punished?"

"No, Mistress," I said. Surely that was an excellent reason. I
was not a free woman. If I were not pleasing, I must expect to be
punished, properly and appropriately, and often immediately.

"You think of punishment," said one of the instructresses,
"in terms of the switch, the whip, close chains, the denial of
clothing, the affixing of a collar with points, a reduction in
rations, being sent naked into the streets, being denied speech,
being put in the modality of the she-tarsk, such things?"

"Yes, Mistress," I said, shuddering. To be sure, I had only
heard about some of these things.

"I will tell you of another punishment," she said, "one you
will not even understand now."

"Mistress?" I said.

"You have sexual needs, do you not?" she said.

"Must I speak?" I said.

"Yes," she said.

"—I suppose so," I said.

One of the instructresses laughed.

I was annoyed that she had laughed.

"Later," said the instructress who had laughed, "you will not
be in any doubt about the matter."

"Yes," I said. "I have sexual needs." I was oddly relieved
to have said this. Indeed, it was the first time I had explicitly

acknowledged this, aloud, before others. I felt an unusual sense of liberation, of freedom, having said this. To be sure, there was no doubt, on Gor, about this matter. My condition, my treatment, my training, my collar, my tunic, my brand, doubtless played some role in an awakening within my body that I sensed, day by day, was becoming ever more obvious and irresistible. I knew, too, of course, that I was not permitted to lie, as I was a slave.

"Your slave fires," said one of the instructresses, "have not yet been lit."

"If you think you are helpless now," said another, "wait until that occurs."

"You do not yet suspect the power that men will have over you," said another.

"I do not understand," I said.

"It will occur sooner or later," said another.

"And from the look of your flanks," said another, "I think it will occur sooner."

"The time will come, Allison," said the first instructress, "when you will want to obey."

"You will be the prisoner and victim of your needs," said another. "You will do anything to have them satisfied, if only for the time, before they again rage within your belly."

"You will beg, grovel, and plead to be caressed," said another.

"As the slave you are," said another.

I found this hard to believe.

Could a woman be so reduced, rendered so needful, so helpless, transformed into so vulnerable and despicable an object, little more than an animal in heat?

Perhaps, I thought to myself, in fear, if she is a slave.

"Some slaves, many slaves," said another of the instructresses, wistfully, "fall in love with their masters."

"It is hard to be at the feet of a man, and be mastered, and not do so," said another of the instructresses, "particularly if he should show you some kindness."

"To be sure," said another of the instructresses, "the slave is not to be loved, as she is worthless, no more than an animal."

"Love is for free persons, companions," said another, "not for animals and their masters."

"Men fear to care for a slave," said another. "Consider how their friends will laugh and make sport of them."

"The girl will soon again be on the block," said another.

"If you should love your master, Allison," said another, "it would be wise for you to conceal your feelings."

"I will never love a master," I said. I was derived from a class of women who did not think in terms of love, but in terms of advancement, in terms of practicality, in terms of position, station, prospects, power, and wealth. What was a woman's beauty for, if not to obtain advantages in a competitive marriage market? This was why Eve, Jane, and I were so terrified that we might be expelled from our sorority. That would have been socially calamitous. The sorority stood as one important step, among several, to a splendid future.

But how could I hope for such a future now, as I was on another world, a collared slave?

Tears sprang into my eyes.

And yet I suspected that a life lay before me, with all its unknowns and perils, which was a thousand times more real than the structured banalities and tediums to which I had been taught to aspire.

"What do you think of this room, Allison?" asked one of the instructresses, one morning, midway in my training. We had paused before an opened door on our way to our usual training room. "What is it for?" I asked. "It is called the Room of White-Silk," said an instructress. "What is it for?" I asked. One of the instructresses laughed. There was not much in the room. A ring, or two, some chains, a trestle or two, and a number of deep, heaped, rich furs. It was certainly not as alarming as certain of the discipline rooms I had seen, with their devices and cages.

It was toward the end of my training, the few days of my training, that I was summoned by my instructresses to one of the training rooms. "Stand," said one of them. "As a slave," said another. "Please no," I said. "Now," said another. So I stood as a slave. "She still must learn to stand appropriately," said another. "Do not fear, Allison," said another. "It will soon be natural for you." "Already," said another, "perhaps unknown to yourself, you are beginning to stand, and move, and kneel, and carry yourself, with the loveliness and grace of a slave, with her subtlety, her lack of pretense, her softness, her deference, her awareness of what she is, her profound and vulnerable, and helpless, femininity."

How terrible, I thought, to be feminine!

"Yes," said another. "She is becoming feminine."

"A slave," said another.

"Yes," said the first.

What was being done to me?

I suspected I was being released, to be myself, not an awkward, clumsy neuter, or a prescribed, facsimile male, but a natural woman in a natural world.

Surely I must resist!

But why, I asked myself. Why should I not be what I truly am?

Because it was frowned upon, or forbidden?

But here, on this world, such things were not frowned upon or forbidden. Here on this world, was I not free, though collared, to be myself?

"First obeisance position!" snapped one of the instructresses.

Swiftly I knelt, my head to the floor, the palms of my hands on the floor, at the sides of my head.

"You are changing, pretty Allison," said an instructress.

"A transformation is being wrought in you, shapely barbarian," said another.

"Are you aware of this, Allison?" asked another.

"No, Mistress," I said. Then, by means of a shadow, I saw a switch lifted. "Perhaps, Mistress!" I sobbed. "Perhaps, Mistress!"

To my relief, the switch was lowered.

"She perhaps does not understand how she is changing," said one of the instructresses.

I feared I was beginning to understand, only too well. The instructresses, of course, could be aware only of attitudes, postures, behaviors, speech, and such. On the other hand, it was becoming clear to me that these externalities, as profound as they might be, were no longer the simple result of intent and design, but were now beginning to emerge as the inevitable consequence of internal realities. My behavior, I sensed, was now becoming less the imitation of a slave's behavior; and more the behavior of a slave.

"Do not be concerned, Allison," said the first instructress. "There is nothing wrong with being graceful, beautiful, vulnerable, soft, passionate, and wholly, wholly female."

"In short," said another, "in being a slave."

"Her transition is well underway," said another.

"Men like women as women," said one of the instructresses.

"And do we not like men as men?" asked another.

"True," laughed another.

"Much of this you do not understand now," said one of the instructresses, "but in time it will become clear."

"Changes are being wrought in you," said another, "that will become part of you, and improve your price on the block, how you move, smile, turn your head, and such."

"You will not even be aware of these things," said another.

"But one can tell a slave by such things," said another.

"Sometimes guardsmen do so," said another, uneasily. "Sometimes they simply command a woman to walk before them, back and forth, and thus detect the slave, even within the robes of a free woman."

"Barbarians, such as you," said another, "are even easier to detect, apart from the marks often placed on your upper arm, or the tiny bits of metal often found in your teeth. You do not know the drapings, the foldings, the layerings, and fastenings of the robes of concealment, the arrangement of the veils, and such."

"There is much more to such things than the donning of a tunic or a camisk," said one of the instructresses.

"Does Mistress know of such things?" I asked.

"Once," she smiled. "But I would not now trade my tunic for the robes of a Ubara."

I could not understand this.

Was not a Ubara a free woman, and one of consequence?

"There are a thousand things a native Gorean would know, of which a barbarian would be ignorant," said an instructress.

"Too," said another, "the Gorean taught to barbarians is often subtly different from that spoken by native Goreans, for example, in the pronunciation of certain words."

"Have you taught me such a subtly different Gorean?" I asked.

"Curiosity," she said, "is not becoming in a kajira."

"Yes, Mistress," I said.

"I wish we had more time to train her," said one of the instructresses.

"Mistress?" I said.

"Market conditions change, orders vary, what is wanted at one time is not wanted at another time, what sold yesterday may not sell today, what sells today may not sell tomorrow."

"I do not understand," I said.

"You are a virgin, are you not?" asked one of the instructresses.

"Yes, Mistress," I said.

"You do not look like a virgin," said one.

"Most do not," said an instructress.

"True," said another.

"Unbeknownst to you," said an instructress, "you have been observed by masters."

"Yes, Mistress," I said. I had not known this, but, surely, I had suspected as much. Would they not observe me, with certain ends in view?

"You have much to gain in attractiveness," said one of the instructresses.

"I do not understand, Mistress," I said. "Am I not beautiful?"

"Her slave fires have not yet been lit," said one of the instructresses.

"Being beautiful and being attractive are not the same thing," said an instructress. "Some extremely beautiful women are not attractive, and some extremely attractive women are not beautiful."

"But I am attractive, am I not?" I asked.

"Do you wish to be attractive?" asked an instructress.

"Do not all women?" I asked. I knew that even cold women, and women who professed to hate men, wanted to be found attractive, if only to torment men, or further their own ends.

"Of course," said an instructress.

"Am I not attractive?" I asked.

"You are attractive," said an instructress. "Otherwise you would not be in your collar. But the masters feel that your current attractiveness does not measure up to your beauty."

My head was at the floor. I had not received permission to lift it.

"Doubtless, in time, it will do so," said an instructress. "We have great hopes for you. You are clearly a born slave. And, eventually, you should be an exquisitely desirable slave."

"Her slave fires have not yet been lit," said one of the instructresses, again.

"Kneel up," said an instructress.

Gratefully I knelt up.

"Belly in, shoulders back, head up," said an instructress.

I complied.

My knees were clenched closely together.

I kept my eyes straight ahead.

"What are you doing, Mistress?" I asked.

"I am removing the white ribbon," she said.

"Mistress?" I asked.

The instructresses were about, looking at me.

"What do you think?" asked one of the instructresses.

"She is pretty," said one.

"Better than a kettle girl, or a pot-and-mat girl," said another.

"A Tarnster, or Drover," speculated another.

"If the price were right," said another.

"Spread your knees, Allison," said an instructress.

"Surely not, Mistress!" I exclaimed.

"Now," she said.

I felt enormously vulnerable, and, oddly, subtly enflamed.

How could I, the former Allison Ashton-Baker be placed in such a position?

What sort of slave would kneel in such a position?

I feared I knew.

She who had removed the white ribbon now approached.

"Do not move, Allison," she said.

I saw that in her hand she had a different ribbon, a red ribbon.

"I am not red-silk!" I said. "I am not red-silk!"

"Do not move," she said, again.

"Yes, Mistress," I said, a slave, commanded.

I was very much aware of the position and attitude in which I had been placed.

To be sure, it could not be appropriate for me.

It must be some mistake.

I was from Earth.

It is strange, how, when one is a slave, small things are

noticed, the nap of a rug, the feel of tiles beneath one's knees, one's body then so alive.

I regarded the instructress, apprehensively.

The red ribbon, of dyed rep-cloth, not silk, was doubled, and then threaded under and over my collar. Its loose ends were then threaded through the loop, and I felt it jerked tight, against the collar.

"There," said the instructress, and stood up. She and the others then stood back, a bit, looking at me. "What do you think?" she asked. "Is she satisfactory, will men like her?"

"She may do," said another.

"Sooner or later," said another.

I did not understand. Had I not been one of the most beautiful girls in my sorority, a sorority noted on campus for its beauties? Certainly I had not lacked for the attentions of young men. A week would not pass without my declining several offers for outings, afternoons or evenings, with such, while I would select from amongst such offers those few which I deemed suitable, those which might prove eventually to be to my advantage, those from suitably positioned young men, young men worth interesting and cultivating, young men whose background and assets exceeded my own. Oddly, though I had pretended to be interested in them, laughed at their jokes, and such, I had seldom received a second invitation from them. I did not understand this. Did they not realize my quality, the honor I paid to them, how fortunate they were, that I would permit them to share my company, however briefly? Surely there were many who would have rejoiced to be granted such an opportunity. How ungrateful, how foolish, how stupid they were!

"Keep those knees split, slave," said one of the instructresses.

"Yes, Mistress," I whispered.

"Wider," snapped another.

"Yes, Mistress," I said.

At least no man was present, to see me so. What would he think, should he see me so? Did I not know? Would it not be clear what I was, and what I was for?

How vulnerable a woman is in such a position!

Too, I felt decidedly uneasy.

I squirmed.

"Steady," said an instructress.

"She is heating," said another.

"Mistress?" I said.

"The little tart is cooking," said another.

"Wait until she knows what a man's touch is," said another.

"She is ready, nearly ready," said another.

"I do not understand," I said.

"She has nice slave curves," said one.

"She has the flanks of a slave who will heat well," said another.

"Mistress," I said.

"Yes?" said the instructress who had placed the ribbon.

"Mistress has erred," I said. "I am not red-silk."

"Who speaks?" asked an instructress.

"Allison," I said. "This slave speaks." I felt tears form in my eyes.

"And what has she to say?" asked an instructress.

"She says," I said, "that she is not red-silk, that she is white-silk."

"The slave is correct," said an instructress.

"Yes," said she who had placed the ribbon.

"Please then, Mistress," I said, "replace the white ribbon."

"It is dirty, grimy," said the first instructress, she who had placed the ribbon. "Surely you do not want such a ribbon on your collar?"

"Perhaps another ribbon then," I said.

"You have another ribbon now," she said.

"A white ribbon," I said, "another white ribbon!"

"No," she said.

"Put back the old ribbon then," I said. "It is all right. I do not mind!"

"It goes to another girl," she said, "one who is white-silk."

"I am white-silk!" I said.

"What are you afraid of?" she asked.

"The men, the guards," I said. "They may think me red-silk!"

"The market," said an instructress, "is now slow for white-silks."

"I do not understand," I said.

"Do you not think you have been white-silk long enough?" asked an instructress.

"Mistress?" I said.

"Oh!" I cried, startled, for something of cloth and leather, enclosing, muchly opaque, was pulled over my head, from behind, by one of the instructresses. I heard it buckled shut, and the sound of a tiny padlock being snapped shut, doubtless linking two rings.

"Steady, steady!" warned an instructress.

"Position!" snapped another.

And then I knelt, as I had before, in position, hooded.

"Should we remove her garment?" asked an instructress.

"The men will do that," said another.

"Stand up, Allison," said the first instructress, gently. I felt her hand on my upper left arm. I was then being guided from the training room, and turned left, and, in a moment, I felt the smooth, worn, flat tiles of the corridor beneath my bare feet. We made two further turnings, and then we stopped.

"Here," said the first instructress.

I heard a door opened, and I was conducted within, and released, some feet within the portal.

Where was I?

"Mistresses!" I pleaded. "Mistresses!"

I heard the door shut, and, from the outside, a bar put in place.

"Mistresses!" I cried.

I stood in the room, perhaps near its center, alone, hooded, frightened, disoriented.

"Mistresses! Mistresses!"

I turned, and felt my way, hands extended, stumbling, toward the door, which was heavy, and shut, and locked, barred on the outside.

I pounded on the door, and cried out, again and again, but, if any heard, none responded.

I attempted to tear the hood from my head, but such are not meant to be removed by such as I.

I, fearing to fall, went to all fours, that I might explore my small world. In short order, I felt a carpet, and then furs, and cushions. Such things seemed luxurious, and abundant. Here and there, too, I felt chains, and wrist and ankle rings. At one side of the room, I reached up, and, bit by bit, felt the structure of a heavy, low, sturdy trestle.

I tore futilely at the hood.

I was in the Room of White-Silk.

"Do you not think you have been white-silk long enough?" had asked an instructress.

I trembled. I heard a soft moan, mine.

Helpless, and hooded, I realized what I was here for, what was to be done to me.

I lay on the cushions alone, for a time.

I supposed the guards, some of them, perhaps some who had noted me, or were curious about me, would visit me, when convenient, perhaps with the turn of the watch, when their duties were done.

I am not sure how long I lay alone in the room, hooded, amidst the cushions and furs.

Bars rang, and midbars.

I was tunicked. I did not know if the tunic would be left to me. It might be. It is a simple thing for a master to thrust up the short skirt of the tunic, to the slave's waist. I wondered if they would be quick.

I clutched at a silken coverlet.

My fingers clenched it.

I dared not cover myself.

The masters might not be pleased.

They might wish to look upon my legs, my ankles, my arms, my throat.

Accordingly, I dared not cover myself.

I knew that a slave is usually expected, on a couch, on a slave mat, on furs, to wait naked, wholly uncovered, for her master.

Tunicked, one is already half naked.

I would not cover myself.

How long must I wait, alone?

Then I seemed suddenly to awaken.

The door had been opened.

I knew they would not talk to me. I must not realize who they were. It is better that way. Awareness is better reserved for a master.

I struggled to my feet.

I sensed there were several in the room.

They must have brought lanterns or lamps. I heard the fire strikers snap more than once. Too, I heard some tiny sounds, some suggesting the placing of lamps on shelves, others the hanging of lanterns on ceiling hooks. I sensed men looking at me, and moving about me. They said nothing. There would not be a great deal of illumination, but it would be soft, and ample, that of lamps and lanterns, two or three, I supposed.

"Masters?" I said.

I was not answered.

I felt my left ankle grasped, and I stiffened. A shackle was closed about it. Some loops of chain were thrown down, beside me. I gathered there was a good length of chain between the shackle and its ring. I do not know why I was shackled. Perhaps because I was a slave, and it was thought fit that I be shackled. I wondered if, later, the wrist rings and ankle rings would be used. I supposed that the length of chain allowed me would not be sufficient to allow me to reach the door, which might now be unbarred. I wondered if others, guards, passing by, might enter.

I knew little of how free women were handled. Perhaps much depends on the caste, or city. I had never encountered a Gorean free woman in any meaningful way, though, from time to time, one had visited the house. At such a time, if one were near, we must kneel in first obeisance position, head to the floor. I had been aware of little more than the almost inaudible sound of a soft slipper on the tiles, a rustle of silks passing me. My knowledge of free women was limited almost entirely to the hints, and gossip, of instructresses, which I had overheard. I gathered that there was little love lost between the slave and the free woman.

I sensed the men standing there, about me.

I did not know if I should kneel, or not.

Should I assume obeisance position, first obeisance position, kneeling, head to the tiles, hands to floor, perhaps second obeisance position, belly to the floor, palms down, beside my head, where one might reach inch forth, to press one's lips to his feet?

How slave I felt, waiting.

I wondered how free women were handled, or if they were handled, so to speak, at all.

Gorean men, I knew, preferred slaves.

That is the way, I gathered, with men.

They prefer us, slaves.

I sensed myself scrutinized.

I was aware of light, dimly, on my right, through the hood. A lamp or lantern was lifted near me. I felt a warmth on my right shoulder. That would be from the lamp or lantern.

I would be in the light.

I knew that men liked to see their slaves.

They delighted in each nuance, and inch, of them.

In the house I had grown accustomed to being regarded openly, and appraisingly, by the guards. How different it was from Earth! There was nothing secret, quick, shy, sly, or furtive about it. We were regarded with the innocence and interest that one might regard an animal, and, in the case of the female slave, an animal which one might consider owning, and having at one's slave ring. At first I had been considerably disturbed at the frankness, the openness, the length, of such assessments, particularly if commanded, turned about, and posed, but of course, a slave, I dared not complain, nor evince, in any way, any objection to such detailed, candid perusals, even handlings. I had no wish to be cuffed, or beaten. This was not Earth, in which a battery of social and legal weaponry might be invoked against any fellow so unwary as to dare to look honestly, openly, frankly, naturally, on a woman.

I, of course, might be so looked upon, certainly here, on this world, on Gor, as I was an animal, a slave.

I was not a free woman, a person, a citizen, the possessor of a Home Stone. I was not a proud creature of dignity and station. I was not the sort of woman who was to be treated with esteem and respect, even awe, to whom would be accorded the many honors befitting her position. I was not veiled in public, that men might not look upon my beauty. I was not wrapped in the lengthy, ornate folds of the Robes of Concealment, that the lineaments of my figure should not betray the delicate canons of modesty, or no more so than might provoke inevitable speculation. I was not encircled with conventions and formalities; I was not one for whom strong men were to step deferently aside, who might be carried in a palanquin, for whom ways were to be cleared, one who was expected, I gathered, at least if of high caste, to speak boldly, even sharply, and with haughty contempt, one expected to hold oneself, and move, in stately disdain, one mighty in presence and power. I had gathered from the instructresses that such women, certainly those of high caste, of such exalted nobility, so taken with themselves, commonly prided themselves on their self-containment, their self-control, their freedom from many human weaknesses, their superiority to many of the elements commonly found in the nature of the female. In particular, many felt they must, as persons, view themselves as above a variety of allegedly lower, or baser, considerations. Accordingly, they would compete with one another, it seems, each attempting to outdo the other with respect to their imperviousness to the liabilities commonly associated with a lower nature, an animal nature. Many, I gathered, particularly of high caste, held themselves superior to sex, which they professed to find demeaning. It is difficult, I supposed, to regard oneself as an equal to, or a superior of, a male when one is smaller, softer, and weaker, and finds oneself clasped in the arms of such a beast, helpless, unable to free oneself, its prisoner, one's softness clasped forcibly, mercilessly, to its hardness, the beast beside itself in its rage of possession and joy. And how unfree then should she feel herself if she sensed what it might be, so held, to be owned and mastered? How she must resist her body, her dispositions, her inclinations, her desires, her emotions, her feelings, lest they betray her, lest they threaten treason to her dignity and personhood. Accordingly, it was said that amongst many free women the taint of carnality was to be eschewed, even violently, as a thing of embarrassment and shame, unworthy of a free woman. One's slave is to be denied, hysterically, if necessary. To acknowledge her, is it not to acknowledge that one should be suitably collared, that one is already, so to speak, in the collar. Accordingly, when the society's demands were to be met, and the more embarrassing, regrettable aspects of companionship satisfied, those having to do with matchings, lines, alliances, and such, the proper free woman was to enter into carnal congress with disdain, resignation, and reluctance, or feigned disdain, resignation, and reluctance, insisting, at least, that such lamentable congress be as brief as possible, and take place in complete dark ess, preferably while substantially clothed, and surely beneath coverlets. To be sure, theory and profession were one thing, and reality another. Upper-caste women doubtless were subject to the same needs and drives as other women, and I would learn that affairs and assignations were not infrequent amongst them, and that many free women, particularly those most sensitive to the demands of their codes, who had most internalized society's expectations with respect to their behavior, often lived a life of frustration, loneliness, and misery, speaking the secrets of their needs only to the silence of damp, tear-stained pillows. Demands on lower-caste women, on the other hand, were less, as befitted their inferior status, and such women were more likely to enjoy a life of open flirtation, even of comparative vulgarity and bawdiness. Indeed, it was often thought that lower-caste women, for all their jollity and looseness, or perhaps in virtue of it, commonly tended to live a more genuinely satisfactory life than their sisters of the higher, nobler castes. To be sure, much depends on the particular woman, the caste, the city, and sometimes, I understand, even the neighborhood or district within the city, as a Gorean city, as many cities, often contains a medley of subcultures. I had encountered something of these distinctions on Earth, and even in the sorority, in which we had tended to pride ourselves on our station, our aloofness, and, in a sense, our frigidity. "No man will ever turn me into something like that," I had heard, "some gasping, whimpering, squirming, moaning, begging plaything!" I had taken her seriously until I had inadvertently come upon her in one of the house's bedrooms, late, during a party, naked, on her knees before a male, his belt wrapped and buckled about her neck, her hands tied behind her with a stocking, leaning forward, kissing at his legs, begging to be touched again. She had turned about, seeing me, tears in her eyes, frightened, agonized, discovered. I had turned away. Oddly, I did not feel dismayed at what I had seen. Rather, as I hurried back to the party I found myself wondering if a woman did not belong at a man's feet, and if I, Allison, did not belong at a man's feet, the feet of some man, or, perhaps any man. I assured her the next day I would keep her secret. She had graduated the following spring.

I stood very still.

The men were about me.

I could sense the light of the lamp through the hood.

There is a joke that in the light of a lamp even a free woman is beautiful.

And I was not a free woman.

I was such that I had been selected for the collar of Gor.

I knew that we were hated by free women.

I knew that men preferred slaves.

"Masters?" I said.

There was no response.

"It is a mistake, Masters," I said. "I should not be here. I am white-silk. I am white-silk."

The tunic was then torn from me.

Chapter Eight

It was two days after my red-silking that I was again hooded. I was aligned with other girls, I supposed some five or six. My wrists were pulled behind me and I was back-braceleted. I had not been permitted clothing after my red-silking. The ribbon, however, was removed from my collar. It is the common presumption that a female slave is "red-silk." My head was forced up, and the house collar, now a new house collar, submitting to a bolt and key, was thrust up, under my chin. This new house collar was quite different from the original house collar in which I had been placed, the high, heavy, iron collar, which had been hammered about my neck. That had been removed in the house's metal shop the morning following my red-silking. I was much pleased to be relieved of the original collar. The new collar was not the light, lovely, secure embondment signification of the common collar but it was a considerable improvement over its high, weighty predecessor. The removal of the original collar suggested that my sale might be imminent. This speculation had proved to be warranted. One role of the original collar was presumably to encourage a girl to do well in her lessons, that she may the sooner be brought to the block. Would such a collar not be likely to produce such an effect? Should it not make one eager to escape the house? Yet I, personally, feared to leave the house, as I knew not what might be found for one such as I outside its walls. In the house there was a certain comfort, and security. One supposes that a girl might be left uncollared, of course, between the conclusion of her training and her departure from the house, as she is marked, and in the house, and her escape

is unthinkable, but Goreans, it seems, do not see it so. They feel
that a kajira should be in a collar, and know herself collared. It
helps her to keep in mind that she is a slave. Too, a kajira soon
comes to understand that it is appropriate for her to be collared,
that she belongs in a collar. Is she not a slave? Too, without a
collar, she might feel naked, insecure, and frightened. What
terrible things might happen to her, were she to be mistaken for
a free woman! I then felt another collar, a coffle collar, for one
could sense the weight of the attendant chain, a light chain, for
we were women, snapped about my neck. The house collar was
then removed.

"What is happening, Masters?" I asked, in the coffle, back-
braceleted, unable to see, for the hood.

My question received in response only the sharp sting of a
switch on my right shoulder.

I realized, then, as I should have before, that I should be
silent. Had I been given permission to speak? Too, is it not said
that curiosity is not becoming in a kajira?

When we began to move we began our climb to higher levels
of the house, and this continued so, for some Ehn. I heard us
pass through some four gates, and, from the sound of it, from
the weight on the hinges, two heavy portals, and then, after the
second portal, the last, I suddenly felt the fresh air, and wind,
of what must be the streets, and I sensed the warmth of the sun,
Tor-tu-Gor, on my body. We were out of the house!

"Surely you know what you are doing here," an instructress
once said to me.

"Mistress?" I had said.

"You are a slave, are you not?" she asked.

"Yes, Mistress," I had said.

"And only a slave?" she said.

"Yes, Mistress," I said, "only a slave."

"And what is a slave?" she asked.

"Mistress?" I asked.

"A property," she said. "Goods, merchandise."

"Yes, Mistress," I said.

"So now you surely know what you are doing here?" she said.

"I am being trained," I said.

"For what?" she said.

"That I may be pleasing to a master," I said.

"We would like you to live past your first night at his slave ring," she said.

"I will try to be pleasing," I said.

"Very pleasing?"

"Yes, Mistress!"

"Wholly pleasing, in every way?" she said.

"To the best of my ability," I said.

"So, then," she said, "what are you doing here?"

"Mistress?"

"You are goods, merchandise," she said.

"Yes," I said, "I am goods, merchandise." It was true; that is what I now was.

"So now you understand what you are doing here," she said.

"Mistress?" I said.

"You are being readied for sale," she said.

I well knew myself a slave, of course. I had sensed this even on Earth, and there was obviously no doubt about it here, on Gor. Here I might or might not wish to be a slave, but, in either case, it was what I was. Here my will was nothing. Whether I might kiss my fingertips and press them to my collar, or sob and scream, and try to tear it from my neck, it was on me. And my thigh was marked, with the Kef, the most common slave brand on Gor, a mark which showed all who might look upon it what I was, and only was, kajira. Still I had not thought, actively, or very actively, of being sold.

Now, as I was being marched through streets I could not see, naked, back-braceleted, a bead fastened in this small slaver's necklace, the wind and sunlight on my bared body, I knew I was being taken, for the first time, to market, a market where I would not buy but be bought, as much as a verr, or a basket of suls.

Still I was delighted to be out of the house.

I wondered who might buy me.

I was soon to be owned, the property of a particular master.

"I regret," had said one of the mistresses, "that we did not have more time to train you."

"You are pretty," said another, "and you will do your best to please, will you not?"

"Yes, Mistress," I said.

"Many men do not object to a half-trained girl," said another. "They are cheaper, and they may train them to their taste."

"There are others coming in," said another, "who must be prepared."

"A city fell," said another.

"You are a barbarian, Allison," said another, "and barbarians are apt pupils, as they are already three-quarters slaves, but the new arrivals will be former Gorean free women."

"I see," I said.

"How we will love to have them under our switches," said another.

"We will teach them that they are now slaves," said another.

It was hard for me to imagine such women as slaves, from what I had heard of them, but I knew, too, that there were few bred slaves, at least in the sense of being the products of the slave farms. The overwhelming majority of female slaves on Gor would have once been Gorean free women, of one caste or another. Too, Gorean free women, whatever might be the expectations of their society concerning them, were surely women, with all the instincts, needs, desires, and drives of the human female, all the complex genetic codings of such latent in each cell of their bodies. And I had heard guards exchanging remarks, after the passage of one free woman or another in the house, perhaps shopping for a serving slave, or a silk slave, speculating on her possible value on the block. It was just as well our exalted visitors had remained oblivious of such conversations. Within the robes of concealment, it seems, following the views of the guards, there was always a slave, lacking only the collar.

"The slave, Allison," I said, "thanks Mistresses for the training they have given her."

They had kissed me, and, shortly thereafter, one of the guards arrived, the hood dangling in his hand.

We continued to make our way through the streets.

At that time, hooded, I did not realize the striking beauty of a Gorean city, how so many of its buildings, the lofty towers and graceful bridges, the spacious porticoes, the splendid colonnades, and such, were bright with color, nor was I aware of the wealth of colors in clothing, both that of men and women. I did realize, of course, from the house, that slave tunics came in a variety of cuts and colors, in samples of which I had been forced to pose before mirrors, but each was commonly of one color. They were, after all, slave tunics. The house tunics, incidentally, those worn in the house, were commonly drab, usually being brown or gray. There are fashions in such things, of course, for both the free and the slaves, with respect to colors, textures, materials, cuts, hemlines, and so on. How and when fashions changed, and why they changed, was not clear. Doubtless there were setters of trends, say, highly placed officials, wealthy Merchants, Actors, Singers, and Poets, certain women of noble family and high caste, and such, but why should one option rather than another succeed in being adopted, however transiently? Perhaps the higher, better fixed, more established or influential members of the Cloth Workers had something to do with it, with hints, with words dropped now and then, with boulevard posters, with some judiciously distributed free garmenture, here and there, and so on. Doubtless each time a fashion changed at least the high Cloth Workers, masters of the foremost garment houses, would sell more garmenture, at least to the fashion conscious, to those who were concerned to keep up with the times, to those who feared to be pitied or ridiculed for being out of style, and such. With respect to slave tunics, for example, it was several years, apparently, since the common slave tunic was white with black striping, usually with a diagonal striping. And, of course, if masters and mistresses might be concerned with the garmenture of their kajirae, as simple and brief, and as revealing and demeaning, as it might be, one can well imagine their concern with their own garmenture, particularly if they were of high caste.

The coffle chain was a girl chain, and, accordingly, light. Nonetheless it would hold us, its prisoners, in a perfect, neck-linked custody. This is not unusual, incidentally, the lightness. The custodial hardware of Gor, where kajirae are concerned, is commonly light. It is also, of course, strong, or strong enough, at least, to well exceed the strength of women. It is also, commonly, graceful, even lovely, and is designed to set off and enhance the beauty of its prisoner, while putting her wholly at the mercy of the free. She is, after all, a slave. Its usual purpose, then, is not merely to hold the lovely prisoner but to make it clear to any observer, casual or otherwise, that she is powerless, vulnerable, defenseless, and unprotected, accordingly, not merely to confine her, but to expose her, or should one say, in the case of a slave, as she is goods, to display her. For example, the slave bracelets we wore, which pinioned our wrists so helplessly behind our backs, were attractive. One might have mistaken them for ornaments or jewelry, were it not for the inflexible metal links which joined them.

I have wondered sometimes if free women do not sometimes wonder what it would be to find themselves in such "ornaments" or "jewelry," stripped and helpless within them.

Did they realize that they might be that beautiful?

Perhaps an iron is being heated, and a collar has already been removed from its peg.

It is common, incidentally, to fasten a girl's hands behind her back. In that way she is more helpless, her arms nicely drawn back, and her beauty, obviously, is better exhibited, more exposed to sight and touch. Too, of course, braceleted as she is, she is incapable of fending away or resisting caresses, even if she, unwisely, should wish to do so. I did not know my place in the coffle, other than the fact that I was neither first nor last, for I could feel the weight of the coffle chain on both the front and back ring of the coffle collar. It was the only collar I now wore. When I had been aligned in the house, awaiting my chaining, I had been hooded. Therefore I was not only ignorant of the number of girls in the coffle, but of the construction of the coffle, as well. Sometimes the most beautiful girl is first on the coffle, sometimes last. Sometimes the coffle is arranged merely in order of height, the tallest girl then placed first.

Interestingly, as I was hooded, I was very little self-conscious in this march. Had I not been hooded I would have been terribly, miserably, self-conscious. Naked slaves are sometimes seen in the streets but that is usually only the case with a new girl or one being punished. Clothing, of course, is at the discretion of the master, whether or not it is to be permitted, and, if so, its nature, whether say, a modest tunic, or a camisk, or slave strip. A new girl, sent into the streets naked, is well apprised of her bondage, and may soon be depended upon to be at her master's feet, zealous to improve her performance and service a thousandfold, that she may be granted a garment, some garment, even the brief, disgraceful tunic of a slave, perhaps hitherto scorned. We are, as it is said, not permitted modesty, no more than a she-sleen or she-tarsk, but we will do much for a garment, however scanty. So much we are in the power of our masters! As I could not see, interestingly, I was concerned very little that I might be seen. Too, I was with others, as bared and helpless as I. In the hood, and with others, I had a sense of anonymity.

By now, I was sure we had been in the streets for at least twenty Ehn. Even coffled we must have been marched for better than a pasang. We had, so far, as far as I could tell, attracted no particular attention. I gathered then that such sights, a coffle of nude slaves, were not uncommon in the streets. Not uncommon, too, might be a line of roped verr, a string of tethered kaiila, or such. Our house was on the Street of Brands but, as I was given to understand, this is more a reference to a district or a part of a district than an actual street. To be sure, apparently several slave houses were in the same vicinity. One also heard of a Street of Coins, of which a similar observation would seem warranted. This, too, seemed to refer more to a particular district, than a particular street, one in which several money houses were to be found. In passing, I will note something of interest, at least to a barbarian. On your world pieces of paper, even with impressive printing on them, are seldom accepted in exchange for actual goods. The Gorean thinks generally in terms of metal, copper, silver, and gold, something obdurate and solid, which can be handled, split, quartered, shaved, and weighed, or else in terms of actual goods. It would be dangerous to try to buy a sleen or slave, or a sul or larma, from a Gorean for no more than a piece of paper. On the other hand, notes are exchanged amongst various coin houses, or banking houses, without difficulty. Sometimes the wealth of a city has been transferred from Jad to Ar, or Ar to Jad, in the form of a piece of paper, sewn into the lining of a robe. In such a way wealth can be exchanged, even back and forth, without a tarsk-bit changing hands.

We continued our march.

We did not know our destination, or destinations. Would you explain such things to sleen or kaiila?

I did note that the footing was now less smooth, less polished, more irregular. Too, more than once I felt dampness, or grime. In this part of the city, wherever it was, it seemed the shopkeepers, or residents, were less scrupulous in their housekeeping. It is understood that the streets in a Gorean city, local bridges, and such, are the responsibility of those in the neighborhood, not of the city or state. The responsibilities of the city and state tend to be limited, mostly to protection, civil and municipal, and arbitration. Whereas a city will often have a coinage, so, too, may private citizens. For example, the golden tarn disk of the banker Publius may be more valuable than that of Ar itself, or, at least, that of the Ar of the occupation, when someone named Talena graced the throne of Ar. Charity, care of the simple, the needy, and such, is handled privately, usually by clan lines, or caste councils. As the city or state is managed by men, and is armed, it is feared. Goreans prefer to be governed as little as possible. The city or state, on the other hand, which has properties, farms, and such, as well as it support from taxes, often supports public festivals, concerts, performances, and contests, competitions, for example, of strength, speed of foot, archery, javelin casting, riding, singing, drama, poetry, dancing, and such.

I occasionally heard men and women about. Conversation. Some bargaining. One fellow was hawking tastas, which is a confection, mounted on a stick. Sometimes female slaves are referred to as tastas.

I could hear the chain on its rings as we moved.

I felt myself prodded by a switch.

In many respects I did not know where I was, not only the district in which I might be, but even the city. I was sure, from the size of the house in which I had been trained, the city was large, at least by Gorean standards. It would take a large city with a substantial commerce to support a house so complex and impressive. I would learn it was Ar. Even were I familiar with the city, which I was not, I would have been thoroughly disoriented given the hood and the many twists and turns of the narrow streets. I was sure, of course, from my secret reading, that I was on Gor. I was still shaken by the comprehension that such a world actually existed. On it I found myself hooded, naked, and coffled, a slave. How could such a world exist and not be known, or, I thought, is it known? Perhaps it is known, but as a guarded secret, official or governmental, to be kept from the general public? Is it the will of the Priest-Kings, the alleged lords of this world, I wondered, that the existence of their world be known or not? Were the Gorean manuscripts intended to be hints of Gor, allusions to that world, a modality by means of which possibly alarming facts, facts for which a general population might not be ready, might be concealed under the veil of fiction? Or were such manuscripts somehow dangerously smuggled to Earth, against the will of, and without the consent of, Priest-Kings? I supposed, on balance, the existence of such manuscripts did not concern entities as mighty and mysterious as the supposed Priest-Kings. Doubtless they knew of them, but thought little of them one way or another. What difference might such thing make to them, the remote and disengaged gods of a world? But I now, at least, was in no doubt as to the reality of Gor. I felt it beneath my bared feet. I twisted my head a bit inside the hood I wore. I could not see. I was helpless. I jerked a little at the bracelets which held my hands behind my back. I, once Allison Ashton-Baker, once a member of a prestigious, wealthy sorority at an exclusive educational institution on the planet Earth, once a scion of the envied upper classes on my world, was helpless, and on Gor, a manacled, hooded, coffled slave!

"Oh!" I cried, suddenly pelted with gravel.

"Kajirae, kajirae!" I heard, a sing-song, mocking chanting of children. "Kajirae, kajirae!" Small stones, stinging, one after another, apparently from almost at my elbow, were hurled against me, and, from the disturbance in the coffle, the rattle of chain, and cries of surprise and pain, I knew I was not the only victim of this petty aggression. "Kajirae, kajirae!" they mocked, running beside us, now on each side. I cried out with pain, struck by a supple, barkless branch, a child's makeshift switch. I heard the sound of such implements strike elsewhere, as well. "Please, no, Masters!" cried out more than one member of the coffle. They had addressed the word 'Masters' to children! Then I realized the children were doubtless free persons. "Please be kind, please be kind, Masters!" I wept, stung twice again. "Be off with you," said one of the guards to our young assailants. "If you would beat a slave, buy your own!" There was laughter, from adults about. We tried to hurry, stumbling on. "Do not gaze upon such worthless, disgusting things!" I heard a woman's voice say, perhaps admonishing a daughter, a child, one paused to look upon the coffle. Then we were beyond the children.

We continued on.

My body still stung.

The coffle was stopped, twice, before discharging one or more of its occupants, once when, apparently, a line of wagons was passing near us. They were probably produce wagons. We were pressed to the side, against a wall to our left. Some such wagons are driven by teamsters, others are conducted by small boys, with sticks. In the better part of the city such wagons move only at night, when they are less obstructive of traffic. I heard the creaking of wheels, their sound on the stones, and some grunting, and snorting, apparently of large beasts. These were draft tharlarion as I now realize, but I had not, at the time, seen such animals. Most Gorean streets are narrow, winding, and crooked. The boulevards, on the other hand, are spacious and straight, often with plantings. Many Gorean streets have no names, really, other than, say, the street of the "smithy of Marcus," the alley "where Decius the cobbler has his shop," and so on. The streets are familiar, of course, to those who live in their vicinity. Others may inquire their way, or fee a guide. The second time we were stopped we were ordered to the side, and ordered to kneel, our heads to the stones. The palanquin of a free woman was passing. It stopped. Perhaps the free woman had parted the curtains of the palanquin for a moment, to regard us. The palanquin then moved on.

"Up, beasts," we heard.

We struggled to our feet.

We continued on, for another twenty Ehn, or so.

In what district of the city might we be?

I was sure we had passed through more than one.

My Gorean was acute enough, now, to detect some differences in accents. The local diction, with its lapses, and grammar, and vulgarities, its rapidities, its simplicities, its contractions, its elisions, unusual words, and vulgarities, was quite other than that of my instructresses, intelligent women who uniformly spoke, as nearly as I could determine, an educated, excellent Gorean. Four had supposedly attained to the "Second Knowledge," whatever that was. All could write. I had some difficulty in even understanding the speech about me. I would learn that some members of some castes even reveled in a deliberately barbarous or vulgar Gorean, as though this were some badge of quality or superiority by means of which they might distinguish themselves from their despised "betters." It was sometimes said that the power of Marlenus, the Ubar himself, rested ultimately on the lower castes, whom he cultivated and flattered. Is it not, ultimately, in the mass that the power lies? Who else, at a word, might swarm into the streets, armed with paving stones and clubs? Woe to the former free Gorean woman of high caste who, enslaved, might fall into the power of her hitherto despised "inferiors." Each Gorean caste, interestingly, regards itself as equal to, or superior to, all other castes. Accordingly, each member of each caste is likely to have his caste pride. In some sense this doubtless contributes to social stability, and, surely, it tends to make the average fellow content with his own person, profession, background, antecedents, and such. He respects himself, and these things. Even the Peasants, commonly regarded as the lowest of castes, regards itself proudly, and with justification, as "the ox on which the Home Stone rests." A casteless society, an open society, in which elevation, wealth, and success is supposed to depend, or does depend, on the outcome of merit and free competition will obviously generate an enormous amount of frustration, jealousy, envy, and hostility. In such a society most will fail to fulfill their ambitions and must almost inevitably fall short of achieving at least the greatest rewards and highest honors which such a society has to bestow. In an open race to which all are invited and in which all are free to run there will be only one winner, and many losers. It is natural then for the loser to blame not himself but the course, the starter, the conditions, the judge, the rules of the race, even that there is a race, at all.

The free woman of a high caste and the free woman of a lower caste commonly have one thing in common which unites them, securely, as free women. That is their contempt of, and hatred for, the female slave.

How strange they find it that men should prefer the helpless female slave, lovely, obedient, needful, desperate to please, to themselves!

How could such a thing be?

But it seems that it might be.

Do the free men not attend the auctions, do they not scout the exposition cages, do they not saunter to the gates, to witness the arriving coffles, to see the former free women of another city being marched naked to local markets, do they not want a shapely collar slut trembling at their slave ring, do they not frequent the paga taverns, and surely not always for conversation or kaissa. How detestable, think the free women, are slaves! How horrifying to want to be owned, to want to belong to a man, wholly, and desire to love and serve him, forever, abjectly, and unquestioningly, to the best of one's ability! And how terrible men are that they should unaccountably prefer a cringing collar beauty, perhaps shackled, desperate to please them wholly, and as a female, to one of their own kind, forward, noble, splendid, proud, and free. What is so special about their terrified, groveling rival, licking and kissing at her master's feet, with her marked thigh, and band-encircled throat? What could she, a slave, an animal, possibly have, or offer, that might begin to compete with the accorded favor of a free woman, standing on her dignity, and jealous of her rights? Why then, given such clear options, between the noble and the worthy, and the despicable and the meaningless, will men seek the despicable and the meaningless, the slave? Why then will they seek so zealously to leash and bracelet her, the slave, to rope her, hand and foot, to kneel her, to collar her? Why will they bid so zealously, and recklessly, to purchase her? Why do they fight to possess such things? Why are they willing to kill for them?

I cried out in sudden sharp pain. I knew the stroke. It was across my right shoulder. I had felt it often enough when I had displeased the instructresses, or made some error in diction, serving, position, or such. It was the result of a blow not from some child's makeshift implement, a plaything, a pretended disciplinary device, but from an actual device of the sort his diversion mimicked, a supple, nicely crafted leather switch, an instrument designed to improve the discipline and service of a female slave. We most fear the whip but it is not pleasant, either, I assure you, to feel the corrective blow of the switch.

We will do much to please our masters!

"Sluts!" I heard, a woman's angry voice. "Sluts! Sluts!"

I heard the sound of more blows, cries of pain.

"Wriggle to that!" screamed the woman. "Jump to the pleasure of that, you filthy sluts!"

"Please forgive us, Mistress!" cried a member of the coffle. But this plea, I gathered, did no more than earn its source another two or three blows.

I had been informed by the instructresses that free women were to be feared. If accosted by one, particularly if accosted unpleasantly, it is wise not only to kneel, as before a man, to ascertain his interests, intentions, or wishes, perhaps he wishes directions, or such, but to put one's head to her feet, to, in effect, assume first obeisance position. In no way, either by word, tone of voice, act, expression, or attitude is one to show the least disrespect. The slightest suggestion of such a thing may result in severe and prolonged punishment. The woman is free, while one is a slave.

"She-tarsks!" cried the woman. "She-tarsks! She-tarsks!"

I heard the sound of more blows, cries of pain.

"Oh!" I wept, struck as well.

"Let them alone," said a man.

"There are better things to do with little vulos than beat them," said a fellow.

"Yes," cried the woman. "You would know about that!"

"Mercy, Mistress!" begged one of the slaves. "Oh!" she cried, struck.

I was silent. I sensed the figure pass me.

Some fellow off to my right began to sing a little song about "Tastas."

"Be silent!" screamed the woman.

"Demetrius will be home soon," said a fellow, reassuringly.

I and one or two others were then struck again. I bent over, as I could, for the chain, cringing.

"Move the chain," said someone to the side. "Move the chain." There was laughter.

"Give me back the switch!" screamed the woman. "Give me back the switch!"

"Move the chain!" a fellow urged, again.

"Step!" said one of the guards, and, gratefully, we moved forward.

"Give me the switch!" demanded the woman, now behind us. We hurried forward, as we could.

I remembered a remark from one of the instructresses. I had not been more than two days in the house. "Be beautiful, and desirable," she had said. "It is the men who will protect you."

"Please the men," said another. "It is the men to whom you will belong."

"They will protect you from the women," said another.

"If you are pleasing," added another.

I was frightened from what I had heard of free women. I resolved to be pleasing to the men, as pleasing as I could be, and I understood what that meant, to be as pleasing as one could, and as a slave.

Soon the coffle was stopped, and, apparently, one individual was removed from it. We then continued on our way

I shortly became aware that another was removed from the coffle. We were apparently being delivered to different addresses. Some of the girls might have been purchased within the house. Usually a girl is sold in-house when the price offered seems clearly superior to what might be expected from vending her off an open block. Too, such a sale requires few arrangements, and little time. Sometimes, too, the capture and enslavement of a woman has been arranged by an enemy or admirer, and, in such a case, it is usually that particular woman that is wanted. She may have been paid for in advance, the price having been earlier negotiated and agreed upon. There is little difficulty in delivering such women through the streets, as they are hooded. Rich men, to whom money is of less interest than what it might purchase, sometimes buy in-house, putting out three or four times what a girl might bring in the open market. But most on the coffle, I supposed, and perhaps all, were being delivered to local markets, some possibly owned by the house itself.

As girls were removed from the coffle, their chaining, with the bracelets and coffle collars, was hung about the neck and shoulders of others. In the vicinity of the Tenth Ahn, as I guessed, I was alone, several loops of chaining, and such, slung about me or wrapped about my body. This was not pleasant, but, too, it was not much of a burden, as the chain was light, being girl chain. We were quite helpless in such bonds, but a man, it seemed, or some men, might have been able to pull apart such links. This is a way in which a woman may begin to understand that she is not a man. The sexes are quite different, and on Gor such picayune details have their role in helping to make the distinction clear. One is suitably master; one is suitably slave.

I was stopped by a hand on my shoulder.

I was also aware that the chaining which I was carrying was being unlooped, and unwound, from my body.

I gathered I was at my destination, wherever it might be. I did not inquire, of course. I did not wish to be struck. I had not been given permission to speak.

There had been two guards with the coffle.

One or both must now carry the chaining and such back to the house.

In the beginning, hooded, I did not know the number of beads on the small necklace. Counting their removal, and adding myself, there had been six.

I felt the coffle collar removed.

I stood there.

Now I was only hooded, and back-braceleted.

I felt a man's hand on my left arm. "There are steps here, kajira," he said. He then guided me, carefully, and assisted me up some five or six steps, onto a circular platform, cement, it seemed, but covered with a carpet, or heavy cloth, and then to the left. I heard a gate open, I would see later it was one of bars, and was conducted through it. Within he removed his hand from my arm, and I stood still. I stood on cement. The bracelets were removed.

"You have the papers?" a voice asked.

"Here," said the guard.

I heard a movement of papers.

"Barbarian," said the first voice.

"Yes," said the guard.

"Is she any good," asked the first voice.

"I do not know," said the guard. "I have not put her to slave use."

"I see she is red-silk," said the first voice. That, I thought, must be on the papers. What right had they to know that?

"Recently," said the guard.

"Good," said the first voice. "There is no place for virgins here."

I heard feminine laughter, from a few feet away.

On the whole, they had not been unkind to me in the Room of White-Silk. I had been handled with authority, of course, and was left in no doubt that I was within the grasp of masters, Gorean masters. I was not sure how many, as I had been hooded, had utilized me for slave pleasure, as some may have done so more than once. It was done to me in various ways. I was not freed of the ankle shackle until they were finished with me, and left, and the instructresses summoned, to unhood me and conduct me to my new domicile, a small, iron cage. I had occupied that cage, at night, until this morning, and my hooding and coffling. The cushions and furs in the Room of White-Silk had been deep. Occasionally the wrist and ankle rings were used, perhaps to accustom me to helpless slave service. I could still remember the feel of the heavy bar of the trestle against my belly. Toward the end, when I was half drunk, lost between confusion and disbelief, with the shocking and flooding of my belly, scarcely able to feel, I was thrown to the cushions and, for a time, left alone.

"Masters?" I said.

Were they done with me?

I was aware of blood on my thigh.

Some of it had been thrust to my lips, and into my mouth, that I might taste my virgin blood, which could be shed but once.

"Masters?" I whispered. Were they still in the room?

Strong hands put me on my back, over the cushions, my head back, and down. My ankles were pulled apart, widely. I left them as they had been placed. I supposed I was again to be put to use, routine, meaningless, forcible use.

I waited.

I did not know how many times it had been done to me. Then I felt a gentle, soft, moist, caressing touch, and I cried out, startled, drew my legs together, as I could, and reached out, and felt my fingers close in a man's hair.

"Oh," I said, softly.

Surely such a caress would never be inflicted on a free woman. It would be disgracefully inappropriate to subject a free woman to such an indignity. It might pull them out of themselves, and make them beg for the collar. It was not for free women. It was fit only for slaves.

"Please, Master," I whispered. "Again!"

"Oh, yes!" I whispered, my fingers in his hair.

At least, I thought, I was not chained helplessly in place. It was hard to imagine what might be the sensations which a master might inflict, even casually, upon a helpless slave, one wholly at his mercy, their subtlety, their variety, their length, and nature.

How helpless she would be, so in his power!

I feared to be so chained. I wanted to be so chained!

How many ways a man has to conquer a woman I thought, the chain, the whip, the switch, the commanding her to her knees, her lips to his feet, a gesture, admitting no questioning, the casting to her of a rag, fit only for a slave, the ordering of her to her tasks, the masterful seizure of her beauty, a kind word, a caress!

"More, more, more, Master!" I begged. "Yes," I whispered. "Yes, Master!"

Well now was I aware of how I might have responded had they been concerned less to routinely open a young slave and had they been more patient, slower, less merciful. What if they had been tortuously slow, reading my body, playing upon it, as on a czehar or kalika, bringing forth what music they wished? Could I help what I was, female, and slave? A thousand modalities attend the mastership, and the slave learns a thousand yieldings, and submissions. She may be seized, and put to use in any place, at any time, in any way. She may be used abruptly, and cast aside, and rejoices to have been granted even so much. Does this not inform her, to her delight, that she is a slave? This thrills her that she is such, only slave, that she may be so used. And she may be utilized at length, should he wish, for Ahn at a time. The master may put aside days for slave sport, mastering her in a hundred ways at his leisure. She learns the blindfold, the gag, ropes, wrapped silken cords, thongs, bracelets, and chains. She learns to bring the master the whip in her teeth, crawling to him, on all fours. She cooks, and sews, launders and cleans, and he may observe her at her lowly, servile tasks, until he summons her to his arms, that she may attend to her truest task, the pleasing and pleasuring of her master. She will bathe him, and he may comb her hair. Her garmenture, if she be granted such, depends upon his will. He may dress her and undress her, considering how she may best be displayed. He is concerned with her appearance. In the promenades she must look well on her leash. Perhaps he will have her taught the kalika, or dance, dance such as is appropriate for such as she, slave dance.

"Please, more, Master!" I begged.

Had I been capable of wondering, on Earth, if I were a slave, a rightful slave, a slave by nature? How foolish now seemed such abstract, idle ruminations! It was now confirmed upon me, that I, the former Allison Ashton-Baker, was a slave, and not only by law, however absolute that legal shackle might be, but by right, by nature! Not only was I slave, but I needed to be a slave!

"Master?" I asked, within the hood, the light of a lamp dimly sensed through the closed, buckled artifact.

I lifted my belly, pathetically, piteously, shamelessly, in the darkness.

"Masters?" I said.

But they were gone.

Later the instructresses came to free me of the shackle, and conduct me from the room. They did not ask me anything. I was left alone with my thoughts.

I stood now, hands free, but hooded, on the cement flooring of what I supposed to be a holding area, or cell, of some sort.

There were some about, at least two men, and some women.

I tried to stand proudly.

I was chagrined with how I had behaved, particularly later, in the Room of White-Silk.

I resolved that I must never again behave as might have a slave.

I must never again let myself be so shamed.

I found it hard to believe that I had begged. How shameful! Happily that lapse would remain a secret of the house. I resolved that that indiscretion must never be repeated.

But even in my righteous self-castigations, which I, of Earth, deemed I should proclaim, at least to myself, and even behind the fragile curtain of that resolve which I thought to interpose between what I supposed I should be and what I suspected I was, there seemed a subtle, elusive whispering, mocking and insistent, kajira, kajira. Then I stood less proudly, and lowered my head. Already, in the scarlet swirl of memory, rising and falling like some warm fluid, I was uneasy. In my belly were clear stirrings. Had I not sensed the beginning of such things, even before my red-silking? Does not being barefoot, tunicked, and collared have its effect, in knowing that one, so degraded, is a slave? What was going on in my body? How was I changing? What had been done to me? I remembered the arms of the guards, so strong about me, I so weak in their grasp. And I remembered those last, brief sensations, casually bestowed on a slave, so unexpected, so different, so startling, so irresistible, which I had so wanted to have prolonged, which I had piteously begged might be continued. Something within me knew, or suspected, that such things might be not only riches in themselves, exquisite and transformative, but were, as well, the promise, the hint, of something beyond them, the explosions and creations of worlds.

What right had I, I asked myself, to arrogate to myself the prerogatives and prides of the free woman?

And the slave, I reminded myself, does not belong to herself. She belongs to her master. She has no self to defend, no honor to preserve, no person to strive to keep isolated and inviolate.

I am not a free woman, I thought.

In a sense, I have never been one.

I was not free.

I did not want to be free.

I was content to be a shamed slave. It was what I was and wanted to be. Then I was no longer chagrined at my behavior in the Room of White-Silk. I regretted only that I might not have been as pleasing as possible to the masters.

Too, I had begun to suspect what I might become, and was willing to become, and wanted to become, in their arms, a slave.

The hood was removed, and I drew in a deep breath, and shut my eyes against the hurtful light.

Some cloth was thrust against me, and I took it.

Blinking, clutching the cloth, I looked about myself.

I was in a cell, a relatively small cell, about eight feet square, with a wall of bars on one side, facing a street. The floor of the cell was some four feet above the level of the street. In this way what was in the cell, given the bars, could be easily viewed from the street. To the left of the bars was a cement platform, at the same level as the floor of the cell, too, about four feet high, on which was spread a worn, soiled scarlet rug. There were steps on the outside leading up to this circular, cement platform, the steps which I had doubtless recently ascended, assisted by the guard. The guards had gone. A barred gate, to the left of the cell, would open to a small passage, which connected with the platform. It was through this passage that I had been introduced into the cell.

I looked about. There were six other girls in the cell. I looked up at a large man, stripped to the waist, who was regarding me.

He would be a slaver's man.

I clutched the cloth.

Each of the girls wore a brief, wrap-around tunic, and each had, either about herself, or at hand, a short, white sheet.

What I held was such a tunic, and such a sheet.

"She is stupid," laughed one of the girls.

I did not know what to do.

I desperately wanted to clothe myself. Now that I was not hooded, I was suddenly muchly aware of my nudity. I stood there in anguish. I did not have even a collar. What if someone should look into the cell, from the outside? I was, of course, well marked.

"How stupid," said another girl.

"She is a barbarian," said another.

"May I clothe myself, Master?" I asked.

"Yes," he said, and turned away. In a moment he had left the cell, closing and locking the gate behind him.

I had remembered, belatedly, that a slave may not clothe herself without permission. Most slaves, of course, have a standing permission to clothe themselves, a permission which is subject to revocation by the master. It is a bit like speech. A slave is not to speak without permission, but many have a standing permission to speak, a permission which may, of course, be revoked at any time. For those who might be interested in such matters, the standing permission to clothe oneself is more often granted than the standing permission to speak. There are few things more likely to convince a woman of her bondage than the need to request permission to speak. Sometimes a standing permission to speak is revoked for a few Ahn or a day, or even a week, that she may be the better conscious that permission is required, and need not be granted. Perhaps she is desperate to speak. "May I speak, Master?" "No," she is informed. She is then well reminded of her collar and mark.

I glanced through the bars, out to the street. There were men, and women, here and there, passing, and, at some stalls, shopping, these on the other side of the street, but none seemed interested in the cell, or its occupants.

I quickly, gratefully, drew the brief, wrap-around tunic about me, tucking it in on the side. It occurred to me how simply it might be parted, and removed. I then clutched the sheet about me. It came midway to my thighs.

The bars were sturdy, some six inches apart, reinforced every ten horts or so by horizontally placed, flat, narrow plates of ironwork. The cell would have held men.

That made me feel particularly helpless.

I looked out, through the bars. Save for the bars the wall was open. It was easy to look out, into the street. And I was very much aware, as well, obviously, that it would be as easy to look within. Anyone outside might simply look within, and see us. Given the shape of the cell, there was nowhere to hide. I was suddenly reminded of a shop window on Earth, a window before which passers-by might stop, and, at their leisure, peruse what might be for sale.

And I, and the others, would be for sale!

I looked to the other occupants, the other merchandise, six girls, in the cell. Each was in a wrap-around tunic. Four were

113

brunets, and two blondes, one a darker blond, one lighter. None
were collared. But I had no doubt each was well marked. Gorean
merchants do not neglect such details.

I folded the sheet, and put it about my shoulders. I was
tunicked, and the tunic, while "slave short," was not unusual. A
girl would not be likely to expect more, unless she were a lady's
serving slave.

I went to the bars, grasped them, and looked out.

I was not pleased with what I saw. This could be no high
market. One might as well have been chained on a slave shelf!

Surely a mistake had been made.

This was not a market in which such as I was to be sold. This
was surely not the Curulean, a market of which I had been
apprised, a palace of an emporium with its statues, carvings,
columns, fountains, tapestries, and cushioned tiers, with its
exposition cages of silver bars, with its great, torch-lit, golden
auditorium which might hold more than two thousand buyers,
with its great central block, with its height and dignity, from
which might be expertly vended even the stripped daughters of
Ubars. I looked about. The slaver's man was nowhere in sight. I
must complain. I must call their attention to their mistake.

I thought of calling out, but thought the better of it.

What if there had been no mistake?

I had been the last on the coffle to be delivered.

I had dared to suppose then that I was the best, that saved for
last. But what if I had been saved for last, as I had been thought
not the best, but the least? Could it be that others might regard
me as less beautiful, less desirable, than I regarded myself? Was
I less beautiful, less desirable, than I had thought? Surely I had
been regarded as one of the most beautiful girls in my sorority!
But, of course, we had never been put beside Gorean slaves. I
did not know my ranking in the coffle, nor if I had a ranking in
the coffle. I had no idea of the quality of the coffle as I had been
hooded.

I looked about.

"What do they call you?" asked one of the girls, one of the
brunettes.

"Allison," I said.

"You are a barbarian," said one of the girls.

"I am from Earth," I said.

"Where is Earth?" she asked.

"It is far away," I said.

"Barbarians are ugly, and stupid," said the darker blonde.

"I am neither ugly nor stupid," I said.

"If she were ugly and stupid," said another of the brunettes, "she would not have been put under the iron, she would not be here, she would not be kajira." I could not place her accent.

"She has skinny legs," said another of the brunettes.

"No," said the brunette, she with the unusual accent, "they are shapely and slender. Many men like that."

"Well," said the first brunette, "they are well exposed."

"True," said the girl with the accent, "and it goes nicely with her height."

I was not especially tall. I was of medium height. Nora was taller than I. So, too, was Jane. I had been a bit taller than Eve. I was pleased to hear that my legs might be acceptable to a man. Some doubtless bought with such things in mind.

"I do not want to be sold with a barbarian," said the light blonde. "It is humiliating."

"I would rather be sold with a barbarian than with you, traitress!" snarled the darker blonde.

"I was high in the Merchants!" said the light blonde.

"And you are now yourself merchandise," laughed one of the brunettes.

Tears brightened the eyes of the light blonde.

"You are fortunate to be such," said another of the brunettes. "You misread your politics. You thought Ar irrecoverably fallen. You betrayed your Home Stone, as much as Talena of Ar or Flavia of Ar. You cast your lot with the occupation, abetting their crimes, conniving with the enemy, flattering officers, feasting and jesting, profiteering, exploiting a starving citizenry, battening on the misery of a confused, leaderless, beaten, subdued populace."

"One must do what one can! One must look out for one's self!" wept the light blonde.

"You did not know Marlenus would return," said one of the brunettes, unpleasantly.

"None did," said another.

"I am not a slave," wept the light blonde. "I am the Lady Persinna, high in the Merchants, the Lady Persinna of Four Towers!"

One of the brunettes laughed. "Listen to the branded piece of collar meat," she said.

"No!" said the former Lady Persinna.

"You are now only goods, goods, slut," said one of the brunettes.

"No! No!" said the former Lady Persinna.

"And you are fortunate to be goods," said the darker blonde. "You were on the proscription lists. You should have been impaled!"

"Perhaps you were saved because you had pretty flanks," said one of the brunettes.

"Perhaps," said another, "because someone wanted you at his slave ring."

She who had been the former Lady Persinna paled. Perhaps she knew of someone of which such a suggestion might be true.

I understood little of this at the time, but it became clearer later. Before I had been brought to Gor it seems a revolution had taken place in the city, Ar, in which upheaval an occupying force deriving from, or given fee by, the island ubarates of Cos and Tyros, and perhaps other states, had been ejected. It seems that a former Ubar, one named Marlenus, had returned from banishment or exile, or some prolonged absence, had rallied the city, and, in several days of fierce and bloody fighting, had cast out the invaders. Even while war was waged in the streets proscription lists had been posted and many traitors, profiteers, and such, hundreds, were seized by maddened citizens and publicly impaled. Later, the invaders flighted and the blood lust of an outraged citizenry largely spent, numbers of surviving profiteers and collaborators, as apprehended, were placed in several underground dungeons scattered throughout the city. Many were later executed by impalement, but others were embonded, men usually destined to the quarries or galleys, and women remanded to slave houses.

"It must be near the Tenth Ahn," said a brunette.

I supposed that so. There were few shadows in the street. So what did it matter, if it were near the Tenth Ahn, noon?

Was that, in some way, important?

One girl, one of the brunettes, went to stand near the bars, sideways, fingering her hair. I saw her smile at a fellow, who seemed scarcely to notice, and did not stop from his way. She tossed her head, annoyed. Her sheet was at her ankles. Another girl stood at the bars, her hands over her head, holding to the bars, her sheet about her shoulders. Her hands might have been fastened there. She had her right cheek pressed against a bar. Another girl, one of the brunettes, now sat a bit back from the bars, her head up and back, leaning back on her hands, her knees slightly bent, her legs extended. Then she would sit differently, her knees drawn up, her hands clasped about them, looking out, between the bars. Her sheet was beside her. The dark blonde now reclined back, a few feet from the bars, on one elbow, on her sheet, her legs partly extended, one more than the other, looking out. She did this in such a way that the view of her between the bars would not be much obstructed by the positions of the other girls. It seemed she would not be much interested in what might lie outside the bars. What was that to her? Her attention seemed casual, at best. I suddenly recalled that I had been taught that pose. It is languid, but seductive. It lifts the hip nicely, in such a way that the hip-waist curve is nicely emphasized, this drawing attention to the promising delights of her love cradle.

I, and two others, were now at the back of the cell, by the rear cement wall. I and the brunette who had spoken for me were standing. To my right, kneeling, was the light blonde, a lovely female, the former Lady Persinna, of the Merchants. I supposed someone would be glad to get his hands on her. She seemed to be trying to make herself small. She was frightened. I, too, was frightened. The brunette with us, too, seemed frightened.

I gathered that this might have something to do with the approach of the Tenth Ahn.

"Look at them," whispered the former Lady Persinna, regarding the others, the other three brunettes, and the dark blonde, all nearer the wall of bars. "See them! See them, the disgusting sluts!"

"They are slaves," said the brunette with us.

"Disgusting sluts!" said the former Lady Persinna.

"You, too, are a slave," said the brunette.

"No," said the blonde. "I am free, a free woman! I am the Lady Persinna, of the Merchants, of Four Towers."

"If you wish to obtain a good master," said the brunette, "perhaps you, too, should strive to present yourself well, subtly, of course."

"No, no!" said the blonde.

"You are not so presenting yourself," I observed.

"No," said the brunette. "I am afraid."

"I, too, am afraid," I said.

"I do not want to be sold," she said.

"Nor I," I said.

Yet what else might we expect, as we were slaves?

My feelings concerning my bondage, at that time, as you may have surmised, were highly ambivalent. I was frightened to be a slave. Did it not hold its terrors, to be a property, to be owned! Yet I knew myself a woman who should be a property, who should be owned! I knew that I was a slave, and should be a slave. My entire Earth conditioning had informed me that I should lament my bondage, that I should regard it as a condition of unmitigated misery and woe. But I knew in my heart this was far from so. I could not, and would not, speak for all women, but I could speak for myself. And why should I allow others to speak for me, to tell me how I should feel, to decide how I should be? I was a female. I wanted to belong to a man, a master, wholly and unconditionally, to be his in the fullest sense that a female can belong to a man, as his rightless slave. Nothing short of this could fulfill the secret needs of my heart. But now, to my terror, on this world, it was done. I was a slave! I would be subject to a collar, and bonds, the rightless chattel of a master! The sense of this was devastating and overwhelming. And I would have nothing to say as to my disposition. This frightened me, alarmed me, terribly, but, too, as I waited with the others, in the cell, filled with a slave's anxiety and apprehension, knowing she may soon be sold, I felt an unspeakable thrill. And then, again, I was terrified! Here, on this world, I was only a slave!

"They cannot sell me, they cannot sell me," said the former Lady Persinna.

"You are mistaken," said the brunette.

"Your accent is not like that of the others," I said to the brunette.

"I am of the islands, from Tabor," she said.

"A tabor is a drum," I said.

"It is from the shape of the island," she said. "I and others were taken at sea, by corsairs of Port Kar, not more than five pasangs from shore."

"They were bold," I said.

"They were of Port Kar," she said.

I knew little of Gor. I had heard of Port Kar. It was well to the north and west, where the waterways of the Vosk's delta drained into the Tamber Gulf, the city's sea walls fronting the gulf on the south, Thassa, the sea, on the west. Was it not from the sea gates of Port Kar that the galleys of the dreaded Bosk, Bosk of Port Kar, clove the dark waters of restless Thassa?

"At least," she said, "I was not sold in Port Kar."

It is said the chains of a slave girl are heaviest in Port Kar.

"You must have been sold, several times," I said.

"From one slaver to another," she said, "not like this."

"It is my understanding that none here are virgins," I said.

"Perhaps the Lady Persinna," she said.

"No," said the light blonde, bitterly. "I was first opened in a dungeon, where I lay chained in the darkness."

"No time was wasted with me, or the others," said the brunette. "We were first used on the deck of the corsair itself."

I shuddered.

"What of you?" she asked.

"In a slave house," I said, "recently, in a room set aside for the red-silking of virgin slaves."

"How was it?" she asked.

I was silent.

"I see," she said.

"Beasts gather," said the light blonde.

I looked out. Some men had approached the circular cement platform to the left of the cell, four or five.

I saw there were tears in the eyes of the brunette. "Who will own me?" she asked.

The brunette who had been seated, her chin on her clasped,

raised knees, now rose to her feet and stretched, lifting her hands over her head, and arching her back.

"The slut!" whispered the former Lady Persinna.

Two or three more men had now joined the few near the platform.

"It is near the Tenth Ahn, I am sure," said the brunette with us.

The girl who was to the left, at the bars, put her hair back, about her shoulders, and then pressed a bit, softly, against the bars.

That, I supposed, the softness against the iron, the helplessness of the softness, confined, and such, would excite a fellow. She was a confined female, who would be for sale. In my training I had been chained from time to time, in one way or another, utterly helplessly, perfectly, by guards. It was clear my helplessness stimulated them. And I am sure that they, Goreans, realized that my vulnerability, my utter helplessness, stimulated me, as well. There are, after all, masters, and there are slaves.

There were now four slaves, the three brunettes and the dark blonde, at the bars. Three were standing, and one kneeling, one of the brunettes, who was clutching the bars.

There were now some ten or eleven men outside the bars. They were close. I was reminded of visitors at a zoo, peering through the bars. The analogy was imperfect, of course, as we were for sale. A better analogy would doubtless be a sales kennel.

One of the fellows reached through the bar and seized a brunette's ankle. "Oh!" she protested, trying to draw back, but she could not free herself of the grip. He then released her, grinning.

"Buy me first, Master," she said.

There was laughter.

They are flirting, I thought, all of them. And is not flirting, I thought, even on my former world, an act of display, hinting, alluding, presenting oneself as something vivacious, attractive, sparkling, as something of interest, something worth investigating, and acquiring, an object of desire? I had muchly enjoyed such games, the suggesting, the teasing, the luring, the playing with the feelings of men, the sensing of the power of my beauty and its effect on them, how it could arouse, disturb, excite, and torment them, and then, when weary of the sport, the pleasure one could take in the chilling, the turning away, the feigned surprise and indignation. How I had despised the boys. How pleasant it was to make them suffer. But now I was a slave, and would probably belong to a man, one who might exact from me, at a mere snapping of fingers, everything that a frightened, docile slave might give. I did remember occasions when it was I who had been rebuffed. How that had stung! Did they think I was unworthy of them, because they were richer, of a better-known, more-distinguished family, or such? How I hated them! I did not think, really, on the other hand, that they were that immune to my charm, my beauty, and such. Now, I supposed, if they might recall me, and find me of some interest, they might buy me, and hide me from their wives.

"See them!" said the former Lady Persinna of the girls at the front of the cell, those near the bars. "Disgusting! Disgusting!"

It is a received wisdom that the higher the price for which one goes the more likely it is to obtain a richer, better-fixed master, and to find oneself in a larger, better-appointed, wealthier household where the labors are likely to be lighter and less frequent. Accordingly, it is recommended, as a prudential matter, to display oneself in one's sale as attractively as possible. There is much to be said for this, particularly when one might be sold at night, under torchlight, and one cannot well make out the buyers, save for some on the first tiers. One often hears only the calls from the darkness. Who is bidding? One might discover one's master only when one is unhooded, in a strange domicile.

It is not unknown, of course, even on my world, for a girl to barter her beauty for gain, for access to exclusive, desirable precincts, to use it in such a way that it might obtain for her advantages and advancement, to win for her wealth and position, and such. Surely I and my sisters in the sorority were well aware of such things. I certainly endeavored to apply my beauty to such purposes, if unsuccessfully, as did they. If one were to obtain our beauty, one would pay our price. We had no intention of selling ourselves cheaply. And how furious I had been when my overtures, so to speak, had been rejected, or worse, ignored.

Could they not see the value of what I was offering? On Gor, of course, to my chagrin, I realized that the profit on my beauty, if any, would accrue not to me, but to another. It is that way when one is oneself merchandise. Still, it is commonly to one's advantage, as noted, to present oneself well on the block, hoping thereby to obtain a richer master, a better house, lighter duties, and such. Yet, at times, how meaningless are these prudential, mercenary considerations! Does the slave not hope that she will be purchased by a strong, handsome, powerful, virile master, rich or not, who will know well what to do with her, before whom she will know herself well in her collar? Are we not all looking for the master who will weaken our knees and heat our thighs, the master before whom we know we can be only slave, and desire to be no more? And what, too, of the love slave and the love master? In such cases, who can understand the mysterious chemistries involved? Let us suppose that a fellow is examining women on a slave shelf. They are kneeling, cringing, shackled, head down. Who can explain how it is that he, pulling up the head of one after another, by the hair, that her features may be examined, suddenly pauses, startled. What is different about this particular cringing, shackled slave? How is she different from another? She looks up, her eyes widened. He sees before him, his hand in her hair, his love slave, and she, looking up, tears in her eyes, for the first time, sees her love master. How is she more than merely another helpless, cringing, shackled slave, and how is he more than merely another male, another possible buyer, in his robes, so free, and strong, looking down on her? But he has found his love slave, and she, to her joy, has been found by her love master. Who can explain such things? Perhaps he has been keeping a collar for just such a one? Certainly a girl can attempt to interest a buyer; consider the differential zeal of the "Buy me, Masters," as one fellow or another peruses a sales line; but, in the end, despite our efforts and hopes, we are not the buyers, but the bought. It is they who will choose, not we.

"Ah!" cried one of the slaves.

The bar had begun its sounding.

Some more men began to move toward us, gathering about the circular cement platform.

"It is the Tenth Ahn!" said the darker blonde.

There were few shadows in the street now. Tor-tu-Gor was at its zenith.

The former Lady Persinna burst into tears, and put her head in her hands. I wondered that one such as she, one apparently once of some prominence, was with us. I clutched the sheet more closely about me. I wished it was longer. My legs were not well concealed. Was it to demean her that she was put with us? Or did some estimate her beauty as equivalent to ours, worthy only of such a vending? I wondered if some might be interested in her, tracking her, informing themselves as to her market, and time of sale. I supposed that some men, for reasons other than her beauty and her promise as a slave, might be interested in obtaining her, perhaps an enemy, perhaps one reduced or ruined by her in her time of power, perhaps one she had once slighted, and did not even recall. Perhaps some lowly clerk once in her employ, mistreated, despised, scorned, and overworked, had saved some money and thought it might be pleasant to have her, once so socially and economically superior to him, chained at the foot of his couch.

I heard the second and third soundings of the bar.

Outside, approaching, I saw the slaver's man, he stripped to the waist.

The bar was struck again.

That sound would carry for better than two or three pasangs, and I could hear, in the distance, other bars, taking up the ringing.

"I do not even know where I am," I said to the girl from Tabor.

"The Metellan district," she said.

"I do not even know the city," I said, in misery. Curiosity, I recalled, was not becoming in a kajira.

"Ar, of course," said she from Tabor.

I had thought that. But why had I not been told that in the house? Was that not a simple enough thing to tell a girl?

Ar, I knew from my reading, was the largest city in the northern hemisphere of Gor. It was the center of many trade routes. I was to be sold in Ar! Given the size of the city, and its many markets, I supposed it constituted a major market.

Certainly it would be a convenient, easy place in which to sell a slave.

"What is the Metellan district?" I asked.

"Look about you," she said. "I am from Tabor."

I groaned.

The bar rang again.

"It is a shabby district," she said, "but there are many worse, worse, and more dangerous. It is not much patrolled. Many free women arrange their trysts and assignations to take place in this district. It is a popular venue for such ventures. Few questions are asked. Little, if any, attention is paid to strangers."

She was surely much better informed than I.

Perhaps her former masters had been less strict with her.

The bar sounded twice more.

Several men, now some twenty or so, perhaps more, had gathered about the circular platform.

"We will soon be on the block," said the girl from Tabor.

"That circle of cement," I said, "that is the block?"

"Of course," she said. "This is not a high market."

"Are we worth so little?" I asked.

"Ask the masters," she said.

The bar rang again.

The former Lady Persinna was weeping.

I saw a small, wiry fellow, with a straggly beard, in soiled blue and yellow robes, approaching. He wiped his mouth with a dirty sleeve. In his right hand he held an implement I recognized well. It was a switch.

"It is he who will auction us," said the girl from Tabor.

That seemed likely to me.

Certainly he wore the colors of the Slavers.

The small fellow, at the foot of the platform, conferred briefly with the slaver's man.

I did not know if the small fellow owned the market, or owned us, or both. For all I knew I was still owned by the house, and I was merely being vended through this outlet, and the small fellow might be merely a professional auctioneer, hired for each sale. I supposed, beside his fee, he might receive some sort of commission on the sales. That meant he would be likely to do his best to get a good price. It also suggested to me that he might, then, be quick with his switch.

"I will not go on that block," said the Lady Persinna, resolutely, sobbing.

"You will," the girl from Tabor assured her.

"No!" she said.

"Have you ever felt the slave whip?" asked the girl from Tabor. The former Lady Persinna paled.

"If summoned, you will hasten to the block," said the girl from Tabor. "And you will smile, pose, and perform."

"As a slave?" she moaned.

"As any slave," said the girl from Tabor.

"No, no," whispered the former Lady Persinna.

I wondered what she would bring, standing on that scarlet rug, on the platform, being displayed.

I recalled that on Earth it had been speculated that I would sell for between forty and sixty. I had supposed, at the time, that meant between forty and sixty thousand dollars. Here I conjectured that I might sell for between forty and sixty pieces of gold, or, given this market, and that I was not much trained, and was a new slave, perhaps only between forty and sixty silver tarsks.

The bar rang again, I think the ninth ring.

Would she bring more than I? I did not think so. She was a mere barbarian, a scion of a primitive culture, and I was a civilized woman of Earth, of the upper classes, young, beautiful, educated, intelligent, sensitive, well-bred, refined, now somehow inexplicably entrapped in a barbarian world, a world where I was denied the protection of the law, a world where my Earth rights were not only ignored, but did not exist. On this world I was a property. Thus, here, the law, in all its power and rigor, in all its weight and majesty, would be used not for me but against me, for example, to hunt me down and return me to a master.

"I can hardly stand," I said. "I can hardly move. I will be unable to perform, even should I try to do so."

"This is a low market," said the girl from Tabor. "They may ask little of us. We may only have to stand, and turn."

"At least," I said, "we have our tunics, the sheets."

"Now," she said.

"Now?" I said.

"Yes," she said.

I recalled that the bar had again sounded.

"The bar rang," I said. "It was the ninth ringing, the ninth stroke, was it not?"

"I think so," she said.

"What if we are not sold?" I asked.

"The masters would be displeased," she said. "It is common to whip a girl who is not sold."

"I see," I said, frightened.

"One then tries, the next time, desperately, to be sold."

I was suddenly overcome with the sense of my helplessness. I was wholly at the mercy of others. Anything could be done with me! How was it that I, a woman of Earth, was here, in a cell, on another world, with a marked thigh, caged with slaves? And how could it be that I, of Earth, was here, on this other world, also a slave, as much as they?

"I do not want to be sold!" I said.

"Do you wish to be whipped?" she asked.

"No, no!" I said.

"Then you should want to be sold," she said.

"I am afraid," I said.

"That is not unusual," she said. "One does not know who will buy one, before whom one must kneel."

Once again the bar rang out.

I seemed to feel the ringing in my whole body.

I looked out, through the bars.

And I said to myself, be silent, slave. You know that it is here that you belong, here with a marked thigh, in a cell, waiting to be sold.

This is right for you.

No, no, I whispered to myself.

Yes, yes, I thought.

Are you a slave, I asked myself, sternly.

Yes, Mistress, I whispered to myself, I am a slave.

I then well knew myself, though of Earth, a slave, a common slave.

I looked to the girl from Tabor.

"Perhaps someone from Tabor will buy you, and free you," I said.

"You know little of Gor," she said.

"He would not free you?" I asked.

"My left thigh bears the slave mark," she said.

"Even so," I said.

"Apparently you know little of Gor," she said.

"I do not understand," I said.

"I was once a free woman," she said. "Men much enjoy keeping former free women as helpless slaves."

"But," I protested.

"I am marked," she said.

"So?" I said.

"My own family would not free me," she said. "They would see that I was sold elsewhere, in my shame and degradation."

I regarded her.

"I am marked," she said. "Are you not marked?"

"Yes," I said, "I am marked."

"Then understand it," she said. "You are no longer what you were."

I suddenly became aware that the bar was no longer sounding.

The short fellow had ascended to the height of the cement platform.

"Noble Masters, noble Masters, noble Masters," he called, "approach, approach, gather about!"

Some twenty, or so, fellows were already clustered about the platform. Some others, from across the street, now approached.

"We have here for your consideration, and delectation, this lovely afternoon, seven beauties!"

There was laughter.

"The finest beads drawn from the finest of the slavers' necklaces, each worthy of the central block of the Curulean, each fit for the Pleasure Garden of a Ubar," said the auctioneer.

There was more laughter.

"Pot girls!" jibed a fellow.

"Have you not, several of you, examined these beauties earlier in the morning, and pondered your bids?"

"Yes," said a fellow, "a copper tarsk for the lot!"

"You may ask," said the auctioneer, "how is it that such goods, goods of such quality, could be offered here?"

"No other market would have them!" called a fellow.

"It is true, noble Masters, that our modest market, as the slave shelves, is noted for its bargains," said the auctioneer, "but that is your good fortune and our pleasure, to serve you better. Would you not prefer to pay less for more? Would you not be pleased to obtain an exquisite pleasure slave, trim, responsive, and vital, for the price of a pot girl, a kettle-and-mat girl? Those who know how to buy know where to buy, and here is where to buy!"

"Begin!" called a man.

"Slaves," called the auctioneer, "come to the bars, smile, press against them, reach out to the noble masters. Good. Can you not see, noble Masters, how ready they are, how they hope to be well purchased?"

I, the girl from Tabor, and the kneeling blonde, shaking with sobs, the former Lady Persinna, of the Merchants, remained at the back of the cell.

I saw the slaver's man looking at us, from the level of the street. I shuddered. The girl from Tabor saw him, too. She then hurried to the bars, to join the other slaves. I saw her straighten her body, and lift her chin. She was beautiful.

"You may plead, needful beauties, to be purchased," the auctioneer informed the girls.

"Buy me, Master," they called to the men.

I saw the dark blonde extending both her hands through the bars, and call out, piteously, to a handsome fellow in the front row, "Buy me, Master!" He smiled. "I am prettier, Master!" called out one of the brunettes. "No, I, I, buy me, Master!" called out the dark blonde. I supposed it was pleasant to be a man, to whom women would beg to belong. I wondered what it would be, to be owned by him. One of my cellmates, I supposed, might learn. Perhaps I would learn! Other girls at the bars seemed to present themselves to one fellow or another. Most, I assumed, would fail to be purchased by the particular master of their choice. They would be purchased by whoever bid the most for them.

It is so with slaves.

It would be so with me.

"Enough!" called the auctioneer, suddenly, sharply. "Be silent. Go back in the cell, away from the bars! Huddle there, together, in the back, away from the bars. As you can, crowd together, and try to hide! Crowd together! Do not speak!"

Frightened, the girls did as they were told. All of us now were together, standing, except for the former Lady Persinna, who still knelt, perhaps unable to rise, toward the back of the cell, away from the bars.

We could not be seen so well now, for the bars, and the distance.

I supposed there was an order to the sales.

The slaver's man entered the cell, took one of the brunettes by the wrist, and drew her from the cell, through the short passage, and led her to the block, where she stood, small, seeming isolated, much alone, though the auctioneer was near, on the red carpet.

The slaver's man, he stripped to the waist, did not bother to close the gate, but none of us essayed the portal. We huddled together, at the back of the cell. One obeys the masters. Too, it would be unutterably foolish, insanity, to try to flee. We were tunicked, sheeted, and marked. What would one do? Where would one go? Where would one run? There is no escape for the Gorean slave girl, and I now well knew myself such.

"A choice item," the auctioneer was saying. He extolled her, the brunette, as he turned her about. Shortly, he removed the sheet which she had clutched about her, continuing to exhibit her. Shortly thereafter he gracefully removed the wrap-around tunic, again turning her about.

She is merchandise, I thought.

It is said that only a fool buys a woman clothed.

He then put her to all fours on the red carpet.

"See her, noble Masters," said the auctioneer. "Would you not like her crawling to your feet, begging not to be whipped?"

He then began to solicit bids.

The dark blonde was next taken by the wrist and drawn to the block. The fellow she had tried to interest did not bid on her. A fat fellow purchased her. I saw her hold forth her wrists and slave bracelets were clapped on them. She then followed her new master. She looked over her shoulder at the fellow she had hoped would buy her, but he did not notice her. His attention was again on the block. I did not feel sorry for her, as she had been unpleasant to me earlier, in the cell.

The girl from Tabor was next brought to the block, and, as the others, exhibited. At one point, she put her hands behind the back of her head, and bent backward. This well exhibited her figure, which was lovely. Bids increased. She would be, doubtless, a good buy. How dare she so display herself, I thought. But, if she were not sold, I thought, she would be whipped. Slavers are seldom lenient with their goods. They are not out to coddle them, but to make coin on them. What if I were not sold? I did not wish to be bound, and whipped. To my right, the Lady Persinna, still kneeling, head down, was weeping, her head again in her hands. I, too, suddenly felt like crying. I looked about, wildly, at the open gate, then through the bars, to the street outside, to the men, intent upon the object for sale. I considered running. Then I moved back, even further. I felt the cement wall of the back of the cage against my back. I would remain where I was. Somehow, the gate open, I felt a thousand times more helpless than before.

I did not see to whom the girl from Tabor went.

The auctioneer, in his introduction of the item which was the girl from Tabor, had mentioned her origin on Tabor, and inquired if there might be any from Tabor present. Apparently there were none. The auctioneer then remarked that her slavery then would doubtless be far easier. Laughter had greeted this remark. I liked the girl from Tabor. She had spoken well to me, earlier in the cell, despite the fact that I was a "barbarian," and, too, we were both, so to speak, far from home.

The slaver's man again entered the cell, and looked about. I was terrified that it would be my wrist which he would seize, in his large, manacle-like hand. But he took another brunette.

She brought less than the girl from Tabor.

Perhaps, I thought, a girl from the islands, with her accent, would have an exotic flavor at a fellow's slave ring.

The brunette was purchased, I gathered, for a restaurant, or tavern, of some sort. "May she serve her goblets well, and nicely grace the chains of your alcoves," had said the auctioneer to her buyer, while his man led her down the steps to the street, into his keeping.

Next, to her misery, the Lady Persinna was seized and drawn to the block. She was clutching the short sheet closely about her, and was shrieking, and sobbing. "I cannot be sold!" she cried. "I am a free woman, a free woman!"

"What is it that she is saying?" asked the auctioneer.

"I am free," she wept. "I am free!"

"Ah!" said the auctioneer. "Can it be that she is free?"

"Yes," she cried. "Yes!"

The slaver's man then, holding her by the upper left arm with his right hand faced her left side to the crowd.

"No!" she cried.

He then, with his left hand, drew up the sheet, and the hem of her tunic, to the waist.

There was much laughter.

"It seems we have here only another slave," said the auctioneer.

The former Lady Persinna fell to her knees before the auctioneer, holding the sheet closely about her. "Do not sell me!" she cried.

"'Do not sell me' what?" inquired the auctioneer.

She looked stricken, before him. "Do not sell me—Master," she said.

There was much laughter.

The slaver's man pulled her to her feet. She clutched the sheet closely about her. It seemed she could hardly stand.

The auctioneer surveyed the crowd.

"What am I offered for this slave?" he asked.

"A tarsk-bit!" called a man.

"Surely more!" laughed the auctioneer. "Surely the sheet does not much hide the legs of this slave!"

She threw back her head, sobbing.

The auctioneer then gestured, annoyed, to his man, who seized the former Lady Persinna by the hair, to hold her in place, and then he, carefully, measuredly, cuffed her, twice, once snapping her head to the right, and then to the left.

"Be silent!" said the auctioneer.

"Yes, Master!" she said.

The slaver's man then released her, and stepped back.

"We have an unusual slave here," said the auctioneer. "This slut was once the Lady Persinna, of the high Merchants, housed even in Four Towers. You know her well for her betrayal of the Home Stone, for her profiteering, for her collaboration with the hated invaders. Recall the shortages, the high costs, the adulterated goods!"

Angry murmurs seethed in the small crowd.

Given the seeming importance of the former Lady Persinna I did not understand how it was that she was being vended in such a market.

Was it, in spite of its appearance, a high market?

Perhaps, I thought, for how could one such as I be sold in any but a high market? Surely I was much too beautiful to be sold in any but a high market. I was now muchly pleased that I had not complained about the market, earlier.

"Behold her," said the auctioneer.

The former Lady Persinna stood, miserable, small, a slave, the sheet clutched about her.

Then, a moment later, looking about myself, at the buyers, the street, the local buildings, the crowded shops across the way, I realized how foolish were my conjectures. In no way could this barred cell and that circular cement platform be thought a high market. We might almost as well have been chained on a slave shelf, where buyers might have examined our teeth, felt our limbs for firmness, and such.

How then, I wondered, could it be that the former Lady Persinna was even now on that simple cement platform, before buyers?

"You know her sycophancy," said the auctioneer, "her privileges, her position in the court of the hated Talena, false Ubara! You know the favors she received, the contracts accorded her by Cos and Tyros."

"Yes," said more than one man.

"She was on the proscription lists," said the auctioneer, "but she has been saved for your pleasure."

The girl held the sheet tightly about her.

The auctioneer lifted the hair of the slave, displaying it.

"Golden hair," he said, "sparkling as ripe Sa-Tarna."

"Shave her head!" called a man.

"Consider it as a sheet of pleasure, which might be spread about your body," said the auctioneer, "or its value as a bond, fastening her wrists behind the back of her neck."

"Cut it off," said a fellow. "Use it for catapult cordage, that she may be good for something."

"Throw her to leech plants!" called a man.

"Feed her to sleen!" cried another.

I knew nothing, at the time, of leech plants, and I had not yet beheld a sleen.

"Come now, noble Masters," said the auctioneer, "regard her ankles, her calves, her small hands, so tight on the sheet, the exquisite delicacy of her features."

The men were silent.

"What are we offered for this traitress?" called the auctioneer.

"Let us see her!" called a man.

The sheet was whipped away from the slave, half turning her about.

Then she was turned before the crowd.

She was praised, as one might praise an animal. Then I realized that, as a slave, she was an animal. And I realized that I, too, was now an animal.

This thrilled me, that I should now be no more than an animal.

The men cried out with pleasure, at the removal of the wrap-around tunic. Now, it seemed, there was no more talk of leech plants, of sleen, or such. What they saw now, it seemed, was a slave.

The former Lady Persinna was put to all fours on the red carpet, while the bids were forthcoming.

A little later, she cried out, in misery, and terror, from all fours, not permitted to rise. "No, no! Not to him! Not to him! Do not sell me to him! Please! Please! Sell me to anyone, but not to him!"

But it was to that fellow that she was sold.

He came to the edge of the platform. "Perhaps you remember me," he said.

She would have scrambled back, on the carpet, but it was too late. The leash had been snapped on her neck.

I saw her being led away.

I now suspected that the fellow who had bought her, despite the shabbiness of his nondescript robes, had come prepared, in such a market, in such a district, to outbid all likely competition. Apparently he had realized she would be sold in this market on this day. I supposed that was not common knowledge. It seemed probable to me that this matter had been arranged, perhaps even with the collusion of a praetor, if not the Ubar himself. Perhaps the fellow had requested, or been granted, such a favor, that he would purchase the former Lady Persinna, to her humiliation, in a low market, for a handful of coins. Indeed, I wondered if the coins, even, were his. Perhaps it amused someone, perhaps an important personage, if the former Lady Persinna should find herself in the collar of that fellow, or someone like him.

Thus, I conjectured a plausible explanation for the apparent anomaly of one such as the former Lady Persinna, of the Merchants, of Four Towers, which, I gathered, must be an exclusive residence, or an exclusive residential area, being vended in such a market. It was to demean and humiliate her. Let her learn quickly, and well, that she was now only a slave.

As the slaves had been sold, even the former Lady Persinna, much in the street had gone on as it had before the Tenth Ahn. Many men, and women, had come and gone, and shopped, and bargained, without attending to, or, apparently, even noticing, what was going on on our side of the street. A sale of slaves, particularly in a low market, was a familiar, commonplace thing, I gathered, worthy of no particular attention. A lad, drawing a cart, had stopped for a time, to look on, but had then gone ahead.

Suddenly I was much aware that only two remained in the cell, myself and another brunette, a darker, taller brunette. I felt the back of the cell wall against my back. I looked to my left, to the opened gate.

The portal was empty.

The slaver's man was at the foot of the circular platform. The auctioneer stood on the surface of the platform. A small breeze moved the blue-and-yellow robes. The auctioneer and the slaver's man, and some of the others, as well, now turned about, were witnessing the departure of the former Lady Persinna, naked on her leash, and her master. Three or four of the fellows who had been at the platform were following the pair, jeering at the miserable slave. I saw her spat upon, and one fellow cast dirt upon her. The only bond she wore was her leash, and, with her hands, and arms, she tried to cover her head. The leash was not taut. She tried to follow her master as closely as she could. It is the master who will protect the slave, as any other animal, should he choose to do so. Her current master, however, seemed not to notice the abuse to which his lovely acquisition was subjected, and she, of course, not having been granted the appropriate permission, would not dare to speak.

Then, after a time, the fellows who had hung about the departing pair stood still, shook their fists, and, looking after the couple, the slave and her master, called out some final words, which, I gathered, may have been foul.

I knew little about the former Lady Persinna, or the affairs, political and otherwise, which had brought her to a tiny, readying cell in the Metellan district, but I hoped that her master would put a different name on her. Given the veiling, and half-veiling, particularly amongst higher-caste women, I would suppose that few in the city would recognize the former Lady Persinna in just another scantily clad collar-girl, one amongst many, hurrying about her errands, fearing to dally, in teeming Ar. Perhaps many might suppose the Lady Persinna had perished in the revolution, or in her imprisonment, in some obscure dungeon, perhaps strangled there, or had perhaps eventually met her end writhing on some obscure impaling stake. Perhaps her secret, that of her former identity, would be known to few. Indeed, perhaps, eventually, for most practical purposes, it would be a secret shared primarily between the slave and her master. Then, as she knelt, and kissed and licked at his feet, she might hope that he would not see fit to reveal her former identity. Could she be so pleasing to him? Too, her life had been transformed. She was now only the slave of a master. Perhaps she might find in this those fulfillments of which a free woman scarcely dares to dream. In the collar she might find her happiness, and a thousand times more freedom, though an abject slave, than she had ever known in her former life. She did have "golden hair," which was rare, but surely not unknown. That would probably not be enough to identify her to strangers. "Golden hair" tends to raise prices in the south, but not in the north, where it is more common. "Golden hair," I suspected, had brought more than one girl into the collar, at least in the south. Interestingly, auburn hair is that pelting, so to speak, which tends to be most favored in the markets. I am not sure why that is. It is probably a matter of its rarity, as it tends to be even more rare than "golden hair." One thing that I learned of your world, which struck me as of much interest, is your preference for honesty, or truth, or your dislike of fraud, or what you think of as fraud. On my former world, for example, it is quite common for a brunette to dye her hair blond, and, so to speak, pass herself off as a blonde. No one thinks much of this, or much objects to this. On your world, on the other hand, at least amongst slaves, such things are taken seriously. If a barbarian slave is brought to the markets and she has dyed hair, this is made clear to possible buyers, and is commonly taken as a defect. Sometimes her head is shaved. If it is thought the girl did this of her own will on her own world, dyed her hair or had it dyed, it is taken as evidence of her deceitful and meretricious nature, and, accordingly, the rightfulness of embonding so duplicitous and worthless a creature. Masters, incidentally, take seriously the moral character of their slaves, and commonly regard themselves responsible for its supervision and improvement, by the whip, if necessary. Interestingly, to me at least, a slaver who misrepresents merchandise, for example, claiming former high caste for a girl who was actually formerly of low caste, or who tries to pass off a dyed blonde for a natural blonde, may be banished and ruined, his goods confiscated, his house burned to the ground. On your world, honesty, truth, and such, are obviously of great moment. Still, I have heard rumors that some free women dye their hair. They may do as they wish, of course, for they are free.

The fellows who had for a time pursued the former Lady Persinna, and discomfited her so cruelly, she now only a slave, were now returning to the area of the block. Too, the fellows there, who had watched, but had not left the vicinity of the block, now turned about again, and began to gather again, now more closely, about the block. Some looked through the bars. We, the other brunette and I, were at the back of the cell, standing, close together. We could be seen, but perhaps not well. Though muchly clothed, as such things go, for slaves, in the wrap-around tunic, and covered as much as possible by the sheet, I was uneasy at how I sensed myself being regarded. In the house I had often found myself well viewed as a slave by men, but here, in the cell, it seemed different, and somehow more meaningful. One of the men outside, looking through the bars, considering my ankles, and such, might buy me. And what would be done with me if I failed to please him, and fully, and as a slave? The slaver's man was on the street level, and the auctioneer, on the surface of the block, looking down, conferred with him.

We, the other brunette, the darker, taller brunette, and I, exchanged glances, but did not speak. At the beginning of the sales, the slaves had been warned to silence. That injunction had not been rescinded. We remained silent.

Was she as frightened as I? Did she, as I, desire desperately to speak, so that we might comfort one another, that we might share our apprehension, our fear? But we, slaves, must be silent.

I smiled at her, timidly, bravely, wanting to be her friend, if only for a moment, hoping for some understanding, some small comfort, in our common plight.

But then she looked away, regally, disdainfully.

Tears formed in my eyes.

I recalled that I was, in her view, a barbarian.

How different was I from she!

Even though we were both slaves, worlds separated us.

When I better learned your language, I was surprised to learn that you tend to regard the women of my world as natural slaves, and thus legitimate and appropriate prey for slavers. There are apparently a large number of reasons for this, aside from such obvious matters as the frequent dying of hair. The fact that women of my world seldom veil themselves, but bare their faces, that often their ankles, their wrists and hands, and such, are bared, that they often conceal soft garments, slave garments, beneath their clothing, is taken as evidence that they are, and should be, slaves. Indeed, some women of my own world have, of their own free will, with their own consent, though you may find this hard to believe, pierced ears, which, on your world, is commonly taken as a sign of the most worthless and degraded of slaves. Without daring to comment on these matters, I have heard, from men, of course, that all women are natural slaves, and should be slaves, that they are the natural properties of the dominant sex, that they are designed by nature to be owned, and pleasing, that they are all slaves, only that some are not yet collared. I dare not comment on so bold, but so common, a view. If there is anything in it, and if it should be true, even obviously so, to an informed view, it may be only that the women of my world, in baring their faces, and such, in presenting themselves as attractive objects, thus encouraging men to their acquisition, are more open about their nature than yours, and, if this is so, would the women of my world not be, on the whole, more honest than yours? I trust my master will not beat me for this speculation. I do not think, ultimately, that there is that much difference, if any, between the free woman of Earth and the free woman of Gor. We are all women, and, being women, might we not be, all of us, appropriately, the slaves of men, the slaves of our masters?

The auctioneer stood up, and the slaver's man ascended the steps of the block, and disappeared into the short passage to the left.

In a moment he entered the cell.

The other brunette and I both shrank back, but he seized her left wrist, and I saw her drawn from the cell. In a moment she appeared on the block before the small crowd, and the auctioneer began her sale.

I was then alone in the cell. I clutched the sheet about me, tightly. My heart was beating wildly.

I closed my eyes that I should not see what was occurring outside, beyond the bars, to the left.

I could, of course, hear the auctioneer.

A murmur of approval coursed through the small crowd.

Then, unable to help myself, I opened my eyes. The slave's sheet had been removed.

The highest price, so far, had been brought by the former Lady Persinna, who had gone for three and a half silver tarsks, three silver tarsks and fifty copper tarsks. Most of the other girls had sold for one to two silver tarsks.

Whereas I had recognized that my cellmates were all beautiful, as was common with Gorean female slaves, I had not regarded myself as inferior to any of them. Indeed, I supposed myself the most beautiful. And had I not been saved for last? Is the very best not saved for last? I was pleased that the masters apparently shared my judgment, as to the quality of my beauty. But, then, was the matter not obvious?

I closed my eyes briefly, and then looked quickly away, to the right, through the bars, that I not see the now-bared slave on the block.

I did hope that I would not be so exposed to the men. I was different. I was from Earth! But then I recalled the saying, that only a fool buys a woman clothed.

How was it that one of my beauty was in this market, such a market?

I wondered how it was that a price, an actual, finite price, could be set on beauty such as mine.

Surely it was priceless!

Then I recalled that only the beauty of a free woman was priceless. But it was priceless only as long as she was free. Once it was embonded, it would have a price, whatever men would pay for it.

I did recall that it had been estimated, on Earth, that I would go from between forty and sixty. Here, of course, I realized they did not deal in dollars, forty to sixty thousand dollars. Here, presumably, one would go for silver or gold. I accordingly had conjectured that I might go from between forty to sixty gold pieces, or, possibly, given my level of training, and such, from between forty and sixty silver tarsks. I was, after all, in their view, a barbarian. Too, although I had begun to sense, to my apprehension and excitement, what might be the whimperings and moanings of an aroused belly, natural to a slave, it seemed reasonably clear to me that I was not yet the helpless victim of what the instructresses had referred to as "slave fires." As a woman of Earth I did not believe that such things could exist. Surely I, of Earth, could never be so victimized. Too, I was sure, even if such things could exist, in some women, I could resist them. I did not realize, at the time, that men might not permit it. I did not realize at the time what they could do to my body, how they could force it to be, as it might please them, irremediably that of a begging, needful slave. And I did not realize at the time that already such things, such fires, slave fires, had been kindled, subtly, in my belly, but, merely, had not yet leaped into flame.

I became aware, suddenly, that the auctioneer was no longer taking bids. I returned my attention to the block. A fellow below the block extended his hand, and assisted the slave down the steps. I was struck with the courtesy, the solicitude, the apparent gentlemanliness, of this gesture. It might have been done so, I thought, by a fellow of Earth. Perhaps I would be so fortunate as to have such a master, though I did not think I wanted such a one. A slave wants to know that she is a slave, that she belongs to a man, categorically, absolutely, wholly. I wondered if he was weak. At the foot of the block, the brunette was facing him, looking up at him. Though taller than I, she seemed quite small before him, he in his swathing of robes. The fingers of her left hand still rested in his right hand. Was that not almost tender? She smiled up at him. I saw that she, as I, suspected that that he might be weak. I sensed that she was confident that her bondage, if she were clever, pouted rightly, and such, would prove to be a lax and light one. She had been unpleasant to me, earlier in the cell, and just before her sale. I hated her. He then put his hands on her shoulders, turned her about, rudely, drew her wrists behind her, and braceleted her. She pulled against the bracelets, startled. Our eyes met, she on the street, I back in the cell, behind the bars. You have a master, slave, I thought. Learn it! You will be well collared, and will know yourself well collared, and you understand, do you not, that I know that you will be well-collared, and know, too, that you will know yourself well-collared, and that that pleases me, much pleases me. Indeed, I was much pleased. She straightened her body, and shrugged her shoulders, and, for a moment, glared at me, wildly, angrily, helplessly, but a word must have been spoken, perhaps sharply, for she swiftly turned about and knelt before her master, her wrists braceleted high behind her, and pressed her lips to his sandals. He then turned about, and strode away, and she rose to her feet, and, casting one look back at me, the look of a now-aware, frightened slave, who might now, I thought, welcome some small token of understanding or sympathy, hurried after him. No longer did I hate her. She was now only another braceleted slave. She increased her pace, to close the gap between herself and her master, that she might follow in prescribed heeling position. Failure to do so may, of course, result in punishment.

I trusted that the sales were over.

There was, at least, a lacuna in the proceedings.

Might I not now be returned to the house?

I had not been offered, so I should not be beaten, having not been sold.

Some men, I was pleased to note, had now turned away, and were leaving the vicinity of the block. Two others, however, I noted, were crossing the street, approaching.

Then the slaver's man had entered the cell, and, taking me by the left wrist, drew me after him, and I was beyond the portal, and in the short passage, and then I was in the sunlight, outside, and I felt the nap of the worn, faded, scarlet rug beneath my bare feet. I blinked against the light, and put down my head. Then I felt the switch of the auctioneer beneath my chin, and I lifted my head, and opened my eyes, looking over the heads of the men.

Much of what then went on remains a blur. At times I did not even understand the auctioneer. This was doubtless in part a function of my Gorean, which was new, and limited, with its unfamiliar grammar, and my vocabulary consisting at that time of only a few hundred words, but, too, I think, part of it was an unwillingness, or refusal, to understand what was being said, or done. My native tongue is called "English," and I am not sure that I would have allowed myself to understand the auctioneer even had he been speaking in that tongue. I had, incidentally, interestingly, understood him quite well, almost always, when he was vending others. To be sure, even if I had known not a word of Gorean, but had found myself somehow on that platform, so clad, so regarded, perhaps having been magically transported from my own world, wafted away, somehow, from chatting, strolling, or shopping, it would not have been difficult to understand what was occurring. I was a female being sold.

The auctioneer was not cruel with me.

The sale proceeds in three phases, in each of which the girl is turned, and exhibited, first in the brief sheet, then, the sheet removed, in the tunic, and, lastly, neither in the sheet nor tunic. The whole process takes no more than a few Ehn. I understood matters in disjointed patches of intelligibility. I did learn, for the first time, that I had been brought from the House of Tenalion, apparently a slaver of Ar. I was clearly identified as a barbarian, which I sensed was of some interest to the men. To be sure, I have gathered that we are no longer the novelties in the markets that we once were. Strictly, a "barbarian," I have been given to understand, is one whose native tongue is not Gorean, a language spoken pervasively but not universally on your world. The pervasiveness of Gorean on your world, as I understand it, has something to do with your gods, the Priest-Kings, laired in the Sardar Mountains. These beings, it seems, encourage Gorean, perhaps that they might the more conveniently make known their will on this world. The caste of Initiates, it is said, act as the intermediaries between Priest-Kings and men, appointing festivals, prophesying, uttering oracles, accepting offerings, selling blessings, performing sacrifices, and such. Much remains unclear, however, as I understand it, concerning the actual relationship, if any, between the Initiates and the Priest-Kings. It is clear, however, that the Priest-Kings are not to be taken lightly. Violations of their weapon, transportation, and communication laws are often, when discovered, followed by sanctions of fearsome import, the destructions of cities, the seizures and flingings of tides, the melting of mountains, the geysers and floodings of fiery magma, inexplicable bursts of flame, and such. The standardization of Gorean is accomplished largely in virtue of the meetings of Scribes four times a year on the neutral ground of the great seasonal fairs held in the vicinity of the Sardar itself. This tends to standardize lexicons and prevent phonetic drift. On the other hand, it is also clear that the connotations of the term 'barbarian', if not its literal meaning, extend well beyond the matter of what might be one's native language. As I have learned, "barbarians" are commonly taken to be simple, stupid, ignorant, uncouth, crude, unrefined, untutored, uncivilized, and, in general, worthless, and far inferior to native Goreans. But even your physicians, your men of medicine and health, the members of your green caste, will assure you that we are much the same as you. Had I been born on Gor and you on Earth, would I not, then, be the Gorean and you the barbarian? It is not our fault if we do not know what you know, your caste customs, your legends, your political arrangements, the histories of your cities, your holidays, your famous generals, musicians, poets, and such. How could we? We may be ignorant, but we are not stupid. To you we may seem lacking, to be simple, primitive, and barbarous, and, doubtless, in a way, we are, but these differences, I assure you, have to do with our history and background, not with what we are in ourselves, apart from such things. If we are so obviously inferior to you, it is a cultural inferiority, and only that. Certainly we have certain qualities which you recognize, which have value. You buy us, do you not? Perhaps in some respects we are objectionable. Yet I do not think you mind us in the furs, in our collars. It is generally understood we beg, squirm, and moan well. If you despise us for this I would suggest you put your precious, priceless, exalted, lofty free women at a slave ring and see if they are any different! Please, Master, do not beat me for this observation.

The sheet was pulled from me.

I was turned about.

"Behold this barbarian vulo," said the auctioneer. "Surely she is of some interest. Might she not be useful as a third or fourth slave in your house, to relieve higher, better slaves of disagreeable tasks? Perhaps she might do as a starter slave, for a son, or a gift for a son or nephew, returning from his studies in Harfax, Venna, Besnit, or Brundisium."

It was called to the attention of the men that I was new to bondage and only partly trained, but these defects were somehow transformed into advantages, that a master might then have the exquisite pleasure of teaching a new girl what it was to be in a collar, that one might then train me more specifically to his own tastes, and such.

"Speculate," said the auctioneer. "Would she not look well in a camisk, or less?"

I recalled I had been put in a camisk by Mrs. Rawlinson at the party on Earth, when I had been forced, as a part of my punishment, for having dared to read of your world, to serve the guests half-naked, as though I might be a slave.

143

"Less!" called a man. "Let us see!"

"Part your tunic, my dear," said the auctioneer.

"Please, no, Master," I said.

Laughter greeted my request.

"Gracefully," said the auctioneer.

I looked over the heads of the men, to the shops across the street. I dared not meet the eyes of any of the men. Tears sprang to my eyes.

"Posture," said the auctioneer.

I straightened my body.

I felt tears running down my cheeks.

"Perhaps you suspect," said the auctioneer, "that this is her first sale."

There was laughter.

I supposed it was obvious.

"Turn about," said the auctioneer. "Now face the masters."

"A bit slender perhaps," said the auctioneer, "but not, I think, disagreeably so."

Surely I had had one of the best figures in the sorority!

"Let us see all of her," said a fellow.

He did not seem excited. The request seemed very matter-of-fact. Were they unaware of my feelings? Did they not realize what was occurring? I was a female! I was a slave! I was being sold!

"The tunic, my dear," said the auctioneer.

"Master!" I begged!

"Gracefully," he said.

The tunic was handed to the slaver's man, who stood to the left, behind, on the platform.

"Consider her," said the auctioneer. "Barbarian. Slim, lovely. Darkly pelted, glossy hair. Partly trained, recently red-silked."

I dared not look into the eyes of any of the men.

"Turn about, slowly," said the auctioneer.

"Surely worth something," said the auctioneer. "She is a barbarian, a mere barbarian. She has been harvested from the slave world for one purpose, and one purpose only, to serve your pleasure, wholly, in all ways. It is all she is for. She has no Home Stone. She has never had a Home Stone. Do what you will with her, without a second thought, use her variously, however you might wish. Keep her nude for a year, if you wish. Conceive of her, neck-chained, ankle-chained, at your slave ring. Consider her soft lips, and tongue, obedient and moist, on your feet, on your body. Is she not of interest? Consider her crawling to you, begging not to be whipped."

I cried out, softly, in misery.

"Forgive me, Master," I said.

"I am now prepared to accept bids," said the auctioneer.

None had been forthcoming yet.

I saw two or three of the men turn about, and leave, chatting.

"Begin, begin, begin," said the auctioneer. "Twenty, twenty, twenty."

I stood there, weak, almost faltering.

The auctioneer occasionally held my upper left arm, steadying me. I might otherwise have fallen.

I knew myself a slave, but, still, the enormity of what was being done to me seemed almost incomprehensible. Where was Earth, my familiar surroundings, the college, the classes, my fellow students, the sorority?

I stood there, under the eyes of buyers.

I wondered if some of the young men I had known might have wondered how I, so aloof, so superior, so unapproachable, might have appeared on an auction block, reduced, rightless, stripped, a slave displayed for the perusal of buyers. I was not so lofty, so proud, now. They might have been amused to see me so, frightened, being vended. I wondered if some might have bid upon me. What if one had purchased me? I would then have been his, helplessly.

"Twenty-five, twenty-five, thirty," was saying the auctioneer.

I feared I might fall.

The auctioneer's hand steadied me.

"Thirty, thirty-five," he was saying.

I heard coins, being rattled against one another, in the palm of someone's hand.

So I stood there, naked, on the platform, only half understanding what was being done.

Was this being done to someone else?

Then I realized that it was I, I, who was being sold!

I recalled Mrs. Rawlinson.

How, in her mind's eye, she must have smiled, considering the fate she was arranging for her lovely, vain, shallow, spoiled charges, the markets of Gor!

In the beginning, we had looked down on her, she merely a house mother, an employee, a servant of sorts, far beneath us, a woman hired to manage the house, to regulate mundane and domestic matters, to look after, even regulate and supervise, to some extent, a number of aristocratic, supercilious, patronizing young women, her social betters. But soon, whether because of the force of her personality, or the uncompromising, confident sternness of her demeanor, we began to fear the influence she might bring to bear, the power she might exercise. We had soon begun to treat her with respect, even awe. We followed her instructions, and did as we might be told. Even Nora feared her. The board, it seemed clear, for we, in our resentment and annoyance, had sought this information, was behind her. It became clear to us that however she had been emplaced, and however she had been empowered, that the house, and its occupants, were hers to rule. In that tiny world her word would be law. The board would accommodate itself to her recommendations, whatever they might be. A word from her, a charge from her, would initiate a sequence of actions which might culminate in one's expulsion from the house, with the shame and ruin which might be consequent on such a disgrace. She might disrupt our plans; she might jeopardize our very future. Imagine then my terror, and that of Jane and Eve, when forbidden literature, secret, suspect literature, literature inappropriate for such as we, improper, scandalous literature, was discovered in our rooms! We were then at her mercy!

I wondered if she thought of us, I and the others, from time to time, now on Gor, owned, doubtless all of us, now the property of masters.

She had done her work well.

Perhaps she was now similarly employed, elsewhere.

That seemed not impossible.

The slave nets are carefully woven, with stout inescapable cordage, and they are cast with skill.

One does not escape their coils.

And so, as I stood naked on a block in the Metellan district, in Ar, the worn carpet beneath my feet, the afternoon sun on my body, warm, shadows across the street, the men about, some people passing by, not noticing me, exposed to buyers, being sold, I thought of Mrs. Rawlinson.

Yes, I thought, Mrs. Rawlinson, you are Mistress. You are a free woman, and here, on this world, as I had not on Earth, I have begun to sense what that might be, its unchallenged force, and pride, and power, and here I am a slave, only that, and here, naked on an auction block, being sold, I have begun to sense what that might be.

"Forty, forty," said the auctioneer. "Forty-two, no more? No more? No more? Done!"

I realized I had been sold.

At least, I thought, I have gone for forty-two. I dared not suppose it would have been forty-two pieces of gold, for I was new to my condition, had not been extensively trained, and had only recently been opened, in what I now had come to understand was the house of Tenalion, in Ar.

I did not fear pregnancy, for early in my sojourn in the house I had been given Slave Wine. Understanding its nature, I had imbibed it willingly enough, as disgusting and foul a brew as it was. Its effects are removed, I am told, if one is given a Releaser, which, I am told, is palatable, even delicious. As a slave, an animal, I knew I could be bred, as any other animal. It is done with us as masters please. But I was not now apprehensive. I had not been administered a Releaser. The breeding of slaves, as you know, as other animals, is carefully controlled. I would be bred only if the masters so pleased.

I took forty-two silver tarsks to be a considerable amount of coin, particularly for a new slave.

My estimation of my extraordinary beauty, I was pleased to note, was now well confirmed, confirmed objectively, in virtue of a block price, in virtue of a sober economic transaction. The matter was now beyond argument. The former Lady Persinna, as I recalled, whom I had thought very beautiful, had gone for only three and a half silver tarsks.

I recalled that it had been estimated, even on Earth, that I would go from between forty and sixty, an amount which I had then mistakenly interpreted as dollars, thousands of dollars, a form of Earth currency.

I heard coins being counted out, one upon the other.

I could not resist looking. Might it not, though improbable perhaps, be gold?

"Master!" I protested. Then I was frightened, for I had spoken without permission. "Forgive me, Master!" I said.

The coins being counted into the palms of the auctioneer were neither of gold nor silver. They were copper.

"Forty-two," said a fellow, thick-bodied, short-bearded, in a brown robe, girded up to his knees. His arms were bare. His left arm was scarred.

"Forty-two copper tarsks," confirmed the auctioneer.

I could not believe that I had brought so little.

"A splendid buy," the auctioneer assured the buyer. "Fortune has smiled upon your bidding."

"An untutored barbarian," said the fellow.

"We had hoped to get fifty for her," said the auctioneer.

"She is not worth so much," said the fellow.

"I trust she will prove satisfactory," said the auctioneer. "If not, we will buy her back."

"For how much?" asked the fellow, warily.

"Twenty," speculated the auctioneer.

"How much Gorean does she have?" asked the man.

"Enough," said the auctioneer. To be sure, I do not know how he knew that. And I surely hoped it would be enough. It is hard to be pleasing, if one cannot understand what is expected of one.

"She will prove satisfactory," said the fellow. "The whip will see to it."

The slaver's man, from behind, took me by the arms, lifted me up, my feet some inches above the surface of the platform, and descended the steps of the platform, to the street, and placed me before the bearded fellow in the short, girded-up robe.

He was looking at me.

I did not know what to do.

"She is stupid," said the bearded fellow to the auctioneer.

I quickly knelt down before the man and, the palms of my hands down on the street, pressed my lips to his sandals, kissing them.

"On all fours," he said.

I had not yet dared to look into the eyes of my master.

As I was on all fours, before him, he removed something from within his robes, and bent down.

There was a click, and a collar had been fastened about my neck. I was now collared. The collar proclaimed me slave, even should I be clothed, and, doubtless, it bore certain information, perhaps something as simple, as "I am the slave of so-and-so," "I belong to so-and-so," or such. If it contained a name, that would doubtless be the name I would be given.

"What is your name?" he asked.

"Whatever Master pleases," I said.

"You see," said the slaver's man, "she is not stupid."

"What are you called?" asked the fellow.

"I have been called 'Allison'," I said.

"A barbarian name," he said.

"Yes, Master," I said.

"You are Allison," he said.

"Yes, Master," I said. "Thank you, Master."

"Look up," he said.

I did so.

It can be frightening to look up, into the eyes of someone who owns you.

"Are you any good in the furs?" he asked.

"I fear not, Master," I said. That seemed the safest response I could manage.

"The whip can change that," he said.

"I will try to be pleasing to my Master," I said.

"You looked well at my feet," he said. "I think you will be responsive."

I shuddered. I feared I might be responsive, and as a slave.

He then turned about, and strode away.

I was not braceleted, or leashed. I hurried after him, heeling him. With two hands I felt the collar on my neck. It was the first standard Gorean slave collar I had worn. It was a flat band which closely encircled my throat. Such collars are common in the north. It was sturdy, but light, and not uncomfortable. Soon I would forget I wore such a device, but it was there. It was, of course, locked. I had determined that, almost immediately.

149

Hurrying behind my master, I did not feel as self-conscious as I might have otherwise. It is hard to go naked in the streets, alone, on errands, and such. Too, there is always the danger that one might encounter a free woman.

I was a little curious as to why I had not been bound, in one way or another, perhaps put on a wrist leash, or something. Did he have such confidence in me, that I would not try to run away? To be sure, I would have been afraid to run away. The instructresses had well impressed on me, in the house, that there was no escape for the Gorean slave girl, barbarian or not. There was nowhere to turn, nowhere to run. In my case, it would not be merely the brand, the garmenture, the collar, the closely knit society, and such, but the very Gorean I had been taught was quite possibly a slave Gorean, subtly different in certain ways from the Gorean spoken by the free. In this respect a Gorean woman enslaved had an advantage over me. But, just as there were barbarian accents, aside from deliberately inserted, betraying subtleties, even the enslaved Gorean girls would usually have an accent different from that of their masters. I recalled that the girl from Tabor, the island, had had a different accent. And I had heard that the island accents of, say, Tyros and Cos, were clearly different from those of, say, Ar or Venna. Turia in the south was different, as well, and surely, so, too, would be those of Torvaldsland, in the north. Still, as I hurried behind my master, I continued to ponder why no bond had been put on me. And then I realized that I did wear a bond, two bonds, the most inescapable bonds of all, a mark fixed in my thigh, and a collar, locked about my neck.

My first master was Menon, of the Peasants. He did not have a holding, nor did he till the fields. If he had, he would have looked for a larger, sturdier girl than I, one who in harness, alone or with another, might drag a hoeing plow. Menon maintained a public eating house near the sun gate, so spoken of because it is opened at dawn and closed at dusk. Several girls worked in the large kitchen, behind the eating hall, amongst whom I was placed. Our Ahn were long, and we were chained at night. I was the only barbarian in the kitchen, and I was much abused. While the kitchen master occasionally put me to his use, I think he preferred others. When I tried to call myself to his attention, placing myself before him, making inquiries, simply to be near him, and such, this was noticed by the other girls, and I paid for my forwardness when we were alone. My hair was jerked and twisted, short of being torn from my head, which would have been a punishable offense, and my body was much bruised, by small, angry fists, and, often enough, from the blows of ladles and stirring spoons. When I put myself to my belly before the kitchen master, pressing my lips to his feet, and complaining, or simply begging to be protected, I would receive little comfort. I was not Gorean. "Masters," he would say, smiling, "do not much mix in the squabbles of slaves." Had there been a "first girl," I might have assisted her in her tasks, done much of her work, flattered her, cultivated her, petitioned her, and so on, but there was no first girl. The nearest thing to a first girl was Marcella, who did not care for me, and was the favorite of the kitchen master. It was not much comfort to me that she might regard me as a rival; rather, it was a source of considerable apprehension.

As you might suppose, girls are eager to escape the labors of the great kitchen, and make the most of their turns at serving the long tables, hoping to come to the attention of one or another of the guests. I, like the others, in such welcome opportunities to enter the eating hall, rare in my case, would hitch up my tunic, and be somewhat negligent in the adjustment of the disrobing loop. It need not be drawn up too tightly, nor knotted too securely. I was learning to move, and smile, and, too, the men, many of them so strong and virile, made me more and more uneasy, and more and more conscious of my bondage. The unquestioning simplicity and naturalness with which they looked upon me, and accepted me, spoke to me, and commanded me, as a slave, and excited me. I was a female slave, and knew myself more so each day, and they were males, and masters. Sometimes I twisted in my chains at night, moaned, and scratched at the straw and the wooden flooring, remembering one or another of them.

As is well known, free women are not permitted in the paga taverns or brothels, and it is dangerous for them to enter them, even for those bold enough to disguise themselves as slaves, but similar restrictions do not apply to the public eating houses. Even so, free women of high caste seldom patronize them, not because of any explicit impropriety in doing so, but, rather, because of the narrowness and plainness of the offerings, the rudeness of the appointments, and the general vulgarity of the diners. Such reservations, however, are seldom entertained by men of high caste, who welcome an opportunity to obtain a cheap, convenient meal, particularly during the workday. Paga may not be served in the eating houses, but a variety of cheap ka-la-nas is usually available.

Long tables are commonly used in the eating houses, with benches, rather as in Torvaldsland. In such an arrangement, the patron usually spends less time eating. There is no lingering over paga, taking time for a game of kaissa or stones, trying out one or another of the proprietor's girls in an alcove, or such. One is usually in and out, without much ado, which usually means more coins per Ahn in the entry kettle. Two ostraka may be purchased. One pays upon entry. The basic ostrakon entitles one to the general meal of the day, with a mug of kal-da, and costs a tarsk-bit. The second ostrakon, or the ostrakon of privilege, costs two tarsk-bits, and entitles the patron to a choice amongst a number of offerings, and a glass of ka-la-na. Most patrons purchase the basic ostrakon. The ostrakon in question, the basic ostrakon or the ostrakon of privilege, is presented to the girl who serves that section of the patron's table.

"Is Master pleased?" I asked.

"You are a pretty slave," he said.

"A slave is pleased should she be found pleasing by a master," I said.

"What is your name?" he asked.

"'Allison', if it pleases Master," I said.

"I have not seen you here before," he said.

"Allison is seldom permitted to serve a table," I said.

"You are a barbarian," he said.

"Yes, Master," I said.

"Are barbarians any good?" he asked.

"Perhaps Master would care to try one, and see," I said.

"You are apparently eager to escape the kitchen," he said.

"Master?" I said.

"Fetch more suls," he said.

"Yes, Master," I said.

At the sorority my sisters and I, as thoughtful, informed individuals, had set ourselves to increase our wealth and advance our station in life. Certainly we had not come to college in order to familiarize ourselves with Medieval French poetry, learn about Roman band instruments, and such. The route to these ends, the assurance of a future of comfort and influence, was obviously to contract a match with a suitable young man, one of wealth and family. Accordingly, in the social circles of an exclusive, prestigious institution, located high in the tiers of a subtly hierarchical society, one given to denying its hierarchicality, and are not all societies inevitably hierarchical, we, and others, competed for the attentions of promising young men. It was a race or game of sorts, but certainly not one of simple vanity, entered into for the sake of outdoing others, of testing one's charms and such, but one, too, with significant consequences, bearing importantly on one's future. The sorority, with its prestige, and its relationship with the most exclusive fraternities, was an excellent platform from which to conduct our operations. In this light, then, as suggested earlier, an expulsion from the sorority, with its shame, and such, would constitute a social calamity to be avoided at all costs. All that, of course, was now far behind me. I was now half-clad in a Gorean eating house, a slave band encircling my throat. Still, I saw, and was well aware, that certain similar constants and practicalities characterized my current existence. Certainly I was not the only girl who hoped to escape the eating house. What means, what tools, or weapons, has a female slave at her disposal? Only her charm and beauty. She owns nothing, not even the collar on her neck. It is she, rather, who is owned. She has little to offer a man but herself. Once again, as before, I was competing with other women for prizes we could not obtain for ourselves, but only through men. The nature of our life would again depend on men. Here the difference was that we were slaves. Men were still the masters, but now not subtly, almost invisibly, as on Earth, but now openly, visibly, in the full force of law. Our futures, our hopes, depended on men. And we were literally collared. How clear then, without obfuscation, the pretenses put aside, the veils now removed, became the nature of reality, culturally, socially, and biologically.

"Hitch up your disrobing loop, properly, pull down the hem of your tunic," said the free woman.

"Yes, Mistress," I said.

I hoped she would finish quickly.

Gorean free women of high caste almost invariably veil themselves in public. Gorean free women of the lower castes tend to be less fastidious, or strict, in such matters. Whereas some will emulate the high-caste women, others will veil themselves more casually, or loosely, exposing more of their features. This is sometimes referred to as half-veiling. In privacy, of course, free women seldom veil themselves. In public, it is easy to eat and drink behind the veil. It may be done with delicacy and grace. It is commonly done in the eating houses. I have seen low-caste free women drink through the veil, but this is rare. It is regarded as barbarous. I have seen some free women, of low caste, on hot days, who will eschew the veil altogether. This is, however, rare. As is well known the female slave may not veil herself even should she wish to do so. That would be an insult to free women. Too, one would not, for example, veil a tarsk.

I moved quickly away from the free woman.

She had come to the eating house alone. I was not surprised. I could see something of her face. What fellow would want her in his bracelets?

There is little room between the tables and one, making one's way, usually slowly, for the crowding, taking orders, carrying platters, and such, often brushes against the patrons. There was a small, oval, bronze mirror in the kitchen, fixed on a wall, and I often regarded myself in its reflection, turning my face one way or another, brushing back my hair, arranging it, and such. It seemed to me that certain changes were occurring in me. It is said that bondage makes a woman more beautiful, and I suspect that that is true. This is doubtless, in part, a function of appearance, and behavior, but I think it extends well beyond a certain deference, a tone of voice, a betraying garmenture, a collar, suitable postures, lowering the head, and such. Bondage, whatever might be its numerous effects, feminizes a woman, radically, and the feminine woman is the most female, the most beautiful, of all women. She becomes soft, graceful, vulnerable, and eager to please. The collar removes many conflicts, which trouble, tighten, and coarsen a woman. She knows what she is, and how she is to behave. Allowed nothing else, and soon desiring nothing else, she accepts herself joyfully as what she is, a female, and a slave, her master's slave, her master's possession. She is radiant. She has never been so happy. She pities the free women, lacking masters. Too, she now understands herself as a natural, intensely sexual creature. The slave's sexual needs are as natural, and persistent and irresistible, as her needs to eat and drink. In one sense she is at peace with her sex, but, in another sense, periodically, if her slave fires burn, she is its helpless victim, a tormented slave, who will crawl even to a hated master, for his least touch. She now not only wants sex, but needs it, and will beg for it, and strive to be sufficiently pleasing, that it may be granted to her. She is grateful, in her chains or thongs, to be her master's pleasure object, his possession, and plaything. She knows herself his property, and would be nothing else. Who can recount the ecstasies of the possessed slave? Knowing herself a slave, she wishes to belong to a master. She could be satisfied with no man who would be contented with less than owning her, wholly. Gorean men are such. She sings at her work.

One cannot help, you must understand, in the closeness of the quarters, the small space between the benches, brushing against a master now and then. There is so little room.

"Oh," I gasped, startled.

His large hand had closed on my leg, above the knee.

"Please, Master," I whispered, smiling, protesting.

Then I shuddered. His grip was strong, commanding. It would be difficult to free myself. I was holding a large platter of strips of roast bosk, fastened in threes with wooden skewers, one of the choices for the second ostrakon.

I saw Marcella approaching, in the narrow aisle. She was carrying a vessel of steaming kal-da.

She did not look pleasant.

"Struggle," said he.

"I might spill the platter," I said.

"You are rather pretty for an eating-house girl," he said.

In the past such compliments had been few. Of late, they had been more frequent. Too, of late, I had been more often assigned to the tables. Who knows how often fellows will come to the eating house, or why they will seek one table rather than another?

"Would Master not like to have me at his slave ring?" I whispered. "I would try to please him."

He grinned, and removed his hand from my leg.

"May I serve Master?" I asked.

"What have you?" he asked.

"Roast bosk," I said.

"I have paid only the first ostrakon," he said.

"Master?" I said.

"Be off, pretty slave," he said.

"Yes, Master," I said.

"Infamous she-sleen!" said a woman.

I had not noticed that the unpleasant free woman, she who, some days ago, had castigated me for a too-casual tunicking, was again in the vicinity. Once again, which did not surprise me, she was alone.

"Yes, Mistress," I said. "Forgive me, Mistress."

I quickly tried to hurry away, and Marcella, who was now near, between the benches, stood to one side, I supposed that I might pass. I smiled at her. Usually she would have expected me to turn about and move back, retracing my steps, removing myself from her path. I did not really want the attentions of the kitchen master, even though he had, of late, discouraged the other girls from bullying me. Surely she must understand that. She could have him. I wanted better game, higher game.

"Thank you," I said to Marcella, smiling, as I went to move past her, anxious to remove myself as quickly as possible from the vicinity of the free woman.

"Oh!" I cried, in misery, stumbling, plunging over Marcella's extended foot, sprawling between the benches, the platter of steaming meat flying ahead of me, meat and gravy showering about, then the platter clattering between the benches. Two or three men stood up, angrily wiping gravy and hot meat from their backs and shoulders. Marcella, simultaneously, had screamed, and turned, as though it might have been she who had been so discomfited. And I, too, screamed, but in pain, as the scalding kal-da soaked and burned through my tunic, and drenched my calves and ankles. "Clumsy slave!" cried

Marcella. "You tripped me!" I cried. "I did not! You tripped me!" she screamed. Several of the masters laughed, some brushing themselves off, some others helping themselves to a three of skewered slices of the roast bosk, which they retrieved from the table, the floor, their laps. I was on my hands and knees, in pain, from the scalding, tears bursting from my eyes. Masters, I knew, did not look lightly on clumsiness in a slave. Too, to make matters worse, if they could be worse, the roast bosk was an item available only for the second ostrakon. I recalled that one of the girls in the kitchen, who had spilled porridge, had been put under the five-stranded Gorean slave lash. I had felt it once, in the house of Tenalion. "You tripped me!" I cried to Marcella. I did not want to be whipped! "You tripped me!" screamed Marcella. "No!" I cried. "Yes!" she screamed. She did not wish to be whipped either. "I saw the whole thing!" said the free woman. "That one," she said, pointing at me, "is to blame!" "No, Mistress," I sobbed. "That one, that one!" repeated the free woman, indicating me. I did not see how she, from her location, could have seen what occurred. I did know that she did not like me. A free woman, of course, may lie, for they are free. Marcella was lying, of course, but she had the words of a free woman spoken on her behalf. "Thank you, Mistress," said Marcella, respectfully, much pleased at the course events were taking. I was sobbing, and still in pain. I did not want to be stripped, tied, and put under the whip. I feared the pain, and terribly, but, too, it is humiliating to be beaten for clumsiness, to be beaten as an inept slave, one who has failed to be pleasing. The slave is to be both beautiful and graceful. If she is not, let the lash instruct her. She is a slave. She is not permitted the woodenness, the awkwardness, of the free woman. "You should be sold for sleen feed!" said the free woman, coming angrily from her place, and hurrying about the table. I was still on the floor, on all fours, miserable, in pain. The boards were greasy. The tunic, in back, was wet, with warm fluid. It clung to my body. My legs hurt.

"Forgive me, Mistress!" I begged.

I felt the slipper of the free woman kick me, twice, viciously, in the left thigh. There would be marks there. I sensed she had spit upon me.

"I am sorry, Mistress!" I said. "Please, forgive me, Mistress!"

I went to my belly, in the grease and scraps, between the benches.

"Oh!" I wept, again kicked.

"Thank you, Mistress!" I said. "Thank you, Mistress!"

Should a slave not be grateful for her improvement?

"Aii!" I wept, again kicked.

"Thank you, Mistress!" I sobbed. "Thank you, Mistress!"

"What is going on here?" demanded a voice. Someone was making his way toward us, pushing, between the benches. My heart sank. It was the voice of Menon, my master. I had been several weeks in his establishment, but he seldom appeared in the kitchen. I was not sure he would remember the miserable, frightened slave purchased in the Metellan district. I struggled to my knees, held them closely together, and kept my head down.

"This slave tripped me, Master," said Marcella, indicating me.

"Have you received permission to speak?" inquired Menon.

"No, Master," said Marcella, turning white, dropping to her knees, head down.

"Well, Masters?" inquired Menon.

"They were passing between the benches," said a fellow. "One of the girls tripped, and fell."

"That one," said the free woman, presumably indicating me, "tripped the other!"

"I see," said Menon.

I kept my head down.

"You saw?" inquired Menon.

"Certainly," said the free woman.

Menon turned about, a bit. I took him to be noting the place, across the table, with its dish and mug, where the free woman had been sitting.

"Did any others see?" inquired Menon.

No one volunteered to speak. Most, of course, would have had their backs turned to the aisle.

"That one," said the free woman, presumably indicating me, "should be lashed bloody, to the bone, and fed to sleen!"

"There would not be much nourishment there," said a fellow.

There was laughter.

I could not help it if I were slighter than many slaves, more slender. Many men, of late, I had been given to understand, did not find fault with me on this score. Certainly I had been one of the most beautiful girls in the sorority, and here, in the garmenture of slaves, what beauty I might possess, as that of other female slaves, left little to conjecture.

"Be silent!" screamed the free woman to the men.

There was silence.

I was afraid. As I was now well aware I was a female slave and what that meant on Gor, I would have been terrified to address a free man or men in that tone of voice, let alone utter words bearing such an import.

What would have been done with me?

But she was free.

There was no band on her neck.

She was not an animal.

She was not purchasable.

She was not owned.

"The house," said Menon, "is distressed that your views have been shown less deference than they deserve."

"You know," said the free woman, "that she, that one, is a she-tarsk, a she-urt, a she-sleen, one who tunics herself provocatively, who brushes against masters, who lingers in serving, who leans too closely to the diners, who puts her half-naked body before them shamelessly, who smiles so prettily, like a paga slut at the loading docks, advertising her master's tavern."

"And she is a barbarian, as well," said Menon.

"Yes," said the free woman, triumphantly. "A barbarian!"

Menon recalled I was a barbarian.

"My Home Stone," she said, "is that of Ar."

Menon nodded. Although his establishment was within the walls of Ar, it was not likely he shared its Home Stone. As he was of the Peasants, I supposed his Home Stone, the community stone, so to speak, not that of his domicile, would be that of some village in the environs of Ar.

"Is there no way to assuage your wrath?" asked Menon.

"No," said the free woman.

Menon drew his pouch on its strings up from his belt, and opened it.

"No," she said.

Menon fetched from within the pouch a handful of copper tarsk-bits.

"Perhaps," said the free woman, "she needs only to be well lashed."

Menon dropped the coins into the palm of the free woman.

"The master, of course," she said, "will decide, as he pleases, what is to be the fate of a neck-banded she-tarsk."

"Thank you, Lady," said he.

I do not know if she looked again at me, but she hurried about the table, to her place and, a moment later, made away.

Menon was crouching near Marcella, who was shaking.

"There is a mark here," said Menon to her, "on the outside of your right leg, above the ankle."

Marcella said nothing.

Menon lifted up my left leg. "This mark," he said, "is on the front of your left leg, just above the ankle."

My heart leapt. It must be, then, that I had struck against Marcella's ankle, thrust into my path, as I had tried to hurry past.

"You must have been hurrying," said Menon to me.

"Yes, Master," I said.

"What happened?" he asked.

I sensed he knew well what happened.

"I stumbled," I said.

Marcella gasped, gratefully, softly.

"I see," said Menon. He smiled. "You should be more careful," he said.

"Yes, Master," I said.

"You, too," he said to Marcella.

"Yes, Master!" she said.

"It would not do," he said, evenly, "for another slave to stumble in your vicinity."

"Yes, Master," she said.

"Do you understand?" he said.

"Yes, Master!" she said, pale.

Menon turned to me. "You are Allison, are you not?" he asked.

"Yes, Master," I said, "if it pleases Master."

"You are to come with me," he said. "Leading position."

I rose to my feet, and bent over, that my hair might be easily grasped. I felt his hand lock itself in my hair. My head was down, at his left thigh.

"Marcella," he said.

"Master?" she said, apprehensively.

"You will return to the kitchen, and return naked, with a pan of water, and no rags," he said, "and clean this mess."

"No rags?" she said.

"Your hair will do," he said.

Marcella had long glossy, dark hair, which fell well behind her. She was very proud of it. We envied her for it.

"Too," said he, "when this is done, you are to inform the kitchen master that you are to serve the tables daily for the next twenty days, but, in this period, you are not to be permitted clothing."

"Master!" she wept.

"And as your hair will be soiled," he said, "you will have the kitchen master crop it short, as short as that of a mill girl."

"Yes, Master," she said.

"And at night, for this period, of twenty days, you are to be put in close chains."

"Please, no, Master!" she wept.

"Would you prefer all this, and the lash, as well, once daily, for the next twenty days?"

"No, Master!" she said.

"Perhaps, in the future, you will be more careful," he said.

"Yes, Master," she sobbed.

"Come along, Allison," said he, and began to make his way between the tables, and I, in the sullied, soaked tunic, stumbled along at his side, sometimes brushing into patrons, sometimes striking against benches, jutting out, in the narrow space between the tables.

"May I speak, may I speak?" I gasped, dragged along, at his side.

"Yes," he said.

"Please do not whip me!" I said.

"Do you deserve to be whipped?" he asked.

"I trust not, Master!" I said.

"Do not all kajirae deserve to be whipped?" he asked.

"I trust not, Master!" I said.

"But they are slaves," he said.

"Even so," I said.

"Surely they know what they have done, or failed to do, even if masters do not," he said, "and thus well know, given their lapses and faults, however infrequent or slight, which may have escaped the notice of the masters, how richly they deserve to be whipped, and, accordingly, should have no objection whatsoever to having the lash at any time well laid upon them."

"I trust Master jests," I said, stumbling along, my hair hurting.

He laughed.

How helpless we are in the hands of men, if they but choose to be masters! How they play with us, and use us as they please! We are so different from them! We are so small, so helpless in their power!

Yet I would not trade the Gorean man, with all his might and will, all his arrogance and power, all his virility and masculinity, all his forcefulness and possessiveness, all his ambition and aggression, all his energy and intelligence, his seeing us as women, and astonishingly different, and rightly, deliciously ownable, for all the males I knew on Earth.

"Surely, surely Master jests," I said.

"Come along," he said.

"Yes, Master," I said, as if I had any choice!

Slaves, as other animals, are seldom whipped on Gor. The reason for that is simple, and obvious. The slave, subject to the whip, and knowing herself so, is careful to avoid it, insofar as it lies in her power. She does her best to satisfy her master, and in all the ways of the slave, all of them. And, obviously, she who satisfies a man fully has little, if anything, to fear. Thus, it is she who is primarily responsible for keeping the whip on its peg. She is, of course, subject to discipline, and this encourages diligence. The female slave is far more likely to be beaten by a free woman than a free man. To the free man she is a joy and treasure; to the free woman she is a hated reproach and rival.

Menon's office was not far from the paying counter, where ostraka were vended, to be redeemed for meals.

He pushed open the swinging partition leading to the interior, and threw me to the floor before a chair.

They are not always gentle with us.

We are slaves.

I kept my eyes down. I had never been in the office before.

"Is this the one?" asked Menon.

"Yes," said a voice.

The back of my legs still hurt, from the scalding of the kal-da.

"Remove your tunic, my dear," said the voice.

I instantly and unquestioningly disrobed. One of the first things a girl learns on Gor is that she is to instantly and unquestioningly obey. It is not Earth, and the college, and the sorority, were far away.

Here men were the masters, at least of women such as I, totally, and absolutely.

One knows oneself their slave, unequivocally, totally, and absolutely.

"Show him something," said Menon.

"Master?" I said.

"As in slave paces," said Menon, "posings, stretchings, curlings, liftings, twistings, floor movements, such things."

"Yes, Master," I said.

After a short time, from the voice, I heard, "Enough."

"Yes, Master," I said.

I had exhibited myself as the slave I now was. How faraway was the college, and the sorority!

"She is blushing," said the voice.

"She is a new slave, and a barbarian," said Menon.

"Yet she did well," said the voice.

"She is born collar meat," said Menon.

"She is of increased attractiveness," said the voice, "different from the Metellan market."

"Yes," said Menon.

I had sensed, earlier, that I was changing. The collar causes such things in a female.

Too, the owner of the voice must have seen my sale some weeks ago.

"How would you like to leave the kitchen, the tables, Allison?" said Menon.

"It will be done with me as masters please," I said.

"Kneel," said Menon. "Face our guest."

I knelt, my knees closely together. I did not cover my breasts, of course, for they were those of a slave.

"How, my dear," asked the stranger, "would you like a new chain, a new cage?"

"It will be done with me as masters please," I said.

"How, my dear," said the voice, "would you like to be chained to a loom in the mills of Mintar, with cropped hair, or be placed in one of the public laundries, or sent to the mines of Argentum, or the tharlarion stables at Venna?"

"It will be done with me as masters please," I said.

"But you would not be too pleased?" he asked.

"No, Master," I said.

"Have no fear," he said, "it is not to such a place I would send you."

"A slave is grateful," I said.

"What would you like?" he asked.

How absurd, I thought, that one should ask that of a slave.

"Perhaps, Masters," I said, "I might be purchased as a private slave, to serve a private master?"

"You would like that, would you not, kajira?" asked the stranger.

"Oh, yes, Master," I said, "yes, Master!"

It was for such a favor, such a delight, such a privilege, that I had plied the tables in my serving. I dared to look up and see the stranger. He was stocky, broad-shouldered, and powerful. He was blond-haired. He was not bad looking. Immediately I began to wonder what it might be, to be owned by him. How glorious, I thought, to have a private master, him or another, to whom one might devote oneself, assiduously, as his slave.

He seemed typically Gorean. He would see to it that a woman served him well, and doubtless with perfection, should she be a slave.

"I would try to serve Master well," I said.

"Astrinax," said Menon, "whom I have long known, is an agent, who receives orders, requests and such, screens merchandise, and buys for others."

"Yes, Master," I said.

"He contracts with several towers, for serving slaves," he said.

"Yes, Master," I said.

I had occasionally been out of the restaurant, on errands, and had marveled at the lofty towers of Ar, so lovely and colorful, and yet so stately, solid, and formidable, each, in its way, a defensible keep, with its reservoirs, and emergency stores. It would take years to reduce even one to submission. These towers, at various levels, were joined by narrow, graceful bridges. In times of peace, one might move from one tower to another, through one tower to another, by means of these bridges, to many parts of the city, without once descending to the streets. The bridges for the most part are unrailed but traversed with ease by urban Goreans used to them. I myself would have been terrified to set foot upon almost any one of them, the streets so far below. They were of different widths, some ten feet in width, many four to five feet in width. They have colored lanterns on them, spaced here and there, which are commonly lit at night. It is very lovely. On my former world, Earth, there are similar walks, but they are on the ground. Few of Earth would think twice about traversing such walks. On the other hand, if such walks were elevated, I suspect few would care to try them. One supposes it is largely a matter of that to which one grows accustomed. In any event, you traverse the high bridges with the same thoughtless nonchalance with which those of Earth traverse their own walks. Your bridges, slender and graceful, are often arched and curved, almost like branches in a forest, for you have an aesthetic sense, it seems, in so much that you do, evinced in things as intricate as the soaring melody of a skyline to things as simple as the carving on an oar or a wooden spoon. To be sure, you have your realms of crowding, ugliness, and danger as well, the dank, odorous, ill-lit insulae, steaming in the summer, clammy and cold in the winter, smelling of offal and urine, and the dark, cluttered, filthy, winding streets of some of the low districts. Sometimes the towers seem to be giants, standing proudly, independent and mighty, soaring to the sky, touching clouds, their feet in garbage. Much depends, of course, on the district. In many respects Ar is a city of wonder, of beauty and grace, of soaring towers, large parks and gardens, and broad boulevards. It is in terms of those that one numbers her amongst the "high cities." But she is, too, a city in which poverty and wealth, surfeit and want, cleanliness and dirt, may be juxtaposed. A silken palanquin, with closed curtains, may be borne through slime. Here and there women, unattended, grace the bridges in their promenades, while below a troop of guardsmen may tread with care. Praetors preside in the markets, dispensing justice, while here and there, beneath their feet, in sewers, like urts, others wait for darkness. Much depends on the district, and the time of day. I suppose that cities are similar, on whatever worlds they may be found. Here a tunicked slave might wander about in the night without fear, there a guardsman is reluctant to enter at the Tenth Ahn. One thing I did not realize originally about your bridges is the military utility involved in their design, that they may be blocked and defended by small groups of armed men; five may defend against a hundred, because of the hundred only five can engage at a time. Too, the bridges may be broken, this preventing access to the towers, turning each into a solitary, soaring, nigh-impregnable citadel.

I supposed then that Astrinax, as I gathered his name was, was jobbing for some tower or another, presumably on the lookout for girls who might make acceptable tower slaves. There tends to be turnover in such slaves, as, in their work, in the corridors, on the stairwells, and in the apartments, they may come to the attention of one fellow or another, who will take them for a private slave. Being a tower slave is usually regarded as a plausible route, even a promising route, to obtaining a private master. Most slaves, as you know, or may suspect, long to be the slave, and wholly so, of one man alone. This is the joy of the slave, to kneel naked at the feet of her master, to lick and kiss his whip, and his feet, and then to lie before him, helpless in his chains.

To be sure, she hopes to be his only slave, as well!

I had occasionally seen tower slaves in the streets, in their white, knee-length, modest, demure tunics.

It was easy to see why a fellow might want to get them out of those tunics. Properly caressed, and long denied passion, it was said they were commonly as hot as paga sluts.

I did not think I would mind being a tower slave.

Surely, as one cleaned an apartment, dusted a bit, arranged furniture, and such, it seemed a clever girl might find ample opportunities for calling herself to the attention of one fellow or another.

A smile, an ankle seemingly inadvertently extended, colored string wound about it, a touching of one's collar, a shy glance, a way of turning, of looking over one's shoulder.

Such things.

"Split your knees," said Astrinax.

"Master?" I said. Then I went to "position," not wanting to be cuffed for dallying.

"Astrinax also," said Menon, "scouts and buys for the taverns and brothels, as well."

"Yes, Master," I said, uneasily.

"Do you think you would make a good paga girl, or brothel slut?" asked Menon.

"I do not think so, Master," I said.

"Do not worry about it," said Menon. "The lash quickly teaches a girl to be accommodating, and grateful."

"Yes, Master," I said.

"The paga slave quickly becomes a passion slut," said Menon.

"Yes, Master," I said.

I already had sensed that such things might be possible. But my body, too, had assured me that not all passion sluts would be in the taverns or brothels. Surely often enough, at night, I had lain uneasily in my chains.

What would it be to be in the arms of a master, my own master?

I would strive desperately to be pleasing to him.

It was not so much that I feared being beaten, should I be found wanting in some respect. Rather it was because I sensed myself a slave, and wanted his touch.

"We are not thinking about the taverns or brothels," said Astrinax.

"Yes, Master," I said.

"Perhaps later," said Astrinax.

"Yes, Master," I said.

"Knees," said Menon, gently.

Quickly I widened my knees again.

I gathered Astrinax was not thinking in terms of tower slaves.

Tower slaves do not kneel so. Another sort of slave kneels so, a familiar form of Gorean slave, the pleasure slave. This was, of course, the sort of slavery for which, on the whole, I had been trained. I supposed the same would be so of my sisters, from the sorority, from the college, doubtless brought to collars on Gor as well as I. I recalled Eve and Jane, from the party, in their improvised camisks. Surely I had seen the eyes of the boys on them, as well as on myself. They were young and beautiful. I did not doubt but what masters would find them pleasing. Too, Nora, and her friends, doubtless, would no longer be so resplendent in those ample, abundant, lovely garments worn at the party, put together to suggest the robes of Gorean free women. Perhaps here, on this world, they would be fortunate enough to be granted a tunic. I suspected that Nora would go for a high price.

I was pleased to think of her as collared, and owned.

So, if Astrinax was not thinking in terms of the towers, and was not thinking, at least at present, in terms of the taverns or brothels, in what terms might he be thinking?

"You are a barbarian are you not?" asked Astrinax.

"Yes, Master," I said.

"Barbarians," said Astrinax, "have inferior moral characters."

"Surely not," I said.

"When you thought yourself free, on your former world, prior to your rightful collaring," said Astrinax, "for you are obviously a slave, you had some sort of relationship with the men of your world, did you not?"

"I was brought to Gor as white-silk," I said. "I was red-silked in the house of Tenalion, Tenalion of Ar."

"I know the house," said Astrinax. "What I have in mind is the nature of your social, economic, and political relationships to men."

"I am not sure I understand," I said. "I think that certain relationships, involving certain intentions, prospects, efforts, plans, ambitions, and such, would have been typical for a young woman of my background, position, wealth, and class."

"But perhaps not for others?" said Astrinax.

"Probably not for all others," I said.

"Tell me something of it," said Astrinax.

"I was of the upper classes on my world," I said.

"You look well in your collar," said Astrinax.

"Thank you, Master," I said. "I belonged to a group of young women chosen, among other things, for their beauty."

"Slaves?" said Astrinax.

"Perhaps," I said. "We were privileged. We were to be sought by men, and would make judicious choices amongst them, seeking thereby our advantage, bartering our beauty for advancement, for greater wealth, more secure position, more power, such things."

"You were calculating in such matters," said Astrinax. "You were selling yourself for profit, for gain."

"Yes, Master," I said.

"In Gorean we have a word for that," said Astrinax.

"Master?" I said.

"'Free woman'," he said.

"Men must try to please us, must pay for our meals, our entertainments, and such," I said.

"There is a politics involved in such things," said Astrinax.

"Yes," I said.

"And to achieve your ends," said Astrinax, "you would do what seemed useful, flatter, pretend, flirt, intrigue, invite, and such."

"Yes, Master," I said.

"Good," he said. "And lie?"

"I am no longer permitted to lie, Master," I said, frightened.

"But then," he said.

"Yes, Master," I said.

"You are not unattractive," said Astrinax.

"Thank you, Master," I said.

"And the men whom you knew had little or no experience with female slaves," said Astrinax.

"No, Master," I said.

"Accordingly then," said Astrinax, "you must have been extremely attractive to them."

"I think so, Master," I said.

"They knew no better," said Astrinax.

"No, Master," I said. Tears came to eyes.

"Do not be upset," said Astrinax. "You now have promise, even as a slave."

"You are much more beautiful than when I bought you," said Menon. "You are becoming slave-beautiful, slave-exciting. Those young men who found you beautiful then, as you were then, on your own world, would scream with pleasure if they could see you now, as you are, as a slave. Slavery much enhances the beauty of a woman. Now, sweet Allison, those young men would sweat, and cry out, and bid recklessly for you, in the hope of bringing you into their collar."

I put down my head.

"I gather you were a true 'free woman' on your world," said Astrinax, "with all her vanities, pettinesses, impostures, ambitions, plans, manipulations, machinations, pretensions, schemes, deceits, and lies."

"Perhaps, Master," I said.

"But now," he said, "you are no longer on your own world."

"No, Master," I said.

"It is common for free women on your world to misuse their power," said Astrinax.

"Perhaps, Master," I said, frightened. I trusted I would not be punished on this world for faults which might have been mine on a former world. But, still, one does not know how men will see things, and they are the masters.

"Free women on Gor," said Astrinax, "misuse their power."

I thought of the free woman at the tables, who had caused me such discomfiture.

"I dare not speculate, Master," I said. "They are free, and I am a slave."

"But stripped and collared, and thrown to a man's feet," said Astrinax, "they are not so different from you."

"I dare not speculate, Master," I said. "They are free, and I am a slave."

"You are all women," said Astrinax. "Nothing more."

"Yes, Master," I said.

"Allison," said Astrinax, "suppose that one of your sister slaves, in the kitchen, had been given a candy, perhaps as a tip from a customer, from waiting on the tables."

"Yes, Master?" I said.

Some of the customers, I knew, kept such small treats about their person, or in their pouches. These were usually hard candies, which might last a long time, slowly savored. Sometimes they would roll them on the floor and have a girl pursue them on all fours, putting her head down, and picking them up, gratefully, in her teeth. Sometimes they would have the girl kneel at the bench, put back her head, her eyes closed, tightly, and open her mouth, widely. She does not know, strictly, if she is to be cuffed or rewarded, but, as you may suppose, she usually has an excellent sense as to how matters will fall out. If her service is thought to have been insufficiently prompt, diligent or deferent, and she is likely to suspect that, she may be struck. "Forgive me, Master," she then sobs, and is hastened about her duties, now intent on improving her service. At least she is not lashed. Usually, however, if so knelt, she is to be rewarded, a candy being placed in her mouth. "Thank you, Master," she breathes, licking and kissing the hand which has deigned to bestow so precious a gift upon her. How proud she is then, the possessor of so rare a treat, and how envied she will be amongst her chain sisters!

How she will nurse that treat, making it last as long as possible!

To be sure, such tipping is frowned upon by the establishment, as the women are merely slaves.

One wonders if the free can understand how important such a tidbit, negligible from their point of view, so tiny, savory, and sweet, can be to one of your despised collar girls.

Even today such a thing is meaningful to me, and my master may or may not grant it to me, as it pleases him, but, at that time, in the place of Menon, so small a thing seemed inordinately precious, and important.

I had not had such a sweet since Earth, since my "harvesting" as one of the ill-protected, exposed, dangling fruits so easily available to slavers in the "slave orchard of Earth," no, not since my acquisition, my capture, my routine snaring, merely another sleek, defenseless animal, ignorant and unsuspecting, easily taken as the prize of methodical hunters.

"Now," said Astrinax, "let us suppose that the girl who has been given the candy wants to save it, to postpone the pleasure of eating it until later, perhaps to when her work is done, and hides it somewhere, perhaps in the straw of her mat, and you, unbeknownst to her, have observed this."

"Yes, Master?" I said, warily.

"Let us further suppose that you might, unobserved, and unsuspected, and with utter impunity, steal it. Would you do so?"

I did not care for this conversation. I was much afraid, to lie, or to tell the truth.

"I must tell the truth?" I asked.

"You are a slave," said Menon.

"And I would not be caught?" I asked.

"No," said Astrinax.

"I am not stupid," I said.

"Of course not," said Astrinax.

It was well known that high intelligence was one of the properties sought in slaves. Who would want a stupid slave? Too, it was well known that highly intelligent women made the best slaves. Of all women they were the quickest to learn that the collar was truly on them, that they were now actually owned by a master, that society wholly supported and approved their condition, and that escape was impossible. They were now slaves, unqualifiedly. Too, once they had been truly knelt, their sexual drives and needs would begin to rage within them; they would become aware of their biological being and its nature, that they were biologically the properties of men; and, pursuant to these understandings and bodily changes, and knowing themselves choiceless, the collar on their necks, they yielded to their being and nature, submissive to, and responsive to, categorical male dominance, yielded helplessly and appetitiously to this, naturally, passionately, and gratefully, it being that for which they had longed for so long, that without they were incomplete, given the radical sexual dimorphism of the species.

They would come to long for the chain, and the caress.

Even to beg for it.

"And she is only a slave," I said.

"Of course," said Astrinax.

"Then," said I, "I would steal the candy. Who would not?"

"Many," said Menon, regretfully.

"I think she will do very nicely," said Astrinax.

"I fear so," said Menon.

"Master?" I said, uneasily.

"Eventually," said Menon, "you will have to grow more moral."

"Master?" I said.

"You are a slave," said Menon. "One expects a greater morality from a slave than a free woman."

"Because they are afraid of being beaten?" I asked.

"Perhaps," he said.

"But, Master," I said, "is the testimony of slaves in courts not taken under torture, that they will not dare to lie?"

"It would be better," said Menon, "for the testimony of free women to be taken under torture, for they are famous for saying whatever pleases them."

"Under torture," said Astrinax, "one speaks not to say the truth, but to say whatever will stop the pain."

"I am disappointed in you, Allison," said Menon.

"Forgive me, Master," I said.

"She is a barbarian," Astrinax reminded Menon.

"True," said Menon.

"I am pleased to hear your response to my question," said Astrinax.

"A slave is pleased if Master is pleased," I said.

Surely a girl is entitled to look out for herself, avail herself of opportunities, improve her place, take advantage of things, and so on.

"I think you are a clever slave," said Astrinax.

"Thank you, Master," I said.

"Though perhaps not intelligent," he said.

"Master?" I said.

"But clever, surely," he said.

"Thank you, Master," I said.

I wished he had said 'intelligent'. 'Clever' had a suggestion of pettiness, of cunning, of smallness about it.

"And pretty," he said.

"Thank you, Master," I said.

"A pretty slave, and a clever one," he said.

"Thank you, Master," I said. I was not sure I had been complimented. Was I not intelligent, was I not beautiful, at least amongst women of Earth, if not compared to Gorean collar girls?

But is the word 'clever' not a mere disparagement, on the part of some, of true intelligence, that which is expedient, and prudentially wise, that by means of which one may pursue one's best interests with the least regard to extraneous impediments, principles, codes, rules, and such?

I was annoyed.

I knew myself to be quite intelligent. The girls in the sorority had not been selected merely on the basis of appearance, carriage, dressing smartly, being economically well stationed, and so on. We were selected, at least in part, to enhance the reputation of the sorority, as an established avenue to wealth and power. Membership, this presenting us as rare prizes in marital competitions, above lesser advantaged girls, much increased the likelihood of our obtaining an enviable match.

"On your former world," said Astrinax, "one supposes you were adept in certain familiar female practices, commonly associated with free women, for example, that you were skilled in flattering males, in teasing them, manipulating them, playing on their feelings, raising their hopes, encouraging them to pursuits in your interest, or perhaps in the interest of your superiors, inducing them to certain activities, by glances, smiles, words, and such."

"Perhaps, Master," I said.

I had enjoyed such games, sometimes for gain, sometimes for sport. It was easy to find gratification in my effect on males, boys, and men.

Then, of course, I was not a vulnerable slave, owned, subject to discipline, and such.

Then I was free. I was not in a collar.

What one did then one might not dare in a collar.

"Do you think you could engage in such activities now," asked Astrinax.

"I do not understand, Master," I said. I did not want to be lashed.

"Could you smile upon men, bring them drinks, brush against them, be at their side, smile, laugh, pretend to share their anxieties, their joys, their disappointments, and keep them engaged in certain activities?"

"Master?" I said.

"Could you lie, if commanded, pretend interest where interest was not felt, simulate affection where none exists, use your beauty, for you now have beauty, yes, beauty, such as it is, to whisper, wheedle, stimulate, instigate, and influence men, even to their ruin, collapse, or destitution?"

"I do not think I understand Master," I said.

"Astrinax," said Menon, "is seeking slaves for a gambling house. It is one of several on the Street of Chance. In such a house, there are commonly slaves, beautiful slaves, to wait upon the men, to serve drinks and food, to contribute to the decor and pleasantness of the setting, to mingle with the patrons, to encourage betting, even to the point of recklessness."

"I see," I said.

"In the beginning," he said, "you would be a lesser slave, though not hard to look upon, and might assist the other girls."

"Yes, Master," I said. I was pleased, at least, to learn that I was not hard to look upon. Perhaps in such a place I might attract a man and win for myself a private master. I could make my choice judiciously, finding a fellow both handsome and strong, and, in such a place, quite possibly one of wealth. A girl has ways of course, of influencing a fellow to think of buying her.

It was lonely in my chains, at night. Sometime I clutched them, hurting my hands, in frustration, those metal fastenings on me so fixedly, and thrashed on my mat.

"I think I know the house," said Menon to Astrinax. "If it is the one I think it is, it is rumored to be dishonest."

"If so," smiled Astrinax, "I think our little Allison might fit in quite nicely."

I remembered my response to the question about the candy.

"Doubtless," said Menon.

I feared I had disappointed my master.

"You understand the sort of thing we have in mind, do you not, Allison?" asked Astrinax.

"Yes, Master," I said.

"Do you think you could well fulfill your duties in such a place?"

"Yes, Master," I said.

"I thought so," he said.

"Slaves, there," said Menon, "exist to loosen the strings on pouches, urge fellows to shower gold on the tables, to risk much, beyond reason, to pout and look away if there is evidence of hesitation or circumspection, to cry out in pleasure if an extra tarn disk is put in the plate, another card drawn, another flash of dice cast."

"Yes, Master," I said.

I did not see that that was my concern.

"Some will ply them with drink," he said, "and bring them food, to keep them at the tables."

"I understand," I said.

"You may be expected to do such things," he said.

"Yes, Master," I said.

"And," said Astrinax, "you would be expected to do such things well, with an appearance of delight and enthusiasm. Do you think you could manage that?"

"Yes, Master," I said.

In such a place might one not secure a suitable master, perhaps even one rich, though, to be sure, I would hope to be his only slave.

"The price agreed," said Astrinax, "as I recall, was a silver tarsk."

I looked up, startled.

I had originally sold for forty-two copper tarsks.

"The price, now," said Menon, rising, looking down on me, "is fifty, fifty copper tarsks."

"Oh?" said Astrinax, smiling.

"She is not worth a silver tarsk," said Menon.

I knelt between them while the tarsks were counted out.

When the transaction had been completed, I dared to look up at Menon. "It is a shame," said Menon, looking down upon me, "that the slavers consider little more than intelligence, beauty, and helpless, latent passion. Perhaps they should concern themselves more with the character of their prey."

"Master?" I said.

"Women such as you," he said, "belong beneath the whip."

"Please do not whip me, Master," I said.

"Take her away," said Menon.

Astrinax stood up, and, from his pouch, he cast me a bit of purple cloth. There was not much to it. It had writing on the back, which I could not read. It barely covered me.

"Stand up, my dear," said Astrinax.

I did so, hip turned, as I had been taught.

Astrinax regarded me, appraisingly. And I think he was satisfied.

"Come along," said Astrinax, holding open the swinging panel, which led from the office.

"I wish you well, Master," I said to Menon.

"Get out," he said.

"Yes, Master," I said, and hurried after Astrinax, sobbing, my eyes filled with tears.

But, I thought, too, I am out of the kitchen, away from the tables. Too, I had little doubt I would be fetching in the sort of tunic I now wore. The angry glance of a free woman, outside the office, reassured me of this.

I felt so superior to her in that moment.

She was only a free woman. I was a slave, half clad, collared, shapely, desirable, ownable, the sort of woman men want, the sort of woman they prize, and buy.

I was a thousand times more than she.

I might be less than the dirt beneath her sandals, but I was a thousand times more than she.

It is no wonder they hate us so, and we fear them so.

How special it was to be a slave, and how right it was for me!

It was what I was, and should be.

If one is a slave, why should one not be a slave?

Chapter Nine

The cages, of heavy, cable-like woven wire, are made for tarsks, not kajirae. One cannot stand in them. They are long, narrow, and low. Thus, more than one can be placed on a sideless, flat-bedded wagon, roped in place. Too, like the common slave cages designed for kajirae, they may be stacked.

I hooked my fingers in the wire, and looked out, frightened, from my knees. The Tarsk Market has its name, obviously enough, I suppose, because it is a general market for tarsks. Certainly the smell of tarsk was all about. And there was little doubt, from the condition of the cage, that the previous occupants of the cage had been tarsks.

Needless to say, it is only low slaves who are vended from such a market.

I lay down in the cage, on my right side, in the straw, facing the back wall of the warehouse.

How vulnerable we were, as slaves!

But, had we been free women I did not doubt but what we would have been abandoned, left in the house, on the Street of Chance, to perish in the flames.

The marks on our thighs, our collars, had saved us. We had been saved, but as what we were, only that, animals.

"That one," said a voice, a woman's voice. I did not place the accent. It did not sound pleasant.

"That one?" asked a man.

"Yes," said the woman's voice. "I would see her."

I felt a stick poke me. "Turn about," said the man's voice. "On all fours!"

I turned about, and went to all fours, my head down, frightened. I would have a bruise on my back.

My hopes of obtaining a handsome, rich master, from amongst the clients of the gambling house, had perished, as had the house, in the furious, vengeful fire, set by guardsmen. No one with money would buy here, I suspected, not in such a place, not in such a market.

I had no doubt I smelled, of the straw, and the dung of tarsks.

Too, it was a woman's voice.

"Let us see her," said the woman.

I heard the gate at the end of the long, low cage unfastened.

"Out," said the man. "Stay on all fours."

I made my way to the end of the cage, and emerged, out, onto the stained, straw-strewn floor.

I kept my head lowered.

"She must be cheap," said the woman.

"She is, they all are," said the man. "We had the lot for next to nothing."

"Twenty tarsks," said the woman.

"Surely not," said the man.

"No more," said the woman.

"She is not bad slave meat," said the man. "Shall I put her in examination position?"

There are various examination positions, but the most common is to stand the slave with her feet widely spread, and her hands clasped behind the back of her neck, or the back of her head. The spreading of the feet makes movement difficult, and the position of the hands keeps them out of the way as the slave is examined. They shall not interfere, nor will there be an impediment to the buyer's vision as the slave is considered. This position also lifts the slave's breasts nicely. Too, the girl is expected to stand erect, her shoulders back, which also accentuates the breasts, and her belly is to be sucked in, this calling attention to the width of her love cradle, the narrowness of a pleasant, trim waist, and the lovely flare of her body, as it rises to the beauty of her bosom. She may be handled rather as the buyer pleases, must open her mouth upon request, that her teeth may be examined, and so on. Sometimes the slave cries out startled, or in misery, for she may be tested for sturdiness of body, for firmness, for responsiveness, and such.

"No," said the woman.

"Shall I have her on her back or belly, and have her squirm for you?" asked the man.

"No," said the woman.

I hoped that the woman might be a slave, buying for a master. I turned my head a little, and my heart sank. I saw no bared ankle, perhaps encircled with a locked ring, nor some loops of binding fiber, suitable for binding a girl, but the hem of a robe, a rich, scarlet robe, and glimpsed the toes of small slippers, yellow, beneath that hem.

It was a free woman!

"What do you want her for?" asked the man.

"Work," said the woman. "Is it true that slaves are lazy?"

I thought that a strange question for a Gorean free woman. Was she a stranger, from some unusual city, away from civilization, unfamiliar with some sorts of animals, ones such as I?

"They had better not be," said the man. "Too, the switch, the whip, encourages diligence."

It suddenly occurred to me that the woman, seemingly unfamiliar with such obvious things, might not be Gorean. Certainly I was unfamiliar with the accent. Perhaps she might buy me and free me?

Then I realized how foolish was such a thought.

I was on Gor.

"Twenty tarsks," said the woman.

"Not enough," said the man.

"Show me something else, cheaper," said the woman.

"There is nothing cheaper," said the man. "She is the cheapest."

"Twenty," said the woman.

"Forty," said the man.

"What was she?" asked the woman.

"A gambling-house girl," said the man.

"What is that?" asked the woman.

"A serving slave, a display slave, a lure slave, such things," he said. "They encourage men to drink, to eat, to spend, to wager, to linger at the tables, to draw further cards, to cast the dice just one last time, and such."

"The gambling," she said, "is not then done with lives, those of men and animals."

"Not in any obvious sense," said the man.

"I see," she said. And it sounded as though she dismissed the bouts of the spinning wheel, the shaken box, the buying of chances, the drawing of cards. The blood shed in such games is largely unseen, doubtless, but, I fear, it is there.

I did know that men bet on tarn races, which could be dangerous at the rings, sometimes a body broken, a limb lost, a wing torn away, and that some cared for arena sports, sword games. Tharlarion races were regularly held at Venna, and other towns. Sometimes, interestingly, fortunes were wagered on kaissa matches.

"I suppose," said the woman, "that a gambling-house girl, one purchased for such a work, would be likely to be of interest to men."

"Very much so," said the man.

"Good," said the woman. "Such a slave upon occasion might prove useful."

I did not understand what she meant.

If she were buying for a brothel, or tavern, it did not seem she would be here, in this market.

"Surely," said the man. "I could let her go for fifty tarsks."

"Fifteen," said the woman.

"Forty-five," said the man.

"Actually," said the woman, "I would prefer a barbarian."

"She is a barbarian!" said the man. "Bring a lamp!" he called.

I was pulled to my knees, and my left arm was seized, and held up. "The barbarian scarring," said the man, indicating my upper left arm. "Many barbarians are so marked, not all." Then he put his hand in my hair, and yanked my head up, and back. "Get your mouth open," he said, "widely, more, more!" I closed my eyes against the light of the lamp, so close to me, held by his fellow. I felt its warmth. My mouth hurt, held so. "See?" said the man.

"I do not understand," said the woman.

"The teeth," he said.

"I see," she said.

"They are in lovely condition," he said.

"No," she said, "the two specks, there and there."

"Of course," said the man, "many barbarians have such things, not all. It is one way of recognizing the barbarian."

"What are they?" she asked.

"I do not know," he said. "Some think they are a decoration, a thing of vanity, like a beauty mark, to call attention by contrast to the exquisite beauty of what is not blemished, others consider them an identificatory device, a subtle one, by means of which a slave may be recognized."

"She is clearly a slave," said the woman.

"Obviously," said the man.

Actually, for those who may be unfamiliar with such things, what they spoke of was a consequence of the work of a form of physician on my native world, one who concerns himself primarily with the health and condition of teeth. The internal damaging of teeth is more common on my former world than on yours, a difference doubtless having much to do with differences in diet. In any event, the damaged tissue is often removed, the resultant opening being subsequently closed.

I looked up, piteously, at the man.

"You may close your mouth," he said.

Gratefully I closed my mouth.

I remained on my knees. Slaves are commonly so, in the presence of free persons. Such things make clear the difference in status between the free and their properties.

And I now well knew myself a property.

The only question was who owned the property, who owned me?

"Too," said the man to the woman.

"'Too'?" she said.

"Yes," he said. Then he said to me, "Say the alphabet."

I could not read, but I had been taught the alphabet, by rote. Interestingly, he had had me recite the alphabet earlier, shortly after my arrival here, before I had been caged. I recited the letters, again, now, which I would not even have known were letters, if I had not been so informed in the house.

"There," said the man, smiling. "Hear?" he asked.

"What?" said the woman, hesitantly.

"The mistakes," said the man.

"Of course," said the woman, but I was confident she was no more aware of the mistakes than I was. Indeed, I suspected she could not read. But the sumptuous raiment she wore surely suggested wealth, if not high caste. The mistakes I had made, I unaware of them, had been taught to me, that they would mark me as a slave. Too, I was certain I had been taught certain pronunciations of words I was not likely to frequently hear, which were also, in their subtle way, entrapments. The free, of course, do not correct such mistakes, and let them pass, deliberately, as a matter of course. In this way it is difficult for the slave to understand what she might inadvertently be doing, which may call attention to her bondage. I had, some days ago, when out of the gambling house on an errand, barefoot, in my short, purple tunic, with its lettering on the back, seen a seemingly free woman, in lovely robes and veils, seized and stripped by guardsmen. Normally, when there is doubt as to the status or condition of a woman she is given to free women, who may then, with respect to her modesty should she be free, examine her body, for a possible collar, or brand. This one, however, was simply disrobed, bound hand and foot, and put in a wagon, for delivery to a market praetor, who would see to her return to her master, or, that failing, to her lashing, fugitive branding, and resale. I would not dare to speak to a free person, but I hurried to a tower slave in the crowd, trying to learn what had happened. The tower slave, however, would not demean herself by responding to the inquiry of a "half-naked, gambling-house girl." A laundress, however, fresh from the troughs and bearing her bundle, looked at me, frightened, and said, "Slave Gorean." "I see," I had said. "It is an extra chain on us," she said, "one we do not even know we wear." "Yes," I had said, uneasily, and hurried on, about my way. I, too, I was sure, wore such a chain.

"I am interested in an ignorant barbarian," said the woman.

"A stupid barbarian?" asked the man.

"No," she said, "one ignorant."

Why, I wondered, would anyone want an ignorant girl? I supposed I was ignorant. I had not been that long on Gor. I hoped she did not want me for a serving slave. I did not even know the subtle fastenings of the robes of concealment, the layerings and arrangements of veils, the order of a woman's bath, or such.

"Girl," said the man.

"Master?" I said.

"When were you first collared?" he asked.

"In En'Kara," I said, "in the house of Tenalion, of Ar."

"That is a good house," said the man to the woman.

"What year?" he asked me.

"This year, Master," I said.

"There," said the man. "This is your slave."

"Twenty tarsks," she said.

"Fifty," he said.

"She is a barbarian, an untutored, ignorant barbarian," she said.

I was not at all sure that the speaker herself was all that informed. Might she be a barbarian, as well? But I did not know the accent. Perhaps it was from the islands, or the far south.

"Barbarians make excellent slaves," said the man. "They come from a world where there is little opportunity for their bondage. Slaves are mostly held in secret. On her world many men are crippled, confused, divided, set against themselves, taught to suspect their most basic, virile impulses. They are taught to fear manhood, and hold it as a thing of regret or shame. Accordingly, the women wander about, neglected, forlorn, lacking masters, denied the chain and whip."

"I see," said the woman.

"I did not, of course, mean women such as you, your graciousness," he said.

"I trust not," she said.

"But the slaves on this slave's world," said the man, presumably indicating me, I kept my head down, "are treated with great cruelty, a cruelty so great that it is difficult for such as we, scions of a high civilization, to even comprehend it, for they are denied what they need, and without which they cannot be fulfilled, their masters. It is little wonder they come hot from the block, tear-stained and needful, to put themselves to a man's feet. They have come from a desert, to the green meadows of

Gor. No longer do they thirst, no longer do they starve. Here they are put in collars."

"Twenty," said the woman, evenly.

"Perhaps forty-five?" suggested the man.

"No," she said.

"Many men are fond of barbarians," he said.

"I am not a man," she said.

"You should have seen her," he said, "in the tunic of the gambling house."

"I am sure she was attractive," said the woman.

"She was almost nude," he said.

"If I buy her," said the woman, "I may put her in a sack, left over from the transportation of suls."

Such sacking is plain, coarse, and ill-woven.

Too, such garmenture is unflattering, and likely to solicit ridicule from one's sister slaves.

"Behold the high slave!" they might laugh. "A slave?" might laugh another. "I must look more closely. I thought it a sack of suls!"

Such cloth, too, scratches.

It is a torment to put a slave in such a garmenture.

Some men avail themselves of such a means to demean or punish a girl.

"If you are interested in her attractiveness to men," he said, "for example, you might wish to give her to one or another, for an evening, or such, for some purpose of yours, you might think in terms of a camisk, a ta-teera, a bit of rep-cloth, such things."

I knew that camisks, and ta-teeras, were frowned on in the streets, in public. The streets of Ar were not the aisles of taverns, the vestibules and stairwells of insulae, the corridors in a military camp. Still one would see them. Indeed, in some of the lower paga taverns, the girls wore only their bells and collars. Little kaissa was played in such taverns.

"Twenty," said the woman.

"Let us say, forty," suggested the man.

"I wish you well," she said, turning about, with a swirl of garmenture.

"Thirty!" he cried. "Yes, yes! Then twenty!"

She spun about. "Done," she said.

I saw a twenty-tarsk piece put in his hand.

I had been sold, again.

"What is your name?" asked the woman.

"Whatever Mistress wishes," I said.

Her eyes narrowed, and I sensed, within the veil, she wrinkled her nose. "What of Dung-of-Tarsk?" she asked.

"Whatever Mistress wishes," I said.

"What have you been called?" she asked.

"Allison," I said.

"I do not know that name," she said.

"It is a barbarian name, your graciousness," said the man.

"Good," said the woman. "We will keep it. That way others will know that she is a barbarian, or no better than a barbarian."

"It will help to keep her in her place," said the man.

"What is your name, girl?" she asked.

"Allison, Mistress," I said, "if it pleases Mistress."

"I will have her picked up later this evening, after dark," said the woman. "In the meantime shave her head and scrub her clean, with kaiila brushes."

"It will be done," said the man.

Why, I wondered, was I to be picked up after dark?

Why would she not take me with her, from the market? The men could thong-bind my wrists behind my back and cord-leash me.

Suitably bound and tethered I could no more escape from her than from a man. A slave is often made helpless, absolutely so.

Surely it would not take long to cleanse a slave, or, if one wished, to shave her head.

Why was I to be picked up after dark?

I was uneasy.

I was looking up, from my knees, these positioned closely together, as though I might still be white-silk, when the woman's veil seemed to slip, as though inadvertently. I think, however, this lapse was not inadvertent, as she did not immediately restore it, but let it lay loose for a moment, as she smiled.

"Aii," said the man, softly.

I myself gasped, as well. She was surely one of the most beautiful women I had ever seen. Her features were exquisite, her eyes a deep, soft, lovely blue. At the side of her hood, there was a strand of bright, blondish hair.

"I am the Lady Bina," she said. "It is in this name that my agent will call for the girl."

She then refastened the veil.

I gathered she had well tested her power, to her satisfaction, on the hapless fellow.

I recalled the sternness of her bidding.

This was no ordinary beautiful woman.

"You may find my agent unusual," she said. "But do not be afraid. He is harmless, save when aroused, or angered."

I did not understand this.

"I have men," said the fellow. "Let them conduct you from this place. It is a low place. The streets are not well lit. It will soon be dark."

"I do not understand," she said, in a way which suggested she well understood.

"The streets are dangerous," he said. "Your graciousness should be guarded."

"I am guarded," she said, and turned, and left.

"She is beautiful enough to be a Ubara," said the man to his fellow, who had held the lamp.

"That is an odd name," said his fellow.

I thought it odd, as well, for 'bina' is a common word for beads, generally cheap beads, of colored wood, slave beads.

"I do not think she is Gorean," said the man.

"What then?" asked the other. "She does not seem barbarian."

"Did you see her?" asked the man.

"Of course," said the other.

"What do you think?" asked the man.

"Ten golden tarn disks, at least of double weight," said the other.

"I think so," said the man.

"Such women are well guarded," said his fellow.

"This is an honest house," said the man.

"Yes," said the other. Then he looked down at me. "So," he said, "twenty tarsks."

I put my head down.

"It is not a bad price for her," said the man.

On Gor, commonly, slaves are cheap, even beautiful slaves. They are easily obtained. Almost anyone may own one, or more. "Allison," said the man, "follow Petranos. He will conduct you to the tubs. There he will shave your head, and then the girls will scour you."

"May I speak, Master?" I asked.

"Yes," he said.

I put my hands to my hair. "Must my head be shaved?" I asked.

He put his left hand in my hair, holding me, as I knelt, and then, first with the back of his right hand, and then with its palm, cuffed me, sharply, stingingly.

"Forgive me, Master," I said.

I then rose to my feet, and hurried after Petranos.

* * * *

I knelt under the sheet, it wrapped closely about me, sobbing, in an outer room, one with access to the street. I could see the street, through the opened door. It was already dark. My left ankle was chained to a ring anchored in the floor.

It is usually the left ankle which is chained.

My body was sore, for the slaves who had cleaned me had not been gentle. They were larger slaves, thick-bodied, and coarse. They tend to have something of the attitude of free women toward slaves of a sort likely to be of greater interest to men. They tend to despise the needful, lovely, feminine slave, the sort men are likely to seek, capture, collar, and put to their feet.

I was now much different from what I had been.

I was now sparkling, doubtless.

The cleaning slaves had seen to that.

The smell of tarsk was no longer on me. Surely that was to the good. But I was miserable. I put my hand to my head. I remembered the feel of the razor on my scalp. I cried out in misery. Petranos had done his work well.

How ugly I now was!

How could I now attract a desirable master?

For what had I been purchased? For the mills, or the mines,

for work at the *carnariums*, the filth pits, for work in the sewers, in the tharlarion stables, at the tarsk pens? I did not know. Clearly I would now be of little interest in the taverns, in the brothels, in the gambling houses, even in the towers, or inns. Who now would want the former Allison Ashton-Baker? Not even the boys I used to torment!

I heard then a cry of alarm from the street.

I jerked against the chain, startled, and nearly rose to my feet, but then swiftly resumed my kneeling position. I was a slave. No free person had given me permission to rise.

We are on our knees as easily, and naturally, and as appropriately, as the free person is on his feet, or sits on his bench or chair, or reclines, at ease, on his supper couch.

Two or three men, from the market, who had been loitering outside, in the warm night, backed through the door, warily.

Something very large, and bent over, boulder-like, was in the doorway. It was huge, the form muchly concealed within the ample, thick, sheet-like, hooded cloak it wore.

The hood moved, from side to side, and I sensed that something deep within the hood was considering the room.

"Away!" cried one of the men.

I then heard a noise, a sort of noise, which, this first time I heard it, dismayed and terrified me. It was a noise such as one might expect from some large, wary, suspicious, predatory, carnivorous beast. It was clearly bestial. But, strangely, it seemed no ordinary noise, some sort of signal, or a revelation of a mood, but a subtly articulated stream of sound, and scarcely had it ceased than I heard Gorean, the words clearly sounded, but oddly spaced, produced, apparently, by means of some sort of device, some sort of machine or contrivance.

"Do not be afraid," it said. "I bear no weapons. I mean you no harm. I come in peace. I come in the name of the Lady Bina, that I might claim on her behalf a female slave."

"Who are you?" said a man.

"What are you?" said another.

"Are you human?" asked another.

"What is human?" rejoined the mechanical voice. "A mind, a shape, a form? Are you human?"

"It is a beast," said another. "They are dangerous. They

189

are hunted. They lurk in wildernesses. Some are north, in Torvaldsland."

"I come on behalf of Lady Bina, to claim a slave," said the voice.

"We await another," said a man, he who had bargained unsuccessfully with the lovely Lady Bina, "her agent."

"I am he," said the voice.

"How do we know that?" asked a man.

"I come in her name," said the voice.

I knelt, chained in place, in terror. I do not think I could have spoken, had I wished to do so.

"What is the name of the slave?" asked the fellow who had dealt with the Lady Bina.

"My translator," said the voice, "does not carry the name."

"Translator?" said a fellow, puzzled.

"The speaking thing," said another.

"Then," said the man who had sold me, "you cannot have her."

At this point a sound came from within that enormous, cloaked, hooded figure which was not translated, but its menace was clear, and the men moved further back.

I found my voice, to scream, and hide my head.

A hairy, large, paw-like thing had come from under the cloak and brushed back the hood, revealing a broad, furred head, perhaps a foot in width, with large eyes. The ears, large and pointed, moved back, gently, against the sides of the head. The mouth opened, enough to see the movement of a large, restless tongue, and afford a glimpse of thick, spike-like, moist, curved fangs.

I had the sense that those massive jaws might have been capable of biting through a beam, and could easily, like tearing paper, snap away a man's head, or woman's.

The beast approached me, the cloak dragging behind it. I could now see its furred chest, and could see, against the chest, the small device, the translator, which was slung about its neck. One massive paw reached toward me.

"Do not!" said the leader of the men, he who had dealt with the Lady Bina. "She is chained! You would tear her foot off!"

The beast reached to the chain that fastened me to the ring, and wrenched it from the floor, with a splintering of wood.

"Stop!" said the leader.

The beast turned and looked at him.

I would not care to have such a thing so look at me.

"I will unchain her!" he said.

"The slave is female," came from the translator, mechanically, unemotionally, a placidity quite at odds with the roiling, tensed power that seemed to rise now like lava within that immense, living frame, "the price was twenty tarsks, and the buyer is by name Bina, and by title, the Lady Bina."

"I will unchain her," said the man. "Forgive us. We wished to be sure of matters. Our mistake is natural. We were not warned, or sufficiently warned. We did not expect an agent such as yourself, noble Master."

I did not think the beast was flattered.

He seemed to be measuring the distance between himself and the rear entrance, leading to the cage area. The ears were lifted. I heard nothing. There was moisture about its jaws and the fangs were wet with saliva.

Words came again from the translator.

"Tell them not to use their bows," it said. "Before they could appear in the portal, I could strike away your head."

"I do not understand," said the man, disconcerted.

"Tell them to put their bows down, in the portal, where I can see them."

The man turned about. "Is anyone there?" he called.

"Now," came from the translator.

"There is no one there," said the man.

"Now," repeated the translator.

"There is no one there," said the man.

"Do you wish to live?" came from the translator.

"Do it, do it," said the man, "put your bows down, in the portal."

Two fellows, whom I recognized from the market, then appeared in the portal, and placed crossbows on the floor.

I had heard nothing, nor, apparently, had the others in the room, only the beast.

Could one hear a step so soft, the drawing of a cable, the laying of a quarrel in the guide?

"You will live," came from the translator.

A key was thrust into the lock on my manacle, and it was turned, moving the bolt, after which the sides of the device were opened, on their hinges.

The sheet was removed from me and I was put to my belly before the beast. I scarcely dared raise my head.

I saw heavy, furred, clawed feet before me.

"Your principal," said the man, rising to his feet, "made an excellent buy. She is a beauty. But perhaps you cannot see that, as you are different."

The large head lifted and regarded him. "I can see that," it said.

I trembled.

"There is an additional charge, of ten tarsks," said the man.

"Perhaps, after all," came from the translator, "you do not wish to live."

"It will be waived, of course," said the man.

The beast then, bent over, wary, began to back toward the street. It paused in the portal. "Come with me," came from the translator.

I saw the large eyes on me.

"What would such a thing want of a slave?" asked one of the men.

"Food?" suggested another.

I screamed in terror, sprang to my feet, and tried to run back toward the cages, but had moved not a step or two before I was caught in the rear portal by one of the fellows there, and held. I struggled, wildly, but my strength was no more than that of a child in his arms. I began to shudder. I turned to look at the beast, saw the eyes and fangs, screamed again, and lost consciousness.

Chapter Ten

I folded the ironed sheets carefully.

Afterwards I would deliver them about. One launders the sheets at the public troughs, and later sprinkles them, and puts them under the handled irons, heated on the plate over the house fire.

The tunic I wore was suitable for a woman's slave, brown, high-necked, and mid-calfed, rather different from what a man would be likely to put on a slave. On the other hand, it was surely not the cruel farce of sul cloth which had been mentioned during the bargaining at the Tarsk Market. In the markets and the streets I had seen the typical garmenture of other women's slaves, following their mistresses, heads down, modestly, supposedly that they might not reflect upon their mistresses by exchanging glances with passing men, garmentures which served to demonstrate at once the status and taste of the mistress and the presumed, irreproachable deportment of her slaves. To be sure, many a quick smile and sly glance was passed now and then between such a putatively virtuous pet and one hardy, bold fellow or another. Occasionally, caught in such a contretemps, I had seen a girl mercilessly switched, until she cowered, rolling under the blows, sobbing and crying out, and I scarcely dared to speculate what might occur when she was marched home to a whipping ring.

In the outer room of the Tarsk Market I had been revived abruptly and unpleasantly by a canister of cold water splashed on my body. It took only a startled, miserable instant to recall the occasion of my loss of consciousness, and one of the first sights to greet me were the eyes of that enormous, crouching beast, regarding me, peering out from within that dark, loose, blanket-like robe and hood within which he concealed, as he could, his massive, but strangely agile frame, that of some sort of hirsute, large-chested, muscular bipedalian, or near-bipedalian, form of life, surely one with which I was unfamiliar. It could rear upright, freeing its grasping appendages for the manipulation of tools, but, as I would later learn, it could also move on all fours, using the knuckles of its forelimbs, with great speed, much faster than a man could run, or a woman. Its entire mien suggested a kind of animal which was predatory, aggressive, and carnivorous. Yet I had gathered from the utilization of the device, or translator, which still hung from its neck, I could see the loose chain, it was rational. Interestingly this reassurance of rationality did not allay my trepidation but increased it, for it bespoke no ordinary beast but one which might pursue its ends not blindly, or even merely cunningly, but patiently, wisely, calculatedly. Surely it was an unfamiliar, fearful robe for intelligence to wear. It was no more than a dozen feet from me. None of the men were near it. I struggled a bit, and fell to my side. While unconscious I had been tightly bound. My wrists had been fastened together behind my back, and my arms had been tied tightly to my sides. Also a leather collar was on my neck, from which a leash dangled, and the end of the leash was clutched in one of the beast's massive paws.

"Please save me, Masters!" I wept to the men about. "I will be a good slave! Keep me! Am I not pretty? I beg to please you, and wholly, unquestioningly, and abjectly, responding to your least whim, in all the ways of the female slave! I will please you muchly. Rescue me! Do not let me be taken by this beast!"

Surely they must have some pity, or feeling, for one who was, after all, a female of their own species, though one with a brand incised into her left thigh.

"Please, Masters!" I wept. "Please, Masters!"

"You have been paid for," said the leader of the men.

"Return his money!" I begged. "Sell me to another!"

"The money was good," said Petranos. "Everything is in order."

"Please!" I wept.

"It is too late," said a fellow.

"Please, please, please!" I begged, thrusting my head to the floor.

"This is an honest house," said the leader of the men.

I felt the leash draw taut and my head was pulled up, and I must, along the length of the leash, regard the beast.

With a last, wary look about the room, before which the men shrank back, he backed through the portal, and I could not gain my feet, and was dragged from the room, my shoulder abrading on the wooden floor, and then I was on the stones of the street.

"Do not eat me!" I begged, from my side, looking to him, frightened, sore, lying on the street, he much as a gloomy boulder in the shadows.

Two or three of the men appeared in the doorway, dark against the light behind them from the room.

A low growl, of obvious menace, was emitted from the throat of the beast, and then men withdrew, and the door was shut, and I heard it bolted.

There was then little light in the street.

The leash was slackened, and gently snapped, twice.

This was a signal, to a trained animal.

I must try to rise to my feet, to be led.

Perhaps, then, I was not the first woman he had had on his leash! Who had taught a beast this? What of the others? Had they been eaten?

I tried to rise, but my legs gave way beneath me.

"Forgive me, Master," I said. "I cannot stand. I am too weak. I am too frightened."

I cowered then, and expected to be beaten with the free end of the leash, but my legs would still not hold me.

"Forgive me, Master," I whispered.

Again he administered the simple leash signal.

I tried to rise, struggling, but again slipped to the stones.

He then approached me, and sat me, facing him. He then crossed my ankles, and, with the free end of the leash, bound them together.

I watched, with an odd fascination.

In the house, of course, the slaves are familiarized with various bindings and tetherings to which they might be subjected. Accustoming them to bonds of various sorts is part of their training. Additionally, they are instructed in various responses to various bindings, for example, how to exploit them to their advantage, how to wear them attractively, how to move seductively within them, how to utilize them to enhance their desirability, how to use them in such a way, by movement and expression, as to excite and stimulate the master, and so on. To be sure, ropes, thongs, bracelets, chains, and such, are not only attractive on the slave, but, as she understands her confinement, her vulnerability, and her helplessness, they have their role in intensifying her sexuality, in heightening her receptivity, her readiness, and passion, as well. A slave will often beg for binding. To be sure, the very condition of bondage itself, aside from questions of restraint, with its signals, rituals, garmentures, behaviors, accouterments, expectations, and such, is richly and profoundly sexual; it is a way of life, a richly sexual way of life, and, given the radical sexual dimorphism of the human species, and the selections of millennia, a very natural way of life, one in fulfilling accord with the biotruths of human nature.

As I watched my ankles being tied I noted the beast was using warrior knots, the sort which quickly and easily secure a woman. As women are common loot on Gor, of greater interest than, say, goblets and tapestries, warriors are instructed in such knots. By their means a woman may be rendered wholly helpless in a matter of Ihn. I moved my ankles a little. They were well tethered.

Where, I wondered, would such a beast have learned such knots? Surely it was not itself a member of the Scarlet Caste. Perhaps it had once known a warrior, somewhere, on some world or other.

I knew little of Gor, but it did not seem likely to me that this form of beast would be indigenous to this world.

"I know you understand Gorean," I whispered.

It looked at me, one lip moving back a bit, revealing the tip of a fang.

"In the Tarsk Market," I said, "the device, the translator, transformed your language into Gorean, but it did not translate the masters' Gorean into your language. Thus, you know Gorean."

I knew that some individuals can follow a language which

they do not care to speak, or are not adept at speaking Too, how could a beast such as this articulate the phonemes of a human language, presumably no more than we could recreate the sounds of its own speech. How could one speak the language of a jard, a vart or tharlarion, even if they had a language? The beast reached to the small device on its chain, slung about its neck. It pressed a portion of the device, at its center. I had the sense that the device had been deactivated.

Then, straightening up, it seemed to growl, a guttural rumbling, some Ihn in duration, perhaps ten or fifteen, above me, and I shuddered. "Please, Master," I said. "Use the device, the translator. You cannot expect me to understand you."

I fought not to understand, for I thought I could not, or should not, understand, and perhaps I did not want to understand, and perhaps I would refuse to understand, and then, to my astonishment, it occurred to me that I had understood.

I looked up at him, in amazement.

He had said that he was Grendel, high Kur, once from the world of Agamemnon, Eleventh Face of the Nameless One, self-exiled from his world, that he might accompany and guard a woman, the Lady Bina, once, too, of that world.

"You understand," he said.

"Yes, Master," I said.

To be sure, I understood very little of what had been said.

"Most of my kind, if I have a kind," he said, "cannot articulate Gorean, or well, certainly not without a translator. My throat is different, and my tongue, a little. There are reasons for this, which need not concern you. I can make myself understood in Gorean, if you will make the necessary adjustments. It is hard, at first, easy later."

"Agamemnon," I said, "was an ancient king, on Earth."

"That is not his name, of course," said the beast, "but you could not pronounce his name. 'Agamemnon' seemed a suitable substitute for the true name. It was suggested by humans, for some reason. They wanted, or needed, some name, it seems. Similarly, you cannot pronounce my true name. But I am called Grendel. That name, too, was invented by humans. I gather it is the name of a monster, a grotesque anomaly, a lonely thing of bogs, and marshes and wildernesses, unpleasant to look upon, hated and feared, perhaps the result of an experiment which turned out badly, so that seems appropriate."

"I am a slave," I said.

It occurred to me an instant later that I might have claimed to be a free woman, and thus, suitably, to be freed. Might I have confused or deluded him? Would he even understand these things? I would not have dared such a stratagem with a native Gorean, of course, even in my terror, for fear of the frightful consequences attendant on being discovered in such a deception.

I did not want to live the rest of my life in ankle chains, my throat locked in a high collar, of weighty iron, with points.

How one would long then for a common collar, and the simple exposure of a common tunic!

"Yes," he said.

But of course I was a slave, and must be understood as such by the beast. I wore no collar, true, for the collar of the gambling house had been removed, but the slave mark was in my thigh, small, lovely, obvious, unmistakable. Too, I had been purchased. And I had been bound, and leashed, as a slave.

There was no doubt as to what the former Allison Ashton-Baker now was. She was slave.

"Sell me, sell me!" I said.

Again the lips moved back a bit, about the fangs.

"Please do not eat me, Master," I said.

"I do not eat human," it said.

I caught my breath. I shuddered with relief.

Was he telling the truth?

The mien of the beast, the size, the fangs, the eyes, set forward in the head, suggested the carnivore.

It reached down and scooped me up, gently, in its arms.

I felt very small within them.

"Please sell me," I begged.

"I do not own you," it said.

I twisted, helpless, in the bonds.

"Lie still," it said.

I supposed that she spoken of as the Lady Bina owned me. Had she bought me for another, I wondered. Had she bought me for the beast?

Had I been bought as food for it, cheap food?

"Be still," it said.

I then lay quietly, enfolded in its mighty arms, miserable, and it moved swiftly, but warily, along the dark street.

Once a fellow appeared, a shadow, in a doorway, but was greeted with so sudden, and fierce, a snarl, that he quickly withdrew.

I think I was as frightened as the fellow in the doorway, who withdrew so quickly, so silently, a shadow vanishing back amongst other shadows.

It was I, after all, goods, who was within the arms of the beast.

We continued on, for better than several Ehn.

I realized, as our journey continued, that I was being carried as a free woman is carried. The slave is commonly carried over the left shoulder, head to the rear, steadied by the bearer's left arm. In this way the slave may not see where she is being taken, what lies before her bearer, and, too, she may understand herself as goods, so carried, as much so as a sack of suls, a roll of matting, a crate of larmas, a bundle of tur-pah. In this way, too, her bearer's right arm is free.

I realized I had spoken, and more than once, without permission.

I had not been punished for this, nor even warned of so untoward an indiscretion, so culpable a presumption.

Too, I was being carried as a free woman.

I was reasonably sure that the Lady Bina, from her accent, was not of Ar, and from her demeanor, perhaps not of Gor itself. I suspected that I, in my ignorance, might be as much informed as she of Gorean ways and culture. Too, the beast, I suspected, was not of Gor. He did not even understand, I gathered, how a slave was to be carried. Thus, he might not understand many things about the treatment of slaves. This I might turn to my advantage. But he had tied me as a slave, and well. Too, had he not spoken of another world? I suspected then that not only the beast but the strikingly beautiful Lady Bina herself might derive from such a world. She, I was sure, was human, quite human. I did not understand the nature of the beast. It was a form of life, a fearful form of life, with which I was hitherto unacquainted.

I lay as quietly as possible in the arms of the beast, being carried through the dark streets.

My hopes of acquiring a suitable master had been muchly dashed after the burning of the gambling house, and my translation, with that of my chain sisters, to the Tarsk Market. What suitable master would have recourse to such a market for a slave? One would hope to find there, if slaves at all, only pot girls, kettle-and-mat girls, she-tarsks, so to speak. I certainly did not consider myself a she-tarsk. I had been popular enough, and as a slave, in the gambling house. Its patrons had not found the former Allison Ashton-Baker, barefoot, collared, briefly and seductively tunicked, remiss as, or displeasing as, a slave. And how she had enjoyed the eyes of the men upon her, well understanding such appraisals as evidence of her value! The free woman is doubtless priceless, but the slave has an actual value, what men are willing to pay for her. My thoughts of a master had varied from time to time. Sometimes it seemed to me that I would like a weak master whom I might control, manage, and manipulate, rather as a typical female companion on my native world was accustomed, given the culture in question, to control, manage, and manipulate their male companions, rather to the unhappiness, distress, and frustration of both. Would it not be pleasant to be owned by a weak man, with whom one would be sure of having one's own way? To be sure, one must be careful. I would be in his collar, and there would be a whip on its peg. But I thought, rather, I must be a true slave, as I wanted a true man, one who would lust after me with power, who would be satisfied with nothing less than owning me, wholly, one who would be to my slave a master, one who would have me kneel before him, naked and collared, perhaps chained, my head to his feet, one who would own me, unequivocally. I wanted to be his, his property, a helpless object, goods, possessed by him, in all the fullness of law, in all the fullness of culture, in all the fullness of nature. I supposed then that I must be in my heart a slave, one radically female, and needful. To such a man I would have no choice but to submit, and wholly, and to such a man I longed to submit, and wholly. It was in the collar of such a man

I wanted to be; it was the collar of such a man I longed to wear. It was the touch of such a man which would make me weak and helpless, a yielding, submitted slave. It was the touch of such a man which would set me afire. It was the touch of such a man for which I would beg. But, alas, how can one's slave be satisfied, as in the lament of so many women of my world, where one has no master?

I was confident that I might exploit the ignorance, the weakness, of those unfamiliar with the nature of Gor.

Could I not win for myself, with a smile, a tear, a word, a frown, an easy life?

But I was unsure of these things, for much here seemed paradoxical, the nature of she who had bargained for me, and bought me, and the nature of he who was her agent, and had claimed me in her behalf.

I was being carried with all the gentleness and courtesy of a free woman.

Had I not seen free women standing as though forlorn before tiny lakes of drainage water and mud at intersections, until a suitable male approached, alert to her seeming distress, to whom she granted the daring privilege of carrying her to safety on the other side of the street? I supposed he knew what was occurring. I hoped so. There is a timing in such matters. Sometimes one had to circle a block in order to strand oneself opportunely.

Yet, though I was carried in dignity, as though I might be free, I was tightly, helplessly bound, bound as a slave.

I was a slave.

Would I be freed?

That seemed unlikely to me. There is a Gorean saying that only a fool frees a slave girl, and I suppose it is true. What man does not want a slave? Even on my native world I was sure that the men and boys I knew would not have minded in the least owning me. That sort of thing had been clear enough in the party on Earth, where they had looked delightedly and unabashedly on the collar on my neck, and my half-naked limbs.

I supposed they thought, how pleasant it would be to own Allison Ashton-Baker. What shall I name her?

Too, I had gathered, during my sale, that the Lady Bina had wished to reassure herself that I might be of interest to men. I did not understand that.

Was a coin box to be chained about my neck and I would be sent into the streets? Was I to be put at the disposal of guests when I had finished serving a supper? Was I to be rented out? To be sure, it is not unusual for a free woman to want her serving slaves to be attractive to men. A double cruelty is involved in this. In this way, by denying her girls the arms of masters she frustrates them, which pleases her, as she hates slave girls, and she also, in a way, punishes, or thinks she punishes, men, to whom she denies her girls, for their interest in slaves, which interest she, as a free woman, resents.

How could one care for a slave when a free woman was present?

But how could one care for a free woman, when a slave was present?

But how, I asked myself, could I now be of interest to men, given the work of the razor of Petranos?

"We are here," said the beast.

* * * *

One commonly irons, as one launders, on one's knees. This is, of course, not different from the usual custom of free women, those of the lower castes. One of the things about your world which I found striking was the paucity of clutter and furniture in your dwellings. You do much with mats, cushions, and low tables, about which men will usually sit cross-legged, and women kneel. Whereas chairs, benches, and higher tables are familiar to you, as in the public eating houses, and common in the north, such things are much more common on my former world. There, almost anyone may sit upon a chair, whereas here, particularly in private dwellings, such an ensconcement is often reserved for individuals of status or importance. And certainly a slave would much fear to take a place on a chair, or, say, on a supper couch. It is not for such as we. Much storage is done in chests, kept at the edges of a room. Perhaps things are different in wealthier domiciles, with their larger kitchens and pantries, their walls, the interior colonnades, the fountains, and gardens, the rooms opening onto them, and such. I glimpsed something of that, once, when a portal had been briefly opened. From the outside, of course, little of luxury is suggested. Much seems drab, and plain, heavy, even forbidding. Sometimes bills are posted on the exterior walls, as though in public places.

I finished folding the sheets.

The Lady Bina had rented the upper-floor of a small, two-floor, common-wall house on Emerald. The front of the first floor, facing the street, was the shop of a pottery merchant, Epicrates, who, with his family, lived in the rear. His companion, Delia, like himself, could read. This is common amongst the Merchants. Indeed, thanks to her instruction, and a handful of coins, distributed over a few days, the Lady Bina was now passably literate. Certainly she could now manage the public boards and, I gathered, typical scrolls. She was apparently an apt pupil. Indeed, I gathered she could already read better than many allegedly literate Goreans. I had no doubt that my Mistress was not only extremely beautiful, but extremely intelligent, as well. She was very quick, and very ambitious. I was unclear as to her background, as much, or more, than that of the beast. It was almost as though she had never been taught, or socialized. There was something about her which, for all her intelligence, suggested the innocence of the animal, something wild and unconstrained, something immediate, direct, and untutored. As nearly as I could tell she was unencumbered by restraints or scruples. What she might want she would see to it, if possible, that she would have. In that small, beautiful body, slightly smaller than mine, there was a nature innocently prudential, vain, self-centered, independent, and calculating. I did not understand her. How had she been raised, or, in a sense, had she been raised at all? In her way she seemed as unsettlingly innocent, and as impatient, occasionally nasty, and possibly dangerous, if crossed, as an urt, or a small, lovely she-sleen. Oddly, I suspected more of humanity, or a sort of humanity, in the beast. It had, for example, or at least seemed to have, a sense of duty, of loyalty, of honesty, of honor. I recalled how my ankles had been bound outside the Tarsk Market. They had been fastened together with warrior knots. Might it be, somehow, familiar with the scarlet codes?

The beast had informed me that it was self-exiled, and had accompanied the Lady Bina to this world, from their former world, as a guard. I had, however, never noted coins passed between them. Guard he might be, but I did not think him a guard in any normal sense. Why, I wondered, had he left his own world, truly, and with her? It did not seem she owned him, or he her. Had he been outlawed, had he fled? What was his relationship, truly, to the Lady Bina? Had others banished him, denying him bread, fire, and salt? Was it substantially a coincidence that they were together, merely fellow expatriates? I did not think so. How had they come here? There must have been a ship. Indeed, how had I come here? There must have been a ship. The translator I had seen suggested a sophisticated technology. Yet here, on this world, I had seen little that would suggest such things. There were mysteries, apparently. And there were the mysterious Sardar Mountains, within which, supposedly, resided the gods of Gor, called Priest-Kings. It seemed a primitive world, but I, and others, had been brought here, and there was the translator.

The beast, in all things, save those in which her safety or health might be jeopardized, would give way to the Lady Bina. She was, of course, a free woman. Sometimes she would stamp her small foot, and pout, in annoyance, but he would be adamant, as a rock, if he feared for her welfare. He would even, with all his size and might, accept abuse at her hands, patiently, unflinchingly. I had seen her, in frustration, strike him, again and again, but he would make no effort to protect himself, or fend her away. I myself would have been afraid to lift my hand to him, lest it be bitten off. I had been purchased, obviously, at least in part, for the work of a female slave, that I might labor on behalf of my mistress, keep the domicile, clean and launder, purchase, prepare, and cook food, as I might, fetch and carry, in particular bringing water from the fountains, run errands, indulge her whims, tend to her wants, accompany her, head down, in the streets, and such. I did not care for the slavery, as I was a female slave, and had no master. It is one thing to perform such tasks for a master, knowing that even in small things I was serving him, each task then being subtly imbued with submission and sexuality, for a woman's sexuality is subtle, warm, profound, and pervasive, and another to perform them for a woman. To the slave, shining the master's boots can be a sexual experience, serving him, and being so close to something he has touched. How privileged is a slave to be permitted to kneel before such a man, put down her head, and lick and kiss his feet! How she hopes to please him! She will fondle the chain that fastens her to the foot of his couch. She is his. May he never sell her! But I had no master.

Lady Bina, I gathered, was proceeding splendidly in her literacy. She could now print, in the odd Gorean fashion, "as the bosk plows," where the first line proceeds from left to right, the second from right to left, and so on. I did not know if the beast could read or not. Certainly it was not taking lessons from the companion of Epicrates. Few instructors, I supposed, would welcome so terrifying a pupil. I could not read, of course, not even my own collar. It said, I was told, "I belong to the Lady Bina, of Emerald Street, of the house of Epicrates." Slaves are seldom taught to read. On the other hand, many are literate, as free women, particularly of the higher castes, are commonly literate. Free women of the upper castes, taken in war, and such, exposed on the block, often bring nice prices. Gorean men enjoy having former free women, particularly those who were formerly rich, or of the higher castes, in their collars. It is probably difficult for one of my former world to understand the awesome dignity and importance, the social and cultural status, of the Gorean free woman, for she possesses a Home Stone, a status incomparably far above that of the usual free woman of my former world. Accordingly, it would be difficult for one of my former world to understand the cataclysmic reversal of fortune involved should such a creature, formerly so powerful, exalted, and revered, suddenly find herself stripped and collared, a caught beast, helpless at a stranger's feet. No longer is she a man's equal, or superior, the haughty, protected possessor of a Home Stone, but a master's property. But in time, they, too, lick and kiss the whip lovingly, for they, too, are women.

There is a common Gorean saying that curiosity is not becoming in a kajira. Certainly few things help us to keep our condition as clearly in mind as our being kept in ignorance. Why should we be informed? We are slaves. Would you speak to your kaiila or sleen about prospects, plans, projects, and such? I think the masters enjoy our frustration. We want so much to know, and feel so keenly our deprivation! How we wheedle, how we lie about the ankles of our masters and beg to be informed! But often our entreaties are greeted with laughter, and a foot may spurn us to the side. Is it not another way to remind us that we are in our collars? So, obviously, keeping a slave illiterate helps to keep her in ignorance. I am, incidentally, highly literate in my own first language, but here, I am only another ignorant slave girl, as it pleases masters I should be. One advantage to having a slave who cannot read is that one may use the girl to carry messages amongst friends or associates, messages which she cannot read. She does not even know if the message pertains to herself or not. More than one girl has been so delivered to a new master. A message might read, "Here is Lana, whom I sold to you yesterday evening. Put her at your ring, that she may know she is now yours." A literate slave may deliver messages placed in a small leather tube, tied by a string about her collar. Her hands are thonged, or braceleted, behind her back. In this way she will be as ignorant of the message's content as an illiterate slave. Messages of great importance, such as might be transmitted between armies, or cities, are carried by free persons, and are sealed with wax, bearing the imprint of a signet ring. In this way one is assured of the sender, and, if the seal is unbroken, of the security of the message.

As the sheets were now folded, and readied for delivery, I put the kerchief about my head.

It had been some weeks now since my purchase from the Tarsk Market. I was still terribly sensitive as to my appearance, following the work of the razor of Petranos. The hair that had been shorn from me had been discarded. That was from the soiling in the tarsk cage, lying on the straw, sleeping there, and such. The most common reason slaves are shorn is for punishment or cleanliness, or both. For example, slaves who work in the tharlarion stables are often shorn, and the girls in the mills, too. Too, when girls are put on slave ships, chained in their wire cages on tiered shelves in a hold, they are commonly shorn, and depilated, completely, to reduce the infestations of ship lice. The shorn hair is often utilized for catapult cordage, as it is much more resilient, and dampness resistant, than common cordage. Too, there are rumors that some shorn hair, taken from slaves, is used for wigs and falls, for free women. Naturally the hair is certified as having been that of other free women. I did not think I was all that unattractive, as long as the kerchief was on me.

Interestingly, the Lady Bina was, in many ways, rather different from the typical Gorean free woman. She had observed other free women, with serving slaves, and so she had me heel her, at the proper distance, on the left, appropriately, head down, but she was not at all strict about my looking about, and I frequently did so. Might I not be of interest to a master, and might not one or another of the fellows about inquire of the Lady Bina, sooner or later, what she might be willing to take for her kerchiefed girl? My tunic was certainly not that of a pleasure slave, a paga girl, or such, or even a tower slave, but, too, it was not as calculatedly concealing as the common tunic of a serving slave. On the other hand, I had seen more than one serving slave, in such a tunic, unseen by her mistress, move in such a way that a passing fellow would be in no doubt that within that tunic there was a slave.

Once, before we were to exit the domicile, Lady Bina instructed me to hitch up the tunic a bit.

"Are you beautiful, Allison?" she asked.

"A little, perhaps," I said.

"Let us see more of your legs," she said.

"Yes, Mistress," I said.

"They are a little thin, are they not?" she asked.

"I do not think so," I said.

"Show more of them," she said.

"Yes, Mistress," I said.

"Good," she said. "I may have use for your beauty."

"Mistress?" I said, uneasily.

"For men," she said.

"Yes, Mistress," I said.

"Come along," she said.

"Yes, Mistress," I said.

As it was daylight the beast did not accompany us. It seldom went out until darkness.

One reason I had been purchased, I gathered, was to have a companion for the Lady Bina when she left the house.

We were in the Sul Market one afternoon.

"Allison," said the Lady Bina, "are you attractive to men?"

"I think so, Mistress," I said, "a little, sometimes, perhaps."

To be sure, I thought myself quite attractive. Had I not been one of the most beautiful girls in the sorority, a sorority in which membership, clearly, was not unrelated to beauty? And now, of course, I was enslaved, and slavery much enhances the beauty of a woman. Collared and slave-clad what woman would not be beautiful? And there is the meaning and nature of the condition which in itself enhances the beauty of a woman a thousandfold, for she is then slave.

To be sure, not every woman is attractive, or particularly attractive, to every man. Too, of course, not every woman who yearns to be at the feet of a man yearns to be at the feet of every man. A woman who might plead for the collar of one man might tremble at being placed in the collar of another.

"Do you like being attractive to men?" she asked.

"Must I answer, Mistress?" I said.

"Certainly," she said, "and remember that you are a slave."

Slaves may not lie.

"Yes, Mistress," I whispered.

Every woman likes to be attractive to men. Even women who hate men like to be attractive to them, if only to humiliate and torture them. In the college I had taken great pleasure in my attractiveness to boys and men, even those I held in contempt. Now, I realized, such might own me.

An important aspect of a slave's life is closely associated with her attractiveness to men. The quality of her life is muchly affected by her desirability. How will she be fed, clothed, treated? Who will buy her? Must she compete with other slaves for the attention of the master? It is no wonder the slave strives to make herself exciting, attractive, and desirable, and as a slave. It is no wonder she strives to be pleasing to her master.

Too, it is not unknown for the slave to discover, sooner or

later, perhaps to her trepidation, that she loves the man whose chain she wears.

Let her hope then that she will not find herself hooded and returned to a market.

"I would make test of your attractiveness to men," said the Lady Bina.

"Mistress?" I said, puzzled.

"It is one thing for which you were purchased," she said.

"There are no men in the house," I said.

"There are many here, in the market," she said, "large men, strong men."

"Mistress?" I said, frightened.

"Have you had what they call Slave Wine?"

"Yes, Mistress," I said, "in the house of Tenalion."

"I shall give you ten Ehn," she said.

"My head was shaved!" I said.

"You now have less than ten Ehn," she said.

"Surely Mistress jests," I said.

"You were purchased for twenty copper tarsks," she said. "I am sure, now that you are cleaned up, and such, I could get at least twenty-five for you, if I sold you to a butcher, for sleen feed."

"Surely Mistress would not do so," I said.

"I could then purchase another girl, perhaps again at the Tarsk Market, one more attractive," she said.

"I do not want to die," I said.

"You are a slave," she said. "You are supposed to want sex, even need it."

"Please, Mistress!" I protested.

Certainly I had felt uneasiness, and, from time to time, after I had been collared, I had felt it acutely.

But, from the lingering effects of my Earth conditioning, and my newness to the state of bondage, I was not yet the helpless victim of the raging slave fires which so frequently tormented and dominated the bellies and bodies of many slaves.

Had I been I would have begged on my knees, or belly, for sex.

"Something like nine Ehn now," said the Lady Bina.

"Please, no!" I cried.

The blue eyes of the Lady Bina regarded me, over the street veil, seemingly pleasantly, seemingly impassively. I did not sense that she was angry, or cruel. Again the mystery of her background alarmed me.

I cried out in misery and fled away, a few yards, and put myself to my knees before a stallsman.

I put down my head and pressed my lips to his sandals. "I am a slave vessel for your pleasure!" I said. "I am docile. I will be obedient. I am sure your touch would heat me, and well!"

"Are you mad?" he said.

"No, Master!" I said. "I beg use!"

"Here?" he laughed.

"Anywhere," I said. "But soon, soon!"

"Where is your coin box, your pan?" he asked.

"I have none!" I said.

"What do you want?" he said.

"A copper tarsk!" I said. I thought it well to say something, that I might be more believable.

He laughed.

"A tarsk-bit, a tarsk-bit!" I said.

"No," he said. "And how do I know you would give it to your master."

"I have no master," I said.

He regarded my tunic. "You are a woman's serving slave?" he said.

"Yes, Master!" I said.

"No coin, no coin, nothing!" I said.

"On your way," he said. "I am selling."

"Master!" I begged.

He then pushed me with his foot to the stones, and turned to a customer, a free woman.

"How disgusting," said the free woman.

The stallsman shrugged. "She is a slave," he said.

I looked back, to where the Lady Bina was watching.

I then leapt up, and looked wildly about.

I next approached a fellow of the Leather Workers, or so I supposed, for he had several loops of harness slung about his shoulders. I barely noticed that several of harnesses slung about his shoulders were slave harness, a form of ingenious harnessing in which a slave might be variously, pleasingly, constrained and exhibited.

In such fastenings, easily and conveniently applied, attractive and adjustable, a slave is well apprised of her bondage, as would be any who might care to look upon her.

"Please, Master!" I begged.

"Why are you wearing a kerchief?" he asked.

Tears sprang to my eyes, and he jerked it away. I heard men laugh. I put down my head, shamed.

When I looked up, he had gone.

Quickly I put the kerchief once more about my head.

"A mill girl," I heard a fellow say.

"She has a serving-slave tunic," said another.

"Probably she looked at a man," speculated another.

There was more laughter.

I had no better fortune with two others.

I rushed back to my Mistress, and knelt and wept, "No one wants me! I am shorn! I am shorn!"

"I am disappointed, Allison," said the Lady Bina. "It seems to me that you would be of interest to men, not that I am a likely judge in such matters."

"I am sure I could be of interest, Mistress," I said.

"I am sure some would find you of interest, Allison," she said.

"Yes Mistress!" I said.

"Perhaps sleen," she said. "Would you like to be thrown, naked and bound, into a sunken sleen cage?"

"No, Mistress!" I said.

"Five Ehn," she said.

I rose up, again, and ran a few feet away. I tried to tear the collar from my neck. It read, "I belong to the Lady Bina, of Emerald Street, of the house of Epicrates." It was locked on my neck.

I did not want to die!

"Four Ehn, Allison," called the Lady Bina.

Then I straightened by body, and, carefully adjusted the collar on my neck, the lock directly at the back. Too, I adjusted the kerchief. I put back my shoulders. I recalled my instructresses from the house of Tenalion. "Remember," they had told me, "you are a female slave, and the female slave is the most helpless, vulnerable, exciting, and desirable of all women." I put up my head, and walked, unhurriedly, in the measured saunter of the slave, proud of her collar, and proud of her womanhood, and well demonstrating it, toward the buildings at the edge of the market. Thus I could be pinned against them. Thus I would have nowhere to run. In its way was this not an invitation? Might it not suggest to someone a convenience, an opportunity? I recalled how the instructresses had drilled me in that gait, at once arrogant, vulnerable, and ready, a gait that said, in effect, "I am a slave, what will you make of that, Masters?" When they were satisfied, they had invited two guards into one of the large training rooms. In this exercise I had been permitted a house tunic. One must learn to wear, and move well within, tunics, camisks, gowns, slave strips, ta-teeras, and such, of various sorts. "Walk," had said the leader of the instructresses, "walk, Allison, in the third walk of the slave."

There are, of course, a repertory of behaviors, walks, postures, prostrations, obeisances, and such, with which a slave is trained.

They are, after all, intended to be sold as dreams of pleasure to men.

"Aii!" had cried one of the fellows, leaping up.

In a moment I had been seized by both. I struggled in their arms. I felt myself being lifted from the floor.

"No, no!" laughed the chief instructress. "She is white-silk, white-silk!"

I was much shaken by this experience, but I had learned something of the power of the slave, for she is not without her power.

The two guards left, disgruntled. Doubtless they felt cheated. I am sure they made the instructresses pay later in the "coin of the furs," not that the instructresses would much mind that. Indeed, I suspected I might have unwittingly figured in their plans.

"Disgusting slut, disgusting, half-naked slut!" hissed a free woman. At least she did not order me to kneel, to be beaten. They so hate us! Or so envy us? She was then away, somewhere. Actually, I was not really half-naked, as many men put their slaves into the streets, but reasonably modestly garbed, as I wore the tunic of a woman's serving slave, to be sure, one rather more revealing than most.

I walked at the edge of the market, the walls of buildings to my right.

I had been told that larls stalking tabuk would sometimes delay their charge until their prey grazed beside a cliff, a wall of stone, a dense thicket. Indeed, sometimes they would herd, and drive, their prey against such barriers.

It was not so strange then that tabuk commonly grazed in open, or lightly wooded, areas.

The walls were at my right, at my right shoulder.

I gave as little evidence as I could of my fear.

I did not know how many Ehn might be left, perhaps two, perhaps three?

Suddenly an arm, abruptly, startling me, blocked my way, the palm of its hand on the side of the building.

"Serving slave," pronounced a voice, a harsh, masculine voice. The arm before me, and the hand, were large.

"Master?" I said, stopped.

"Where is your Mistress?" asked the man.

"Somewhere," I said.

"You do not walk like a serving slave," he said.

"Forgive me, Master," I said.

"Are you running away?" he asked.

"No, Master!" I said, frightened.

I was well aware there was no escape for the Gorean slave girl.

"But you have slipped away," he said.

"Perhaps, Master," I said.

He removed his hand from the wall, so it no longer blocked my passage. But he now stood before me. I did not try to move about him, or turn, or run away. I was a slave.

He pulled off the kerchief, and freed it of its knot.

"I see this is not the first time you have slipped away," he said.

I did not respond to him. I let him think that my shearing was a punishment shearing, perhaps from some indiscretion, for which a woman's serving slave might be punished.

"Perhaps," he said, "you were also well lashed."

"Perhaps, Master," I said.

My kerchief dangled in his right hand.

"Turn about," he said, "and place your hands, crossed, behind your back."

"Master!" I protested.

"Now," he said.

My hands were then tied behind my back. He tied them tightly.

"Kneel down, and put your head to the stones," he said.

I obeyed, a slave, but I expected my Mistress, at any moment, to intervene.

Surely she was about!

"Aii!" I cried, startled. "Oh, please, oh!" Then I cried, "Master! Master!"

He then turned me about, and tore my tunic down, to the waist.

I was then thrown forward, on the stones.

"Is this your slave?" asked the man.

I looked up, from my belly.

"Yes," said the Lady Bina.

"I return her to you, for the lashing she deserves," he said.

I gathered the fellow had a righteous, proper streak. I was, after all, a woman's serving slave.

"Did you find her attractive?" asked the Lady Bina.

"What?" he asked.

"Did you find her attractive?" asked the Lady Bina. "Could you conceive of men wanting her? Willing to buy her? Do you find her well shaped? Did she squirm well?"

I kept my head down. I had been given little opportunity to squirm.

"What are you asking me?" he asked.

"You are a man," she said. "I am asking for your assessment of the girl."

"She was made for the collar," he said.

"Good," she said.

"But she is to be as a woman's serving slave, is she not?" he asked.

"No matter," she said.

"I do not understand," he said.

"She is a barbarian," said the Lady Bina. "Does that dismay you, or give you pause?"

"No," he said. "Barbarians make excellent slaves."

"Good," she said.

"They kick and juice as well as any other woman," he said.

"Forgive me, Lady, as well as any other slave."

"Of course," she said. "I now bid you good-day."

"May Tor-tu-Gor warm you," said the man.

"Thank you," she said. "Come along, Allison."

"My tunic, Mistress," I said, "and I am bound."

"No matter," she said, "come along."

So I followed her through the market, my head down, until we reached a stall, where the Lady Bina, I standing beside her, bargained for a stone of suls. It was late in the day, and the prices tend to be lower at such a time.

"I will need you," she said, "to carry the suls."

She looked about. "You," she said to a tall, strapping fellow, in the gray and black of the Metal Workers, "untie this slave."

He came to stand before me, and I felt his eyes, Gorean eyes, peruse me. I lifted my head, and turned away, angered. He looked at me as though I might have been on a block.

"You are in the presence of a free man," he said. "Get on your knees."

I suppose few women of Earth had heard such commands, but, hearing them, and in such a tone, I expect there would be few who would not obey.

I, collared, a slave, knelt immediately, frightened.

I looked up at him, from my knees, and our eyes met. I suddenly had the strange feeling that I was kneeling before my master.

I turned aside my head, no longer daring to look into his eyes.

Was I before my master?

"Untie her," said the Lady Bina.

"I do not free slaves," he said. "I bind them."

Then he turned away.

I sensed he was a master who would well know what to do with a slave.

"You," said the Lady Bina to the stallsman. "Untie her."

He looked at her.

"The knots are tight," said the Lady Bina. "I am a woman, with only a woman's strength."

"Surely," said the stallsman, and freed my hands.

I rose to my feet, and tied up, as I could, the torn tunic, and replaced the kerchief. I then, carrying the suls, heeled my Mistress from the market.

"May I speak?" I asked.

"Yes," she said. "You have, as of now, a standing permission to speak."

"Thank you, Mistress," I said.

"So speak," she said.

"Is Mistress pleased?" I asked.

"You may put that differently," said the Lady Bina.

"Is Mistress pleased with Allison?" I asked. I feared that the Mistress was learning more of Gor each day, perhaps, in part, from Delia, the companion of Epicrates.

"Yes," she said, "I am pleased. I think you did very well, Allison. I am quite pleased. I think you will do very nicely."

I was not clear as to Mistress' intentions.

I followed behind her, carrying the suls.

I could not forget the Metal Worker, who ordered me to his feet. I thought I had seen him before, and more than once.

How strange had been the moment when our eyes had met.

Could I be, I wondered, his slave?

I was sure that, in his collar, I would indeed be his slave, and might not any woman?

In him I sensed a strange sense of power. I had the feeling that if I knelt before him I would lift my wrists to him, closely together, that they might be braceleted. Was his the leash, I wondered, which belonged on my neck?

How his eyes had roved me, my tunic half gone from me! What a beast, and monster, he was! How I scorned him, the large, callous, appraising, imperious brute! What could a woman be to such a man but a slave! His collar would be well locked on a woman's neck! How he had looked upon me as a mere object, and yet, I sensed, as an object which he might find of some interest, slave interest. How I loathed him!

Then I dismissed these thoughts, for we had turned onto Emerald, and would soon be at the domicile.

* * * *

As the sheets were now folded, and readied for delivery, I put the kerchief about my head.

I then lifted the bundle, and held it on my head, steadying it with both hands.

It was in this fashion that I had seen tunic-clad girls bearing burdens.

It was my impression that my Mistress, and her guard, the beast, Grendel, had come to Gor, and, later, to Ar, with considerable resources, and might still retain an ample portion of these. These were in the form, I gathered, of jewels, in particular, rubies. I had accompanied the Lady Bina to the Street of Stones, actually a tiny district, only a few establishments, near the Street of Coins which, in effect, is itself not truly a street, but a district, where banking is done, credit extended, loans made, moneys changed, and such. In this "Street of Stones" she had exchanged a single ruby, which she had earlier shown to me, proud of its size, cut, luster, and hue. "This would purchase ten or more of you," she said, "even if you were a silver-tarsk girl." "Yes, Mistress," I had said. I supposed it true, and that her estimate might well have been conservative. I do not know what she received for the stone, as I was not permitted in the shop. I must kneel outside, in the sun, head down, chained by the neck to a public slave ring. Such things are apparently common in Gorean cities, at least in the high cities, the tower cities, for the convenience of masters and mistresses. As slaves are animals it is easily understood that there are many places in which they are less than welcome. One would scarcely, for example, bring a kaiila into a shop. In particular, slaves are not permitted within the precincts of temples, lest these edifices be considered defiled by their presence. A free person might seek sanctuary in a temple, but a slave might be killed, if found within one, after which the temple must be purified.

I avoided, whenever possible, the bridges. This was usually possible as, in times of peace, one may enter most towers at the level of the street, and use the stairwells within them, to gain access to the various levels, with their corridors, from which one might reach apartments, ranging from simple one-room cubicles to large, elegant suites. Laundering is done variously in the cities. Most cities have public laundries to which garments, sheets, linen, and such, may be taken, weighed, and washed, and, for an additional fee, ironed. On the other hand, the public laundries do not deliver. There are, in addition, public laundering troughs, which are divided into those reserved for free women and those accessible to slaves. Women of high caste seldom launder, but women of low caste often do. If a household contains a slave or slaves they will do the laundry, as well as other domestic tasks. Many lower-caste households do not contain slaves. There are two primary reasons for this. Whereas slaves are abundant and cheap, it costs to keep them. Most obviously, they must be fed and, to some extent, clothed. Secondly, if the household is small, and a free companion is in the household, she may not care to have a slave on the premises. For example, Delia, the companion of Epicrates, was such a woman. In the towers there are often "tower slaves," most often owned by the management of the tower. These slaves will launder, amongst attending to other domestic duties, sweeping, dusting, polishing, cleaning, scrubbing, and such, but there is an additional charge for such services. Accordingly, some residents in the towers rent work slaves whose services, being more intermittent and casual, are less expensive. Advertisements for such may be found on certain of the public boards. It was through Delia that the Lady Bina was first apprised of such matters.

It seemed important to the beast, and this did not much please the Lady Bina, who would surely have preferred a suite in a lofty tower, and an opulent mode of life, that they should live obscurely and appear impoverished. I supposed the beast's desire for privacy was easy enough to understand, given its unusual nature and appearance. In the streets it would surely be noted, watched, followed, called to the attention of guardsmen, and so on. It would no longer be possible to move freely. It might be subjected to ridicule, derision, and abuse. Too, it was scarcely the sort of thing to parade on the bridges or keep in some exclusive residential tower. So, it was thus that it had taken up residence over a small shop on Emerald. Its existence, of course, was not entirely concealed from the world, as Delia and Epicrates were obviously aware of its presence, and it was occasionally seen in the streets, usually after dark. It was understood to be an unusual pet of the Lady Bina. Few understood it as a rational form of life. In some respects, despite its tendency to indulge the will of the Lady Bina, it ruled, and categorically, and the Lady Bina, however fretful and resentful, must abide by its will. Their housing was one such instance. The point of appearing impoverished was involved in this, as well, as the impoverished attract less attention and are less likely to be the target of aggression. Few thieves will rob where robbery seems pointless. It is a fool who dips his bucket in a dry well. To be sure, the Lady Bina did insist on raiment befitting a free woman of station. But the beast would seldom let her out at night, and, when he did, he was often in the vicinity, beside her, or following, sometimes lightly, stealthily, watchful, on the adjacent roofs.

Goreans tend to be curious as to whence one's income is derived. If one has no obvious means of support suspicion is aroused. Few would suspect that the Lady Bina might have at her disposal a cache of rubies, or similar stones. And it would be well that such suspicions were not entertained, lest they provoke the interest of the unscrupulously acquisitive.

Indeed, I was not sure what resources the Lady Bina and the beast retained. Had the aforementioned ruby been their last? They had no new source of income of which I was aware, lest it might be from investments in the Street of Coins, but I knew of no such investments, and I suspected they would not wish their principal to be tethered to a particular location, nor, perhaps, would they care to have their wealth, if wealth they had, recognized.

In any event, whether as a mere aspect of their disguise, or because the pittances of my earnings might actually be important to their economy, I found myself serving as a work slave, a laundering slave, several customers having been located on the public boards by Delia, companion of Epicrates. The inference to be drawn, correctly or not, was apparently that the Lady Bina was so tragically impecunious that it seemed advisable for her to take in laundry, by means, of course, of her slave, the girl, Allison. I was never permitted of course, to touch this money. Delia would collect coins from some customers, the richer ones, and others, the ones less well off, would deliver the coins to the shop of Epicrates.

And so it came about that the former Allison Ashton-Baker, once of the upper classes of her world, once so superior and haughty, once so special and important in her own eyes, once one of the beauties of an exclusive sorority, at one of her country's most selective and expensive schools, now tunicked and barefoot, carried laundry in Ar.

I had at first rebelled at this suggestion.

This had occurred after the incident of the Sul Market, that dealing with the Metal Worker. I was still smarting from that episode. I recalled my humiliation, my helpless fury, on my knees before him, put there by his words, half stripped and bound, and he one of lesser caste, only a Metal Worker! This may have motivated, at least in part, my transient, foolish recalcitrance. Did I think I was still Allison Ashton-Baker? Did I not know I was now a slave? I would be reminded. I would be left in no doubt. I would test my limits. I would be taught them.

When I had first been brought to the house of Epicrates I suspected little more than the fact that the Lady Bina and the beast were not native to Gor. I thought this might constitute my opportunity for a manipulable, easy bondage. Certainly neither the beast nor the Lady Bina had treated me as I might have expected to be treated in a Gorean household, at least at first. For example, I had not been carried across the portal bound, thrown to the floor, and put under the whip. This is sometimes done to inform the slave that this is a household in which she is truly a slave, and must understand herself as such. Subsequently there is likely to be little doubt about the matter. And if doubts persist, they may be quickly dispelled. I took this lapse, if lapse it be, on the part of the beast, as an indication of indulgence or weakness, or perhaps merely a lack of interest, and, on the part of the Lady Bina, to be a consequence of ignorance, of her lack of familiarity with Gorean customs, and the attitudes and behaviors expected of a free woman. For all her petulance, pettiness, willfulness, vanity, and nastiness, she did not yet have the acculturated arrogance and sense of social power of the typical Gorean free woman. To be sure, she was highly intelligent and might be expected to learn such things. Delia, I am sure, would be an excellent tutor in such matters. She, like Epicrates, was of the Merchants, and the Merchants often take themselves as a high caste, though few others do. The five traditional high castes are the Initiates, the Scribes, the Builders, the Physicians, and the Warriors. Many would prefer not to count the Warriors as a high caste, but there are few who would openly deny their title to the status, as they are armed.

"I do not do such things," I had told them, "launder, and such."

"What?" had asked the beast.

"Grendel?" had said the Lady Bina, puzzled, turning to the beast.

I was standing, facing them.

"I was an important person on my world," I said. "I am not the sort of person who is set to such tasks." Then I straightened my body. "You must find another," I said.

I would never have had the courage, or the stupidity, to speak so in a normal Gorean household.

In such a household, I would have been only too aware of what I was.

Before a man, for example, I would have knelt, head down, waiting to be commanded, hoping, at any cost, to be found pleasing.

A bit of lip pulled back about a fang on the beast's jaws. In this instance, it had an unpleasant look about it.

I thought it best to kneel.

"What?" said the beast.

I lifted my head.

"I was an important person on my world," I said, falteringly. "I am not the sort of person who is set to such tasks."

From the throat of the beast their emanated a low sound, scarcely audible to me, though doubtless quite audible to the beast.

It was not a pleasant sound.

"You must find another," I said, boldly.

Then I was frightened, for I suddenly feared that the beast, though only a beast, might be familiar with how slaves were to be treated. Why might he not know such things? He may have learned them from others, or another.

I remembered then not the gentle graciousness with which I had been borne here from the Tarsk Market, carried nestled in its arms, as though I might have been a free woman, but remembered, rather, the perfection with which I had been bound, bound as a slave. And the knots had been warrior knots!

I was scarcely aware of its movements so swift it was, and I felt myself seized up, lifted, in mighty paws, and I sensed nails within them, and heard a roar of rage, and I was flung a dozen feet across the room, striking into a wall. Then I was pulled back, by one foot, to the center of the room.

I was on my belly.

The beast, with its size and weight, knelt across my body.

I was pinned to the floor.

It leaned forward.

"Do not! Do not!" I heard the Lady Bina scream.

It was my first experience of the sudden rage of that form of life, a rage easily aroused, swift, unexpected, unpredictable, terrible and overwhelming, a rage almost impossible to subdue.

I would learn later that it was the rage of the Kur.

Whatever might be the nature of that body in it coursed the blood of the Kur.

I felt massive jaws close about my head. I felt the tongue, and saliva, of the beast, its hot breath.

"No, no!" screamed the Lady Bina.

The jaws seemed to tremble. They tightened, relaxed, then tightened again. Had they closed my head would have been bitten away.

"No! Stop!" screamed the Lady Bina. I sensed she was dragging at the fur on the beast's back.

I sensed a titanic struggle being waged within the beast.

Then the jaws were removed from my head.

"Good, good," said the Lady Bina, soothingly.

"It seems you do not know you are a slave, and are in need of discipline," said the beast.

"No, no!" I said. "I am a slave. I am a slave, only a slave! I am not in need of discipline, Master! I will obey! I beg to obey!"

"Cord," said the beast to the Lady Bina.

A Gorean male might have so spoken, calmly, one recognizing what must be done.

Then, as I lay on my belly, helplessly, pinned down, I felt my wrists drawn up, over my head, behind me, and then, held, they were bound together.

"You will beg on your belly," said the beast, "for the privilege of serving your Mistress, and other free persons, as they might please, in whatever manner they might please."

"I am on my belly, Master!" I cried. "I so beg! I so beg!"

My hands were still held up, bound, behind my head.

He then rose up and drew me to my feet, and to the side of the room, where there was a slave ring fastened in the ceiling, some two or three feet in from the wall. I was then bound to the ring, my hands high over my head. I could barely reach the floor, with my toes.

"Go downstairs," said the beast to the Lady Bina. "Fetch a slave whip."

"They have no slave," she said.

"They will have such a device," he said.

I did not doubt it.

Such things are common in a Gorean household. Delia, companion of Epicrates, a free woman, I was sure, would not be without one. Who knew when a slave, perhaps near the shop, at a fountain, on the street, might be displeasing? Free women, abroad, often have a switch about their person.

The Lady Bina scurried away.

I heard her descend the stairs.

I half turned about, muchly suspended from the ring. "It will not be necessary to whip me, Master," I said. "I was foolish! I am sorry! I will obey, unquestioningly instantly. I am a slave. I beg for the privilege of serving masters and mistresses to the best of my ability!"

"I see you have felt the whip," said the beast.

"Yes, Master," I said, "in the house of Tenalion of Ar!"

I had no wish for that experience to be repeated.

Soon the Lady Bina had returned.

"Please do not whip me, Master!" I said.

"But you have not been pleasing," he said.

I was then whipped.

When I was released from the ring I fell to the floor, on my belly, my hands still bound.

"Have you anything to say, Allison?" inquired the beast.

"Yes, Master," I wept. "I am on my belly. I beg for the privilege of serving masters and mistresses, unquestioningly, instantly, as they might please, in whatever manner they might please."

"Anything else?" he asked.

"Yes, Master," I said, recalling my training. "I thank Master for my whipping. I hope that it has improved me."

"Has it?" he asked.

"Yes, Master," I said.

"Go downstairs," said Grendel to the Lady Bina. "Return the whip. But buy one. We should have one here."

She left.

"You will not need a whip, Master," I said.

"That is for me to say," he said.

"Yes, Master," I said.

I later learned that the beast had indeed learned how to treat slaves, and that he had learned this on another world, a steel world, the former world of Agamemnon, Eleventh Face of the Nameless One.

He was, of course, a beast, only a beast. I wondered what it might be to have a human master. That I thought might be even more frightening, for the human would be of one's own kind, selected for according to the radical, dimorphic relationships of master and slave over countless generations, one well aware of, and sensitive to, the psychology, the needs, the fears, the vulnerabilities, the tricks, the wiles, the vanities, the pettinesses, the weaknesses, the helplessnesses of his natural prey and possession, the female slave.

How terrifying, I thought, it would be to belong to a Gorean male, a natural male, one by whom one would be uncompromisingly exploited and mastered, as, of course, in one's secret heart, one would wish to be.

I thought of the Metal Worker, in the Sul Market. How arrogant and hateful he was! How I loathed him!

My wrists were freed by the beast.

"What are you going to do now, Allison?" he asked.

"Prepare supper, Master," I said.

* * * *

I made my way toward the tower of Six Bridges.

I was wary, as I did not wish my laundry to be soiled.

There was a reason for my fear.

All this was before the incident of the blind Kur.

I had had no idea, of course, when I and my sisters were transported to Gor where we would be sold. I was delivered to the house of Tenalion of Ar. Had others been, as well? I did not know. The house was large. And in a city the size of Ar there are many slave houses, many markets. The most famous is the Curulean. And, of course, there are hundreds of cities, mostly small, even in known Gor, and each would presumably have its emporium for collar-girls.

Still, upon reflection, though one supposes the catch from the sorority, the harvested items in that particular "slaver's basket," so to speak, would be distributed about, it is also plausible, upon reflection, that it might be more convenient to the masters, from the point of view of transportation, that several, if not all, might be disposed of in one location, or a limited number of such locations. From such a location, or locations, they might then be distributed variously. In this way, the wholesaler, so to speak, need not march coffles about, bundle his beasts into closed slave wagons, ankles chained to the central bar, ship them bound hand and foot in tarn baskets, and so on. Such things may be done by retailers.

I had hopes, of course, at least at first, that I might meet some of my sisters in Ar.

Surely that was a possibility.

Ar is large, but the number of laundry troughs, with their flowing water, is limited. So, too, is the number of wells and fountains, where water may be drawn. Kajirae, as is well known, though I think we are no different in this from many of our sex, delight to chat, gossip, observe, speculate, exchange views, recount anecdotes, waft rumors about, and so on. And the foremost gathering places for this sort of thing, for kajirae, at any rate, as they are not allowed in the baths unless they are bath girls, are the laundering troughs, those to which they are permitted access.

In any event, I had hoped, at least at first, that I might, at the troughs, or fountains, or in the markets, or on the street, encounter some of those I knew from the sorority, but I had not done so.

Then later it seemed to me that it was just as well, and perhaps better, that we not encounter one another again.

I assumed they would not have been freed. They were comely, and it is said that only a fool frees a slave girl.

How could I bear that they might look upon me now, in my shame and degradation, now no more than a barefoot, tunicked, collared slave? And what of them? How could I bear to look upon my former sisters, shamefully garbed, their necks clasped in the circlet of bondage?

Yet I knew I would be thrilled to see them so, owned, but, too, so free, so natural, so alive, so basically and radically female.

But how could I bear to have them see me, as a slave?

It was no dog collar now buckled, and locked, about my neck, as at the party, but, on my neck, now, a true slave collar, marking me as what I now was, a true slave.

Yet somehow, though I scarcely dared admit it to myself, I had never felt so healthy, so alive, so excited, so meaningful, so female, as here. I suppose this had something to do with the air of Gor, and the food, fresh, wholesome, tasty, and uncontaminated. But even more, I thought, it had to do with the culture, and the ethos, in which I found myself. These were so natural, so open, so innocent, so honest, so real. Here I could be what I always sensed I was. Here it seemed I had found myself. I found I loved what I was. And there was no doubt about what I was, no confusion, no uncertainty, no ambiguity. I was slave. Here, in a collar, I felt myself a thousand times more free than I had on my own world. Forgive me, Mistresses, if you are reading this, but it is true. I must speak the truth, for I wear a collar.

Whereas the Lady Bina was extremely intelligent, she was not always well informed, nor always realistic, and, I fear, she was not always wise.

She thought very highly of herself, and justifiably.

But she knew very little of Gor, or, I suppose, of any other complex human world.

From what sort of world, I had often wondered, had she been derived.

She was certainly well aware that she was unusually beautiful.

Indeed, she seemed to believe that she might well be the most beautiful woman on Gor.

For all I knew she might be, but, too, I had little doubt that there were thousands of other quite beautiful women who entertained the same suspicion, if not conviction. It was rumored that the former Ubara, Talena of Ar, daughter of Marlenus, the current Ubar of Ar, until disowned, might have regarded herself, or been regarded by many, as the most beautiful woman on all Gor. To be sure, given all the veiling of free women, and the dispersal of the population, who can speak practically of such things? Perhaps the most beautiful woman on all Gor is in some tiny village in Torvaldsland or herding bosk on the plains of the Wagon Peoples. Too, I had little doubt there were thousands of fellows about who thought that their companion or slave was the most beautiful woman on all Gor, for any woman, even ones whose appearance might frighten tharlarion, may appear beautiful when seen through the eyes of love. No one knew where Talena might now be. A large reward had been offered for her capture and return to Ar but the reward had never been claimed. I supposed she was in a collar somewhere. Certainly if she were as beautiful as many said, it would be almost certain she would have a collar on her neck. For some fellows, Goreans, having such a woman in a collar might be worth more than what she will bring in gold, thrown stripped and shackled to the foot of a Ubar's throne. But, of course, for others, the gold might be preferred. Much would depend on the man, and here men are the masters. I was pleased I was not Talena of Ar.

I have suggested that the Lady Bina, my Mistress, while highly intelligent, may not have been as informed as would have been desirable, or as wise as might be desired, or such. In some respects she was an interesting, indeed, a remarkable, combination of vanity, ambition, and naivety.

I dared not speak to her of such things, even in hintings or allusions, as I was only a slave, and was now well aware of that, and her mind was muchly made up, and even the concerned, well-intentioned counsels of the beast were ineffective. He, though a stranger to Gor, was at least no stranger to matters of rank, distance, and hierarchy, no stranger to questions of status, no stranger to probabilities, nor to politics and political relationships.

In short, the Lady Bina, counting on her unusual beauty, and well aware of its usual effect on men, and bolstered by an unchastened vanity, one as yet little bruised by the contact with reality, planned to become, however unlikely or incredible it might seem, literally the Ubara of Ar, Gor's greatest city, unless it be rivaled by Turia, in the far south. She seemed to believe that little more would be necessary to bring this astonishing elevation about than bringing herself to the attention of the Ubar or his advisors.

"Do not proclaim such ambitions," warned the beast. "You will be thought mad."

"But I am not mad," she said.

"No," said the beast, "but you do not understand these things, at all."

"How so?" she asked.

Once again I wondered about her background, her seeming lack of socialization, and such. How could she understand so little? Might it not have been better if she had undergone some frustrations and disappointments? Had she no sense of her place, or her limitations, or that limitations even existed? Did she think that only a dozen or so individuals might be involved, as in a tiny village? Ar was profound and complex, socially and economically. Her population consisted of hundreds of thousands of citizens. Most did not even know one another. What were her antecedents? What had been her experiences? Again, from what sort of world had she derived? It was as though she had been told of something important and precious, say, a particular jewel, and had decided she would have it. Did she not know that a jungle, formidable and dangerous, exacting and competitive, existed in the streets of Ar, a jungle which, as in many communities, for all its reality, was invisible?

"A Ubar, a great lord, a potentate," said the beast, "does not companion casually or lightly. There are slaves for that sort of thing, hundreds, scattered about in various pleasure gardens. He companions to forge alliances, protect borders, acquire cities, extend dominions, obtain access to trade routes, a port on the shores of Thassa. You are unknown, and unconnected, you bring no cities or armies into his grasp, no fleets, or cavalries of tarns. You do not even have a Home Stone."

I knew little of Home Stones, at that time.

Nor would I be permitted one, as I was a slave. Sleen, kaiila, verr, and such, other animals, too, have no Home Stones.

"I see," said the Lady Bina. "Things would then be difficult."

"A Ubar might companion a Ubara from another city, a coveted city, one of wealth and power, or companion the daughter of another Ubar, of such a city, such things."

"I see," she said, not pleased.

As I knelt in the background, inconspicuous but at hand, I saw that the Lady Bina was not so much dissuaded of her astonishing ambition, as convinced that its realization might be less easily achieved than hitherto anticipated.

"Occasionally," said the beast, "a Ubar may companion the Ubara of a captured city, forcing companionship, however unwelcome, upon her, making of her free spoils, so to speak, thereby, as she is then companioned, entitling himself legally to the wealth of her treasury and the allegiance of her subjects. In such a case she may sit beside him, on a throne, within her fine robes, chained."

"I suppose," said the Lady Bina, "he may do this severally."

"No," said the beast, "for one may have but one companion, at one time."

I had no doubt, of course, that a Ubar, or, indeed, any person of means, might have several slaves.

"What if a second Ubara is conquered?" asked the Lady Bina.

"You are thinking of companioning?" asked the beast.

"Yes," she said.

"Then the Ubara of less consequence," he said, "will be demoted to bondage, and then kept, or put up for sale, or such."

"But surely," she said, "companioning is not always involved in such matters."

"Certainly not," he said. "The conqueror holds rights to all in virtue of the right of conquest, in virtue of war rights. The usual ensuance in such matters is that the conquered Ubara will be marched naked in the triumph, chained to the stirrup of the victor's tharlarion or kaiila, after which she, and the women of her court, similarly paraded, will serve naked at the victory feast, during which they will be enjoyed, and after which, in the morning, they will be lashed and fitted with their collars."

"I see," she said.

"Accordingly," said the beast, "abandon your unrealistic ambition."

"Perhaps if I presented myself at the Central Cylinder," she said.

"I would not do so," said the beast. "You lack a Home Stone."

"So?" she said.

"You might be collared," he said. "Sometimes unauthorized women are rounded up and held for bidding, house biddings, thence to be distributed amongst the various slave houses of the city."

"I suppose there are others of wealth and power," she said, "other than Ubars, in a city such as this."

"Doubtless," said the beast.

"But," she said, "I think a throne would be nice."

"Perhaps," said the beast.

The Lady Bina then cast me a glance, which made me uneasy. That night, when the beast was absent, the Lady Bina summoned me to her.

She entrusted to me a message, which was written in black ink on cheap rence paper, in simple block letters, at that time almost childishly formed letters, as she, for all her dexterity and intelligence, was still far from adept in Gorean. Certainly she was not yet the mistress of cursive script.

I had learned from the laundry troughs that a lady's notes, having to do with her small secrets, private exchanges, intrigues, affairs, arrangements, assignations, rendezvous, and such, were generally carefully crafted, written in a tasteful, dainty script, usually on small sheets of fine linen paper, or parchment, subtly scented, and attractively sealed. There would be no doubt that their authors were women of refinement, breeding, sensitivity, taste, and intelligence. Surely much thought went into these things, well beyond the delicacy of the message itself. After all, the ink, the paper, or parchment, the script, the perfume, the seal, and so on, are, I suppose, in their way, a part of the message itself. Do they not themselves convey much without a word being spoken? In content the letters were often carefully ambiguous, designed to seem to promise much but guarantee little. I supposed the Gorean free woman was entitled, as with her veils and concealing robes, to balance concealment with revelation, mystery with the hint of possible abandon, even rampant disclosure.

A Gorean saying, seldom heard in the presence of free women, has it that beneath the robes of every free woman there is a naked slave.

These notes, of course, are commonly carried about by the woman's slaves, often concealed within their tunics.

Discretion is of the essence.

And then one hears about it at the laundry troughs.

I had no doubt that many a fellow's breath came faster, and his heart beat more rapidly, when he received such a note.

"May I inquire, Mistress," I asked, "the content of the note which I am to carry?"

At that time I did not realize how unwise was such a question. Happily, at least at that time, the Lady Bina lacked many of the habits, dispositions, and responses of the Gorean free woman.

"Certainly," she said. "I am proposing myself to be Ubara of Ar."

"I see," I said. "Is Master Grendel to be informed of this?"

"No," she said. "He might not approve."

I did not doubt that.

"You will leave in the morning," she said, "at dawn, as though on a common errand. Indeed, I will give you two tarsk-bits and you may later purchase some larmas which we may press for breakfast."

"Yes, Mistress," I said.

In that way, I supposed, my true mission, that of import, might be judiciously veiled.

"Now," she said, "relieve yourself, and we will chain you for the night."

"I need not be chained, Mistress," I said. "I will not run away." Indeed, where would one run? By noon I had little doubt but what I would be returned, bound, on a leash, to the house of Epicrates.

"I suppose not," she said. "But the Lady Delia has told me that a slut like you belongs on a chain."

"Yes, Mistress," I said.

I knew that males commonly kept their girls chained at night, usually to the foot of their couch, where they might be conveniently at hand, if desired in the night. In larger houses, girls were sometimes slept in their cages, perhaps to help them keep in mind that they are animals, and thus suitably caged.

The Lady Bina, perhaps on the advice of the Lady Delia, chained me so that my mat would lie across the threshold, at the height of the stairs. My left ankle was chained on one side of the portal and my right wrist on the other side. In this way an intruder would have to pass me, indeed, step over me, and, in this passage, would be likely to be discovered. The left ankle is the ankle most commonly chained, probably because most masters are right-handed. Too, it is the ankle most often fitted with bells or an ankle ring, presumably for the same reason. And I was right handed. Master Grendel slept on the roof. Were I a slaver, or a raider, I do not think I would have cared to have my tarn alight in his vicinity.

Master Grendel, as the Lady Bina apparently was not, was well aware of the possible jeopardy in which an unguarded free woman might find herself on Gor. Too, she had no Home Stone, no family, no clan, no caste.

I wondered if the beast was aware of how beautiful the Lady Bina actually was, how attractive she might prove to a human male. Probably not, I thought. She was not of his kind. He, a beast, would be unaware of such things.

The next day, about the Seventh Ahn, miserable and sore, walking stiffly, I had returned to the second floor of the house of Epicrates.

"What is wrong?" asked Master Grendel.

"Put the larmas here," said the Lady Bina. "Is there change?"

"A tarsk-bit," I said.

"You are improving in your bargaining," said the Lady Bina.

"I did not let them know I had two," I said.

"Excellent," she said. "She is clever," she said to the beast.

One learns such things.

"Why are you bruised?" asked the beast.

"No matter," said the Lady Bina.

"No," said the beast. "Why?"

I looked to the Lady Bina, frightened.

"You may speak, Allison," she said.

"Soldiers," I said.

I had not been within a hundred paces of the Central Cylinder when a lowered spear had blocked my way.

I had made clear my business, that I was to deliver a message to the Ubar, or to some high officer, who might then convey it to him, and the note was then taken from me by an officer, not of high rank, perhaps the commander of a ten, who read it, laughed uproariously, slapped his thigh, and then, to my unease, shared it with others, while I knelt.

It, and its bearer, were obviously the cause of much amusement.

"Is there an answer, Master?" I had asked.

"Yes," he said, and availed himself of a marking stick, and wrote something on the back of the note.

Still kneeling, I took the note.

"Thank you, Master," I said.

"Is your 'Mistress' free?" asked the officer.

I fear he thought some jest was afoot, perhaps sprung from the humor of some fellow officer.

"Certainly Master," I said.

Surely a mistress would be free.

"We will give you something for her then," he said. Then to four of his subordinates, he said, "Seize and spread her wrists and ankles and belly her."

"Master?" I said.

"This," said he, "is for your Mistress."

He then, and some others, with feet and spear butts, belabored a slave.

I wept with misery.

"Here is one for your Mistress!" said a fellow.

"And here is another!" said another fellow.

"And another!" said yet another.

"Aii!" I cried. "Please no, Masters! Please, no, Masters!"

Then I was released, and lay before them, on the stones, sobbing, and bruised, a beaten slave.

One may not, of course, strike a free woman. They are not to be struck. They are to be held immune from such corporeal indignities. They are free. Indeed, there are penalties for such things. On the other hand, I then learned, and later confirmed, that a slave may stand proxy for a Mistress's punishment.

Supposedly this is disconcerting to the free woman, and she much suffers, being outraged, scandalized, and humiliated at her subjection to this vicarious chastisement.

The Lady Bina, however, who knew little of Gorean culture, failed to detect the insult intended, and bore up well under the ordeal.

"I do not think anything is broken," said the beast.

"No," I said.

When a slave is beaten the point is usually to correct her behavior, or improve her, not to injure or maim her.

Still they had not been gentle.

"It is past the Seventh Ahn, Allison," said the Lady Bina. "Did you dally, flirting about the stalls and shops?"

"No, Mistress," I said. I had been pleased, incidentally, that I had seen nothing of the offensive Metal Worker, for whom I had looked, the better to avoid him, of course. Certainly I would not have wished him to see me as I was then, stiff and aching, miserable and bruised.

"Four larmas for a tarsk-bit, especially in the morning, is quite a good buy," said the Lady Bina.

"I did smile at the stallsmen," I said.

"Excellent," said the Lady Bina. "Men are such manipulable weaklings."

"Some men," said the beast.

"Squeeze the larmas," said the Lady Bina. "There are biscuits, and honey breads, in the pantry."

"Yes, Mistress," I said.

"Wait," said the beast. "There was a response to the note?" he said.

"Written on its back," I said.

"It will not be important," said the Lady Bina.

The large paw, five-digited, like a human hand, was thrust toward me, and I withdrew the note from my tunic, and, head down, handed it to the beast.

The beast perused the note.

Apparently he could read, unless he was merely taking the scent of the hand which had written the note.

"Oh!" I said, for the beast then did something which seemed shockingly incomprehensible. The lips of the beast drew back about its fangs, and it uttered a snorting exhalation of air, and then, three or four times, it leapt into the air and spun about.

I was muchly alarmed.

The beast was very large, and I did not know its ways. Had it gone suddenly, unexpectedly insane the apartment might have been damaged, and life lost. How long might such a behavior, or fit, endure? I backed away, on my hands and knees, terrified. The Lady Bina, on the other hand, seemed more annoyed than frightened.

I gathered she was familiar with such spontaneous, apparently irrepressible, exhibitions.

"Surely," she said, "it is not so amusing as all that."

Apparently the beast could read.

Such exhibitions I would later learn may, with slight variations, betoken enthusiasm or jubilation, high spirits, the appreciation of a deft witticism, an excellent move in a game, pleasure at unexpectedly glimpsing a friend, a fine shot in archery, a victory in the arena, one's foe slaughtered at one's feet, a splendid jest, and such.

"What does it say?" asked the Lady Bina, for the beast seemed in no hurry to surrender the paper.

"'Put on a collar, and visit the barrack'," read the beast.

"Do you think that would further my project?" she asked.

"No," he said. Then he turned to me. "Squeeze the larmas," he said to me.

"Yes, Master," I said.

* * * *

And so I made my way toward the tower of Six Bridges.

I was wary, as I did not wish my laundry to be soiled.

There was a reason for my fear.

All this was before the incident of the blind Kur.

I had taken a roundabout way to Six Bridges, to avoid

encountering the laundry slaves of the establishment of the Lady Daphne, a private laundering house in the vicinity of Six Bridges. In Ar there are several private laundering houses and they tend to live in an uneasy truce with one another, allotting districts amongst themselves. Six Bridges was in the district of the house of Lady Daphne. These houses do not relish intrusions into their territory, either by other houses or by independent services. Two of her girls, large girls, for such are best at such things, had intercepted me twice, once a month ago, and once last week.

"Discard your laundry," had said one last month.

"No," I had said. "Go away. Let me alone."

"A barbarian!" had said the other.

"What do you have under that kerchief?" inquired the first. She yanked it back, down about my neck.

"Nothing!" laughed the second.

"Go away!" I had implored them, tears springing to my eyes.

"As bald as a tarn's egg!" said the first. "She must have been quite displeasing."

I was not bald now, but there was not much hair there either, little more than a brush of darkness, soft to the touch. Still I was happy to have so much.

"She does not please me," had said the second.

"Is the laundry heavy?" asked the first.

"No!" I said, frightened.

"Yes it is. It is too heavy for you," said the first.

"Stop!" I said.

The bundle was pulled away from me and cast into the gutter, which, in this district, runs through the center of the street. The two then trod it underfoot, into the drainage and mire.

"You are to accept no more customers here," said the first girl.

"The tower of Six Bridges," said the other, "belongs to the house of Daphne."

I had then recovered the garments and returned to the house of Epicrates.

After that, for four trips, though I was terrified of the bridges, I had ascended a tower several Ehn from that of Six Bridges and warily made my way, by stairwells, and connecting bridges, to the tower of Six Bridges. Once I had seen the two ruffians lurking below in the street, presumably alert to intercept either me or another.

I kept to the center of the bridges as much as possible, kneeling to the side if a free person was passing. The bridges I utilized were not really narrow. Most were two to three paces in width. But they were high, and railless. Sometimes I became dizzy. It made me sick to look over the edge of such a bridge. I stayed as far from their edges as possible. "A barbarian," laughed more than one person passing me. How superior they felt to me! How superior they were to me! Too, you tread roads, paths, and bridges to the left. I suppose this is natural, and rational. In this way your right hand, which might wield a weapon, a dagger or staff, faces the stranger whom you pass. Thus, on the left, you are better positioned to defend yourself, if necessary. On the other hand, in the part of my old world, that called Terra, or Earth, that part from which I derived, one treads to the right. How uneasy that would make you! Presumably there are historical, political reasons for that, perhaps involving a blatant declaration of differences amongst states, different symbols, different currencies, different customs, different practices, different ways of doing things. One does not know. In any event treading on the left, for a long time, made me uneasy, particularly on the high bridges.

To be sure, it was easy enough, soon enough, for the delivery girls of the house of Daphne to ascertain, from amongst their customers, that competition lurked about.

Accordingly, it took Lady Daphne's ruffians, both natively Gorean, little time to extend their surveillance to the local bridges, this easily done from a higher bridge, or even from the roof of the tower of Six Bridges itself.

Accordingly, last week, seeing one of the two approaching rapidly on the connecting bridge, I turned about to flee, only, to my consternation, to see the other, who had been following me.

Caught between them, on the high bridge, I sank to my knees, dizzy and sick, and put down the bundle, frightened, trembling.

I knew, weak and unsteady, I could be easily swept from the bridge, and might even, trying to stand and move, stagger, and precipitate myself over the edge.

I began to shudder.

How close the edge seemed, the sharp drop much closer than it could have been in reality.

I could then not even manage to kneel.

So I lay on my belly, my hands at the side of my head, unable to move. I just did not want them to touch me. I felt wind on my tunic, I saw a wisp of cloud pass by.

"What is wrong with her?" asked one of the girls.

"I do not know," said the other.

I was aware of the laundry being lifted, and, piece by piece, cast from the bridge, doubtless fluttering to the street far below.

The two girls from the house of Lady Daphne then withdrew.

I lay there for a long time, not daring to move, while occasionally a man or woman moved past me.

"Are you all right?" asked a man.

"Yes, Master," I said.

"Do you want me to carry you into the tower?" he asked.

"No, Master," I said.

Later, inch by inch, I crawled on my belly to the edge of the bridge and looked over the edge.

Here and there below, on a lower bridge, and on the street, I could see bits of the laundry, cast about, scattered, and crumpled. While I watched, a sheet was taken by a wind and swept from the lower bridge, whence it fluttered to the street below. An occasional person looked up, and then moved on.

After a time, I backed away from the edge, and then, on my hands and knees, carefully made my way to the security of the tower and the descending stairwell.

I recovered what laundry I could from the lower bridge, and the street, and returned to the house of Epicrates. I was not beaten. Lady Delia, companion of the pottery merchant, Epicrates, with coins received from the Lady Bina and the beast, later remunerated a number of customers who had lost their goods.

"It would be better, in the future," said the Lady Bina, "if you kept to the streets, for it would then be easier to recover lost articles."

"Mistress wishes to continue her enterprise?" I inquired.

"Certainly," she said.

"Perhaps we could avoid the district of Six Bridges," I said.

"If it were not the district of Six Bridges," said the Lady Bina, "it would be another district."

"Yes, Mistress," I had said, in misery.

"Too," she had said, "Six Bridges houses several of our best customers."

"Yes, Mistress," I had said.

And so it came about that I was taking a roundabout way to Six Bridges, this time, at least, again on the street level. Once more I was hoping to avoid the laundry slaves of the establishment of the Lady Daphne. I had first encountered them a month ago on the street, and then, more frighteningly, on the bridge last week. Usually, of course, I did not encounter them. Had I done so regularly our service would have been irreparably disrupted. Twice I had been accompanied in my rounds by the Lady Bina, and once by the Lady Delia. If the laundry slaves had been about then, and noted my passage, they had not disturbed me, as I was accompanied by a free person. The beast, of course, did not accompany me. It seldom went out while Tor-tu-Gor reigned amongst the towers. Had he been with me I would have had little doubt but what the laundry slaves of the Lady Daphne would have kept their distance, if not have fled altogether back to her house. Men sometimes became embroiled, as mercenaries, in the disputes between the laundering houses, but the routine policing of territories was generally entrusted to slaves.

I was within fifty paces of one of the lower entryways, a back entryway, to Six Bridges when, to my dismay, I saw my two nemeses, one emerging from a doorway to the left, the other from a doorway to my right. I had little doubt they had been waiting there, watching, for me to come close enough to surprise. Carrying the laundry, a rectangular bulk of it, steadying it on my head with two hands, I could not well have turned about and fled.

They were too close.

Both were smiling.

Both were carrying a peeled, supple branch.

I did not know how long I could hold the laundry, if those branches were laid against the back of my thighs, or across my arms and shoulders. They would avoid my face, I was sure, lest I be permanently marked or damaged.

I was, after all, goods, perhaps goods of some value.

The first of the two laundering slaves whipped her branch viciously through the air, twice. I heard its swift rush through the air. The other slapped her branch in her palm.

"Why are you not on the bridge?" laughed the first.

"You looked well, paralyzed, unable to move, cowering on your belly," said the second.

"She is a barbarian," said the first.

"I will enjoy this," said the second.

"I mean you no harm," I said. "Please! Please let me pass. I must do as I am told."

"So, too, must we," laughed the first.

"You were warned," said the second.

They then, improvised switches at the ready, stepped forward. They lifted their arms, eager, grinning, but then, to my amazement, they stopped, and turned white.

"First obeisance position," said a voice behind me, sharply, a male voice, "switches in your teeth."

The two laundry slaves swiftly went to first obeisance position, kneeling, head to the ground, palms of their hands on the ground, the switches crosswise in their teeth.

Both were discomfited, frightened, in the presence of a man, presumably a free man.

"You, you with the laundry," said the voice. "Remain standing, where you are, and do not turn around."

I think the man then withdrew a few feet behind me.

Then he said to the two laundry slaves, "Get on all fours, and approach me, the switch in your teeth, both of you."

I watched them, frightened, crawl past me. The first one cast me a look of terror, of misery.

In the house I had been trained to crawl thusly to a man, humbly, the switch held crosswise between my teeth. It is one way in which a slave may bear the whip or switch to her master.

She does not know how, or if, it will be used.

She will soon learn.

I did not turn around.

"Now turn about, and belly," said the voice.

Then I sensed that the slaves had been put to their bellies, their heads toward me.

I then heard some small, frightened sounds, as though limbs had been jerked about, behind backs, and then tiny noises, as though wrists had been thonged together, and not gently.

I then heard two small cries, accompanying a ripping of cloth.

"Now," said the voice, "let us see about these switches."

"Mercy, Master!" said the first of the two laundry slaves.

"Were you given permission to speak?" he asked.

"No, Master, forgive me, Master!" said the girl.

A moment later I heard the switch being applied to the two slaves, a blow for one, and then a blow for the other, and so on.

There was much sobbing.

"Knees," said the voice.

"Henceforth," said the voice, "you are not to bother this slave, or any other, as they are about their work. If you do, you will be placed on a slave ship for Torvaldsland or Schendi. Do you understand?"

"Yes, Master," they said.

Then they cried out with pain, as though they might be being dragged at a man's hip, in leading position.

"Move," he said, and I saw the two slaves pass me, on the right, tied together, closely, head to head, by the hair, their tunics torn to the waist, their hands thonged tightly behind them, their backs and the back of their thighs richly striped from the blows of a switch.

"Stop!" he called.

Instantly they stopped.

"Tell your Mistress," said the voice, "that this district is open, and will not be defended, or contested. It, and its pricings, are not to be managed, or controlled. If the Lady Daphne does not find these arrangements acceptable, her house will be burned to the ground."

"Yes, Master!" they said.

"Now, go," said the voice.

The two bound, chastised slaves then, awkwardly, as they could, uncomfortably, half stumbling, fled down the street.

"Do not turn around," said the voice behind me.

I remained still, looking ahead, frightened, balancing the laundry, holding it in place with my two hands.

"A slave thanks Master," I said. "A slave is grateful."

I trusted he would not now, himself, take the laundry and cast it to the gutter. Would that not be a rich Gorean joke, at the expense of a helpless slave, a joke worth recounting in the taverns?

"You are Allison, the barbarian slut of the Lady Bina, are you not?" asked the voice.

"I am Allison," I said, "girl of the Lady Bina, who resides in the house of the pottery merchant, Epicrates."

"The barbarian slut," he said.

"I am barbarian," I said, "Master."

"A barbarian slut," he said.

"If Master pleases," I said.

I sensed I was being regarded, from behind, as a slave may be regarded.

"How is it that Master knows a girl's name, and that of her Mistress?" I asked.

"Hold still," he said.

I stiffened, angrily.

I felt his hands at the side of my body, and then at the sides of my waist, and then at my hips, and then a bit down, at the sides of my thighs.

Had I been on Earth, and free, I would doubtless have spun about, and struck him. But I was on Gor, and a slave.

"Not bad, for a barbarian," he said.

"I assure Master," I said, "that many of us are quite as good as his native Gorean girls."

Certainly we were all of the same species, and all in our collars.

"I am told we sell well," I said, angrily.

"For copper tarsks," he said.

My fingers dug into the laundry, angrily.

Did he know of the Metellan district, or the house of Menon?

"Do not turn around," he said.

"No, Master," I said.

"Straighten your body, girl," he said.

"Is Master pleased with what he sees?" I asked.

"I have seen worse," he said.

"A slave is pleased, if Master is pleased," I said, acidly.

I was sure now whose was the voice whose face I could not see.

It was he from the Sul Market, he whom I loathed.

I had seen him about, from time to time.

"It seems Master follows a slave," I said. "Perhaps Master will make an offer for her."

"You are a vain slut," he said. "What makes you think anyone would want you?"

"I am lovely," I said.

"That is all you are," he said.

"At least that is something," I said.

"Certainly," he said.

"How did you know my name, and that of my Mistress?" I asked.

"Curiosity is not becoming in a kajira," he said.

"Forgive me, Master," I said.

"Are you any good in the furs?" he asked.

"Perhaps Master would care to try me, and see," I said.

"You are boldly spoken," he said.

I shrugged.

"Perhaps I will try you," he said, "and see."

"I am owned by another," I said, quickly.

"But a woman," he said.

"She might hire men," I said.

"If she could hire men," he said, "you would not be doing laundry."

"Surely a barbarian slut could be of no interest to Master," I said.

"Barbarians look well," he said, "naked, collared, chained, licking and kissing at one's feet, bringing the whip to a fellow in their teeth, and such."

"I have laundry to deliver," I said.

"Remain where you are," he said.

"There is another, of course," I said.

"I know," he said.

"Oh?" I said.

"What do you know of it?" he asked.

"Very little," I said. "It is the pet of Lady Bina."

"Do not be naive," he said.

"Master?" I asked.

"Do you know what form of life it is?" he asked.

"No," I said.

"It is Kur," he said.

So he knew that word.

"I know little of such things," I said.

"What," he asked, "is it doing on Gor, and what, too, is the Lady Bina doing on Gor?"

"I do not know," I said.

"You are stupid," he said.

"I find Master hateful," I said.

"You would look well at my feet," he said.

"I have laundry to deliver," I said.

"Do not move," he said.

"Yes, Master," I said.

"You would find out what it is to be owned by a man," he said.

"A slave thanks Master," I said, "for his intervention in her behalf, in the matter of the laundry. With his permission, she now begs to be dismissed, that she may be about her work."

"Are you red-silk?" he asked.

"Of what business is that of Master?" I asked. Then I said, quickly, "Yes, I am red-silk."

One must be careful how one responds to a Gorean male, if one is a slave.

"But perhaps not yet," he said, "in frequent, desperate need."

"It seems not," I said.

"You look well," he said, "your arms up, bearing your burden."

I was silent. I did not dare release the laundry and yet, holding it, my arms were lifted and, in effect, held in place, as much as though they were at the sides of my head, held in shackles, chained to a ceiling ring.

"Do women of your world bear burdens thusly?" he asked.

"Some do," I said, "but not in the part of my world from which I derive."

"You do it attractively," he said.

This was partly an effect, I supposed, of the position of the arms, and its effect on the girl's body. A common examination position, as noted earlier, requires the hands to be placed behind the neck, or at the back of the head. Too, there are chaining arrangements which fasten a girl's wrists together, at the back of her neck.

"On my world," I said, "I did not bear burdens."

"You were of high caste?" he asked.

"I was well placed," I said, "and of high social station."

"And now you are a mere slave," he said. "Excellent."

"'Excellent'?" I said, angrily.

"Certainly." he said. "That makes you more interesting, once of superior station, now a reduced, meaningless chain slut."

"Please release me, Master," I said, angrily.

To this plea, there was no response.

I dared not turn my head.

"Master?" I said. "Master?"

He then came about, and was facing me.

It was indeed he of the Sul Market!

He was close to me, very close.

"Steady," he said.

I turned my head away. There was a faded, stained, half-torn poster, advertising a carnival, on the wall opposite.

He then gently took my head in his hands, turned it to him, and held it, and I tried to pull away, but could not do so.

"No!" I begged.

He drew me to him.

"No," I said, "no!"

Then I felt his lips on mine.

I tried to pull back, but could not do so.

"Part your lips, more," he said. "Get your mouth open, more."

I tried to shake my head, negatively, but could scarcely manage it.

"I want to feel your teeth," he said. "Do not bite, of course, or your teeth must be torn from your head."

I tried to protest, but could not well form words.

"You have good lips," he said, "sweetly soft, bred for a master's kiss."

I struggled, futilely.

"Touch teeth, gently," he whispered. "Now," said he, "tongue, tongue. Surely you have been trained."

"Please, no, Master, please, no, Master," I murmured.

Then suddenly, unexpectedly, tears ran from my eyes, forcing their way between the clenched lids.

"You are in a collar," he whispered.

"Yes, yes," I said. "I am in a collar!"

My body then shook, and I felt weak, and I pressed my lips to his, piteously. But almost at the same time, suddenly, unexpectedly, spasmodically, I thrust myself against him, needfully, beggingly.

I recalled slaves in the house, moaning in their kennels.

I remembered the kitchen of the eating house of Menon, at night, late at night, how I had thrashed in my chains.

I pressed myself against him, my fingers clawing into the laundry I carried.

"Interesting," he said. "I suspect our barbarian slut is now just another well-oiled, nicely lubricated, juicing slave."

"I hate you!" I said.

"You might do for a paga tavern," he said.

How I hated him, but might he not be my master?

I knew I was ready, open, wet, gaping, and a master's.

"Yes," he said, "you are red-silk."

"I am yours, I know I am yours!" I said. "Buy me, buy me, Master!"

"You are anyone's," he said.

He then thrust me back, away from him, and held me at arm's length.

"I have now established what I wished to ascertain," he said. "You are, as I thought, just another piece of collar meat."

"Yours," I said.

"Anyone's," he said.

"I cannot help it if I am a woman!" I wept.

"Nor should you," he said.

"Buy me!" I begged.

"Only a slave begs to be bought," he said.

"I am a slave!" I said.

"Obviously," he said.

"Master!" I wept.

"It is a pity to waste you on a woman," he said. "You are a man's slave."

"Yes," I said, "yes, Master!"

"I thought you might be a hot little thing," he said.

"Master," I said, but I could not reach him.

"You have laundry to deliver," he said.

Two or three fellows were standing about, smiling.

"You have aroused me, as a slave!" I said.

"You are scarcely warmed," he said. "You do not even suspect what might be done to you."

I knew Goreans sometimes set aside two or three days for a slave. It was common to devote a day, a morning, or an afternoon, to dalliance, a dalliance in which the slave, from time to time, might scream her need. But, too, of course, the use of a slave could be brief, dragging her to oneself by her leash or chain, throwing her over a saddle, or the arm of a couch, thrusting her, as one wished, to the carpet, kneeling, head to the floor, hands clasped behind the back of her neck, and such. Too, of course, the slave may be commanded to serve her master in a medley of modalities, at so little as a hand sign or a snapping of fingers.

"You have made me show myself slave," I said, "publicly, in a street. I have been humiliated! I have been treated with contempt, I have been scorned!"

"All women are slaves," he said. "You are no different."

"I hate you!" I cried.

"Though not all are in collars," he said.

"I hate you!" I screamed.

"You, at least, are in a collar," he said.

I shook with frustration.

"Be careful of the laundry," he said.

He then turned about, and left.

I turned to look after him.

After a bit, he turned, looking back. "Perhaps sixty copper tarsks," he called. "Not a silver tarsk!"

Tears burst from my eyes.

He then resumed his departure.

After I had delivered the laundry, I returned to the street, to make my way back to the house of Epicrates.

On the wall opposite the back entrance, one of several, to Six Bridges, there was a faded, half-torn poster.

I had seen it before, but had paid little attention to it.

But, somehow, I had not forgotten it.

I now went to it, and, for the first time, regarded it with care. Amongst the animals portrayed on the poster, snow larls, large, striped urts, snarling sleen, performing tharlarion, prancing kaiila, there was another, where the poster was half torn. It was a beast, much like Master Grendel. It was clearly Kur.

Then I dismissed the matter from my mind.

As I made my way back to the house of Epicrates I recalled the Metal Worker. What a hateful brute he was. How I loathed him!

How he had humiliated me, and taught me my collar!

But it was nice of him, was it not, to have protected me from the girls of the house of Daphne? He needed not have done that. And how had he been there so opportunely? Was that a coincidence? I did not think so, which thought gave me considerable satisfaction. Too, I was sure I had seen him, from time to time, even before the Sul Market. It seemed likely that, at least from time to time, he had followed me. Certainly some men will so follow a slave about, or even a free woman. What then might be his motivation? Might he have some interest in a slave, even one who might be a mere barbarian slut?

Surely he was muchly different from most of the men I had known on my former world.

He was Gorean.

And I was a slave.

On the way back to the house of Epicrates, I hummed, and sang.

Chapter Eleven

"We think it is in the sewers," said Antiope, rinsing a master's tunic, at the public troughs, late in the afternoon.

"What?" I said.

I knew little of what might be about. Perhaps my mistress, the Lady Bina, and her escort, or associate, or colleague, or guard, whatever he might be, the beast, Grendel, might know, but they had not spoken to me of such things, nor before me of such things. I think the Lady Bina may have been as uninformed as I. I was less sure of the beast.

"It," she said, "the thing, or things."

Shadows were long, near the troughs, at this time of day.

Patrols of guardsmen were more frequently about, of late.

"You know something, or think something," I said, "I am sure of it. Tell me."

I had been trying to cultivate her, and some others, for several afternoons now.

"You are a barbarian," she said.

"Forgive me," I said.

"Soak, and rinse, these coverlets for me," she said.

"Yes," I said, adding, "Mistress."

This pleased her.

A few Ehn later I mentioned, "I have a candy."

"Oh?" she said.

"It is as large as a tiny tospit," I said, "hard, and yellow-and-red striped, and has a soft center."

"Curiosity," she said, "is not becoming in a kajira."

I had wheedled this prize from Grendel, who sometimes

purchased such things for the Lady Bina. After my beating, following my brief essay at assertiveness, and discovering that even the least impertinence or forwardness was not acceptable in a woman who wore the collar of Gor, I had gotten on quite well with the beast. The beast was male, and, as with other males, males of the Gorean type, it is easy to get on with them, provided one is, so to speak, at their feet, intent to please and zealous to obey. On its peg hangs the whip. One hopes to keep it there.

"But not unknown," I said.

Neither the Lady Bina nor the beast were particularly cruel or demanding. I rejoiced that the Lady Bina had not been acculturated as a Gorean free woman, with their usual contempt for, and hostility toward, female slaves. Accordingly, she saw no point in the exercise of arbitrary, gratifying authority, nor in the infliction of humiliation or pointless pain. Part of this may well have been because it never occurred to her, in her unquestioning confidence in her own beauty and intelligence, to think of me, as other free women might, as some sort of rival. "The beauty of a free woman," she once said to me, perhaps having acquired such views from Lady Delia, downstairs, the companion of Epicrates, "is a thousand times beyond that of a mere slave. It is as the moons, and the stars, and other things, which I forget. A slave's beauty, on the other hand, is that of a mere accessible, squirming beast, chained at a man's ring." "Oh?" I said. "What do you think?" she asked. "Perhaps it depends on the woman," I said. "Quite possibly," she said. "I shall soon deliver the laundry," I said. "Good," she said. I did not doubt but what the Lady Bina, herself, properly stripped and collared, would make an exquisite little bundle at a man's feet. Perhaps she might then better assess the views of the Lady Delia, whom, I suspected, might not do all that well at a man's slave ring. It was fortunate, I thought, that she, the Lady Bina, had not ventured herself to the Central Cylinder several days ago, when I had been belabored with boots and spear butts in proxy for her naive importunity. She would doubtless have been recognized as barbarian, suspected to lack a Home Stone, and one thing might have led to another. To be sure, I would not, in such situation, have cared to deal with a pursuing, vengeful beast. And with the beast, as I have suggested, I had little, if anything, of which to complain. Despite his hirsute, ferocious, dangerous appearance, he was invariably kind to me, and was extraordinarily understanding, patient, and gentle with the Lady Bina, who seemed, if anything, to despise him for this indulgence. I often wondered about the nature of the beast, and his unusual devotion to her, a devotion so profound, it seemed, that he would abandon a world for her. It sometimes seemed to me that he was almost human, and then I recalled his fangs, and how I might once, in a moment of rage, have had my head torn from my shoulders. He was clearly Kur. All in all, as you may have surmised, my bondage in their loft, if one may so characterize it, was a fairly light one, save, of course, for labors involved in the business of the laundering, which business did accrue, from month to month, a small store of copper tarsks, some delivered, some collected, for her commission, by the Lady Delia.

As the weeks had sped forth, however, particularly at night, when I was chained across the threshold of the apartment, at the head of the stairs, I had grown increasingly uneasy. It was sometimes difficult to sleep. I would sometimes twist, and sweat on my mat. Sometimes I would pull a little at the chain on my left ankle, fastened on one side of the threshold, and that on my right wrist, fastened to the other side. I knew myself chained, and as a slave. Chains are arousing to a female who knows she is a slave, and what she is for, and yet these were not the chains of a man, a master whose helpless possession and plaything one might know oneself to be, but those of a mistress and a beast, to neither of which, I gathered, was I of more interest than a small, silken, pet sleen.

I would with my left hand sometimes touch the collar on my throat. Sometimes I would try to pull it off, but it was locked on me. What is the point, I wondered, of being in a collar, if it were not the collar of a master?

I was uneasy.

My belly, my thighs, were restless.

I remembered the kitchen of the eating house. There, at least, from time to time, men would put me in their hands, and do astonishing things to me, which left me in no doubt as to my bondage. Too, in the gambling house, though seldom, for we were not to distract the men from the tables, I was put to a customer's pleasure, usually when it was feared he might be on the point of leaving. At such times a copper tarsk was often put in my mouth, to be retrieved by the customer when done with me, a tarsk which might be redeemed for tarsk-bits, to be spent on the tables, tarsk-bits which might, soon, result in the loss of tarsks, even of silver.

I do not think I was truly suffering from the fiercer conflagrations of slave fires, not as they so acutely tormented some slaves, thrashing about, and crying out with need, but I had little doubt that the former Allison Ashton-Baker, so refined, cool, and lovely, was now muchly different than she had been on her native world. She was now a half-clad, collared Gorean slave girl, and her belly needs, as those of others, were beginning to assert themselves, muchly troubling her.

It is no wonder free women thought themselves so superior to us.

Or were they so superior? Perhaps they just had not yet been awakened. And what, I wondered, if anything, did they whisper to their pillows and coverlets in the night?

"You have a candy?" said Antiope.

"Yes," I said.

"Let me hold it in my mouth for a time," she said. "I will not steal it."

"What is going on in the city?" I asked.

"Curiosity," she said, "is not becoming in a kajira."

"You are kajira," I said.

"Yes," she said, "but I know."

"Tell me," I said.

"Perhaps you will let me have the candy, just for a little while," she said. "I will not run away."

"I have finished this laundry for you," I said, rinsing the coverlets.

"Thank you," she said.

I envied Antiope. She had a master. I had seen him once, when he, from some yards off, had summoned her. How delightedly, how swiftly, she had run to him. He was a handsome fellow.

I envied Antiope. I suspected she was excellently and wholly mastered. She had that look about her.

"There are the extra guardsmen," I said, "the additional patrols, the uneasiness, the early closure of some stalls, some markets, the curfew."

"It is understandable," she said.

"I think," I said, "you do not really know what is going on."

"Oh?" she said, archly.

"No," I said.

"Give me the candy," she said. "Just for a little bit. I will not keep it. If it is hard, as you say, it will last a long time. I will give it back to you."

"It has a soft center," I said.

"No matter," she said.

"Very well," I said, and I freed the small candy from its wrapper, the candy and wrapper extracted from a tiny sleeve inside the hem of my tunic.

Antiope looked about.

We were the only slaves at the troughs now, and it was late afternoon. In an Ahn or so the curfew bar might sound.

Our laundry was piled to the side.

I shivered a little, as it seemed to be cooler now.

"You know about the killings?" asked Antiope.

"Very little," I said.

"Some beast, or beasts, is in the city," she said. "Eight or ten men, some women, have been torn to pieces, in different places, in different districts."

"Could a larl be in the city," I asked, "or a wild sleen?"

"Unlikely," she said. "The work does not suggest the attack of such beasts."

"Something different?" I said.

"What is wrong?" she asked.

I must have turned white, for I thought of the beast, Grendel. Such a thing would be fully capable of such work. How did I know the beast remained on the roof of the dwelling of Epicrates? It would be easy for something of its size, agility, and power to descend to the street. I knew it tended to leave the domicile only at night.

Antiope, holding the candy delicately, touched her tongue to the candy, her eyes closed.

"The bodies were not robbed," she said. "They were partly eaten."

"A larl then," I said, "or a sleen?"

"No," she said, "the larl, the sleen, kill in their own ways. Some of the bodies were crushed, others had the neck broken."

"You thought it came from the sewers?" I said.

"It is thought so," she said.

The candy disappeared into Antiope's mouth. "Good," she said.

"Make it last," I said. I wanted some of it back.

"I will," she said. She then removed it from her mouth, and again savored it, tongue-wise. In this way it would last a very long time, as it would not too soon melt away. It is a trick of slaves.

"Then tharlarion," I said.

Some tharlarion, usually found in rivers, or along shores, are squat, heavy, sinuous, patient, and capable, under certain conditions, of brief bursts of speed.

"It does not seem so," she said.

"Why do they think the sewers?" I asked.

"Where else?" she said. "Too, some thieves, some well known, in broad daylight, even within view of the praetor's platform, pushing aside a grating, rushed from a sewer, to be shortly apprehended by rings of spear-bearing guardsmen. Shortly were the thieves manacled and neck-chained."

"Why did they so emerge?" I asked.

"Something in the sewers they feared, and never saw," she said.

"It was the beast, or beasts?" I said.

"Perhaps," she said.

"Guardsmen, with lanterns, have surely traversed the sewers," I said.

"It seems they found nothing," she said. "Two never returned."

I conjectured then that two had apparently found something, or had been found by something.

"There is one thought, but much rejected," she said, licking at the candy.

"What is that?" I asked.

"Some months ago," she said, "hunters in the Voltai, seeking larl, found an unusual beast in their net, almost man-like, but larger, covered with hair, large-jawed, fanged and clawed, fierce, twisting, and howling. Such a beast had never been seen. It was returned, caged, to Ar, and purchased for a carnival."

I immediately recalled the faded, half-torn poster, the remains of which were affixed to the wall opposite one of the rear entrances to Six Bridges.

"It was a large, dangerous, stupid, simple thing," she said, "and, as it proved, at least at the time, untrainable, it was kept for exhibition."

"It was irrational?" I said.

"Clearly," she said.

I was not sure of that.

"It then seemed docile, and bided its time," she said. "Then, one day, when it was to be fed, it reached through the bars and seized a keeper's arm, and broke him against the bars, and tore at his belt, where dangled his keys, but others intervened with spear butts, striking at the beast, and it, roaring, tore away the keeper's arm, and fed on it, and the keeper died moments later, of shock and loss of blood."

"It was reaching for the keys," I said.

"No," she said, "it only seemed so, as it was naught but a mindless, violent beast."

"It later escaped?" I said.

"Its danger was recognized, and the owner of the carnival, who was also its chief trainer, to neutralize and pacify it, had it blinded, with hot irons."

"What then?" I said.

"Weeks went by," she said. "Then it was noticed one evening that the blinded beast was turning about, and moving, in time to the carnival music, when the kaiila were performing, and later, the striped urts. This was brought to the attention of the owner, the chief trainer, who brought a flautist to the vicinity of the cage, and, behold, the beast danced to the music of the flute. Thereafter this was one of the attractions in the carnival. Further, this suggested to the chief trainer that the beast might now prove susceptible to training. Apparently this proved to be the case, and, eventually, the beast, led on a leash, was brought regularly, in its turn, to the area of performance, surrounded by the crowd. There it performed simple tricks, to the snapping of a whip, jumping up and down, rolling over, turning about, climbing on boxes, and such. Then one evening, it turned on the chief trainer and tore out his eyes, and then, blindly, awkwardly, rushed through the crowd. Guardsmen, and others, were about, and the beast was wounded, cut, and slashed time and time again. Then it disappeared, bleeding, and limping, into the darkness."

"Then it escaped," I said, uneasily.

"In its flight," she said, "it killed four, and injured several others."

"It escaped," I said.

"It is thought not," she said. "It was struck many times. It is thought nothing could long live so grievously wounded, so copiously bleeding."

"The body was not recovered," I said.

"Blood led to the sewers," she said. "It doubtless died in the sewers."

"But that is not known," I said.

"No," she said, "that is not known."

"One is then left with the mystery of the killings," I said.

"Yes," she said.

"What sort of beast was it?" I asked.

"Of an unusual sort," she said.

"What was it doing in the Voltai?" I asked.

"I do not know," she said.

"It is growing cold," said Antiope.

"It is getting late," I said.

I shivered, again.

We saw two guardsmen some yards away.

"Ho, kajirae," called one of the guardsmen.

"Master?" said Antiope.

"Is your work done?" he inquired.

"Yes, Master," said Antiope.

"Dawdle not then," he said, "lest your collars be read."

"Yes, Master," we said, and hurried to gather up the laundry.

In leaving, it seemed we must pass them. Sometimes it is

difficult to pass a free male, under certain conditions, without a kiss or a slap.

"Give me back the candy," I whispered to Antiope.

"We must not dawdle," she said.

"I am not dawdling," I said, standing up.

"There is not much left," she said.

"Give it to me," I said.

"The masters may be displeased," she said, uneasily.

"Approach," called one of the guardsmen.

"They are displeased," said Antiope, apprehensively.

We were then standing before the guardsmen. One of them had lifted his right hand, slightly, the palm up, so we did not kneel. I, and perhaps Antiope, as well, was uneasy at this, as one commonly kneels before a free person, often with the head down.

It was obvious to us that we were being looked upon, as the slaves we were.

Antiope was quite attractive, and I, surely, had often enough seen the eyes of men upon me.

"What is in your mouth?" asked one of the guardsmen of Antiope.

"A candy, Master," she said.

"It is mine, Master," I said.

"Please do not take it away from us," said Antiope.

"Who would wish a candy which has been soiled by the mouth of a slave," said a guardsman.

"You are dawdling slaves," said the other. "You should be switched."

"No, Master," we assured them.

"The streets are dangerous," said the first guardsman. "The curfew bar will sound in a bit."

"Hasten to your cages," said the other. "You will be safe there."

"My master does not cage me," said Antiope.

"Surely a manacle awaits," said the first guardsman, "hoping to be warmed by your slender, lovely ankle."

"Thank, you, Master," said Antiope. "A slave is pleased, if she finds favor with a master."

"Go," said the first guardsman.

"Oh!" said Antiope.

"Oh!" I said.

Then we hurried on.

"He does not own me!" said Antiope, smarting.

"Nor the other, me," I said.

Still, we knew such things were done only when a slave was found attractive. One supposed one should find some gratification, or reassurance, in that.

We were then about a corner, and out of the sight of the guardsmen.

"Give me the candy," I said.

"I fear," said Antiope, "it is gone."

"I see," I said. To be sure, we had been delayed by the guardsmen.

"But I will tell you a last thing," said Antiope.

"What is that?" I said.

"Of all the killings, in the streets, men and women," she said, "all were free."

"No slave was set upon?" I said.

"No," she said.

"Why is that?" I asked.

"I do not know," she said.

"It is a coincidence," I said.

"The attacks are commonly at night," she said. "I think, then, slaves would be on their chains, in their kennels, in their cages, such housings."

"That is doubtless it," I said.

"But sometimes," she said, "attacks are in the day, particularly in less frequented districts, and sometimes slaves are abroad at night."

I supposed that were so.

Usually, of course, they would be in the company of their masters, or, say, keepers, if they might be returning late from feasts, serving slaves, flute slaves, kalika slaves, brothel girls, dancers, or such.

Too, it was not unknown for a neglected slave, if unconstrained, to prowl the streets, hoping for a secret tryst, to relieve her needs.

Sometimes, too, they might be dispatched under the cover of darkness to carry messages for their mistresses, pertaining to projected rendezvous.

To be sure, it was unusual for an unaccompanied slave to be abroad at night. But then, indeed, few, slave or free, if solitary, essayed the streets after dark, particularly in certain districts. One, if sufficiently affluent, and lacking his own men, might hire guards, and a lantern bearer. There were establishments to provide such a service. Too, such conveniences were sometimes available, gratis, to the clientele of certain residences. One such residence was Six Bridges.

"No slaves have been attacked?" I said.

"Not to my knowledge," said Antiope.

I found that of interest.

"It will soon be curfew," said Antiope.

We then wished one another well, and, bearing our laundries, took leave of one another.

Chapter Twelve

I dipped the first of the two buckets into the fountain of Aiakos, where I usually drew water. It is at the intersection of Clive and Emerald, and is the nearest fountain to the shop of Epicrates.

It, as many fountains, has two basins, water flowing first into the high basin, and then running over to the lower basin. As an animal I was permitted to drink only from the lower basin, but there was no difficulty in filling the buckets in the upper basin, and we invariably did so, as it was deeper and fresher. The water entered the fountain through eight spouts, oriented to the eight major points of the Gorean compass. Below each spout, on the adjacent stone rim, there are two shallow depressions, or worn areas, the one on the right deeper than that on the left. This difference takes place over generations, as right-handed persons tend to brace the right hand on the rim while leaning over to drink, and left-handed persons tend to place their weight on the left hand as they lean forward to drink. Similar worn places do not appear on the lower rim as slaves, sleen, kaiila, and such, are expected to drink while on all fours. The water is brought in from the Voltai Mountains, or Red Mountains, which at that time I had not seen, far north and east of Ar, by means of long, towering aqueducts, most of which are more than seven hundred pasangs long. The Builders, the "Yellow Caste," one of the five castes commonly regarded as high castes, engineered these remarkable constructions, and are charged with their supervision, upkeep, and repair.

"Step aside, girl," said a woman's voice, and I backed away, my head lowered. The free woman then dipped her pail into the water, and left.

Some free women are cruel to slaves.

I was pleased she had not switched me across the back of the thighs.

I dipped the second bucket into the water.

Men prefer us, I thought.

"Where is Lord Grendel?" the Lady Bina had inquired, unfastening the shackles which held me in place, across the threshold of the apartment.

"Is he not on the roof, Mistress?" I inquired, rubbing my right wrist. To be sure, it was light, and, by now, one would expect him here, below, in the loft, or apartment.

"No," she said.

"I do not know, Mistress," I said.

"It is not like him to be absent," said the Lady Bina.

"No, Mistress," I said.

I feared he had departed from the roof, after dark, after the curfew had sounded.

I feared there might have been another killing in the streets.

"I would be spoken to," I said to the Lady Bina.

"To what end?" asked the Lady Bina.

"Things have been muchly different, of late," I said.

She did not respond.

"There has been much reticence in the household," I said.

"It has to do, I think," said the Lady Bina, "with the curfew, the killings. Lord Grendel has been uneasy."

"There is much unease in the city," I said.

"That is clear in the streets, the markets," she said.

"Something is out there, at night," I said.

"Not always at night," she said.

"May I speak?" I said.

"Surely," she said.

"I do not understand Lord Grendel," I said.

"How so?" she said.

"In the past," I said, "he cleaned his own body, oiling the fur, washing it, brushing and combing it, with particular care, and, of late, he has had me much attend to him, sometimes an Ahn at a time, often concerning myself with such things."

"You are grooming him," she said, "cleaning the fur, and such. Have you encountered small forms of life in the fur?"

"No," I said.

"Good," she said. "He is a cleanly brute, and, for his kind, fastidious."

"I do not understand," I said.

"Pets," she said, "are often used by his kind to groom their masters. Much is done with the fingers, and the lips, and teeth. The small forms of life, caught in the fingers, or between the teeth, are eaten."

I felt ill.

"I am not a pet," I whispered.

"Of course not," she said, "or, at least, no more than any other slave is a pet."

"Who is he, Mistress?" I begged. "Who are you?"

I expected to be told that curiosity was not becoming in a kajira, but the small, exquisite Lady Bina, despite her selfishness and vanity, her almost charmingly innocent lack of concern with the feelings and lives of others, was often pleasant, and communicative. Too, she was not natively Gorean. That, I thought, quite possibly, was relevant.

"There are metal worlds, large metal worlds," she said, "like small planets, inhabited by Kurii, rather like Lord Grendel, though he is not truly Kur."

"No?" I said.

"Lord Grendel," she said, "is the result of an experiment, one which apparently did not turn out well."

As far as I could tell, Grendel, or Lord Grendel, was Kur. I recalled he had identified himself as such, on the very evening he had brought me to the domicile, the first floor of which held the living quarters and shop of Epicrates.

"I myself," said the Lady Bina, "was originally a Kur pet."

"A pet?" I said.

"There is nothing wrong with being a pet," she said. "Indeed, on the world once of Agamemnon, Eleventh face of the Nameless One, it was a great honor to be the pet of a Kur, particularly if one were only a human being, and not a female Kur, defanged and declawed, kept in chains and chastisable by the rod. I myself had the privilege of being the pet of Lord

Arcesilaus, who now, as I understand it, is the Twelfth Face of the Nameless One, Theocrat of the World, that world. Pets are not taught to speak, but I learned to do so; the mechanical translators, and Lord Grendel, and some others, were helpful; and, after the dislocations of an insurrection, and the downfall of Agamemnon, Eleventh Face of the Nameless One, former Theocrat of the World, that world, learning of this world, a beautiful, natural world, not a small world and one of metal, and ships which might voyage here, I decided to embark, reach this world, and make my fortune here, in particular, becoming a Ubara, a ruler or consort of a ruler, of some great city - I had heard of Ar - or, possibly, of the planet itself."

How naive she is, I thought.

Again I tried to envisage what might have been her socialization, her acculturation.

Then it occurred to me that, from what she had said, for most practical purposes, she had had little in the way of such customary amenities.

"You spoke of an experiment," I said.

"Yes," she said.

"It did not turn out well?" I asked.

"Apparently not," she said.

"I do not understand," I said.

"You should speak to Lord Grendel of that," she said.

"Might he not kill me?" I asked.

"You could ask him, and see," she said.

"I do not think I will do so," I said.

"I do not think he would hurt you," she said. "At most you would be well lashed, perhaps several times, over several days, and warned not to speak of it again."

"You speak of Lord Grendel," I said. "I gather, then, he was important on his world."

"He came to be so," she said. "Muchly so, in power and prestige, and, if he had been interested in such matters, and wished it, might have become so in wealth, as well."

"Why then would he leave?" I asked. "Why would he give up so much?"

"To accompany me," she said.

"To a new world, a strange world, an unfamiliar, perhaps hostile world?" I said.

"Yes," she said.

"Forgive me, Mistress," I said, "but why would he, so strange and different a form of life, do so?"

"I have never inquired," said the Lady Bina. "He insisted on doing so."

"Here," I said, "he is feared, even loathed."

"That is because he is not a true Kur," she said. "The true Kur is beautiful, large, agile, proud, long-armed, glossy, wide-nostriled, with six-digited appendages, with a voice a larl might envy. Grendel has deformed paws, with only five digits, and the throat, and tongue, the oral orifice are different, and the eyes, too. He can even approximate human sounds."

"I think," I said, "he is devoted to Mistress."

"I have never objected to his presence, despite his appearance," she said. "He is useful to have about, and I am fond of him. He cannot help his ugliness. Too, I suspect his presence, like that of a pet sleen, would encourage predators, thieves, or such, to circumspection."

I had no doubt about that.

"I do not understand," I said, "why, of late, Lord Grendel has had me attend to his grooming."

"Nor do I," she said.

"Mistress is well aware of the killings," I said.

"Surely," she said.

"Some fear a Kur may be involved," I said.

"There are no Kurii on Gor," she said.

"Lord Grendel," I said.

"Not a true Kur," she said.

I was not so sure of that. I had sensed that the beast regarded itself as Kur, and prided itself on the possession of that dark, dangerous blood. As noted, he had certainly, and, indeed, unhesitantly, identified himself as Kur.

"There was one, I think," I said, "who performed in a carnival."

"It died, did it not," she asked, "in the sewers?"

"It is thought so," I said.

"Then a larl, a sleen, or such, perhaps a sewer tharlarion, must be about."

"Kurii are dangerous," I said.

"They must eat," she said, "and sometimes, it seems, they want blood."

At that moment we heard a movement, above us, as of a large body turning about, moving, on the roof.

"Ah," said the Lady Bina, pleasantly, "Lord Grendel has returned."

* * * *

I was readying myself to return to the shop of Epicrates, with the two buckets, freshly filled, when I became aware of a shouting about, and I saw several citizens hurrying to join a cluster of others, gathered near the double doorway of an insula on Clive, not more than a hundred paces from the fountain.

I saw a slave rushing past, hurrying away from the insula.

"What is going on?" I cried.

"A body!" she cried. "Another killing!"

"Wait!" I called, but she had sped past.

I remained at the fountain, the buckets put to the pavement, beside me, shading my eyes.

The crowd parted a bit, as four guardsmen, summoned, I gathered, pressed through the gathering.

I saw them pull part of a body by one foot toward the center of the street. More than one free woman wrapped a veil more closely about her face, and backed away.

Guardsmen were motioning to the crowd, to disperse. The body, what I saw of it, was placed in a mat, which was folded about it.

A Tarnster, come from the crowd, was passing. Near him, similarly withdrawing, was a fellow in the brown of the Peasants, a bundle of the leafy vangis over his shoulder.

"Masters," I called.

"A larl is loose in the city," said the Tarnster.

"It was no larl," said the Peasant.

"A sleen then," said the Tarnster.

They had then moved past.

I then rose to my feet.

"Persinna!" I called to a shapely slave, in a brief gray tunic, with a tiny, locked message box, chained to her collar.

Her eyes were suddenly wild with fear. "Be silent!" she said, looking about her. "Do not speak that name, I beg of you."

"Do you not remember me?" I said. "I am Allison. We were sold together, in the Metellan district."

"I am not Persinna," she said.

"You are, or were," I said.

"You see my tunic!" she said. "I am a state slave. I am owned by the state of Ar!"

"Now," I said. "And that is ironic, is it not?"

"Be merciful," she said, looking about.

"I thought you had a private master," I said.

"I did," she said, "but he sold me to Ar, as a joke, for a pittance."

"Doubtless there are some in Ar," I said, "who would like to see you adorn the spike of impalement."

"Do not reveal me," she begged.

"There is doubtless an anonymity for you," I said, "being chained amongst state slaves."

"Please," she said.

"But, of course, if you are discovered," I said, "you would be nicely at hand, on a chain."

"Worthless barbarian!" she hissed.

"I think I shall call out your name," I said, angrily.

"Please do not," she whispered, "—*Mistress*."

"I am not a Mistress," I said. "We are both now no more than collar sluts." I could conceive of a fellow in whose arms I thought I might now well be no more than an eager, grateful, squirming collar slut. How far I was now, a slave, from the cool, smug, haughty, so-self-satisfied Allison Ashton-Baker!

"You perhaps," she said, "not I."

"Wait," I said, "until you are put out for public use, with a hundred others, on a feast day."

"Let me go," she begged.

"What is going on, down the street?" I asked.

"Curiosity—" she began.

"Speak," I told her.

"A body was discovered," she said, "thrust between buildings."

"From last night?" I said.

"One supposes so," she said.

"Then the larl must be about," I said, frightened.

"If it is a larl," she said.

"What else could it be?" I asked.

"I do not know," she said. She touched the message box chained to her collar. "Please," she said. "I must be back within the Ahn."

"Who was killed?" I asked.

"Did you not see the garmenture?" she asked.

Somehow I had refused to see it, or, better, to see it for what it was. Too, of course, I had only glimpsed it, some shreds, and at a distance. I suddenly felt very much afraid. "Yes," I said.

"A Metal Worker," she said.

"What is wrong?" she asked.

I could form no words.

"I am Mina, Mina," she said. "May Mina go?"

"Forgive me, Mina," I said. "I wish you well."

The former Lady Persinna then turned about and, gratefully, hurried away.

There would be, of course, hundreds of Metal Workers in Ar.

"Do you dally, Slave?" inquired a free woman, come to the fountain.

"No, Mistress!" I said. "No, Mistress!"

I then seized up the handles of the buckets and, step by step, slowly, carefully, for the weight, and that no water be spilled, frightened, miserable, made my way toward the shop of Epicrates.

Chapter Thirteen

I had fled through the streets, terrified.

"Come back, Allison!" had called the Lady Bina, but I had rushed, weeping, past her, down the stairs, and emerged on Emerald.

It was now late afternoon, and I was in the closest, sizable market to the domicile of Epicrates, the market of Cestias, in one corner of which was the Sul Market. It was there, in the market of Cestias, we commonly shopped. It was there I had been commanded by the Lady Bina, when she, for whatever reason, was intent to satisfy herself that I might be found acceptable to men. Well did I remember the ten Ehn she had given me, within which time, as she was not a patient woman, I was to satisfy her curiosity. It was there that I, hands bound behind me, in half a tunic, had been ordered to my knees by a surly, imperious stranger, he who had later protected me at Six Bridges, but had seen fit to take his reward from my lips, I helpless to prevent his arrogant presumption.

Surely I must despise him!

Yet he had protected me, from the girls from the house of Daphne.

From the fountain I had made my way, sick and fearful, to the domicile, and, step by slow step, had brought the buckets upstairs.

"Lord Grendel," had said the Lady Bina, "wishes water. Carry one bucket to the roof."

"Yes, Mistress," I had said.

"Too, he wants cloths," she said. "Take these."

"Yes, Mistress," I had said.

The trap opening to the roof was open, and I climbed the stairs, and, the cloths over my shoulder, and two hands on the bucket handle, emerged on the roof.

The beast was crouching in one corner of the area, concealed from the street by the wall surmounting the roof. Given my height, I could look over that wall. It came about to my shoulders.

It was there the beast slept.

It turned about, and lifted its head, and I saw those large, glinting eyes upon me.

I half dropped the bucket, and water splashed to the sun-hot roof. I threw down the cloths, and backed away.

"Do not speak of what you have seen," said the beast.

"No, Master," I said.

I then turned about, and fled, running down the stairs to the apartment, and then, past the Lady Bina, down stairs, to the street.

The paws of the beast had been covered with dried blood, stiffening and matting the fur.

Now I had been searching the market of Cestias, and nearby streets, how long I did not know. I did not see him! It was growing late. Where might he be? Was he no more? Had he met his end on Clive? Who had been in those bloodied shreds of black and gray, the colors of the Metal Workers? Could it have been he? To be sure, what could he, a stranger, be to me, and what could I, a slave, be to him, a free man? Were we not muchly disparate, he a free man, a citizen, doubtless the possessor of a Home Stone, and I, a lowly barbarian beast, brought from a far world to the markets of my superiors, my masters? I tried to remind myself that I should hate him, the callous brute, that I should loathe him, he so arrogant and supercilious, he who looked upon me so casually and saw me as nothing, only a meaningless Gorean kajira, fit only to be at a man's feet. But I recalled he had ordered me to my knees before him, when I was helpless, wrists fastened behind me, and half-stripped, and I had knelt, as I had no choice but to do, as a slave, and had looked up at him, and suddenly, startled, wondered if it might be he, my master, before whom I knelt. And I remembered, too, the intimacy of the kisses forced upon me when I, as a slave, dared not, and desired not, to resist. I must have passed given stalls and vendors, given shops, an indefinite number of times. Surely I attracted curious glances, in the nearby streets, and, time and time again, in the market plaza. More than once I had been regarded by guardsmen. What business had I there?

I did not know where else to look for him. Indeed, I feared he had been cruelly slain, even dismembered. What had been folded in the mat by the guardsmen on Clive had not been a whole human being. Parts, I supposed, must have been eaten, or disposed of, elsewhere.

And I remembered the blood on the paws, and arms, of the beast, and how it had lifted its head, and regarded me, on the roof. "Do not speak of what you have seen," it had said.

I had then, in horror, and hysteria, fled from the roof, and the domicile.

I hoped it would not be thought I had run away.

I knew I could not elude the consequences of the collar, the brand, the tunic. There was no escape for such as I, the Gorean slave girl. At most, one might fall into a heavier, more severe, more terrifying bondage.

But I had been unable to help myself, and had fled the house.

I had not truly intended to run away.

I knew the penalties which might be inflicted on a fugitive slave, the lashings, hamstringing, being cast amongst a foliage of leech plants, being butchered for sleen feed, even being cast alive to such beasts.

"Kajira," said a guardsman.

"Master?" I said, kneeling.

"Are you lost?" he asked.

"No, Master," I said.

"What are you doing here?" he asked.

"I am looking for someone," I said, "a Metal Worker."

"Your master?" he said.

"No, Master," I said.

"What is his name?" he asked.

"I do not know," I said.

"You have been summoned to a tryst?" he said.

"No, Master," I said. I realized that free persons do not always reveal their names to slaves. Many Goreans, too, I understood, particularly of the lower castes, had "use names," to conceal their real names, lest their real names, it seemed, might supply ill-wishers with grist for spells and sorceries.

"Today," said the guardsman, "a Metal Worker was killed, in the vicinity of Clive."

"I fear it might be he," I said.

"Your tunic," he said, "suggests that you are a woman's slave."

"Yes, Master," I said.

"Many of the stalls and shops are closing," he said. "You are to be off the streets by curfew."

"Yes, Master," I said.

"Do you know your way home?" he said.

"Yes, Master," I said.

"Go home," he said.

"Yes, Master," I said, and rose to my feet.

Chapter Fourteen

"Groom me," said the beast.

I brought the brushes and combs to his side, and began at the sides of the head, brushing downward, toward the shoulders.

"You tremble," said the beast. "Your hand shakes."

"Forgive me, Master," I said.

"Do not be afraid," said the beast.

"Forgive me, Master," I said.

"You barely arrived home before curfew," said the Lady Bina.

"Where were you?" asked the beast.

I drew the brush downward.

"The market, the market of Cestias," I said.

"Good," he said. "You are familiar, then, with the market."

Why should he be pleased with that, I wondered. I had not been given permission to go there. Commonly, just as a slave may not clothe herself without her master's permission, so, too, she may not leave his domicile without his permission, and it would then be expected, of course, that her destination would be specified and her anticipated time of return. She is not a free woman. She is his possession, his animal, his slave. I, on the other hand, in my misery and terror, hurrying past the startled Lady Bina, had precipitously fled the domicile. Such leave takings are not permitted slaves. When I had returned, by then much aware of the enormity of what I had done, I had been contrite and fearful. My lapse had been significant, and I was owned. I had crept up the stairs, and knelt, head down, before the Lady Bina and the beast. "Forgive me, Mistress. Forgive me, Master," I had said, pressing my lips first to the Lady Bina's slippers, and then to the clawed feet of the beast. Interestingly, I was not beaten. I was not even scolded. Had I a male master, I am sure I would have been tied and lashed. Male masters tend to be exacting of their girls. I wished I had such a master, who would be firm, and severe, and see to it that I would be an excellent, and pleasing, slave. That is what I wanted, and had always wanted, to be well owned, and wholly mastered. To be sure, I had arrived back before curfew.

"We shop there, frequently," said the Lady Bina.

"Do you know the praetor's platform, by the coin stalls?" asked the beast.

"Yes, Master," I said.

There were two market praetors in the market of Cestias. One was near the coin stalls, and Sul Market, the other, rather across the plaza, not far from the Paga and Ka-la-na Markets.

The coin stalls were, in effect, exchanges, as, in a market of the size of that of Cestias, in a city such as Ar, buyers and sellers from diverse cities might mingle and carry diverse currencies. As would be expected, the most common denominations in the market were those of Ar, her tarn disks, and her tarsks, of copper, and silver and gold. But coins of many cities circulated. Occasionally one encountered a disk from far-off Turia. Some prized coins were the silver tarns of Jad and, on the continent, the golden staters of Brundisium. Many of the transactions were conducted by means of scales. One often encounters, for example, clipped or shaved coins. The professional in shaving keeps the roundness of the subject coin as perfect as possible. Sometimes it is hard to tell, by eye, that a coin has been shaved. Clipped coins are easy to identify but then, of course, one must bring forth the scales, and, not unoften, as well, rough silver or gold, unminted, is presented, perhaps melted droplets, or pieces cut from silver or golden vessels and goblets, which items will also require judicious determinations. Negotiations and bargainings, over the scales, often grow heated. The advantage, of course, lies with the stallsman. Complaints may be lodged with either of the two praetors, who, interestingly, though magistrates of Ar, apparently strive to adjudicate matters to the best of their lights. Their efforts not only redound to the honor of Ar, but, too, one supposes, tend to preserve the value and integrity of the market, which, in the long view, is doubtless in the best interest of the city's commerce. To be sure, major transactions often take place near the walls, and outside them, in the wholesale markets.

"I have an errand for you to perform," he said.

The beast's wide nostrils flared slightly, as though scanning the room. I wondered what might be the consciousness of the beast.

"Master?" I said.

"I will explain it to you later," he said.

I continued to brush his fur.

"Why are you afraid?" he asked.

How could he ask such a thing? Had he not recognized my horror at the sight of his body, earlier today, in the late morning, the matting, the caking, the stiffened fur?

"Tonight," he said, "you will not be chained."

I was then more afraid than before.

Is there not, on the chain, some security?

"Why is that?" asked the Lady Bina. I was sure it made little difference to her whether I was chained or not. Indeed, I was sure that my chaining had more to do with the recommendations of the Lady Delia than any interest which the Lady Bina might have in the matter. The Lady Delia, a Gorean free woman, had definite views as to the proper treatment of female slaves. To be sure, men often chain their female slaves, perhaps because it pleases them to have their animals on a chain. A discrepancy in a routine, on the other hand, would be of interest to the Lady Bina, for, as a highly intelligent woman, such things were likely to provoke curiosity, and require some explanation.

"Because it is my will," said the beast.

"Very well," she said.

The beast was commonly concerned, sometimes almost pathetically so, to please the Lady Bina. It would unprotestingly accept her pettinesses and abuses, which were not infrequent, would seek to attend to her wants, which were frequent, and, to the extent practical, would indulge her every whim. Sometimes it seemed as though it were no more than a large, agile, hideous, somewhat terrifying, but devoted and harmless pet. At other times, however, one sensed an adamancy in that imposing form, an alarming core of bestial will which would brook neither compromise nor deviation, no more than tides and seasons, a will behind which lay the instincts, the blood, the fangs, and claws, of Kurii. At such times, the Lady Bina would remain silent, and, resignedly, gracefully, withdraw. She was apparently familiar with such things from the metal worlds of which she had spoken. To what end might one remonstrate with a living anvil, or winter, or hunger, or a quiescent volcano which, jarred, might speak with fire?

The Lady Bina had now left the room, crossing the threshold to her chamber.

It was at such times that it seemed to me that it was she, and not he, who was the pet. In any event, I had long been aware that in matters of moment, or times of crisis, there was but one voice and one will in the domicile, that of the beast.

I did not think the beast would kill me in the presence of the Lady Bina.

She was no longer present.

"Do not be afraid, Allison," said the beast.

"I am afraid," I said.

"Why?" he said.

"The roof," I said, "what I saw."

"I see," he said.

"There was a killing," I said, "on Clive."

"I know," he said.

I continued to brush him.

"From last night," I said.

"From shortly before dawn," he said.

"I will not speak what I saw," I said.

"I know you will not," he said.

I felt cold.

"I think the comb now," he said.

"Yes, Master," I said.

"You are trembling," he said.

"I think Master was not on the roof last night," I said.

"No," he said. "On several nights I have departed the roof. One may move from roof to roof, occasionally descending to the street, then climbing to a roof anew."

I thought of that agile, large form on the roofs, in the streets, moving about, lightly for its bulk, a shadow amongst shadows.

"Master has been about," I said.

"Yes," he said.

"There have been killings," I said.

"They must stop," he said.

"A larl, in the streets," I said.

"No," he said.

"What then?" I said.

"The Lady Bina is sleeping," he said.

I could hear nothing, but I gathered that the beast had no difficulty in making this determination.

"I will now explain to you what you are to do," said the beast.

"Master?" I said.

"You understand that you are a female slave," he said.

"Yes, Master," I said. On Gor, I had no doubt of that.

"And how is a female slave to obey?" he asked.

"Instantly, unquestioningly," I said, "and, to the best of her ability, with perfection."

"If you obey with perfection," he said, "you will not be hurt. If you do not obey with perfection, you will undoubtedly die a quick and most unpleasant death. Do you understand?"

"Yes, Master," I said.

"You will not wear your kerchief," he said. "In that way, your head bare, you will not be confused with a free woman."

"I do not understand," I said.

"As a collar girl, I know you are vain," he said.

"I am a woman," I said.

"Your hair," he said, "is still quite short, but, over the months, it is not badly grown out. And some masters have their girls wear it that way, that the girl, and others, may understand that every aspect of their appearance is at the master's discretion."

I supposed such girls would beg, and perform desperately, that their hair might be permitted to grow "slave long."

"I do not understand what is going on," I said.

"Your hair is now attractive," he said.

"How would Master know?" I asked.

"You are no longer permitted to wear the kerchief, unless given explicit permission," he said.

I was silent.

"You are a pretty slave, Allison," he said. "If you were also helpless in the furs, you might go for better than a silver tarsk."

I was silent.

"Your helplessness would doubtless be assessed," he said, "before you were brought to the block. Buyers are interested in such things. One wants not only a pretty girl, but a hot girl."

"Oh?" I said.

"One uncontrollably hot, helplessly hot," he said.

"I do not think I am 'hot'," I said.

"Coolness, inertness, and such, are acceptable in a free woman," he said, "but not in a female slave."

"Yes, Master," I said.

"I will now explain what you are to do," he said.

"Why have I not been chained?" I asked.

"Because," said he, "you are leaving, almost immediately."

"Surely not, Master," I said.

"But, yes," he said.

"It is night," I said. "It is after curfew."

"You will go into the streets, alone," he said, "and do precisely what I shall explain to you."

"There are guardsmen," I said.

"You must elude them," he said.

"I do not know what is out there, in the darkness," I said.

"If you obey properly," he said, "I think you will learn."

He then rubbed his heavy paw about my head, my neck, and shoulders, and drew me against his side, and then put me from him.

"Master?" I said.

"If all goes well," said he, "you will not have to groom me after this."

"As Master pleases," I said.

"You do not do it all that well," he said.

"I am sorry," I said.

"Perhaps," he said, "you are curious as to why I have required that service from you so frequently of late."

"Yes, Master," I said.

"You cannot smell it," he said, "but my scent is now muchly upon you."

"I know nothing of these things, Master," I said. "Be merciful to me! I am only a poor slave, a thigh-marked girl, nothing, a beast, a property, only another poor, helpless kajira, fastened in her collar."

"Be pleased you are collared," he said. "It is that which I anticipate will save your life."

"Keep me here until morning," I said. "Chain me, chain me!"

"Here are your instructions," he said.

Chapter Fifteen

I heard footsteps, and crouched down, small, in the doorway. Shortly the guardsmen, with their lantern, had passed. There were not many guardsmen about, after curfew, but this was the second pair I had encountered, on the way to the market of Cestias.

"I will not speak what I saw," I had said to the beast in the domicile.

"I know you will not," he had said.

I had learned his scent was on me, and I was sure I might be followed, in the darkness, as easily as by a sleen. Too, I had little doubt that my slightest footfall might be marked by the hearing of the beast.

I feared he wanted me to proceed some distance from the shop of Epicrates, and then, when I was far enough away, away from the neighborhood of the shop, he might appear from the side, about a corner, or drop down beside me, from a roof, and, before I could cry out, bite through the back of my neck. I supposed, were I clever enough, I would have remained in the doorway of the shop of Epicrates, forcing him to kill me on the premises, or to refrain from doing so, for the proximity to his own domicile. Too, I thought of surrendering myself to the guardsmen, and accepting the consequences, whatever they might be, for violating the curfew.

"I know you will not," he had said.

How could he know that, if he were not going to assure himself of it, with, say, a swift blow, a grasping paw on the throat, an embrace which might break a back?

The tiniest sound, the scuttling of an urt, the fluttering of a vart, come over the walls from the countryside, almost made me scream with fear.

I could not escape from the city at night, for the closure of the gates. Might I not hide by a gate, and then run when it was opened?

Could I traverse a hundred paces before being pulled down by boys?

I feared to inform on the beast, for it might escape, and seek me out. Too, oddly, I did not want to inform on him. I had agreed that I would not speak of what I had seen. Why had I done that?

I knew what I was to do, elude guardsmen, and go to the market of Cestias, near the praetor's platform near the coin stalls.

But what then?

The market would be deserted at this hour, and ill-lit, if lit at all. Certainly the goods, the currencies, and such, would be withdrawn and locked away.

There were few in the streets, and they were furtive, indeed. And I suspected this had less to do with the curfew, than with the fear of what might be loose in the streets, moving in the darkness.

The beast, I was sure, might have most of the city at its disposal, moving from roof to roof, traversing the darkness, saving perhaps the towers and bridges.

Why was I obeying the beast?

Why was I moving, as I could, toward the market of Cestias? Would it not have been better to flee anywhere else? Why would he want me there, rather than somewhere else? Was it in the market, near the praetor's platform that he wished to apprehend me?

Was I proceeding blindly, foolishly, toward a predesignated place of execution? But why there, rather than a hundred other places?

What might be special about that place?

Indeed, why did he not simply kill me in the domicile, bloodlessly, strangling me, breaking a neck, and then carrying me to some other part of the city, far from the shop of Epicrates, to be discovered in the morning?

But, I recalled, from Antiope, that slaves, or, at least, it seemed so, had not been set upon. To be sure, perhaps no other slave had seen paws, and arms and fur, matted thickly with dried blood.

I knew little of the Lady Bina, nor of the beast, nor of the world, or worlds, from which they had come.

I was sure, if the Lady Bina were not, that it was Kur.

Why was I obeying the beast?

Was I moving to my death?

But, if so, why had he given me the instructions he had? Would that not have been meaningless, and excessive, or might it have been calculated, to assuage my anxieties, to put me off my guard? He had informed me that I would not be hurt, unless I disobeyed. But that was hard to believe. Were the streets themselves not a danger? Who knew what might lurk around the next turn? Might one not be slain by a guardsman's spear, a frightened guardsman striking at a movement in the darkness, the source of which was unknown?

I felt the soft brush of hair on my head, for I wore no kerchief now. That had seemed important to the beast. I touched my collar. That, too, it seemed, might have some significance, that my neck was so encircled, that I was thus identified as no more than kajira.

I was terrified of the beast, but, oddly, I was not at all sure he wished me ill. If he wanted to kill me, he could have done so, a number of times, conveniently, and with impunity. He had treated me, surely usually, with solicitude, even kindness. He had disciplined me only once, and that lesson needed not be repeated. The former Allison Ashton-Baker was an intelligent slave, and she learned quickly, very quickly. My bondage in the domicile had been a light one. He seemed, in many ways, despite his size and appearance, more sensitive, more rational, more human than the Lady Bina. Surely I could never have supposed he would have given me ten Ehn, in a public place, to demonstrate that I might be of interest to men, and, failing that, be sold to butchers for sleen feed. I wondered if the Lady Bina would have done so. Certainly I would not have liked to make trial of the matter. I suspected she might have done so, if I had failed to satisfy her curiosity in the matter, and not because she was thoughtless or cruel, but, rather, simply, because she was concerned with the matter. If one object proved unsatisfactory, it could be discarded and replaced with another, one more satisfactory. I wondered sometimes if she were fully aware, other than intellectually, casually, or abstractly, that other human beings existed, had feelings, and such. Doubtless she understood such things, but perhaps did not see them as having much, if any, importance. Interestingly then, she who appeared most human might seem in some ways less human, and that which appeared least human might seem in some ways more human. But what is "human"?

I recalled that I had been told his "scent" was on me. What significance might that have, if any?

Certainly I was unaware of the scent, at least on my own body, or of any significance which it might have.

My bondage in the domicile of the Lady Bina and the beast was, as noted, a light bondage, but, too, I found it dissatisfying. On this world my slavery, and its appropriateness, had been brought home to me. I had seen hundreds of Gorean men about, as I had scarcely on my world understood such men could exist, so large, strong, and powerful, so naturally self-satisfied, so unassumingly proud, and arrogant, possessive, aggressive men, unconfused and unconflicted, so clear-eyed, easy-moving, and large-handed, so innocently and unquestioningly virile, before whom my slightness and softness, so different from them, seemed theirs, an appropriate prize and acquisition of their desire and might. In the very sight of such men I felt it natural that I should kneel and bow my head, hoping that I might be noticed, might be found acceptable, might be found such that they might deign to snap their fingers and indicate that I might follow them, hoping to be eventually awarded their collar. As a woman, or a sort of woman, I felt weak before such men. I did not desire pain but was prepared to accept it if they imposed it on me. It was to male dominance that I thrilled. How natural and whole, and right, and happy, and grateful, I felt in such a relationship. One supposes this harkens back to remote antiquities in which certain acquired females, as opposed to others, responded to male dominance, surrendered to thongs and masters, and, generation by generation, were preferentially bred. And so it is not so strange that in women, or many women, one might find the readinesses and hopes of slaves. Let each ask herself what she desires to be, what she is. Celebrate the free woman, but take in your arms the slave.

I was now in the vicinity of the market of Cestias.

I recalled the beast had told me not to be afraid, but I was afraid. Who would not be?

I touched my collar.

Are we not, in our way, bred for the collar?

On my old world I had not worn it, unless invisibly. But here, on this world, I wore it. It was real, and fastened on me.

Any of this world who might see me would see me, and understand me, and instantly, as what I was, kajira.

The market was muchly dark.

To one side, my right, at the far edge of the market, there was a pole, on which was suspended a single lantern.

It flickered, and moved a little, in a moment of wind.

I went to all fours.

I would make my way, slowly, carefully, toward the coin stalls, now deserted. I took advantage of what cover might be available. There were, of course, empty stalls, to which produce might be brought near dawn, come before light from the local villages. But there were also, here and there, baskets, boxes, occasional chests and cabinets, presumably empty, and some bare, tiered shelves, which might be lodged against the back of a stall, or, often enough, behind a spread mat or rug.

I nearly cried out for a small urt, presumably startled, had darted by. I could have held two or three in the palm of my hand.

One of the moons emerged from behind a cloud, and, for a moment, the market was eerily lit in its pale light.

I saw, some fifty or so paces to my left, the platform of one of the two market praetors. It bore a single curule chair. The platform is reached by a set of wooden steps. Sometimes an awning is stretched over the platform.

It was close to that platform that the coin stalls, perhaps advisedly, were stationed.

I did not move until the clouds once more obscured the moon.

In a bit, as I moved, listening, a few horts at a time, my hand suddenly rested on an iron ring, anchored in the stone. It was a slave ring. Such rings are often found in public places, in markets, near shops, along boulevards, and such, furnished by the municipality as a convenience. Girls such as I may be chained to them, while masters shop, or otherwise pursue their various concerns. The girl is usually fastened by the left ankle, or the neck, to such a ring. Usually she is left to her own devices there, but sometimes the masters require a certain position, most often kneeling, head down. Sometimes boys enjoy tormenting the slaves at the rings. This is particularly the case if the girl is a new slave, fresh to her collar, brought in from an enemy city. This sort of information seems somehow to travel rapidly about, perhaps as a result of a master's seemingly casual or inadvertent remark, overheard by some unpleasant urchin, a snide observation by another slave, one informed, and perhaps jealous of the beauty of the new slave, perhaps as the result of the ridicule of some inquisitive free woman who has taken it upon herself to inquire into such matters, a ridicule perhaps administered to the strokes of a switch, such things. Sometimes a master's vanity is involved, and he chains the girl publicly in order to display her, that he may be envied, that his good fortune may be recognized, or such. If the day is hot and sunny, the girl may be chained in the shade. Perhaps a pan of water will be placed near her. Too, of course, a girl may be so chained in order to elicit bids on her. If that is the case, there will usually be a sign to that effect hung about her neck. The commonly proffered reason for using a slave ring, of course, is to prevent the theft of the slave. I realized that I had never been chained to such a ring. This produced a certain amount of annoyance. Did it never occur to my mistress, or the beast, that I might be stolen, that someone might regard me as worth stealing? My own suspicion in these matters, of course, was that the public chaining of slaves was likely to have less to do with the dangers of slave theft, and more to do with the gratification of masters. Masters seem to enjoy chaining their slaves. Aside from the indubitable perfection of the custody involved, it is also a ritual of the mastery, in which the master shows the slave that she is a slave, an animal, and a possession, which may be chained at his pleasure. She will remain where she has been placed, helplessly so. It is his will. Too, of course, the chaining has its effect on the slave, who is fully aware of what is involved. In this act, she understands herself owned, and who is her master.

I suddenly stopped, absolutely, straining my hearing. I thought that I might have heard a sound, some paces to my right. But it was then quiet. I must have been mistaken. I think the slightest scratch of a leaf on the stones, perhaps even the gentle alighting of a scrap of paper borne by the tiniest whisper of wind, curling about a corner, would have alarmed me. I could see the lamp, on its pole, far to the right. It was dim. It swung a little. I then began, again, my progress, bit by bit, toward the praetor's platform, and the empty coin stalls.

I remembered that, days ago, some thieves, fleeing, had emerged from a sewer in the vicinity of the praetor's platform, and had been apprehended by guardsmen. The grating, of course, would have been replaced.

I trusted it was securely in place.

At last, to my relief, I came to the coin stall nearest the praetor's platform. I understood I was to wait there, or in the vicinity.

For what was I to wait?

Was it here I was to wait for Lord Grendel to arrive and, at his leisure, kill me?

Without rising to my feet I pushed open the half-gate of the stall and crawled inside.

I then closed and latched the gate.

I huddled within.

The wooden sides of the stall were comforting. If affording little protection, they would, at any rate, as they were surmounted, or thrust aside or splintered apart, warn me of his approach.

It was very quiet.

I heard nothing.

As time went by, more and more time, I began to suspect that some mistake, or misunderstanding, had taken place.

Far off I heard the bar for the First Ahn.

It was still early then, very early.

Later I heard the sounding of the bar for the Second Ahn.

Was I to stay here all night?

I then became afraid, even though it was the middle of the night, that I might be apprehended in the market, in the morning, when guardsmen, at the praetor's signal, opened the market to the stallsmen, merchants, and dealers.

That would not be pleasant.

Still, as individuals milled about, early, I thought, perhaps I could mix in, and, unnoticed, make my way back to the domicile.

I heard, far off, the ringing of the Third Ahn.

Perhaps, I thought, I should return home.

It is lonely here, and dark, and cold, but, clearly, if something were to happen, it would have happened by now. I was heartened. Now, I was sure, reasonably sure, nothing would happen.

Return to the domicile, Allison, I said to myself.

No, I said to myself. I will stay, if only a little longer.

Again the clouds parted, and, again, one of the moons was visible. I rose up a little, and looked over the counter of the stall. The market was again bathed in cool light, and then, again, with the rolling of clouds, the moon was obscured, and the market became once more a jumble of shadows, a weird terrain of the night, a frightening desert of darkness, so different from the brightness, the bustle, the noise and tumult of the day. Across the plaza the lamp, on its pole, was still lit.

I will go back to the domicile, I thought.

It was at that moment that I heard a heavy, grating sound, a scraping sound, some yards away.

Something heavy, and metal, was being moved, shaken, being wrenched, and then was forced free, and thrust to the side.

A moment later I heard it replaced.

I knew I was to wait, and stay in place.

But I could not have run then, even had I wished to do so.

Run, I thought, run, but I could not do so.

I sensed something was outside, being very still.

Then I sensed something moving toward me. I had tried to be silent, but it was approaching.

Then something struck against the side of the stall. Had it not seen the barrier? It is clumsy, I thought.

I looked up, toward the ridge of the counter and there, a

darkness against a darkness, I saw a wide, shaggy, massive head.

It is Lord Grendel, I thought, come to kill me.

I heard a snuffling sound, as though scent were being taken. A dark tongue moved about fangs. Broad ears, pointed, like lifted hands, seemed to emerge from that head, against which they must have been laid. They turned toward me, as though they might have been eyes, inclining downward, peering downward.

I knew that I was not to cry out, and that I was not to struggle. The instructions of Lord Grendel had been clear on that point. Oddly, I did not think I could even whisper, or speak, let alone cry out, nor could I move.

I was terrified.

Suddenly the stall's frontage was torn away, from before me, and struck clattering to the side, and I saw the large shape there, intent, crouched down. Then it moved a little forward, reaching out, moving its arms back and forth, uncertainly, as though it could not see for the darkness, but even I could see that much.

I sobbed as it scrambled forward, and seized me.

It held me tightly, clutching me to it, and I sensed filth, and slime, from the sewer, and was almost overwhelmed by the smell of Kur. I was aware of a broad, deep chest, hot and covered with damp, matted hair. In some parts of its journey it must have moved through water. I sensed a mighty heart beating within that expanse. I heard again the snuffling sound and felt the broad, distending nostrils of the beast moving about my neck and shoulders. Then one paw was placed on my head, carefully, and I felt it moving about, through my hair. I wore no kerchief. Then I felt the paw, feeling about, clumsily, under my chin. I feared then I was to be strangled, or that my neck was to be broken. I now knew this was not Lord Grendel for Lord Grendel was not awkward; for all his size, and power, he was remarkably graceful; his movements were as sure as those of a stalking sleen; too, he was dexterous; the same paw which might tear the iron handle from a gate could lift a pin from the floor, and fetch a stone of choice from a lady's jewel box. But the paw did not crush me, but thrust up, seizing the collar, briefly, which it then, almost immediately, relinquished.

It then thrust me back, away from it, against the back of the stall. My shoulder was bruised.

I half lay against the wood, regarding it with horror.

I had not cried out, I had not resisted.

Then there issued from that monstrous thing on the other side of the stall a series of low noises, almost as though they might have been those of larl, or sleen. There was nothing human there, but the stream of sound was clearly articulated, and I knew it was speaking to me. I understood nothing. Did it hope I might understand it? Did it think I might have a translator?

The scent of Lord Grendel, I knew, was on me. At least he had said so. Had that encouraged it to speak? Did it suspect that something was in the vicinity, or even in the stall, which might understand it? Could it not see we were alone?

"I do not understand you," I whispered, though I was as sure it could not understand me as I knew I could not understand it.

Lord Grendel, I knew, had superb night vision. The Kur, like the sleen, I suspected, might be at home in the night. What then, I wondered, is wrong with this terrible thing, scarcely a body's length away? Why is it so tentative, so uncertain?

Then again, as it had from time to time, one of the moons, white and cold, the only one now visible, was discernible, if only for a moment, but the moment was enough to tell me that the thing so near, so near I could almost touch it, was blind. There were twin darknesses in that massive head, flesh, and hair, where eyes, large, bright and glistening, must once have been but no longer were.

The thing then, as grievously wounded as it might have been, had not died in the sewers, as conjectured, but somehow survived. Blind, unable to defend itself save erratically, awkwardly, it must have been struck an innumerable number of times. Trails of blood had led to a sewer, the grating of which it must have felt with its feet. None had cared to follow it into that darkness. It had been supposed it had bled to death somewhere below the streets.

Its eyeless head was facing me.

How could it be alive?

But it was alive.

It must be hard, I thought, to kill such things. It was hard to conceive how tenaciously and unsurrendering, how difficult to quench, how stubbornly, the fires of life might burn in so mighty a frame, in the dark, sheltered furnace of so awesome a physical engine.

It did not move.

Was it waiting for me to move?

It would be difficult to catch urts in the sewers, so alert and quickly moving. It would have to feed. It would come, occasionally, out of the sewers, however clumsily, to seek slower, easier game.

It was blind, but it could smell, and it could hear.

I remembered the last instruction of Lord Grendel. I was to hurry home.

I suspected that Lord Grendel would have been almost certain that the killings in the city were the results of the attack of a Kur. Indeed, he may have examined bodies. Perhaps that explained the blood on his paws, and arms, which had so dismayed me. Certainly he would, in any case, well know the work of a predatory Kur, the nature of its stalking, its strike, how it was likely to feed, and such. As the Kur from the carnival had disappeared into a sewer, that clear from the trail of blood, Lord Grendel, in his peregrinations at night, may have scouted various accesses to the sewer system of Ar, of which there are a great many. Then there had been word of the seemingly rash flight of the thieves, seemingly so inexplicable, emerging in daylight in the market of Cestias, in the vicinity of the very platform of a praetor, with guardsmen aplenty about, amongst the vendors and stalls. He must have come, then, I supposed, after dark, to the deserted market. There he may have established, to his satisfaction, by the trail of scent, that the Kur may have emerged, even frequently, perhaps habitually, from this particular opening, which, at night, would be in an area unlikely to be traversed by humans. I recalled he had said, "The killings must stop." Too, I supposed, some relationship must exist, or be supposed to exist, amongst Kurii. Might not a human, or some humans, be disposed to aid another human, in similar straits? Perhaps he and the Kur shared a world, or a sort, a kind of being, or a blood. Were they not, despite the views of the Lady Bina, both Kur?

I knew I was to hurry home.

But might it not, if I should move, leap forward, reach out, and seize me?

I unlatched the half-gate of the stall. Surely I was not going to exit the stall where the one side had once stood, until broken away by the beast, for that opening was behind it. I would have to pass the beast. I was very quiet in unlatching the gate, but there was a tiny sound, and the ears moved alertly, slightly, forward, toward that tiny sound.

I rose to my feet, and, not taking my eyes off the large, crouching, dark shape across the stall, opened the gate, and backed through. I was then a few feet outside the stall. I heard the beast strike against the wood, and then, feeling for the opening, pull the gate from its hinges. A sweeping paw convinced it that the opening was not to its liking. Wood was torn aside, and the thing was outside the stall.

There had been noise when it had torn away the frontage of the stall, a brief, clear shattering of the market's silence, which I trusted no one heard, and now, too, though less, when it tore away the gate and forcibly enlarged the threshold, that its bulk, paws extended before it, might exit frontally. Kurii, I would later learn, tend to avoid constricted spaces, and will seldom enter a space which has but a single opening. A narrow space is one in which it may be difficult to defend oneself, and a space with but a single opening is a space in which one might be cornered, or trapped.

The beast and I, separated by some feet, faced one another.

I heard a voice, behind me, one I recognized.

"Get behind me," it said.

"Master!" I breathed. "You live!"

"The thing is dangerous," he said. "Get behind me."

"I feared you slain," I whispered.

There was a low, growling sound from the beast. Clearly it was uncertain as to what was occurring.

I did not turn around. I did not wish to take my eyes from the beast.

"Please, leave, Master," I whispered. "I am sure it is more dangerous to you than to me."

"Oh!" I said, startled, for a leash loop was dropped about my head, pulled close, and snapped shut. I was leashed!

"I see, barbarian," he said, "you must be taught to obey."

How I would have been terrified to hear those words, under different circumstances! But I needed not be taught to obey; the former Allison Ashton-Baker, on Gor, had well learned how to obey!

"Flee, Master," I whispered. "It may not kill you. I think myself in small danger. I think you are in great danger."

A hand on my arm, my right arm, jerked me to the side, and back, over an extended foot, and I sprawled, twisting, to the stones of the market. It is a simple, effective, unpleasant, crude way to put a slave to her belly. The leash was now behind me, looping up to his hand. I twisted about, to my side. "Run, Master!" I said. "I have no way to communicate with it. Run, run, Master!"

But he stood between me and the beast.

He cast down the leash, back. The strap was over my legs.

"Run, Master!" I begged.

He stood between me and the beast.

He was unarmed!

There could be no mistaking then the menace in the sound which now emanated from the throat of the beast.

It did not know what was occurring. It was impatient. It was growing angry. It was displeased.

He waved his arm, angrily. "Begone!" he said. "Away! Away!"

"Run, Master!" I begged. "Please, run, Master!"

But he stood his ground, and would not abandon me.

Clearly the beast, blind as it was, must be aware that I was not in motion, and that something, with a different scent, a different voice, belligerent and obstructive, now stood between us.

I would have given much for a translator.

"Away!" he cried to the beast.

At that moment the beast hurled itself forward, with startling, incredible swiftness, and I saw him whom I had earlier sought, him whom I had earlier feared lost, dismembered, on Clive, struck to the side with a reckless, wide, sweeping, indiscriminate, mighty blow, one that might have loosened or dislodged planking or a beam. The Metal Worker was flung a dozen paces to the side, to strike amongst chests and boxes beside a stall. I saw him struggle to his feet, amongst the debris, waver, and then fall.

I had heard no snapping of a neck or spine.

I think he was then unconscious, or half unconscious.

I feared the beast might then go to the body and, while it yet lived, begin to feed, but, rather, it turned, again, to face me.

I rejoiced, even in my terror for his life, that the Metal Worker lived. It was not he then but, I supposed, one of his caste, who had perished on Clive, or in the vicinity of Clive.

But then I recalled that he was naught but another arrogant Gorean brute with little respect for women, a natural master, who would survey women appraisingly, conjecturing what value they might possess, if any, in a collar. There was a leash on my neck. I pulled at it. It was his! I feared it was locked there.

I tore, futilely, at the leash!

I was pleased that he lived, if only that I might despise him the more, and loathe him ever the more deeply.

How dared he put me on a leash?

But I was, of course, a slave.

I was thus fittingly to be leashed, thonged, braceleted, roped, chained, gagged, blindfolded, should masters please.

The beast was facing me.

I had a sense of its power, from the stall, the broken wood, from the strength of Lord Grendel, as one of its sort, from killings in the streets of Ar, from the improbable, sightless blow it had delivered, which had struck a large, grown man stumbling, reeling, yards to the side.

I fear I then lost what little nerve or courage I might have had, for I turned about, and, frantic, wanting only to escape, sped toward the perimeter of the market. I knew I could not outrun the thing, but I could see, and it could not. Surely then one might be able to elude it!

I kept hearing it behind me, and then I did not hear it, and, then, suddenly, it was almost at my side, reaching out.

I realized then how foolish my flight had been.

It might not be able to see, but it could hear, and it could take my scent, mine, I suppose, and, more importantly, that of Lord

Grendel. Indeed, why else, unless to feed, would it follow me? It smelled Kur about me, and was following me, to make contact with another, or others, of its kind.

How it must have welcomed the message which I bore, a message I would not even have known I bore, had it not been for the words of Lord Grendel.

Did it know I had tried to escape?

If it did, it did not seem to object, perhaps for it knew also that I could not escape.

I feared I might be killed, for my flight, but it was crouched near me, unperturbed, expectantly. From my experience with Lord Grendel, I realized it was not angry.

Then I realized it would not kill me, of course, at least not now, for I was the link between it and one or more of its kind, the key to its rejoining one or more of its kind.

I sank weakly to my knees.

I became aware that the beast had picked up my leash. I was then startled, for it had snapped the leash, twice. I responded instantly, as the trained beast I was. When I was standing, and I stood very straight, shoulders back, belly in, slender, and slimly erect, as one must, for one is a slave, the leash was snapped again, once. That is the signal to move. It is common, as in promenades, when the slave is to precede her master. If the slave follows her master, no such signal is required. The pressure on the collar ring makes clear that she is to move, as any other owned, tethered beast. I then began to make my way, preceding the monster, on its leash, toward the shop of Epicrates. I now knew it, as Lord Grendel, was not only rational, but informed. It knew how to manage slaves, how to handle and control them, and what to do with them. Perhaps, on some world or other, it even owned slaves. I was also now more willing to credit Antiope's conjecture that slaves were exempt from the predations of the beast, or beasts, in the street. The slave, after all, as the free woman does not, has uses. Of what value is a woman, save for her pretensions and vanities, until she is collared, after which she will learn there are uses, a large number of them, to which she may be put? The free woman may be beheaded or impaled; the slave, an animal, will be preserved and protected, to be distributed or sold.

How was it, I wondered, that the Metal Worker had been in the vicinity of the market of Cestias tonight?

He stalks me, I thought. He finds me of interest. He wants me. It is not unusual, of course, for a man to want a slave. What male does not want one or more slaves?

Well, I thought, he, the arrogant brute, will never have me!

He knew my name. I recalled that from the vicinity of Six Bridges. So he must have made inquiries. Yes, I thought, the curves of this slim barbarian have intrigued the mighty master.

Let him pine then in vain!

I recalled how he had commanded me to my knees in the Sul Market, leaving me half-stripped and tied at his feet, how he had pressed himself upon me in the vicinity of Six Bridges, I unable to resist.

I did not even know his name.

I wondered if he were truly of the Metal Workers.

How I despised him!

He would never have me. I would run away. To be sure, it is hard to run farther than the length of the chain on one's ankle.

I wondered what it would be like to be in his arms.

Would he find me pleasing, acceptable, as a slave? I knew that I, a slave, would have to do my best to please him, and in all the ways of the slave. The slave has no choice in such things, nor does she want one. She soon learns to beg, even pathetically, that she may be permitted to so serve.

How humble, and hopeful, she is, at the feet of her master!

Once, but only once, we were in the vicinity of guardsmen, two, one with a lantern. The beast would not know they were guardsmen, but he must have heard their footsteps, and voices, two voices, male voices. He drew me back, into a small side street, little more than a space between buildings, from which we had just emerged, for I had sought a most clandestine, unfrequented route to the shop of Epicrates, and, holding me tightly against him, covered my mouth tightly with one vast paw. I could not have begun to utter a sound.

The guardsmen passed.

I thought the guardsmen were fortunate that they had not discovered us. Even blind I had little doubt that the beast, from a small sound, the scrape of a boot on the stones, from the movement of a weapon departing from a sheath, from breathing, might locate an enemy. In such an altercation I would run or throw myself to my belly and cover my head with my hands. In such an altercation three might die.

We reached the shop of Epicrates well before the bar signifying the end of curfew. In another Ahn or so, some of the smaller gates would open, and many Peasants, with their baskets and sacks of fresh produce, would begin to make their way to the various markets in the city.

It was with relief that I, on the beast's leash, it following me, slipped into the doorway to the left of the shuttered front of the shop, and climbed the stairs to the domicile of the Lady Bina and Lord Grendel.

The Lady Bina was asleep, but Lord Grendel was waiting for us.

I collapsed to the floor of the domicile.

I was aware of low noises from the beasts, conversing in Kur.

Shortly after dawn the lantern on its pole at the edge of the market of Cestias would be extinguished, and, a bit later, the market pennon would be hoisted to the height of the pole, above the lantern arm, after which, at the praetor's signal, guardsmen would open the market.

There would doubtless be some speculation as to the damage undergone by one of the coin stalls.

I then fell asleep.

Chapter Sixteen

"Are you comfortable?" he asked.

"You!" I cried.

His head was thrust through the curtain, at the front of the wagon. His smile was that of a master, gazing on a slave.

I drew back, with a rattle of chain in the wagon bed, the chain sliding along the central bar. I was the only girl in the wagon. It was drawn by a tharlarion. The canvas was a common white, not the blue-and-yellow covering, sometimes silk, usually decorating, covering, a slave wagon. The central bar runs linearly the length of the wagon bed. It is hinged at the forward end and fits into a coupling, within which it is commonly locked, at the back end of the wagon bed. My ankles were shackled, and a foot of chain joined them, the chain looped about the central bar. If one wishes to remove a girl from such a wagon, one either unshackles her, or, more commonly, that she remain ankle-shackled, for example, in a camp, one lowers the back of the wagon and unlocks the bar from the coupling at the rear of the wagon, which, lifted, allows the girl to leave the central bar and wagon.

I moved toward the rear of the wagon and covered myself, as I could.

"Do not bother," he said. "I like you naked."

"Brute, beast, monster!" I said.

"Do not tell me the little barbarian is modest," he said.

"I am untunicked," I said. "Do not look at me!"

"Do you really think a tunic, a slave tunic, makes all that much difference?" he asked.

"Go away," I begged.

"To be sure, it is nice to see you slave naked," he said.

"Please leave," I said.

In slave wagons, girls are nearly always transported naked.

He did not ask me to uncover myself. I was somewhat annoyed, as I think he gathered, at this. Did he not really want to see me bared before him, as the slave I was?

"I saw you at the road camp," he said. "Your new tunic is quite nice, much better than the one you wore in Ar."

"Go away," I said. "Please."

Five days ago, for whatever reason, the tunic to which I had become accustomed in Ar, one suitable for a woman's serving slave, was taken from me.

"Put this on, Allison," had said the Lady Bina, and handed me what seemed little more than a tiny scrap of rep cloth.

"Surely not, Mistress," I had said.

"Yes, yes," she said. "It is time you were put in a more revealing garment, one more suitable for a pretty slave."

"But, Mistress," I said, "this is the sort of garment in which a strong man might choose to display a slave, to boast of the beauty and pleasures he has at his disposal."

"We have business," said the Lady Bina, "and we must recruit some fellows to help us with it. If you are about, one of our beasts, especially so clothed, we anticipate things will proceed apace."

"Mistress?" I had said.

"You will remember," she said, "that I was concerned, even at your purchase, with your attractiveness to men."

"Yes, Mistress," I said.

I recalled, too, her test in the market. How frightening had been that experience!

"It might serve my purposes," she said.

"Yes, Mistress," I said.

I did not inquire what purposes she might have in mind. The services and use of a slave, of course, may be bestowed as the master or mistress might wish. One advantage of a private male master is that they are commonly rather proprietary where their slaves are concerned, even jealous. It is a common act of courtesy at a feast, or a visit, to offer a guest the use of a slave, but too, it is understood that the sensitive guest will graciously forgo this gift. It is different, of course, with the girls kept at inns, and such, for such purposes. Also, feast slaves may be cheaply rented for the night, and longer. The Lady Bina, of course, was not a male master, let alone a jealous, possessive one, and I was afraid she might be generous, perhaps excessively so, in such matters. To be sure, I had not been put to slave use since the eating house and the gambling house, and that was long ago. I was uneasy, of course, for a master's hands on my body, for which I subtly longed, but I was in no way in the sorry straits of many miserable girls, the conflagrations of whose slave fires periodically plunged them into acute torment.

And so I would have a new tunic.

To casually glance upon me, I supposed most would assume that I was a man's slave. They enjoy putting us in such things. It was the sort of garment which, in Ar, might elicit a switching from a free woman.

"Too," she had said, "we may buy two or three other girls, stupid girls, barbarians, as you."

"I am not stupid, Mistress," I said.

"Then uninformed, ignorant girls," she said, "as you."

"Barbarians, then?" I said.

"Of course," she said.

"May I inquire," I had asked, "the nature of Mistress' business?"

"No," she said. "Now put this on, and we will put you before men, and see if it should be shortened, or altered, a bit, perhaps slit at the hems, torn down some about the neck, such things."

"Yes, Mistress," I had said.

At least, I had thought, it is not a camisk.

I did not mention this, of course, for fear I would be camisked.

* * * *

"Please do not look at me in that fashion," I said.

I drew up my legs further. He did not require that I change the position of my hands.

"Yes," he said, "I like you slave naked."

"What are you doing here?" I said.

"Looking at a naked slave," he said.

"Master!" I sobbed.

"I am of your party," he said. "Perhaps if you are very nice, I will let you cook for me."

"I would salt your food so that you could not eat it," I said.

"Then," said he, "it would be you who would eat it, after which I would have the pleasure of lashing you."

"I see," I said.

"Your ankles look well in shackles," he said.

"Where are we going?" I asked.

"You may thank me," he said.

"Thank you, Master," I said, drawing my ankles a bit further back, with a rustle of chain.

"We are north of Ar, on the Venna road," he said.

"We are bound for Venna?" I said.

"Doubtless for the tharlarion races," he said. "It is the season."

"I see," I said.

"Actually," he said, "I do not know."

"I see," I said.

"If you were to peep out, between the side boards and the canvas, you might occasionally see a tharlarion ranch."

"Oh?" I said.

"But doubtless you are afraid to do so," he said.

"Perhaps," I said.

I did not know how long he had been with us. Perhaps he had noted, for all I knew, several times, the tiny lifting of the canvas. If the wagons were in the care of slavers, I supposed girls might be punished for such things. Slavers like to keep the girls in their wagons ignorant of their surroundings, their destinations, and such. Indeed, even in coffles the destination of the coffle is seldom made explicit to, so to speak, the "beads on the slaver's necklace." Native Gorean girls, of course, coffled, are rampant in their speculations in such matters. Here, however, in our party, there seemed to be permissiveness in such matters. Even so, I did not care to be discovered in my small, furtive reconnaissances.

"You have probably never seen a racing tharlarion," he said.

"No," I said.

"Perhaps they do not have them on the barbarian world," he said.

"Perhaps not," I said.

"Some," he said, "are quadrupedalian, others bipedalian."

"I do not even know your name," I said.

"Why?" said he. "Do you want it on your collar?"

"No!" I said.

"Perhaps I will buy you," he said.

"Do not!" I said.

"Are you comfortable?" he inquired, reverting to his initial question.

"No," I said. "I am naked, the boards are hard, the Ahn are long."

"Be glad," he said, "the road is smooth. It may not be so later."

"Master?" I said.

"I think we are going beyond Venna," he said.

"Where?" I asked.

"Somewhere in the Voltai," he said.

"What is there?" I asked.

"I do not know," he said.

"Please, Master," I said.

"Mountains," he said.

I suspected that I might know more than he. There were three wagons in our small party. In the first, the stateliest and most comfortable, was the Lady Bina, and, possibly, Lord Grendel. I, as yet alone, occupied the second wagon, and, in the third wagon, its covering drawn tight, I was sure, was the blind Kur. It had been captured in the Voltai, and, I suspected, it was the intention of Lord Grendel to return it to its savage haunts, if savage haunts they were. Presumably, it might have fellows in the Voltai, who might look after it, if Kurii were concerned with such things.

"It is warm, and close, in here, is it not?" he asked.

"Master is perceptive," I said.

"Beware you are not cuffed, girl," he said.

"Forgive me, Master," I said.

He seemed more amused with my insolence than annoyed. How, from the heights of his freedom, he looked upon me as nothing, only a slave! I was pleased, however, that he was not angry. I was quite certain that if a girl deserved a cuffing, or, in an ambiguous situation, it seemed she might deserve a cuffing, she would receive one, and sharply, at his hands. She must strive to keep things clear. It is dangerous for a slave to approach such borders. It is not wise for a girl to test the limits of a master's tolerance. They do not care for such games, and the whip is theirs.

He smiled upon me, the beast!

I did not care to be so looked upon, as a meaningless chit. But before such men what could women be but meaningless chits?

"Perhaps Master has duties to which he might attend," I suggested.

I was furious.

I lacked no confidence in my own excellencies, in my own qualities, and such, which I had deemed considerable, certainly for my former world, but I sensed, too, to my fury, that he, this brute, like so many Gorean men, was in many ways, and by far, my superior.

What could we be to such men but meaningless chits?

How angry that made me!

And yet, too, it made me want to yield to them, and serve, and please them.

How different he and so many others were from most of the men I had known on my former world. What had been done, I wondered, to the men of my former world? How superior to me, in so many ways, were these brutes of Gor! How slave I felt before them! Were such as I not fittingly owned by such as they, as the females of so many species of my former world were, in effect, owned by their males? To my chagrin such things were now, on Gor, indisputably obvious to me. I was unable to deny them, as much as I might wish to do so. And such relationships on Gor were institutionalized, fixed in law! I was collared! I sensed that I belonged on the block, stripped, before such men, who might, fittingly, purchase me as an object, or toy. It is strange how one can sense such things, but, to my irritation, I was in no doubt about it. Before such men women could be but properties; they belonged at the feet of such men, as slaves.

But if one were a slave, why should one not be a slave?

Is there not a freedom, a liberation, a relief, in such an acknowledgement?

Are the miseries of a free woman so superior to the joys of a mastered, loving slave?

Let each consider the matter for herself.

With two hands, he thrust open the canvas curtains at the head of the wagon and light, and fresh air, surged into that narrow, rectangular, hitherto oppressive wood-and-canvas enclosure.

I blinked against the light. I could see, over the wagon box, the broad, arched back of the plodding tharlarion which was drawing the wagon. It was tied by its nose ring to the back of the preceding wagon. Its reins were looped about a hook to the left of the wagon box. The Metal Worker, if that were indeed his caste, was on the Teamster's bench, which was, too, the lid of the wagon box. Within it, parts, harness, and other tackle can be stored. Within it, too, I supposed, would be other sets of chains and shackles, should other girls be added to the party. I had gathered that two or three might be purchased in Venna, though I knew not for what purpose, if we were proceeding to the Voltai. Slave girls do, however, I knew, make lovely gifts.

I was at the back of the wagon bed, to which I had retreated, drawing back along the central bar, to distance myself from the Gorean scrutiny of the unexpected, offensive intruder.

I hated him.

I wondered what it would be, to have his collar on my neck. I knew it would be easy enough to put there.

I recalled he had stood between me and the beast nights ago, in the market of Cestias. It was fortunate for him that he had not been slain. What had he been doing there? I smiled to myself. He might have followed me there, as a man might follow a slave. If he were tangled in the coils of my beauty, such as it might be, fastened there, he might prove to be the slave and I the mistress! Much power I knew could reside within a collar. Have not Ubars succumbed to the smile of a kajira? I could taunt and torment him, I suspected, if I were clever, to my heart's content. As long as he did not own me, I could enact a girl's vengeance on the hapless tarsk. I reminded myself that I despised him, that I loathed him. I was sure I could make him suffer. But then I wondered what might be the feel of his bracelets on my wrists. If he were kind enough to bracelet my hands before my body I might, when no one was about, lift them to my lips and kiss them.

Strange, I thought, how a woman can desire to be owned, and helplessly so.

"Girl," he said.

"Master?" I said.

"The air, and light, is better forward, and there is not much dust."

The countryside was beautiful, mostly meadows. The road stretched ahead, a gleaming line between hills, beyond the first large-wheeled, lumbering wagon, that of the Lady Bina, and, perhaps Lord Grendel, a road, I learned, of layers of fitted stone blocks, feet deep. Like the Viktel Aria, the road was designed not to last some years, or a decade, but centuries, even millennia.

"With Master's permission," I said, "I shall remain where I am."

He reached to the side, and bent down, and, from in front of the wagon box, lifted up a carefully folded blanket. My body roughened, and sore, I eyed it covetously. He dropped it inside the wagon, to the right of the central bar, just behind the wagon box. He then turned away, to look down the road.

The blanket lay there, neatly folded.

Why did he not cast it back to me? I knew.

"Oh!" I said, for the wagon had lurched.

The Venna road is smooth, but even so it has its irregularities. Indeed, over the years, its surface, in shallow grooves, records the passage of countless wagons. A wheel may scrape into, dip into, or climb from, such a groove. Too, the shifting of the earth, the occasional softening of the soil by rain, differences in weathering, various temperature changes, and such things, may produce a shifting of one stone in relation to another.

I crawled forward, to the back of the wagon box, the chain sliding along the wooden floor, along the metal bar.

I seized the blanket there and spread it beneath me. It was but one blanket, but it was welcome. I did not take it to the rear of the wagon, as it seemed clear its placement was meant to bring me, if I wished its comfort, to the front of the wagon. I was then close enough that he might turn and touch me, but he did not do so.

Was I not smooth, and attractive? Why did he not reach back and touch me? What difference would it make? Was I not a slave?

"A slave is grateful for the blanket," I said.

"It rained a while ago," he said.

I knew that, from the sound, earlier in the afternoon, the light patter on the canvas. It darkened, but, closely woven, it had not leaked.

"I think it will rain more, later," he said.

"Perhaps," I said.

"It rained last night," he said.

"Yes," I said.

"This morning," he said, "I saw strange prints about the edge of the camp. Do you have an account of such things?"

"No," I said. How would I know what beasts might lurk about the camp? I suspected, of course, that they might be the prints of Lord Grendel, or his fellow, the blind Kur.

"Perhaps you have a conjecture?" he said.

"Curiosity," I said, "is not becoming in a kajira."

He had seen the blind Kur in the market of Cestias, though I suspected he had not realized it was blind. If he had been with the party, with the wagons, I suspected he knew of the presence of one, or both, of the beasts. Presumably, as might others, he thought them some sort of pet, or guard animal. I doubted that he recognized them as a form of rational life, of fearfully rational life.

I wondered if he had been testing me. Certainly he knew I would be aware of the existence of such things, from the market of Cestias that earlier night, some days ago.

I supposed that I had inadvertently told him what he wanted to know, that the wagons undertaking this mysterious journey might harbor secret denizens, of which I, and others, were not to speak, denizens which might be embarked on projects of a nature best concealed from public scrutiny.

"Tomorrow, we should reach Venna," he said. "Have you ever been to Venna?"

"No," I said.

"Nor I," he said.

"Can you cook?" he asked.

"I am not a cook slave," I said.

"What sort of slave are you?" he asked.

"I am a woman's slave," I said.

"You should be a man's slave," he said.

"What sort of man's slave?" I asked.

"You have the curves of a pleasure slave," he said.

"Oh?" I said.

"Are you hot?" he asked.

"Perhaps Master remembers, from Six Bridges," I said.

"As I recall, you begged, liked a piteous little bundle of collar meat, to be bought."

I was silent.

How he demeaned me!

How I loathed the brute!

But I knew I was a slave, in need of a master. What would it be, I wondered, to be his slave? I had little doubt I would be an excellent slave to him. He would see to it.

"I wager," he said, "in a matter of Ehn, I could have you kicking and squirming, and moaning, and begging for more."

"I am stronger now," I said.

"No," he said, "you are weaker now, and more needful, for you have been longer in bondage."

I feared it was true. Slaves need their masters.

"I am a free woman," I said, "who has had the misfortune to be placed in a collar."

"No," he said, "you are a slave."

"Oh?" I said.

"You were never a free woman," he said. "You were always a slave, though perhaps not always in a collar."

"I see," I said. How often I had sensed that true, even from girlhood.

"I tasted your lips, at Six Bridges," he said. "They are those of a slut, and slave, a slab of worthless, needful collar meat."

"I see," I said.

I well recalled, to my humiliation, how he had aroused me, so profoundly, so quickly, so easily. But I, a slave, had been unable to help myself, even had I desired to do so.

"It is fortunate," he said, "that you were captured on the barbarian world and brought to the markets of Gor. Otherwise you might never have fulfilled your birthright, heritage, and destiny, that of a female, to be a slave, to be owned, and mastered."

"Perhaps you believe all women are slaves," I said.

"Yes," he said.

"I am not your slave," I said.

"You would be, if I bought you," he said.

We then drove on, for a time.

He pointed to the side, to the left. "There is a pasang stone," he said.

"I cannot read," I said.

"Fifty," he said.

On the Venna road, from Ar, there is usually a well every ten or twenty pasangs. Sometimes there is an inn, or a camping ground, where there will be shops.

"Fifty pasangs to Venna," I said.

"Yes," he said.

"We will camp tonight," I said.

"Yes," he said, "in an Ahn, or so."

"I am in your care, I gather," I said.

"Yes," he said.

"Will you let me leave the wagon?" I asked.

"Certainly," he said.

"When I am out of the wagon, will you remove my shackles?" I asked.

"No," he said.

"'No'?"

"No," he said. "Do not be concerned. There will be many wagons there, and there will doubtless be other kajirae there, several more closely shackled than you."

"More closely shackled than I?" I asked.

"Yes," he said.

"Why?" I asked.

"Presumably because they will be regarded as more valuable," he said.

"I see," I said.

"A single chain, run through their shackle chain, and fastened between trees, will secure the lot. You may be added to such a chain."

"My Mistress," I said, "usually buys at the camps."

"I know," he said. "I have been with the wagons since Ar."
"Why are you with us?" I asked.
"I have taken fee," he said.
"And why have you taken fee?" I asked.
"I thought it might be nice to see Venna," he said.
I smiled to myself. I thought I might be able to manipulate him. But then, too, I thought, it is difficult to manipulate a man when one is chained at his feet.
"You can cook, can you not?" he asked.
"On my former world," I said, "I did not do such things."
"But here," he said, "you find that the lowliest, the most trivial and servile of tasks, are yours to perform, unquestioningly, and perfectly."
"Yes," I said.
"So?" he said.
"Yes, Master," I said. "I can cook, a little. I was taught in the slave house, that of Tenalion of Ar."
"I know the house," he said.
"Then Master knows it handles the most beautiful, and prized, slaves in Ar," I said.
"All the houses do," he said. "The house of Tenalion is also known for distributing she-tarsks amongst minor markets, for quick, cheap sales, some even in the Metellan district."
"I see," I said.
I recalled the small cell, facing the market area, behind the bars of which I, with others, as merchandise to be vended, were publicly displayed to passers-by, and then my sale, being turned about, exhibited naked, on the small cement sales dais.
"I am thinking of having you prepare my food tonight," he said. "Do you think you could do it, passably?"
"A slave must do her best to please," I said.
"If I am not satisfied," he said, "you will be beaten."
"A slave will do her best," I said.
"If I am satisfied," he said, "I will let you feed."
"A slave is grateful," I said.
"Would you prefer," he said, "to have the food cast to the ground, or to take it, kneeling, or on all fours, from my hand?"
"From Master's hand," I said.
He well knows, I thought, how to teach a woman that she

is a slave. I recalled a lesson in such things from the house of
Tenalion, in which I fed, kneeling, leaning forward, from the
hand of a guard, my right hand clasping my left wrist behind
my back. Such things can enflame the belly of a woman.

"Master?" I said.

"Yes?" he said.

"I think my tunic may be in the wagon box."

"So?" he said.

"May I wear it, outside the wagon?" I asked.

"Do you beg it?" he asked.

"Yes, Master," I said, "I beg it."

"Very well," he said.

Chapter Seventeen

It was hard not to be excited by the roar of the crowd. I leaped to my feet, with thousands of others. "Hurry on!" I thought to myself, feverishly, with respect to the blue colors. He in whose care I was favored them. Perhaps, then, I thought, as I hated him, I should favor another color, say, yellow, or red, just so that it would be different, to spite him, though it would not do, of course, to call such a discrepancy to his attention. It could be my private concern. But I did not. He had wagered on blue, he in whose charge I was. Thus, insofar as I might have a color, which, of course, I was not permitted, it was his color, blue. How strange! His desire was my desire, his wager as though my wager. Odd, I thought. As I loathed him, what difference was it to me, his fate, his fortune? To be sure, it occurred to me that if he lost, he might be displeased, and I might be beaten. "Hurry on, blue!" I thought, rising to my tip toes. Across the track it was hard to see for the dust. Much was the noise about me. Some had glasses of the builders, though shorter than the usual glass. I felt myself immersed in the surf of screaming, shouting, cheering adherents. I did not cry out, of course. I had not been given permission to speak. We were in the high tiers. There were five in our party, if I include myself. I pulled a little at my wrists, which were braceleted behind me. It is only so that my sort were permitted in the stadium. To be sure, if the master lacks bracelets, one's wrists may be thonged or corded behind one, or, with a strip of cloth, tightly scarfed in place. Venna was far more permissive than Ar, for in Ar slaves, unless discreetly concealed, were not permitted in the stadiums, let alone theaters. For example, one would almost never see them at the pageants, the plays, the concerts, the song dramas, the epic readings, the great kaissa matches, and such. This was in deference, supposedly, to the feelings of free women, whose sensibilities might be offended by the presence, in their vicinity, of the half-clad, shapely beasts of masters. One sort of slave, however, is likely to be more visible in a stadium, a certain sort of stadium, a "stadium of blades," a more vulgar, violent milieu, the sort helplessly chained naked to a post, a sack of gold tied about her neck, she and it prizes to be awarded to a successful fighter.

"Hurry on, red!" cried another slave, two rows below me.

She had permission to speak, to cheer for her master's favorite! I felt like pulling her to the ground by her hair, but I would not dare to do so. I knew it would be I who would soon be weeping, and pleading for mercy! It would not be another, but I, I knew, who would soon be the cringing, beaten slave. This was clear to me, even from my former world. I had sensed this ever since the party on my former world, when I had been disgracefully camisked and forced to serve, in a locked leather collar, and had found myself tearfully, stung again and again, helplessly groveling under the switch of the imperious Nora. It takes but one such experience to realize that one is a slave. I still, after all these months, dreaded and feared Nora, terribly. She was Mistress and I was slave. She had taught me that.

As you know, as in the tarn races, there are various factions, the blue, the yellow, the orange, the red, and so on.

Many Goreans take their allegiance to a given faction with great seriousness. This may continue for generations in families. There are sometimes riots between the adherents of these factions.

Orange won the race.

I sat down, on the tier. Many filed down the tiers, to place new bets. Hundreds clutched programs, which listed the mounts, and their riders.

The last race, just witnessed, was one of quadrupedalian tharlarion. These are bred for endurance and speed, but, even so, they are ponderous beasts, and no match for the more typical racing tharlarion, which is lighter and bipedalian. It is also carnivorous and more aggressive. In the race they commonly have their jaws bound shut. There have been several cases in which such beasts, before a race, or in the stable or exercise yards, have attacked their competitors, even their handlers. They are occasionally used for scouting or communication. Some hunt wild tarsk with lances from their saddles.

"Orange won," said he in whose charge I was.

"Yes, Master," I said.

There were five in our party at the stadium, the Lady Bina; Astrinax, who was our jobber; a man named Lykos, hired, I think, for his sword; he in whose keeping I was; and myself. I remembered the man, Astrinax, from Ar, as it was he who had arranged my sale to the gambling house. He had been hired in Ar by the Lady Bina to facilitate our journey, buying tharlarion and wagons, hiring teamsters, putting in supplies, arranging the stages of our journey, and such. Clearly such matters could not have been well handled by the Lady Bina, Lord Grendel, or myself.

I was pleased to have been permitted to come to the stadium. It would have been easy enough to have left me in the wagon, in the fenced-in wagon lot, shackled to the central bar.

I looked about myself. As I, the other slaves I noted in the audience were tunicked, and some more scantily than I. One, I saw, who regarded me disdainfully, and tossed her head proudly, was even camisked. How proud her master must have been of her, the arrogant brute, to so display her. And how smug, and how vain, she was, how proud of her beauty, to be so displayed, camisked.

"I am going below, to bet anew," said he in whose care I was.

"Yes, Master," I said.

I felt my left ankle gripped, and, a moment later, it was shackled to the iron ring anchored in the cement under my seat.

He then departed, to seek the betting tables beneath the stadium tiers. The Lady Bina, Astrinax, and Lykos accompanied him.

I sat on the tier, alone, moved my ankle a little, and pulled a little at the bracelets. Had my hands been free, I would have better adjusted the tunic at my left shoulder.

I was an unattended slave. I was apprehensive. I realized

what that might mean. Such a slave might be accosted, even fondled, with impunity. Still, there were many about.

We had arrived in Venna early this morning.

Apparently the small collation I had prepared for the Metal Worker yesterday evening had proved satisfactory. In any event, after he had eaten for a bit, I kneeling back, he signed me to all fours, a simple gesture, and indicated that I might approach, beside the small fire. Then, from time to time, as he fed, he held out tidbits to me, and I fed, too, delicately, from his hand. Afterwards he permitted me to lie by his side, "bound by the master's will," I crossing my shackled ankles, and holding my hands behind my back, my left wrist held in my right hand.

He said, "Speak."

"Surely Master is not interested in hearing a slave speak," I said.

"Speak," said he.

"Of what shall I speak?" I said.

He then told me to speak, as I would, telling him about my former world, my former life, my capture, my training, my sales, my owners, even my thoughts and feelings.

I fear much that was foolish gushed forth from me, but words had tumbled forth, seemingly endlessly, for Ahn, even amidst grateful tears.

"What have you done to me?" I said, at last, lying in the dirt beside him, by the reduced embers of the fire, looking up at him from my side, bound by his will.

"Is it not clear?" he asked.

"Master?" I said.

"I have stripped you," he said.

"I see," I said.

"It is time to put you on the common chain," he said. "You are unbound."

I struggled to my feet, and he then conducted me, his right hand on my left upper arm, to the common chain, on which several girls were already placed. He sat me by the chain, removed the shackle from my right ankle, looped it about the chain, and fastened it on me again, thus tethering me to the common chain. In this camp it was strung not between two trees, but between two heavy posts, to which it was bolted, the posts some twenty paces apart.

"So, Master," I said, "the slave is stripped."

"There are many ways to strip a slave," he said.

"I understand," I said.

"Ordering her to disrobe, or tearing away her tunic, are but two," he said.

"I understand," I said.

"To be sure," he said, "that is pleasant."

"Doubtless," I said.

After I had confessed so much of myself to him, so revealed who was in my collar, I had almost hoped I would hear the issuance of a disrobing order, or that his hands, at my neckline, would have torn away my tunic.

But he had conducted me to the girl chain.

"It is all of the slave which is owned," he said.

"That is understood by the slave," I said.

"The slave's every thought," he said, "even her subtlest, least feeling, is owned by the master."

"Yes, Master," I said.

He rose to his feet. I swiftly knelt, and looked up at him.

"Master," I said.

"Keep your knees closed," he said, annoyed, his voice brusque.

I quickly closed them. I smiled to myself, a little. I do have power, I thought.

"It seems this slave is in the care of Master," I said.

"Yes," he said.

"You hold the key to her shackles?"

"As of now," he said.

"You knew the slave's name, 'Allison', even from Ar," I said.

"So?" he said.

"But the slave," I said, "does not even know Master's name."

"Desmond," he said.

"That is not a Gorean name," I said.

"It is," he said, surprised.

"Surely not," I said.

"It is, in the vicinity of Harfax," he said.

"Oh," I said.

"My Home Stone," said he, "is that of Harfax."

"What was Master doing in Ar?" I asked.

"Curiosity," said he, "is not becoming in a kajira."

"Yes, Master," I said.

"I have heard," said he, "there are tharlarion races in Venna tomorrow. To be sure, it is the season. Would you care to attend?"

"Yes," I said, "yes, Master!"

"You may, if you wish," he said, "remain chained in the wagon, with the curtains tied shut."

"I beg to accompany Master," I said.

"If you do so," he said, "you will do so as a kajira."

"What does that mean?" I asked.

"You will see," he said.

"Yes, Master," I had said.

* * * *

The crowd milled about, some descending the tiers, others climbing them.

The robing of a Gorean crowd is colorful, particularly on holidays, or in attendance at public events, races, and such. Doubtless that is all very familiar to you, but perhaps, as it is so familiar to you, you do not much note it.

Some slaves, as I, were on short ring chains, but many were loose, wandering about, though back-braceleted. I supposed it would then be difficult for them to pilfer small objects, dared they to do so. On the other hand, I suspected there were subtler reasons underlying this lovely constraint. Does it not remind the girl that she is a slave, and only a slave? Certainly she is constrained as one. But men, too, the monsters, seem to enjoy having women helpless before them, fully at their mercy, and what woman, rendered so helpless, does not then the better understand that she is a woman. Too, of course, it helps to draw a sharper distinction between us and free women, as though the scantiness of our tunics, and the obviousness of our lovely, slender, locked collars, compared to the richness of their robes, and veils, and half veils, were not enough!

I saw a lovely-legged, long-haired girl in a brief blue tunic. I did not know if that were because her master favored the blue, or if he might be a scribe.

A vendor went by, just below our level, on the walkway, hawking tastas.

I wished he in whose charge I was, Desmond, in the black and gray of the Metal Workers, would return. Though I hated him, I wanted to be helpless near him. I wanted to be such that he might exploit me, as he pleased.

Far below, on the broad, level area, inside the rail, I saw two girls, in tunics of yellow and blue, the Slaver's colors, back-braceleted as other slaves, but also, interestingly, joined together, neck to neck, by a yard of chain. I stood up, to get a better look. There seemed something different, or interesting, about them, or something familiar, something I could not place. Perhaps, I thought, I had seen one or the other, perhaps both, somewhere in Ar, perhaps at the laundry troughs, or in a market. Perhaps in some way they were a matched pair, and were to be sold as such. It did not seem likely, on the other hand, they were twins, as one was blonde and the other darkly haired, rather like myself. Perhaps, then, they were matched in some other sense, or, even, not really matched at all, save in the sense of each being undoubtedly of slave interest.

After the rescue, if that be the word, of the blind Kur, I had learned more of the past of Lord Grendel. Some I had learned from the Lady Bina, but more, interestingly, from the translator. As the newcomer to our domicile was incapable, for most purposes, of uttering intelligible Gorean, Lord Grendel taught me the use of the translator, so that I might have a means of understanding the newcomer, and communicating with him. The Lady Bina was already familiar with the device. Interestingly the Lady Bina seemed muchly to esteem the newcomer, and even to stand in some awe of him. "He is true Kur," she had whispered to me. Certainly she showed him more respect, or deference, than she commonly accorded to her own colleague, or friend, or guard, Lord Grendel, for whom she often seemed to entertain, for all his devotion to her, and for all her dependence on him, something like a patient, tolerant, pitying contempt. She regarded him as imperfect, and malformed, as if he might be a monstrosity or cripple of some sort. Perhaps, in some sense, he was. I did not know. To be sure, she realized that he had his uses. Sometimes, before we had left the domicile,

I had lingered in the vicinity of Lord Grendel and the blind Kur, whose name I had heard many times, but could not begin to say. No equivalent to it, in Gorean phonemes, had been programmed into the translator. When it was pronounced in Kur the translator, in Gorean, would be silent. I had sometimes stayed by the two beasts while they spoke in Kur, turning on the translator, but lowering the volume, putting my ear to the device. They could hear the Gorean from the translator, even from across the room, and probably more clearly than I, who was adjacent to it, but it was of no interest to them, and they paid it little, if any, attention. After a bit, it was probably not even noticed by them. The blind Kur had expressed interest, in the beginning, in the machine's being on, but Lord Grendel had authorized the harmlessness of its use with the explanation that "they are curious little beasts." "Yes," had said the newcomer, "they all are." It seemed then that he knew something, as I had earlier suspected, about human female slaves. The newcomer had never seen me, of course, but I had no doubt he could have picked me out promptly from a hundred slaves by scent. To be sure, I had no doubt he could have performed the same feat with the Lady Bina, from, say, a hundred free women. So, too, of course, and more fearfully, might have a sleen, put on our scent. Much from the Lady Bina and from the translator I did not understand, that having to do with distant worlds, exotic engineerings, unusual weaponries, strange customs and holidays, diverse races and cultures, troubled histories, and such, and with mysterious projects, factions, and wars, seemingly current, but some things were clear, or reasonably so, that they were the remnants of advanced peoples who, having destroyed their ancestral world, and having migrated to the exile of artificial spheres, uncontaminated and unpolluted, livable and unradiated, coveted new and better worlds. I did learn, in passing, something, too, of Lord Grendel. In the plans of some Kurii, it had been hoped that an alliance might be formed between themselves and the humans of Gor, that the surface of Gor might be shared, putatively in peace, for a time. Supposedly this would be acceptable to those who were the guardians of two worlds, my world, called Earth in my native language, and Gor, the Priest-Kings of Gor, a mysterious set of beings regarded with great awe, both by humans and Kurii. Supposedly the Priest-Kings, whoever or whatever they might be, concerned to protect the two worlds of Tor-tu-Gor, in particular, Gor, a generally undamaged world, and their own, would allow this alliance, provided their weapon and technology laws were respected, laws designed to keep dangerous power out of the hands of species too aggressive, or stupid, to manage it with intelligence. Lord Grendel speculated that the Kurii would begin in peace, and then, bit by bit, eliminate Gorean humans, save perhaps for those which might be kept as work beasts and food, and have the surface of the world for themselves. The next phase would be when Kurii were abundant on Gor, and suitably emplaced. Then, by means of smuggled weapons, and the aid of the technology of the metal worlds, the Priest-Kings themselves might be attacked and eliminated, following which the world would belong to Kurii, who might then, with their various, competitive factions, contest it as they might. As a phase in this program, in order to facilitate an approach to humans, a series of experiments were to be performed, producing a set of hybrids, part Kur, part human, who, hopefully, could profitably interact with Gorean humans. This program was abandoned, after one such experiment, the result of which was the supposed monstrosity, Grendel, later Lord Grendel. He had several fathers, interestingly, as the genetic materials of several male Kurii were injected into, and fused within, a single human egg, which was eventually brought to term in the human female from whom the egg had been originally extracted. She, after the offspring was shown to her, had killed herself. Lord Grendel, part Kur and part human, was apparently not found acceptable by humans, and so the program was discontinued. Interestingly, for most practical purposes, he was not found acceptable by Kurii either, and became, in effect, an outcast on the steel world of his birth. A second plan was formed, to convert, bribe, or suborn, and then support, with power and riches, a human to further their projects. There was an attempt to recruit a disaffected human, one alienated from, and inimical to, Priest-Kings, a warrior, whose name was not spoken. Apparently this warrior not only declined to accept this commission, but became involved somehow in the politics of the steel world itself, participating in a revolt which brought about, in the steel world in question, a change in governance.

I, personally, saw little difference between Lord Grendel and another Kur. To the Kur, on the other hand, certain differences were apparently offensively obvious. For example, the paws and feet of Lord Grendel had but five digits, rather than the six found in the paws and feet of a normal Kur. There were other apparently subtle differences of appearance, as well, but these, or most of them, seemed negligible to me. Perhaps most interestingly, Lord Grendel could approximate human phonemes. One supposes, of course, that there might also be other differences, internal differences, of a sort less easy to detect, in physiology, and, perhaps, in sensibility, disposition, consciousness, and such. Lord Grendel, as I have mentioned before, claimed to be Kur. The newcomer accepted him as Kur. But the newcomer, of course, was blind.

I looked about myself.

The next races were with bipedalian tharlarion. Such races, given the beasts, are faster, rougher, and more dangerous. Such races are apparently difficult to anticipate and analyze, presumably from the unpredictability of the beasts, which are sometimes refractory, and sometimes wayward and aggressive. Sometimes a favorite will balk, and an unknown bound to victory. Some people will not bet on such races.

I could no longer see the two back-braceleted, neck-chained kajirae. As they had been in a blue-and-yellow livery, the colors of the Slavers, I supposed they might have been brought to the races to be offered. I supposed them such then that men might bid well on them. I suspected that if I were to be put up now, men might bid well on me, as well. Was I not different now than I had been, now that I was collared? Had I not been stalked by the Metal Worker? Had he not stood between me and a beast? To be sure, he had treated me with abruptness and authority in the market of Cestias, long ago, and had availed himself of my lips near Six Bridges, taking so presumptuous a liberty, when I was in no position to resist. He had given me a blanket in the wagon. But he had forced me to cook for him, the same night, and had put me to the indignity of all fours, as though I might have been a she-tarsk, and had fed me by hand. To be sure, I was grateful for the food. He had then had me lie beside him, "bound by his will," reclined as the mere slave I was, and had had me speak, and speak. I had told him so much, and revealed so much of myself, baring myself, my past, my thoughts, my hopes, fears, and feelings before him, as only a slave might bare herself before a master, and then, when I was so open, so confessed, so exposed, so vulnerable, so helplessly exhibited, he had informed me that he had "stripped me." And well then had I been stripped, stripping myself, before that man! How well he then knew me! What had I left to hide from him, but then it is all of a kajira that is owned. He had then put me on the girl chain. But as I lay there that night, in the dirt, shackled to the common chain, I was pleased, so pleased, that I had been able to speak. But, I wondered how it was that he, a master, should be interested, if indeed he had been, in the thoughts and feelings of a kajira. Surely we kajirae were only beasts to be worked and put to use, and to be whipped if we were not pleasing. But, I thought, perhaps he is the sort of master who would be satisfied with owning nothing less than all of a kajira. The kajira, of course, knows that it is all of her that is owned. That is clear in law. But how frightening it sometimes is for her to realize that that is true, that it is all of her that is owned.

I supposed the saddle beasts, the racers, were now being prepared for the final races, which would culminate the day.

Tor-tu-Gor was still bright, but there were long shadows, from the awnings, lying across the nearer track. Across the way, at the far track, male work slaves were scattering water on the track.

People were now beginning to return to the tiers.

I sat there on the tier, tunicked, my legs closely together, my hands braceleted behind me, my left ankle fastened to the tier ring. I picked out the slaves in the crowd, in their colored tunics. I saw one slave in a short tunic which was white, with broad, diagonal black stripes. Her master, I thought, must be an old-fashioned fellow, a traditionalist, or such. Such tunics, it seemed, were once quite common, indeed almost a universal uniform of kajirae, but, later, happily, a great deal of variety had been introduced into slave tunics, in color, cut, neckline, and such. Masters now had a great many options at their disposal when it came to clothing their properties, if they chose to clothe them. We girls, muchly concerned, like all women, with enhancing our appearance, with being attractive, even beautiful, muchly approved this state of affairs. And, of course, though the final word is the master's, it is a rare master who is immune to the delights which a lovely slave might choose to present for his consideration. Surely he does not wish his girl to be out of fashion, which might cast discredit on his taste, or wallet, or both. And now we might compete in a hundred new ways with one another, almost like free women who compete by means of the many luxurious varieties of their own bright, colorful, beautifully draped garmentures. To be sure, there is no danger of mistaking the brief, slight, dramatically revealing tunic of a slave with the concealing robes and veils of a free woman. I noted, again, the slave in the white, black-striped tunic. It was not unattractive. She had good legs.

I pulled a little at the bracelets which held my hands confined behind my back. How different this is from my former world, I thought. Here one thinks nothing of lovely, collared, back-braceleted, briefly tunicked slaves moving about in a crowd. Such a striking contrast with the others about, those well robed, so fully clothed! But how taken for granted here such beauties are! It is no more than a cultural commonplace. But on my former world this sort of thing would attract a great deal of attention, say, the appearance in a crowd of a lovely young woman, barefoot or sandaled, half naked, briefly tunicked, her neck in a collar, clearly locked on her neck, her hands braceleted closely, helplessly, behind her, perhaps even on a leash.

"Oh!" I said, for a cloth had been, from behind, suddenly slipped over my head. It was looped twice about my head and knotted in the back. I was blindfolded! "Master?" I said.

There was laughter from about.

I felt my head pulled back by the hair, and I was then, head back, facing upward, toward the billowing, striped awning, which I could not see.

I felt harsh masculine lips crush my lips.

I could not move, for the hand in my hair.

I could not speak, for the pressure.

Too, I had not been given permission to speak.

Then I moaned, and squirmed, and fought, and feared, and involuntarily trembled, for I sensed my body might yield to him.

How could I help myself?

I was a slave!

I feared that, in a moment, I might, to the amusement of those about, press myself piteously against him.

Had he touched me, as one might touch a slave, so confidently, so certainly, and possessively, I feared I would have leaped to his touch, even spasmed.

Then the lips were gone, and I heard more laughter from those about.

I leaped to my feet, in consternation, in misery, unable to see, helpless, jerking against the bracelets.

"Kneel down, slut," said an unpleasant masculine voice, and I instantly knelt, frightened, before the tier, putting my head to the cement.

"She is indeed a slut," said another voice.

Had they detected the incipience of my response?

"Worse," commented another, "a slave."

"How helpless they are," said another.

"She is a hot little beast," said another.

"Ten tarsk-bits for her," said another.

There was more laughter.

I heard, amongst the laughter, the peels of feminine mirth. I thought, angrily, put you in a tunic, and blindfold you, and subject you to such attentions, and see if you are any different!

A bit later, I felt myself drawn up, kneeling, and hands undid the blindfold. "Master," I cried, "what was done to me!"

I was quickly, brutally cuffed.

My face stung. Tears sprang to my eyes.

"I do not recall," said he in whose charge I was, "that you were given permission to speak."

I looked at him, wildly, pathetically.

"You may speak," he said.

With him were the Lady Bina, with her program, Astrinax, and the guard, Lykos.

"What was done to me!" I exclaimed, tearfully.

"You were put to lip rape," he said. "You were not used under the tier, were you?" he asked.

"No, Master," I said.

"It does not matter, anyway," he said, "as you have had, as I understand it, your slave wine."

"Yes, Master," I said.

He held up, before me, a tarsk-bit. He handed it to the Lady Bina, who placed it in her pouch.

"I did not see who did it to me," I said.

"No matter," he said. "The tarsk-bit was paid."

"The tarsk-bit?" I said.

"Look there," he said, "and there," pointing.

I followed his direction, and, in two places, I saw a slave on a tier, one below and well to my right, and another down, four tiers, to my left. They were blindfolded. I then saw another slave, looking down the tiers toward a vendor, which slave suddenly stiffened, fighting a blindfold wrapped about her face. I saw a large fellow hold her head back, and feast, at his pleasure, on her lips. She struggled, helplessly. I wondered if it were the same fellow who had pressed himself upon me.

"It is a jollity of the Vennan races, a game," he said, "to harvest kisses from the lips of unattended kajirae."

"So why was I unattended?" I asked.

"I do not understand," he said.

"I am in your charge," I said. "Why did you leave me? Why did you not stay, and protect me?"

"The tarsk-bit was paid," he said.

"I see," I said.

"You are not a free woman," he said. "You are kajira. Surely, on the street, in the market, or elsewhere, you have received a sudden slap, or pinch, on the fundament, when unattended, even though you were in the tunic of a woman's slave?"

"Yes," I said, angrily.

"Perhaps, even," he said, "an occasional kiss."

"Perhaps," I said. It did not seem to me that he, or the Lady Bina, or the beast, needed to know about such things. Occasionally a fellow had taken me in his arms, suddenly, unexpectedly, held me to him, and kissed me. Such things were done almost as one might glance at a sunset, ruffle the fur of a pet sleen, or bestow a familiar slap on the flank of a kaiila. I was, after all, goods, a property girl, a collar girl, a vendible animal, a purchasable, perhaps lovely, thigh-branded beast, a female slave, a mere kajira. Once a ruffian, lounging against a wall, as I made my way to the market, summoned me to him. As he was a free person, I had to obey, of course. He put me before him, and said, "Clasp your hands behind your back." I did so, of course. Much may be done with an unattended slave. Is she to disobey a free person? He then put his hand under my chin, lifted it a little, and said, "Slave lips." He was very close to me. I complied, and waited, eyes closed, and then he took my head, and pressed my lips to the wall. "Kiss it, slut," he said, "for three Ehn; then be about your business." I remained thusly, my lips pressed against the wall, my hands clasped behind my back, for three Ehn. I counted the Ehn, for fear he might be behind me, watching. Some passers-by laughed. Doubtless I was not the first slave they had seen, so discomfited. I then, tears in my eyes, my fists clenched, then better aware of my slavery, left. Too, I was distraught. He had been cruel, but had I been found wanting? Was I so poor a slave, so unattractive a slave? Had my lips not been formed, at his command, as a slave's lips, readied for attention? Had I not, eyes closed, waited, until I had been ignored or rejected, and my pursed lips put to a stone wall, against which I foolishly stood, my hands clasped behind my back, while strangers, some amused, passed by? How helpless, weak, and meaningless I felt! I had been neglected, ignored, and scorned, and not scorned as any slave is scorned, for she is a slave, but scorned even for the purposes of a slave! Is a woman fastened in a collar only to be fastened in a collar? Is its placement meaningless? Is that all she is to be left with, that there is a collar on her neck which she cannot remove? Was I such as to be put aside, dismissed, collared? Was I adjudged of no interest? Could I be so lacking? Was I so poor a slave? Was I not attractive, even beautiful, at least a little? My sense of my own worth, as a woman and a slave, was shaken. Was I so lacking? The young men I had known on my former world would have sought my kiss. Had I been interested in such things they would have been eager to pay for it! If I were truly of no interest to men why would I, and my sisters of the house, beauties all, have been brought to this world, for its girl markets, to be stripped, trained, caged, exhibited, and sold? I recalled a paga girl I had seen soliciting outside her master's tavern. I had thrilled to her profound, vital, needful sensuousness. I felt a need to reassure myself, perhaps because I was a woman's slave, and not a man's slave. Of what value is a slave if she, in her collar, is not of interest to masters? I waited in the street for a time, and then chose a handsome, young Tarnster. Such, I was sure, would be interested in the lips of a slave. I trusted he would not strike me from him. I hurried before him, and knelt down, blocking his way, humbly, and seized his left leg, and pressed my head, lowered, against his leg, as I had seen the paga girl do. I then lifted my head and eyes to him, and said, as she had, "A slave would be kissed, Master." "Very well," he said, and lifted me up, and spent a few Ihn with me. "Is Master pleased?" I asked. "Very much," he said, "which is your tavern?" "Ela, Master," I cried, hurrying away, "I have only the tavern of my beauty." I was much pleased, but, too, I was uneasy, for his touch had made me restless. I had suffered little in the way of slave fires, but I was a slave, and well aware of the deeper meanings of my collar. My most memorable experience along these lines, of course, was the interlude with the Metal Worker himself, in the vicinity of Six Bridges. After he had saved me from the girls of the house of Daphne, he had dealt with me at his leisure, and as he pleased, my hands incapacitated, unable to interfere, held over my head, balancing the laundry, my fingers, as he went about his inquiries, clawing into that large, soft bundle of sparkling sheets and linen which I dared not release lest it fall and be soiled, arousing me until, I fear, I had well shown myself, to his satisfaction, as he had apparently intended, slave.

"You were not concerned," I asked, "with what was done to me?"

"The tarsk-bit was paid," he said.

"Did you see?" I asked.

"Yes," he said.

"All of you?" I asked.

"Yes," he said.

"I see," I said.

"The Lady Bina," he said, "was quite pleased."

"Oh?" I said.

"Yes, Allison," said the Lady Bina. "I was curious to see if you would be selected for the game."

"Mistress?" I said.

"Yes," she said. "It seems clear that you are of interest to men, or to some men."

I was silent.

"I think," said Astrinax, "we will need two or three more."

I gathered then that I might not be the only slave for whom the Lady Bina might have use. I gathered, too, that one's interest to men might be pertinent to the use, or uses, she might have in mind. But that is common to kajirae, that they are of interest to men. Why else would men brand and collar them?

"Did you note the behavior of our little barbarian?" Desmond asked the Lady Bina.

"Oh?" said the Lady Bina.

"She started to squirm," said Astrinax, "and was on the verge of beginning to yield, as the collar slut she is."

"Mistress!" I protested.

"In another moment," said Desmond, "she would have thrust her pretty little body, bare under the nothing of rep cloth, against him."

"Master!" I said.

"Come now, pretty slut," said Astrinax, "it was obvious. Many about noted it."

"What do you think, noble Lykos?" asked the Lady Bina.

"She has nice thighs," he said. "She might, in a good market, bring nearly a silver tarsk. She is a hot little tart. That is important. I think she would do well on an alcove chain."

"The taverns are interested in such girls," said Desmond.

"Have your slave fires been lit?" asked Astrinax.

"No!" I said.

Desmond was looking upon me, grinning.

"No!" I said.

I knew, of course, that I would be no more immune than any other slave should men decide to do such things to me, making me then irremediably their needful, begging slave.

"It is pleasant," said Desmond, regarding me, "to stoke such fires in a slave's belly."

I looked away.

How I hated him!

He saw me as what I was, a slave.

And never had I met a man before whom I felt weaker, more helpless, more slave.

"We will need some more men, too," said Astrinax.

"Why is that?" asked the Lady Bina.

"For the wagons," he said.

I did not understand that, as it seemed one driver for a wagon, particularly as the wagons were small, would be sufficient. There were, as of now, three wagons. Astrinax drove one, Lykos the last, and Desmond mine, the second wagon. Indeed, the tharlarion of the second wagon, my wagon, was attached, by its nose ring, to the back of the first wagon, and the tharlarion of the third wagon was attached, by its nose ring, to the back of my wagon. Accordingly, it seemed three Drovers, or teamsters, would be enough. To be sure, I knew little about such matters, and, possibly, Astrinax might be returning to Ar, rather than accompanying us into the Voltai.

"The race is about to begin," said Astrinax.

"On what have you wagered, Desmond?" inquired the Lady Bina.

"Blue, as I would in Harfax, Lady," he said.

"I thought, this time, I would hazard yellow," she said.

"An excellent wager," said Astrinax.

"Loyalty is admirable, Desmond," said the Lady Bina, "but not invariably prudential."

"One supposes not," he said.

"Is this all there is to it," I asked, "that I was taken in hand, blindfolded, and kissed, and that is all?"

"The tarsk-bit was paid," said he in whose charge I was.

"All?" I asked.

"Yes," he said.

"I," I said, "would favor red."

"Why?" asked Desmond.

"Because it is not blue," I said.

"I see," he said.

"What are you doing, Master?" I said.

I was turned about, and the blindfold, retrieved from his belt, where he had placed it, keeping it at hand, was again wrapped about my head, twice, and knotted, behind my head, and I was, as before, securely and perfectly blindfolded. I jerked at the bracelets which held my hands behind me, in frustration.

"I will be unable to see the races," I said.

"Possibly," he said.

"It matters not to me, Master," I said.

"And what does that matter?" he asked.

"Master!" I said.

"Your permission to speak has been rescinded," he said.

I felt tears spring to my eyes, dampening the cloth of their prison.

I was not permitted speech!

On the tier, I writhed in helplessness, and fury, back-braceleted and on the short ring chain, and then the race began, and I could not see it. I heard movements about me! I sensed the agitation, the diverse partisanships abounding about, the excitement of the crowd, heard the cries, the cheering, the stamping, the screams and shouts, and I could see nothing!

It does not matter I said to myself, reassuring myself of my lack of interest in such things.

I sometimes heard cries of protest, even of rage, for some reason, which I did not understand, and, twice, I heard gasps of dismay, or of fear, perhaps as a beast fell, or was forced from the track.

It was nothing to me, of course.

I had never seen the bipedalian tharlarion compete. Also, actually, as a matter of fact, I had never seen the smaller, quicker quadrupedalian tharlarion compete either. There are classes of such beasts. I had seen, earlier, some races of the heavier-class quadrupedalian tharlarion, the larger, more ponderous beasts, the maneuvering, the shifting about for position, the lurching, thrusting, and buffeting, the grunting, the crowding. Below, near the rail, one could sense the ground shaking beneath their tread. These were similar to war tharlarion whose charge can shatter phalanxes, breastworks, palisades, and field walls.

You must understand that I did not care that I was blindfolded.

Who was interested in such things anyway?

I sensed people rising up, screaming, about me.

How helpless and frustrated I was! How I loathed the brute

in whose keeping I was. I would be treated not as I might wish or please, but precisely as he would wish or please.

I was collared!

How excited was the crowd!

How often might a kajira have the opportunity to see such things? Did I prefer the shackles looped about a central bar, and the tied-shut canvas of a wooden slave wagon?

Too, this was all new and different, and thrilling, to me. I was not natively Gorean. I was only a slave girl, brought from a different world. I so wanted to see, to realize what was going on, to be a part, if only as a slave, of what was going on about me.

I tried to put my head back, and peep beneath the blindfold, if only to perceive an undecipherable line of meaningless light, but I could see nothing. The device, twice wrapped and then knotted, had been put about my head broadly, in the Gorean fashion.

I moaned to myself, helplessly.

I decided I must not yield, I must give him no satisfaction.

But I realized, almost simultaneously, that my concerns, so important to me, would be absolutely immaterial to him.

I might remain in darkness, or petition him for relief, as a slave her master.

I endured my privation for two races

Then, wildly, desperately, in misery, I threw myself to my knees at the feet of he in whose keeping I was, pressed my sodden cheek to his leg, and then began to kiss his leg, repeatedly, beggingly.

I felt his hand in my hair, not tightly, but holding my head in place.

"I beg to speak, Master," I said.

"Speak," he said.

"I would see," I said.

"Do you beg it?" he said.

"Yes, Master," I said. "Oh, yes, Master!"

He then undid the blindfold.

"A new race will soon begin," said Astrinax, turning to Desmond. "May I place a bet for you?"

"On blue," said he at whose knee I knelt. A coin passed from him to Astrinax.

The Metal Worker put his hand near me, and I put down my head, and kissed it. "Thank you, Master," I said.

"You are a pretty little thing, Allison," he said.

"A slave is pleased if Master is pleased," I said.

"Master," I said.

"Yes," he said.

"I am pinioned," I said, "helplessly so. Perhaps Master might adjust my tunic at the left shoulder."

I had been concerned with this for some time.

"No," he said.

"'No'?" I said.

"No," he said. "I like it the way it is."

"I see," I said.

"Perhaps it might improve your price, a tarsk-bit or two."

"As Master pleases," I said.

He was a beast, of course, but then what girl would object to her price being improved a bit?

"I am sure," he said, "the fellow who pressed himself upon an unattended kajira did not object."

"Doubtless not," I said. "Perhaps it was to that tiny inadvertence of habiliments that I owed the attention bestowed upon me."

"Not at all," he said. "Even in a serving slave's tunic you would be an attractive little prey animal."

"'Prey animal'?"

"Yes," he said. "An interesting little quarry beast."

"I see," I said.

"Surely you are aware of how men see women," he said.

I was silent. I was afraid. But, too, I was thrilled. We are sought, hunted, captured, and owned, possessed by masters, who will deal with us as they please. They make us theirs, in reality, and law.

"The day is warm," he said.

"Yes, Master," I said.

"Who would you favor in the next race?" he asked.

"Blue," I said. "Blue, Master."

That seemed to me appropriate, as it was in his keeping that I was.

"An excellent choice," he said.

"Thank you, Master," I said.

"Allison," he said.

"Yes, Master," I said.

"Your permission to speak is revoked," he said.

"Yes, Master," I said.

So I was not then to speak. He did not care for me to do so. It was then as before. I was silenced.

There were four more races, and in some there were as many twenty or thirty tharlarion encircling the long track as many as five times. The competitions were at times unruly, even violent, but no riders or beasts were lost. There are, of course, races of different length, and some beasts are favored in shorter races, and some in longer races, depending on differences in speed and stamina. It is similar with racing slaves, bred or otherwise, and kaiila. Some are superior at short distances, others at longer distances.

For the remainder of the day, to my relief, I was not left unattended. Either Astrinax, Lykos, or Master Desmond remained with me. When the Lady Bina went below to the tables, the shops, or such, she was always accompanied. I gathered that she was never to be left unattended. In this I suspected something of the will of Lord Grendel.

At the end of the day we were making our way from the tiers, descending toward the broad open area between the rail and the stands, from there to exit toward the wagon-and-cart yard, some adjacent inns, and some of the closer camps. Indeed, during the races, it is often crowded, for many prefer to watch from there, possibly for the better view of the beasts, and the greater proximity to the betting tables.

Debris was about, useless betting tickets, discarded programs, tasta sticks, food wrappers, and such. Such things would be cleaned up by male work slaves. I saw such a fellow, brawny, with a heavy collar on his neck. Such as I were not for such as he. To be sure, we might be cast to one or more, as a punishment, or, perhaps, put at the disposal of one, as a reward for, say, a successful fighting slave. Interestingly, we had the sense that such as they, even in their collars, were our masters. On Gor, I had the sense that, in some natural sense, perhaps in the order of nature, we belonged to men. Not all of us, of course, were owned, and collared.

I suddenly stopped, startled, and almost cried out, but realized I could not do so, as I had not received permission to speak.

"What is wrong?" asked Desmond.

I wanted to weep with elation. I jerked at the bracelets, holding my wrists behind me.

The two of them regarded me, disbelievingly.

Then, wisely or not, but unable to help ourselves, we rushed to one another, they in the brief blue-and-yellow tunics, the Slaver's colors, the chain on their neck, joining them, and I.

They, too, had their small wrists pinioned behind their back, as was required of kajirae in the Vennan stadium.

But, weeping, sobbing with joy, we kissed one another, I them, and they me, again and again.

I realized, suddenly, that they, too, as I, did not have permission to speak. They, as I, doubtless in their training, had learned fear, and discipline. In my joy, overwhelmed with emotion, I had inadvertently fled from my heeling position, behind and to the left of he in whose charge I was, to approach them, but he did not rebuke me. I think all there were surprised, the Lady Bina, Master Desmond, Astrinax, and Lykos, and the keeper of the pair on the chain, with his switch, who was in his holiday regalia, that of the Slavers. Often enough, they wear dark robing or tunics, with only a small pair of chevrons visible, one blue, one yellow, on the left sleeve of their robe, near the wrist, to indicate their caste. Sometimes they do not identify their caste, as when, say, approaching free women.

We pulled futilely at the bracelets on our wrists; were it not for the obdurate impediments of masters imposed upon us, we would have doubtless embraced one another, joyfully.

As it was, tears streamed down our cheeks.

Perhaps it was the slaver who first saw fit to impose order on this small scene.

"Down!" he snapped, and his two barefoot charges, in their tiny tunics, immediately knelt, with their heads lowered.

How moving it was to see them as slaves!

And how well they had been trained!

And doubtless this was the first time they had seen me, as well, as what I now was, barefoot, tunicked, and collared, a slave.

"Let us see them," said the Lady Bina.

"Lift your heads," said the slaver, and his two charges complied, instantly.

"Pretty," said Astrinax, appraisingly.

I noted that their knees were placed closely together. I wondered how long that would be permitted to them.

Our eyes met, those of the two slaves, and mine.

Each was nicely collared, the thin, flat band, encircling the neck, closely. Their collars would be fastened on them, the lock at the back of the neck.

Both were now kajirae, and lovely. I thought they were now even more attractive, as I thought myself to be, as well, than they had been before, in the house, in the sorority, on Earth.

"You may speak," said the slaver to his charges.

"Allison!" they cried.

I looked wildly, piteously, at he in whose charge I was. "You may speak," he said.

"Jane!" I cried. "Eve!"

"Get on your knees," said he in whose charge I was.

I knelt, instantly.

"Jane, Jane!" I said. "Eve! Eve!"

"Allison!" they cried, joyfully.

Chapter Eighteen

The road here was narrow, and rough.

I looked up, at the stone channel of the aqueduct, some hundred feet over my head.

I do not think the road really has a name, or, if it does, I did not know it. It is called, however, like other such roads, the Aqueduct Road, for it follows the line of the aqueduct, to enable the approach of crews and service wagons, which tend regularly to the massive conduit, bringing fresh water from the snows and streams of the Voltai to Ar. This was the Vennan aqueduct, one of some five supplying the city.

Master Desmond had informed me that the Vennan aqueduct, the third longest, was some eight hundred and ten pasangs long.

Eve, Jane, and I were identically tunicked, as I had been before, in brief white rep cloth. Too, we now had identical collars. Given the roughness of the terrain, we were now sandaled. We were grateful for this.

We had left Venna four days ago.

"I cannot read my new collar, Master," I had said to Master Desmond.

"No," he said, "you are illiterate. I like you that way. It makes you more helpless."

"A girl," I said, "would like to know what is on her collar."

"Come closer," he said.

I then stood close to him, and lifted my chin, that he might the more easily read my collar.

"You seem uneasy," he said.

"Master is very close," I said.

"You are very close," he said.

"Yes, Master," I said.

"You would like to know what is on your collar?"

"Yes, Master," I said.

"You may then," he said, "petition me properly. Kneel, kiss my feet, and make your request."

I knelt, and pressed my lips to his feet, and kissed them.

I was thrilled to do this, before this man. How right it seemed to me that I should be so before him. But what was he to me? Could he be, I wondered, my master? Again and again I kissed his feet, I now only a slave, and he so far above me, standing, formidable and powerful, a Gorean male. How far I was now from my former world, from the former Allison Ashton-Baker.

"I would know what is on my collar, Master," I said.

"Do you beg it?" he said.

"Yes, Master," I said.

He then indicated that I should stand, and he took my collar in his hands, and lifted it a little.

"Master?" I said.

"It is very simple," he said. "It says only 'I belong to Lady Bina'."

"There is nothing about the house of Epicrates, or Emerald Street?" I asked.

"No," he said, "but do not be concerned. Many collars are similarly simple."

"And if I were in your collar?" I asked.

"You are a bold slave," he said. "It would presumably be something like 'I am the property of Desmond of Harfax'."

"It would not even contain my name?" I said.

"One may then change your name as often as one might wish, without changing the collar," he said.

"It is fortunate I am not in your collar," I said.

"It is perhaps more fortunate than you realize," he said, quietly.

"I hate you," I said.

"That might make it more pleasant to have you at my feet," he said.

* * * *

334

The day's races had been recently finished and our party, the Lady Bina, Astrinax, Lykos, Desmond, and myself, had descended the tiers, and were preparing to leave the grounds when we had encountered a neck-chained, matched set of slaves, both barbarians.

"In what way," inquired the Lady Bina, "is this a matched set?"

"They are both barbarians," had said the slaver, "and, apparently, speak the same barbarous tongue. Your girl seems to know them."

"Can you speak to them, Allison?" asked the Lady Bina. "In their barbarous tongue?"

"Yes, Mistress," I said. "It is called English."

"There are several barbarian languages, Lady," said the slaver.

"Speak to them, a little, in that English," said the Lady Bina.

Words burst forth amongst us, eager, wild, grateful words. "We are all collared, all slaves!" I cried. "Yes, yes," cried Jane and Eve. It seemed that my apprehension, which had been separate from the others, had been an accident of my location in the house. The rest had been brought to the parlor, stripped, bound hand and foot, gagged, and placed in a truck, as though they might have been kindling, and taken to a transportation point. Apparently Mrs. Rawlinson had much enjoyed the scene, observing the reduction of her former charges to the status of captures destined for Gorean markets. Jane and Eve had been brought to Venna. I, and perhaps others, had been delivered to Ar. Others must have been variously distributed.

"That is enough," said the Lady Bina, sharply. We were then silent, frightened. One obeys free persons. One hopes to please them. One does not wish to be punished.

"Interesting," said the Lady Bina.

"Yes," said Lykos, regarding Eve.

The fair Earth-girl slave put down her head.

"Yes," said Astrinax, scrutinizing Jane, as a slave may be scrutinized.

I saw that Jane knew herself so scrutinized. She looked to the side, her lip trembling.

I then saw my friends, Jane and Eve, familiar from a thousand interactions on a former world, afresh, as they now were, as I had never thought of them before, as mere slaves, as lovely, exquisite, delicate animals, half naked, purchasable, timid under the eyes of men. But why not, I thought. They were young, they were beautiful, they were desirable. And they were now, as I, on Gor.

How different were things now, from my former world!

How far were we all, now, from the banalities, the boredoms, the competitions, and trivialities of the sorority!

How meaningless we had been, how worthless!

We now had worth, some value, at least what coin we might bring. And we must strive to please!

We were now such that men would have their will of us.

We were slaves.

And had I seen something in Eve's eyes, before she thrust down her head, frightened, before Lykos, and had I not noted a momentary start in the eyes of Jane, before hurrying to look away from the gaze of Astrinax?

How can a kneeling slave, looking up, not wonder if he who looks down upon her is not her master?

Surely she knows she has a price.

Perhaps he before whom she kneels will pay it. She does not know. She will then be his. She will then be bought.

The Lady Bina then addressed herself to the men. "Can you understand them?" she asked.

"No," said the slaver. "No," said the others.

"Nor I," said the Lady Bina.

"I assure you that they are competent in Gorean," said the slaver.

"I trust so," said the Lady Bina.

"It is certified," said the slaver.

It was in no way unusual, after the brief indulgence accorded us, consequent upon the curiosity of the Lady Bina, who was apparently curious as to the nature of our native speech, that we had been abruptly silenced.

In the presence of masters it is expected, of course, that the slave will speak in the language of the masters. Not to do so is to invite the lash. Whatever she says is to be comprehensible to the master. In all ways, verbal and otherwise, the slave is to be open to the master. This is fitting, as she is a slave.

"You are offering them, I take it," said the Lady Bina.

"Certainly," said the slaver.

"But you have failed to sell them," she said, "and the races are over."

"For the day," said the slaver.

"But you do not wish to return to the house with them still on your chain," she said.

"I would rather not," he said.

"I wonder," said the Lady Bina, "if these two slaves might be of interest to men."

"Certainly they would be of interest to men," said the slaver. "They are lovely. They would grace any block."

"Astrinax," she said, "do you think these two slaves might be of interest to men?"

"Yes," he said.

"Assess them," said the Lady Bina.

"Remove their bracelets, and the neck chain," said Astrinax.

This was done.

"Tunics off," said Astrinax.

I turned aside while they were assessed.

"Oh!" said Jane.

I heard Eve whimper.

"Kneel," said Astrinax.

Both, I gathered, were found suitable for slave meat.

"I will let you have both for ten silver tarsks," said the slaver.

"One, for both," said the Lady Bina.

"Impossible," said the slaver.

"You may as well debracelet Allison," said the Lady Bina to Desmond. "We are leaving the grounds."

I rubbed my wrists, the bracelets removed.

"Both for five silver tarsks," said the slaver.

"They are barbarians," said the Lady Bina.

"Then four, for both," said the slaver.

"We are looking for cheap girls," said the Lady Bina, "for we are going into the Voltai."

"No, please, Mistress!" cried Jane, and then, frightened, put her hand before her mouth. "Forgive me, Mistress!" she begged.

Clearly Eve was in consternation, as well.

"You may speak," said the Lady Bina.

"Not the Voltai!" said Jane, kneeling with Eve, wearing only their collars, their knees in the dirt. "There are beasts, bandits!"

"You need have no fear," said the Lady Bina, "for obviously you are not to be sold for a reasonable price."

"Surely you could not be thinking of taking merchandise of this quality into the Voltai?" said the slaver.

"One silver tarsk for both," said the Lady Bina, "if you throw in the tunics. They will do until something more suitable may be arranged."

"More suitable?" said the slaver, looking at me, grinning. I stepped back. My tunic was such that I might have easily been thought to be a man's slave.

"Let us return to the wagons," said the Lady Bina.

"Three," said the slaver. "No? Very well then, one for each!"

I was not a good judge in such matters. A girl often does not know what she will bring until she had been thrust from the block. I did know that I had never brought as much as a full silver tarsk.

I looked upon Jane and Eve. Slaves are often naked, and one thinks little of looking upon them, and, commonly, they think little of being so looked upon. Still, I had known them from my former world. Our eyes met, and they lowered their hands. I saw that they now realized they were slaves.

"The tunics must be included," said the Lady Bina.

We were at the gate of the grounds when we heard the slaver's exasperated cry, "Hold! Done!"

We turned about and watched him approach. He had Jane's upper left arm in his right hand, and Eve's upper right arm in his left hand, and was conducting them toward us. Each had her tunic thrust crosswise in her mouth.

The Lady Bina withdrew a silver tarsk from her pouch and gave it to the slaver.

"They will be reluctant to enter the Voltai," the slaver warned the Lady Bina.

"We will keep them well chained until we are well in the Voltai," said the Lady Bina. "Then we will unchain them and they may run off, if they wish, to be eaten by animals."

Jane and Eve knelt before the Lady Bina, looking up at her,

pathetically, and, against the tunics thrust in their mouths, whimpered.

"Of course," said the Lady Bina. "You may clothe yourselves."

The two slaves gratefully slipped into their tunics, drawn over their head, fastened at the left shoulder, with a disrobing loop. Their tunics, I noted, were not much more ample than mine. When one is offering a woman, of course, one wants it to be clear that she may be worth buying. To be sure, long ago, at the party, we had, all three of us, been even more scandalously clothed, for we had been camisked.

Desmond, at a nod from the Lady Bina, fastened Jane and Eve together with the bracelets which he had removed from me a bit ago, the left wrist of Jane fastened to the right wrist of Eve.

Astrinax removed his belt, briefly, and, looping it, struck Jane twice, sharply, across the back of the thighs, and then served Eve identically, and they cried out, softly, and better understood themselves slaves. Astrinax then replaced his belt, and we continued on our way.

I went beside Jane and Eve, at Eve's side. "We are slaves," said Eve, "slaves!" "We are all slaves," I said. "We are afraid to enter the Voltai," said Eve. "It will be done with us as masters please," I said. "Yes," said Jane, "it will be done with us as masters please."

* * * *

Lykos was a spare fellow, dark-haired, familiar with the wicked blade, called the *gladius*, who had been hired by Astrinax in one of the camps between Ar and Venna. He was, as far as I knew, a mercenary, with a possible background in the Scarlet Caste. It was well that we had at least one such with the wagons, for the two beasts, Lord Grendel and the blind Kur, who were usually concealed, or shadowing the wagons from a distance, could scarcely accompany the Lady Bina about, for example, to the races. I did not know the caste of Astrinax, but it seemed likely, if he had caste, that he was of the minor Merchants. Master Desmond, of course, as far as I knew at the time, was of the Metal Workers. He was seldom visibly armed, but I supposed that he would have a weapon somewhere, perhaps in his pack, at least a knife, as few male Goreans are likely to be without a weapon of some kind. Slaves, of course, are seldom permitted to touch weapons. They might lose a hand for doing so, if not be cast to leech plants or sleen. This had been so ingrained upon me, in my training, that I was afraid even to look upon a weapon, beside a chair, hanging on a wall, or such.

Astrinax, I recalled, had wished to hire two or three more men. It did not seem likely, however, that he would be successful, as few fellows, even of the Scarlet Caste, cared to enter the Voltai, particularly on some obscure mission which might prove to be of some indefinite duration.

So it was our last night in Venna, before leaving for the Voltai.

Astrinax would make one last try, it seemed, in one of Venna's larger, more popular paga taverns, The Kneeling Slave. He would be accompanied by Desmond and Lykos. The Lady Bina would remain near the wagons, in the camp's "palace of free women," a small, closely guarded area, scarcely a palace, more a small house, supplied with certain amenities, cakes, ka-la-na, and such. It was also within earshot of our wagons, within one of which was Lord Grendel. The Lady Bina enjoyed the company of free women, which she found instructive, and, in its way, profitable. I well recalled Lady Delia, the companion of the pottery merchant, Epicrates. As a slave, I trusted that the Lady Bina, who was an apt pupil in many things, would not learn too much about the character and behavior of Gorean free women, or, at least, would not strive to adopt or emulate it. In the house of Tenalion, I had heard certain slaves, being readied for their sale, beseeching Priest-Kings that they not fall into the clutches of a free woman. I had gathered, more than once, that I was fortunate to be owned by the Lady Bina, who, while often demanding, petty, and vain, entertained toward me, as far as I knew, not the least animus or hostility. This was quite different from being the slave of a typical Gorean free woman, particularly if one should be attractive. Such slaves, it seems, can seldom please, and they are often scolded, humiliated, and beaten. If they so much as look at a man they may be tied and lashed.

So I had learned, earlier in the day, that Astrinax would visit one of Venna's more patronized taverns, The Kneeling Slave, to search again for two or three fellows to join our small caravan. He would be accompanied by Lykos, whose opinion, because of his blade skills, it seems, would be relevant and perhaps important. Indeed, from what I had heard of the Voltai, I gathered that blade skills might be as important as wagon skills. Too, I learned that Master Desmond would accompany them. "I need a goblet of paga," he had told me. "And what of me, Master?" I had inquired. "Am I to be put on the common chain at the camp, or am I to be fastened to the slave post, nearer the wagons, with Jane and Eve, or am I to be merely left in the slave wagon, shackled to the central bar, or what?" "Have you ever been in a paga tavern?" he asked. "Certainly not," I said. "Would you like to see one?" he asked. "If I were to exhibit enthusiasm," I said, "would you then be certain to shackle me in the wagon?" "And tie shut the canvas?" he asked. "Yes," I said. "Not necessarily," he said. "Then," I said, "Master, I would very much like to go." "Do you think you can take it?" he asked. "I would suppose so," I said. "I would think so, too," he said, "as The Kneeling Slave, as I understand it, is a large, clean, expensive, well-appointed, superior sort of establishment, one catering to an elegant, elite sort of clientele. The girls may be belled, but they are not even chained, and they are clothed." "I see," I said. "It is not like the dingy holes in which one such as you might serve as a paga girl, nude and chained." "Oh?" I said. "I understand it that one may even stand upright in some of the better alcoves," he said. "I see," I said. "I will take you along," he said, "that you may see some truly beautiful slaves." "And at what time," I asked, "will Master call for the girl." "You will be unshackled after supper," he said. "Will Lady Bina accompany us?" I asked. "Certainly not," he said. "Free women are not permitted in paga taverns." "Oh?" I said. "Rejoice," he said, "it is one place kajirae need not fear free women." "I do not fear free women," I said. "That is because you have never been owned by one," he said, "that is, a typical free woman." "I see," I said. "It is dangerous for a free woman to enter such a place," he said. "They may be marked by slavers. It is commonly supposed that a free woman who enters such a place courts the collar, and wants her bare feet in the yellow-dampened sawdust of the slave block. Sometimes a free woman, as an adventure, will disguise herself as a slave, even to the collar, and enter such an establishment." "How bold they are," I said. "And sometimes," he said, "they end up in a different collar, one to which they have no key." "I understand," I said. "It is easy," he said, "to transport a woman from a city, nude, bound, gagged, in a slave sack." "Doubtless," I said.

* * * *

It was after dark when I approached the slave post.

"Who is there?" whispered Jane.

"It is I, Allison," I whispered. "I have brought you something to eat."

I could not well see the slaves, but, when they moved, I could hear the linkages which secured them to the post. Each was on a chain which led to a collar. Further, the left ankle of each was chained to the post, as well. Accordingly, they were twice secured. Beyond that, each was ankle shackled and wrist shackled. The Lady Bina, it seemed, had taken the warning of the slaver seriously.

"We have taken our gruel, face down, from the pans," said Eve, bitterly.

"I have brought you some tiny honey cakes," I whispered, "from the food cart of the masters."

"You will be beaten," said Jane.

"No," I said. "It is with the permission of the Lady Bina."

"The Mistress?" said Jane.

How easily, I thought, that word now comes to us!

"Yes," I said. "Do not be concerned. They were left over. No one wanted them."

"Garbage," said Jane.

"I suppose so," I said, "in a way."

"Then when crumbs are found on our mouth, we will be whipped!" said Jane.

"I will take them away," I said.

"No!" said Jane. "Please, no!"

"We have not had a sweet in weeks," said Eve.

"Perhaps you remember how, on Earth," I said, "we might indulge ourselves as we pleased."

Small hands, shackled, reached toward me. "Please, Allison," said Jane. "Please, please, Allison," begged Eve.

I had brought four of the small honey cakes, and I gave two to each of the slaves.

They thrust them into their mouths, with soft cries of gratitude, and pleasure.

"Thank you, oh, thank you!" they breathed.

Simple things, a sweet, a kind word, a comb, a scrap of cloth, can mean much to a slave.

Then they shrank back, with a rustle of chain, frightened, for the light of a lantern had fallen upon us.

"What is going on here?" asked a voice, that of a camp guard, on his rounds.

"I am bringing food to the slaves, Master," I said.

He held the lantern high, regarding us.

"Food is included in the post fee," he said.

"This is extra, Master," I said. "Tomorrow they are to be taken into the Voltai."

"And what is in the Voltai, for pretty slaves?" he said.

"I do not know, Master," I said.

Eve and Jane knelt by the post to which they were fastened, their heads down. I, too, remained kneeling, as I had been, as I was in the presence of a free man, though I lifted my head to the lantern. I could not well see the guard's face.

He did not lower the lantern.

"Get your heads up," said the guard to the chained slaves.

Instantly they complied.

At the post slaves are chained nude. A nude slave is quickly noticed. It is another way in which escape is made more difficult.

I remembered Eve and Jane from Earth, from the college, from the house. Here they were Gorean slave girls, naked, chained to a post.

"The Voltai," said the guard. "Too bad."

He then left.

"Tomorrow," I said to the slaves, "you will receive new tunics, and collars. We are to be identically tunicked and collared."

"You are well exhibited," said Jane.

"As will be you," I said.

"Mrs. Rawlinson arranged things well, did she not?" said Jane, shaking her chains.

"Yes," I said.

"Do not let us be taken into the Voltai," begged Eve.

"As I understand it," I said, "we are to be back-braceleted and chained by the neck to the back of a wagon. At night, we will probably be shackled to the central bar, in a slave wagon. After a day or two, you will be released, to accompany the wagons."

"We might then run," said Eve.

"To be taken by bandits, or eaten alive by beasts," said Jane.

"Stay near the wagons," I said.

"There is no escape for us," moaned Jane.

"No," I said, "we are kajirae."

I then prepared to withdraw.

"Thank you for the cakes," said Jane.

"Yes," said Eve, "so much!"

"You might remember," I said, "that at the party we had been refused permission to feed, and had been denied lunch that day."

"We were so hungry," said Eve.

"Nora cast you some scraps to the floor," said Eve, "on which you must feed, as a slave."

"Yes," I said.

"And she placed a pan of water on the floor from which you, head down, not using your hands, on all fours, were to drink, as a she-beast," said Jane.

"I recall," I said.

"Which water she spilled," said Eve, "for which you were punished."

I shuddered, and put my arms about me. How I had been punished, so mercilessly, so richly, switched! I had then, groveling and weeping under the blows, sensed that I was a slave, and should be a slave. I still feared Nora, terribly. I still thought of her as Mistress and myself as slave.

"Tonight," I said, "I am to be taken to a paga tavern."

"To be sold?" said Jane.

"I do not think so," I said.

It could, of course, be done to me. It would have to be at the instructions of the Lady Bina, of course, my Mistress.

"I must let you rest," I said.

"Here in the dirt, nude, in our chains," said Jane.

"Do you not feel," I whispered, "that they are right on you?"

There was a pause, in the darkness.

"Yes," Jane whispered.

"Yes," Eve whispered.

I then withdrew.

* * * *

"Now those are slaves," said Master Desmond, with an expansive gesture about the room, he in whose keeping I was.

"Yes, Master," I said.

I knelt beside the low table, about which Masters Desmond, Lykos and Astrinax sat, cross-legged.

It was a high tavern.

"Not one would go for less than two silver tarsks," he said.

"Perhaps," I said.

I supposed men had much sweated in their bidding on them. I saw one fellow knot the wrists of a slave behind her and thrust her toward an alcove.

I recalled that he in whose keeping I was had said that in some of the alcoves a man might stand upright. The alcoves, I understood were furnished with a variety of conveniences, bracelets, chains, thongs, cords, scarves, hoods, switches, whips, and such, by means of which a girl might be encouraged to perform excellently, to do her best for one of her master's customers. It was in her best interest to see that no client was disappointed, in the least.

I looked about. The girls were belled, on the left ankle. Each was clothed, in a sense. Each was silked, but diaphanously. In my brief, rep-cloth tunic, kneeling by the table, I felt myself less exhibited than they, in their soft, colorful, swirling silks.

I could understand how it was that men would seek the paga taverns.

Still, to one side, at more than one table, fellows were intent upon a game of kaissa.

How could that be? Were the slaves not beautiful enough?

I knew that a yearning slave, to one side, lying in her chains, must often await the outcome of such a game

There was music in the tavern, a czehar player, a drummer, utilizing the small tabor, two flautists, and a pair of kalika players. He with the czehar was the leader. That was common, as I was given to understand.

I could smell paga, and roast bosk.

A bit of silk flashed by. I drew my head back, for it had brushed across my face.

He in whose keeping I was laughed.

I did not care for that.

"Master?" I said.

"You were insulted," he smiled.

"What flanks!" said Astrinax.

"Why do you not pursue her and tear her silk from her?" asked Lykos.

"She would tear out my hair, and beat me," I said.

Master Astrinax had been, so far, unsuccessful in his recruiting. He had approached more than one table, without success.

Master Desmond, I noted, had an eye for the paga slaves. That was nothing to me, of course. Why, then, was I so angry?

"I have brought Allison here," said Master Desmond, "that she might see what true slaves are like."

"My collar is on my neck as well as theirs are on theirs," I said, angrily.

"Then," said he in whose charge I was, "you are a true slave, as well?"

"My thigh is marked," I said, "my neck is collared, I am owned."

"Then you are a true slave?" he said.

I looked at him. "Yes, Master," I said, "Allison is a true slave."

"Look at me, and say it," he said.

"I am a true slave," I said. "Allison is a true slave."

"That is known to me," he said.

"I hate you," I said, tears in my eyes.

"Put your hand on her," said Lykos.

"No!" I said.

"How would you like to be taken to an alcove?" asked he in whose charge I was.

How I had dreamed of being in his power, as a slave is in a master's power.

"No," I said, "no!"

"Why not?" he asked.

"You do not own me!" I said.

"True," said Master Desmond.

"I have seen her like," said Lykos. "Put her in your chains, and she will leap, begging, to your touch."

"No, no!" I said.

"She would be an easy one to master," said Lykos, "a little resistance, and then she is yours."

"No, Masters!" I said.

"See that one!" said he in whose charge I was, pointing toward the paga vat.

She was indeed beautiful.

"See that auburn hair," said Astrinax.

"That color," said he in whose charge I was, "is prized in the markets." Then he looked at me. "It is not common," he said, "like brown hair."

"Brown hair is beautiful," said Lykos.

I cast him a look of gratitude.

"But common," said he in whose charge I was. How angry I was with him.

"The hair of the Lady Bina," said Lykos, "what I have seen of it, is beautiful."

That was true. I had often seen the Lady Bina unhooded, unveiled, and her hair was strikingly blond, and her eyes were a soft, sometimes, sparkling blue. She was exquisite, in face and figure. I supposed, though the speculation was inappropriate, as she was a free woman, that she might bring a fine price off a block. I had sometimes wondered what she would look like, if marked and collared.

She with auburn hair, the paga slave, had dipped her goblet into the vat, and then, holding it with two hands, had turned, and conveyed it to a table.

"There is another beauty," said Astrinax, gesturing with his head to another slave.

She had a swirl of long blond hair.

"That hair color is similar to that of the Lady Bina, is it not?" said Lykos.

"Perhaps, Master," I said. It did not seem fitting to me, to speak of such things, to speak of the Mistress. To be sure, at the troughs, and in the Sul Market, I had heard more than one woman's slave excoriate her Mistress, in the most detailed and vivid terms.

I noted that Master Desmond, whom I supposed of the Metal Workers, certainly he in whose charge I was, to my annoyance, was still appraising various paga slaves, as masters look upon such women.

"Master considers slaves," I observed.

"See that one," he said to me, pointing.

"Perhaps Master would care to gaze upon a slave closer at hand," I said.

"Where?" he said.

"Here," I said.

"You?" said he.

"Perhaps," I said.

"Surely you do not think to compare your beauty with that of the paga girls of The Kneeling Slave," he said.

"On my former world I was thought quite lovely."

"Perhaps for such a world," he said.

"If we were such poor stuff," I said, "we would not have been brought here, to be put in the collars of brutes such as yourself."

"Some barbarians are of interest," he said.

"You might learn much from the men of my world," I said.

"Oh?" he said.

"They are sweet, pleasant, kind, gentle, sensitive, solicitous, accommodating, and wonderful, and they do what we want," I said.

"Is that why the women of your world make such excellent slaves, why they lick and kiss our whips and feet, why they beg to be subdued and chained, owned and mastered, why they writhe in grateful ecstasy in the thongs and silken cords that render them helpless?" he asked.

"Ah!" said Astrinax. "See that one!"

"But, yes!" agreed he in whose care I was.

ple see a woman as their slave, as delicious, incomparable collar meat, special to them, and will not rest until she is chained at their feet."

"And I have heard," said he, "that some women, for whatever reason, look up at a fellow, from their knees, and recognize him as their master."

"There is another beauty," said Astrinax, indicating another paga girl.

"She has brown hair," I said.

"At least," said he in whose charge I was, "it is more than a hort or two in length."

"My hair will grow," I said.

"I think," said he, "I will ask the Lady Bina to have it shaved off again."

"Please do not, Master!" I said.

"You are going to be deferent, docile, obedient, humble, zealous, eager to please, and such, are you not?" he asked.

"Yes, Master!" I said.

"What lovely girls," said Astrinax.

"Superb," said he in whose charge I was.

"But we have obtained no new men, no new swords," said Lykos.

"Are all taverns like this, Master?" I asked Astrinax. I suspected not, for the apparent quality of the girls.

"No," he said. "The prices here are such that the place should be burned down. In a typical tavern a drink is a single tarsk-bit, with which drink a girl may go, if you want her. Here, a drink is five tarsk-bits, five! And for all I know, the girl is extra."

"No," said Lykos. "She goes with the drink."

"But five tarsk-bits!" said Astrinax.

"True," granted Lykos, resignedly.

At that moment there was an exciting skirl of music, a flash of bells, a burst of color, a jangle of beads, and a cry of enthusiasm from the patrons, and a dancer was on the floor. After her entry

349

she stood silent, not moving, posed, ready, on the floor. I could sense the anticipation, even the difference in breathing, of the men. Then the music began, softly, slowly, and the dancer, looking about herself, began to move, obedient to the melody of masters.

"Is she a slave?" I asked.

"Certainly," said he in whose charge I was. "It may be hard to see, beneath the necklaces, so many of them, but there is a collar there, close-fitting, steel, and locked."

"Much as mine," I said.

"Yes," he said.

"She is so beautiful," I said. "She is so soft, so feminine, so utterly female, so vulnerable, so needful."

"A slave," said Lykos.

"It is so beautiful," I said. "What is it called?"

"It is a form of dance fit for slaves, is it not?" he said.

"Yes," I breathed, awed, rapt.

"Slave dance," said he in whose charge I was.

"Slave dance," I whispered.

"Yes," he said.

"I have seen something like it," I said, "on my former world, but I scarcely dared look upon it."

"It spoke to you of things which stirred you, things for which you longed, but which you feared, spoke to you of a distant, or forgotten, world, one a thousand times more real, I suspect, than that which you knew. It spoke to you of how women might be before men, as slaves, and how men might look upon women, as masters."

"Yes," I whispered, "but here it seems somehow different."

"It is different here," he said, "for this is such a world."

"I think I know this dance, or sort of dance," said Astrinax. "It will have its phases, its swiftness, and its slowness, its emotions, insolence, pride, defiance, apprehension, recognition, fear, struggle, defeat, surrender, and submission."

I heard, it startling me, the cracking of a whip. The dancer reacted, as though struck, but the blade had not touched her. Occasionally it snapped again, and again, and, at the end of the dance, as is often the case in such dance, the dancer is prostrate, clearly submitted and owned. In this particular dance she was kneeling and the fellow with the whip was behind her. He placed the whip, coiled, against the back of her neck, and she lowered her head. The men about voiced their approval, and several smote their left shoulders with their right hand. Others uttered trilling noises or staccato bursts of sound. Others pounded on the tables. She then sprang to her feet and hurried from the floor, followed by the fellow with the whip.

"Paga, Master?" asked a girl.

She had not been summoned to our table!

Sometimes a master will summon a particular girl to his table. Masters have choices, of course, even if they are interested only in paga. I suppose it is natural for a master to wish to be served by one girl, rather than another. On the other hand, more than paga might be involved. The particular girl, summoned, is well aware that the fellow may be considering her for alcoving, as well.

The slave had addressed herself to he in whose charge I was! To be sure, a girl might approach a table, unsummoned. But how dared she? I remained, of course, on my knees. I had no permission to rise.

She glanced at me, condescendingly, and smiled, with the look of a high-priced girl upon one of lesser value, perhaps one who might regard herself as fortunate that men had deigned to put a collar on her, at all.

I recognize her soft, light, loose sheen of swirling, diaphanous yellow silk. It had been insolently cast before me earlier, and drawn across my face.

It was doubtless her way her of showing contempt for a lesser girl, and calling Master Desmond's attention to the difference amongst slaves.

He was a handsome fellow. Might he not be interested in buying her?

"Yes," said Desmond, "paga."

She then backed away, smiling, and then turned about, making her way to the paga vat.

"An excellent choice, Kalligone," said a tavern's man, as the five tarsk-bits were placed in his hand. Before he left, he dropped a slender silken cord, short, coiled, on the table. There was little doubt what such a cord was for. Most masters, on the other hand, brought their own cords, bracelets, laces or thongs to a table. The tavern's man then left the table.

"Master!" I protested, tears in my eyes.

"What is wrong?" asked he in whose charge I was.

"Nothing," I said.

Shortly, the slave, whose name I took to be Kalligone, returned, and, two hands on the goblet, knelt before Master Desmond. Her knees, beneath the sheen of silk, were clearly spread. Of course, I thought, angrily, she is a pleasure slave! But then are not all paga girls pleasure slaves? Was pleasure not what men paid for? Was it not with pleasure in mind, inordinate pleasure, that men put collars on such women?

Kalligone did not neglect to glance at the cord, and smiled.

"Here," said Master Desmond, holding out his hand.

"Master?" she said, startled.

"Here," he said. He then took the goblet, and placed it on the table.

"Master?" she asked, again.

"Leave," he said, "but remain on the floor. I may want you later. Go, quickly, on your pretty little feet, and jangle your bells."

"You refuse Kalligone?" she said.

"Go," he said, "while I permit you to retain your silks."

"Yes, Master," she said, frightened, and withdrew, to a jangle of bells.

"They are belled, like animals," I said.

"Be quiet, or you, too, will be belled, little beast," he said.

"I thank Master," I said, looking after Kalligone.

"I think now," he said, "you are avenged."

"Well avenged!" I laughed. "Allison thanks Master."

To be sure, how could a man refuse the tavern's gift of a Kalligone? Perhaps, I thought, because there is another slave who, for whatever reason, is a thousand times more desirable, at least to him?

"But who, now," he asked, "will serve me paga?"

"Allison," I said, happily, reaching for the goblet, and holding it out to him.

"Put it down," he said.

I placed it, puzzled, on the table. Astrinax and Lykos laughed.

I did not care for the sound of their laughter. Some others, too, at the nearby tables, were looking on.

"Master?" I said, uneasily.

"Remove your tunic," he said.

"Here," I said, "Master?"

"Now," he said.

I was then naked. Some had gathered around, amongst them the girl, Kalligone.

"What was your former name?" he asked.

"Allison," I said. "Allison Ashton-Baker."

"You are a barbarian, are you not?" he asked.

"Yes, Master," I said.

"What were you on your former world?" he asked.

He knew, surely, for I had spoken to him of such things, in the camp, when I had lain beside him that night, "bound by his will," when he had, so to speak, stripped me of myself, and I had lain open before him, in so many ways.

"A student," I said, "at a small school, called a college, an expensive, exclusive college, and a member of an organization at the college to which only women might belong, called a sorority, and it the most expensive and exclusive of the college's sororities."

"You stood high in your world," he said.

"Yes," I said.

"You had position, station, resources," he said.

"Yes," I said. "I was of what one spoke of as the upper classes."

"And you stood high in such classes," he said.

"Yes, Master," I said. "Quite high."

"Very high?" he said.

"Yes, Master."

"And what are you here?" he asked.

I touched my collar. "Kajira, Master," I said.

There was laughter from those about.

"Excellent," he said.

"Yes, Master," I said.

"You are now going to serve a man paga," he said.

"I know nothing of such things," I wept.

"Take the goblet in two hands," he said.

"Yes, Master," I said.

"Now back away a little," he said, "and spread your knees."

"I am not a pleasure slave!" I said.

"Are you white-silk?" he asked.

"No, Master," I said.

"Spread your knees," he said.

"Yes, Master," I said.

"Good," said Astrinax.

"Good," said Lykos.

"Now," said he in whose charge I was, "I could not tell you from a pleasure slave."

"See her turn red!" laughed one of the paga girls.

"Now take the goblet," said he in whose charge I was, "and press it firmly, deeply, into your lower belly."

The goblet was metal, and hard, and cold, and, within it, the paga swirled.

"Do not spill it, or you will be beaten," he said. "Now," said he, "lift the goblet, and touch it lightly to your left breast, and then to the right breast, and then lift it, and, looking at me over the rim, lick and kiss the goblet, slowly, softly, tenderly, lingeringly, and then, after a time, extend the goblet to me, arms extended, head down, bowed, between your extended arms."

"As a submitted woman!" I said.

"As far more than that," he said, "as one who is only a slave."

I felt him remove the goblet from my hands, and then I knelt back.

"Now," said he, "close your eyes, turn about, put your head to the floor, and place your hands behind you, wrists crossed."

I glanced, frightened, at the coil of cord on the table.

I then obeyed.

"Alcove her," said a fellow.

I remained for a time, eyes closed, as I had been placed, but I felt no bit of cord whipped about my wrists, fastening them together.

"You may open your eyes, Allison," said Astrinax, "and kneel at the table, as you will, knees together, if you wish."

I knelt up, blinking, just in time to see a frightened, stripped Kalligone, cast me a look over her left shoulder. Her hands were tied behind her. She was thrust, stumbling, toward an alcove. I did not think Master Desmond would be easy with her. He had, of course, paid his five tarsk-bits, and she, if wanted, would go with the drink.

"Masters!" I said.

"Do not be concerned," said Astrinax.

"He does not own you," Lykos reminded me.

"I was afraid he was going to alcove you," said Astrinax. "You are not an unattractive little slut."

"I hate him, I hate him, Masters!" I said.

"Put your tunic on," said Astrinax.

I did so, in humiliation, and rage. I feared I tore it a bit, in my haste. A typical Gorean free woman, I was sure, later, had I belonged to one, would have lashed me for that, for such clumsiness. The Lady Bina, on the other hand, would simply locate me a needle and some thread.

"I must be about my recruiting," said Astrinax.

"May fortune be with you," said Lykos, but he did not seem hopeful. It was growing late.

* * * *

"Dear friends," said a tavern's man, "we must, in ten Ehn, extinguish the lamps."

I was half asleep, lying beside the table.

I did not so much as glance at he in whose charge I was, Master Desmond, whom I supposed of the Metal Workers. He had returned from the alcove, after an Ahn or so, in a splendid mood. Certainly I well loathed him, he in whose charge I was. Might I not be better placed in the charge of another, but who? Jane, as I understood it, would report to Astrinax, and Eve to Lykos. Both, of course, as I, were owned by the Lady Bina. In Venna I had seen nothing of Lord Grendel or the blind Kur. To be sure, I had not sought them. A few Ehn after Master Desmond had emerged from the alcove, a slaver's man had entered, and freed Kalligone, who, perhaps as specified by Master Desmond, was to return on all fours to her cage, her silk clenched between her teeth. It would be removed, doubtless, before the cage door would shut behind her. Such cages are tiny, as I understood it, and this encourages the girls, for an additional reason, to be zealous in the alcoves, that they might strive to obtain a private master. Certainly Kalligone had approached Master Desmond without having been summoned. I supposed I should feel sorry for her. Rather, I was pleased that she was back in a cage. I hoped that it was small. In most, as I understood it, a girl can do little more than kneel, or sit or lie down, with her legs drawn closely up. In such constraints a girl is kept well apprised that she is a slave. To be sure, such a cage is luxurious compared to the "slave box," usually used for punishment. Even the proudest and most recalcitrant of slaves, usually a recent free woman, of high caste, is quickly broken in such a device, and emerges a readied, humbled, and trembling slave, fearful only that she will not be found fully pleasing, and in all ways. In the kitchen, at the eating house of Menon, we had our chains and mats. Menon was a kind man. He was often criticized for being too lenient with his girls. There was, of course, a whip in the kitchen.

"Probably we should return to the wagons," said Desmond.

"I have failed," said Astrinax, wearily. "We have offered good fee, but none seem interested in essaying the Voltai, at least as of now."

"Perhaps it is the season," said Lykos.

"Wake up, Allison," said Master Desmond.

"I am not asleep," I said, acidly, rising to my knees.

I had resolved never to speak to him again, unless, of course, commanded to do so. I was not eager to sustain the attentions of a displeased free person. They tend to be quick with instruments of correction, usually of braided leather.

"What is wrong?" he asked.

"Oh, nothing," I said.

"Good," he said.

"I do not like her tone of voice," said Lykos. "Beat her."

"Please, no, Master!" I said, quickly, frightened.

It had been made clear to me, quite clear, in the house of Tenalion, that a slave must speak to free persons as the slave she is. She is not to forget that. She is not a free woman, who might speak in any way she wishes. She is a slave, only that. A sharp or unpleasant word may bring her a lashing. Her voice, as her behavior, as a whole, must show that she is a slave, and knows herself such. She is to speak softly, politely, respectfully, humbly, and clearly, with excellent diction. She is not allowed the mumbling, the indecipherable gibberish, the ambiguities, the false starts and stops, the slovenliness allowed to the free woman. She is to address free persons always in the clear understanding that there is a collar on her neck, that she is subject to discipline, and that it will be inflicted upon her if he is found in any way displeasing.

"Please do not whip me," I said.

"Is there something wrong?" asked he in whose charge I was.

I looked away.

"Beat her," said Lykos.

"Please, no!" I said.

"Did she not fail to answer a question?" asked Lykos.

I knew Eve was to report to Lykos. I did not envy her.

"What is wrong?" inquired Master Desmond.

"How do you think I feel," I asked, "kneeling down, my eyes closed, my head to the floor, my hands behind me, wrists crossed, and then you abandon me."

"And alcove the girl, Kalligone," laughed Astrinax.

"You were not abandoned," said he in whose charge I was. "Astrinax and Lykos were here."

"And no one cares how you feel, girl," said Lykos. Again, I did not envy Eve.

"Have you no interest in my body?" I asked he in whose charge I was.

"Of course your body is of some interest," said he in whose charge I was. "For example, your ankles shackle well. Of greater interest is the whole of you, which I think it might be interesting to own."

"Master," I said, uncertainly.

"To own the whole of you," he said, "as a slave is owned."

"So completely?" I said.

"Of course," he said.

"That goes far beyond law," I said.

"No," he said. "It is in law, as well, that the whole slave is owned."

"I see," I said.

"She needs a beating," said Lykos.

"Quite possibly," said he in whose keeping I was.

"No!" I said.

"She is a trim little thing," said Lykos, "and I suspect, with a bit of proper stimulation, she would be writhingly helpless."

"Surely not!" I said. To be sure, what did I know of such things? I did sense that if he in whose keeping I was were to touch me, I might cry out helplessly, and, a grateful, shameless slave, press myself piteously to him.

But I hated him!

He had knelt me, eyes closed, head to the floor, wrists crossed behind me, awaiting their pinioning, and then, when I had been released from this custody, I had seen him thrust a stripped, frightened, thonged Kalligone before him to an alcove!

I was quite angry.

How I had been treated!

I resolved to speak as little to Master Desmond thenceforth as possible. I would have to be subtle, of course. The lash is unpleasant. Let him then, over the coming days, puzzle over my coolness, my distance, my aloofness. Surely a free woman could make a man so suffer. Why then might not a slave? Let him try to fathom the mystery of my remoteness, my indifference, my troubling, inexplicable detachment. Perhaps he would then, eventually, regret his treatment of me!

"Allison," said he in whose charge I was, "I have not been fully satisfied with your behavior, as of late."

"Please do not whip me," I said.

"You are hereby sentenced to the modality of the mute slave," he said. "You are herewith denied permission to speak. You are silenced. You may not, even, in language, beg for permission to speak. As when gagged, one whimper will serve for 'yes' and two for 'no'. Do you understand?"

I looked at him with misery.

I would not even be permitted to speak to Jane or Eve, or even to the Lady Bina or Lord Grendel, unless I was commanded to do so, which commands were highly unlikely of issuance, as free persons tend to be consistent where the discipline of slaves is in question. Indeed, if I were to attempt to circumvent the discipline of Master Desmond by an appeal to Lord Grendel, I had no doubt he would lash me well, and if I were to attempt to appeal to the Lady Bina I was sure she would make inquiries as to what was appropriate under such circumstances, and then, when informed, as custom recommended, would have me lashed as well.

"Do you understand?" he asked.

I whimpered once.

* * * *

The road here was narrow, and rough.

I looked up, at the stone channel of the aqueduct, some hundred feet over my head.

We had left Venna four days ago.

The first two days Jane, Eve, and I had been chained to the back of the last wagon. This was done by each of us having her hands braceleted before her, and a chain run from the bracelets to a ring on the back of the wagon, three chains, three rings, this permitting us to walk abreast.

On the first day, as we were attached to the wagon, Jane and Eve had been in consternation that I could not speak with them. "Speak to us!" said Jane. "We are your friends!" I could do little more than shake my head, tears running from my eyes. "I do not understand," said Jane. "What is wrong?"

Eve tried even to communicate in our native tongue, which you would understand to be a barbarian language. Forgive me, Masters and Mistresses, it is, of course, a barbarian language! But she was seized by Trachinos, cuffed brutally, and thrown to the dirt, in her bracelets. "Gorean!" he said. "Gorean, slave slut!" "Forgive me, Master!" she wept, kneeling and pressing her lips, again and again, to his feet. It is a common placatory behavior of slaves. Slaves are expected to speak in the language of their masters. This helps them remember that they are slaves. Too, of course, the masters wish to understand whatever slaves may say. This is an additional form of control, and surveillance. Trachinos then fastened Eve's bracelets to the ring chain, and turned away. "Please, forgive me, Master!" she called after him. "So," said Jane, "even when we are alone, we must speak in Gorean!" I nodded. I was pleased that she had said that in Gorean. We were learning well that we were slaves! "Can you not say something to us?" asked Jane. I shook my head, negatively, tears running down my cheeks. Jane was already on her chain. "What did you do?" asked Jane. I shook my head, again. "Surely," she said, "you may use language to petition to speak." I shook my head, again. Jane looked at me, disbelievingly. Commonly, of course, a slave will have a standing permission to speak. This permission, of course, is revocable at will, by the master or the mistress. Thus, in a very real sense, the slave requires permission to speak. This is similar to clothing. Usually, the slave will have a standing permission to clothe herself, if a slave garment can be dignified in such a way. On the other hand, some masters require a slave, each day, to explicitly request permission to clothe herself. This tends to impress her bondage on a girl. If she does not receive the permission, of course, she may not clothe herself. Her clothing, like her speech, is at the discretion of the master. Some masters expect a slave, each day, as in the matter of clothing, to request permission to speak that day. If she does not receive that permission, she may not speak. "May I clothe myself, Master?" "You may." "May I speak, Master?" "You may." What Jane had in mind, of course, were the usual formulas by means of which a slave, denied speech, may request to speak. Some typical petitionary formulas would be "I beg to speak," "I would speak," and "May I speak, Master?" The common understanding here is that the slave requires the master's permission to clothe herself and to speak. She is, after all, a slave. The master's permission is, actually, implicitly involved in many aspects of the slave's life. To be sure, most of these permissions are standing permissions. And much depends on the particular master and slave. For example, it is almost universal that the slave may not leave the domicile without requesting permission, and it is often required that she will state the purpose of her departure and make clear her expected time of return. The master will be the first to partake of food, and his permission may be required before the slave is permitted to feed. The slave will commonly kneel when a free person enters the room, and, if knelt, will usually await permission to rise. If a slave is ordered nude to the furs she will remain there until the master sees fit to join her, or, if he wishes, put her about, say, her domestic labors. Sometimes the slave, nude and bound, must await the pleasure of the master. This can well heat her.

I heard, ahead, at the first wagon, the voice of Trachinos. The wagons were soon to move. Both Jane and Eve, in their brief tunics and close-fitting collars, were already attached to the back of the wagon, the last wagon, each by a chain looping up from their braceleted wrists to a wagon ring, bolted into the back of the wagon. I was with them, my wrists braceleted before my body, but was not yet on the wagon chain.

I heard steps approaching.

It was he in whose keeping I was! I instantly knelt, and lifted my braceleted wrists to him, pathetically, tears on my cheeks. I pointed to my mouth with my pinioned hands, and whimpered, pleadingly. It was only last night, in the paga tavern, that I had been put in the modality of the mute slave, but almost from the first moment I was suffering. I had struggled again and again last night, in the tavern, on the way back to the wagons, when my shackling was being attended to, to make clear my contrition, and my resolve to be more pleasing. I so desperately wanted to speak to him, to return myself to his favor, such as it might be, to express my shame and sorrow at my overweening, unconscionable pride, my insolence. I so wanted to prostrate myself before him, to lie before him on my belly, to cover his feet with kisses, to beg his forgiveness. I was in a collar! I had failed it! Did I think I was a free woman? I was no longer a free woman, if I had ever been a free woman. I was a slave, and knew myself a slave. And yet I had been a poor slave. I had not been pleasing! Did I not know I belonged in my collar? Yes, I knew I belonged in it. I had learned that well on Gor. Did I not know then how to behave in a collar? Yes, I knew! How then could I have behaved so ignorantly, so foolishly, so stupidly, so badly? I pleaded as I could, without words. But my protestations had been ignored. Master Desmond had declined to relent. It is hard to make clear, one supposes, to one who has not been put in such a modality, one who has never been "gagged by the master's will," how this deprivation can so sorely affect a woman, particularly a slave, the most helpless and vulnerable of women. We are not men, with their large bodies, their strength, their ferocity, their callousness, their speed, and power. We are different, so different! What have we, in our collars, what means, to win our ways? We have our slightness, our softness, our wit, our beauty, and our speech. Is not our speech our delight, our pleasure, our joy, our recreation, our weapon, our instrument, our gift? Is it not that whereby we can make known our feelings, our hopes, and fears; that whereby we can express ourselves, plead our causes, make known our wants, needs, and desires, that by means of which we can petition, influence, and wheedle? Is it not that by means of which we may beg for mercy, hope to be heard and understood, hope to placate the large, dangerous beasts who own us? Without it we are muchly helpless; without it how even can we best surrender and submit; without it how can we best acknowledge and serve our masters? Without it how can we well profess our love?

I knelt before him, pathetically, tears on my cheeks. I pointed to my mouth, with my braceleted hands, and whimpered, pleadingly.

He stepped back.

I threw myself to my belly before him, and reached with my closely linked hands, to seize his ankle, that I might hold it, and press my lips to his feet, kissing them, again and again. Do men not enjoy having women so before them, as helpless, prostrated slaves? But he seized the linkage between the bracelets and pulled me to my knees, and then to my feet, and then snapped the wagon chain on my bracelets. I whimpered, pleadingly, but he had turned away.

Again I had failed to please him, a free man.

* * * *

I looked up, at the stone channel of the aqueduct, some hundred feet over my head.

Such structures are majestic, the products of, to me, almost incomprehensible feats of engineering, and I had wanted to express my wonder and awe at them, their size and massiveness, their efficiency, their beauty, the loveliness of the sky and mountains behind them, but I was not permitted to speak.

How helpless and alone, how miserable, one soon is, if placed in the modality of the mute slave!

He in whose care I was, and the others, the free persons, ignored me. Would it not have been more merciful if they had lashed me? I was no longer on the wagon chain, nor were Jane or Eve. They, at least, were kind to me, and spoke to me, though I could not speak back. They no longer spoke of running away. The country now was lonely. The small villages were far behind. The terrain grew steeper, and more formidable. Twice we had heard, at night, when we were shackled in the slave wagon, from somewhere back in the mountains, the roar of a larl. During the day we remained close to the wagons.

We had left Venna four days ago.

The last night at Venna we had visited the paga tavern, The Kneeling Slave. Master Astrinax had been unsuccessful in his recruiting. I had apparently displeased he in whose care I was, for I had been put in the modality of the mute slave. A tavern's man was extinguishing the lamps.

The masters were preparing to rise from the table when suddenly a flat, linear object of metal clattered, ringing, on the table.

"That is the sword of Trachinos, he of Turia," said a fearsome voice, that of a large, bearded fellow, clad in the brown of the Peasantry.

But I feared this was no Peasant.

Certainly he carried no staff, no great bow, no sheaf of long arrows, at his left hip.

The blade was the gladius.

"That blade," said the fellow, pointing to it, "is for hire."

"We are hiring," said Astrinax.

"You are far from Turia," said Lykos.

Turia, I knew, was far to the south, even beyond the equator.

"What brings you this far north?" asked Lykos.

"Sword pleasure," said the stranger.

I gathered then he was a soldier of fortune, a mercenary, or perhaps a fugitive.

"Your accent," said Astrinax, "does not sound Turian."

"Do you dispute me?" inquired the fellow.

"Not at all," said Astrinax.

"I might," said Lykos.

"Outside?" asked the stranger.

"If you wish," said Lykos.

"Whose girl is this?" asked Trachinos.

"She belongs to a woman, the Lady Bina, one supposes of Ar," said Astrinax.

"In that tunic?" laughed Trachinos.

"Her Mistress might wish to put her out to men, for girl use," said Astrinax.

"Good," said Trachinos.

I trembled, and looked down. I was afraid to meet his eyes. Too, some masters do not permit their girls to meet their eyes, unless commanded to do so.

"She cannot speak," said he in whose charge I was.

"You have cut out her tongue?" said Trachinos.

"No," said he in whose keeping I was. "She has merely been placed in the modality of the mute slave."

"Is that true, girl?" asked Trachinos.

It was surely a test. I kept my head down. I whimpered once.

I sensed Astrinax was relieved. He in whose charge I was was impassive. Lykos had moved his robes a little. I could then see the hilt of his gladius.

"She is pretty," said Trachinos. This pleased me. I received few compliments. To be sure, I knew I was attractive. Otherwise a collar would not have been put on my neck.

Still I had no desire to lick and kiss the whip of Trachinos, though I would do it fearfully, and well, if it were pressed to my lips.

"Can you handle a wagon?" asked Astrinax.

"But she does not have much hair," said Trachinos.

"There are two others chained to a slave post, in our wagon camp," said Astrinax.

"I know," said Trachinos.

"You have looked upon them?" said Astrinax.

"Yes," said Trachinos. "They are pretty."

"You seem to know something of us," said Lykos.

"I am told you are going into the Voltai," said Trachinos.

"Yes," said Astrinax.

"That is why you have few fee takers," said Trachinos.

"We will pay well," said Astrinax.

"For what purpose are you entering the Voltai?" asked Trachinos.

"That has not been disclosed to us," said Astrinax.

"Does it matter, if you are well paid?" asked Lykos.

"No," said Trachinos.

"It seems you have brought a sword to the table," said Lykos.

"You are going into the Voltai," grinned Trachinos.

"We need drivers," said Astrinax.

"I can drive, and so, too," said Trachinos, "can my fellow, Akesinos." He indicated a fellow standing in the shadows, just within the large double doors of the tavern.

"Forty copper tarsks each week," said Astrinax.

"That is good fee, indeed," said Trachinos.

"Perhaps you think us rich?" said Lykos.

"A lowly driver does not inquire into such things," said Trachinos.

"You are aware there are dangers in the Voltai?" said Lykos.

"I do not fear them," said Trachinos.

"He is our man!" said Astrinax.

Lykos rose to his feet, and thrust his robe back, behind his shoulder. He indicated the blade, flat, on the table. "You can use that?" he asked.

"Let us make trial of the matter," said Trachinos.

"That is not necessary," said Astrinax.

"Here is the last lamp," said the tavern's man. "The tavern is closing."

Trachinos, not taking his eyes from Lykos, bent down and retrieved his blade. It seemed almost small in his grasp. He was a very large man.

"Is blood to be shed?" inquired Trachinos.

"Certainly not!" said Astrinax.

"If you wish," said Lykos.

"Surely outside, outside, noble Masters," said the tavern's man.

"Do not extinguish the lamp," said he in whose charge I was, he who had silenced me.

"Please, Masters!" protested the tavern's man.

"Who shall move first?" asked Trachinos.

"I," said Lykos.

I backed away, on my knees.

I could not follow the movement of the blades, so sudden, so swift they were, but, a moment later, I realized they had crossed six times, from the sound.

"Well?" grinned Trachinos.

"Hire him," said Lykos.

"I vouch for my fellow, Akesinos," said Trachinos. "He has killed four men."

Lykos sheathed his blade, and nodded.

"We leave tomorrow, at dawn," said Astrinax.

"Whose caravan is it?" asked Trachinos. "Who is in charge, who stands the fee?"

"You will report to this man, Astrinax," said Lykos.

"Very well," said Trachinos.

I had now regained my composure, after my withdrawal from the vicinity of the blade engagement, and was now kneeling beside the table.

I sensed I knelt within the regard of the stranger.

I did not look at him.

Then I felt his boot put against my upper right arm, and I was thrust to my side on the floor. "And what of this little vulo?" asked Trachinos. "Is she with the wagons?"

He had not hurt me, nor had he intended to. His action had been no more than a way of calling attention to me, as a slave might be indicated.

None of the men at the table objected.

I, of course, was well reminded, first, of my bondage, and, secondly, of the power of men, who might do with us, with women, if they pleased, what they pleased.

"Yes," said Astrinax.

"Then her Mistress, as well?" asked Trachinos.

"Yes," said Astrinax. "The Lady Bina."

"And she is a she-tarsk, is she not?" asked Trachinos.

"Not at all," said Astrinax. "She is thought to be marvelously, extraordinarily beautiful."

The Lady Bina, perhaps in her vanity, or perhaps because she was not natively Gorean, was often careless in her veiling. I recalled that from as long ago as the Tarsk Market. Too, like many beautiful free women, I suspect she enjoyed seeing her effect on men. Certainly I, on my former world, before I was collared, had very much enjoyed that sort of thing, a form of amusing play, exciting boys and men and leading them on, and then, when well reassured of my attractiveness, pretending to dismay or annoyance, putting them from me, dismissing them. Then, of course, I was not in a slave collar. It is my suspicion that the free women of my former world and those of Gor, forgive me, Mistresses, are much the same. Do you not enjoy such games? And are you not, as much as we, prepared upon occasion to put your beauty to use, to barter it for position and wealth? For example, it is my supposition that, in the markets, and on the boulevards, and elsewhere, handsome slavers, perhaps disguised in the robes of rich Merchants, do not encounter with you in fact the difficulties which one might expect them to encounter in theory. Forgive me, Mistresses.

"Excellent," said Trachinos.

He then, with his fellow, left the tavern. We followed them shortly, and the lamp was extinguished behind us, and the large double doors were closed and barred.

"I feel safer now," said Astrinax.

"Do you?" asked Lykos.

"It would be better, of course," said Astrinax, "if we could have had two or three more."

"I do not trust Trachinos," said Lykos.

"To be perfectly frank, my dear Lykos," said Astrinax, "I do not trust you, either."

"Oh?" smiled Lykos.

"No," said Astrinax. "What do I know of you?"

"Probably little more than I of you," said Lykos.

"It is hard to get men to go into the Voltai," said Astrinax.

"It is perhaps the season," said Lykos.

"No," said Astrinax, "it is the Voltai."

* * * *

We had left Venna four days ago.

With the wagons were three slaves, Jane, Eve, and Allison, the latter not permitted to speak, not even to request permission to speak. One free woman was with the wagons, the Lady Bina. There were five free men with the wagons, Astrinax, who was much as our caravan master; Desmond, thought to be a

Metal Worker, in whose care I was; Lykos, whom I supposed a mercenary; fierce, bearded Trachinos, clearly skilled with the gladius, at whose background I could scarcely guess; and his fellow, thin, reticent Akesinos, who spoke little, but watched much. And somewhere there were perhaps two beasts, though, as far as I could tell, they were not now with the wagons.

It was now near the Tenth Ahn.

The wagons were stopped.

"It is the six hundredth pasang stone," said Astrinax, indicating a marker, across the road from one of the arched pylons supporting the aqueduct. "It is here we must wait, for a guide." I had been interested to learn that pasang stones are found on many Gorean roads; commonly they contain a number, and an indication of a direction and destination. For example, on the Vennan road, as it is called in Ar, a stone is erected midway between Ar and Venna, lists a number, and points in two directions. Closer to Ar, the number lists the pasangs to Ar, with an indication of the direction of Ar. Closer to Venna, the number lists the pasangs to Venna, with an indication of the direction of Venna. To be sure, there are many varieties of pasang stones, and some list only the distance to a given point, as though the road had but one destination. Many roads, particularly small ones, lack pasang stones altogether. Either they are too short or too unimportant, or, perhaps, it is supposed the stones are unnecessary, given the supposed familiarity of the terrain to any who might be in the vicinity. Here, beside the Vennan aqueduct, the stones contained only a number, and no further indications. This was because here the pasang stones measured the length of the aqueduct from Ar, and the pasang stones were largely a convenience to the caste of Builders, concerned with the care of the aqueduct.

I did not know how Astrinax knew we were to stop here, or that a guide would appear.

I did know he commonly held the late watch when we camped.

Having shared the domicile of the Lady Bina and Lord Grendel in Ar, I probably had a better sense of the purport of this journey than the free men with the party. Surely it had to do with returning the blind Kur to his fellows. Whether it had a purpose beyond that I did not know. I did know that there had occasionally been conversations between the Lady Bina and the blind Kur, through the intermediation of the translator, when Lord Grendel had been absent. At such times I would be dispatched on one errand or another. The Lady Bina, as I indicated earlier, had a great respect for, and admiration of, what she regarded as true Kurii, in which category she placed the blind Kur, and from which category she excluded Lord Grendel. This went back, apparently, to a remote, metal world. Accordingly she endorsed the scheme of Lord Grendel's assisting the blind Kur to regain his haunts in the mountains. On the other hand, she, herself, was reluctant to exchange the delights and comforts of Ar for the hardships of some distant, possibly hazardous journey far from civilization. She had little sense of the risks to which she might be exposed as a defenseless woman in Ar, a barbarian lacking a Home Stone. Lord Grendel, however, had informed her, despite his usual complaisance, that she would accompany him, if necessary, in chains. "I see," she had said, annoyed. I was intrigued by the thought of the Lady Bina in chains. I sometimes thought she did not understand the extent to which she was actually in the power of Lord Grendel. If she felt his chains on her pretty limbs it would doubtless be clearer to her. I thought she would look lovely in chains. But then does not any woman? In any event, she later withdrew her objections to the journey, and, indeed, soon seemed eager to be on her way. This change in disposition followed, I think, the aforementioned conversations with her large, savage house guest, the blind Kur. She it was who contacted Astrinax, possibly through the eating house of Menon, with which establishment she was familiar, and engaged him to assist in the venture, buying tharlarion and wagons, putting in supplies, and such.

Lykos was standing on the wagon bench of the first wagon, with a Builder's glass, scanning the horizon.

"What do you see?" asked Astrinax.

"Nothing," said Lykos, closing the glass.

"How long must we wait here?" asked Desmond.

"I do not know," said Astrinax.

"But you do know we must wait?" said Desmond.

"Yes," said Astrinax.

Jane, Eve, and I, the wagons halted, had come forward. When Master Desmond turned about, I knelt near him, that I might be before him. This required courage, more courage each day. I shook with fear. I knew that I had been found displeasing. I did not wish to be intrusive, and be punished. Too, I had the natural temerity of the slave before the free person. If a slave lacks this temerity, it is something she soon learns. A slave may desire her master, long for him, want more than anything to surrender herself wholly and unquestioningly to him, ache for him with all the flames of love, yearn to submit herself to him as no more than a negligible, meaningless, helpless, loving beast, be willing to die for him, but, too, she may well fear him, for the whip is his, and he is master.

But I was desperate.

Please, oh, Master, I thought, be kind. See Allison! She is here, before you. See her!

I looked up at him.

I could hardly catch my breath before him. Had I been able to speak, I would scarcely have been able to form words. Surely I would have stammered. I fear my lip trembled.

How different he was from the men of Earth!

How helpless, and slave, I was, on my knees before him.

I wanted him to pay me attention. I wanted him to find me acceptable once more, as he had before, as the animal I was, a slave, but perhaps one of some interest. Please, oh, Master, I thought, let me speak, let me speak! I have so much I want to say, so much I want to tell you, so much for which to beg forgiveness! Yes, I so wanted to be permitted to speak, and yet, now, some days since my sentencing, I feared even to beg mutely for the restoration of that coveted privilege, lest even that might displease him. It would be done, the sentence's rescinding, if at all, at his wish, not mine. But as much as I wished to be allowed to speak, and as much as that deprivation cost me in helplessness and misery, what hurt me most was his neglect, his ignoring of me. I think I would have rejoiced had I been cuffed or kicked, or tied to a ring and beaten, for then, at least, I would have known myself as a reality, however negligible and contemptible, in his world. Even a girl in a collar wants to be seen, to be recognized, and noticed, even be it to no greater extent than being mocked, humiliated, and scorned.

Jane and Eve were present, with me, near the first wagon.

He turned away.

"Please, Master!" cried Jane, falling to her knees. "Master!" said Eve.

Master Desmond turned to regard them.

"Please, Master," said Jane. "Please permit Allison to speak! I do not know what she did, but I am sure she is sorry. She has suffered much. Please let her speak!"

"Yes, Master," said Eve. "We beg it for her, as she cannot speak! Please let Allison speak."

"She is only a slave, a collar girl, as we! Please be kind, Master!" said Jane.

"Forgive her, Master," said Eve. "She is miserable! She is penitent! Please, Master!"

"It seems," said Master Desmond, "that you two wish to be placed in the modality of the mute slave, as well."

"No, Master!" said Jane.

"No, no, Master!" wept Eve.

"There is a wide place here, a clearing, for wagons," said Master Desmond. "We are not the first wagons to stop here, nor will we be the last. Work parties camp here, perhaps others, hunting parties, and such. There will be a well about. Find it. Fetch water, water the tharlarion, and rub them down."

"Yes, Master," said Jane, leaping up.

"Yes, Master," said Eve, leaping to her feet, as well.

He then turned to me.

He was looking upon me!

"Your friends are foolish," he said.

I made a tiny sound, a grateful, single sound. Tears were in my eyes.

Had they thought to sway a Gorean male? Had they no sense of the discipline under which their chain sister had been placed? How dared they think of interceding, of interfering? Did they not know the risk they undertook? I supposed not. Perhaps they did not yet understand they were slaves. Had they not yet ascertained the significance of their collars, what it meant to be in a collar? Many masters, I was sure, would have had them bound and lashed for their temerity. The will of masters is not to be questioned. The head is to be bowed before the master's will.

"I would not have thought," said he, "that a slave such as you would have had friends."

I did not understand his words. How was it that he might think so of me? Ela, I could not speak!

Then I recalled that Astrinax, now with the caravan, long ago, had arranged my purchase from Menon, on behalf of the gambling house. I recalled both Astrinax and Menon had thought I would be a good buy for such a place, a girl willing to wheedle and smile, to pretend to emotions of excitement and enthusiasm, one who could adroitly feign dismay and sympathy, one who would ply customers with drink, urge them to remain at the tables, encourage them to recklessness in wagering, though it might lead to the loss of estates and honor, to shame, vagrancy, and destitution.

But surely they must realize that I was in a collar, that I had no choice in such matters!

Did they want me to do such things poorly? Such duties were easy, and silken. Did they want me to risk the fields, the laundries, the public kitchens, the stables, the mills?

And I remembered the test of the candy.

Of course, I would have stolen the candy, if such might have been accomplished with impunity. What intelligent girl with her wits about her would have forgone such an opportunity? What rational girl, in the conjectured circumstances, would not have done so?

And Astrinax had doubtless brought he in whose charge I was, Master Desmond, into fee!

"Put your head to the dirt," said Master Desmond. "Keep it there for ten Ehn, and then you may rise, and do as you wish."

He had not even seen fit to assign me a duty!

As I knelt so, different people passed me, Jane and Eve, with their buckets, and one or two of the free men.

When I rose up, I was crying.

I walked along the side the wagons, toward the back of the wagons. It was hot. Usually there is no one there. It is usually a good place to hide, to be alone. Suddenly I stopped, for, visible from where I stood, under the high channel of the aqueduct, on a distant hill, I saw a sharp flicker of light.

"Ho, slave," said a voice behind me, that of fierce, bearded Trachinos.

I turned about.

A slave grows accustomed to being looked upon as a slave, having her lineaments frankly appraised, being undressed with a glance, and such.

I was taken in his arms.

He then took a free man's liberties with the lips of a helpless slave. I whimpered, a weak, half-intended protest. I feared the responsiveness of my body. How weak we are, how needful we are, once a collar is fastened on our neck! Would you be different, noble Mistresses, were one fastened on your neck? Of course, for you are not slaves! Once before, at a night camp, our second day from Venna, he had put his hands on me, as well, and thrust me, standing, back against one of the mighty columns, or pylons, supporting the aqueduct. Astrinax had summoned him to the wagons, and, when he had flung me from him, he had had but a taste of slave.

"Yes," he grinned, now holding me out, a tiny bit, from him, "you would be a hot little tasta."

I squirmed a little, but was helpless in his grasp. How could he say such a thing? Surely I had given him no satisfaction, or only a little. I was a collared female. How could I help such things?

Do we not belong to males, such males?

There was sweat on his arms, and my tunic was damp from the heat.

"What did you see?" he whispered.

I shook my head, frightened. Surely he knew I stood under the sentence the mute slave.

He thrust me back against the broad, high wagon wheel, and I saw the point of a knife at my lips.

"Ah, yes," he said. "You are silenced." He then said, "It is difficult to speak when one is silenced. And, of course, it is difficult to speak well, if one's tongue is slit. And it is impossible to speak, if one's tongue is removed. Do you understand?"

I whimpered, once.

"And," said he, holding the blade crosswise, I felt it touch my throat, under the collar, "it is quite impossible, as well, if one's throat is cut. Do you understand?"

I whimpered, again, once, desperately, plaintively.

He then turned about, and left me.

I looked back, beneath the loftiness of the aqueduct, to the hills in the distance. There was no longer a flicker of light.

"Ho, Astrinax," called Lykos, ahead in the wagons.

I, and others, including Jane and Eve, went to the first wagon, where Lykos was again standing on the wagon bench, the glass of the Builders once more in his hands.

"What is it?" said Astrinax.

"I am not sure," said Lykos. "Join me. See what you make of it."

"I see nothing," said Astrinax.

Lykos took back the glass. "It is gone," he said.

"What was it?" asked Astrinax.

"Something alive, more than one, several perhaps," said Lykos.

"Larls?" asked Astrinax.

"I do not think so," said Lykos.

I noted that Akesinos, the fellow of Trachinos, had joined the group. I had not noticed his arrival. I did not know how long he had been there. But Akesinos was the sort of fellow who might be somewhere, and not be noticed.

"The shadows in the Voltai can be deceptive," said Akesinos.

"It was doubtless a trick of the light," said Lykos.

"It is no trick of the light behind us, nor to the left, approaching," said Master Desmond.

"Dust," said Astrinax, shading his eyes.

"Wagons," said Lykos, handing the glass of the Builders to Astrinax.

From the left a small group of riders, on bipedalian saddle tharlarion, were approaching.

There were five in the group. Each carried a lengthy lance.

"Tal!" called Master Desmond to the leader of the small group. The wagons, down the road, behind us, approaching from the direction of Venna, might not reach the six hundredth pasang stone until dark.

"Tal!" called the leader of the riders cheerfully to Master Desmond.

"They are hunters," said Astrinax. "Wild tarsk, Voltai tarsk." The Voltai tarsk, as some forest tarsk, are much larger than the common tarsk. They are often ten to twelve hands at the shoulder. The beast tends to be territorial and aggressive. It is particularly dangerous when wounded.

"Racing tharlarion," said Astrinax, considering the bipedalian mounts of the newcomers.

"No," said Lykos. "Racing tharlarion are longer-legged, and finer-boned."

"True," said Astrinax.

"Those are rugged, powerful animals," said Lykos.

"Hunting tharlarion," said Astrinax.

"Consider the saddles," said Desmond, "there are five boots to a side, as for javelins."

"So?" said Astrinax.

"Perhaps then," said Desmond, "cavalry tharlarion, war tharlarion."

"Let us make festival," said the leader of the newcomers. "You have meat and paga, I trust, and we have coin, though doubtless your hospitality may be depended upon, and wagons approach, as well, doubtless well supplied."

"Welcome," called Astrinax.

"Tonight we drink," said the leader of the hunters. "Tomorrow we hunt."

"And tomorrow night," said one of his fellows, "who knows?"

I felt slightly chilled, even in the day's heat, and despite the newcomer's jollity. The results of addressing oneself to the pursuit of wild tarsk, I suspected, were difficult to anticipate.

I trusted such animals would not be in the vicinity of the wagons.

"This is a strange juncture for festival, the clearing at the six hundredth pasang stone, is it not?" asked Trachinos.

"It would seem so," said Desmond.

Trachinos then turned away.

The newcomers, whom I took to be hunters, had dismounted, and were conversing with Astrinax, and Lykos.

Far down the road, behind us, one could make out a darkness, some dust rising from the road.

Master Desmond, shading his eyes, watched it for a time. He then turned to me. His eyes on me, I immediately knelt, and lowered my head.

It is appropriate for a female slave, gazed upon.

"Lift your head," he said.

I did so, but feared to meet his eyes.

"You may speak," he said.

I then looked at him, disbelievingly, my eyes wide.

"I saw you in the arms of Trachinos," he said.

"Forgive me, Master," I whispered. It seemed I could hardly form words. In a moment I was sure that this would pass. How strange it seemed, after several days, to hear my own voice.

"I think you will do very well for what I have in mind," he said.

"There was a flickering of light, in the hills," I said.

"I know," he said.

"I tried to resist," I said.

"But you were not entirely successful," he said.

"I am a slave," I said.

"It is interesting what the collar does to a female," he said.

"Yes, Master," I said.

Certainly it informs us that we are females, and properties, the properties of men.

"Perhaps Trachinos will buy you," he said.

"I would rather be purchased by another," I whispered.

"You once served in a gambling house, did you not?" he said.

"Yes," I said, "on the Street of Chance, in Ar."

"Good," he said.

"Thank you for permitting me to speak," I said.

"I may have need of you, tonight," he said.

Chapter Nineteen

"A kiss, barbarian slut," said the driver, reaching for me.
"You have had your kiss, Master," I laughed. "I must now serve another."
"You should be lashed to the bone," he said, but then fell to his side, asleep.
"Paga!" called another driver.
"I hasten, Master!" I said, and conveyed the damp, bulging bota to him.
"To me!" called another.
I hurried to him.
"What is your use fee?" he asked.
"That would have to be arranged with my Mistress," I said.
"Mistress?" said a fellow, drunkenly.
"Yes, Master," I said. "I am a woman's slave."
"Your tunic," said a fellow, "is that of a man's slave."
"I must be tunicked as my Mistress wishes," I said.
"She is renting you out, to make coin," said a fellow. "What is her price for your use?"
I hurried away from him.
"Give me the bota!" cried a driver, and pulled it away from me.
"Master!" I protested.
"Here, by the fire!" called a fellow. "On your back! Lift your right knee. Roll over, in the dirt! On your back now, squirm, to your side, draw your knees up. On your back! Arch your back!"
It was hard to know what I might look like to them, half in the firelight, half in the shadows.

Men enjoy mastering kajirae.

"Stand!" said a fellow. "Examination position."

"Please, no, Masters!" I said.

One is so helpless in that position!

"Good," said a fellow.

"Oh!" I said.

"A silver tarsk!" said a fellow.

I was startled that he had said this.

"It is a barbarian," said another.

"So less," said the fellow.

Of course, I thought, a barbarian, so less!

"Pass her about," said a fellow.

"No, Masters!" I begged.

Two men seized me and I was put to my back in the dirt, beside the fire. I felt my ankles seized.

Then a fellow was pulled away from me. Then another.

"Ho, lads," said he in whose keeping I was. "It is late. It is time for her shackling."

"No!" cried several fellows.

By the hair, he drew me to my feet.

"Is she to be so tunicked, so collared, and put to serving so, and for two Ahn, and then simply to be wafted away, as might be a tower slave?"

"She is a woman's slave," Master Desmond reminded them.

"See that face and figure," said a fellow, "those legs, and ankles."

"Nonetheless," said Master Desmond.

He kept my head at his hip, his right hand in my hair.

"She is a little thin," said a fellow.

"Obviously," said Master Desmond.

Many Goreans, I knew, preferred a little more body in a woman.

Still, I was sure, few of them would have any objection to this slave.

With the wagons there had been four slaves, former state slaves, as it turned out, purchased cheaply in Ar. But these were chained to a tree, off in the shadows, a guard set over them. Apparently these, for some reason, were not for the use of the drivers. I did not understand why such slaves would be brought into the Voltai. Indeed, I was not clear as to the reason the arrived caravan might be here. It was not a Builder's caravan, with its tools and work crews.

"Leave her here," said a fellow, staggering to his feet. He had a knife half drawn from its sheath.

Happily, he was drawn back by one of the other drivers. None of them were entitled to my use. None owned me, nor did he in whose care I was.

The fellow who had half drawn the knife was not alone in his disgruntlement. It is common for a camp girl in a feast or festival, after a time, to be handed about, from fellow to fellow.

"Line up!" called he in whose care I was. "A last kiss."

There were some fifteen or twenty drivers, tending the ten or so wagons which had come to the clearing shortly after dark.

I was stood, and he in whose charge I was corded my wrists behind my back.

Then, in the helplessness of a tethered kajira, I was enfolded into the arms of each, one after the other, some gently, some fiercely, some closely, some more closely.

"Kiss well, Allison," said he in whose charge I was.

I then, helpless, was well reminded of my hatred for this brute who could deny me speech, who could punish me, who could do much what he wished with me, and would, and to whom I suspected I belonged.

"Consider her lips," said he in whose charge I was, "are they not helplessly moist, open, soft, sweet, and full, yielding, and ready, and eager, just right for a collar slut."

"Ah!" said a fellow.

"Look there," said he in whose charge I was. "Did you not detect a movement of her small body within that tunic?"

There was laughter.

"I am sure I saw a movement of her thighs," said he in whose charge I was.

"No, no," I said, but my protest was futile, and undecipherable, mumbled, beneath the pressure of the lips pressed to mine.

"Enough," said Master Desmond, pleasantly, and pulled me back, and forced my head down, it held by the hair, again, to his right hip, and then, the slave in leading position, her hands fastened behind her, tied with a short cord, took his way from the fire.

Behind us, the men began to sing songs.

"The master of the wagons," said Master Desmond, "is of Ar. His name is Pausanias. The leader of the hunters, or supposed hunters, is Kleomenes. Pausanias spent the evening in card-sport, with Kleomenes."

His hand was still tight, almost absently so, in my hair.

"I would be interested in seeing the cards," he said.

I did not understand his interest there.

"You are familiar with card-sport from the gambling house, are you not?" he asked.

"No," I said. "I did not know those games. Some were played at tables in the back."

There are different decks of cards, containing different numbers of cards, with different markings, and such. The most common deck of cards is thick, and contains a hundred cards. For the most part there is little standardization on Gor, and many things differ from city to city. One game does tend to be standardized, or relatively standardized, however, and that is kaissa. The kaissa of Turia is apparently identical with that of Ar, and that with that of Port Kar, Ko-ro-ba, Anango, Tabor, the island ubarates, and so on. This probably has to do with the Sardar Fairs. As you know, there is literally a caste of Players, generally itinerant, which makes its living by "the Game." The charge for a game can range from a tarsk-bit, which is common, to a golden tarn disk, of double weight. Important kaissa players are celebrities, welcomed in a hundred cities, and entertained at the courts of Ubars. They have a status comparable to that of conquerors and poets.

"Was the card-sport honest in the gambling house?" asked he in whose care I was.

"I do not think so," I said.

"No more than other games?"

"One guesses not," I said.

"You seem to know little of it," he said.

"I am a slave," I said.

Such things were managed by the masters. They were seldom made clear to slaves. Our concern was to keep men at the tables.

"Here we are at the wagon," he said. He then released my hair, and I stood up, stiffly. "Go over there, beside the clearing," he said, "where I can see you, and relieve yourself, and then return to be shackled."

In a bit he lifted me in his arms, to place me in the wagon.

I felt small in his arms, and he seemed very strong. I lifted my head to him. "Perhaps Master would care, as several others, to sample the lips of a slave?" I said.

"No," he said.

"You did in Ar," I said.

"Only to establish that you were vain, petty, and meaningless, and, of course, a true slave slut," he said.

"Perhaps this vain, petty, meaningless slave slut is of interest to Master," I said.

"Perhaps," he said.

"Kiss me!" I said.

"No," he said.

"I am tunicked," I said.

"So?" he said.

"It seems Master is distracted," I said. "Perhaps it is because there is a slave in his arms."

"Oh?" he said, annoyed.

"In slave wagons," I said, "kajirae are commonly kept naked."

He put me on my feet.

"Remove your tunic," he said.

"That will be difficult," I said, "as my hands are tied behind me."

He then unbound my wrists, and I slipped the tunic from my body. I stood before him, in the moonlight. "Perhaps the body of a lithe slave pleases Master," I said. I had little doubt that the answer to that speculation would be affirmative, given the diet and exercises imposed on a female slave. Astrinax, two days ago, had lined Jane, Eve, and I up before him, and regarded us. "Excellent," he had said, "three pretty little vulos, all ready for a block." We trusted, of course, that there were no blocks in the Voltai.

"Are all the women of your world slave sluts?" he asked.

"I am sure I do not know," I said.

"You are, clearly," he said.

"I am in a collar," I said.

"The collar," he said, "does not make the slave slut. It releases the slave slut."

"I see," I said.

"Yes," he said.

"We do not wish to be lashed," I said.

"That is only an excuse," he said.

"I see," I said.

It was true that I felt extraordinarily free, marvelously liberated, in a collar. How right I felt in it! It was as though the sign of something inside of me had been put on the outside of me, for all to see, something which was now obvious, something it was no longer possible to deny.

"I am now ready to be shackled," I said.

"Not quite," he said.

"Master?" I said, hopefully. I approached him, closely, with slave closeness. It seemed my body was afire.

I felt weak and slave before him. He could dominate me with a glance, a word, a gesture. I sensed myself his.

Then I was turned abruptly about and, to my consternation, my wrists were again corded behind my back.

I was then, again, lifted lightly into his arms.

"I am bound," I said.

"Kiss me," he said.

"Oh, yes, Master!" I said.

"You do that well," he said.

"I have been trained," I said.

Again our lips met.

"Buy me, buy me, Master!" I whispered. "Please, buy me!"

"Only a slave begs to be bought," he said.

"Yes, Master," I said. "Buy me! Please buy me!"

Shortly thereafter I was shackled to the central bar. Jane and Eve were asleep.

"Will Master not unbind me now?" I said.

"No," he whispered.

He then prepared to slip from the wagon.

I jerked at my bound wrists. What a monster he was, to leave me in this fashion, not only naked and shackled, but bound helplessly, as well!

He was Gorean.

He knew what might be done with women, with slaves.

"What was Master doing, earlier?" I asked.

"Examining the contents of the new wagons," he said. "They contain no common haulages. There are various metals, subtle metals, alloys, and such, with not all of which I am familiar, coils of wire, unusual machines, unfamiliar tools, boxes of tubing, canisters of diverse powders, and other objects, crated and secured, which I could not examine. I suspect that Pausanias, and his drivers, do not even understand the cargo they carry."

"Do you understand it?" I asked.

"No," he said, "but I suspect its nature."

"You are not of the Metal Workers," I said.

"No," he said.

"What is your interest in the card-sport of Pausanias and Kleomenes?" I asked.

"Import I am sure is borne within those cards which has little to do with the games of men."

"If not of men," I whispered, "of what?"

"Of things other than men," he said.

"Games?" I said.

"Dark games," he said.

"From Ar," I said, "you know of Kurii."

I recalled this from Six Bridges.

"Yes," he said.

"And doubtless you know of the beast, who resided with the Lady Bina?"

"Of course," he said. "Many did."

"A guard animal," I said.

"Perhaps," he said.

"I understand now," I said, bitterly, "your presence here, which has in fact little to do with a slave. I understand now the interest you have feigned in me, following me about, as though you might have been intrigued, aroused, slave stimulated, perhaps even a prospective buyer or slave thief. I understand now your protecting me, your petitioning for my charge, why you have attached yourself to our party! It is not to be near me! It is to pursue some other purpose, one of your own!"

"Do not underestimate your slave interest, barbarian," he said.

"It is true, of course, that a useful confluence of conveniences has occurred here."

"Would not any girl do?" I asked.

"Yes," said he, "but not as well."

"I see," I said.

"I find it difficult to understand my interest in you," he said, "given the pettiness and mediocrity of your character."

"Surely my beauty is not negligible," I said.

"No," said he.

"I have seen myself in the mirror," I said.

"There are many women more beautiful," he said.

"What, then?" I asked.

"I do not know," he said. "Your ankles look well, shackled, of course."

"You do not care for me," I said.

"A slave is not to be cared for," he said. "She is to be purchased and owned, worked and enjoyed, tied and mastered, humiliated and ravished, reduced to needful, whimpering meat, writhing helplessly in her chains, crying, begging for another touch."

"Yet," I said, "some men care for their slaves."

"Perhaps," he said.

"Suppose," I said, "these matters of alleged import did not obtain."

"Then," said he, "you would by now be cowering at my slave ring in Harfax."

"I see," I said.

"You would find yourself, ignorant barbarian," he said, "as you would never have dreamed on your old world, mastered."

I knew that any woman can be mastered.

I had already been mastered, and thoroughly, in the house of Tenalion, in the eating house of Menon, in the gambling house, on the Street of Chance. Indeed, I now realized that I had been mastered, as I had lain naked and bound, in the conveyance which had transported me from the house on my former world to some collection point, from which I had been shipped, as one of several captured beasts, to the markets of Gor.

"You would kneel me and put your whip to my lips?" I asked.

"And you would lick and kiss it lengthily, devotedly, splendidly," he said.

"And if not?"

"Then it would be used upon you."

"I would try earnestly to please my Master," I said.

"And I would see to it that you were successful," he said.

"Yes, Master," I said.

"You are a meaningless barbarian slut," he said.

"Yes, Master," I said.

"Now sleep," he said.

"I love you, Master," I said.

"A slave's love is worthless," he said.

"But I do love you!" I said.

"Beware that you are not lashed," he said.

"Yes, Master," I said.

"Sleep," he said.

"Will Master not unbind my wrists?" I said.

"No," he said.

"Yes, Master," I said.

Chapter Twenty

I was kneeling on a mat, near the forward, right wheel of the first of our three wagons, that usually driven by Astrinax. Its tharlarion, hobbled, was grazing nearby. I was oiling its harness, softening it.

Now that I was permitted speech I, as Jane and Eve, was employed about the wagons. This morning we had made several trips to the local well with our buckets, and, returning, had filled our water barrels. We had also gathered forage for the tharlarion, and firewood. We surmised, then, that we might soon leave the six hundredth pasang stone, and the Aqueduct Road. I had hoped, after all this time and distance, we would have returned to Ar. On the other hand, the forage and firewood we had gathered suggested that we might be venturing further, and higher, more steeply, into the Voltai. As one goes higher into the mountains vegetation grows thinner. After a time, one is likely to encounter little but wild verr, and tiny snow urts, amongst the crags. Water, on the other hand, if one is high enough, may be obtained easily enough from snow, which commonly lasts all year on the summits of many peaks. I did not know the location of either Lord Grendel or the blind Kur. As we were far into the Voltai, perhaps it had already made contact with its fellows. But if that were the case it seems we should be returning to Ar, which seemed, patently, not the case. The five hunters had left before dawn, presumably to seek tarsk. From what I knew of Voltai tarsk I did not envy them their enterprise. I wondered sometimes why men did such things. Clearly they are different from us, in a great many ways. More significantly, perhaps, the ten wagons, there were ten, of the caravan of Pausanias had also departed, something like an Ahn before noon.

Astrinax, the Lady Bina, and Master Desmond, he in whose keeping I was, were conversing on the other side of the wagon.

I rubbed oil carefully into the harness, a bit at a time. Softening the harness makes it more supple, and prolongs harness life. It also tends to protect the leather from long exposure to sunlight, particularly at high altitudes. Similarly, if the harness is wet, as from rain, it may dry stiffly. Under both conditions it is more likely to weaken and crack from the strain of haulage.

Last night words had escaped me, inadvertently, unaccountably. Allison, a slave, had confessed her love for Desmond of Harfax, a free man. What presumption, what insolence! Did she think she was a free woman, whose love was of inestimable value, a priceless gift, a love worth having? She was a slave. A slave is less than the dirt beneath the sandals of a free person. What could her love be but a foolishness, a joke, a source of merriment, an absurdity, an insult, an embarrassment? How fortunate she was that she had not been beaten. Had he been her master, as he was not, she might have been sold the next morning. Is the slave not to keep her thoughts to herself? Is she not to conceal her love for her master? And yet I knew, from a hundred slaves, in the house of Tenalion, and in Ar, from the streets and markets, and from the camps, and elsewhere, that it was common, almost universal, for a girl to love the man at whose feet she knelt, he in whose collar she was fastened. This has to do, doubtless, with a great many things, but, one supposes, it has to do, given its pervasiveness, with nature, nature given the institutional enhancements of civilization. One owns and one is owned; one is master and one is slave.

A woman wishes to be reassured of her value, and on the block she is in no doubt as to the matter, as men bid on her. Of course, she is of value, for men have seen fit to buy and sell her, as goods. A woman wishes to be attractive, and she knows that she is attractive, for she has been marked and put in a collar. A woman wants to be wanted, and she finds she is wanted, as men most want a woman, as what is theirs, as a property. The woman longs to belong, and in bondage she finds herself a belonging, a rightless belonging. It is hard to wear a man's collar and chains, his thongs and bracelets, and not be his, helplessly so, and in so many ways. It is hard to sustain the despotic depredations lengthily imposed on her, the exploitations which she must frequently and helplessly endure, without crying herself subdued, conquered, and submitted, as she longs to be, and begging for yet more, another intimacy, another caress, another ecstasy.

How innocently and hopefully we crawl to the feet of our masters!

The well-owned slave is the most content, and happiest, of women, the most sexual, and utterly female of women.

How tragic then that so frequently she dares not confess her love for her master, but must conceal it, to her misery, in the depths of her heart.

We long for our love master; might he not then, in some sense, long for his love slave?

To be sure, he must not then be weak with us!

Let him treat us as more of a slave than ever. It is what we want to be, his slave, for we are females.

Before he had joined Astrinax and the Lady Bina by the wagon box, he in whose care I was, Desmond of Harfax, had passed me.

"Tal, Master," I had said to him, my head down, not looking up from my work.

"Tal, kajira," had he said to me, not pausing.

He had not ignored me, so hurting me, as he had when I was under the sentence of the mute slave, but, too, he had given me no more attention than he would have given Jane, or Eve. A tear coursed down my cheek. Surely I should not have let those fateful words slip out. "I love you, Master." But it seemed that I had not said them, so much as that they had said themselves. I knew, of course, that a slave's love was worthless. Who did not know that? It had been fortunate that my boldness, my lapse, had not been rewarded with a whipping!

I rubbed the oil, in small, firm circular motions, into the broad harness.

It is not as though I myself, upon reflection, had said those words, I thought. I am not really responsible for them. They had spoken themselves. They were meaningless, in that sense. It is as though they had not been spoken, though, it was true, they had been uttered. Thus, I thought, I do not really love him. It could not be! It is a misunderstanding. How could I love him, truly? Had he not, on many occasions, treated me as what I was, a slave? Had he not been abrupt, cruel, not caring? Had he not cuffed me? Had he not, for no adequate reason, inflicted upon me the dreadful modality of the mute slave? Had he not, on many occasions, treated me with contempt? Had I not many reasons to despise him? I should hate him, I thought. I should loathe him, I thought. Too, had he not scorned me last night? Had he not left me bound? How embarrassing that was when Jane and Eve, shackled to the bar, awakened, and found me similarly shackled, but, too, with my wrists bound behind me. "What did you do?" asked Jane. "Nothing," I told them. "Why, then, did he bind you?" asked Eve. "It pleased him to do so," I said. "Ah!" said Eve, happily. "He well reminded you that you are a slave." "Yes," I said, "he well reminded me that I am a slave. Now untie me." "You must be very proud," said Eve. "Proud?" I said. "To bind a woman," said Eve, "is surely to show that she has been found of slave interest, and, is it not, in its way, a way of putting a claim on her?" "Untie me," I said. "That is for Master Desmond to do," said Jane. "Then you would let him find me as I am, still bound?" I asked, my wrists angrily, futilely, fighting the cording, my ankles, as I was sitting, jerking back, again and again, in frustration, rattling the shackle chain looped about the central bar. "Yes," said Jane. "Let me see the knots," said Eve. I turned about, holding out my wrists. "Look," said Jane. "Yes," said Eve. "I do not think we could undo the knots," said Jane. "In any event," said Eve, "it is not for us to do. Master Desmond will soon be here, to unshackle us. Then, he may attend to the matter." "Or, if he wishes," said Jane, "he may have you feed, as you are, kneeling, from a pan." Desmond of Harfax had untied me, but, too, he had tied me! I had no doubt that he found me of slave interest, but then, so, too, did many men, certainly the drivers of the caravan of Pausanias. But I did not see that his binding of me had any particular significance of making a claim. It was not as though I was a free woman, amongst others captured in a city being sacked, and a captor had tied my wrists behind me with his own colored cords, different from those of his fellows, that I might be sorted out appropriately in the temporary slave pens outside the city. If there was any significance to his binding, I think it was merely to teach me better, as though I needed the lesson, that I was a slave. Certainly he had no claim on me, as I belonged to another, the Lady Bina. To be sure, I did not doubt but what it pleased him to bind me. Goreans seem to enjoy making a woman helpless.

What brutes they are!

How they own and master us!

How helpless we are in their hands, those of our masters!

How unfortunate had been those foolish words, "I love you, Master." They could not be mine. They had slipped out. Surely I could not have meant them! Still, I often dreamed of myself at the foot of his couch, naked, fastened to a slave ring.

What an inexplicable dream!

I wondered if I were capable of loving.

Could I love?

I recalled myself from Earth. It seemed to me unlikely that that Allison Ashton-Baker could have loved. She had been too selfish, too egotistical, too self-centered. She had been too ambitious, too opportunistic, too calculating, too rational. Her relationships with men and boys, when not addressed to her amusement, had been invariably shrewd, prudential, and exploitative.

Much had changed since then.

Now she was on Gor, a marked, collared slave girl.

She was softer now, more helpless, more vulnerable, more dependent, now without status, now scarcely clothed.

Much had changed.

I sensed that the former Allison Ashton-Baker, now in a collar, might now love. I had the sense that when one is locked in a collar, it is easy to love. One hopes for love, one wants love, one needs love.

But how frightful that one might not dare to express this, lest one be beaten or sold!

Desmond of Harfax, I was sure, thought me incapable of love. He thought me too vain, too petty, too shallow.

He was perhaps right.

But, of course, he found me at least of slave interest. He enjoyed, for example, tying my hands behind my back.

He had reservations, too, I knew, pertaining to some further aspects of my character. But why should anyone be expected to sacrifice themselves, or act against their own best interests? Was that not foolish, stupid, irrational? What had that to do with character? Surely a girl has a right to look out for herself. What is wrong with, say, the theft of a candy, if one may manage it with perfect impunity? One would not wish to be caught, of course. That might mean the switch or lash, close chains, an unpleasant roping, short rations, a slave box, such things.

She is not a free woman.

Strange, I thought, how a better character is expected of a slave than a free woman.

The masters attend to our character, and are concerned with it, in their training, rather, I suppose, as they would attend to, and be concerned with, the character of any animal, a sleen, a kaiila, or such.

Soon we wish to improve ourselves.

We wish to reflect credit on our masters.

We wish to be worthy of our masters.

I suddenly stopped working the oil into the harness leather, as something on the other side of the wagon had caught my attention, without my really being aware of it.

"How long do you think it might be, before we receive our guide?" asked Desmond of Harfax.

I knew curiosity was not becoming in a kajira, but I crawled a little closer, and listened intently.

"We have received him," said Astrinax.

I remembered that Astrinax commonly held the late watch.

"Where is he?" asked Desmond.

"He has gone," said Astrinax.

"How then can he guide us?" asked Desmond.

"Easily," said Astrinax.

I heard the Lady Bina laugh.

"I do not understand," said Desmond.

"Our guide," said Astrinax, "is Pausanias, who recently left with his caravan."

"Pausanias?" said Desmond of Harfax.

"He does not know it, of course," said Astrinax. "He is an unwitting guide."

"And how," asked Master Desmond, "does Pausanias know his way?"

"It was conveyed to him by Kleomenes, of the hunters," said Astrinax.

"Then," said Master Desmond, "Kleomenes, at least, knows the way."

"No," said Astrinax, "he does not. He merely conveyed the way."

"I do not understand," said Desmond of Harfax.

"Pausanias, of the caravan," said Astrinax, "had the key, without the lock, so to speak, whereas Kleomenes had the lock, so to speak, but lacked the key."

"Can you not speak more clearly?" said Desmond of Harfax.

"I think you suspect more than you pretend," said Astrinax.

"It has to do," said Master Desmond, "with a deck of cards?"

"Precisely," said Astrinax.

"And how do you come by these things?" asked Desmond of Harfax.

"I am told," said Astrinax.

"Oh?" said Desmond. "By whom?"

"By one who sees much but knows little," said Astrinax.

"And who might be his informant?"

"One who sees little, but knows much," said Astrinax.

This must be, I thought, Lord Grendel and his fellow, the blind Kur he had brought safe from Ar to the Voltai.

"They have not been with us for days," said Desmond.

He must know then of the two beasts. He might not know that one was blind.

"They have been about," said Astrinax.

"You are contacted during the night watch?" said Desmond.

"During some night watches," said Astrinax.

"I think I will keep the night watch tonight," said Desmond.

"I would not do so," said Astrinax.

"Why not?" asked Desmond.

"You might be killed," said Astrinax. "These are dangerous times, and this is a dangerous place. Serious matters are afoot."

"As you will," said Desmond.

"I will tell you something else of interest which has been

conveyed to me," said Astrinax. "Trachinos and his fellow, Akesinos, are outlaws, and lately in contact with their band, recently come from Venna. The rendezvous was to be held, it seems, in the vicinity of the six hundredth pasang stone."

I recalled the flickering light. Master Desmond had been aware of it, too.

"An ambush is planned," said Astrinax.

"How many in the band?" asked Desmond.

"Nine, not counting Trachinos and Akesinos," said Astrinax.

"Your information is detailed," said Desmond.

"It is apparently easily gathered by an informant with excellent night vision and unusual hearing," said Astrinax. "Too, apparently the outlaws cooked and kept an animal fire."

"We cannot well defend ourselves against eleven men," said Desmond.

"I do not think it will be necessary to do so," said Astrinax.

"I do not understand," said Desmond.

"The outlaws will live as long as they pose no threat," said Astrinax. "It will be in their best interest to abandon their plan. Once they prepare to attack, I fear it will be too late for them."

"Why have they delayed this long?" asked Desmond.

"Trachinos is waiting," said Astrinax. "He suspects we are projecting a rendezvous, perhaps with others as rich as we, or that we may lead them to a cache of concealed wealth. The purpose of our venture, as you well know, seems mysterious, even to you and me. Why would one venture so into the Voltai if riches, perhaps a buried horde, or a secret mine, were not somehow involved?"

"I see," said Desmond.

"They will bide their time," said Astrinax.

"It is like an ax, which may fall at any time," said Desmond.

"The ax," said Astrinax, "may be in greater danger than we."

"How is that?" asked Desmond.

"We are not the only ones in the Voltai," said Astrinax.

"I wonder if we are watched?" said Desmond.

"Possibly," said Astrinax.

"What of the caravan of Pausanias?" said Desmond.

"I have little doubt that it is watched more carefully than we," said Astrinax.

"How so?" said Desmond.

"It is apparently far more important than we," said Astrinax.

"Why?" asked Desmond.

"I do not know," said Astrinax. "But I gather it is of great importance to someone."

"Or something," said Desmond.

"I do not understand?" said Astrinax.

"It is nothing," said Desmond, dismissively.

"I," said the Lady Bina, who had been present, I gathered on her cushion on the wagon bench, but muchly quiet, "have something of interest to convey as well, but I must ask you to hold the matter in confidence for a time."

"Lady?" asked Astrinax.

"I am to be the Ubara of a hundred cities, and then, later, when the planet is properly unified and organized, the Ubara of all Gor."

I heard no response from the men.

"That is what I have been given to understand," she said.

"From whom, Lady?" asked Astrinax. I feared he and Master Desmond might think the Lady Bina joking, or mad. More frighteningly, I did not think she was either.

I sensed, as naive or unrealistic as she might be, there might somehow be a world at stake.

"Oh," she said, "someone, but someone of importance."

I was sure this illusion, or fantasy, had been implanted by the blind Kur who had guested with us in the house of Epicrates.

What was involved here, I was sure, had less to do with the Lady Bina than with one with whom it was thought she might exercise great influence.

"When I am suitably emplaced," she said, "I will not forget my friends."

"We hope to be numbered amongst them," said Astrinax.

Poor Astrinax, I thought. He thinks she is insane.

"We are to follow the caravan of Pausanias," said Master Desmond.

"Yes," said Astrinax, "but, obviously, not that closely."

"It should be easy enough to do," said Desmond, "ten wagons, heavily laden, even should there be torrential rains."

"I think so," said Astrinax.

I hoped that we might return to Ar, quickly and safely, once the blind Kur had been reunited with his fellows. On the other hand, it seemed clear that this practical expediency, as sensible as it might seem, might not be congenial to either the Lady Bina or to he in whose charge I was. They might have subtler, deeper interests in this wilderness.

"The caravan of Pausanias left the Aqueduct Road," said Desmond.

"There are hundreds of trails in the Voltai," said Astrinax.

"And thousands of places where there are no trails," said Desmond.

"Call Lykos, Trachinos, Akesinos," said Astrinax. "We must harness the tharlarion and be on our way."

It would take some time to do this, and turn the wagons, to follow the tracks of the departed caravan. I did not care to leave the road. I stood up, by the mat and harness, and jar of oil, and the rags, and looked about myself.

The Voltai Mountains are called the Red Mountains. Their color, dull and reddish, is doubtless a consequence of some property of the soil. They are, I think, the most extensive of Gor's mountain ranges. They may also be the highest and most rugged. There are villages here and there in the Voltai, usually of herders of domestic verr. These are generally, though not always, in the foothills. I know of only one city in the Voltai, like a remote tarn's aerie, and that is the bandit city of Treve.

The mountains are beautiful, but forbidding. They contain larls and sleen, and, in the lower ranges, wild tarsk, as well. As noted, at the higher altitudes, there is little to be found but wild verr and tiny snow urts.

The sun was high.

I could see snow on some distant peaks.

I did not care to leave the road, the aqueduct. I was afraid, very much afraid. Had I known more of this world I would have feared even to enter the Voltai. Certainly many did. Even Jane and Eve, untutored, illiterate barbarians, as myself, had known enough to fear the Voltai. They had been double chained to the slave post in the Venna camp. And Astrinax had been largely unsuccessful in recruiting drivers and guards for our small caravan.

I did not wish to go further into the Voltai.

I was terrified to do so.

Perhaps some of you feel that under the circumstances, so threatening and uncertain, I should have considered flight, but I did not do so. I would stay with the wagons. We all would, Jane and Eve, as well. I do not think it was merely that we knew ourselves safer with the wagons, though that was surely true. Certainly we did not wish to be eaten by animals. It was frightening enough, sometimes, just to gather firewood. Too, of course, we accepted that there was no escape for the Gorean slave girl. Marked, collared, and slave-clad, and given the culture, the best she might hope for, if she were not bound and returned to her master, would be, as a fugitive, to fall into a harsher and more grievous bondage. Men like to own us, and have us in collars. Too, one did not care to be hamstrung, fed to sleen, or cast to leech plants. We were aware of all these things. Too, for whatever reason, I was reluctant to leave the vicinity of the brute I so hated, Desmond of Harfax, he who had treated me so badly, who held me in such contempt, who had so scorned me. Perhaps my lips had been bred to be pressed to the leather of his whip. Might I not belong in his slave bracelets? Might he not be my master? But aside from all these things, I think, rather, primarily, and more profoundly, the reason we would not run away was quite simple, that we were now quite other than we had once been; we now well knew what we had become, and were. We now clearly understood, in every fiber of our bodies, in the bottom of our bellies and in the depths of our hearts, that we were no longer those cultural artifices which are called free women, but now something quite different, something more natural, more ancient, more biological, that we were now belongings and properties, that we were now slaves. This understanding brings about a radical transformation in a woman. She is no longer the same. She cannot be. We would not run away. We could not run away. We were owned.

I gasped, and drew back, from half under the wagon.

"Have you finished with the harness?" asked Desmond of Harfax. He had come about the wagon. I had not realized his presence until he spoke.

"Nearly!" I said.

I scrambled back, to return to the mat. I knelt, of course, as I was in the presence of a free person.

"Who gave you permission to stop work?" he asked.

"No one, Master," I said.

"Why then did you stop work, before you were finished?" he asked.

I put my head down.

"You were listening," he said.

"Yes, Master," I said. "Forgive me, Master."

"Curiosity is not becoming in a kajira," he said.

I kept my head down.

"Should you not be tied to a wagon wheel and lashed?" he asked.

"It will be done with me as masters please," I said.

"Do not speak of what you heard to Jane and Eve," he said.

"No, Master," I said.

"There must be no changes in their behavior which might arouse the suspicions of certain others in the party."

"I understand," I said.

"And you," he said, "have heard nothing."

"I understand," I said.

"In particular," he said, "you are not to avoid Trachinos."

"Master?" I said.

"Trachinos," he said, "finds you of slave interest. He may seize you, may press himself upon you, fondle you, and such. You are not to resist his advances."

"A slave dare not resist the advances of a free man," I said. "She is a slave."

"Respond to him," he said.

"Master?" I said.

"Have no fear," he said. "You will not be able to help yourself."

"I see," I said. I feared it was true. I was a slave.

"You are a pretty slut," he said.

"And might not others find me of slave interest, as well?" I said.

"Certainly," he said. "Many men would find you of slave interest."

"Why?" I asked.

"Because you are of slave interest," he said.

I, kneeling, clutched my collar, with two hands, as though I would tear it from my throat.

"Rejoice," he said, "not every woman is of slave interest."

"I hate you!" I said.

"How long will it take you to finish the harness?" he said.

"I am nearly done," I said. "Two or three Ehn."

"Finish it," he said, "and then deliver it to Master Astrinax."

"Yes, Master," I said.

"We will leave within the Ahn."

"Yes, Master," I said.

He then left.

I was so pleased that I was such as might be of slave interest. What woman does not wish to be of slave interest?

And I knew I was such, for I had been collared. It was for women such as I that men had constructed the elevated slave block, that we might be exhibited and sold.

I then bent again, to my work. I began to hum. It was only later I realized that it was a slave tune which I had heard, long ago, in the house of Tenalion.

Chapter Twenty-One

"Please," I said, turning my head away, and I felt his mouth on the side of my neck, above the collar, and then at the side of my face, fierce, under my ear.

It was the heat of the day. We had stopped, for two Ahn.

It was the fourth day we had been following the caravan of Pausanias.

I was pinned against the wagon wheel. At least he had not tied me to it.

"No!" I begged. I felt his hand on my left thigh. "Please, do not, Master!"

I had seen both Jane and Eve fastened at a wheel, but, in each case, for discipline. Eve had been tied with her back to the wheel, her wrists bound widely apart to spokes, and her legs widely spread, fastened, too, to spokes. She, in the care of Lykos, had dared to speak without permission, when she had not received a standing permission to speak. She had perhaps been testing him, to see, as the saying is, how many links of chain were permitted to her, which is an unwise venture with a Gorean male. She had discovered, so to speak, as she should have known, that the chain was quite short. Afterwards she had been almost inseparable from him. Sometimes he had had to order her from his presence. "I want him to buy me," she had later whispered to me, in the darkness, in the wagon, when Jane was asleep. "I think I am his slave." Jane, who was in the care of Astrinax, had been tied facing the wheel, naked, wrists widely apart, ankles widely apart, fastened to spokes. She had been lashed. She had tied a narrow, folded strip of cloth about her head, to hold back her hair and keep sweat from her eyes. This could be interpreted as a talmit, which is a common sign of a first girl, the girl in charge of other female slaves, who usually reports directly to a master. First girls are common when there are many slaves in a group, or household. They keep the other girls in order, assign tasks, settle disputes, and such. Many masters, if several girls are involved, do not care to involve themselves in such matters. It is enough for him to issue instructions to the first girl, usually in the morning, as she kneels before him, and she, according to her lights and biases, her choices and favorites, sees to their implementation. In a house containing a hundred or more slaves, there may be more than one first girl, there being various groups of slaves, and these first girls, in turn, will report to the first girl of first girls, so to speak. She, in turn, of course, reports to the master, or the master's representative. In such a household the lower first girls will wear a talmit of one color, and the high girl, or first girl of first girls, she who reports to the master or his representative, the kajira sana, will wear one of a different color. The colors depend on the customs of cities, the whims of particular masters, and such. In any event, Jane, who was not first girl, as we had no first girl, had seemingly, without permission, arrogated to herself a talmit, commonly understood as a badge of authority. I had no doubt this was done in all innocence, and I am sure Astrinax himself thought it to have been done in all innocence, as well, but, still, it had been done, and the prestige of the talmit was deemed to have been compromised. Certainly Jane, and Eve and myself, who, to our misery, were forced to be present at the lashing, had had well impressed upon us the significance of the talmit. One lives in terror of it. She who wears the talmit is as Mistress to the other slaves, who will address her as Mistress. Slaves often live in terror of the first girl, speak deferently to her, kneel to her, and such. As is often the case, as with free women, we hope that men, given our beauty and sex, will protect us. Jane, like Eve, it seemed to me, should have known better. It is easy enough to knot a cloth about one's neck and use it to wipe away sweat, and men, for some reason, seem to find sweat-wet hair, loose about a kajira's features, attractive. Are they not lovely, even when hot and working?

"Please, stop, Master," I begged Trachinos.

I heard a tearing of cloth.

"Please do not strip me, Master," I begged, "not here, beside the wagon."

"Elsewhere then," he said.

"Please, stop, Master!" I said.

"You must have a use fee," he mumbled, the words now blurred against my bared shoulder.

"Oh!" I said.

"Ah!" he said, triumphantly.

"Please, stop, Master!" I begged.

"You want it, slut," he said.

"Please release me, Master," I said.

"Do you resist?" he asked.

"I may not," I wept. "I am a slave."

"Do you doubt that I could make you leap to my touch?" he growled.

"No, no," I said. I knew any man could do this to me. I was kajira.

How defenseless we are, in our collars!

"You do not own me!" I said.

"Who will dispute my use?" he said. "A woman, a Metal Worker?"

"Honor, honor!" I said.

"Honor," said he, "is for fools."

I was miserable, and his hands were strong, and I was kajira!

"Allison," said a voice, pleasantly. "You have torn your tunic."

I pulled away from Trachinos, and slipped to the side. I held the tunic, as I could, about me.

Trachinos had turned about, angrily, to see Desmond of Harfax.

"Be off," growled Trachinos, "Metal Worker."

Desmond of Harfax was unarmed. Trachinos, claimedly of Turia, had his blade at his left hip, suspended from the belt slung over his right shoulder.

"Do you find her pleasant to hold?" inquired Desmond. "I would think she would be such."

"Go," said Trachinos.

"It is not I alone with whom you might deal," said Desmond, "but with Lykos, and Astrinax, and perhaps others."

"Others?" said Trachinos, uneasily.

"I believe so," said Desmond, politely.

I noted that Akesinos, lean and swarthy, as though from nowhere, was now in the background, rather behind Desmond. His shadow, however, was on the wagon, so I am sure that Master Desmond was aware of his presence. I supposed he was not so much concerned to conceal his presence as to have Desmond placed between him and Trachinos. One can face in only one direction at a time.

"What is her use fee?" asked Trachinos, angrily.

I suspected Trachinos was unwilling to bring his enterprise, his band in the hills, to a premature closure, thus perhaps precluding an access to a greater wealth, one which might await a more patient man.

"That would have to be arranged," said Desmond, "with the Lady Bina, but I think I can speak for her, and that she would support my recommendations in the matter."

"So?" said Trachinos.

"For most," said Desmond, "I would suppose her use fee should be a tarsk-bit. Unfortunately there is no smaller coin. Perhaps one might split a tarsk-bit in two."

I backed against the wagon, clutching my tunic to me. The boards were rough and hot.

How angry I was!

How I hated Desmond of Harfax! Was I, the former Allison Ashton-Baker, worth so little?

To be sure, she was now only kajira.

A tarsk-bit is not unheard of for a use, but the use would presumably be brief, as, say, for a coin girl, used on the stones of a street. It might be two or three tarsk-bits if one is going to keep a girl for the evening. To be sure, a slave may be rented for a day, or two or three, at some negotiated rate. Sometimes this is done to try out a prospective slave, to see if she is worth buying. If she wishes to be bought, she is zealous to please her rent master. If she is bought, and is truly owned, she may be sure that her former rent master, now her owner, will see to it that she is now held to standards of performance which she had scarcely dared to conjecture might exist when she was a mere rent girl. This is to be expected, of course, as he then owns her. The rent fee, incidentally, is often applied to the purchase fee. Apparently this encourages sales.

"A tarsk-bit then," said Trachinos.

"For most," said Desmond of Harfax, "but for you, a golden tarn disk, of double weight."

Trachinos smiled.

"It is not that I think her worth that, of course," said Desmond. "I would suppose her use worth would be something like a quarter or an eighth of a tarsk-bit, if that. Indeed, one would be embarrassed to charge anything for the use of such a slave, so inferior she is, but it is, rather, that, this afternoon, I do not feel disposed to deal with fellows from Turia."

"I am not from Turia," said Trachinos.

"You said you were," said Desmond.

"Teletus," he said.

"I see," said Desmond.

"So?" said Trachinos.

"And I am even less disposed to deal with liars," said Desmond of Harfax.

The blade of Trachinos leapt from its sheath.

I screamed.

At that moment, from somewhere on the other side of the wagons, I heard Jane scream, and Astrinax cry out, "Tarsk, tarsk!"

Trachinos turned about, startled.

I heard something, several things, seemingly large things, scrambling, and grunting and squealing, descending the hillside on the other side of the wagon.

"Into the wagon!" said Desmond.

Something from the other side buffeted the wagon, and it tipped toward us, and I heard a squeal, angry and piercing. Then, emerging from under the wagon, half lifting the wagon with its passage, was a large, hairy, humped, four-footed form, shaggy and immense, and it sped past. The wagon righted itself. I had had a glimpse of tiny, reddish eyes, a wide head, and a flash of four curved, white tusks, two like descending knives, two like raised knives, on each side of a wide, wet jaw.

Trachinos ran to the left, and Akesinos darted to the first wagon, and drew himself within.

"Into the wagon!" cried Desmond.

Dust was all about.

I coughed. It was hard to see.

The tharlarion had been unharnessed.

Master Desmond seized me by the upper right arm and right ankle, and thrust me into the wagon, over the wood, under the canvas, and I found myself on all fours, over the central bar. In a moment he was beside me.

The wagon shook, as it was struck again.

I heard Eve scream. She was sheltering herself behind the first wagon.

The wagons for the most part divided the running tarsk, like rocks dividing a stream.

These were the first Voltai tarsk I had seen. Though they were shorter and squatter, they were like small bosk. Several might have come to my shoulder. The wagon, struck, tipped again, and I cried out, but it settled back into place. Then it was half turned about, in a swirl of dust. There had been a splintering of wood. The wagon tongue had been half snapped apart.

Desmond of Harfax lifted the canvas and peered out.

I could see past him.

Suddenly a new form came bounding down the hillside, scattering rocks, and I put down my head as a bipedalian tharlarion, mounted by a brightly capped, lance-bearing rider, literally leapt over the wagon, and landed on the far side.

"Hunters," said Desmond.

I was close to him. I wanted to be close to him.

Following were four other riders, similarly mounted.

One tarsk, snorting, spun about, head down, to face the riders. They were then about him, lances thrusting. I saw blood on the hump, running in the dust with which the beast was covered, and the beast then, with an enraged squeal, charged the nearest hunter. The tharlarion, its jaws unbound, moved to the side, and bit at the tarsk as it lunged past. The rider lost his saddle, and plunged to the dirt. The tarsk spun about to charge, again, but the tharlarion, apparently trained, interposed its body between the tarsk and the rider, its head down, jaws gaping. The beast never reached either the tharlarion or the rider, for its body had been penetrated by three lances, which pinned it in place. The dismounted rider then hurried about the beast, and leapt on it from behind, seized its long hump mane, and plunged his dagger into its side. The lances, which are smoothly pointed, to allow for an easy retrieval, were removed from the animal. The dismounted rider then regained his saddle and he, and the others, sped about the wagon, raising dust, following the first rider, and the running tarsk. The struck beast rolled in the dirt, bleeding, blood coming in gouts from its mouth, as the heart might beat, reddening the tusks, and then, after a time, it lay still, beside the wagon.

"Tarsk normally do not cluster and run like that," said Master Desmond.

"Master?" I said.

"They were herded," he said. "Our friends, the hunters, are suggesting that we discontinue our journey."

"I hope we are all well," I said.

"We shall hope so," he said.

"Even Trachinos and Akesinos?" I said.

"Certainly," he said. "We may need them."

"I am afraid," I said.

"The wagons provided cover," he said, "and some were probably away from the wagons."

"Thank you for rescuing me from Trachinos," I said.

"I thought I told you to be responsive to him," he said.

I was silent.

"Some men," he said, "speak freely when a slave is in their arms."

"I hate you," I said.

"Did you wish to be rescued?" he said.

"Of course!" I said.

"Pull up your tunic, what is left of it, slut," he said.

"Yes, Master," I said.

"I saw you in his arms," he said. "I saw your readiness. I heard your little, begging cry. In another handful of Ihn, with a proper caress or two, you would have melted to him, whimpering and begging like a paga slut."

"I cannot help myself, Master," I said. "Have you not noted I am in a slave collar?"

"Beware," he said.

"And I am still in one," I said.

"The collar," he said, "does not make the slave. It merely identifies the slave."

"Yes, Master," I said. "Master," I said.

"Yes?" he said.

"I note," I said, "that you did, in fact, interfere. You did, in fact, interpose yourself."

"True," he said.

"Perhaps," I said, "Master does not truly desire to see me in the arms of Trachinos."

"I thought," he said, "it might be amusing to frustrate Trachinos."

"Perhaps there is another reason," I said.

"What might that be?" he asked.

"Perhaps Master can guess," I said.

"Oh?" he said.

"You inquired of Master Trachinos," I said, "if he found me pleasant to hold, and, as I recall, you expressed a view that you would think me such."

"Certainly," he said. "If you were not such you would not have been put in a collar."

"I think Master finds me of slave interest," I said.

"I do," he said, "though I also think you are worthless."

"I am here," I said, within reach, slave-clad, if that. "Perhaps Master would like to take me in his arms."

"Perhaps," he said.

I inched more closely to him.

"I may not resist," I whispered. "I am a slave."

He thrust me back, rudely, away from him.

"Master!" I said.

"I do not own you," he said.

"What difference does that make?" I asked.

"You are indeed worthless," he said, "and not simply worthless as any slave is worthless, as a meaningless property-girl, an article of collar meat, a vendible beast, but beyond that."

"I do not understand," I said.

"Astrinax was right about you," he said, "even from Ar."

"Master?" I said.

"Honor," he said.

"Is honor not for fools?" I asked.

"Some men are fools," he said.

"And perhaps Master is amongst them!" I said.

"That is my hope," he said.

"You kissed me in Ar," I said. "You even made me respond to you, and as a slave!"

"You were not then in my keeping," he said.

"I want you to own me!" I said. "What are you doing?"

"Shackling you," he said. "I think the hunters will return. I think they will want a feast, with roast tarsk. You and the others, later, will be needed to prepare and serve the feast."

"Can you not understand, Master?" I wept. "I want you to own me. I have wanted this from the beginning, even from the Sul Market! I want to be at your feet. I want to be yours, helplessly so, to be done with as you will. I want your collar, the stroke of your whip, should you be pleased to lash me! Whip me if you want, but I want to be yours! I beg you to buy me!"

"Only a slave begs to be bought," he said.

"I am a slave, and I want to be yours! Please, Master, buy me! Buy me!"

With two clicks my ankles were fastened in the shackles, the chain looped about the central bar. Then he was gone. I jerked at the shackles and chain, but only abraded my ankles, and then I wept, for a slave is not permitted to lessen her value, in even so small a way. I trusted I would not be struck.

Chapter Twenty-Two

"You must forgive us," said Kleomenes, leader of the hunters, to Astrinax. "We had no idea your wagons were in the path of our drive."

"It is nothing," said Astrinax. To be sure, his right thigh, beneath his tunic, was bandaged, as it had been gashed by the tusk of a running tarsk in the confusion at the wagons.

Surely the hunters had seemed concerned, even contrite, and had not made their own camp, but dragged, on ropes, through the dust, the bodies of two slain tarsk back to our wagons. They had also assisted in the repair of the wagon tongue.

Grease from the tarsk, on the spit, dripped into the fire, hissing there. Eve and I turned the spit.

Jane carried the bota of paga, hurrying about, as she might be summoned.

How far we were, marked, collared, barefoot, half-naked, from our former world, from the exclusive college, from the elegant, prestigious sorority. I thought the boys who had known us might not have been displeased to see us so. I think they would have been delighted to see us so, and, particularly, to understand the collars were truly on us. Is this not how males want us? But if this was so, why had they not kept us so? Surely they had the power to do so. In any event, on Gor, it would be done with us as men pleased. On Gor, men did as they wished, at least with such as we.

Firelight well illuminated the nearby wagons, and shadows danced on the wood. The evening was, as far as one might suppose, one of innocent merriment. The men sat cross-legged, but a chair, of branches, had been arranged for the Lady Bina. Had she been natively Gorean she would presumably have knelt sedately, in the manner of the free woman, doubtless, here, in such a place, on some mat or blanket. She chatted with the men, her veil casually loose. Lord Grendel, in the domicile, had warned her about irresponsible veiling, but the Lady Bina, as many free women, did much as she pleased. They are, after all, free. Lord Grendel, it seemed, regarded her with almost proprietary attention. Were he not a beast and thus incapable of such emotions one might have supposed he was in love with her. She would lift the veil to drink demurely behind it, her blue eyes sparkling over the cloth. Some women of low caste drink through the veil, which stains the cloth. That seemed to me unrefined. I needed not be concerned with such things, of course, as we must go about face-stripped, as the animals we are. One of the most disconcerting and shocking things that can happen to a free woman is to have her veil taken from her, bearing her features to a public gaze. Slavers, and conquerors, will often tie a free woman's hands behind her before removing her veil. How helpless she is then, unable to prevent her face-stripping. Sometimes raiders are displeased with what they behold when the veil is torn away. Then it is not unknown for some to leave the woman's hands tied behind her and to strip her, and tie a sign about her neck, as, for example, "Poor stuff," "Rejected for bondage," "Not to be collared," "I am unworthy of being a slave," or such. When she is again returned to her robes, and status, rejected and humiliated, woe to any girls whom she might own. The Lady Bina drank not paga, but ka-la-na, with studied delicacy. I think she was more concerned with presenting the image of a Gorean free woman than with the drinking itself. The Lady Bina was an avid pupil of what she took to be cultural proprieties. Certainly she had carefully attended to the instructions of the Lady Delia, the companion of Epicrates, in Ar. She was, incidentally, drinking what you know as a "soft ka-la-na." In most Gorean houses, I had learned, to my interest, there is a mixing bowl, in which the stronger, or "hard," ka-la-nas are mixed with water, the proportions determined according to the household, the occasion, the wishes of guests, and such. It would be an orgy indeed to distribute an unmixed hard ka-la-na amongst the supper couches. Normally this would take place only at private parties for high-spirited males, rash, reckless, rowdy fellows, garlanded revelers, the sort of parties at which one might encounter flute girls, slave dancers, and such. Sometimes such parties spill into the streets, resulting in disturbances of the peace, vandalism, and such.

The roast done, Lykos, with a two-edged blade, cut portions which he placed, from the knife, on wooden trenchers borne by myself and Eve. These we delivered to the men, kneeling, head down, between our extended arms.

I made certain to be the first to serve Desmond of Harfax. I thought I knelt well, gracefully, properly, subserviently. My posture and attitude, my entire deportment, as was appropriate, expressed the submissiveness of the slave. What he could not see, of course, was that, inside, I was also submissive. My heart was submissive. I wanted to be submissive. Many women of my old world would have scorned me for this, castigated me for being what I was, myself, would have insisted instead that I share their views and values, would have dictated to me, with terrible social and economic sanctions for noncompliance, would have demanded that I emulate them, and I had tried to do so, despite their obvious wretchedness, their forlorn misery and unhappiness, but I had found such things empty. Rather, I longed to be defeated; I wanted to be conquered and owned; I wanted to have no choice but to obey with perfection; I wanted to be subject to discipline; I wanted to submit; I wanted a master.

Desmond of Harfax took the trencher.

I did not expect to be thanked, of course. I had learned, shortly after my arrival on Gor, that one does not thank a slave. It is what she is for. If she does not serve humbly and well, she may be punished. Indeed, a slave is likely to be frightened, if thanked. Something is different. She does not comprehend it. What does it mean? Is her master, perhaps absently, distractedly, not noticing her, or no longer thinking of her as a slave, as his slave? Is she to be sold? Has she already been sold?

Although I had not expected to be thanked, I had, looking up, hoped to have from him some acknowledgement of my existence, an expression, the hint of a smile, a possible frown, an annoyed gesture, suggesting he was displeased with me, from my behavior in the wagon, a sense that his needs might be upon him, and he would like to have his hands on me, and as what I was, a slave.

But I saw nothing.

He had taken the trencher. It might have been given to him by any slave! Perhaps he was not even aware of who had brought it to him!

What a beast he was! Again I hated him. In the wagon, I had presented myself to him as, in effect, a begging slave, and I had been rejected!

I was sure, from a thousand things, here and there, now and then, large and small, that he found me of slave interest.

I think he wanted this slave.

I think he burned for her.

Why then had he not seized me, and cast me to his feet, and pointed to his boots that I might lie on my belly before him, and cover them, as I wished, with the kisses of a trembling, submitted slave?

Why had he not done so?

What an absurd excuse, honor!

What was honor?

There was blood, steel, and gold, and the might of masters, and the soft flesh of helpless, collared slaves! Where in all this was honor?

What was honor?

"I do think, friend Astrinax," said Kleomenes, leader of the hunters, "that it would be unwise for you to proceed further into the Voltai."

Kleomenes, as would be expected, assumed that the leader of our expedition was Astrinax. For example, the Lady Bina deferred to him. And, presumably, he would be unaware of what might lurk in the night, somewhere beyond the light of the fire.

"We thank you," said Astrinax, "for your concern."

"Today," said Kleomenes, "you were fortunate, but the Voltai is dangerous. There are beasts, some quite dangerous. There might be avalanches, suddenly flooding streams, dislodged boulders, tumbling, fallen trees, trails might be lost, faded or washed away. It is even possible gangs of ruffians are about, seeking refuge in the wilderness from the guardsmen of a dozen cities."

"You are right," said Astrinax, "we must think of turning back." Trachinos looked up, quickly, suspiciously. If we did turn back, there might be little point in delaying the strike of his band, somewhere in the mountains. Could this whole venture be some meaningless lark, pointless, one without a horde, a concealed treasure, a vein of gold somewhere?

"Why are you in the Voltai?" Kleomenes inquired, pleasantly.

"We are instructed," said Astrinax, guardedly.

"By whom?" asked Kleomenes.

"Would you care for a game of cards?" asked Desmond of Harfax.

"No," said Kleomenes, "I do not gamble."

I was frightened by the sound of that.

"Come now, Kleomenes," said one of his men, jocularly, "you do cards."

"Ah, yes," said Kleomenes, "now and then, but not now."

Shortly thereafter the Lady Bina, perhaps drowsy from the ka-la-na, had retired.

When I was serving, my ankle was suddenly grasped by Trachinos. I could not move. "Ho, noble Desmond," said Trachinos, "do you not think this ankle would look well in a pretty anklet?"

"She has trim ankles," said Desmond. "They shackle well."

"Would you not like, kajira," said Trachinos, "to have a pretty anklet? You might then be the envy of your sister slaves."

I did know such things, an anklet, a bracelet, an armlet, could be prized amongst kajirae.

"It will be done with me," I said, "as masters please."

He then released my ankle, and I hurried away.

"Paga!" he called to Jane.

"Yes, Master," she said, hurrying to him.

The men continued to converse, about many things, things of interest to men, techniques of hunting, the best seasons and terrains, the politics of mighty Ar, the taverns of Venna, the Vennan races, the breeds of tharlarion, the kaiila and slaves they had owned, and such.

Jane, Eve, and I knelt in the background, close enough to be easily summoned, far enough away to be unobtrusive.

I had tried, in my serving, to catch the eye of Master Desmond, to avoid the eye of Master Trachinos.

As the evening wore on one or another of the hunters cast us a glance. I became more and more aware that the Lady Bina had retired.

"Do your girls dance?" asked Kleomenes.

I was startled. I had never thought of dancing, certainly not as a woman might dance before Gorean males.

I wondered what it might be, commanded, to dance before such males, and as a slave.

"Ela," said Astrinax, woefully, "no. They are all ignorant barbarians."

"Barbarians?" said Kleomenes.

"They are cheap," said Astrinax.

"Some barbarians are quite expensive," said Kleomenes.

"These were cheap," said Astrinax.

"What of their use?" asked Kleomenes.

"They are owned by the lady," said Astrinax, "and I fear she has retired."

"Well," said Kleomenes, pleasantly, "there are many such vulos in Venna."

"You are returning to Venna then," said Astrinax.

"Early," said Kleomenes, "probably before you rise."

"What of the meat?" asked Astrinax.

"Some we will put over our saddles," said Kleomenes, "some we will leave for you. We will break the tusks loose from the jaws. The tusks of Voltai tarsk sell well in Venna."

"You are professional hunters then," said Astrinax.

"No," said Kleomenes, "we hunt for the sport, the chase, the kill."

"It is a dangerous sport," said Astrinax.

"So, then," said Kleomenes, "it races the blood, it sharpens the eye, and is thus, for that, the better sport."

"And the tusks sell well," said Trachinos.

"That, too, noble friend," said Kleomenes.

"Possibly there are even more dangerous sports," said Desmond of Harfax.

"Possibly," said Kleomenes.

"I fear it is late," said Lykos, "and we, too, must depart early."

"You are proceeding then?" said Kleomenes.

"I think so," said Astrinax.

"Then we shall wish you well," said Kleomenes.

"And we, you," said Astrinax.

"We have," said Kleomenes, "a rare liqueur of Turia, which we were saving for the night of victory, the celebration of a successful hunt."

"This night, then?" said Desmond of Harfax.

"Why not?" said Kleomenes.

"What liqueur?" asked Trachinos.

"That of Falnus," said Kleomenes.

"Aii!" said Trachinos.

"You know the liqueur?" asked Kleomenes.

"I am from Turia," said Trachinos.

"I understand," said Master Desmond, "it is known even in Teletus."

"It is worth a golden tarsk in Ar," said Trachinos.

At a sign from Kleomenes one of his men left the fire, to seek the vicinity of their packs.

Shortly thereafter he appeared in the firelight bearing a small flask, sealed with golden cord.

The seal was undone, and Kleomenes handed the flask to Astrinax.

"It is your victory, your hunt celebration," said Master Desmond. "You should drink first."

"But you are our hosts, and it is our gift to you, to share this rarity with you," said Kleomenes.

"Nonetheless," said Desmond of Harfax, politely.

"Very well," said Kleomenes, and drank from the flask.

"Give it to me," said Trachinos.

He received the flask.

"Do not drink it all," warned Astrinax.

The flask was then handed about, amongst the masters, the hunters, and those of our party.

"Ah!" cried Astrinax.

"It is from the house of Falnus," Kleomenes reminded us. "Raiders of the Wagon Peoples sometimes raid Turian caravans for this, and, of course, Turian women, to be put in the chatka and curla, the kalmak, and a nose ring."

I understood little of this. I gathered it had to do with a garmenture in which slaves might be kept. I did understand the concept of a nose ring.

"Superb," said Lykos.

"Quite good," said Desmond of Harfax.

Even taciturn Akesinos, who had scarcely spoken the entire evening, seemed pleased.

"And you," said Kleomenes, rising to his feet, stumbling a little, "the three of you, pretty kajirae, put your hands down on your thighs, put your heads back, far, and open your mouths, widely!"

"Master!" we cried, gratefully.

How fortunate we were, how privileged, how generous the master! Many free persons, doubtless, had never tasted a Turian liqueur, not to speak of that of Falnus.

"Enough, enough," said Kleomenes.

"Thank you, Master!" we breathed.

It was like a sweet, burning drop of liquid fire, flavored with flower herbs and, detectably, tospit and larma.

Warm words of pleasant parting were exchanged, and the hunters withdrew to their camp, and tethered tharlarion.

"I will shackle you for the night," said Desmond of Harfax.

I tried to press myself against him, but he thrust me away.

He turned about. "Come along," he said.

I stumbled.

"What is wrong?" he asked.

"Nothing," I said. "I am unsteady."

He leaned against the side of the wagon. Then he struck his fist against the wood.

"Astrinax!" he called. "Lykos! Trachinos, Akesinos!"

There was no reply.

He clutched the side of the wagon, trying to hold himself upright.

"Fools, fools, fools!" he said.

I went to my knees, and then to all fours. I shook my head. Then I must have slipped to the ground.

Chapter Twenty-Three

It was hard to see, against the pounding rain. The pack I bore was sodden. Water ran down the side of the mountain. The trail beneath our feet was half washed away. The sky was again black with a mountain storm. It was the third day of rain. We all, men and slaves, bore our burdens, with the exception of the Lady Bina, for she was a free woman. The heavier burdens were borne by the men, the lighter by myself, and Jane and Eve. Our tunics had not been dry for days. Our legs were run with water and mud. We had salvaged what we could from the three wagons, which we had left behind. In the third wagon there had been some weaponry, some spears, two swords, a crossbow with a dozen quarrels. None of the men, I took it, knew the Peasant bow, the great bow, else such a formidable weapon would have been carried, one of rapidity of fire, of remarkable penetration. Had Trachinos been truly of the Peasants, as his garb suggested, he would have known that weapon, and not been without it. Peasant boys, from childhood, are trained in the use of bows, preparing them for the day when they will have the strength to draw the great bow, on which day they are accounted men, suitable for mating with free women. Our weaponry, of course, was borne by the men. It can be death for a slave to touch a weapon.

"Oh!" I cried, and Desmond of Harfax spun about, seized my right arm, and steadied me. "Watch your footing, clumsy slut," he said. He then turned away, to fight his way further through the rain and mud.

"I am not a slut, Master," I called after him, plaintively.

"You are," he snarled.

"Yes, Master," I moaned.

"And lower, and worse," he called back, "a slave!"

"Yes, Master," I said, in misery. I feared I had displeased Desmond of Harfax. If only I were a free woman, and worthy of him!

A few steps forward, and he called back, cheerily, "I like sluts!"

"I am one!" I called out, in the rain.

"That is known to me," he said.

"And a slave!" I cried.

"The least and best of sluts," he called back.

"Would you not rather I were a free woman?" I called ahead.

"No," he said, "free women are boring."

"Why is that?" I asked.

"You cannot buy them," he said.

"I am not free!" I called out, happily.

"No," he said. "You are a slave, and should be a slave."

"I know, Master," I said. "I have known that for years, long before I was put in a collar."

"Good," he said.

"May I not heel Master?" I said.

"No," he said, "the trail is too narrow." One heels on the left side, usually a little behind. Much depends on the master, the terrain, the crowding, or such.

"If you owned me, would you march me on your leash?" I laughed.

"Certainly," he said, "and possibly naked."

"In public?" I said.

"If it pleased me," he said.

"Yes, Master," I said.

In Ar, and even in Venna, I had seen several girls on their leashes, some naked. Some had had their wrists braceleted or thonged behind their back. Masters are beasts and sometimes enjoy displaying their properties. How proud some of those girls had been, particularly when marched before free women. It would not do, of course, for some of those girls, even if tunicked, to encounter one of those women later, if her master were not present. She might be knelt and well switched. That is sometimes the penalty for being desirable and beautiful.

I wondered if I would be switched.

The liqueur of Falnus, as was now obvious, had been drugged. It had been drunk largely because of the seal on the flask and, far more importantly, the freedom with which the hunters themselves had partaken of the fiery delicacy. It now seemed clear the seal had been broken earlier, and then, after the contents had been tampered with, had been restored, or at least given the appearance of having been restored. More interestingly the hunters must have prepared for the evening's work, either by, over time, building up an immunity to the drug, or, more likely, by imbibing a counteragent to its effect, prior to its distribution at our camp. Our tharlarion had been driven off in the night.

"We must turn back," had said Trachinos. "The tharlarion are gone. The Voltai is dangerous. We cannot carry enough supplies for an indefinite journey forward. We must try to find our way back to the Aqueduct Road. Even so, we may starve."

"The wagons of Pausanias," said Desmond of Harfax, "are ahead. They must have a destination, some village, or stronghold. I think it best to continue our journey."

"Afoot?" asked Lykos.

"Yes," said Desmond of Harfax.

"What shall we do, noble Astrinax?" asked the Lady Bina.

"We shall go forward," he said.

"Good," she had said.

He had seemed resolute on this. He still kept the night watch.

We now heard a rumbling, from somewhere above us, through the rain.

I saw a frightened mountain urt scurry past. Higher in the mountains the urts have a mottled pelt, or one which is white.

Desmond of Harfax, who led our column, stopped, and lifted his hand. "Hold, hold!" he cried.

I tried to peer upward, through the rain.

A pebble bounded past.

"Back, back!" cried Desmond of Harfax, and we turned, all, and fled back, slipping, half sliding, along the trail.

"Hold!" called Desmond.

We turned about.

His hand was again raised.

Shortly thereafter a vast, loose quantity of mud, some fifty paces wide, and perhaps fifteen deep, moved past us, before us, downward, slowly, then more rapidly, to plunge into the valley below, perhaps a quarter of a pasang distant.

Before us the trail had disappeared.

"We shall have to make our way around this," shouted Desmond of Harfax, trying to wipe rain from his eyes.

"I have had enough," shouted Trachinos. "I am going back."

"I wish you well!" called Desmond of Harfax.

"What?" shouted Trachinos.

"I wish you well," called Desmond of Harfax, again.

Trachinos cupped his hands to his mouth. "We must all go back!" he shouted.

"Come closer," called Desmond of Harfax.

A cold wind began to blow.

The free persons gathered together. There was a wide spot on the trail here. It had a fair steepness on one side, a chillingly sharp drop on the other. Jane, Eve, and I, shivering in our soaked tunics, our sopped burdens tied to our back, stood to the side. As animals we must wait to see where we would be taken.

"The weather must break," said Lykos.

"A Voltai storm can last for weeks," said Trachinos.

"That is rare," said Desmond of Harfax. "You are not out on Thassa."

"It has rained for three days and three nights," said Trachinos.

"I think the weather will break," said Lykos. "It must break."

"The wind is rising," said Astrinax. "It will move the storm to the west."

"Ah!" said Lykos.

"And there is a greater darkness in the east, yet to come!" said Trachinos.

"We are going forward," said Desmond of Harfax. "The mountain is less steep ahead. Climb carefully. Do not slip. We will go above the slide and around it."

"You are a fool," said Trachinos.

"You are free," said Desmond of Harfax. "You may depart when you wish."

"Alone?" asked Trachinos.

"Be patient," said Akesinos. "We have come a long way. The weather is sure to break."

"It is dangerous to go alone," said Trachinos.

Desmond of Harfax scrambled up the side of the mountain. I gasped, as I saw his foot slip.

In a moment he had rejoined us.

"Rope," he said to Astrinax.

"Go back," said Trachinos, angrily. "You do not even have the trail of Pausanias."

"How is that?" asked Astrinax.

"The trail is too narrow for wagons here," said Trachinos.

"Not when Pausanias passed," said Astrinax.

"How do you know?" asked Trachinos.

Astrinax was silent.

"The trail is narrowed," said Desmond, "slides, the rains."

"They would be insane to have ventured here," said Trachinos.

"They have directions," said Desmond.

"How so?" inquired Trachinos.

"It has to do with a deck of cards," said Desmond.

"You are mad," said Trachinos, against the rain.

"One man might be mad," said Lykos. "It is unlikely that some twenty men with ten wagons would be mad."

"How could they get back?" asked Trachinos.

"Easily," said Desmond. "They might no longer need the wagons. They could return on foot. If they wanted them, they could return differently. There is no dearth of routes. Too, with the men they have they could fell trees, bridge gaps, smooth passages, widen trails."

"You have lost them," said Trachinos.

"No," said Astrinax. "Did you not note evidence of their passage just this morning?"

"No," said Trachinos.

"A mark on a boulder to the right, a fresh mark, the mark of a wheel hub scraping the stone."

"Absurd," said Trachinos.

Desmond fastened the rope about his waist, and then about mine. I looked at him, but his eyes did not meet mine. Next came Astrinax, and then the Lady Bina and Jane, and then

Lykos and Eve, and then, however reluctantly, Akesinos, who looped the extra coils about his shoulder. In this way, if one member of the party fell, there would be others to draw him to safety. The women were largely centered, and staggered with the men, who were stronger. This was clearly done with the safety of the women in mind. This solicitude was interesting to me, considering that three of us were slaves. Women are special to men, it seems, even when they are in collars. To be sure, the free woman is priceless, and the slave does have a value, as she may be sold.

"I am leaving," shouted Trachinos.

Desmond of Harfax waved a farewell to him, and turned, bracing himself, into the wind and rain, and then, slipping some, began to ascend the mountain. I followed, the rope grasped in two hands, the pack on my back, Astrinax and the others, on the same rope, following. Shortly thereafter, in a momentary stop, steadying myself on the slope, my left foot lower than my right, I turned to look back. I shook my head and hair, and tried to wipe the rain from my eyes with the back of my right hand. It was hard to see, for the rain, and the shadows, but there was a new last figure on the rope. Trachinos was now behind Akesinos, and the coils of rope were now slung about his shoulder. So Trachinos was again with us. He had not left. He had one of the two spears tied across his pack. The other spear was similarly borne by Lykos. The spear is the weapon of choice against a charging larl, or, I suppose, Kur.

Chapter Twenty-Four

"Dear Trachinos," said Desmond of Harfax.

Trachinos, who had gone a little ahead, about a bend in the trail, spun about, wildly, almost dropping the mirror he held.

It had rained for two more days, and then the weather had cleared.

"I would discontinue your signaling," said Desmond of Harfax. "You will endanger your cohorts."

"I saw flashes in the hills," said Trachinos. "I know not their source. I thought them possibly those whom you might be seeking. I responded."

"The signaling," said Desmond, "was from your band, from Venna, who have been with us for some time, at least since the six hundredth pasang stone of the Aqueduct Road."

"I do not know what you are talking about," said Trachinos.

"There are nine in your band," said Desmond.

The right hand of Trachinos moved to the hilt of the blade slung at his left hip.

"There is an informant," said Desmond.

"A spy!" exclaimed Trachinos, angrily.

"No," said Desmond, "not as you would think of a spy."

"How long have you known?" asked Trachinos.

"For days," said Desmond.

"Akesinos!" called Trachinos.

Akesinos, then, like a sudden shadow, was at his side.

"We are discovered," said Trachinos.

"Why now have you signaled your people?" asked Desmond.

"You are unarmed, Metal Worker," said Trachinos.

"It would seem so," said Desmond.

"We have waited long enough," said Trachinos. "We are far into the Voltai. The journey back will be difficult and dangerous. There seems to be no clear end to your journey. Perhaps you have no rendezvous in mind. Or perhaps it is with the wagons of Pausanias, or some fortress or lair shared with them, and, if so, we would be considerably overmatched. Should we not, by now, if it exists, have reached some cache, some horde, or mine? Perhaps you are mad. We do not know. We have waited long enough."

"It was a mistake to signal your band," said Desmond.

"We think not," said Trachinos.

"Was there a response to your signal?" asked Desmond.

"Look!" said Trachinos, pointing to the mountains.

"I see," said Desmond. "It is unfortunate."

I could see a flickering for a moment or two, and then it ceased.

"We bear you no ill will," said Trachinos. "We will spare you your lives. We will merely take what you have, your coin, your supplies, your weaponry, the women."

"The Lady Bina," said Desmond, "is free."

"We will have her marked, collared, and sold in Venna," said Trachinos.

"You would leave us here, defenseless, with larls and sleen about, and without food?" said Desmond.

"It would not do, to have you return to Venna," said Trachinos.

"May I inquire the purport of your recent signal to your band?" asked Desmond.

"I told you," said Trachinos. "We have waited long enough. Too, the band grows restless. That is clear in the signals. They wish to act. These are not fellows of the Scarlet Caste. Discipline is fragile."

"Do not signal them to act," said Desmond.

"It is done," said Trachinos.

"I am sorry," said Desmond.

"They will be here, within two Ahn," said Trachinos.

"Lykos may be dangerous," said Akesinos.

"I do not think he will attack both of us," said Trachinos.

"He will not," said Desmond. "I spoke to him of this several days ago."

"He will be reluctant to be disarmed," said Trachinos.

"He does not expect to be disarmed," said Desmond.

"I do not understand," said Trachinos.

"Let us prepare our noon meal," said Desmond. "After that we will try to ascertain the fate of your band."

"What?" said Trachinos.

* * * *

I later regretted accompanying our party higher into the mountains, not that I had any choice. Jane, Eve, and I had been roped together. Master Desmond thought this a wise precaution, given what might be found. Perhaps we might have scattered, or fled back down the slope. When we came over the rise, to a level place, where there were the ashes of an extinguished fire, and the signs of a small camp, I had quickly looked away. I do not think that either Jane or Eve were any more pleased. Trachinos was stunned, and white-faced. Even dark Akesinos had paled. The men examined the bodies, and parts of bodies, of nine men. The Lady Bina joined them. It seemed that she was less distressed than we. I sensed she might be familiar with such sights, from her former world. There had been, as I understood it, a revolution there, perhaps replete with such incidents.

"This is not the work of Grendel," said the Lady Bina.

"Grendel?" said Lykos.

"My guard," said she, "come with me from a far place."

"Kur," said Astrinax.

"In part," said the Lady Bina.

"My informant," explained Astrinax.

"What is Kur?" said Trachinos.

"A higher form of life," said the Lady Bina, "compared to which we are but weak, disarmed beasts."

"Surely not," said Desmond.

"No," she said, "it is not the work of Grendel."

"Are you sure, Lady?" said Astrinax.

"There are nine men here," she said, "and Grendel is but one, and it is daylight. He might kill nine at night, in the darkness.

It is not likely he could kill nine in the bright day. Surely some would arm themselves, and manage to slay a single foe, or, at least, cry out, scatter, and escape, perhaps to be hunted down later."

"He was with another, surely," said Astrinax to the Lady Bina.

"The other," she said, "would be left behind. It would be useless here."

She referred, doubtless, to the blind Kur. Astrinax, I gathered, and perhaps Desmond, as well, did not realize the other Kur was blind. Desmond of Harfax had encountered it only in the darkness of the market of Cestias, long ago.

"This is the work of a larl," said Trachinos, "a pride of larls."

"Who did not eat the kill?" said Desmond.

"It must be," said Trachinos, "heads bitten away, an arm gone, part of a leg."

"That is not the way a larl kills," said Lykos. "Commonly it pounces from behind, and bites through the back of the neck, or, approaching frontally, sinks its teeth in the shoulder, and, with its rear legs, disembowels the prey."

"Kurii can do that," said the Lady Bina.

"It must have been he whom you call your guard," said Astrinax.

"You have that in your mind, my dear Astrinax," said the Lady Bina, "doubtless from your night watches, so much so that you have not looked about you. Note some of the wounds here, the penetration and withdrawal of a single object. There is nothing of larls or Kurii there. Too, at the edge of the camp, and elsewhere, you will see tracks."

Desmond and Lykos moved about.

"Tharlarion!" said Desmond.

"Tharlarion are not native here," protested Astrinax.

"You are perceptive, Lady Bina," said Desmond, admiringly.

I was suddenly jealous of the Lady Bina.

"A quality of perception is not involved here," said the Lady Bina. "As I recognized it could not be the work of my guard, Grendel, I merely looked further."

"Bipedalian tharlarion, hunting tharlarion," said Lykos, "lancers."

"I think now it is reasonably clear," said Desmond of Harfax, "from the tracks, the grouping of the bodies, their attitudes. It was a simple closure attack. The lancers appeared there, and the men turned and fled, and encountered the waiting beasts."

"You are no Metal Worker," said Trachinos.

"You, and your fellow, good Akesinos," said Astrinax, "must now decide what you will do."

Trachinos and Akesinos backed away, a little, drawing their weapons.

Astrinax and Lykos, too, released the birds of steel from their housings.

"The odds," said Desmond, "are no longer heavily in your favor."

"We fear only Lykos," said Trachinos. "And we are two."

"And Astrinax," said Desmond, "might engage, delay, or even strike, one of you, while Lykos and the other tested blade luck in the dark game."

"I do not rely on blade luck," said Lykos, measuring Trachinos.

"We would have given you your lives," said Trachinos.

"To perish in the Voltai," said Desmond.

"Give us your coin, and half the supplies," said Trachinos.

"Surely you do not think Lykos is going to put down his weapon," said Desmond.

"And the women," said Trachinos.

"Take them, if you can," said Lykos, eagerly.

As women we could be taken. My hands went to the rope about my neck, which held me to Jane and Eve.

"My blade is thirsty," said Lykos.

"My dear Lykos," said Desmond, "it would be better if it were to slake its thirst at another time, and from some other fountain. I would suppose we need every blade at our disposal."

"Attend to Desmond of Harfax," said the Lady Bina.

"Why should one attend to one who is not armed?" asked Trachinos.

"Look about you," said the Lady Bina. "These bodies, as I understand it, are all of the band of Trachinos. If that is true it is quite possible that their assailants are not diminished in number. If they managed this carnage, nine men, quite possibly with ease, with little or no cost to themselves, it seems they might do as well with, say, five men. Accordingly, I think it would be wise, at least until we know differently, to regard them as strangers."

Trachinos returned his blade to the scabbard. Akesinos did so, as well. Then, with a glance at Desmond of Harfax, so, too, did Lykos.

Chapter Twenty-Five

"Ho," said Trachinos, pointing, "is that not the Crag of Kleinias?"

We had come to a high point in the trail, which, with the edge of the mountains, the slopes, and valleys, had numerous ascents and descents.

From here one could see for several pasangs about.

"I have heard it described," said Astrinax, "described variously," joining Trachinos, at the front of the column. Shortly thereafter, he was joined by the other men, followed by the Lady Bina, and the slaves.

"Might that not be the Crag of Kleinias?" asked Trachinos.

"What think you?" Astrinax asked Desmond of Harfax.

"Perhaps," said Desmond. "I do not know the Voltai."

"I see no higher mountain about," said Lykos.

The mountain, whichever it might be, was very beautiful. Much snow lay sparkling about its heights. As it was early in the month of En'var, there were darknesses about the lower slopes of the mountain, where snow was melting. The higher elevations, as with many mountains in the Voltai, might be bright with snow all the year. Here and there tiny rivulets of water had cut channels in the trail. Some days ago we had evaded a mud slide which might have been released, given the melting of an ice ridge or wall.

The Crag of Kleinias, I had heard, was one of the higher elevations in the Voltai. Supposedly few but prospectors and hunters penetrated this far into the Voltai.

"Is it not like a ship," asked Trachinos, "sailing through the snow? Can you not see sails, the jutting prow?"

"I would see the head of a tarn," said Lykos, "with the wings spread behind it."

"I wager," said Desmond, "one of Teletus might see it as a ship, and perhaps one familiar with the rage, the size, the terror of tarns, see it as one of those formidable monsters."

Both Trachinos and Lykos were then silent.

"And what would you see it as?" inquired Astrinax of Desmond of Harfax.

"I do not know," said Desmond. "If I had heard it described as a ship, I suppose I would see it as a ship; if I had heard it called the Tarn of the Voltai, or such, I would probably see it as a tarn."

"It is clear, at least," said Astrinax, "why it might be called the Crag of Kleinias. It clearly involves a mighty crag, and, one supposes, it might have been named after some fellow named Kleinias, perhaps he who first saw it, or, at least, saw fit to speak of it, to call attention to it, or such."

"I think," said Desmond of Harfax, "we are near the end of our journey."

"How so?" asked Trachinos.

"Is that mountain not both prominent and unusually shaped?" asked Desmond.

"Assuredly," said Astrinax.

"Presumably there are few such mountains in the Voltai."

"One would suppose so," said Astrinax.

"It may be the only mountain of its configuration for hundreds of pasangs," said Desmond.

"Quite possibly," said Astrinax.

"And much of the Voltai is utter wilderness, much of it trackless," said Desmond.

"True," said Astrinax.

"Did Pausanias seem to you a skilled navigator, one who might read charts, lay out courses, determine positions by the stars?"

"I would think not," said Astrinax.

"His directions, then," said Desmond, "would be relatively simple. He would require little more than a set of distances, a guiding needle, and a goal, or marker, one which might be difficult to miss."

"It would be difficult to miss the Crag of Kleinias," said Astrinax.

"Precisely," said Desmond of Harfax.

"If you are correct," said Astrinax, "we may soon turn back to Ar."

"How so?" asked Desmond.

"I have gathered from my informant," said Astrinax, "we have been engaged in a mission of honor, or mercy, to return a lost beast to its fellows. Once that is done, our work is finished."

"I have further interests here," said Desmond of Harfax.

"I do not," said Astrinax.

"I have further interests here, as well," said the Lady Bina.

"I do not understand," said Astrinax.

"They have to do with politics, and power," she said.

"You did not speak to me of such things," said Astrinax.

"One seldom speaks of everything to everyone," said the Lady Bina.

"My informant did not speak to me of such things," said Astrinax.

"Your informant is not fully informed," said the Lady Bina.

"Is he not first in this party?" asked Astrinax.

"He will do as I wish," said the Lady Bina.

"Is there wealth ahead, Lady?" inquired Trachinos.

"Yes," she said. "Great wealth."

"Let us proceed," said Trachinos. Then he turned to Desmond of Harfax. "I wronged you," he said, "you are not the fool I thought."

"I may be a bigger fool than you thought," said Desmond of Harfax.

"How so?" asked Trachinos.

"I am not interested in wealth," he said.

"Then you are a fool," said Trachinos. "What are you interested in?"

"The fate of a world," he said, "perhaps two."

"You have been very helpful to me, Desmond," said the Lady Bina, "I am thinking of giving Allison to you."

"Lady?" said Desmond of Harfax.

"One often gives female slaves as gifts, does one not?"

"It is done frequently," said Desmond of Harfax. "They make lovely gifts."

"Lykos," asked the Lady Bina, "would you like Eve?"

Eve gasped, and put her hands to her mouth.

"I would find her acceptable," said Lykos.

Eve knelt and put her head to his thigh.

"And, my dear Astrinax," said the Lady Bina, "I am thinking of Jane for you. Do you think you would like her?"

"I would think so," he said.

"You may, of course, sell her," said the Lady Bina.

"Of course," said Astrinax.

"This is no time to think of slave girls," said Desmond of Harfax.

"True," said the Lady Bina. "They are unimportant."

"What of Trachinos, and Akesinos?" asked Trachinos.

"With sufficient wealth," said the Lady Bina, "you may buy several such women."

"Good," said Trachinos.

"I gather we are to proceed," said Astrinax.

"Yes," said the Lady Bina.

"To the Crag of Kleinias?" said Astrinax.

"Yes," said the Lady Bina.

Chapter Twenty-Six

"Hold. Do not move. Be quiet," said Desmond of Harfax. "I do not think she sees us."

Four days later we were much closer to the Crag of Kleinias. The men had speculated we might reach it by noon, tomorrow.

"From here," said Trachinos, shading his eyes, "she looks like a nice one. I like them camisked."

I saw her in the distance, stumbling, trying to run.

She frequently turned, and looked behind her.

"I think she is weak," said Master Desmond. "I think she is tired, and hungry. She may not have eaten in two or three days. She has probably been trying to hide."

"She should be apprehended, and punished, terribly," said Trachinos.

"Perhaps for a time she was not missed," said Astrinax.

"It seems she now fears herself pursued," said Desmond.

"I think she has been flushed," said Lykos.

"I think so," said Astrinax.

"If sleen are on her," said Lykos, "she is caught."

"I see no sleen," said Trachinos.

"Others," said the Lady Bina, observing the approaching figure, small in the distance, stumbling, seemingly forcing itself to move, "can trail nearly as well as a sleen."

"She is coming this way," said Lykos.

"She will run into our arms," said Trachinos.

"That," said Master Desmond to me, pointing, "is a runaway slave."

"Yes, Master," I said, frightened.

I thought there was little doubt about that. She was closer now. She was alone, distraught, apprehensive.

"She is a fool," he said.

"Perhaps she is frightened," I said.

"There is no escape for the female slave," said Desmond of Harfax. "I trust you know that, pretty Allison."

"Yes, Master," I said. "That is known to me."

"What a fool she is," said Desmond of Harfax, regarding the pathetic, approaching figure.

"Perhaps she was frightened, terribly frightened," I said.

"She has good legs," said Trachinos. "Perhaps she will not be killed."

The slave running toward us had her head muchly down, and turned, frequently, to look behind her. Suddenly, she lifted her head, and saw us, and stopped, and cried out, piteously, half fell, and then turned, and fled to the side.

"Bring her in," said Astrinax, and Trachinos and Akesinos darted from our side in pursuit of the fair quarry.

In a matter of moments they returned with the slave, one on each side, holding an arm. She struggled weakly, futilely. Her hair was about her face. Then they flung her to her knees before Astrinax.

She looked up.

"You are caught, girl," said Astrinax.

There was a dark collar on her neck, of a sort with which I was not familiar.

"I know this slave!" I exclaimed.

She shook her head negatively.

"Who is she?" asked Desmond of Harfax.

"I am Mina, Mina!" she cried.

"Who is she?" Desmond of Harfax asked again.

"Mina," I said.

The slave sobbed, and drew in a deep breath.

"How do you know her?" asked Desmond of Harfax.

"We were sold together, in the same auction, in the Metellan district in Ar," I said. "Too, I met her in Ar, near the fountain of Aiakos. She is a state slave."

"State slaves are not camisked," said Astrinax.

"What is she doing here?" asked Desmond.

"Speak," said Trachinos.

"I was a state slave, in Ar," she said. "Each month there is an auction of selected state slaves in Ar. I was purchased, with three others, by Pausanias of Ar, and brought in caravan to the Voltai."

"For what purpose?" asked Astrinax.

"To serve, to serve!" she said.

"Why are you camisked?" asked Astrinax.

"It is how we are kept," she said

The common slave garment is a brief tunic, of which there are several sorts. Some masters camisk their slaves. Others give them less, and others nothing.

"You are a fugitive slave," said Astrinax.

She put down her head.

"Who is your master?" asked Astrinax.

She kept her head down.

"Read her collar," said Astrinax.

"I cannot read," said Trachinos.

Master Desmond crouched by the slave, and examined the collar. "It is not Gorean," he said.

"Look up, girl," said the Lady Bina, and she bent forward, and looked at the collar. "It is in Kur," she said, "but I cannot read Kur."

"You see," said Master Desmond to me, "we are near our goal."

"Your goal," I said, "not mine."

"What is the name of your master?" asked Astrinax.

"Lucius," she whispered.

"Lucius of Venna, of Ar, what?" asked Astrinax.

"Lucius, of the Cave of Agamemnon, Eleventh Face of the Nameless One," she said.

"I do not understand," said Astrinax.

"She cannot say the name," said the Lady Bina. "She is a lesser form of life. Her speech cannot make the sounds. Accordingly a name is provided which it is possible for her to speak."

"Rescue me!" begged the slave. "They are monsters, beasts, not human. They can see in the dark! They can kill with their teeth! The strength of one is that of a hundred men! They think less of us than we of tarsk! They kill without compunction, and feast on their kills! Save me! Keep me! Sell me! But do not send me back."

"It is a lair of beasts," said Astrinax.

"No," said Desmond. "I am sure there is more to it. No simple lair or den is involved."

"My men," said Trachinos, "were not eaten."

"And there are doubtless men involved, as well," said Lykos. "Else why would kajirae be brought to the Voltai. Surely to content, please, and serve men."

"Pausanias, and his crew, and Kleomenes, with his men, are surely human," said Desmond of Harfax.

"Yes," said Lykos.

"And there are doubtless others," said Desmond.

"I would suppose so," said Lykos.

"And supplies, fit for Builders, were brought in the wagons of Pausanias," said Desmond.

"I did not know that," said Lykos.

"The slave is frightened, beside herself," said Desmond. "The beasts doubtless have excellent night vision, but so, too, has the sleen. They would not be wreaking havoc amongst human allies. That would subvert the purpose of such an alliance. They are powerful, and dangerous, but their strength, though considerable, would not begin to approximate that of a hundred men, though perhaps that of five or ten. Being newly amongst such creatures she may have become confused, bewildered, disconcerted, mad with fear."

"I gather they are dangerous enough," said Lykos.

"Surely," said Desmond of Harfax.

"Do not send me back!" begged the slave.

"I fear something mighty is afoot," said Desmond of Harfax.

"Perhaps in this wilderness of danger and loneliness," said Lykos, "one might incur some favor, and generate some good will, were property to be returned."

"No!" wept the slave.

"I think so," said Desmond.

"Please, no!" she wept.

"What do you know of decks of cards?" asked Desmond.

"What?" said the slave.

"Apparently little," he said.

"Keep me, handsome Master," she said. "I will be a slave of slaves to you! I will please you in a thousand ways!"

"As a slave?" asked Desmond of Harfax.

"Yes, Master, beggingly so!" she cried.

I decided that slave fires had not yet been lit in the sweet belly of the slave, or she would indeed serve zealously, and beggingly, but for the assuagement of her own needs, as well as those of the master.

I also decided I would hate the former Lady Persinna of Ar.

"What of me?" said Trachinos.

"Yes, yes!" she said.

"You have good legs," said Trachinos.

"Thank you, Master," she said.

A Gorean slave tunic leaves little to conjecture about concerning the quality of a slave's legs, and the camisk even less.

"I would hope to please Master," she said to Trachinos.

She smiled at Trachinos, as though from a slave shelf on which she might be chained, on a fellow she hoped would bid on her. I saw that she had proceeded far in learning her collar since that hot afternoon we had been dragged from the cell in the Metellan district and marketed off the low, circular stone block. Had she smiled so at Desmond of Harfax I would have been tempted to leap to her and yank her about, by the hair. To be sure, I did not doubt but what, in a little time, it would have been I who would have been crying for mercy. Surely I would not have done well as a female fighting slave, those large, misshapen female creatures, some bred, who strike and mangle one another for the entertainment of bettors, and free women.

"Are you hungry, thirsty?" asked Desmond of Harfax.

"She is a runaway slave," said Trachinos. "Let her be lashed."

"Her master may attend to such things, as he wishes," said Desmond of Harfax.

"I am very hungry, very thirsty, Master," said Mina, the slave, the former Lady Persinna of Ar.

"Tie her ankles together," said Desmond to Trachinos.

In a bit this was done.

I gather he tied them well, for the awe with which she

regarded him. Had she never been bound by such a man, as the slave she was?

"Allison, Jane, Eve," said Desmond. "Bring her food, and water, and a blanket."

The binding of a female slave's ankles is normally quite sufficient in the way of slave security, if the slave is under surveillance. She cannot rise and run, and it would take time to undo the tie, within which time her efforts would be clear to any about. And should the slave so abuse the privilege of having her hands free, she may be bound instead in total slave helplessness. She may then on her belly feed from a pan as best she can, be fed by hand, or, more likely, not be fed.

I recalled how she had viewed Trachinos with awe. Her ankles had been well fastened. I was not sure she could even manage to undo the knots herself.

"It is late," said Desmond. "Let us camp here tonight."

"This has to do with the slave," said Trachinos. "You are feeding and watering her, and then you wish to allow her to sleep."

"Yes," said Desmond.

"You seem unduly solicitous for the welfare of a slave," he said.

"I want her in good condition, in the morning," said Desmond.

"To be returned to her master?"

"Of course," said Desmond.

After the abandoning of the wagons, several days ago, after the tharlarion had been driven away, we could no longer be shackled to a central bar. Accordingly the masters had made use of small trees as slave posts, about which we would be ankle-shackled. If no such "post" were available, we were shackled to one another, Jane's left ankle to my right ankle, and my left ankle to Eve's right ankle. With the addition of Mina to the "chain," things were the same, except that Eve's left ankle, formerly free, was now was fastened to Mina's right ankle. In this fashion we were all shackled together. I do not think that any of us, saving Mina, were interested in trying to escape, for by now we were well aware we were slaves. On the other hand, we were still shackled. This is not that unusual, even within fortresses, and walled cities. Whereas security and convenience are obviously involved in these matters, I suspect that masters enjoy chaining their slaves. Is there not an uncompromising, ruthless claimancy in such an act, signifying, with heat and pleasure, his absolute possession of the slave? Certainly it well reminds slaves of their bondage. Interestingly, whereas it is seems clear that masters, or many masters, enjoy chaining their slaves, what may be less clear, or more surprising, is that many slaves, indeed most, welcome their chaining; they are grateful for it; what an honor it does them; what a compliment it pays them; they have been found worthy of being chained; they love belonging to their master, and, accordingly, rejoice at, and revel in, their chaining, which is proclamatory of his ownership of them. There is the joy of the mastery, but, too, there is the complementary joy of the submission. They want to submit to a man. They are not happy, fulfilled, and whole until they do so. Hopefully he will keep them, and not sell them. On the chain, they know they are kept. Chaining, too, as is well known, as bonds on the whole, probably because of its relationship to male domination and female responsiveness to male domination, enflames the female, sexually. The most sexual of all females is obviously the female slave. At the feet of a man she learns new worlds of desire and responsiveness. Does this practice, chaining, not say for the master, "You are mine," and does it not say for the willing, helpless slave, "Yes, yes, Master, I am yours!"

In the morning things proceeded much as usual, except for the addition to our party, Mina. Jane, Eve, and I were unshackled, and set about our morning duties. Mina must assist us, but her ankles were shackled together, with something like a foot of chain. The men were taking no chance that she would run.

When the breakfast was done, the fire extinguished, and the packs readied, Astrinax directed Trachinos to bring Mina, the former Lady Persinna of Ar, this known only to me and the slave, to him.

Trachinos knelt her, shackled, before Astrinax.

She looked up at Astrinax, whom she took, naturally, to be the leader of our party.

She was certainly well-formed, and the camisk, even in its looseness, concealed little. She was blond-haired, and blue-eyed, and collared. I supposed she was very beautiful. I recalled that she had sold for considerably more than I had in the Metellan district. I did not know if that would still be the case. Bondage, commonly, as is well known, softens a woman, and increases her desirability. An owned woman is quite different from one who is free. Indeed, simply that she is a slave increases her desirability. In bondage, she comes closest to the natural woman, and farthest from an engineered product of cultural conditioning, whichever product, whichever manufactured article, it might be, given the particular culture; she becomes a more natural woman, richer, deeper, more profound, ever more real, ever more biological, and ever less an artifact. In bondage, she finds herself. In bondage, she becomes the most radically female of women. It is no wonder that free women, with all their conventions, prescriptions, restraints, and frustrations, hate her so.

Mina looked up at Astrinax.

"What are you going to do with me?" she wept.

"Return you to your master, of course," said Astrinax.

"No, no!" she begged.

She tried to spring up, but stumbled, shackled, and was then again on her knees before Astrinax.

"It is the law," said Astrinax.

"Please, no!" she wept.

"We could keep her and sell her," said Trachinos.

"Yes, yes!" she begged.

"No," said Astrinax. "She is to be returned to her master. That is the law."

The slave put down her head, shuddering, weeping.

"Have pity on her!" I said to Desmond of Harfax. "They will listen to you! Tell them! You cannot return her to beasts!"

"It is in accord with my plans," he said.

"You are heartless," I said.

"Much is at stake," he said.

"Hide her!" I said.

"That is not practical," he said.

"Please!" I said.

"She is a female slave," he said. "She ran away. She is to be returned to her master."

"I heard Master Lykos," I said. "You hope to be welcomed,

to incur favor, to generate good will, or such, by returning the slave!"

"Certainly," he said. "Would you have us incur disfavor and generate ill will, thus jeopardizing our enterprise?"

"What enterprise?" I said.

I then found myself beneath the frown of a free person.

"Forgive me, Master!" I said.

"Would you have us release her here, into the mountains, to die?" he asked.

"Bind and leash the captive," said Astrinax. "Then unshackle her."

Desmond of Harfax approached Mina with a short thong. I saw Trachinos drop a widened leash collar about the head of the slave, and then adjust it to her neck. He grinned. Clearly it pleased the brute to do this. Many masters enjoy having slaves on their leashes. It certainly makes clear the relationship involved, both for he who holds the leash and she who is leashed. I wondered if she had ever been promenaded in Ar. Many masters, I supposed, would have been pleased to walk such a slave. She looked ahead, not meeting his eyes, frightened. He jerked the strap twice, against the leash ring. She whimpered. It was a tiny sound. It could scarcely be heard. Almost at the same time Desmond of Harfax drew her hands behind her, and thonged them together, snugly. This made me angry. I did not like to see him tie another woman's hands behind her. Certainly a woman understands what it means to be tied by a man. It was I who wanted his thongs!

The slave now stood, leashed and bound, her head down.

Lykos crouched down, and removed her shackles.

I recalled that the former Lady Persinna of Ar had sold for more than I, considerably more.

"You are heartless," I said to Desmond of Harfax. "You have tied her too tightly!"

I was suddenly cuffed, struck to the dirt. I looked up at him, frightened. The left side of my face stung, terribly.

"We leave," said Astrinax.

"Proceed," said Desmond of Harfax. "We shall join you shortly."

I struggled to my knees, and watched our party proceed down the trail. Once Jane and Eve looked back at me, frightened.

They were last in the march. Trachinos, who held the leash of the former Lady Persinna of Ar, was forward. This was, I supposed, that the leashed slave would be prominently displayed, to make it clear that she was not being concealed, or such. One might suppose, then, that our party would be amenable to returning her, now captured and helpless, to her rightful owner or owners. Astrinax and the Lady Bina were also forward.

I looked up, at Master Desmond.

"Why did you speak as you did?" he asked.

"I hate you," I said.

"I find it difficult to understand you," he said. "Perhaps it is because you are a barbarian."

"Do you find it difficult to understand Jane and Eve?" I asked.

"No," he said.

"They are barbarians," I said.

"True," he said.

"Why, then," I asked, "am I so difficult to understand?"

"I do not know," he said.

"I thought it was easy for a man to understand a woman who was in his collar," I said.

"You are not in my collar," he said.

I looked up at him, tears in my eyes. "Am I not?" I said.

"You are jealous of Mina?" he said.

"Perhaps if I were in a camisk," I said, "you would find me more attractive."

"Your tunic," he observed, "conceals little."

"Our party advances," I said.

"Do not concern yourself," he said.

"I loathe you, I hate you," I said.

He looked down at me, thoughtfully.

"What are you going to do with me?" I asked.

"Perhaps bind you, hand and foot," he said, "and leave you here, on the trail, for larls or sleen."

"You cannot do that," I said. "I am not yours! I belong to the Lady Bina!"

"I could do that," he said. "But I would not do it."

"Why?" I said.

"Because," said he, "you are not mine. You belong to the Lady Bina. Too, you are in my care."

"Yes, Master," I said.

"I could, though," he said, "give you a good lashing with my belt. I think you would profit from such a lashing."

"I trust that you will not do so," I said, uneasily.

"You said that you and Mina were sold together," he said.

"Yes, Master, many months ago, in the Metellan district."

"It is strange that she would have been sold in the Metellan district," he said.

"How so?" I asked.

"She is quite beautiful," he said.

"But not so strange that I would have been sold there?" I asked.

"She brought a higher price," he said.

"Yes," I said.

"Much higher?" he asked.

"Yes!" I said.

"I begin to see your concern," he said.

"Master is perceptive," I said. "Please do not strike a kneeling slave!" I said.

He lowered his hand, and I breathed more easily. I could still feel his former blow.

"You regard yourself as far inferior to her?" he asked.

"I merely, as a pitying slave," I said, "dared to call attention to your cruelty, your heartlessness, the way you bound her wrists behind her."

"It is merely the way one binds a slave," he said. "It is not done with excessive cruelty. It is merely that a slave is to be made utterly helpless, that she be bound with perfection, and that she will know herself utterly helpless, and bound with perfection."

"I see," I said.

"She has more body than you," he said, "but I do not see that you are all that inferior to her."

"Oh?" I said, angrily.

"You are generally worthless," he said. "You are stupid, vain, petty, selfish, deceitful, and, if the opportunity should present itself, I fear dishonest. I have serious reservations concerning your character."

"I am not stupid," I said.

"Still," he said, "your face and figure, and something indefinable about you, are not without interest."

"I rejoice," I said.

"Remove your tunic," he said. "I want to see you in nothing but your collar."

"Surely Master has seen me often enough in the slave wagon," I said.

"In nothing but your collar," he said.

"You would have me strip myself here, in the open?" I asked.

"Now," he said.

I slipped from my tunic, a slave.

I straightened my body. "Is Master pleased?" I asked, acidly.

"No!" I cried. "Please, no!"

Then I was kneeling down, head down, to the dirt, muchly cuffed, twice kicked. "It is my hope that Master is pleased," I wept.

"You had best hope that I am pleased," he said.

"Yes, Master," I wept. "Yes, Master!"

"We shall see," he said.

"Master?" I said.

"Perform," he said.

"Please, no, Master!" I said.

"Roll about," he said. "Writhe! Pose. Assume attitudes. Display your limbs! Various positions. Show what you have, slave! Perhaps someone will buy you. Perhaps you will not be beaten. Perhaps you will not be thrown to sleen!"

The dust, scattered and stirred, was wet with sweat and tears.

"More!" he said. "More frenziedly, more pathetically, more wildly, more boldly, more violently, more desperately!"

"Yes, Master," I wept.

"And so," he said, "the slave performs before the loathed, hated master, frantically hoping to be found pleasing."

"I do not hate you Master!" I cried out, an outburst breaking from my tortured body.

"Enough," he said, angrily.

I crawled to him on my belly, weeping. I pressed my lips to his boots and kissed them, again and again.

"I do not hate you, Master," I said. "I love you!"

"Your hair is growing out," he said.

"I love you," I said. "I love you!"

"Of what worth is the love of a worthless slave?" he asked.

"Of no worth, Master," I said.

I rose to all fours. I dared not meet his eyes.

"Garmenture," said he. "And fetch your pack. We must join the others."

Shortly thereafter I stood on the trail. I was now tunicked. I stood very still. Our party must be a pasang, or so, ahead. He adjusted the pack. That is sometimes done.

"I do love you, Master," I whispered to him. "I think I have loved you since the Sul Market, in Ar, when I was half-stripped, with my wrists bound behind me, and you, a stranger, ordered me to my knees before you."

"I see," he said.

"I looked up, and feared you were my master, and, I fear, I desired it so."

"I see," he said.

"And perhaps," I said, "as you gazed upon me, a kneeling slave, with your master's appraisal, you wondered how I might appear, naked, chained at a slave ring."

"That sort of thing is common with any fellow," he said, "looking on any woman, slave or free."

"Yes, Master," I said.

"And," said he, "as you were at the time, that conjecture required little imagination."

"Did my performance please you?" I asked.

"Yes," he said.

"You made me perform well," I said.

"That was my intention," he said.

"You humiliated me," I said.

"You enjoyed it," he said.

"Oh?" I said.

"What woman does not enjoy displaying herself, naked, as the slave and slut she is?" he asked.

"It is my hope," I said, "that the Lady Bina will give me to you, or sell me to you."

"Do not concern yourself with such things," he said.

"Such thoughts occur to a slave," I said.

"Matters of moment abound," he said.

"Please care for me," I begged.

"Though you be but a slave," he laughed.

"Though I be but a slave!" I said.

"We must hasten, to rejoin the group," he said.

"Master!" I begged.

"Slave girls are unimportant," he said.

"Yes, Master," I wept.

"One does not care for the female slave," he said. "She is no more than a beast. For her it is the whip, bonds, the collar, service, ownership, work, and the inordinate pleasures which she must frequently and unquestioningly provide."

"Yes, Master," I said.

"Why else do you think women are collared?"

"Yes, Master."

"Surely you learned such things in the slave house," he said.

"Yes, Master," I said.

"What was your name when free?" he asked.

"Allison Ashton-Baker," I said.

"Well," said he, "does the former Allison Ashton-Baker understand these things?"

"Yes," I said, "Master."

"Heel," he said.

"Yes, Master," I said, and hurried to follow him, a bit behind, on the left.

* * * *

We made our way along the trail.

We were well behind the party, but I had little doubt that we, a free man and one slave, might shortly overtake it, possibly within the passage of an Ahn. The Lady Bina was robed, though less decorously than would have been thought proper in Ar, and Mina, our captive, was leashed and bound. Such things commonly reduce the speed of a march. Moreover, the party would presumably proceed slowly in this unfamiliar terrain, and certainly with the Crag of Kleinias in the offing, rearing up before them, into the sky.

"I am lovely, am I not?" I asked Master Desmond.

"Yes," he said, "and vain, and such."

"Might I not now bring a good price?" I asked.

"Forget about Mina," he said.

"Master!" I begged

He did not look back.

"I would suppose so," he said.

"Better than Mina?" I said.

"Do not be absurd," he said.

"Might Master bid on me?" I asked.

"Many men might," he said, "who did not know your true nature."

"My true nature?" I said.

"Your pettiness, and such," he said.

"My belly wants you," I said.

"Do slave fires burn there?" he asked.

"Not yet," I said. "I do not think so."

"It is easy enough to ignite them," he said.

"Ignite them!" I said.

"No," he said.

"You did such things to me in Ar, by Six Bridges," I said, "with your kiss, your touch."

"It is pleasant to do such things to a slave," he said, "to render her helplessly responsive, whether she wishes it or not."

"I wish it, Master," I said.

"Even a petty slave," he said, "of little worth, may bring a good price if she kicks, and squirms, and gasps and moans, and writhes well."

"Allison begs Master for his touch!" I said.

"You are in my care," he said.

"No one would know!" I said.

"I would know," he said, "and the slave would know."

"Oh, yes," I said, angrily, "honor! Honor!"

He did not respond, but I saw a fist clench.

"But Master is tempted, is he not?" I said.

"Yes," he said, "Master is tempted."

I smiled to myself, and was well satisfied with this answer.

We continued on, and then he said, "Do you think you would be any good in the furs?"

"I would do my best to be pleasing to my Master," I said.

"So, too," said he, "would any slave."

"Yes, Master," I said.

After a time, I called out, "I think Master would bid on me!"

"Perhaps," he said.

"Hold!" he said, stopping. "Ahead!"

"Yes, Master," I said.

Ahead, on the trail, was our party, Astrinax; the Lady Bina; Lykos; Trachinos, his leash on Mina, the former Lady Persinna of Ar; Akesinos, the confederate of Trachinos; and two slaves, bearing packs, Jane and Eve.

With them, before them, and about them, were several other figures. Several of these figures were human. I recognized Kleomenes amongst them. Several were not human. They were large and shaggy. Some carried long-handled, double-bladed axes. These were Kurii.

Chapter Twenty-Seven

"All hail Lady Bina, future Ubara of all Gor!" said Kleomenes, lifting his goblet. The humans about the long table rose, lifting their goblets, facing the Lady Bina, who sat in a curule chair at the head of the table, as though enthroned. She bowed her head, graciously, acknowledging the toast.

Men through back their heads and downed the contents of the goblets.

About the table, mixed in with the others, were Astrinax, Desmond, Lykos, Trachinos, and Akesinos. They were not so placed that they could speak to one another.

Far down the table I saw Pausanias, whose caravan we had followed to the vicinity of the Crag of Kleinias.

His men were doubtless about, though I did not see them.

Doubtless there were some humans of the "Cave," too, so to speak, lesser allies of the Kurii, who were also absent.

I did see the men who had accompanied Kleomenes.

All the slaves present, including myself, Jane, and Eve, were camisked. That was how the men of the Cave of Agamemnon, Theocrat of the World, Eleventh Face of the Nameless One, would have us. I knew nothing of this Agamemnon, though I gathered he must be Kur, nor what might be involved in the associated titles. In the banquet hall there were three prominent, visible Kurii, he referred to as "Lucius," who seemed to be first in the Cave, and two who crouched in the background, like beasts of prey, surveying the festivities. These, in human sounds, were said to be Timarchos and Lysymachos. On a shelf above and behind them there was a metallic box, which, I supposed, given the care with which it had been handled, and the watchfulness with which it was regarded, must contain some precious substance, a treasure of some sort, perhaps gold or jewels. If so, I did not understand why it should be placed as it was, on a shelf in the open. Would it not have been wiser to have locked it away somewhere? The box seemed a strange one for a strong box, as it bore no bands of iron, nor a heavy lock, or locks. Rather it had certain projections fixed in its surface, and what appeared to be screens or lenses. The three Kurii, Lucius, Timarchos, and Lysymachos, all had translators slung about their large necks, on golden chains, by means of which, doubtless, they followed the progress of the feast, and by means of which they might, if they desired, communicate with the humans present. I would learn that the status amongst the Kurii was indicated, to themselves, at least, by differences in harnessing, and by rings worn on the left wrist. These rings were earned, or won, I gathered, in some sort of contest. To humans, those who wore the golden chains were of highest rank, those who wore silver were of the next rank, and those whose translator chains were of common metal, usually closely meshed links of iron, were third. Below these were most of the Kurii of the Cave, who carried no translators. These, I discovered, were generally avoided by the humans. I did not know how many Kurii inhabited the Cave, but I would have supposed some forty or fifty. Many Kurii I could not tell apart, for days. Even then I sometimes made mistakes, or became confused. Interestingly, though I suppose it was only to be expected, many Kurii had a similar difficulty distinguishing humans, particularly slaves, for we were similarly garbed. They could, however, easily distinguish men from women, given the radical sexual differences of form in our species. I later learned there were no female Kurii in the Cave. Apparently there are three or four sexes amongst the Kurii, depending on how one understands such things. I know little about this so I will simply recount what I gathered from conversations amongst the Kurii's human allies in the Cave. There are the males, and the conceiving females, and the nurturing "females," or "wombs," which are irrational and sessile. As a fourth sex, or a latent first sex, there are the Nondominants, which, I gather, are males of a sort. These are generally despised, supposedly, by the conceiving females, while the nurturing "females," eyeless, and mindless, would not know they exist. Occasionally, under certain circumstances, physiological or social, perhaps the lack of a Dominant, the Nondominant may occasionally become a Dominant, in effect, a true male. Thus, there is an ambiguity amongst Kurii with respect to something which one would suppose would be easy to determine, namely, the number of sexes in the species.

I have mentioned the three prominent, visible Kurii in the hall, Lucius, Timarchos, and Lysymachos. There was another in the hall who was visible, but, clearly, not prominently placed. I knew him from before. He was the blind Kur. We were given no human name for him. He crouched in a darkened corner of the hall, and some meat had been thrown to the floor before him, for which he must reach about, scratching here and there, and find.

I saw no sign of Lord Grendel.

There were several slaves in the room. Others were elsewhere. All had been brought to the Voltai to serve and content the human allies of the Kurii. Gorean men do not wish to be without female slaves. Four additional slaves had been brought to the Cave by Pausanias, girls bought at a state auction in Ar, amongst whom was Mina. She had fled, been recaptured by our party, and returned to her master, Lucius. It was his intention to have her fed, alive, to lesser Kurii. Trachinos, however, learning her projected fate, had cried out to Kleomenes, "No! I will buy her! Sell her to me!" Kleomenes arranged this matter with Lucius, and Lucius, who took little interest in the affairs of humans, turned the coin over to Kleomenes, a silver tarsk.

I myself had never sold for so much but I suspected that I might now, myself, sell for as much. To be sure, one does not know what one will sell for until, say, the auctioneer closes his hand, and cries, "Done!"

Mina had thrown herself to the feet of Trachinos, seized his knees, and pressed her face against his thigh.

She knew he tied women well.

I had little doubt she would be excellently mastered. She knelt behind him, so close that she might have reached out, and touched him.

She was far from the glories of her freedom in Ar.

I was not permitted to kneel behind Desmond of Harfax, or even behind the Lady Bina. Similarly, Jane was not permitted to kneel behind Astrinax, nor Eve behind Lykos, whose slave she knew herself, and whose slave she longed to be.

We served as though we might be common slaves, no different from the others.

Indeed, it was not clear to us, after some days, to whom we belonged. We knew, of course, we belonged to someone, or something, for we were slaves.

* * * *

"Nora!" I had cried.

Our party had been intercepted on the trail to the Crag of Kleinias, and we had been conducted by a party of humans and Kurii to the opening of the Cave of Agamemnon, Theocrat of the World, Eleventh Face of the Nameless One, which lay secretly within the massive vastness of the Crag of Kleinias. The Cave was partly natural, but had clearly been enlarged, extended, and considerably modified by some form of technologically advanced engineering. Concealed then within the Crag of Kleinias was a labyrinthine complex of considerable proportions. There was housing within that complex sufficient for a thousand men and a thousand beasts, but no such numbers were present. I would have supposed, rather, that its occupancy was no more than some fifty beasts and less than some seventy or eighty men. We discovered that the wagons of Pausanias had been drawn up, inside. The wagons, as we noted in passing them, had been emptied. The tharlarion, the draft tharlarion, and the mounts of Kleomenes' riders, the bipedalian tharlarion, were stabled, though separately, within a hundred yards of the wagons. We would learn later that there were laboratories and workshops in the complex, as well as kitchens, storerooms, feast rooms, pleasure rooms, punishment rooms, exercise areas, an infirmary, conference chambers, and such. Also, there were tarsk pens, verr pens, and vulo cages. There were also illuminated internal gardens and growing areas, some utilizing large, shallow trays of water. Something approximating a small, self-sustaining world appeared to be involved. It seemed forms of life might exist there, almost indefinitely, without importing food from the outside. The Crag of Kleinias itself provided water. Many areas were restricted, humans and most Kurii not being permitted in them. These were usually the laboratories and certain workshops. There were also slave quarters. The facility had contained fifteen slaves. This number had been augmented by the four brought from Ar, and, if we were to be counted, the three who had accompanied Astrinax and the Lady Bina into the Voltai, Jane, Eve, and Allison. One would then have had some nineteen slaves, or, if we were to be counted, twenty-two slaves.

When we had approached the mouth of the Cave, a further number of Kurii and men had emerged to greet us. Many of these, men and beasts, were wearing wreaths and garlands. Pennons and streamers, too, were about, and flowers, seemingly anomalous in the terrain, for we knew not then of the illuminated gardens within the Cave. Some of the beasts were striking on small bars, which, we gathered, constituted a form of music. It was made clear to us that these arrangements were in honor of the Lady Bina, welcoming her to the household of Agamemnon. This seemed to please, but did not seem to astonish, the lovely Lady Bina, who may have been led to expect something of the kind, given her conversations long ago in Ar with the blind Kur. It was my supposition, of course, that all this had much more to do with Lord Grendel than with the Lady Bina, who, for all her remarkable intelligence, was in some ways astoundingly naive; certainly she knew little of Gor, little of the channels of politics, little of the springs of power, little of the motivations and plans of men and Kurii.

The earlier attempt on the part of Kleomenes and his hunters to dissuade us from proceeding farther into the Voltai and the attack, if it were an attack, and not an unanticipated consequence of the hunting, of the wild tarsk at the Wagons, suggested that, at that time, the blind Kur had not made contact with his fellows. Certainly now, Kleomenes, and the others, seemed well disposed to our party, welcoming us on the trail, helping us to the Cave, and such.

There were various levels in the Cave, at least four. These were connected by ramps. The Cave, on each level with which I was familiar, possessed a large number of wide corridors. The walls and ceilings of these corridors were largely of natural rock, but the floors had been leveled and smoothed. The Cave was lit, where lit, by illuminated globes, which, interestingly, seemed self-sufficient. Clearly they did not use fire, as you are likely to think of it, as in, say, candles, lamps, braziers, torches, or such. The lighting tended to differ from area to area, depending on whether the area was largely utilized by humans or Kurii, humans desiring more light, and Kurii needing less, or wanting less, at least as compared to the humans. Coming from one of the darker corridors to the vicinity of the Cave's opening, as in carrying a message, or provender, to the guards, I was sometimes dazzled, painfully so. Kurii apparently make the adjustment more quickly.

Led within the Cave we marveled.

Long and broad were the corridors, high the ceilings, refulgent the lighting. Numerous were the portals about, and abundant the passageways. I doubt that any of us, unless the Lady Bina, from her conversations with the blind Kur in Ar, had suspected that anything like this might exist on Gor, and surely not within the terrifying, rugged wilderness of the mighty Voltai. Yet, too, we would discover that other portions of the Cave, some of them, were far less awesome to humans, but, one supposes, more congenial to Kurii. I know little of the biology, or history, of the Kur species, but I have gathered that it, perhaps like the human species, long ago in its past, may have frequented caves, using them as dens or lairs. In any event, perhaps due to the warmth of their pelting and the excellence of their dark vision, for the Kur can hunt in the night as well as in the day, they seem, even today, to find, unlike the human, cave-like surroundings congenial. There is little which can surprise one in the twisting, confining narrowness of a cave, and it can be dangerous to enter one. I have been told that even on the metal worlds, the steel worlds, the engineered dwellings of Kurii are often reminiscent of dens or lairs. A building, for example, with its halls, may resemble a maze of tunnels. In any event, whatever may be the truth in these matters, the decor and structure of the vast "Cave" was not uniform, and, from the human point of view, certain areas were more pleasant than others. Interestingly, most districts within the "Cave" seemed to have been constructed with humans in mind, perhaps to suggest a kinship of outlook and values betwixt the species. Humans, I gathered, might be important in the plans of Kurii, at least initially.

Shortly after we had entered the Cave, a Kur took Mina's leash and dragged her away. At that time we did not know if we would ever see her again. Following this our party was divided into three groups. Astrinax and the Lady Bina were conducted, almost ceremoniously, in one direction by Kleomenes. The men other than Astrinax, namely, Desmond, Lykos, Trachinos, and Akesinos, were then led away in another direction, by one of the men of Kleomenes, presumably to their quarters. The third group consisted of Jane, Eve, and myself. We were not to be led, but to precede another of Kleomenes' men. All of us, men and slaves, had earlier been relieved of our packs. Our men, however, were permitted to retain their weapons. I do not think that Lykos, Trachinos, or Akesinos, would have cared to have been disarmed.

"Move, kajirae," said the fellow behind us, and we hurried before him, down a side corridor.

"Hold!" he said, and we stopped, instantly, not looking back.

He then came about, before us.

"Do not kneel," he said.

How naturally we, as kajirae, had been on the point of kneeling. I felt decidedly uneasy, being on my feet before a free man. I suspect Jane and Eve felt similarly. I did not wish to be switched, or lashed. He had, of course, told us not to kneel. The three of us standing there, in our collars and tunics, were small before him. Much depends on context, of course, and one grows sensitive to what the master may wish. Sometimes one will stand before him but then, commonly, with the head bowed. If the master is sitting, one might, too, sit, but on the carpet, or tiles, at his feet. Too, one might lie before him, or near him, perhaps beside him, as might another animal, curled, or languid, or such, and so on. We are taught much in the slave house, how we should be. Sometimes one might await him, naked, in the furs, spread on the floor, at the foot of his couch. We flame, in need. One hopes he may deign to caress us.

"There!" he said, indicating a portal, to our right.

Jane thrust open the door, which was heavy, and she, followed by Eve and myself, entered. Behind us we heard the door close, and heard a bolt thrown into place.

We looked about ourselves, apprehensively, but there seemed little in the room to suggest a cause for alarm. It was a large room, well lit, with red walls and a yellow ceiling. Its floor was also yellow and formed of what appeared to be smoothed wooden beams, fitted closely together. There were two doors, that through which we had entered, and one at the far end of the room. The room was bare, containing no rugs, no hangings, no draperies, no furniture.

"What are we to do?" asked Eve.

"What is there to do?" said Jane.

We would wait. After a time, weary from the trail, and perhaps worn from the fear and amazement generated by our new surroundings, we lay on the beams of the yellow wooden flooring.

I am not sure how long we waited, but I do not think it was long, only longer than we might have anticipated.

Perhaps ten or twelve Ehn.

"Perhaps they do not know we are here," said Eve.

"Perhaps you would like to call out, or pound on the door," said Jane.

"No!" said Eve.

We waited a little longer.

"I do not think we are to be housed here," said Eve.

"No," said Jane, "I do not think so. I see no blankets, no slave mats, no rings."

"Or cages," I said.

A bit later the door at the far end of the room opened, and a large-handed, brawny fellow, bearded, with a leather cap, entered, carrying a lidless tool box by its triangular handle. As soon as we saw that the entrant was male we went to first-obeisance position, kneeling, head to the floor, hands, palms down, at the side of our head.

The tool box was set down near us and we, not looking up, heard the fellow reaching into the box, moving one or another of its contents about.

A bit later I heard Jane gasp, heard a sharp, cutting sound, and, a bit later, the dropping of a light metal object into the tool box.

"May I speak, Master?" I begged.

"Yes," he said, moving toward me.

"There is some mistake," I said. "We are the slaves of the Lady Bina, honored guest in this household. We belong to her!"

"There is no mistake," he said. "Keep your head down."

I felt a thick, curved blade thrust between my neck and the collar, and knew this was matched with a similar blade, one with which it was paired. The tool had two stout handles which were spread, and would then be brought muchly together. The fellow held the two handles rather at the ends, where the most leverage might be exerted. I sensed him strain, then apply more pressure, and then I heard the breaking of the metal. He put the tool down and spread and pulled the sides of the rent collar from my throat. I heard it put into the tool box. In a moment or two Eve had been similarly served.

"Kneel up," he said. Then he said, "Beg me to accept your tunics, and then present them to me, properly."

I was frightened, without my collar.

We slipped from our tunics.

"I beg you to accept my tunic, Master," said Jane. She then held it to him, her arms extended, her head down between her extended arms.

Eve and I then uttered the identical ritual phrase, and, as had Jane, proffered our tunics, and properly, to the fellow, who then turned about and left the room.

We looked at one another.

"I am afraid," I said.

"I, too," said Jane, uneasily.

Eve smiled, and stood up. She posed, and pointed to her throat. "Look," she said, "I am a free woman!"

"Show me your left thigh," said Jane, angrily.

Eve then knelt beside us, quietly.

She was well marked, as were we.

A few Ehn later the far door opened once more, and a fellow we recognized, one of Kleomenes' hunters, entered, but not the one who had brought us earlier to this chamber. We went to first obeisance position. I was vaguely aware that a woman had entered behind him.

"Kneel up," had said the man. The woman was at his side, a little behind, on his left.

"Nora!" I cried.

"Nora!" exclaimed Jane, joyously.

"Nora!" wept Eve, with relief.

Then I saw the look in her eye, and I shrank back, a Gorean slave. Her first reaction, when we knelt before her, our faces clearly to be seen, was one of astonishment, but then, almost immediately, one of pleasure, and gratification, and then, as her eyes fell on me, one of hostility and triumph.

"These slaves know you?" said the man.

"Yes!" she said.

"'Yes'?" he said.

"Yes," she said, quickly adding, "Master."

She was a strikingly beautiful slave, with lovely features, long dark hair, and a figure that would easily bring silver on the block. As with the rest of us, masters had seen to it that she would be improved. She had been stunningly attractive on Earth, and I thought her more so now. And I was certain that I, and others, such as Jane and Eve, had become more attractive on Gor, as well. I am not sure to what factors, perhaps several, these transformations might be attributed, but I suspected they might, at least in part, have something to do with the naturalness, the openness, the honesty, the lack of hypocrisy, of the Gorean world itself. She was camisked, as Mina had been. On her neck there was a dark metal collar. Mina had worn such a collar. From what the Lady Bina had said on the trail, based on the lettering, I took it to be a Kur collar.

"You know me, Nora!" said Jane. "I am Jane, Jane, from the house!"

"Remember me!" said Eve. "I am Eve! Eve! From the house!"

"We are so happy to see you!" said Jane.

Eve began to weep with joy.

Nora regarded us. She carried some objects, some of cloth, some of metal. About her right wrist, from its loop, dangled a switch. Across her forehead, bound there, tied at the back of her head, was a talmit.

I looked upon this simple, narrow folding of cloth, and was terrified.

"I am so happy!" said Jane.

"I, too!" cried Eve.

If a free man had not been present I feared Jane and Eve might have leapt to their feet to gather Nora into their arms.

"And you, Allison," said Nora, "are you not happy to see me, too?"

I put down my head, afraid.

"Kneel up, straightly, more straightly," said Nora. "Heads up!"

We knelt properly, our heads raised.

She cast three objects, circular metal objects, to the floor before us.

"Collar them," she said.

The collaring of a woman is almost always done by a man. There are few things which make a woman more conscious of her sex than being collared by a man. The collar functions on many levels. It is an identificatory device, of course, which proclaims her bondage, and often identifies her master. But more subtly it is a symbol of her womanhood, what she is, what she is for, and such. It is a symbol of a natural relationship, the female in submission to the male, or, within the institutions of a natural civilization, within the legalities of a natural culture, the relationship of the slave to the master.

We were not collared gently.

Each of us heard the snap of the collar lock.

Each of us was now recollared.

Each of us wore a Kur collar.

I supposed it was no coincidence that the fellow who had collared us was one of the hunters of Kleomenes. From the wagons, days before, we knew the sort of men who might dare to mount and manage the bipedalian hunting tharlarion, the sort of men who, armed with a slender lance, would match themselves against Voltai tarsk. We were females, small and soft, perhaps lovely, so different from them; they are large, strong, impatient, possessive, demanding, uncompromising, and dangerous. It was obvious with such men, as with Goreans generally, that it was we who would be owned, and collared.

The hunter, done with our collaring, took his leave, paying

no attention to Nora. She wore the talmit but, to him, she was only another slave.

The door closed behind the fellow.

"He is gone!" cried Jane, delightedly, in English, one of the barbarian tongues, one we shared. "Dear Nora! Dear Nora!" she exclaimed.

"Yes," cried Eve, happily, "dear, dear Nora!" She, too, had spoken in English.

"Remain kneeling," said Nora. "Keep your hands down, on your thighs." It took me a moment to realize that she had spoken in Gorean.

Jane and Eve, puzzled, knelt back, on their heels.

We then felt bits of cloth with tangles of thong thrown against our bodies.

We let them fall, against us. They lay upon our thighs. We did not pick them up. We had not received permission to do so.

"Nora?" said Jane.

"Nora?" said Eve.

"Put them on," said Nora.

We slipped the narrow rectangles of cloth, with their simple, centered, circular openings, over our heads, and then wrapped the long leather thong twice about our waist, and knotted it at our left hip. The knot is to be a simple bowknot, so that it may be easily loosened by a man's casual tug. It is at the left hip because most men are right handed. The length of the thong, or cord, or binding fiber, whatever is used, is intended to allow for a variety of slave ties, or tetherings, hand and foot, or whatever the master may please.

"Nora?" said Eve, uncertainly.

"Be silent," said Nora.

Nora then surveyed us.

"You are to speak in Gorean," said Nora, "for it is the language of your masters."

I sensed that Eve wanted muchly to speak, but she did not do so.

"It is my understanding," said Nora, "that you have been named Jane, Eve, and Allison."

These were now, of course, slave names, only that, no more.

The slave, as an animal, has no name in her own right, but, as any animal, may be given any name the master pleases.

"Those names will do," she said. "I am Nora," she said.

She walked about us, and then was again before us.

"It is a long time," she said, "since I have seen you three in camisks. It was at a party, as I recall. You looked well in them. You are the sort of women who should be in camisks. All of you! They are suitable for such as you."

Did she think of herself as a free woman, I wondered. Did she not know that she, too, was now camisked, now collared?

"Allison," she said, "straighten your body."

I knelt more straightly.

"Is that how you belt a camisk?" she asked. "Belt it more closely, more snugly. Men prefer it that way."

I fumbled at the thong,

"Must I do it for you?" she asked.

"No!" I said.

"'No'?" she asked.

"No, Mistress," I said.

Jane and Eve gasped.

I then drew the double thong more tightly about me, and knotted it, closely, at the left hip.

"You may thank me," she said.

"Thank you, Mistress," I said.

"Who thanks me?" she asked.

"Allison, the slave, thanks Mistress," I said.

"You are here, all of you," said Nora, "to work, and please men. Do you understand?"

"Yes, Mistress," we said.

"Who is first girl?" she asked.

"You, Mistress," we said.

Nora then held the switch to our lips, those of Jane, Eve, and Allison. We all kissed it, with deference.

Nora wore the talmit. She was first girl.

"Jane, Eve," she said. "Go through the far door. You will find the slave quarters. You will find three empty cages there, with the gates ajar, against the left wall, as you enter. Jane, enter the first, Eve, the second. Once within, pull the gate shut. It will lock, automatically. Go."

Jane and Eve, confused, shaken, distraught, disbelieving, rose up. I would have risen, too, but Nora's switch, lightly on my left shoulder, indicated I should remain where I was. "The slave girl, Allison, will follow you shortly," she said.

Nora waited until Jane and Eve had disappeared through the far door which, as it had been closed, they closed, again, behind themselves. Nora and I were then alone in the large room. She walked about me, and then, again, stood before me. I think she was pleased to do so. Too, I had the sense that I had been assessed, as a slave.

She struck the switch into the palm of her left hand, sharply. I winced.

"Do you wish to be switched?" she asked.

"No, Mistress," I said.

"On the old world, in the house, on the campus, at the college, in the town," she said, "you thought yourself more beautiful than I, more attractive."

"You were always more beautiful than I," I said. "Perhaps I was more attractive."

"More fit for a collar, at a man's feet," she said.

"I do not know," I said.

"I wear the talmit!" she said.

"Yes, Mistress," I said.

"How annoying and contemptible I found you," she said, "laughing and smiling, so pretentiously suave, so fraudulently refined, so feignedly clever, so aristocratically chatting and gossiping, so pointlessly sparkling, so calling attention to yourself, so posing and posturing, so carrying on, and, too, so irritatingly and prescribedly slender, just as the fashion magazines would require, so pert and trim, so well-dressed, so tasteful, so refined, so chic, not a hair out of place, your makeup invariably subtle, scarcely existing, and perfect, looking about, over your shoulder, those glances, what an actress, your little movements, flirting with the boys, leading them on, amusing yourself at their expense, rebuffing them when your sport was done."

"Were we all so different," I asked, "even Mistress?"

"You were pretty," she said, "but petty, too, and empty, shallow, a nothing, a sly, selfish, cunning, opportunistic, calculating, vain, egotistical, little chit. And how popular you were with the boys, and, oh yes, how aware of it you were! How many envied you!"

"Surely as many, or more, envied you," I said.

"What a match, with such delightful charms, might you not have garnered for yourself."

"I had few repeat dates," I said, "of the sort I wished."

"A serious male," she said, "soon saw through your shallowness and hypocrisy. At best you might be of some transient interest at a slave ring."

"Perhaps I am different now!" I said.

"You are," she said, "you are now, as you should be, branded, and collared."

"What of you?" I demanded.

"You dared to think of yourself as my equal, my rival," she said.

"Was I not," I asked, "and one or two of the others?"

"You were never my equal," she said. "I was always, by far, your superior."

"Yes, Mistress," I said. I supposed it was true.

"How I hated you, how I despised you!" she said.

I put my head down.

"And now," she said, "it is pleasant to see you again, and as you should be, and are, kajira."

"A slave notes," I said, looking up, "that Mistress is camisked, and collared."

"Do you think you are clever?" she asked.

"Mistress knows I am intelligent," I said, "just as I know that Mistress is intelligent."

"I wonder what Mrs. Rawlinson saw in you," she said.

"Doubtless the same that she saw in you, and the others," I said, "that we might do, as slaves."

"What do you know of Mrs. Rawlinson?" she asked.

"Nothing," I said. "Doubtless she is on our former world, going about her work, abetting slavers, locating and assessing other girls such as we for the chains of Gor."

"Some of us wear the talmit," she said.

"I know one," I said.

"I trust you have been red-silked," she said.

"Yes, Mistress," I said. "White-silk slaves are rare on Gor."

"I would have enjoyed seeing you in the hands of a man," she said.

"It is possible I might not appear that much different from Mistress," I said, "were she in the hands of a man."

"Beware," she said.

"Perhaps Mistress has been red-silked, as well," I said.

She slashed down with the switch, striking my left shoulder.

"Forgive me, Mistress," I begged.

"Now I have you amongst my girls!" she said.

"Please be merciful, Mistress," I begged.

"Who would have dreamed of this, pretty Allison," she said.

"Please be kind, Mistress," I said.

She then cried out in rage, and a storm of blows fell upon me, and I went, gasping and sobbing, to all fours, and then to my belly, trying to cover my head, and then, struck repeatedly, I was twisting on the floor, back to belly, then belly to back, and then to belly, again, and then the blows stopped, and I was on my belly, trembling, my hands beside my head, my body a raging tissue of fire.

"Who is Mistress, and who is slave!" she demanded.

"Mistress is Mistress, and I am slave!" I wept. My insolence, my forwardness, my boldness, was at an end. I was then only a beaten slave, cringing before her Mistress, fearing to be further punished.

This was Gor, and I was kajira.

"You are going to be well worked," said Nora, "and often in shackles. You will know the heaviest of labors and the lowest and most repulsive of chores. If you are in any way lax or deficient you will be whipped, as you deserve."

"Yes, Mistress," I sobbed, almost a whisper. I was scarcely able to speak.

"And recall," she said, "that you exist for men!"

"Yes, Mistress," I said.

"Do you understand what that means?" she asked.

"Yes, Mistress," I said.

"And if I hear of the least dissatisfaction," she said, "it will mean the whip. Do you understand?"

"Yes, Mistress," I said.

"Now," said she, "kajira, to all fours, and crawl to the slave quarters, through that door. The last cage on the left is yours. Enter it, and draw shut the gate. It will lock automatically."

"Yes, Mistress," I said.

"Hurry," she said. "Hurry! Faster! Faster!"

"Yes, Mistress!" I wept.

Chapter Twenty-Eight

"Have you not finished yet?" asked Chloe.

"Do not tell the Mistress," I begged.

"Only if she asks," said Chloe. "I do not wish to be lashed."

Chloe bit into a larma, and the juice ran down her chin. "Where is your camisk?" she asked.

"In the slave quarters," I said. "It is not to be soiled."

"You had best hope that no men traverse here," she said. She took another bite of the larma, and sucked the juice into her mouth. "Why are you shackled?" she asked.

"It pleased the Mistress," I said.

"She is Mistress to us," said Chloe, "but she is slave to the men. She is as much in a camisk and collar as the rest of us."

Chloe then went her way.

It pleased me to think of the proud Nora on her knees, her lips pressed to the feet of men.

I was on my hands and knees, and I dipped the heavy, thick-bristled brush into the soapy water again. The strokes are to be firm, and circular. Later one rinses with rags and clear water. As I moved, I heard the chain linking my ankles move on the wood.

Nora would usually give me my assignments in the morning, as I knelt before her, specifying the times they should begin and the times within which they were to be completed. This was usually done in such a way that I could not complete the task in the allotted time. I would then be punished. Usually the punishment was not as serious as a lashing, though I had been bound and lashed twice. More often I was given a harsh scolding before the other girls, concluded with a stroke or two of the switch. The point of this was more to demean and humiliate me before my sister slaves than really hurt me. Indeed, Nora would have been treading a thin and dangerous line if she were to diminish my value. Often my punishment would consist of nothing more than being ordered to enter my small cage well before locking time, or being denied a meal. One expects a first girl to have her favorites, and those she least favors, but, I think, it was clear to all that for some reason I was very much in our first girl's disfavor, and indeed, unusually so. I suppose most of the other girls thought me indolent or lax, or my work slovenly, but Jane and Eve, at least, realized that this hostility had nothing to do with those matters for which I was commonly castigated, but was of long standing, dating back, even, to a distant venue, one on another world. As long ago as my former world, I had sensed myself a slave, and this intuition or comprehension had been explicitly and undeniably confirmed at the party. Under Nora's switch, she clad in regalia akin to that of the Gorean free woman, I actually camisked at her feet, I had cringed as the slave I was, being beaten. I had feared her afterwards, on my former world, and even here, on Gor, as Mistress, and knew myself fittingly a slave at her feet, or at the feet of any such as she. I wept at my work. How cruel she was! How helpless I was! Surely she must understand that I was trying to please her, and was striving desperately to do so. Could she never be satisfied? Could she not understand I was no longer what I had been, her haughty, pretentious, shallow, despised rival, Miss Allison Ashton-Baker, but was now only a humbled, helpless kajira at her mercy?

"Allison," said a voice.

I went immediately to my belly on the wet, slick floor. I was terribly frightened. "Please do not beat me, Mistress!" I begged.

"How is the task proceeding?" she asked.

"I have not yet finished!" I said, trembling.

"That is obvious," she said. "When was the task to be finished?"

"The Fourteenth Ahn," I said.

"It is past that time," she said.

"I have not even begun to rinse the floor, Mistress," I said.

"That is obvious," she said. "Do you think you could finish by the Seventeenth Ahn?"

"Yes, Mistress!" I said.

"Do not dally," she said.

"No, Mistress!" I said.

"Have you pleased men?" she asked.

"As they have summoned me," I said.

"Have they been pleased?" she asked.

"It is my hope that they have been pleased," I said. "I have striven to please them."

"Have slave fires begun to burn in your belly?" she asked.

"A little, Mistress," I said.

"I see," she said.

"I cannot help myself, Mistress!" I said.

"Have you been in the hands of Kleomenes?" she asked.

"No," I said.

I went to my knees before her, as was appropriate, for she was first girl. I looked up. She touched her collar, dreamily.

"Mistress?" I said.

"We are all kajirae, Allison," she said.

"Yes, Mistress," I said.

"Am I beautiful?" she asked.

"Extremely beautiful, Mistress!" I said.

"Today," she said, "I was put to the slave ring of Kleomenes."

"Chained?" I said.

"Of course," she said.

"Your beauty would grace any ring," I said.

"Do you think so?" she said.

"Yes, Mistress," I said.

"I have been severe with you, Allison," she said. "Tomorrow you will be unshackled. Tomorrow it will be with you, as with the others."

"Mistress!" I exclaimed.

I threw myself to my belly before her on the wet floor, and pressed my lips to her feet, again and again. My eyes were flooded with tears. "Thank you!" I said. "Thank you, Mistress!"

"There is to be no slacking in your work," she said, "or in the pleasures you give the masters. If I am not satisfied, or if I hear complaints, you will lashed, and well."

"Yes, Mistress," I said. "Thank you, Mistress!"

"Now return to your work," she said, "and do not dally."

"Yes, Mistress," I said, and seized up the brush, immersed it in the soapy water, and bent again to my task.

"I will have Jane and Eve hold a plate for you," she said.

"Thank you, Mistress," I said.

The strokes are to be firm, and circular.

Chapter Twenty-Nine

"Lord Grendel!" I exclaimed.

He lifted his head, behind the heavy bars, but did not otherwise acknowledge my outburst.

A Kur guard crouched, as though somnolent, a few feet behind me, near the gated portal through which I had been admitted to the place of cells, the prison area, bearing the tray of food and drink. It was my first visit to this place.

"What are you doing here, Lord Grendel?" I asked. "The Lady Bina is in this place. Others, too. Where have you been? What has happened to you? I do not understand. I am sure the Lady Bina would desire to speak with you. I have seen the blind Kur in a feast room, but not you. How is it you are here?"

I heard sounds of Kur from the guard. They had a hint of menace about them. Though the guard seemed quiescent, even distant, I knew that those huge shaggy forms, sometimes almost like an enormous ball of muscle and fur with eyes, could spring alive in an instant, raging and snarling.

With an easy movement, and an extension of his long arm, the guard, turning about, unhooked a translator hanging on its chain of iron links from a peg on the wall behind him.

Again I heard some sounds in Kur, to my ears still little more than a bestial rumbling, reminiscent of sounds which one might expect from something like a larl, or sleen, but, oddly enough, different, seemingly articulated. Shortly thereafter, I heard, in Gorean, "You need not speak to him, kajira. He cannot understand you, he has no translator."

"Yes, Master," I said. "Thank you, Master. Forgive me, Master."

The tray I bore was heavy.

The guard, who now had the translator slung about his neck, presumably that it might be convenient, as I was about, reached back and, with a small mallet, removed from a peg, struck a hanging bar, which emitted a sharp, clear note, in response to which signal a second Kur shortly appeared at the portal and, the gate open, entered. He carried a large bow-like device, with four tiered, horizontally placed quarrel guides, each guide containing its missile. There were four triggers on the device. The slotted quarrels were heavy, and of iron, almost like short javelins. The four cable tensions, tiered, were such that I supposed few but a Kur could have readied the weapon. It seemed to me a terrible weapon, one which might splinter beams, perhaps shatter rocks, but, also, I supposed that it complied with the weapon laws of the Priest-Kings. It was, in its way, a form of complex crossbow. It would have been difficult for a human to lift, and, if it were not mounted, to fire.

The guard, backed now by the second Kur, the armed Kur, motioned that Lord Grendel should retreat to the rear of his cell, which he did. The gate to the cell was then opened and I entered, bearing the tray. I put it down on the floor toward the center of the cell. Lord Grendel's eyes watched me, closely. I knew he required no translator to understand me, and I knew, too, he could speak, in his way, Gorean. Clearly these things were not understood by the guard.

As I was preparing to withdraw, Lord Grendel said something in Kur to the guard.

The guard stood at the gate to the cell. I tried to slip past him, but was prevented from doing so. "Master?" I said.

"The prisoner would be groomed," said the guard, by means of the translator. "Do you know how to groom?" he asked.

"Please, let me go," I said.

"Human females on the steel worlds," he said, "are often kept as pets, and groom their masters. I see no reason why a kajira, who is even less than a pet, might not do so, as well."

"I am afraid," I said.

"Do you not groom your masters?" he asked.

"We attend to them in all the ways of the slave," I said. "We may dress them, tie their sandals, bathe them, and such."

"It is an honor for you to do so, is it not?" he asked.

"Yes, Master," I said. "It is a great honor and privilege for a slave to be permitted to serve her Master."

"How much more so then," said he, "for you to serve a Kur."

"Let me go!" I begged.

I was thrust back in the cell.

"Groom him," said the guard.

"How is this to be done?" I asked.

"You will be instructed," he said.

He then backed through the gate and swung it shut. I ran to the gate and extended my hands and arms through the bars. "Please let me out!" I begged. "Let me out! Do not leave me alone with him! I am afraid!"

"I hope," said the guard, "that the meal you brought is sufficient for the prisoner. Otherwise you may be eaten."

"Let me out!" I begged.

I trusted this was a joke on the guard's part, but I was not altogether sure of it.

"If you groom well," said the guard, scratching at his side, "I may permit you to groom me, as well. On this world we miss our pets."

He then spun about, hopping a little, which I took to be a sign of amusement. Shortly thereafter, the prisoner's meal having been brought, and delivered, he, and his fellow, the large bow cradled in his arms, took their leave.

I hurried to Lord Grendel, and knelt before him. "Master," I said.

"You are a clever slave," he said. "You did well. I will be able, I am sure, to request your presence from time to time. You will be my eyes and ears."

"I am only a slave," I said.

"But a very pretty one," he said.

"How would Master know?" I asked. He was, after all, a beast.

"I am part human," he said. "You must forgive me. I cannot help that."

"Can you see me, as a human male might see me," I asked, "and have emotions, feelings, desires, such things?"

"Of course," he said.

"I am afraid," I said.

"Do not be afraid," he said. "Why should I not be able to see how attractive you are, and how stimulating is your body?"

"Master!" I protested.

"Stimulating, indeed," he said. "I expect that it, stripped and exhibited, well posed, well presented, would bring a good price off the slave block."

"I did not know this sort of thing," I said.

"What sort of thing?" he said.

"How you might see me, or others," I said.

"You did not anticipate it?" he said.

"No, Master," I said.

"You are quite fetching as you are," he said, "your lineaments scarcely concealed, your neck in a collar."

I began to tremble.

"That you are pretty, that you might be of interest to men, was important from the beginning to the Lady Bina," he said, "who thought it might occasionally be found useful, for her purposes. Renting you out, or such. Now it seems I may rejoice in your charms, for I might, too, find some application for them."

"I do not understand," I said.

"Where men are," he said, "kajirae are welcome."

"Master?" I said.

"You, and through you, Jane and Eve, too, may prove useful."

"I am afraid," I said.

"You remember how to groom me?" he asked.

"Surely Master," I said, "from the domicile, in the house of Epicrates, before contact was made with the blind Kur."

"That was largely to leave my scent upon you," he said, "which was done that my fellow, who was blind, would know a Kur scent, and follow you, and, of course, not be likely to kill you. Now, of course, it will be necessary to give you some training, as an actual Kur pet, the biting, the nibbling, the use of your teeth, the swallowing of lice, and such."

"I could pretend that," I said.

"With me, yes," he said, "but with others, not so."

"Others?" I said.

"My brethren," he said, "miss their pets and the services performed by them. The kajirae here are for the men, and that has been made clear to my fellows, which intelligence does not please them."

"I see," I said.

"I trust it will not come to that," he said. "But if they know you groom me, it may be easier for you to move about, amongst them. They are likely to think no more of you than the speechless Kur pets with which they are familiar."

"'Speechless'?" I said.

"Yes," he said. "Who would teach an animal to speak?"

"I see," I said.

"The Lady Bina was once such a pet," he said.

"She speaks well, beautifully," I said.

"I, and others, taught her," he said.

"She can even read Gorean," I said.

"She is quite intelligent, and quite beautiful as well," he said.

"'Beautiful'?" I said.

"Yes," he said.

"I cannot understand Kur," I said.

"Much might be gathered by what you see," he said.

"I do not know where the Lady Bina is being kept," I said. "I think she may be with Astrinax. Our men may be domiciled separately, kept from one another. I am not sure. Perhaps they have liberty. I do not know. Jane, Eve, and I are mere kajirae. Little, if anything, is told to us."

"We must learn what is going on in this place," he said.

"Many areas are closed," I said. "I think it will be impossible."

"You saw the weapon borne by the second guard," he said.

"Yes," I said. I shivered.

"Thus," he said, "Priest-Kings are still feared. Thus, there may be time to intervene."

"In what?" I asked.

"That we must learn," he said.

"I saw the blind Kur in the feasting room," I said. "He was put apart from the others. Food was thrown to the floor, which he must strive to find."

"His name," said Lord Grendel, "is," and then followed a syllable or two which was unintelligible to me.

"I cannot say that," I said.

"They have given him no name for humans?"

"No," I said.

"I feared so," said Lord Grendel. "They are most likely done with him."

"Jane knows of him, saw him in the feasting hall, and such," I said. "She calls him Tiresias."

"Let us so refer to him then," said Lord Grendel.

"It is an ancient name, from Earth, she told me. From stories one supposes, but from a city which did exist, Thebes, the name of a blind soothsayer."

"Very well, then," said Lord Grendel, "Tiresias."

"How is it," I asked, "that he is free, and you are encelled?"

"Betrayal," said Grendel. Then he said, abruptly, "Groom me!"

I heard the outer gate opened. Lord Grendel gathered me into his arms, and I thrust my face into his fur, biting and nibbling.

I lifted my face from the fur, to look through the bars. The two guards were there.

"Groom well, little kajira," came from the first translator, "and perhaps you will not be eaten."

I thrust my face again into the fur.

I then heard from a second translator, apparently back a little farther than the first. "Enjoy the tiny, furtive, crawling things."

"Crack them between your teeth," came from the first translator.

"Are they not delicious?" came from the second translator.

Shortly thereafter I heard the gate closed.

"They are gone," said Lord Grendel.

I was terrified.

"You did well," said Lord Grendel. "If we were home, I would cast you a pastry."

"Tell me of your doings, Master," I said. "How is it that you are here?"

"We must inform one another," he said. "As you know I wished to save Tiresias, as we shall call him, and, too, end his killings in Ar. Accordingly, we brought him to the house of Epicrates. I wished to return him to his fellows, but not leave the Lady Bina unattended in Ar. She was reluctant for a time to leave Ar, but then, rather surprisingly, she found the journey congenial."

"She expects, somehow," I said, "with the help of Kurii, to

become the Ubara of all Gor, an idea undoubtedly suggested to her, implanted in her, in your absence from the domicile, by Tiresias, an idea congenial to her naive and unrealistic ambitions."

"Actually," said Lord Grendel, "it is not as unrealistic as you might think. If Kurii should win Gor, they might indeed make her the Ubara of the planet, but, of course, they would not do so. They would no longer need her. She then, with other humans, would be enslaved or eaten."

"There are humans here," I said.

"Mercenaries who know nothing, who do not look beyond their fee," he said, "or fools who believe they would be enriched by a Kur victory, in a world to be shared."

"You figure in this somehow," I said.

"I was prominent in the revolution," he said. "I am well-known and influential on one of the steel worlds, the steel world of Arcesilaus, Theocrat of the World, Twelfth Face of the Nameless One. That world might be important for supplies and support, and exerting a broader influence on other steel worlds."

"You could be important, as an ally," I said.

"Perhaps," he said.

"They would expect," I said, "to reach you through the Lady Bina."

"I have not heard from her," he said.

"They might expect you to pacify and humor her, to bow to her whims, to cooperate with the plans of these conspirators, to please her."

"I fear more," he said, "that they might harm her, if I should be reluctant to cooperate."

"To avoid that," I said, "you would do much."

"Perhaps everything," he said.

"You were betrayed," I said.

"The wagon caravan, a small one of three wagons, was organized by the jobber, Astrinax. Tiresias and I, for a time, rode in the third wagon. Later, that we might be able to range more freely, and be less likely to be discovered, we left the wagons, but remained aware of their progress. In a sense I was their guard. Tiresias I kept with me most of the time. A tether would fasten us together. Many nights I made contact with

Astrinax, during the night watch. In the mountains I discovered an outlaw band of nine men, and warned Astrinax. It turned out that he had hired, in Venna, two outlaws, in league with that band. In the night, at their camps, it was easy to overhear their speech. I warned Astrinax, and I think he warned two of his hires, Lykos, a mercenary, and Desmond, a Metal Worker."

"I am not sure that Master Desmond is a Metal Worker," I said.

"What then?" he asked.

"I do not know," I said.

"I think," I said, "they had an overweening confidence in your capacity to attack and destroy the band of the outlaw, Trachinos."

"It seems, then," he said, "they were in more danger than they realized."

"I suspect they did not know that Tiresias was blind," I said.

"At night," he said, "it would not have been difficult, in the darkness, moving from body to body. In the day, without suitable weapons, it would have been more difficult, if not impossible."

"I think they did not understand that," I said. "I think they thought there were two of you, armed, whole, and dangerous."

"I would, of course," he said, "have done what I could."

"An attack, it turns out, was to have been made, and was signaled, but it never took place. Men and Kurii from here, this facility, destroyed the outlaws."

"I could not have prevented the attack," said Lord Grendel. "I was taken into custody, and chained, shortly after returning Tiresias to his fellows."

"He betrayed you," I said, "you who had saved him."

"Do not think ill of him," said Lord Grendel. "He knew things I did not. I had no idea what was going on in the Voltai. He was thinking clearly. Worlds are at stake."

"He is not being treated as a hero," I said.

"He is now useless to them," said Lord Grendel.

"He has done much for them," I said.

"He will be put out for larls."

"I do not understand."

"It is the Kur way," said Lord Grendel.

"I think one human, at least," I said, "had some notion as to what might be afoot, somewhere, if not in the Voltai."

"Some probably suspect," said Lord Grendel.

"Master Desmond of Harfax," I said.

"Interesting," he said.

"He knew of your existence," I said.

"Many did," said Lord Grendel.

"He may have thought you implicated somehow, in something," I said.

"And would spy upon me?"

"Or others, too," I said.

"You have often heard, have you not," he asked, "that curiosity is not becoming to a kajira?"

"Many times," I said.

"Perhaps there should be another saying, too," he said, "that curiosity in many places and at many times can be extremely dangerous, to anyone."

"Do not kill him," I said.

"Why not?" asked Lord Grendel.

"I want his collar," I said.

"I must attend to my meal," he said. "Go to the gate, as though you could not be too near to it."

I hurried and knelt near the gate.

Shortly thereafter the two guards appeared. I gathered that Lord Grendel had heard their approach.

I put my hands through the bars, pathetically. "Please let me out, Masters," I begged.

In a short time Lord Grendel had finished what provender had been provided him, and finished the tankard of water which, too, had been on the tray.

"Fetch the tray," said the first guard, by means of the translator.

"Please do not make me approach him," I begged.

"Now," came from the translator.

I crept back and, as though frightened, retrieved the tray, the plate and tankard, and then rose to my feet, and backed toward the gate, which was opened for me, and I exited the cell, following which the gate was again closed.

"Did she groom well?" the first guard asked Lord Grendel. He had apparently left the translator on. It still hung about his neck, on its simple iron chain. Lord Grendel responded, and, a moment later, I heard, "Yes."

"That is fortunate for you, kajira," came from the translator.

I was silent.

I wanted to leave the area of cells.

"Perhaps," came from the translator, "you will sometimes groom me."

"I would be honored to groom Master," I said, and then, as I was not detained, hurried past the second guard, with his heavy weapon, exiting through the outer gate.

Chapter Thirty

"Ho, kajira," said a voice, not heard for days.

I spun about, delighted, and rushed to Desmond of Harfax, knelt before him, pressed my lips quickly to his sandals, knelt up, and then knelt close to him, holding him about the legs, and putting my turned head humbly against his legs, rather as I had seen Mina do with Trachinos.

"Here, here," he said, surprised.

I supposed many women of my old world would not have understood something this meaningful, and simple, the love and gratitude, the pleasure of a slave in the presence of a master. Perhaps that is because they do not know themselves slaves. Perhaps that is because they have never met a true male, so mighty, so innocently and naturally the master of such as we. Perhaps they have never met a male before whom they could hope to do little but kneel, and hope to be found pleasing.

"Here, here," he said. "You are not my slave."

I looked up at him. How did he know whose slave I was?

"Stand up, back away," he said. "Let me see you."

I obeyed, smiling. I pulled down the camisk a little, self-consciously. How meaningless that gesture was when camisked!

"Turn," he said.

I turned, and then, again, faced him.

"Lovely," he said, admiringly. "The camisk becomes you."

A slave, I was muchly pleased. We love our bodies, and our beauty, and are thrilled to be choicelessly displayed as the slaves we are. What free woman would not, in our place, wish to be brazenly exhibited to the eyes of men as the treasure she is?

Too, what woman, I wondered, would a camisk not become?

"In the past weeks," I said, "I have not seen Master."

"Nor I you," he said.

"I trust Master is well," I said.

"Yes," he said, "and you?"

"Yes, Master," I said.

"You are looking well," he said.

"We are carefully dieted and routinely exercised," I said.

"That is common with animals," he said.

"Yes, Master," I said.

"Your hair," he said, "is far from slave long, but I have seen many barbarians whose hair, in their first sale, was no longer, or not much longer."

"Many barbarian females," I said, "wear their hair as they please."

"When they are collared," he said, "they will wear it as their masters please."

"Of course, Master," I said.

He then approached me, and my body tensed. I hoped he would gather me into his arms.

He placed his hand, lightly, on the side of my waist, on the left. I made a tiny, inadvertent noise, and drew back a little, my eyes, wide, regarding him, my lips parted.

"From so little?" he said.

"Forgive me, Master," I said.

"Your slave fires," he said, "have begun to burn."

"It is being done to me, Master," I said. "Please, forgive me."

"It is acceptable," he said. "Indeed, it is desirable."

"I cannot help myself, Master," I said.

"Nor should you," he said. "Kneel."

Immediately I complied. Kajirae are to obey unquestioningly, and instantly.

"I see," he said.

"I must now kneel like this," I said.

I was before him in the position of the pleasure slave, in nadu, back straight, head up, hands palm down on thighs, belly in, shoulders back, kneeling back on heels, knees spread. This was common nadu. Some masters prefer the hands behind the back, the right hand grasping the left wrist, if the girl is right handed, and the left hand grasping the right wrist, if the girl is left handed. Some masters, too, prefer for the head to be bowed, in subservience. In the common nadu, as required in the complex, and insisted upon by Nora, the hands are to be visible and the head raised. Some say the hands are to be visible in order that the slave cannot conceal within them a package, a pellet, a powder, a weapon, or such. One supposes that may be a consequence of the position, but, one supposes, as slaves could scarcely have access to such things, that one must look further. Aside from the aesthetic aspects of the matter, namely revealing the small, sweet loveliness of a woman's hands, the small wrists, almost asking to be bound, and such, it facilitates a common begging gesture, one which is lovely and subtle. One merely changes the position of the hands, by turning the backs of the hand to the thighs. This exposes the soft, concave, curved tenderness of the palms, open, sensitive, and vulnerable, to the master. Another subtle device is the simple bondage knot, loosely tied in the hair. In both these ways, and others, the slave may make her needs known. Perhaps, when she is expected to be tunicked, she appears in a camisk, or naked; perhaps she is discovered, as suggested earlier, stripped, at the foot of his couch; perhaps she kneels before him, bringing him a whip, or rope. Or perhaps she merely kneels, or bellies, and begs to be caressed. Numerous are the variations which might appear in such matters. The point of having the head raised is presumably that the beauty of her features may be well displayed. Too, of course, it makes it easier for her to apprise herself of her surroundings, the master's moods, and such. It is common with slaves, as with other animals, that they are trained to the master's tastes.

"You serve, in the complex?" he asked.

"Assuredly," I said. "I even, from time to time, groom Kurii."

"You may groom all the beasts you wish," he said.

"I must also please men," I said.

"Doubtless," he said.

"Master does not seem pleased," I said.

"I dislike the naked feast of you in the arms of others," he said.

"Master does not own me," I said.

He made an angry noise, which pleased me, though I attempted to conceal my pleasure.

"Who owns you?" he asked.

"I no longer know," I said.

"Legally," he said, "you must belong to the Lady Bina."

"I do not know," I said.

"Master," I said.

"Yes," he said.

"The beast who attended on the Lady Bina, he in which you seemed to be interested," I said, "is here, imprisoned."

"I had not seen him," said Desmond. "He is not one of them, then?"

"No," I said. "Far from it. He was ignorant of this place. As nearly as I can determine, he is opposed to their projects, whatever they may be."

"They have to do with worlds," said Desmond.

"How does Master know these things?" I asked.

"Curiosity—," he said.

"Surely Master does not think we cease to be women when we are collared."

"No," he said. "I think that is when you begin to be women."

"Perhaps Master will one day speak to a slave," I said.

"Perhaps," he said.

"I think you would find the imprisoned beast," I said, "is your ally."

"How so," he said.

"He is reluctant to abet the projects of this place," I said.

"There are many beasts," he said. "What is one more, or less?"

"He may have influence in a far place, an important place," I said, "one from which support would be solicited."

"I see," said Master Desmond.

"And it is hoped he will solicit this support."

"And he declines?"

"As of now," I said.

"Of now?"

"I think they hope to secure his collaboration by means of the Lady Bina," I said, "one supposes either by means of her influence upon him, or by means of her jeopardy."

"They would threaten her?"

"I think he would do anything to protect her," I said.

"Why?" he asked.

"How could a slave know?" I said. "He is a mere beast."

"The key then," he said, "is the Lady Bina."

"I am sure the beasts flatter her, and enflame her ambitions."

"She thinks she would be the Ubara of the planet?" he asked.

He must have recalled such remarks from the journey.

"The prisoner, Lord Grendel," I said, "perhaps better apprised than we of possible Kur power, thinks that would be within the realm of possibility, but would not be likely to take place. He thinks, rather, following a Kur victory, after which she would no longer be needed, she would be enslaved or eaten."

"I see," he said.

"Perhaps it is the Kur way," I said. I thought of Lord Grendel's speculation with respect to the likely fate of Tiresias.

"She must be informed," he said.

"I do not think she would believe the informant," I said, "especially if it were the prisoner, Lord Grendel, whom she suspects would wish, for personal reasons, for selfish reasons, to deny her such an exaltation, such station, and grandeur. She might well suppose him jealous of such fortune, and that he would prefer to keep things as they were before, to keep her in modest circumstances, and to keep her muchly dependent upon him."

"If she would not believe the prisoner, who is Kur, and known to her, who would she believe?" he asked.

"I do not think anyone," I said.

"Where is the Lady Bina?" he asked.

"Somewhere here, in this place, I would suppose," I said, "but I know not where."

"The complex is large," he said.

"Many areas," I said, "are closed to us, and many even to lesser beasts."

"I have not seen Astrinax," he said.

"He may be with the Lady Bina," I said.

"Occasionally I see Lykos, Trachinos, Akesinos," he said, "but muchly we are apart from one another."

"Even so," I said, "you must know more than I."

"I doubt that," he said. "In some respects kajirae come and go more freely than free persons. They may be less noted, and are likely to arouse fewer suspicions."

"As pet sleen, wandering about," I said.

"Precisely," he said.

"I see," I said.

"Certainly the beasts notice them scarcely at all," he said.

"That is true," I said. Certainly he must be aware that men often took note of kajirae. This was particularly the case in the feast halls, the guard stations, the gaming rooms, their quarters, when we were cleaning them, and so on. At certain Ahn walking down certain corridors, as when carrying provender to the guards at the outer gate, given the accostings, hootings, stolen kisses, playful slaps, and such, it could be something of a gauntlet. To be sure, such things remind a woman of her interest to masters. Sometimes a fellow's superiors would permit him to write with a grease pencil on a girl's thigh something like, "Tonight I belong to Leucippus," to whom that night the girl would report, to give him pleasure, of the sort expected from a woman who was no more than a slave.

"Who is Agamemnon?" he asked. "I have heard this name."

"I do not know," I said. "This place is named for him."

"Have you seen him?"

"I do not think so," I said. "I have seen high Kurii, whose translators are on golden chains, such as Lucius, Timarchos, and Lysymachos, and several silver-chain Kurii, and a great many iron-chain Kurii, but, as far as I know, I have not seen a Kur named Agamemnon."

"He may not be here," said Desmond.

"There was a revolution on a far world," I said. "He may have perished there. These Kurii may be the remnants of a force which was once his, one still loyal to a politics, or a memory,"

"I see," he said.

"I think the golden-chain Kur, Lucius, is first here," I said.

"Perhaps," he said.

"It is late," I said. "I must report back to the slave quarters. It is nearly locking time."

"Then you are caged?" he said.

He looked at me as though he did not disapprove of that.

"We all are," I said, "even our first girl, Nora, though she is the last caged and the first released."

"Who does this?" he asked.

"A Kur," I said. "We are Kur girls. I am told our collars make this clear."

"Are the cages large?" he asked.

"No," I said. "One can do little more than kneel or sit in them."

"I see," he said.

"Perhaps Master would like to see me in my cage," I said.

"You are naked in the cage?"

"Of course."

"Good," he said. "I like to see naked, caged women."

"Have I permission to withdraw?" I asked.

"Somehow," he said, "we must gather information, somehow we must make contact with the Lady Bina."

"I see no way in which these things can be done," I said.

"Nor I," he said.

Chapter Thirty-One

In the early afternoon Nora entered the slave quarters, humming an Earth tune. Her switch dangled jauntily on her wrist.

"Tal!" she said.

"Tal, Mistress," Jane and I said to her. We were sewing some garments of the men, earlier washed, which had been torn in man sport, in this case hunting wild verr on the passes about the Crag of Kleinias, rents mostly from thorn brush, some, it seemed, from climbing, a loss of footing on rocky slopes, or such. Men are rash and careless beasts. If they had to sew their own garments I supposed they would be more careful. I had never sewn on my former world, but I had learned to do so in the house of Tenalion, for some skill in such matters is expected of a slave. Certainly she is expected to be good for more than bucking and squirming, and crying out, at the end of a chain. I had come to be rather proud of my skill in this humble matter. And it seemed a task appropriate for a slave. Certainly one would not expect a free man, or many free women, at least of upper caste, to do such things. Too, it gave me pleasure to do such things for the masters, to wash and iron their tunics, to sort their clothes, to polish their boots, and such. Interestingly, as a slave, the pleasure I found in these tasks was undeniably sexual. I found such tasks subtly arousing, and sometimes more than subtly so. Sometimes I squirmed doing them, and moaned, for I knew I was doing them as a slave. Eve was elsewhere, in one of the kitchens.

"Behold," smiled Nora, indicating her left thigh, below the brand.

None of us, including Nora, of course, could read. Of the Kur girls housed in the quarters only Chloe could read. She had been a free woman of Cos, captured at sea by a corsair from Port Kar, as had been the girl from Tabor with whom I had been sold in the Metellan district, though much farther from shore, had been sold to rencers in the delta of the Vosk, who had sold her at a profit to a camp of slavers at the delta's edge, with its wooden cages, a camp transient, seasonal, in nature, by means of which slaves from Thassa might be brought eastward into the Vosk basin, and slaves from the Vosk basin might be brought westward, through the delta, to Thassa. The rencers often sell and trade in both directions. Sometimes the slaves, stripped, a rope on their neck, in the keeping of a master, are made to pole the light reed boats through the rence. Sometimes they are merely kept, lying naked, bound hand and foot, in the craft, while the men propel the craft. A common practice is to keep them bound at the eastern and western edges of the delta where, new slaves, in their naivety, they might be tempted to think of escape. Poling in the trackless delta, the rope on their neck, they are well aware of the wilderness, the vastness, the treacherous byways, the quicksand, the heat, the insects, leeches, delta sharks, winged, predatory uls, and, in particular, marsh tharlarion, which often scout the boats, and accompany them, little but the eyes visible, for pasangs. Chloe had changed hands several times in her eastward journey on the Vosk, town to town, but, in the end, she had been sold in the great clearing station of Victoria, from which point she had been sold southeast to Torcadino, and then, eventually, in Ar, where some agent of the Kurii had apparently purchased her for the Cave.

Jane and I regarded Nora's left thigh, as she had prompted us, just below her brand, the common Kef, as ours.

"What does it say?" asked Jane.

"I am told," said Nora, happily, "it says 'Tonight I am the property of Kleomenes'."

"Marvelous," said Jane.

"You are highly favored, indeed," I said.

"How beautiful and desirable you are," said Jane, "to be called to the slave ring of such a man."

"I sold for two silver tarsks," said Nora, "and in my first sale."

"That is more than I was sold for," I said. I saw no point in telling her how much more it was.

"And more than I and Eve," said Jane.

I had little doubt that all three had brought more off the block than I, and certainly Nora, but then they had not been put up in the Metellan district.

"Do you think he will buy me?" asked Nora.

"He is a fool if he does not," said Jane.

"You are very beautiful," I said.

"How could he hope for anything better on his chain?" said Jane.

"On Earth," she said, "I never told you, but I was frigid, and did not care for men, and despised them, and had no feelings for them, but here I find myself weak, and warm, and confused in their presence. Here I kneel, and hope that they will find me pleasing, not because I am afraid, though I am afraid, but because I want to be found pleasing—as a female."

"It is so!" said Jane.

"Yes!" I said.

"When they look upon me," said Nora, "I want to yield. I want to be owned. I am ready to be mastered, and I long for my mastering. I think, 'Master this slave! Take her! She is yours!' When Master Kleomenes touches me, I am a lost slave, hoping that I will not be shown mercy. I did not know on Earth that feelings such as these could exist. When he touches me, I am his, whether I will it or not, though I will it, a thousand times so!"

"Do you cry out, and beg?" asked Jane.

"Yes, yes," she said.

"Let us hope," said Jane, "he does not tire of you."

"No, no!" said Nora.

"If so," I said, "you could always be sold to another."

"No!" she wept.

"You are a slave," I said.

"Yes, yes," she wept, turning away. "I am a slave! A slave." Then she fell to her knees, facing away from us, weeping.

Jane and I then returned to our sewing.

"Allison," said Nora, rising, wiping her eyes with her forearm, and facing us.

"Mistress?" I said.

"A Kur," she said, "one called Grendel, wishes to see you."

I put down the sewing. "I hasten," I said. "He is in the place of cells. Am I to go to the kitchen first? Am I to carry him food or drink?"

"He is not in the place of cells," she said. "He is in the Golden Corridor, in the fourth compartment."

This startled me. The first compartment in the Golden Corridor was that of Lucius, putatively first in the Cave, the second and third were occupied, respectively, by Timarchos and Lysymachos. All three were what we might call "golden-chain Kurii," namely high Kurii, their station witnessed by the golden chains from which depended their translators.

* * * *

"Master?" I said.

"You will accompany me," said Lord Grendel, "as a grooming slave, heeling me."

"Yes, Master," I said.

"Few have grooming slaves," he said.

I supposed that was true. It seemed to be generally understood that the kajirae in this place had been purchased for men, not Kurii.

"You have groomed Lysymachos, too, have you not?"

"And some others," I said. "Mostly iron-chain Kurii."

Interestingly, the iron-chain Kurii seemed to wish to keep me much for themselves. I think little love was lost between the iron-chain Kurii and the golden- or silver-chain Kurii.

"How is it, Master," I asked, "that you are free. I do not understand."

"Some other slaves may be present, as well," he said.

"You are free," I said, uncertainly. "How is this?"

"You are a clever slave," he said. "Surely you can speculate."

"I dare not," I said.

The beast's lip curled up a little, about a fang. I conjectured this was a sign of amusement. I had accounted it so, in the domicile.

"You are even housed in the Golden Corridor," I said.

"I have my freedom," he said. "I may even leave the Cave, to venture about, should I wish to do so."

"I understand nothing of this," I said.

"While I was incarcerated," he said, "you were to be my informant, my eyes and ears for the outside."

"Yes, Master," I said.

"Now," he said, "I will still have use for your eyes and ears, and perhaps for your hands, as well."

"How is it that you are free?" I asked.

"I have become rational," he said. "I am no longer foolish. You, if anyone, Allison, given your nature and character, must understand this."

"No," I said.

"Who," he asked, "would reject untold wealth, and almost absolute power?"

"They threatened to torture and kill the Lady Bina," I said. "Under this duress, you succumbed to their importunities."

He looked at me, his head slightly to one side.

"Poor Master," I said.

"Not at all," he said. "It is rather that I see, clearly, eventually, the Kur conquest of this world, and, indeed, later, of another. Humans are a weak and inferior species, a vermin species, appropriately to be supplanted by a superior life form. Do not fear. Some role may be found for select humans, grooming, fetching, carting wastes, perhaps decorative objects, as exotic fish or colorful birds, and, certainly, for those who enjoy the taste, food. And for their part, Priest-Kings, whatever they may be, such passive, inert, aloof, sessile creatures, they may be ignored or, if one chooses, destroyed."

"Surely all this is to preserve and protect the Lady Bina," I said.

"Do not concern yourself," he said. "She will be quite happy. We will give her the title Ubara of Gor, and I will govern the planet, under the authority of Agamemnon, Theocrat of the World, Eleventh Face of the Nameless One."

"But surely all this is for her?" I said.

"No," he said. "It is for me, and my superiors. We may, however, while it pleases us, amuse ourselves at the pretensions of a naive young woman."

"Surely this cannot be Master Grendel, Lord Grendel," I said.

"You now see Lord Grendel," he said, "as he is."

"Yes, Master," I said.

"We are not so different from humans, are we?" he asked. "I am told that Priest-Kings regard us as rather equivalent species."

"Please, let me go," I said.

"I do not wish to destroy you," he said. "You do not wish to be destroyed, do you?"

"No, Master," I said.

"Prepare to accompany me," he said. "You will enhance my prestige amongst the others. Few have grooming slaves."

"I am not a grooming slave," I said. "I am a kajira, intended for the use of my masters."

"Nonetheless," he said, "this afternoon you will appear as a grooming slave."

"I will be a display item," I said.

"A modest one," he said.

"But one redounding to your dignity?"

"In your small way," he said.

"I see," I said.

"This sort of thing is not that unusual," he said. "For example, many rich men keep display slaves. Have you not seen chains of them in Ar, lightly tunicked, back-braceleted, neck-coffled, perhaps double strings of them, chained to the back of a palanquin?"

"Where are you taking me?" I asked.

"To the audience chamber of Agamemnon," he said, "Theocrat of the World, Eleventh Face of the Nameless One."

"Was there not a revolution fought against this Agamemnon?" I said.

"A tragic misadventure," he said. "Had it not taken place, we might now be the masters of all Gor."

"Yes, Master," I said.

"Let us be on our way," he said.

"Yes, Master," I said.

Chapter Thirty-Two

I shall now speak of him simply as Grendel. I heeled him into the large room, and, when he crouched down, at ease, before the broad dais, I knelt behind him, on his left.

It took some time for my eyes to grow accustomed to the light, as, for a human, it was almost dark, at least until this adjustment took place.

If humans of interest or importance were to be present, I supposed that the room would have been better lit.

I did not know how deep the room was, for, at the front of the room, at the back of the dais, there was a heavy, drawn curtain. To our right, crouched on the dais, at its edge, before the curtain, was Lucius, whom I recognized, partly from his size, and partly from the glint of the golden chain from which hung his translator. Looking about myself, as inconspicuously as possible, I noted that almost every Kur in the room was a silver-chain Kur. I saw few iron-chain Kurii. Although almost every Kur in the room bore a translator, and in spite of the fact that there were several kajirae, some six or seven, in the room, none of the translators would be activated. What took place was entirely in Kur. Accordingly, my account of what occurred is based almost entirely on what I saw, and my interpretation of what I saw. Had there been human males in the room, perhaps the translators would have been activated, but there were not. There were only a few humans in the room, the human animals known as kajirae. The absence of human males in the room I later thought not only interesting, but perhaps significant. Perhaps it was thought that some, at least, of what took place in the room may not have been judiciously shared with the Kurii's human allies. Had human males been in the room they would doubtless have requested that, or insisted that, they be provided with a translation of the proceedings. Kajirae, of course, would make no such request, or demand. They would remain silent. There were already some twenty Kurii in the room when Grendel entered and took his place, a prominent place, near the front of the room, before the dais.

A number of the other Kurii witnessed his arrival, and there was a stirring amongst them.

Grendel, I gathered, was noteworthy, perhaps important.

A few Ehn later, there was a sharp, ringing sound, resulting one supposes from the striking of one of the small bars, to the sounds of which the Lady Bina, amongst other festal tokens, had been welcomed to the Cave.

Timarchos and Lysymachos then emerged through the curtain and, one on each side, drew back the curtain, revealing a passage behind it.

I did not know how deep the passage was. It was dark.

In a moment I thought I sensed something within the passage, back in the darkness. I rose up a bit, off my heels, and strained my eyes. Then I was afraid, an Ihn or two later, that there was indeed something there. Then I heard a sound which was difficult to interpret, like a metallic scratching, interspersed, now and then, with a sudden, quick sound like a wheel of rotating metal spokes moving on tiles.

I was then sure there was something in the passage, but it had stopped. Then it had moved rapidly forward, then stopped again. I saw a glint of metal. It was a machine of some sort. At least it was not alive. Then it darted forward, onto the dais, and I screamed. Other kajirae, too, screamed, or cried out, startled, in fear. Then I heard a cry of pain as one of the kajirae was seized by the hair, and had her head forced down to the floor. It was a machine, clearly, but, in a moment, I was not so clear that it might not be alive. It was poised on the dais, alertly, and then sank downward, resting its belly on the dais. It had four eyes, or eye-like things, two mounted on its front, and two on metallic stalks which were lifted above the body, and could rotate about. The thing, then, could look behind itself without turning its body. The Kurii present, including Grendel, were unperturbed. One gathered they had seen this, or things like this, before. Oddly, though it was merely a machine of sorts, they accorded it respectful attention. It is difficult to describe the machine, which seemed so animate one might almost have thought it alive, even conscious, even intelligent. It had a generally crab-like look about it, a flattish, rounded, heavy, disk-like, metallic body, four jointed appendages in virtue of which it might move, and, most crab-like, emerging from the body on each side, two large, metallic arms, each terminating in giant bladed pincers. There was also, in the front of the body, below and to the sides of the lower eyes, those not on stalks, two capped apertures, the function of which I did not immediately discern.

Timarchos, and then Lysymachos, began to chant in Kur, and this chant was taken up by the Kurii in the room. Then, a few moments later, Lysymachos began to utter a series of short noises, and each of the attending Kurii responded to each of these noises with the same, brief response. Meanwhile the eyes on the stalks lifted and surveyed the room. I sensed them peering at Grendel, briefly, and then I half froze when I sensed them pointing in my direction, and was relieved, overwhelmingly, when they slowly, gracefully, moved to another perspective. One had the sense that the machine, unconcerned with the chanting, and the subsequent utterances with their unmistakably repetitive, identical, rote response, was noting, and counting, each form in the room.

I heard another note on the bar, and the room was then quiet, redolent with an expectant silence.

I began then to feel hair rising on the back of my neck, and on my scalp, and forearms.

Noises, clearly Kur noises, though with a sense of having been artificially produced, had begun to emanate from the machine.

One had the unmistakable sense, a terrifying illusion, that the machine was alive, though one knew this to be impossible. Something, however, somehow, was surely controlling the device, expressing itself through the device, perhaps perceiving through the device.

Dialogue apparently took place, largely between Lucius,

Timarchos, and Lysymachos, and the machine. Certainly they spoke to it, regarded it, and treated it, as though it were alive, rational, conscious, and such. And, too, it seemed to regard them, relate to them, and interact with them, eerily, as though it were sentient, conscious, and rational. At one point the machine addressed itself to Grendel, who rose in response to its attention. It spoke for a short time to Grendel, and, at one point, Grendel stepped back, startled, seemed almost to fall, and began to tremble. He did not seem frightened, but I had never seen such a reaction in the beast. Then, after a bit, at the conclusion of the machine's address, he resumed the crouching position, so common to Kurii at rest.

There was then a commotion in the rear of the room, as a door was opened, and, in the threshold, feeling about, appeared, to my amazement, a figure I well recognized, one with which I had, in the past, become familiar, that of the blind Kur, whom we have decided to call Tiresias. It was prodded forward by two iron-chain Kurii with pointed sticks. By means of these sticks, striking and jabbing, Tiresias was guided to the foot of the dais, where he stood, lost, and forlorn, turning his head about, as though he were trying to see through the seared holes in his face. As he had been driven forward the other Kurii had hastened to clear him a path, as though they were loath to make contact with him.

He was addressed by the machine, to the utterances of which he made no response, but crouched down, and lowered his head, as though in shame.

Lucius then scrambled forward and began to snarl and hiss at Tiresias, and address him violently. He then struck at him, and then, carefully, firmly, perhaps ceremoniously, clawed him, on both sides of his face. There were then twelve streams of blood about the side of the Tiresias' face. Tiresias made no attempt to resist, protect himself, or retaliate. Then all the Kurii in the room began to direct what I took to be abuse on the injured Kur. Grendel, too, sprang up and contributed to the opprobrious uproar, and it was only then, when this was done, that Tiresias reacted. He turned his bleeding, eyeless head to Grendel, and then, with his wide paws, covered the holes where his eyes had been, as though he could not bear to see what he might have seen, could he have seen. Tiresias was then, with the sharp sticks, striking and jabbing, hurried from the room.

While this took place the machine had been quiescent, though, I supposed, from the gleam of the eye-like things, not unaware of what had occurred. Next two Kurii came before the machine, and stood before it, side by side, each, in turn, with great agitation, addressing it. One of the Kurii wore a silver chain. The other wore an iron chain.

When they were done, the machine, which had shown no sign of interest or emotion during what I took to be the protestations of either, turned slowly toward the Kur who wore the silver chain. It began to back warily away. Then it howled, as though in rage.

I do not know if it would have fled, or not, but it had no opportunity to do so. The two capped apertures below and to the side of the lower eyes, those mounted in the face or chest of the machine itself, snapped open and two, javelin-like, barbed darts burst out, each trailing a light, supple metal cable. These darts caught in the chest of the Kur, who wrestled to draw them forth, but, a moment later, he was drawn stumbling forward, toward the dais, as the cables were being reeled back into the machine. He was thus brought within reach of the gigantic pincer-like claws of the machine. I turned my head away. I only looked back in time to see that the silver chain, now dripping blood, had been removed from what lay about on the dais, and was being, by Lucius, put over the head of the other Kur. It was no longer an iron-chain Kur. It was now a silver-chain Kur. Timarchos and Lysymachos placed garlands on the shaggy head, and the assembled Kurii, including Grendel, rose up, and, as nearly as I could determine, congratulated, and saluted, the Kur about whose neck there now hung, I supposed for the first time, a silver chain.

I felt sick.

I wanted desperately to rise up, and flee through the halls, back to the slave quarters.

A noise came from the machine, and Grendel rose to his feet, facing the machine.

Many of the Kurii leaned forward.

The machine then, again, began to speak. It spoke for more than three or four Ehn. Now and then, at the conclusion of one phrase or another, several of the assembled Kurii uttered sounds which I took to be sounds of agreement, or approbation. Following the remarks of the machine, or those which were transmitted by means of the machine, Lucius brought forward a golden chain, which he placed over the head of Grendel. He then brought forth two garlands, giving one to Timarchos and one to Lysymachos. Each of these Kurii then placed his garland on the head of Grendel. Following this the assembled Kurii rose up, and, as nearly as I could determine, congratulated, and saluted Grendel.

I scarcely noted, in the celebratory milieu, that the machine had backed away, vanishing down the dark corridor behind the dais. Timarchos and Lysymachos, who seemed to attend on the machine, went behind the curtain and drew it shut.

After a time Grendel and I alone were in the room. He stood, and I looked up at him, from my knees. There was a golden chain, with a translator, looped about his neck. On his head were two garlands.

"Soon," he said, "we will have work to do."

"Might Master not use another girl?" I asked.

"No," he said.

"Yes, Master," I said.

"Go to your cage," he said "and draw shut the gate."

"Yes, Master," I said.

I must remove my clothing before entering the cage. I would then draw shut the gate. It would lock automatically.

Chapter Thirty-Three

"Provender, Masters," I said, "and ka-la-na."

I set down the tray on the table-like shelf to the right of the great portal, as one looks out, toward the Voltai. There is a small, open guard station there.

"How red your body is," said one of the two guards.

This was so, even though I knew myself collared kajira.

"Some of the ka-la-na is spilled," said one of the two guards.

"It was difficult coming through the corridors," I said. "The masters, their hands!"

"Shall we beat her?" asked one of the guards to the other.

"Let us have a kiss instead," said the other.

He opened his arms, and I hurried to him, and I was enfolded in his arms, and our lips met. I was held very tightly, and the kiss was a typical claiming kiss of a master. He then thrust me away, I half turning, into the arms of his fellow, and I found myself again handled as what I was, a slave girl.

"Shall we mark her thigh?" asked the first guard.

"It is early," said the other. "There may be others. We can search her out later."

"She may then be marked for another," said the first guard.

"Then another day," said the second guard.

The guards then turned to the tray.

I stood before the wide, double-gated portal, looking out onto the sunlit mountains. It was very beautiful.

It was doubtless through this portal that Mina, weeks ago, unnoted, had slipped from the Cave.

Through this same portal, too, weeks ago, the Lady Bina had been welcomed to the Cave, together with her party.

Through this portal, too, recently, Tiresias had been driven from the Cave, to wander sightless amongst the escarpments, the peaks, and crags.

It was chilly by the portal, but I dallied, for the bright, sharp air, and the vista. I did not, of course, cross the threshold.

It was now early in the fall, the second week in Se'Kara. We were aware that the wagons of Pausanias, now substantially emptied, were being refitted for a return journey, possibly to Ar. I did not know when they would depart. He would certainly wish to leave, however, before the late fall, and the commencement of the first snows. In the winter the Voltai is, for most practical purposes, impassable. I supposed he would not return, if he were to return, until the spring. I was not clear, nor was Master Desmond, as to the role the unusual cargo which had been borne by the wagons was to play in the affairs of the Cave. It did seem obvious that most of these goods, or supplies, had been transferred to the more restricted zones of the Cave, where there lay, supposedly, various laboratories and workshops. I speculated that the cargo, which I had gathered from Master Desmond seemed curious and exotic, might be expensive. This suggested substantial economic resources at the disposal of the Cave. Too, of course, it would be expensive to transport any cargo over long distances through dangerous, uninhabited areas, over perilous routes. I supposed it was unlikely that large quantities of gold or silver, for obtaining goods, would be carried in the wagons, as such an indiscretion, difficult to conceal, would be likely to attract the attention not only of outlaw bands but of some of the less savory "free companies," assemblages of mercenaries, usually under a captain, who fought for fee, whose services were usually available to the highest bidder. Sometimes sides were changed in the midst of a single war. Who knew what clandestine gold might now have found its home in a new purse? Might the fellow beside you suddenly turn on you? Accordingly, much of the financing involved in such matters would doubtless be accomplished by means of drafts, notes, letters, and such, things mysterious, even unreal, to many Goreans, but familiar to the Merchants of the coin streets, pieces of paper which, like birds of the air, might only occasionally light upon a silver branch or rock of gold.

"Masters!" I cried, pointing.

The two guards came to my side, shading their eyes.

"What is it?" I asked.

"It is a big one," said the first guard.

"Masters?" I said.

"It is far off, kajira," said the second guard. "It is much larger than it appears."

"It is a larl," said the first guard.

It was the first larl I had seen, though I had heard much of them. It is a much larger animal than the sleen, and it has four, not six, legs. It lairs in dens, and does not burrow like the sleen in the wild. It is carnivorous, and it most commonly hunts in the day. The sleen, in the wild, is predominantly nocturnal. The larl is probably the most fearsome land predator on Gor. The sleen, on the other hand, is Gor's finest tracker. Domesticated sleen, tracking sleen, hunting sleen, herding sleen, guard sleen, war sleen, are relatively common on Gor. Domesticated larls are rare. Few people have seen one.

I stepped back a bit, behind the threshold.

"Do not be afraid, kajira," said the first guard. "There is little to interest a larl here."

"Except perhaps a tasty kajira," said the second guard.

They laughed.

"They do not approach the portal," said the first guard. "They do not understand it. It is different, unfamiliar, to them. Perhaps they fear being trapped. It is aversive to them."

"Perhaps one will be more curious than another," I said.

"Or more hungry," said the first guard.

I shivered. I put my arms about my body.

"Do not be afraid," said the first guard.

"I am not afraid," I said. "I am cold."

"You may withdraw," said the first guard.

"You may return later for the tray, the utensils," said the second guard.

"Or send another for them," said the first guard.

"A pretty one," said the second guard.

"I shall stand back a bit, if I may," I said.

"As you wish," said the first guard.

They then went again to the shelf to the right, where reposed their small meal.

I had been cold near the entrance, as it was a brisk day in Se'Kara, and I was camisked. Later in the year a camisked girl in the Voltai would presumably die of exposure, if she were not first devoured by beasts which, in the late fall, winter, or early spring, being half-starved, become unusually aggressive. I was not uncomfortable, back from the portal. The temperature in the Cave is kept equable by the Kurii, largely for the sake of their human allies, as Kurii, given their pelting, can easily sustain temperatures which, to a human, would be not only uncomfortable, but dangerous. In any event the Kurii, who seemed to tolerate a wide variety of atmospheric conditions with equanimity, had apparently arranged the Cave's temperature and humidity with the comfort of humans in mind. Indeed, I thought the temperature in the Cave, if anything, might be a bit warm. But what do Kurii know of humans, or care to know of humans? In any event, one would think nothing of encountering half-naked kajirae in the Cave even should the outside temperatures be freezing and the cold winds moan and roar about the peaks. The girls, of course, will be well aware of the contrast between the scantiness of their garmenture and the nature of the outside world.

I stood there, back from the portal, and listened to the chatting of the guards, mostly dealing with racing tharlarion and the price of women in Venna, and the small noises of utensils.

In the place of cells, where I had first encountered Grendel in the Cave, I had learned something of the politics of worlds. Those Kurii of the Cave, stubborn refugees of a putatively lost cause, impenitent and undissuaded, I had gathered, hoped to enleague themselves with one or more of the remote steel worlds, with the end in view of a conquest of Gor, and, perhaps eventually, if wished, of Earth. It was thought that Grendel, who stood high on one of these steel worlds, and was a hero of a recent revolution, might further this project. Doing so, of course, would be to repudiate the ends and principles for which he had earlier fought, and to ally himself with the very forces which had sought to destroy him and his party. The Grendel I had thought I had known, of matchless courage, integrity, and honor, would rather have perished uncomplainingly beneath the knives and irons of his enemies. I had feared only that he might be torn between the clear demands of honor and his troubling, profound solicitude for a single human female, the naive, unrealistic, ambitious, frivolous, charming Lady Bina. This solicitude was hard to understand, as he was a mere beast, and she was clearly human. If he had been human, or fully human, which he was not, the dilemma might, at least in principle, have been comprehensible. As it was, it made no sense. If it were not absurd, so out of the question, biologically, and such, one might have thought some sort of infatuation, even love, was involved. Certainly human history was filled with men who had betrayed a family, a party, a state, friends, allies, principles, honor, themselves, for the sake of an affair, a dalliance, a smile, a kiss. Surely the sparkling eyes of a free woman, and the hint of lips beneath a veil, had brought more than one general to defeat, more than one Ubar to ruin. It is said the man conquers with a sword, the woman with a kiss. How different from the slave who may be merely whipped and bought.

My fears in this matter had been twofold; first, that the Lady Bina, having succumbed to the blandishments of Kurii, might prevail upon Grendel to join their party, and, second, she being in their power, he might, to procure her comfort and safety, perform whatever tasks they might ask of him. I recalled his fear that she might be harmed if he refused to cooperate. To avoid that, I had speculated that he might do much. "Perhaps everything," he had said.

What I had failed to anticipate were his revelations to me prior to our entry into the so-called Audience Chamber of Agamemnon, spoken of as the "Theocrat of the World," and the "Eleventh Face of the Nameless One." There I had understood, for the first time, that he had no more respect for, or feeling for, the Lady Bina than the other Kurii. She had been for them no more than a piece in their games, of value only for her possible effect on Grendel, but now, given his lack of concern for her, even his contempt for her, she was no longer even that. His motivations, made clear to me, were wealth and power. How clever he was! His initial reluctance to further their cause, as one might see now, had been no more than a ruse to raise the stakes, presumably to the governorship of a world. I had been wrong about Grendel. I saw him now as he was, ruthless, cruel, treacherous, ambitious, and greedy. Part Kur, he was perhaps more than Kur, adding to the horror of one species the worst of another.

"One comes!" called the first guard, looking about, pointing toward the trail outside the portal.

Each seized his spear.

"Beware," said the second guard. "Do not challenge. See! It is a golden chain!"

Only four in the Cave wore the golden chain, Lucius, putatively first in the Cave, Timarchos, Lysymachos, and, of late, some days ago, Grendel.

The guards uneasily drew back their spears, and stepped aside.

I knew the entering beast. For me to effect this recognition it was not necessary for me to note a golden chain, nor hear him speak. I could recognize him easily, from Ar, from the domicile of Epicrates, from the place of cells, from the audience chamber. After weeks in the Cave, where Kurii were frequently encountered, I could also easily note the subtle difference about the eyes, and, of course, if one looked, that of the appendages, for the hands and feet of the entering beast were five-digited, not six-digited. These differences would have been instantaneously obvious to a Kur, but I am sure that many humans would have seen little or no difference between Grendel and a purely bred, or full-blooded, Kur. There would also, of course, if the beast were to speak, be a difference in the sounds uttered. They were neither purely human nor purely Kur. A human first encountering Grendel's Gorean might find it difficult to understand but, after a short while, with certain adjustments, it was easily intelligible. I gathered that his Kur was closer to Kur, than his Gorean to Gorean. In any event, however it might seem to a Kur, I saw little difference between the Kur of Grendel and that of his Kur fellows with whom he readily and frequently conversed.

Grendel growled as he passed the guards, and they drew

back a bit more. They would have been more at ease had they kept their spears at the ready, drawn back, in the two-handed thrusting position.

He had entered from the outside. I recalled that he had told me, before the meeting in the audience chamber, that he had been given his freedom, and might even leave the Cave if he wished. His natural pelting would protect him from the weather. I envied him his capacity to come and go as he might please. Aside from the question of garmenture, a kajira who left the Cave might be accounted a fugitive, and hunted down, as such. Mina, as I recalled, was to have been fed alive to lesser Kurii until Trachinos, pleased with her lineaments, had purchased her.

When Grendel turned to me, I dropped to my knees, and lowered my head, fearing to look into the eyes of such a monster. I remembered a glimpse of the golden chain swinging against that large, dark chest, the translator dangling from it, and then he had passed.

A bit later, the first guard said, "Kajira."

I then gathered up the tray, utensils, goblets, and the emptied bottle of ka-la-na, and made my way back to the kitchen.

As I passed the wagons of Pausanias, drawn up within the portal, I noted some of his men inspecting an axle, the wagon raised a few horts from the level.

Chapter Thirty-Four

"What is Chloe doing?" I asked, puzzled.

Chloe was the only girl in the slave quarters who could read. Mina, the slave of Trachinos, a former free woman, could also read, but she was not kept in the slave quarters. She now had her own collar, and was slept at the slave ring of Trachinos, who, as Lykos, Desmond, and Akesinos, now had a small, private room assigned to him. The kajirae who had been with the wagons, Jane, Eve, and myself, were forbidden to tend these rooms. We seldom saw the masters. Interestingly, these rooms could all be locked from the outside. Thus, they might serve as cells. I did not know the location of Astrinax, but supposed that he might be, as earlier, in attendance on the Lady Bina.

"I do not know," said Nora.

"Is it not obvious?" asked Chloe, not pleased.

"I see what you are doing," I said. "But I do not know what you are doing."

"Barbarian," said Chloe.

"So what are you doing?" I asked.

"Look," she said.

"I see that you are kneeling at a small desk," I said, "and are making marks on large sheets of papers, papers covered with squares. Beside you is a helmet, containing many small scraps of paper. You draw forth one small scrap of paper, look at it, and then write something in a square on one of the larger sheets, and then you put the small scrap of paper aside, and keep doing this."

"Very good," said Chloe.

"Do not be angry," I said.

"Why should I not be angry?" she said. "I am literate. Why should I be put to this nonsense. You could do it, as well."

"Let me try," I said.

"Are you serious?" she asked, alertly, brightly.

"Certainly," I said. "Why should an exalted literate slave, such as yourself, be put to such puerile endeavors?"

"I suppose you are right," she said.

"I am literate in my own language," I said to her, annoyed.

"A barbarian language," she said.

"True," I said.

"I am tired," she said. "Look what I have done." She pointed to several sheets, each square of which had been filled in. There were several more, beside her. I supposed it was a boring business, or might become so, after a time. On the other hand, I thought I might enjoy it, certainly for a while. I had no objection to its clerical aspect, and it was certainly very different from the tasks I commonly performed.

"Explain it to me," I said. "Let me help you."

"These large sheets," she said, "are each marked off into a hundred squares, ten on a side."

"That is like a Kaissa board, is it not?" I asked.

"Yes," she said. "And on most of the small scraps of paper is a letter, an Al-ka, a Ba-ta, and so on, though on some, for some reason, there is nothing but a meaningless mark. What one is to do is to take a paper from the helmet which bears a letter or the meaningless mark, and transcribe it onto one of the squares on the large sheet. There are also one hundred such scraps. After transcribing the letter or meaningless mark one puts it aside until later. When a large sheet is filled, the last letter or meaningless mark placed in the last square, one replaces the scraps of paper in the helmet, shuffles them about, jumbles them, and then, with a new large sheet, one begins again."

"How many large sheets are there?" I asked. Chloe had, clearly, filled in several already.

"One hundred," she said.

"It is clearly a great deal of work," I said.

"You offered to help," she said.

"I am happy to do so," I said, "at least for a time."

506

"You do not have to recognize the letters," she said. "Just transcribe them."

"I understand," I said. "What is the point of all this?"

"I do not know," she said. "As there are a hundred squares and letters, and such, I suppose it is some sort of game."

"Might it be a form of decoration, or an eccentric oddity for display?" I asked.

"Perhaps," she said, rising from her low desk and stretching.

"Where are you going?" I asked.

"I will wander about in the halls," she said.

"Beware that your thigh is not marked," I said.

"Why do you think I am going to wander about in the halls?" she asked.

"Oh," I said.

Chloe went to Nora, knelt before her, lowered her head, and requested permission to leave the slave quarters, which permission received, she exited. I knew that Chloe was not happy that our first girl should be a barbarian. Indeed, I had gathered, from remarks by our Gorean chain sisters in the quarters, that such an appointment was rare. It was their surmise that Nora's position was intended to affront and demean them, that they should be under the authority of a barbarian. Would this not make their collars more meaningful to them? It is hard to know about such things. I supposed it was also possible that Kurii, subversives, traitors, conspirators, and such, those who might wish to conceal the nature of their activities and plans, might have less to fear from an ignorant barbarian, at a loss in an unfamiliar culture, than a native Gorean. On the other hand, it is my surmise that to the masters, inspecting the available slaves, it had been a simple matter; Nora had been the obvious choice for first girl, the best choice for a girl to intimidate, control, and manage lesser girls.

For better than an Ahn I continued the work which Chloe had relinquished to me. I did not even know the names of the letters I was transcribing. In a sense they were simple designs, or mere marks, to me, though I knew them to be letters, or most of them. Chloe had said that some of these marks, or designs, were meaningless. I did not know for certain which were letters and which were not. If I were familiar with the alphabet I could probably have done the work more quickly, knowing that, say, that was an Al-ka, that a Ba-ta, and so on, and then quickly transcribing them. On the other hand, to me they were mostly marks or designs, and so I was careful to try to reproduce each as carefully as I could. I placed each mark or design in the center of a square, neatly.

"Master!" I heard, a girl's warning cry.

Instantly we all went to first obeisance position.

"I hoped more would have been done," said a masculine voice, almost at my side.

"Master!" I said, lifting my head. It was Master Desmond. Then I said, "Chloe is gone. I am doing the work."

"I will take these," he said, picking up the sheets which had been finished, Chloe's and mine.

"I am not authorized to surrender them!" I said.

"What are they?" he asked.

"I do not know," I said.

Nora called from her knees. "May I inquire the name of Master?" she asked.

"Desmond," said he, "Desmond of Harfax."

"You may not carry such things from here, Master," she said.

"Who has said so?" he asked.

"Pausanias, master of the Wagons," she said.

"I herewith countermand his order," said he.

"I fear to report Master," she said.

"You are first girl?" he asked. Surely he knew that, from the talmit, from the switch on her right wrist.

"Yes, Master," she said.

He put down the sheets, and strode to her. She cowered back.

"Talmit!" he said.

She reached behind her head and undid the talmit, and handed it to him. He cast it to the floor.

"Camisk off!" he said.

"Master?" she said.

"Now," he said. Then he said, "Switch."

He then looked down upon her, as she now was, the switch in his hand.

"Please, no, Master!" she said.

I then saw the proud Nora under the switch. In a moment

she was only a cringing, beaten slave, no different from others. He then yanked her to her feet by the hair, and held her head to his right hip, following which he dragged her, stumbling, to the nearest empty cage. There he threw her to all fours and, with his boot, hastened her into the cage, the gate of which, as she turned about, on her knees, he flung shut. She grasped the bars, trembling, tears coursing down her cheeks, looking out.

"Are you a slave girl?" he asked.

"Yes, Master!" she said.

"Anything more?" he asked.

"No, Master!" she said.

"Do you want your tongue slit, or removed?" he asked.

"No, Master!" she said.

"Do you intend to interfere further in the matters of masters?" he asked.

"No, Master!" she said.

Nora, I was sure, would remain silent.

Desmond of Harfax then returned to my side. He picked up the sheets which had been finished. "Continue your work," he said. "Make haste."

"Yes, Master," I said.

"Do not fear that Pausanias will soon call for the sheets," he said. "I encountered Chloe in the hall. She will see to it, in the manner of the slave, that Pausanias marks her thigh."

"Is that not dangerous?" I said.

"She will do much for a sweet," he said.

"I, too, would like a sweet," I said.

"You have not earned one," he said. Then he said, "Keep working. I shall return these sheets before locking time. Hopefully this business will be finished by tomorrow."

"Yes, Master," I said.

"Hopefully, Pausanias will not be satisfied with but one taste of Chloe," he said.

"Perhaps not," I said.

"It seems you sluts know how to manage such things almost off the block," he said.

"We are women," I said.

"And slaves," he said.

"The most female of women," I said.

"Certainly," he said.

"Perhaps Chloe will earn another sweet," I said.

"Perhaps," he said. "Are you jealous?"

"No," I said.

"Are you a liar?" he said.

"Yes," I said.

"You are pretty in your camisk," he said.

"Thank you, Master," I said.

"Continue your work," he said.

"Yes, Master," I said.

Chapter Thirty-Five

I paused, frightened, before the door to the Punishment Room, to which a white-faced Nora had instructed me to report. Nora's discipline, of late, while remaining strict, was no longer vindictive or arbitrary. This had much to do, I supposed, with having been shackled at the slave ring of Kleomenes. I still feared her, and mightily, but I knew now I would be punished only when I might be displeasing.

But I had been instructed to report to the Punishment Room. Who then had arranged this? Who might I have displeased?

I had no idea what might lie within the Punishment Room, and I was not eager to find out.

The door of the room was slightly ajar. I could see that the wood was thick, presumably that the cries from those within might not resound in the hall outside.

I was then conscious of a figure behind me. I could not kneel for a hand on my upper right arm held me on my feet.

"Shall we enter?" inquired Desmond of Harfax.

I was conducted within the room, and looked about myself. The room was lit with energy bulbs, as were the numerous chambers and labyrinthine halls of the Cave. The room was relatively bare. I saw no chains, whips, pincers, tongs, irons, boots, crowns, knives, and such, no miscellany of paraphernalia or furniture designed to produce pain of one sort or another, to one degree or another. I detected not even a brazier, within whose coals implements of one sort or another might be heated, nor a tank within whose iced waters implements of another sort might be chilled.

Desmond of Harfax closed the door behind us, and bolted it shut, from the inside.

There was a long table in the room, with benches. Master Desmond took a seat on one of the benches, and indicated that I might kneel beside him. In the presence of a master a kneeling or lying position is common with female slaves. For example, one might lie on the floor on one's side, looking up at him, at the foot of his couch.

"I cannot withstand torture, Master," I said, kneeling at his knee. "I do not know what I have done, or what I might be supposed to have done. I know nothing."

I did know that testimony from a slave, at least in a court of law, is commonly taken under torture. As noted before, the theory is that the slave may be expected to tell the truth only under duress. In fact, of course, the slave is likely to say, and quite soon, whatever the judge wishes to hear.

"Look about you," said Master Desmond. "Do you think this is a Punishment Room?"

"It does not look like one," I said.

"It is not a Punishment Room," he said. "It is a room called a Punishment Room."

"I do not understand," I said.

"Would you like to see a true Punishment Room?" he asked.

"No," I said.

"Calling this a Punishment Room," he said, "discourages entry, and increases privacy. It gave us a place where Jane and Eve might work undisturbed, copying the sheets Chloe, and you, prepared for Pausanias."

"You have bolted the door," I said.

"We may then speak in privacy," he said.

"I am at Master's mercy," I said.

"Are you alarmed?" he asked.

"A little," I said. "But I think Master is generally disposed to be kind to an animal."

"Unless she is in the least bit displeasing," he said.

"Of course, Master," I said. I was well aware of what might occur if a Gorean master found one less than fully pleasing. Accordingly, one attempts to be fully pleasing.

"We find this room a great convenience," he said.

"We?" I asked.

"It has been arranged by another," he said.

"Why have Jane and Eve been copying the sheets of Pausanias?" I asked.

"That we may have copies, of course," he said.

"I understand little of this," I said, "nothing of this."

"Let us suppose," he said, "that there is a vast conspiracy afoot, with one or more worlds at stake. Let us also suppose that this conspiracy's projection is threefold, one of alliance, one of extermination, or virtual extermination, and one of ultimate victory."

"I am only slave," I said, frightened.

"You already know Kurii have designs on this world," he said.

"I am only a slave," I said.

"The first phase," he said, "is likely to be securing the surface of Gor, with the exception, perhaps, of the Sardar Mountains, taken to be the range of Priest-Kings. The Priest-Kings, as is well known, tend to refrain from interference in the affairs of both Kurii and men, provided their weapon and technology laws are respected."

"Do Priest-Kings exist?" I asked.

"Yes," said Desmond of Harfax, "though their nature is little known. We think them to be much like men. Kurii perhaps think them much like Kurii. Their power makes clear their existence, for example the Flame Death, selectively used, usually to enforce the weapon and technology laws, the policing of the skies, to seek out and destroy intruding ships, the inability of tarns to fly over the palisaded Sardar, and such things. In any event, the first phase will presumably be the conquest of Gor, its surface, so to speak, largely within the circumscriptions of the laws. Given the limited numbers of Kurii on Gor at this time, they will begin by forging alliances with dissident elements in given cities, the resentful, envious, and jealous, those of thwarted ambition, and such, for there are always such, to bring them to power in their own cities, and then it will be these cities against other cities, the Kurii surreptitiously abetting their allies, as before, to the extent possible, with forbidden means. These means, together with numerous supplementary Kur contingents, as possible, will be obtained from one or more of the remote habitats of Kurii. Thus, at the end of the first phase one would have a conquered world putatively shared by men and Kurii, men who have served Kurii, and Kurii who have directed and managed men, the men unaware of their manipulation, all this theoretically achieved in compliance with the weapon and technology laws of Priest-Kings. The next phase, which I have referred to as that of extermination, or virtual extermination, would be that of the now-augmented numbers of Kurii turning on the considerably war-reduced human population of Gor, perhaps in a hundred coordinated nights of massacre, perhaps in a set of campaigns, in which Kurii, in virtue of their size, strength, agility, savagery, sharpness of sensory perception, and such, would presumably overmatch similarly numbered forces of humans in the field. Then, with a Kur Gor, so to speak, with large amounts of smuggled weaponry in place, the way would be cleared for a massive invasion fleet from the remote habitats, one unlikely to be significantly deterred by Priest-Kings. Lastly, the Sardar would be entered, and the Priest-Kings destroyed. The Kurii would then have their planet, all of Gor, with all its resources, from which, if they wished, they might seek other worlds. All this would be seemingly done within the weapon and technology laws of the Priest-Kings, until the final phase, the invasion of Gor from the remote habitats, abetted by the numerous emplaced Kurii, with their contraband weaponry."

"This is too bold, too far reaching, too daring," I said.

"Let us hope so," he said.

"Surely such things could not occur," I said.

"Let us hope not," he said.

"What is being done here?" I asked.

"We are on the brink of the first phase," he said, "in which dissident elements in various cities, or, I suppose, even minor, frustrated, ambitious Ubars, are to be contacted, encouraged, enflamed, and supplied."

"Would one or more of what you have called the remote habitats not be involved in this?"

"Certainly," he said. "If even one were secretly involved here, providing ships, supplies, personnel, weapons, and such, matters might precede apace, and if one were to be successfully involved, it seems then there might be another, and another, and so on."

"But would not Kurii, given their dispositions, and such, then contest Gor amongst themselves?"

"Yes," he said, "and then with weapons of enormous power, such as might turn the world into a cinder, such as might alter the axis of the planet itself."

"Such weapons should be denied them," I said.

"That is the view of the Priest-Kings," he said.

"And perhaps to us," I said.

"That is the view of Priest-Kings," he said.

"I know a world where there are no Priest-Kings," I said.

"Perhaps you are curious as to why you have been ordered to report here," he said.

"Yes, Master," I said.

"It has to do with your experience in the house of chance, in Ar," he said.

"I was only a serving slave, an entertainment slave," I said. "My role, and that of the others, was primarily to keep men at the games."

"While your masters ruined them," he said.

"They were free to leave whenever they wished," I said.

"But perhaps their luck would change," he said. "And how, if they left now, could they recoup their losses? And might their departure not dismay the pretty kajira who has been so delightedly and enthusiastically at their side, encouraging them to spin or choose once again, and then again, one sharing so sympathetically in their fortunes? Could they, if they were to leave, brave that tiny exclamation of disappointment, a pout from such pretty lips, a turning aside to another fellow, one of greater interest?"

"Master has been in such a house," I said.

"Perhaps," he said.

"Please do not look at me like that, Master," I said.

"Your pretty body," he said, "should be lashed, and lashed."

"I am no longer in such a house," I said. "A kajira must do as she is told!"

"Yes," he said, "but I suspect some are better at doing what they are told than others."

I was silent.

"I learned from Astrinax," he said, "from your test in the office of Menon, which you passed easily, that you, a nasty, deceitful little kajira, were an excellent choice for such a slave."

"Master!" I protested.

"Ah, yes," he said, "you, with your smiles, your expressions, your laughter, your body movements, your inadvertent touchings, your little cries of pleasure and disappointment, would do very well at keeping a fellow at the tables, in prompting him to continue, even be it into penury or destitution."

"I am different now, Master," I said. "I have learned much in the collar."

"But I have not brought you here," he said, "to castigate you for the worthless, shameful slut you are."

"Allison does not want to disappoint Master," I said. "She has learned much in her collar. She wants to be as Master would have her be. She wants to please Master."

"You think you have learned a little in your collar?" he said.

"Yes, Master," I said. "Very much, Master!"

"How to be a better animal?"

"Yes, Master," I said.

"Kiss my hand," he said.

I quickly kissed it.

I looked up him. I felt myself his slave. I wanted to be his slave. Then I put my head down. "Master has suggested that my presence here has to do with my having served in the house of chance, in Ar," I said.

"Yes," he said.

I lifted my lips to him, the offering of a slave.

He looked away, across the room.

I knelt back, a tear forming in my eye.

"I do not see how I can help Master," I said.

"First," he said, "I will give you a sense as to what is involved."

He rose from the bench and went to a shelf to the side, from which he drew forth a large leather envelope, and returned to the table.

"You recall the sheets with squares, on which you, and Chloe, inscribed various letters, signs, and such," he said.

"Certainly," I said.

516

He then extracted a small sheet from the envelope. "Do you know what this is?" he asked.

"No," I said.

"Do you play kaissa?" he asked.

"No," I said.

"But you have heard of it, you have seen a board, some pieces, such things."

"Yes," I said, "in the house of Tenalion, in Ar, even here. Some men play it."

"Many men play it," he said. "Records are kept of some games. Some games are annotated, criticized, discussed, and such."

I looked at him.

"In order to do that," he said, "obviously the pieces, which have rules for movements, and commonly accepted values, must have names, and there must be a way of designating the areas to which they might be moved. The squares of the board are numbered, and named for the initial placement of certain pieces, those on the first row. Each player has twenty-three pieces, but only ten are placed on the first row; the squares take their designations from the initial placement of these ten pieces. For example, from left to right, on the first row, one would have the Ubara's Initiate, the Ubara's Builder, the Ubara's Scribe, the Ubara's Tarnsman, and then the Ubara. Next comes the Ubar, and then, in order, the Ubar's Tarnsman, the Ubar's Scribe, the Ubar's Builder, and the Ubar's Initiate."

"This sounds complex," I said.

"It is not really complex," he said. "It is only that it is unfamiliar to you. For example, the fifth square in the Ubara's Initiate's column would be Ubara's Initiate Five, the seventh square in the column of the Ubar's Builder, would be Ubar's Builder seven, and so on."

"Yes, Master," I said.

"Now," he said, holding the small sheet removed from the leather envelope before me, "this resembles a game's annotation. Indeed, the first entries might occur in a game, for example one beginning with the opening called the Ubar's Tarnsman's Flight. On the other hand, if one examines the sheet carefully, most of the later entries would be impractical, even illegitimate, in an actual game. Accordingly, the first level of concealment is that the sheet is not what it initially appears to be, and might not attract particular attention, certainly not from those unfamiliar with kaissa, and probably not from your average player, who would not be likely to inquire into the annotation of a game in which he would not be likely to have much interest. It is not as though it was a game from the records of Centius of Cos, Scormus of Ar, Corydon of Thentis, Olaf of Tabuk's Ford, or such. And even if he looked at the sheet he would presumably soon cast it away as some sort of hoax or joke, perhaps even a jibe from some critic of kaissa, who thinks too much time and attention is devoted to the game. The second level of concealment, of course, is that these seemingly meaningless signs are mostly related to the alphabet."

"Surely the alphabet does not contain a hundred letters," I said. My own alphabet, incidentally, in my own native language contains twenty-six letters. A typical Gorean alphabet, as I understand it, though this seems to differ a bit in one place or another, contains twenty-eight letters.

"Of course not," he said. "Certain letters occur in Gorean more often than others, for example, Eta, Al-ka, Tau, and so on. Thus, there may be several variants for those letters."

"Chloe can read," I said, "and she did not understand some of the signs on the scraps of paper."

"Those are meaningless," he said. "The kaissa squares in which they are inserted thus constitute no intelligible part of the message. Thus, those who are attempting to unravel the message by means of considering the relative frequency of signs will have a difficult task, as some letters are represented by more than one sign and some signs represent no letter."

"And the way to compose a message, or to understand a message, has to do with the large sheets of squares which Chloe and I filled in."

"Precisely," said Desmond of Harfax. "It is only necessary that the sender and the receiver of the message use a corresponding sheet of squares, of which there could be an indefinite number, but which, to date, seems to consist of one hundred sheets."

"There must be a way," I said, "to know what sheet to use, as there are so many."

"As you cannot read," said Master Desmond, "this is not

obvious to you, but the small sheet which seems to be a game's annotation and the large sheet, whose squares contain letters, or meaningless marks, are both numbered."

"The numbers are then matched," I said.

"Yes," he said.

"Perhaps a message could be unraveled."

"But not easily, or quickly," he said. "By the time the message is understood it might be too late. More importantly, it is difficult to unravel such things unless one has a large amount of material at one's disposal, which allows for more attention to letter frequencies, hypotheses as to possible meanings, testing these hypotheses against additional material, and such. The large number of sheets, different sheets being used for different messages, means any given message is likely to afford the interpreter little to work with."

"I could not begin to unravel these things."

"You cannot even read to begin with," he said. "It would be enough to give you a nice clear message in simple Gorean."

"It is not my fault," I said, "that I have not been taught to read."

"Why should an animal be taught to read?" he asked.

"You like me illiterate, do you not?" I asked.

"Yes," he said. "If I owned you, I would keep you that way."

"You like an illiterate girl at your feet," I said.

"Actually," he said, "it is a great pleasure to have a highly intelligent, well educated, literate girl at one's feet. It pleases one to have her lips and tongue on one's boots."

"Perhaps then," I said, "you should teach me to read."

"It is also pleasant to have an illiterate barbarian at one's feet," he said. "Her simplicity and ignorance is charming."

"I assure you," I said, "I am highly intelligent, and well educated, and, in my own language, literate."

"Good," he said, "then, if I owned you, I would have both pleasures."

"I hate you," I said.

"Did you not lift your lips to me, but moments ago?" he asked.

I looked away, angrily.

"Even if I could read," I said, "I do not think I could unravel these things."

"Few could," he said. "Presumably some can, given enough

time, and enough material. There are much more complex and subtle ways to conceal meaning, of course, but the device I have explained to you is simple, easily understood, and likely, as far as they know, to be secure. It would not do, of course, for them to know we have copies of the sheets."

"No, Master," I said.

"To be sure," he said, "this advantage is not likely to be of long duration. New sheets would presumably be prepared from time to time, to continue to pluralize possibilities, and, if it were suspected that copies of the original sheets were in the possession of an enemy, new sheets would be instantly prepared, or, more likely, an entirely different method of communication and concealment would be adopted."

"At least now," I said, "I have some sense of what Chloe and I were doing."

"It is not necessary to explain these things to Chloe, or others," he said.

"I understand," I said.

"These concealments, of course," he said, "are intended to be of use to the conspirators in their communications within and between cities, between cities and the Cave, and so on."

"Why has Master explained them to Allison?" I asked.

"To give you a sense of what intrigues abound, and what projects are afoot," he said.

"Master is not alone," I said.

"No," he said.

"I shall not inquire the name of his confederate, or confederates," I said.

"I would not want your pretty body torn apart on the rack," he said, "while you are crying out their name, or names."

"I understand," I said.

"Do you remember my concern with cards?" he asked.

"Yes," I said.

"You served in a house of chance," he said.

"Until it was burned, and I, and others, were sold in the Tarsk Market."

"That seems a suitable place to sell one such as you," he said.

"Doubtless," I said.

"In the house of chance," he said, "there were games involving cards, were there not?"

"In the back of the large room, at the far tables," I said, "but I did not attend on those tables. Most of us attended on the gaming tables, with the wheels, and the dice, where most of the men were."

"But you must have heard things," he said.

"One always hears things," I said, warily.

"I am not an investigating magistrate," he said, "with a rack in the next room."

"I understand," I said.

"Presumably," he said, "those gambling on behalf of the house would wish to have some advantage in the matter."

"Otherwise," I said, "they might lose money, unintentionally."

"'Unintentionally'?" he smiled.

"It is important," I said, "for the patron to win occasionally, else he might abandon the game, or grow suspicious."

"And how," he asked, "does the house obtain its advantage? Are there apertures in the ceiling through which an accomplice, perhaps with a glass, might somehow signal the house's player, are there loitering observers nearby, in a position to read cards, and convey signals?"

"I do not think so," I said.

"The advantage then," he said, "lies in the cards themselves."

"That is my understanding," I said. "But I did not, personally, attend on the far tables."

"There would be calls for new decks, sealed decks," he said.

"I think that decks were prepared, and then sealed," I said.

"The house's player could recognize the nature and value of an opponent's card from the back," he said.

"There were intricate designs on the back of the cards," I said, "apparently identical on each card."

"But not identical," he said, "for those who knew what to look for."

"I think the differences were subtle," I said, "very subtle."

Desmond of Harfax then reached again into the leather envelope. He produced another sheet of paper. It was as unintelligible to me as the first, which had resembled, as I had been given to understand, the record, or annotation, of a kaissa game, but it was clearly different.

"What do you make of this?" he asked.

"I cannot read," I said.

"This appears to be a list of cards," he said. "But I am not sure what it actually is. I suspect a concealment is involved."

"Perhaps in the manner of the preceding concealment," I said, "a different card standing for a different letter, more than one card for a single letter, perhaps some cards standing for nothing."

"Possibly," he said. "But there are no doublings, or repetitions."

"That is important?" I asked.

"I think so," he said. "Surely it would severely restrict the potentiality for communication."

"Perhaps it is an inferior device," I said.

"We are not dealing with fools," he said.

I was silent.

"In the case of the kaissa concealment," he said, "we were fortunate enough to obtain, and later copy, crucial sheets, materials in virtue of which the message might be concealed, and then, later, revealed. But we have nothing similar here, no such sheets, no materials in virtue of which the message might be concealed or revealed."

"In the first case," I said, "you may have been fortunate."

"I have a principal," he said, "who is highly placed, who would have access to such things, if they existed."

"Perhaps not," I said.

"Yes, perhaps not," he said.

"I fear I can be of little help to Master," I said.

"Perhaps there is something simple here," he said, "so simple we cannot see it."

"Perhaps a single explanatory sheet, to which we lack access?" I suggested.

"Possibly," he suggested, "but I do not think so."

He reached again into the leather envelope. He drew out a deck of cards. He handed me the deck. "I want you to examine these cards, and see if anything occurs to you."

"I suppose you have arranged the deck in the order prescribed by the sheet," I said.

"Yes," he said.

"And that did not prove illuminating?"

"No," he said. "But I did not expect it to. It tells no more than the sheet itself."

"They are very plain," I said. "If they are prepared in such a way as to admit reading their values from the back, it must be very subtly done."

"We are not concerned here with cheating at cards, but with concealed messages," he said. "Does anything about the deck strike you as different, or unusual?"

"No," I said. "You are thinking of something like the kaissa concealment."*

"That would be the initial conjecture," he said, "but it seems unlikely, as each card is different."

"Then the order of the cards must be important," I said.

"I think so," he said, "but what is the relevance of the order? What would it mean if, say, a Physician's Vulo is succeeded by a Scribe's Tarsk?"

"Perhaps that would stand for an entire message," I said, "something like 'Meet at dawn', 'Bring gold', 'Depart on the morrow', such things."

"That is far too complex in one sense," he said, "for it would require a storeroom of messages, and too simple in another, as one might wish to express something not in the stock of messages."

"The arrangements of the cards would be limited," I said.

"That is not the problem," he said. "You are dealing with sixty cards. Consider the matter. The formula is simple and involves diminishing multiplications. If there were two cards, there would be two arrangements, as in two times one; if three cards, six arrangements, as in three times two times one; if five cards, one hundred and twenty arrangements, as in five times four, times three, times two, times one. If there were ten cards, in this fashion, there would be over three million arrangements, and so on."

"On my former world," I said, "I left such things to others."

"You doubtless left many things to others."

---

* See Appendix

"Yes, Master," I said.

"You were substantially useless, were you not?" he asked.

"Perhaps," I said.

"But one can find uses for such women," he said, "whether of your former world or of Gor, when they are collared."

"Yes, Master," I said. On Gor I had found myself owned, under discipline, and put to work. On Gor women such as I were good for something, indeed many things. Masters saw to it. And one of the things a slave was to be good for, indeed usually the most important thing, was to give her master incredible pleasure. Surely she was expected to do more than cook and clean, shop, fetch sandals on all fours, bringing them to a fellow in her teeth, and such. Why then, I wondered, with all his opportunities, even in the slave wagon on a blanket, had he never put the slave, Allison, to use, full slave use, in the fullest sense that is understood on Gor. Ah yes, I thought, honor, honor! Mina, at least, I thought, had the reassurance and comfort of her shackle at a slave ring. To be sure, there was a difference. Trachinos had bought her.

Sometimes it is hard to be a slave. One is so much at the mercy of the free. May one be clothed? Will one be caressed, will one be given a sweet? Will one be allowed to crawl, begging, to the feet of the master?

"But even so," he said, "even with so many possibilities, it is almost certain one would often wish to express something new or different."

"Yes, Master," I said.

"More importantly," he said, "Kleomenes, in the camp, I am sure, conveyed something secretly to Pausanias by means of cards, furnishing him with instructions, directions, or such. Surely Kleomenes had no bundles of messages to rummage through, in the saddle bags of his tharlarion, looking for a card equivalent, nor had Pausanias a wagon load of card equivalents by means of which he might locate messages."

"I do not think so," I said.

"So there must be something simple here, so simple that it is hard to see, so obvious that it is not noticed."

"Perhaps you do not have the right deck," I said.

"Perhaps," he said. "Yet this deck was furnished by my principal."

"Can he not explain these things?" I asked.

"He is as baffled as we," said Desmond of Harfax. "He has tortured himself to make sense of the possible meaning of the list, the meaning of the individual cards, their order, and such."

"Perhaps there is no meaning," I said.

"Are you serious?" he asked.

"Perhaps the cards are a diversion, a false trail, a distraction of sorts, something to consume time, while the actual messages are conveyed in some other way, as by the kaissa concealments."

"That seems unlikely," he said, "for, as far as we know, the conspirators feel themselves unidentified and secure at present. Into whose hands would they wish such a thing to fall, and for what purpose, at present?"

"Perhaps into your hands," I said, "and that of your principal."

"If we were suspected," he said, "I do not think we would find ourselves at liberty."

"Perhaps," I said, "it is not that the cards are meaningful, but that they are not yet meaningful, that they might become meaningful."

"They must now be meaningful," he said.

"Why?" I asked.

"Because we have the list," he said, tapping that small sheet of paper on the table.

"I thought poorly," I said.

"No, no," he said. "Any thought is welcome."

"Why am I here?" I asked.

"You served in a house of chance," he said. "I thought you might be helpful."

"The door is bolted," I said. "Was there no other reason?"

"No," he said.

I put my cheek on his knee. "I am uncomfortable," I said. "My body whispers to me."

"Do not tell me that the little barbarian's slave fires have begun to burn," he said.

"Men have done things to me," I said.

"The cards," he said, "the deck, the order. Think, think!"

"My presence here has been unavailing," I said.

"Tell me about the tables, the play, everything," he said.

"I know nothing," I sobbed. "They invite men to the tables, some seek them by themselves, games are suggested, drinks are brought, decks are produced, and opened, men divide the decks, disarrange the cards, distribute them to the players in certain fashions, depending on the game. Other cards may be drawn, such things."

"Of course!" he said.

"Master?" I said.

"That is it!" he said. "You have it!

"What?" I asked.

"It is so simple, so deceptively simple!"

"I do not understand," I said.

"We were looking for the wrong things in the wrong places!" he said. "We were too sophisticated, too devious, too clever, too stupid! It was there before us, all the time!"

"What?" I asked.

"The list is the preparation for a message, not the message," he said. "You were right. It is not that the cards are meaningful, but that they might become meaningful, and easily so."

"I do not understand," I said.

"Remind me to give you a sweet," he said.

"For what?" I asked.

"You have solved our problem," he said.

"How?" I asked.

"'How'?" he asked.

"Yes, how?" I asked.

"I thought you were intelligent, Allison," he said.

"It seems not, Master," I said.

"Nonetheless," he said, "you remain of slave interest."

"I do not understand," I said.

He rose and went to the door, unbolted it, and held it open.

"Return to the slave quarters," he said.

"Yes, Master," I said.

I paused in the threshold. "Master finds Allison of slave interest?" I said.

"Perhaps," he said.

"Allison is pleased," I said.

"And run!" he said.

"Yes, Master," I said, hurrying through the portal. If one runs quickly enough, it is unlikely that one will be caught, and one's thigh marked. It is easy to mark a thigh, of course, when one is in a camisk. Sometimes one's leg is held. The writing is then boldly visible, for all to see. In this way it is clear to everyone that the girl has been reserved for that evening, and also clear who has reserved her.

Chapter Thirty-Six

"You know the master named Desmond, do you not?" asked Nora. She sounded frightened.

"Yes, Mistress," I said. "I was even in his keeping, on the journey to the Crag of Kleinias."

Nora clutched a small package in her hands. "I have been instructed by him to deliver this to Master Kleomenes," she said.

"That is understandable enough," I said, "as you are frequently called to the slave ring of Master Kleomenes."

"This Desmond of Harfax," she said, "knows you. Why would he not have you deliver it to Master Kleomenes?"

"I do not know," I said, though I could easily speculate as to a possible motivation.

"It is clear the matter is sensitive," said Nora. "If you were to deliver it, it might be noted. Curiosity might be aroused."

"Perhaps," I said.

"I am afraid," she said.

"I would not disobey a master," I said.

"I do not want my tongue slit, or removed," she said.

"No," I said. I recalled such threats were made once to her by Desmond of Harfax. Since then she had lived in fear of him. It pleased me, somehow, that Nora, so proud, severe, and magisterial with us, so imperious and exacting a first girl, was no more than a cringing slave before Desmond of Harfax. I recalled her in the small slave cage into which he had forced her, kneeling, naked, clutching the bars, looking up at him in fear.

"What is in the package?" she asked.

"It is loosely wrapped," I said. "There seems no secret about it. Why not look, and see?"

We turned back the wrapper.

"It is a deck of cards," she said.

"You see," I said, "there is nothing to worry about."

She almost fainted with relief.

"May I see it?" I asked.

I took the deck of cards in my hand, and moved the cards about a little. I detected no slips of paper hidden amongst the cards, nor anything on the cards that was foreign to the expected designs and markings. As far as I could tell, it was a normal deck of cards. Perhaps, I thought, there is nothing more here than what appears to be here. Might this not be innocent? Perhaps Kleomenes had expressed an interest in play, which interest had come to the attention of Desmond of Harfax, who had somehow located and supplied a suitable means for exploring this interest? Certainly they knew one another from the time of the caravan. Kleomenes had been twice at a camp of ours, when we first met him and his hunters, and, second, when he had visited us after his hunt, the night the tharlarion had been driven away. The one difference in this deck of cards from the deck which I had earlier seen in the keeping of Desmond of Harfax was the attractive speckling on the edges of the deck, a sort of design with which I was familiar from the house of chance. Goreans tend to be fond of beauty and color, in garments, architecture, paving stones, utensils, tableware, and such. Often even the cords and straps, the binding fiber, and such, and sometimes even the chains with which slaves are bound, are colorful.

I closed the wrapper.

"You had best deliver it," I said.

"Perhaps you would like to do so," she said.

"Are you prepared to disobey a master?" I asked.

"No!" she said.

"Have you ever disobeyed a master?" I asked.

"Once," she said, "in the training house. I never dared to do so again."

"You have never disobeyed Master Kleomenes?" I said.

"I do not want to disobey him," she said.

"What would happen if you did?" I asked.

"He is not man of Earth," she said. "I am a slave. He is a Gorean master."

"You would be punished?" I said.

"Of course," she said. "If it were not the case, how could I yield to him with the trembling helplessness of the eager slave?"

"You had best deliver the package," I said.

She sped from the slave quarters. It pleased me to see the proud Nora, whom I remembered from Earth, running as a slave.

She was well submitted, I gathered, to Master Kleomenes. I was sure he well knew what to do with a woman.

Chapter Thirty-Seven

"I have explained to you my understanding of things," said Desmond of Harfax.

There were eleven men in the room, and four slaves, the three who had been in the party of the Lady Bina, Jane, Eve, and myself, who had either prepared or copied the kaissa sheets, and Mina, formerly the Lady Persinna of Ar, who had been purchased by Trachinos. Amongst those in the room were Astrinax, Lykos, Trachinos, and Akesinos.

"Astrinax!" I had said, seeing him in the room.

I had inquired after the Lady Bina.

"She is essentially a prisoner," said Astrinax. "For some reason they are holding her."

"Is the throne of a Ubara still in her thoughts?" I asked.

"If so," he said, "she no longer expects it from Kurii. Her rations have been reduced, and she is no longer treated with the respect with which she was originally received."

"She has been repudiated by Grendel," I said, "whose true feelings have now been revealed. She served his purpose as a pretext for hesitation in allying himself with Kurii, to win himself a more estimable offer of wealth and power. That received, she is no longer of use to him."

"I fear she will be killed," said Astrinax.

"No," I said. "She is beautiful. She would bring a high price on a block. Let her be collared."

"You do not understand, dear Allison," he said. "That is because you are a barbarian. She is not an animal, such as you, which might be roped and claimed as such, bought and sold as such. She is a free woman. Thus, she is far more likely to be slain."

"Might not Grendel speak for her," I asked, "that she might be simply marked and collared?"

"She is of no concern to him," said Astrinax.

"How treacherous and hateful he is," I said.

"How is he different from any other of these beasts?" he asked.

"How, Desmond of Harfax," inquired Kleomenes, "have you arrived at your understanding of things?"

"I prefer, at present," said Desmond, "to keep my source confidential."

"How can you expect us to believe you?" asked Kleomenes.

"I give you my word," said Desmond.

"The word of many in this Cave," said Kleomenes, "is worthless."

"Obviously," said Desmond, "I am willing to risk much. Even summoning you to this secret meeting is fraught with danger."

"You have placed us all in jeopardy," said Kleomenes.

"Yet you have come," said Desmond. "And no one has left. To have come shows that you have suspected what might be afoot, that you have remained shows you suspect what I say is true."

"There may be spies amongst us," said a man.

"If so," said Desmond, "they are fools, for they would be involved in the common peril."

I noted that one or two of the fellows in the room held what appeared to be a deck of cards.

"If what you say is true," said Kleomenes, "what can we do?"

"Pausanias, with his drivers, and wagons, has already left," said Desmond. "That means, I believe, that things have begun. I do not expect them to return in the spring. I think they will scatter and initiate the intrigues I spoke of in a hundred cities."

"Then it is too late," said a fellow.

"No," said Desmond, "for a hundred cities might be warned."

"I see," said Kleomenes.

"It is too fanciful," said a man.

"We would not be believed," said another.

"We must try," said Desmond of Harfax.

"The snows will soon commence," said a man.

"The passes will be closed," said another.

"It will be safest to pretend we suspect nothing of this," said a man, "and wait until spring."

"That would give the conspiracy a start of months," said Desmond.

"I am not eager to be hunted down by Kurii," said another, "now, later, in the cold, in the snow, in the thaws of spring, in the heat of summer, anytime."

"The beasts have use for us, for a time," said another. "Is it not better to live for a time, than not to live, at all?"

"The beasts are formidable," said Desmond, "but, within the laws of Priest-Kings, they are not invincible. The spear and sword, the bolt and arrow, speak to them as well as to us."

"The hunted larl, the hunted sleen," said a man, "often becomes the hunter."

"Who would pursue the Voltai tarsk into a thicket, the wild bosk into the high grass?" said a fellow.

"Good, good!" said Desmond.

"How are we to proceed?" asked a fellow.

"We must enlist who we can amongst the humans," said Desmond. "Gather supplies, secretly, and flee."

"Soon," said a fellow, "—the winter, the snows."

"Yes," said Desmond.

"But Kurii, the Cave, will remain," said a fellow.

"Would it not remain a center for subversion and intrigue?" asked another.

"Quite possibly," said Desmond. "But before we leave we might be able to inflict a crushing blow, one of great strategic importance, on the hopes of Gorean Kurii, on the very conspiracy itself."

"Speak," said a fellow.

"Who is high Kur in the Cave?" asked Desmond.

"Lucius," said several of the men, without hesitation.

"How many of you have heard of the Kur, Agamemnon?" asked Desmond.

"He was a leader, faraway," said a fellow.

"The Cave is said to be the Cave of Agamemnon," said a fellow.

"Theocrat of the World, Eleventh Face of the Nameless One," added another.

"That is nonsense," said a man.

"Not to Kurii," said Desmond, soberly.

"I have heard remarks," said a man. "There was a far world, a war, and this Agamemnon perished in that war."

"Perhaps," said Desmond, "Agamemnon is still alive. Perhaps only one or another of his bodies perished. Perhaps he is here, alive."

"This is madness," said a man.

"How many of you have seen the small metal chest, sometimes on display, that tended so carefully by two golden-chain Kurii, Timarchos and Lysymachos?"

"I have seen it," said a fellow.

"I, too," said another.

"As it is guarded," said another, "it must contain riches."

"Diamonds," speculated another.

"If we are to flee," said a fellow, "perhaps we could steal it, and take it with us."

"We might all be rich," said a fellow.

Interest coursed amongst the men.

"What has this treasure chest to do with Agamemnon?" asked a man.

"I think it is Agamemnon, or contains Agamemnon," said Desmond of Harfax.

"I think you are mad," said Kleomenes.

"I have gathered certain things, some rather obliquely, not openly stated, from my source," said Desmond.

"Which is to remain confidential?" said Kleomenes, skeptically.

"I will now," said Desmond of Harfax, "command an unlikely speaker to address you, the barbarian kajira, Allison, whose thigh some of you may have marked."

There was some laughter.

"Master?" I said.

"Do not insult us with noises from the mouth of a slave," said a fellow.

"Slaves know nothing," said a man.

"She is a barbarian," said another.

"If she is to speak, let instruments of torture be brought," said another.

"How else could one believe the words of a slave?" asked another.

"A meeting was held," said Desmond of Harfax, "at which none of us, and no free man, was present, but some kajirae were present. The meeting was held in Kur, without translators, but the kajirae, of course, could witness what occurred. I have learned that Allison, whom I have had in my keeping—"

There was laughter at this point, which annoyed me, for they doubtless supposed that Desmond of Harfax had reaped much pleasure from the rich and frequent use of the slender, barbarian brunette in question, whereas the slender, barbarian brunette in question had been scarcely touched, and had been, so to speak, muchly deprived. How often she had longed for his touch, even wept for it, and had been denied!

"—was present."

I was not sure how Master Desmond knew I had been at the meeting in question, but it seemed likely he had obtained this information, and some sense of the nature of the meeting, from one of the other kajirae who had been present. Of the four kajirae in the room I was the only one who had been at the meeting.

"Allison," said Desmond of Harfax.

I kept my head down, frightened.

"She fears to speak before free men," he said.

"If she is to speak," said a fellow, "then let her fear not to speak."

"Do not be afraid, Allison," said Desmond of Harfax.

I looked up at him, him to whom I wished to belong. How could he not know that?

"We have mentioned a box, a case, a chest, a container, of some sort, which is usually found in the company of two golden-chain Kurii, Timarchos and Lysymachos, a container which it seems they guard zealously. Are you familiar with that object?"

"Yes, Master," I said. "I have seen it."

"What do you think it contains?" he asked.

"I do not know, Master," I said. "A treasure perhaps, surely something very precious."

"Did you see this container at the meeting in question, that at which there were no free men present, that conducted entirely in Kur?"

"No, Master," I said.

"But you did see Timarchos and Lysymachos?"

"Yes, Master."

"Without the container," he said.

"Seemingly so," I said.

"Tell us about the meeting," he said.

"It was in Kur," I said.

"Tell us a little about it, what you can," he said.

"Only Kurii and some kajirae were present," she said, "I suppose grooming slaves."

"Are you such a slave?" he asked.

"No," I said. "But I have groomed."

"You were brought by Grendel," he said.

"Yes, Master."

"Why?"

"I do not know," I said. "I think it was that he would appear to have a personal grooming slave, which would seem to enhance his prestige, and suggest importance. Few of the Kurii, on this world, have such slaves."

"Continue," said Master Desmond.

"I understood little of what was occurring," I said. "Grendel, near whom I knelt, was prominently placed, before a dais at the front of the room. Timarchos and Lysymachos emerged from behind a curtain at the back of the dais, which curtain they then drew aside. Shortly thereafter, frighteningly, apparently emerging from a deep recess behind the dais, taking its place on the dais, was a large machine, behaving as though it were alive. It had jointed metal legs, and a metal torso, but no obvious head, unless the head and torso were one. It had things like eyes, four of them, two of which were on metal stalks. These eyes could turn about. The device was very large, and doubtless heavy. It was crab-like, a large, metallic crab-like thing. Attached to it, or part of it, were two metallic arms, each terminating in heavy, pincer-like objects."

"Let her be lashed for lying," said a fellow.

"Who dares to subject us to the ravings of a mad slave?" asked another.

"Put her out of the Cave, naked and bound," said a man.

"Master?" I said, frightened.

"Continue, Allison," said Desmond of Harfax.

"There were chantings," I said, "and, later, what appeared to be a number of utterances, all of which received the identical response from the assembly. Then commenced what seemed to be a dialogue between Timarchos and Lysymachos, and the machine."

"The machine spoke?" asked a man.

"It seemed so, Master," I said.

"Bring a whip, that a lying slave may be suitably chastised," said a man.

"Continue," said Master Desmond.

"Master!" I begged.

"Or I will use the whip on you myself," he said.

"One Kur, Grendel," I said, "was singled out, and addressed. I know not what transpired."

"What then?" said Master Desmond.

"Some will recall a blind Kur," I said. "He was brought into the hall, was apparently denounced, and seems to have been condemned, and sentenced. He was driven from the hall, and, as I understand it, from the Cave. Following this two Kurii were presented to the machine, one a silver-chain Kur and one an iron-chain Kur. Each addressed the machine, which appeared to listen, perhaps deliberate. The silver-chain Kur was then slain, and his chain given to the other, who was also garlanded by Timarchos and Lysymachos. Following this the machine spoke for some Ehn, remarks which, I took it, related to Grendel. At the end of this, amidst apparent approval, Grendel was given a golden chain, and received a garland from both Timarchos and Lysymachos. Shortly thereafter the machine withdrew, followed by Timarchos and Lysymachos. The meeting had ended."

"These things are hard to understand," said Desmond of Harfax, "but it is my conjecture that the Kur, Agamemnon, did not perish on a far world, but is alive, and on Gor."

"And living in a little box?" laughed a man.

"He must be very small," laughed another.

"Living, yes," said Desmond, "but not as you think. The natural body of Agamemnon, limbs and organs, may have perished centuries ago."

"Then he is dead," said a man.

"There are devices, technologies, here," said Desmond of Harfax, "with which we are unfamiliar. What feels, and thinks, and sees? Surely you are aware that he who has lost a leg or an arm may continue to feel them, though they no longer exist. Sometimes a body may be subjected to torture and ruin and no pain is felt. You thrust a stick against the ground and say you have felt the ground, and it surely seems so, but it is an illusion. The most you could feel is a pressure on your fingers or hand. In sleep, do you not see, hear, feel, and experience, though you do not leave your couch? That the body be protected it is surely desirable that you should seem to feel, say, a pain in an injured limb, that you will remove it from danger, or tend to it, but the limb may be felt when it no longer exists. Without these illusions, these precious, invaluable, wonderful illusions, how could one exist? You open your eyes and see a world, but how could this be? The world somehow stimulates you in such a way that you produce a representation of the world. Your eyes do not throw nets out and draw trees and mountains into your head. Remember the dreams. The world which causes you to see and feel may be quite other than the seemings and feelings which it produces, and yet, surely, it is somehow related to those seemings and feelings, else we could not survive. Experience is internal, not outside the body. It is centered in the brain. It is the brain with which you think, see, and feel."

"Absurd," said a man. "I open my eyes and see the world before me. So do we all."

"Yes," said another fellow.

"I see you," said a man.

"Yes," said Desmond of Harfax, "but the seeing is within you, the seeing is not outside of you. What is within you cannot be identical with what is outside of you. They are different. They are two things."

"This is all nonsense," said a man.

"Let us suppose that the account rendered by a slave is true," said Desmond of Harfax. "Presumably Timarchos and Lysymachos, who seem to be in constant attendance on the container, who are its devoted companions or faithful guardians, would not have abandoned it, or its occupant, at such a meeting. As the container was not in view, it is my suggestion that it was somehow incorporated in the machine, connected to it in such a way that whatever was within the container could see, feel, think, speak, and communicate by means of the machine."

"It would be the brain then," said Kleomenes, "the living brain, related somehow to the outside world."

"That is my belief," said Desmond of Harfax. "Moreover, I believe there must be some way in which the brain, in its container, by means of its container, or its construction, can communicate with the outside world. Thus the container, itself, is a machine, a body, for the brain. And the container, I suspect, given the report of the slave, Allison, might be incorporated in a variety of bodies, with various capacities."

"This is absurd," said a man.

"Consider," said Desmond of Harfax, "the brain of a mighty, fearsome, almost legendary leader, gigantic and formidable, a Kur of Kurii, kept alive, revered, obeyed. Consider the terrible centrality of sensation in that brain, the enormity of ambition which might linger, the rage at the loss of its body, the force of a focused, extraordinary rationality, unwilling to accept compromise or limitation, a will determined to have its way, a ruthless mind resolved to affect worlds, an incomparable intellect, unconquered, commanding, devoted to power, stung by defeat, desiring to recoup losses, fanatically committed to pursue ends, to return from exile with the resources of a planet at its back."

"Absurd," said the fellow, again.

"Titanic forces could be locked in battle," said Desmond of Harfax, "forces compared to which men are small, weak, and fragile things, little more than field urts scampering about in the grass, amidst the tread of trampling tharlarion."

"We are well paid," said a man. "Let us collect our gold, and let the future care for itself."

"It would be a future in which you would be unlikely to participate," said Desmond of Harfax.

"Yet," said Kleomenes, "if two mountains were balanced in the scales, the smallest weight might tip the balance."

"Yes!" said Desmond of Harfax.

It was his whip beneath which I wished to cower.

"And what small weight might tip so great a balance?" asked Kleomenes. "What small blow might affect so great a war?"

"Perhaps none," said Desmond of Harfax. "But I can think of one blow, small, but easily struck, which might possess an immediate effect."

"What is that?" asked a man.

"The assassination of Agamemnon," said Desmond.

"You are mad," said a fellow.

"He is not here," said a man.

"If he were here, we would have seen him," said a man.

"Lucius is high Kur in the Cave," said another.

"Agamemnon died long ago," said another.

"All know that," said another.

"How can you assassinate someone who is dead?" asked a man.

"The container of which we have spoken must be seized," said Desmond of Harfax.

"Diamonds are in the container," said a man. "You want them for yourself."

"No!" said Desmond of Harfax.

"Who will trust a mad Metal Worker, and a lying slave?" asked a man.

"I would trust them before Kurii," said Kleomenes.

"You have taken fee," said a fellow.

"Not to throw myself on my own sword," said Kleomenes.

"We should not be met here," said a man. "It is dangerous."

"The beasts do not look lightly upon treason," said another.

"Let us leave singly, and inconspicuously," said another.

At this point we heard a rushing about in the hall outside, a snarling, much roaring, and the jangle of weapons.

"Ela!" said a man. "They have come for us!"

"No," said Desmond. "Listen! Weapons clash!"

Chapter Thirty-Eight

"Beware! Back!" cried Desmond of Harfax, thrusting me to the side of the hall.

Four Kurii, claws scratching on the smooth tiles of the hall flooring, hurried by. They carried improvised shields of nailed wood and spears. One turned about, surveying us, eyes bright, determined that we were human, growled, and rejoined his fellows. A kajira, Chloe, sped past us, in the other direction.

"What is going on?" I asked.

"War," said Master Desmond, "but it seems one in which we are not implicated."

"I do not understand," I said.

"One in which we are not yet implicated," he said.

Astrinax appeared at our side.

"This is our opportunity," he said, "to escape the Cave. I have been to the great portal. It is no longer guarded."

"What of the guards?" asked Desmond.

"One is dead," he said. "I do not know the whereabouts of the other."

"Four Kurii, armed, passed us, a moment ago," said Desmond.

"I think some beasts have left the Cave," said Astrinax. "I fear chaos reigns."

"Back," said Desmond, and we shrank back against the wall.

"What is it?" said Astrinax.

"I do not know," said Desmond.

"The machine," I said. "You have not seen it. I know the sound. It is the machine!"

Approaching down the corridor, moving carefully, the

stalk-like eyes rotating about, scanning, came the machine, accompanied by two shield-bearing, ax-carrying Kurii, Timarchos and Lysymachos.

"Aii!" said Astrinax.

The machine paused, and the stalk-like eyes turned toward us, but then it, and its fellows, passed us, as had the previous Kurii, but in the other direction.

I supposed that it was reconnoitering or looking for isolated foes.

I did see that the large pincer-like appendages were wet with blood. If the barbed darts with their thin cables had been fired, they had now been withdrawn into the torso of the device.

"It does exist," said Astrinax.

"You see," said Desmond. "Slaves can speak the truth, without the assistance of torture."

"That is Agamemnon?" said Astrinax.

"Yes," said Desmond.

"He is a machine?" said Astrinax.

"Now," said Desmond. "He might have many bodies."

"Let us gather men, who will be our allies," said Astrinax, "acquire supplies, warm clothing, and depart. Pausanias and his wagons have gone. We have the kaissa sheets. They must be distributed. Gor must be warned."

"We must exercise caution," said Desmond.

"The great portal is clear," said Astrinax.

"It is not obvious we may leave with impunity," said Desmond. "Too, I suspect most of the men will not care to desert their gold."

"Some may flee," said Astrinax.

"Alone, into the mountains, with gray winter on the horizon?"

"Before the snows," said Astrinax.

"Let them," said Desmond. "I will remain."

"Why?" said Astrinax.

"To kill Agamemnon," said Desmond.

Chapter Thirty-Nine

I clutched the bars of the slave cage in which Desmond of Harfax had placed me. I shook the bars, as I could. "Come back, Master!" I had cried. "Come back, release me, Master!" But he had gone.

He had thrust me into the cage, and then swung shut the gate, securing me within. How helpless one feels in such a cage! I had turned about, quickly, to regard him. He was standing back, contemplating me. The shadow of the bars fell across my body. He was grinning. He liked to see me so, naked, caged. "I hate you!" I said.

"Lie down," he said. "On your side. Curl, kajira."

I did so.

"You are a pretty little bundle," he said. "How high your hip, the lovely curve to your love cradle, your calves, your small feet."

He smiled.

My eyes must have flashed fire.

"Yes," he said, "pretty."

"I hate you," I said. "I hate you!"

He had then turned away.

It was then that I had risen to my knees, clutched the bars, and called after him, but he had not come back.

He had left me in a cage, a cage, as it had pleased him!

I recalled how he had looked upon me! How boldly! He had looked upon me as what I was, an animal, a pretty animal, which might be bought and sold, which might be done with as a master might please. I held the bars. I pressed myself against them.

I was caged, and helpless.

How strong are men! How they look upon us! How much we are at their mercy! How I hated him! How I wanted to kiss his feet. How I wanted to please him, as a naked slave!

* * * *

We had not anticipated a Kur revolt, the rising of several of the iron-chain Kurii against the silver- and gold-chain Kurii. Indeed, we had not been clear, for more than a day, what was occurring. We did know that there was skirmishing in the halls, and that some Kurii had attacked others. The humans in the Cave, I am sure, would have been muchly pleased to have remained neutral in such an altercation, as a single human, or even two or three, was a sorry match for a Kur. But, as may often be the case in such affairs, neutrality was not acceptable to committed belligerents. The choice accorded to humans was, in effect, certain death or participation in the conflict, supporting one faction or the other. I suppose this had partly to do with Kur distrust of humans, partly with an unwillingness that some might profit in safety and comfort from the pain and blood of others, and partly with the fanatic conviction of each party in its righteousness, which justified the impressment of reluctant allies. Which side a given fellow found himself on seemed to be largely an accident, a matter of vicinity. Master Desmond, though, with his fellows from the secret meeting, including Astrinax, Lykos, Trachinos, Akesinos, and Kleomenes, had worked his way through to the positions held by the adherents of Agamemnon. The point of this, I gathered, was to gain access to the container so that he might, when the opportunity afforded itself, open it and destroy its contents.

It was four days into the revolt before we learned that the leader of the revolutionaries was Lucius himself, whom many of us had taken to be high Kur in the Cave. His ambition it was, it seems, to replace Agamemnon, and further the schemes which Agamemnon had put in place. It was not a question of overthrowing a state, or relinquishing its intrigues and projected imperialisms, but appropriating a state with its established strengths. He was less interested, so to speak, in overthrowing a throne than in changing its occupant. I had been aware, for some time, of the jealousy, envy, and resentment felt by many lesser Kurii for those placed above them, for whatever reason it might be, intelligence, energy, vision, some conception of merit, success in some form of competition, blood connections, the machinations of politics, the accidents of time or place, or simple fortune. If they could not wear a golden chain why should anyone? Let there be a golden chain for everyone, or no golden chains. I supposed that golden chains, so to speak, would always exist, though perhaps not always be displayed. They did not realize that not every golden chain is visible. The imposition and consolidation of equality requires equality enforcers, and this introduces a new inequality. But that would become visible only when the new establishment was in place. Order is essential; it is only a question as to who will impose it. The mass, manipulated and utilized, aroused and employed, harrowed and bled, when the disruption and killing is done, when the entertainment is over, remains the mass.

Chapter Forty

I lay, naked, in the cage.

Other kajirae, as well, were so incarcerated. As animals, we would await the decisions of masters.

Things were muchly unsettled in the Cave.

The door of the slave quarters moved a little, not much. Then I heard Jane scream. I forced my face against the bars to my right, trying to see to the door. Jane was across the room, and could easily see what was in the threshold.

I heard another girl scream.

Then I saw it, large, four-legged, some six or seven feet at the shoulder, with a wide, triangular-shaped head, lowered now, sunk now between its shoulders. It had a heavy, silken, reddishly tawny coat. Its paws were broad and thickly matted. Such a creature could move comfortably on rocky slopes, on ice, through snow. For all its size it moved with the sinuous, stealthy grace one might have expected of a smaller animal. The eyes were large, and the ears, tufted, bent forward. It sunk to its belly, and its long tail moved back and forth. The beast seemed passive, except that the agitation of the tail bore witness to an inward excitement. I had never seen such a beast this close. I had seen one, perhaps this one, weeks ago, on a slope across from the Cave's main portal, perhaps three or four hundred paces away.

I suspected that the portal now was not guarded, or only sporadically guarded.

I shrank back in the cage, as the beast, head down, moved a little toward me, and then crouched down. It moved a little more toward me, again, and was then again still. It did not pounce or charge. It did put its broad face near the bars. I saw its nostrils widen. It then put its snout literally against the bars, while I stayed as far back as I could. It made a small noise, as if puzzled. One large paw was put to the bars, but they were closely enough set that it could not enter the cage. I did see fangs. There was no blood about them. It then backed away, looked about the room, and exited through the gate. My heart began to pound. I gasped, trying to breathe. Then I think I lost consciousness.

Chapter Forty-One

In fifteen days the revolt was muchly suppressed.

Many of the iron-chain Kurii had not supported the insurrection organized by Lucius. There were presumably several reasons for this, but one supposes loyalty and discipline were significantly involved. Many Kurii recognized the need for societal order, and recognized their role in maintaining that order. Rather than regarding themselves as the oppressed and exploited dupes of a tyrannical establishment, as they were encouraged to do, they saw themselves as the reliable and confident defenders of a valuable, proven tradition. Too, one supposes that the charisma of the almost legendary Agamemnon, whom many had followed on another world, was unlikely to be eclipsed by a renegade upstart. The fact that Lucius had been a golden-chain Kur, too, might have given some cause for reflection. He was not truly of the iron-chain Kurii. But is it not often the case that a disgruntled scion of the elite, one of station, if not of principle, eager for greater power, will seek to exploit the discontent and resentments of others for his own purposes? Demagogues are unstinting and lavish, careless and generous, in expending the blood of others. It is not their own. Behind how many gleaming veils, emblazoned with rhetorical embroideries, lurk secret, unbespoken realities? Too, societal life, like organic life, I supposed, had its inertias and habits, and balances, emerging over generations, sustained over time, vindicated in practice. Perhaps such things are best changed only incrementally, and then only with circumspection. Change is part of life; but an advantageous metamorphosis is rare. How simple the complexity of the world seems to the simple, and arrogant. The law of gravity may be objectionable, but with what is it to be replaced?

In any event, whatever might be the cause, most insurrections fail, and those that succeed seldom do more than restore the past with new bodies and different labels.

We kajirae had been uninvolved in the small war in the Cave. We, as vulos and verr, were not combatants. We were generally confined to the slave quarters, and sometimes caged. As indicated, men had been recruited, or impressed, by each faction and some, forced into battle, had been slain in the fighting. On the other hand, it was clear to the Kurii that humans made indifferent allies in a quarrel that had little, if anything, to do with them. That, doubtless, was the motivation for Agamemnon's issuance of an amnesty for all humans who had served under Lucius or his lieutenants. Their coming, weaponless, to the lines of Agamemnon, had been a not inconsiderable blow to the insurgents. A similar amnesty had been granted to the Kurii who had served with Lucius, but only five availed themselves of this offer. These, as we learned later, had been disemboweled and strangled with their own intestines.

In any event, after some fifteen days, the fighting had diminished to an occasional skirmish in the halls. Lucius, and his followers, now reduced to a small number, were still at large in the Cave, but it was not clear where. Lucius, from his former position of authority, was extremely familiar with the Cave, not only with its open halls, and its less open, or more restricted, halls, but, too, as it turned out, with a diversity of less recognized passageways, several of which were obscure and unfamiliar, if not secret.

The greatest victory of the insurgents had occurred on the ninth day of the insurrection, when they had managed to trap, attack, and destroy the most recent body of Agamemnon, the large, mobile, crab-like machine which had been, as it turned out, fearsomely effective in the halls. A portion of the corridor had been undermined, to the degree that it could not withstand the weight of the machine. Moreover, the ceiling above this point had been prepared in such way that when the trap was sprung the ceiling, connected to the trap, would collapse. Kurii concealed nearby were then to rush forth and attack the device with axes. Agamemnon had sent two of his cohorts forward to scout his path. The floor, of course, could sustain this weight, even of two large Kurii. The bait for the trap was Lucius himself who let it appear that he was surprised in the corridor, and had then fled. To secure the very leader of the enemy was seemingly too great a prize to be ignored, and the machine, following its two scouts, abandoned its hitherto stately pace. The result was that the machine dipped into the trap, stalled, and, a moment later, was half buried in the rubble of the collapsing ceiling. The two scouts, advanced, unable to block the charge of several ax-bearing Kurii, were cut down in place, and the machine was struck by blow after blow of the axes. The machine, of course, was supported by Kurii loyal to Agamemnon, including Timarchos and Lysymachos, and the ax-bearing Kurii were soon forced to withdraw. The container which had been incorporated within the steel body of the machine was rescued by Timarchos, who bore it to safety. The machine, however, which apparently contained a large amount of intricate circuitry, could not be repaired. We did not know, after that, whether or not Agamemnon possessed another body. Doubtless, on his former world, he may have had a variety of bodies. Here, however, in effect, in exile, his resources were presumably limited. He did retain, of course, the loyalty of his followers, who doubtless associated him with a body, but no particular body.

I knocked, lightly, on the door of the small room which had been assigned to Desmond of Harfax. In my hands I held a deck of cards. It had been given to me by Astrinax, and I was to deliver it to Master Desmond.

"Who is there?" said Desmond.

"Allison," I said.

"Is that how you identify yourself?" he asked.

"Forgive me, Master," I said, frightened. I knew that I could be punished, if I had not been found pleasing, and I feared I might not have been found pleasing. How different it is with free women!

"Knock, again," he said.

I did so.

"Who is there?" he said.

"Allison, a slave, Master," I said.

"What is your errand?" he asked. It would be a bold slave, indeed, who would approach a free man, unbidden, without suitable justification. To be sure, a slave may approach her master thusly, perhaps to beg to be caressed, but I was not his slave.

"I bring a deck of cards, from Master Astrinax," I said.

"Are you kneeling?" he asked.

The door was between us.

"I am now," I said.

Thus, when the door was opened, I would be suitably positioned, slave before free, property before person.

He opened the door, and I lifted the deck of cards to him.

"Head down," he said, "arms extended."

I then lowered my head, humbly, between my two arms, and lifted the deck to him, it held in two hands.

He looked about, and then said, "Inside." Then he said, "Kneel there."

"It is an ordinary deck of cards," I said.

"Do not be foolish," he said.

I did know that messages were somehow conveyed in some decks of cards, but, as far as I could tell, this was an ordinary deck. It did have the speckling about the edges of the deck, which I had seen in the Cave, but I had seen such cards, as well, in the house of chance. Indeed, many decks came decorated, in one fashion or another.

"You are illiterate," he said.

"Yes," I said.

"But you can read cards, can you not?"

"I can tell the colors," I said, "and recognize the pictures, the Tarn, the Sleen, and such."

"The deck is presumably arranged in order, as might be a new deck, a sealed deck," he said, "from White Tarn to Red Ost."

"That would be Initiate's Tarn through Warrior's Ost," I said.

"Yes," he said, "and that will make your work easier."

"My work?" I said.

He drew forth a small sheet of paper, with tiny writing on it. It was one of several such sheets. These were removed from a small chest, which contained some tunics, and, in a drawer-like tray, a handful of nondescript objects. The room was very bare. It contained this chest, a stool, a small table, and a simple couch. I did note that the couch did contain a slave ring, with a loop of chain. Also, on the wall, on its peg, there hung a slave whip. I had never been in this room before. And I hoped no kajira had been fastened at the slave ring, at least by Desmond of Harfax. The sheet of paper, one of several, which had been removed from the chest, had been taken not only from the tray, but from beneath a paper which had seemed to floor the tray. Thus, a cursory search might not have revealed these papers.

He held the small sheet of paper which he had extracted from the tray before me.

"I assume you cannot read this," he said.

"No," I said.

"Moreover," he said, "the list is in cursive script."

I was not sure that the Lady Bina could read cursive script. She could read printing. She could read the public boards.

"I can see it is not printed," I said. "I would not have been sure that it was a list."

The lines were horizontal, not vertical.

"It would be convenient," he said, "if you could read."

"Perhaps Master could teach me to read," I said.

"As I do not own you," he said, "that would be a waste of time."

"Perhaps if you owned me," I said.

"Then," he said, "I would keep you illiterate."

"You like me that way," I said, "even more slave."

"More barbarian slave," he said.

"I see," I said.

"Free women prefer for barbarians to be illiterate," he said. "It helps the barbarian to keep in mind that she is a barbarian."

"We are unlikely to forget that on this world," I said. "We learn it from the first chain put on us."

"Do you know the nature of this list?" he asked.

"It would seem to have to do with the cards," I said.

"It has sixty entries," he said, "each pertaining to a card. I shall read the list to you, and you will arrange the cards in the order of the list."

"It will take a little time," I said.

"Spread the cards in five columns, in order, from Tarn to Ost."

"Yes, Master," I said.

He then began to read the list to me, card by card, and I drew forth the pertinent card, rearranging the deck, card by card, to comply with the list. This simple task actually took very little time. In a few Ehn it had been completed.

"We now have the message," he said.

I looked at the face of the first card in the deck, and moved the cards about, a little, examining the face of several of the succeeding cards.

"I see no message," I said. "Doubtless the order is somehow relevant."

"Quite relevant," he said.

I handed him the cards.

"Note," he said.

"Ah!" I cried, softly.

"It was there," he said. "In a moment you would have detected it. Your mistake was a natural one, namely to look for meaning where it would seem most likely to lie, on the face of the cards. It, however, lies on the edges of the cards, on sixty edges, each one meaningless in itself, a meaning which manifests itself only when the sixty edges are suitably aligned."

"It is so simple," I said.

"That is one of its beauties," he said.

"After the message is written," I said, "the cards are rearranged, and the message disappears."

"To reappear when the proper order is restored," he said.

"I cannot read the message, of course," I said.

"I cannot either," he smiled.

"Master?" I said.

"But it can be read shortly," he said. "The substitutions are simple. It would present no great problem to one adept in these matters, provided he had enough material to examine."

"Do not explain to me how the substitutions are made," I said.

"There are an indefinite number of ways in which it can be done," he said. "I suppose that is obvious."

"I do not want to know," I said.

"Have no fear," he said. "I have no intention of informing you."

"Thank you, Master," I said. What I did not know I could not reveal.

"Besides the substitutions may be easily changed, and are, from time to time."

"I see," I said.

"There are several levels of security here," he said. "First, and perhaps most effective, it is not clear that a message is involved, at all. Who would suspect a message concealed in a harmless deck of cards? It is not like a discovered, suspicious piece of paper with strange symbols or letters inscribed on it. Second, if one suspects a message is conveyed, it is not easily discovered what the message is. Thirdly, the message itself is not obvious, even if discovered. Fourthly, once the message is delivered, the deck is cleaned, and all that remains is a simple deck of cards, to be sure one now ready for a new message."

"A slave should now withdraw," I said.

"Remain on your knees," he said.

He then placed the deck of cards on the small table, and regarded it thoughtfully. He was, I supposed, unraveling the message in his mind, bit by bit. He drew forth no paper nor a marking stick from the chest. I thus supposed the substitutions were indeed simple, perhaps as simple as a reordering of the alphabet. In any event, there would be no lingering physical record of the message, no ashes suggesting its destruction, or such.

While he worked my attention strayed to the slave ring, and its loop of chain, at the foot of his simple couch. It was such as might be fit for a simple girl, a low slave. Yet so simple a device might confine a captured, stripped Ubara as well. I looked to the slave whip, suspended from its peg on the wall. I feared that simple implement, so useful in establishing and maintaining diligence amongst kajirae. It is seldom used, if ever, but it will be used, we know, if we are not pleasing. We do our best to be pleasing. We are not free women.

I wondered what it would be, to be whipped by Desmond of Harfax. I would then be well assured of his attention. Would that not put the seal of my slavery upon me and the badge of his ownership? Surely it would well remind me of my bondage, and make clear to me who it was who owned me.

In a few Ehn, with a cloth, he rubbed clean the edge of the deck, and the speckling was gone.

"Master?" I said.

"My principal," he said, "is preparing to conclude his business, and leave the Cave."

I assumed his principal must be Astrinax, or in communication with Astrinax, as the message I had brought had been from Astrinax.

"We will then try to escape?" I said.

"One should," he said, "before the snows."

"Men are with us?" I asked.

"Several," he said.

"I rejoice," I said. "What is wrong?" I asked. "Master seems distressed."

"The project of my principal," he said, "seems unduly limited."

"How so?" I asked. "Surely the kaissa sheets will be brought to the cities, surely men will be warned?"

"All that," he said.

"What more?" I asked.

"There is nothing here," he said, "pertaining to the destruction of Agamemnon."

Chapter Forty-Two

As noted, Lucius, and some few cohorts, had, as yet, escaped apprehension. On the other hand, for most practical purposes, order had been restored in the Cave, and matters, with some exceptions, were much as they had been earlier, before the revolt. Three differences, or obvious differences, for I did not know what others might be being enacted privately, were that the container thought by some to be pertinent to the person of Agamemnon was now seldom publicly visible, the men in the Cave had been disarmed, even to knives, and policing in the Cave was assigned exclusively to Kurii, for example patrols in the halls, and the guards at the great portal.

Prior to the revolt I had often brought provender and drink to the guards at the great portal, at that time men, usually two in number. This task remained mine, though the nature of the guard had changed. It was one morning in the Seventh Passage Hand, I think the second day, shortly before the Ninth Ahn, that I approached the great portal. The day was bright. Sometimes, when Tor-tu-Gor was almost overhead, the slopes of the Voltai, beneath its blaze, seemed almost white, which anomaly, I took it, had to do with some aspect of reflected light. The shadows of the valleys and crevices then could seem like black wounds. I bore no tray now, but a yoke, from each terminus of which was slung a skin of water and a haunch of tarsk. It was heavy. My shoulders would ache. The feeding of Kurii often reminded me of the feeding of carnivores.

Sometimes, in discharging this errand, I would see Grendel returning from the outside. I knew he had the freedom to come and go, as he might wish. I did not understand the nature of these excursions, but I supposed they might be explicable in terms as obvious as escaping the tedium of the Cave, a zest for movement or fresh air, and perhaps even some light hunting. Grendel tended to enjoy open vistas and the sun; most Kurii, it seemed, felt more at ease in closed spaces and conditions of reduced light.

My yoke, with its burden of food and drink, was heavy, at least for me. I hoped I would not see Grendel returning from the outside.

One of the guards waved me forward, impatiently. He did not bother to use his translator, nor was there any need to do so. I tried to hurry, but not so much that I might fall. I was sure that would displease the beasts. What might be a simple cuff from a man might break my neck if it were delivered by a Kur. The yoke cut across my shoulders.

When I encountered Grendel, either in the vicinity of the portal, or in the large halls, I kept my head down, and pretended not to see him. I did not want our eyes to meet. Had they met I would have had to assume first obeisance position, and then hold that position until summoned, or he had passed. I do not know if he looked upon me, or not. I was helplessly and futilely angry with Grendel, whose faithlessness, and treachery, cruelty, and ambition, so shocking and dismaying me, had betrayed his friends, his principles, his honor, his allies, his brethren of a far world, Grendel who had used his cleverness to win greater prospects from the conspirators, Grendel who was willing to recruit allies on a far world to provision and support a war which might reduce, if not destroy, the humans of Gor, and perhaps, later, of another world, as well. Too, his pretense of loyalty to, if not affection for, the Lady Bina had been a sham. He cared no more for her than any other Kur, to whom humans might seem at best little more than temporarily useful vermin.

The guard waved me forward, again.

I did not want to fall. I could move only so quickly. The weights on the yoke swung. I feared to be pulled off balance.

Then I had come to the portal and the guard, with one hand, lifted the yoke from my shoulders, and flung it, and the suspended meat and skins of drink, to the table-like shelf at the right side of the portal.

I backed away a little.

I expected to receive back the yoke, with its hooks.

This morning something was different at the great portal. There were two guards, as usual, but, rather back and to the side, there were two other Kurii, each armed with one of the large, four-quarreled crossbows, which I had seen in the place of cells, weapons which a man could have hardly lifted, let alone load and accurately fire.

I did not think those two beasts could have been easily seen, from the outside. Certainly I did not understand their presence.

One of the guards lifted a haunch of tarsk and tore at it with his teeth. I saw a fang sunk deep into the meat, anchoring it, and then a huge piece was wrenched free, and the long, dark tongue wrapped itself about this, and thrust it back, into the toothed darkness, and, in a moment, I witnessed its passage, sliding downward, under the fur of the throat. Kurii were no more likely to chew food than a larl or sleen. It looked at me, while it was disposing of this gorge of meat. I supposed that a carnivore, in the wild, is likely to eat quickly, to eat while it can. Time might be lost in careful chewing. There appear to be compensations involved in this sort of thing. Such a piece of meat, even one much smaller, would choke a human; on the other hand, the structure of the human throat is such that it is capable of assisting in the utterance of a subtle and theoretically infinite variety of sounds. It seems thus that in nature an organ which may constitute a danger or increased hazard in one respect may in another respect confer a significant advantage.

I looked away from the feeding Kur.

Normally, particularly when humans had been at the portal, I had enjoyed lingering in its vicinity, to look outside, and draw in the fresh air. With the Kurii, on the other hand, I thought it best to withdraw as soon as it was practical. I was much aware that some Kurii looked upon humans as food.

I backed away a few more steps.

The haunches of tarsk freed from the yoke's hooks, and the skins of drink put on the shelf, one of the guards picked up the yoke, and flung it over my head, behind me, several paces, to the side of the hall.

I supposed this was an act of contempt, like brushing aside a plate or dashing a tray to the floor, but I did not object. I preferred to retrieve the object at a distance from the Kur. The last time it had been extended to me, but, when I had grasped it, the beast had not released it, but had held it. I had feared to let it go. There was then, by means of the device, a fearsome connection between us. His eyes were upon me. I looked down, and saw his two six-digited, tentacle-like paws move a hort on the yoke, toward me, and then another hort. He was, bit by bit, moving closer to me. I then cried out in alarm, released the yoke, and fled back some paces, and then turned, to see him. He had put the yoke down before him, at his feet. He pointed to it. I must fetch it. Crouching down, watching him, I moved warily toward the yoke; when I had it in one hand, he made a sudden move toward me, and roared, and I went to my stomach, shrieking, covering my head with my hands. I feared I might have died. When I lifted my head he was turned away, conversing with his fellow. I had seized the yoke and crept away, and had then run down the hall, toward the kitchen where I had received the provender and drink. It had been, I gathered, a Kur joke.

I went to the side of the hall, back several paces from the portal, and retrieved the yoke.

Before returning to the kitchen, that from which I had received the provender and drink, I heard harsh Kur sounds, and spun about. Grendel was in the portal, and the two Kurii who carried the large crossbows had them trained upon him. I then saw the two guards roping Grendel's arms to his body. Then, bound, he was brought down the hall. I knelt as they passed, Grendel preceding the two Kurii with crossbows, with their tiered firing guides. Our eyes met, but I could read no expression in that dark, broad countenance.

I did not understand what was occurring, other than the fact that Grendel had apparently fallen from favor.

Chapter Forty-Three

"All is lost," said Desmond of Harfax.

"How so, Master?" I inquired.

"Grendel has been seized," he said. "His execution has been arranged. He will be taken outside the Cave and killed, his body left for sleen and larls."

"He is a traitor to our cause," I said. "He was to have garnered remote support for the conquest of Gor."

"You camisked, collared little fool," he said. "It is from Grendel that we have learned of the conspiracy, its plans, and its projected ends. It is from Grendel that we learned of the kaissa sheets, and were supplied with the materials, the privacy, and time required to copy them. It was thanks to him that we came to a clearer understanding of the card codes, though he was not then clear as to how the messages were conveyed. Thanks to him, we later managed to adopt the very Kur device, the card codes, to our own purposes. We can order cards with subtle and clandestine intent as well as they. And the Kurii are, or were, unaware of our capacity to do so. Grendel supplied us regularly with information. It was he who was essentially behind our small counter-conspiracy. I was his factor. It was he who was my principal, communicating commonly through Astrinax."

"Why Astrinax?" I asked.

"In order that he might the more closely monitor the condition and safety of the Lady Bina, for whom I suspect he would willingly die."

I recalled that she had been placed largely in the keeping of Astrinax.

"He spoke to me," I said. "He cited complacent treachery, greed, contempt for the Lady Bina."

"And you, fool, believed him."

"Yes!" I said.

"You belong in a collar," he said.

"Not for such a reason," I said.

"And you will be kept in one," he said.

"Why?" I asked.

"Because you belong in one," he said. "Get on your belly!"

"Yes, Master," I said.

"You are unworthy to kiss my feet," he said. "Kiss the floor before me."

I obeyed. Also my thighs were heated. I felt helpless.

"How else could he obtain his release from his cell?" asked Desmond of Harfax. "How else could he secure the liberty to move about, to organize an opposition, to attempt to frustrate and oppose the dark schemes of Agamemnon?"

"I did not know," I whispered.

"And it was well you did not," he said. "Were you conscious of the duplicity you might well have ruined it, behaved suspiciously, gave some revealing sign that might have been noted by the adherents of Agamemnon."

"Yes, Master," I whispered.

"Things began to go badly several days ago," said Desmond of Harfax. "Much of this had to do with the revolt of Lucius. Grendel refrained from participating in this small war, on either side. This displeased Agamemnon and his cohorts, who had naturally expected him to ally himself with them, to kill without question, and such. More seriously, Grendel refused to execute the Kurii of Lucius who availed themselves of the supposed amnesty. This aroused suspicion amongst the adherents of Agamemnon. Had it not been for his projected value as an influencing emissary to a steel world, he would doubtless have been immediately killed."

"Why has he just now been taken?" I asked.

"I do not know," said Desmond of Harfax. "Perhaps the patience of Agamemnon and his cohorts was finally exhausted."

"I do not think so," I said, "with so much at stake. Who but Grendel might plausibly, and with a better prospect of success, conduct Agamemnon's embassy to a certain far world?"

"A certain far world?" he said.

"Yes," I said.

"I have heard such talk," he said. "Grendel himself has spoken in such a way."

"You are skeptical?" I asked.

"There are things here which I find it hard to understand," he said. Then he said, "Kneel up. I want to look at your eyes, slave."

I obeyed immediately, as one obeys a Gorean master. I did not look forward to being under his scrutiny.

"Where is Earth?" he said.

"Master?" I said.

"Is it north of the Vosk?" he asked. "Is it east of the Barrens?"

I looked at him. Surely he knew Earth was another world. Did he not have access to the Second Knowledge? Perhaps he was indeed a Metal Worker, one of a lower caste, and had attained only to the First Knowledge. It is said there is a Third Knowledge, but that is reserved to Priest-Kings. He must know of other worlds. Had he not spoken of a steel world, one flung farther away than Tor-tu-Gor itself? Was he testing me, somehow? I supposed he might well not be aware of how such worlds might be reached.

"No," I said.

"It is another world?" he said.

"Yes," I said.

"You are not lying?" he said.

"No, Master," I said.

"How did you come here?" he asked.

"I do not know," I said. "I was rendered unconscious on my former world, and when I awakened I found myself on Gor, in a small, dark cell, naked and chained, hand and foot."

"There was a ship?" he said.

"Doubtless," I said.

"I am told," said he, "that there is a strange ship in the higher levels of the Crag, a ship which might sail amongst mountains, a ship borne not by water, but by air, or less."

"Such things are possible," I said.

"I learned of this from Grendel, through Astrinax," he said.

I supposed the lair of this ship, perhaps somehow housed within the crag, had been discovered by Grendel. Certainly he had been often enough out of the Cave.

"Doubtless it was in such a ship," I said, "that he was to be envoyaged to the distant world, one of metal, where he was to plead the cause of Agamemnon, acquire resources, and enlist allies."

"Four times," said Desmond of Harfax, "before the revolt of Lucius, despite the importunities of Agamemnon, Timarchos, Lysymachos, and others, Grendel sought to postpone this journey, meanwhile laboring on our behalf."

"I understand," I said.

"One pretext after another was proposed, each more exasperating to Agamemnon and his adherents than the other. Then, before we were well organized, the abortive revolt of Lucius took place. The aftermath of the revolt has been unfortunate. The movements of Agamemnon have become more guarded, men have been disarmed, and Kurii patrol the Cave and guard the great portal."

"Things would be difficult," I said.

"Even with Grendel, and some trust in him by Agamemnon and his cohorts, I fear they would have been impossible."

"I saw him taken," I said, "by the great portal."

"Why now?" he asked.

"I do not know," I said.

"Nor I," he said.

I recalled Grendel, roped, being led down the hall, preceding his captors, bearing their primitive but terrible weapons.

"Our plans have come to naught," he said.

I was silent.

"There is another danger," he said.

"What is that?" I asked.

"Given the suppression of the revolt, and the increased security in the Cave," he said, "the increased suspicion and watchfulness, the fear of further disruption or dissension, the intensified vigilance, our small organization of men, secret and subversive, intent on exposing the machinations of Agamemnon and his cohorts, is in ever greater jeopardy. How can it not be discovered, if not now, tomorrow, or the day after?"

"Perhaps all will survive," I said.

"It is clear how at least one might survive," he said.

"How?" I asked.

"By betraying the rest," he said.

Chapter Forty-Four

"I recognize you," said the guard. "You are his grooming slave."

"I am not such a slave," I said. "I have groomed him. Will you deliver the tray to him?"

"No," said the guard.

"I fear to approach him," I said.

"He will not hurt you," said the guard. He then sounded the small bar in the background and, in a bit, another guard appeared, carrying one of the bulky, complex crossbows. The door to the cell was then opened, and I was ushered within. I did my best to appear reluctant. I heard the gate close behind me.

"Groom him," said the guard. "He dies tomorrow."

All these remarks from the guard, of course, were transmitted by means of his translator.

The two guards then withdrew.

If the prisoner had cared to tear my head from my shoulders, my arms from my body, there would have been nothing to prevent it.

"Tal, Allison," said Grendel.

"I beg your forgiveness, Master," I said, "for doubting you."

"You were supposed to doubt me," said Grendel.

"How is it," I asked, "that they have turned on you?"

"The matter was simple," he said. "It was inevitable that their suspicions would be aroused. I would not fight for Agamemnon, I would not execute those who were foolish enough to avail themselves of the amnesty. I sought excuses for delaying my departure for the steel world of Arcesilaus. Indeed, I was surprised at their patience. One does not expect such of my fellow Kurii."

"You were crucial to their plans," I said. "You were not to be lightly expended."

"Apparently," he said. "But they then devised a test, one I must refuse to pass, to see if I were sincerely of their camp."

"They threatened the Lady Bina," I said.

"Nothing so simple," he said. "One might always negotiate, delay things, make promises, fail to keep them, make new promises, fail to keep them, and so on."

"That might have earned enough time to escape the Cave," I said.

"That would have been my hope," he said. "As you know, matters were moving forward. Supplies might have been gathered, warm clothing found for the humans, the Lady Bina freed, and the guards at the gate dealt with, hopefully benignly. It might well have been dangerous, particularly if we were pursued in force, but the stakes were high, and there seemed little choice."

"What happened, then?" I asked.

"Returning to the Cave," he said, "I was apprehended, bound, and conducted into the presence of Agamemnon, and confronted with the test."

"I saw you arrested, at the great portal," I said. "What was the test?"

"Bite at the fur," he said. "Appear to groom me."

I obeyed, and, shortly thereafter, the two guards returned. Grendel had doubtless heard their approach.

"Feed," ordered the first guard.

I drew back, and Grendel, humbly, turned to the tray. The guards then, again, withdrew.

He then faced me, and I went close to his muzzle.

"The test was a simple one, exquisite, worthy of Agamemnon," said Grendel. "The Lady Bina was present. I was instructed to kill her, immediately. I refused, and that was the end of the matter. Thus were my lies and ruses exposed. My pretense of being of the party of Agamemnon was proved fraudulent."

"The Lady Bina must have been terrified," I said.

"Not at all," he said. "She fears nothing from me."

"How is that?" I asked.

"I am her guard," he said.

"You are to be executed tomorrow," I said.

"Agamemnon will have to find another envoy to the world of Arcesilaus," he said.

"I do not think there is another," I said, "and certainly none who might be expected to be taken as seriously as you, nor exercise an influence such as yours."

"Perhaps," he said.

"You have dealt a great blow to the plans of Agamemnon," I said.

"With respect to remote support, at least for a time," he said.

"Master Desmond," I said, "without your leadership, despairs of escaping the Cave, of braving the Voltai, of counteracting the conspiracy. Pausanias and his wagons may already be near Venna."

"Desmond is a fine leader, one of intelligence, power, and honor," said Grendel.

"He puts me in a cage when it pleases him," I said. "If he owned me, I have little doubt but what I would be well corded, well roped, and chained."

"I take it you hate him," said Grendel.

"Yes!" I said.

"And how is it then," he asked, "that you love him?"

"I, love?" I said.

"Yes," he said.

"On Earth," I said, "I did not love. I did not know what love was. But here, with a collar fastened on my neck, I know."

"You love Desmond of Harfax," he said.

"Yes," I said.

"With the love of a free woman?" he asked.

"No," I said. "I love him with the most profound and deepest love a woman can know. I love him with the love of a helpless, yielding slave for her master."

"Tomorrow, at the Ninth Ahn," said Grendel, "I am to be taken from the Cave and executed. Perhaps you might leave the Cave a few Ehn before the Ninth Ahn and walk to the Sixth Ahn."

"I do not understand," I said.

"There is no escape for you, of course," he said. "If you were not caught, you would die of cold, or be eaten by animals."

"What are you saying?" I asked.

"You would be well advised to return promptly," he said. "You might not even be missed. If you returned soon, and of your own accord, you might not even be switched."

"There are guards," I said.

"They might not be observant," he said. "In any event, they are not likely to leave their post."

"Why should I do this?" I asked.

"Perhaps you thought to run, and then wisely changed your mind," he said.

"Master?" I said, puzzled.

"Remember," he said, "walk to the Sixth Ahn."

"How can I walk for so many Ahn," I asked, "if I leave before the Ninth Ahn?"

"You will only have to walk a little," he said, "only a few Ehn."

"To the Sixth Ahn?" I said.

"Precisely," he said.

"I understand nothing of this," I said.

"It is better that you do not," he said.

At this point the two guards entered the outer chamber. Shortly thereafter I removed the tray, the plate, and tankard from the cell.

Chapter Forty-Five

Shortly before the Ninth Ahn, I was in the large hall, leading to the great portal. I moved very carefully, my back to the wall on the left, as one would approach the great portal from the inside. I was several yards from the opening. One of the guards turned, regarded me for a moment, and then turned back, to his fellow. Shortly thereafter, some yards back from the opening, two slave girls, Jane and Eve, began pushing one another, and screaming at one another. In a moment, they were rolling on the floor of the hall, seemingly intent on tearing out one another's hair, seemingly clawing at one another like embroiled she-sleen, while the male crouched nearby, waiting to pull the victor to his burrow by the fur at the back of the neck. The two guards turned about, to watch the sobbing, screaming, seemingly tearing, seemingly scratching slaves. Altercations amongst slave girls can be nasty things. Kurii, and, I fear, some men, find them amusing.

I slipped through the portal, unnoticed. I was frightened. I had crossed the threshold, without permission. In theory I knew I could be lashed, hamstrung, or slain. Mina was to have been fed alive to Kurii until Trachinos had intervened with coin, purchasing her.

I looked about, wildly.

I normally told Gorean time by the ringing of the bars, often public bars, but sometimes bars within a house. Grendel, however, in the domicile, had taught me to read time from the small chronometer he kept in his pouch. He doubtless would have recalled that he had done this. That was undoubtedly important. In the night I had pondered his strange words, about walking to the Sixth Ahn. Clearly, as he had told me to walk for only some Ehn, he had not meant that I should try to walk for several Ahn, until it was again the Sixth Ahn, almost a day later. What then could be meant? I was unfamiliar with Gorean directions, which I found complex, and, in any event, I not only lacked a compass, but would not have been able to read one if I had had one. I did know that the Gorean compass needle always pointed to the Sardar Mountains. It seemed clear then, upon reflection, that Grendel had given me a direction in which to proceed. It was also clear that he took it for granted that I would understand him. His confidence in this matter, although flattering, was not obviously warranted. Various difficulties obtained. I thought of time in terms of the bars, and not chronometers. I was not all that familiar with Gorean chronometers, and his casual lesson in the domicile had been brief. I tried to remember it. Most dangerously the chronometers with which I was familiar on my former world not only divided the day differently, but marked the divisions in a different order. On my former world the hands of chronometers begin to rotate to the right, whereas in your chronometers they begin to rotate to the left. Your concept of "clockwise" is thus opposite to that with which I was familiar. When I thought of Gorean time, as it might be measured by a chronometer, I always thought of it analogously to the chronometers of my former world; thus, in my mind I would think of the Fifth Ahn as to the right of the Twentieth Ahn, rather than, as you would think of it, as to the left of the Twentieth Ahn. Grendel, of course, would be thinking in terms of the Gorean chronometer. Accordingly, if a large Gorean chronometer had been placed flat before the great portal, and one was to move toward the Sixth Ahn one would go to the left and not the right. In any event, I sped from the portal, aligning myself with where the imaginary Sixth Ahn would lie.

I heard no cry, or roar from behind me, and so I supposed the attention of the guards might still be focused on the amusing spectacle of two squabbling slave girls.

The terrain was uneven and treacherous.

There were many rocks, and crevices about, and narrow

passageways between boulders and out-juttings. In places ascending and descending narrow ledges skirted cliff-like projections. Here and there there were spears of stone. The morning sun would be bright before me, on rock, and then, in a moment, one would confront almost impenetrable, cave-like shadows, indicating recesses of an undisclosed depth. In such a place anything might hide. Occasionally, from a high place, I looked back, to see the great portal. I tried to keep the direction, I hoped it was correct, which I understood Grendel to have given me. I recalled I had seen a larl from the great portal once, perhaps one at much this distance from the Cave. I swallowed, and continued on. My feet hurt, for I had no sandals. Too, camisked, I began to shiver. I nearly slipped into a crevice, but pressed myself against the rock, and, bit by bit, made my way forward. Mighty boulders were scattered about, some jagged, and young, and some worn smooth by centuries of wind and rain. Might the knives of expanding ice in fissures have broken loose stones, some like small mountains? I wondered if, in its long past, the Voltai had witnessed the passage of oceans of ice at its feet, oceans which might bear ships of stone. I wondered what forces might have given birth to the mighty Voltai.

I hurried about a boulder, turning, and screamed in terror, for I had plunged into the outstretched arms of a large, hairy shape, which clutched me to itself, its nostrils dilating and closing, and dilating and closing again, sucking in scent from about my neck and shoulders. A massive paw closed over my mouth. I could barely squirm. Then, gently, it released me, and I stepped back. There was no mistaking the seared pockets of tissue marking where once large, glistening eyes had glowed.

"You are alive!" I said.

It could not understand me, of course, for it had no translator. But it might have detected something of the shock and amazement in my voice. Certainly it was familiar with the sounds humans made, from its captors, from the carnival, from the house of Epicrates, perhaps even from before its capture, from the Cave, and from after its brief return to the Cave, before its banishment into the wilderness. Looking on this beast, not on the brink of starvation, not half dead, but alert and sound, I realized the explanation for Grendel's many departures from the Cave. He had fed it, and kept it alive. It was one of his own, even though it had betrayed him, a treason which Grendel had understood, and had not resented. It had been to return this ruined, blinded beast to his fellows in the Voltai that Grendel had undertaken our perilous expedition to the mountains, which expedition had unexpectedly revealed large secrets of political and military significance. I was sure now, of course, that the point of my mission into the mountains was precisely to contact this beast, whom we spoke of as Tiresias.

The beast regarded me.

I was sure it would not attack me. I was sure, too, that it recognized me, by scent. Had I not been sent for it once before, in Ar, and had encountered it in the market of Cestias?

But how could I make clear to it the plight of Grendel, and even if I could manage to do so, of what help might be so powerful but so handicapped an animal?

"Lord Grendel," I said, again and again. And again. I thought it possible he would recognize this name, for he had heard it often enough, from the Lady Bina and from myself, in the house of Epicrates. And, hopefully, he could recognize the apprehension, the frantic concern, the pleading note in my voice.

The beast growled suddenly, and lifted its sightless head. I saw fangs bared. I turned away, and retraced my steps, just a few steps. I thought it might follow me, if it understood. In any event, I had given him a direction. Suddenly he sprang forward and, as I cried out in fear, he took me in his left arm and nestled me against that broad, hirsute chest. I sensed the large heart beating within it. My feet were cold and bleeding. I pressed myself against that large body, half hidden in its long fur, perhaps its winter coat, grateful for the warmth. Its right paw extended before it, and sometimes brushed to the side. It began to move rapidly down the trail I had ascended. I realized then that it was extremely familiar with its immediate environment. Just as a blind human might negotiate its own house with relative ease, knowing the thresholds, the location of furniture, and such, so, too, the beast was at home in what, over the weeks of its exile, had become its territory. Indeed, it may have come this route many times, to meet Grendel. At the high points in this sometimes frightening trek, for it occasionally negotiated ledges which I, sighted, might have been reluctant to traverse, I could make out the great portal. At one point I cried out in fear, and clutched the beast's fur, for, not more than a dozen paces from us, over a shelf of rock, I saw the lifted head of a larl, broad, triangular, quizzical. The beast was fully aware of it, for its head turned in that direction, its ears inclined to that place, and its nostrils drew in the alien scent, and then the beast, with no further action, either of a monitory or preparatory nature, continued on its way. The larl had not charged. I supposed it was recently surfeited. Like most carnivores, and unlike men and Kurii, it hunts only when hungry. I would discover later that more was involved. In much less time than it had taken me to rendezvous with Tiresias, he had brought me to a passageway which debouched onto a relatively flat slope of rock no more than a hundred paces from the great portal. This was the point, I gathered, at which Grendel and he might have met. In any event, I think it might have marked the end of its territory. The beast remained behind a turn of rock. It would not be visible from the portal. Released, I regained my footing and went cautiously to the opening of the passageway, and, shielding myself with the rock as much as possible, looked back to the portal.

"Grendel," I whispered. I was sure the beast knew that name.

Emerging from the portal was Grendel, bound, and on a leash. With him were two Kurii, each with a large ax.

The beast pushed his paw toward me, opening and closing the digits. "Counting," I thought. "He wants me to count." I took one digit in my hand, and then I took another, and then I held them together, and pressed the two, twice.

A small soft noise greeted this action.

I did not know where the execution was to take place, but I supposed it would not be all that far from the portal.

Grendel and his two guards continued for a time to approach our position, and then, some sixty or so paces from the portal, some forty or so from our position, they halted. I saw them kneel Grendel down. One of the Kurii pushed his head down, further, that the back of his neck would be the better exposed. It was clear to me that it would not be practical for Tiresias, blind, to attack two armed Kurii, let alone across an expanse of relatively flat rock in daylight.

Tiresias could tell me nothing, but he did look at me, and I thought the expression was almost human.

I stepped out from behind the rock. "Tal!" I called, lightly.

The two Kurii were clearly startled, at seeing a human, and a kajira, here, outside the Cave.

Neither Kur carried a translator, nor did Grendel. Indeed Grendel had been divested of most of his usual harnessing. I supposed it had been appropriated.

"Tal," I said, again, approaching more closely.

I had been seen in the company of Grendel more than once, and I hoped I might be remembered as a putative grooming slave. On the other hand, as I have suggested, many Kurii are not that interested in distinguishing one human from another. This is particularly the case when they do not deal closely with them. Probably they could not have easily distinguished me from several other similarly clad, brunette kajirae. Could you, for example, easily distinguish one urt from another, mixing together, if they were similarly sized and pelted?

In a moment I was sure that neither recognized me, save, of course, as a human female, and one, of course, who was a collared slave.

I did not want to approach too closely, for I must be able to turn, run, and reach the cover behind me.

One of the Kurii gestured with his ax toward the portal. I gathered that he was ordering me to return to the Cave.

Instead, I remained where I was.

He repeated the gesture and, again, I remained where I was.

"Must a command be repeated?" is a question which strikes terror into a slave girl's heart, for a repeated command is commonly a cause for discipline. The usual answer to that question is a hasty "No, Master," followed by immediate compliance. It is another thing, of course, if the command has not been heard, is not clear, would be impractical to obey, or such.

"You are stinking beasts!" I called out. "You are cowards! You are the sons of urts, the brothers of tarsk!"!

There were no translators about, so neither the guards, nor Tiresias, could understand me.

Grendel, of course, who was at home with untranslated

Gorean, could understand me, but he had the good judgment not to furnish the guards with a translation. Had he done so the execution might have been unofficially, infelicitously expedited.

My attitude, however, my tone, and the grimaces, and gestures with which I saw fit to accompany my address, would, I was sure, suffice.

I turned about and fled back toward the passageway amongst the boulders. I trusted this, following my insulting, truculent provocation, would initiate a chase response. This response, common to many animals, is familiar even to humans. I further trusted that only one would follow me. One would surely remain with Grendel, whose legs were not bound.

I had not realized how swiftly a Kur can move. I heard the scratching of claws behind me on the upward slope of rock. When the Kur drops to all fours, it can move faster than a man can run. Fortunately the beast kept his ax, and this kept its passage in the bipedalian mode. Even so, of course, few humans could outrun it. I had, of course, by design, a much shorter distance to traverse than the pursuing Kur. Even so I barely managed to swing about the rock behind which Tiresias was waiting. And I suddenly became aware I was no longer followed.

I turned about, and then turned away. Tiresias was slowly twisting the beast's head from its body. Shortly thereafter he put the body and the head in a side passage. They would not be visible from the opening to the passageway.

It was then I dared to look.

I made as though to move to the opening between the rocks, but Tiresias growled, and I stopped. He charted my movements by the sound. He pointed behind him, and I went back in the passage, some twenty or thirty feet back, away from the opening. He then felt about and picked up the guard's ax. I then lost sight of him, as he disappeared behind some rocks. I was not much pleased by his disappearance as I would have preferred to have him, blind or not, between me and the opening, as I expected the other guard, wary and curious, to appear there, once Grendel had been secured, presumably by using the leash to tie his ankles together. I was familiar with such ties, as I had sustained them in the house of Tenalion. It is a common way of rendering a back-bound slave immobile and helpless. I did not think the guard, alone, would strike Grendel, who might move, even leap up or flee, until he was secured, and when he was secured, there would be no hurry about the matter. Too, he would be curious, I supposed, as to the whereabouts of his fellow guard. Might he be still pursuing an annoying, wayward kajira?

I waited an Ehn or two, and then I heard the other guard calling out, in raucous Kur. After another Ehn, he called out again, less temperately.

There was then silence, and I could scarcely breathe.

I was sure that he was approaching.

I sensed then that he was at, or near, the opening. I saw the blade of the ax first, and then saw the shaft, and then the whole weapon grasped in his paws, and his body crouched over it. I did not think I could have run, even if I had wanted to.

Clearly the beast was puzzled. It saw me, standing back a few feet in the passageway, and it saw nothing of its fellow.

Irrationally, it said something to me in Kur.

I shook my head. I could not understand it, nor, had I spoken, could he have understood me.

He came toward me a pace or two.

Then, suddenly, he lifted his head, and those wide dark nostrils distended. I was sure he smelled blood.

I then screamed and covered my eyes, for the ax of the first guard, in the grasp of Tiresias, from behind, from where he had come about the boulder, smote down on the second guard, hemmed in by the narrow passageway. The blow, I took it, was not a good one, as Tiresias could not see his target, though he must have been aware, reasonably closely, of its position. The blade missed the center of the head, and clove downward, through the side of the skull, close to the left ear, and continued through the shoulder, and half into the ribs. I am sure the ax had been well sharpened for an execution. Still I think it was a blow such that few but a Kur could have struck.

I was back several feet and yet the rocks near me were spattered with blood. The entire end of the passageway, where it opened onto the sloping rock, about the fallen Kur, was run with blood. Tiresias was crouching over his kill, divesting it of harnessing. He cast the harness toward me, impatiently, growling. Grendel had not yet joined us. Thus he must have been unable to do so. "Yes," I whispered, "yes." I removed from the sheath a Kur side knife. The blade was some fourteen horts in length, and double-edged, but the handle, made for the grip of a Kur, was large for my hand. I seized it with both hands. Again, with a growl, Tiresias admonished me for what he must have interpreted as dalliance. It was with exquisite care that I made my way about the body in the passageway. Tiresias was less fastidious and the fur of his feet, and his paws, were soaked with blood. In a moment or two I had made my way from the passageway to where Grendel was secured, and, with the knife, slashed apart the leash strap which had bound his ankles together. Another moment and the ropes which had bound his arms to his sides were lying about his feet, as he crouched down, looking back to the portal. He put out his paw and I surrendered the knife. That handle would be comfortable in his grasp. He looked behind himself again, and then thrust me toward the passageway from which I had emerged.

When we reached the passageway Tiresias had dragged away the body of the second Kur, presumably to place it with the body and head of the other. I went several feet away from where the fearsome blow had been struck, that which had felled the second guard. I stood there, shaken, trembling, while speech in Kur passed between Grendel and Tiresias. Each took the hand of the other in his mouth, and I shuddered, as those massive, fanged jaws closed about the other's hand, but not even the skin was broken. This was, I took it, some sign of confidence, of fellowship, of respect, perhaps even of affection. Each might have torn away the hand of the other, but not even the skin was broken. Suddenly Grendel turned toward me, and I went instantly to my knees, and put my head down. He stood then before me. I lifted my head, and smiled. Was he not pleased? Would he not be grateful? Had I not done well? Had I not played a part in saving his life, at least for the moment? I waited for him to speak. Then he turned away, again to speak to Tiresias.

I regarded him disbelievingly, he facing away from me.

Tears sprang to my eyes.

I was then acutely conscious of my camisk, of the collar on my neck, the mark borne by my thigh.

I was a slave!

One does not thank a slave. Would one thank an animal?

I had done, in effect, what I had been expected to do, what, in effect, I had been instructed to do. I had, in effect, obeyed. One does not thank a slave for obeying. It is what she must do.

How conscious I was then of my bondage!

Indeed, it can be frightening for a slave to be thanked. What might it mean? Is it a warning, a criticism, that she is behaving too much like a free woman, who would expect to be thanked? Is it a trick? Is he thinking of her in terms of close chains, or the slave whip? Is he thinking of selling her? Has she already been sold, or given away?

"Master," I said, softly, "may I speak?"

Grendel turned to face me. "Yes," he said.

"What occurred may have been seen from the portal," I said. "It may be supposed that the guards took you into the mountains, but, in time, when they do not return, an investigation will be made. There will be a search, a pursuit in force. You must flee."

"I have not finished my work," he said. "There is more to do."

"There is nothing you can do," I said. "They will hunt you down. They are merciless. You must flee."

"What of you?" he asked.

"I am freezing," I said. "I am half lame."

"We will build a fire," he said.

"You must not," I said. "Smoke will be seen. You must flee!"

"When they come to the fire," he said. "We will be gone."

"The fire," I said, "will be a distraction?"

"There will be a better," he said.

"Master?" I said.

"After dark," he said, "you will go by the portal, but keep against the wall, to the right, where you will not be seen. Then, when it is opportune, slip into the Cave."

"How will I know when it is opportune?" I said. "There are guards, Kur guards."

"It will be clear," he said. "The matter will be arranged by our friend, Tiresias."

"You must flee, both of you," I said.

"We will hide," he said.

"Where?" I asked.

"Where," said he, "they will not look."

"Flee!" I begged him.

"I have work to do," he said.

I saw Tiresias approach, some short, gnarled branches in his grasp, and some shrubbery, dirt still about the roots. I also noted he was now in harness, as well. Grendel fetched the ax of the second guard, and lifted that long-handled, double bladed, weighty weapon. He handled it as I might have wielded a stick.

"Master," I called to him.

"Yes?" he said.

"Tiresias cannot understand us," I said. "He has no translator."

"So?" said Grendel.

"Did I not do well?" I asked.

"You did splendidly," he said.

"Is Master not pleased?"

"I am pleased," he said.

"Should I not be thanked?" I asked.

"Are you a free woman?" he said.

"No, Master," I said.

"Are you a slave?" he asked.

"Yes, Master," I said.

"Then you should not be thanked," he said.

"I see," I said.

"I am not sure you do," he said.

"I do not understand," I said.

"It is a kindness," he said.

"I do not understand," I said.

"It is a lesson," he said. "It may save your life."

"Master?" I said.

"The slave," he said, "is not to be self-concerned, self-seeking, or self-interested. That is for the free woman. The free woman thinks of herself. The slave thinks of her master, and hopes to be found pleasing. The slave serves selflessly, surrendering herself wholly to the master. She belongs to him, as a tarsk or a sandal. She does not obey to be rewarded. She does not serve to be thanked. She is a slave. It is hers, his animal, to obey unquestioningly, immediately, thanklessly. It is what she is for."

"Surely a master might throw her a candy, or give her a caress," I said.

"Yes," he said, "but such things are not owed to her. Rather, let her be grateful for any attention the master may give her."

"I want to serve so," I said, "helplessly, mastered!"

"On Gor," he said, "you will have no choice but to serve so."

"Yes, Master," I said.

"So," said he, "do you still wish to be thanked?"

"No, Master," I said.

"But," he said, "you would perhaps like to know that you have been found pleasing?"

"Oh, yes, Master!" I said.

He then put a great paw in my hair, and shook my head, affectionately, as one might the head of domestic sleen.

"You have been found pleasing," he said.

"Thank you, Master," I said.

"We will now light a fire," he said. "You must be cold."

"Thank you, Master," I said.

"But you must understand," he said, "that I am part Kur. A human master might not be so tolerant."

"I understand," I said.

"What do you think they buy women for?" he asked.

"To be slaves," I said.

"And what sort of slaves?" he asked.

"Perfect slaves," I said.

"Keep that in mind," he said.

"Yes, Master," I said.

Chapter Forty-Six

Much frustration, fury, and rage coursed through the corridors of the Cave.

Two Kurii, those assigned to execute the prisoner, Grendel, had disappeared. Later, their bodies and parts of bodies, for wandering animals had fed, were discovered near the ashes of an abandoned fire. It was then supposed that the prisoner, presumably somehow abetted, was in flight. Two axes were missing, and two sets of harnessing. A dozen armed search parties were dispatched, over a period of several days. Some of these smaller, more rapidly moving parties may have ranged a quarter of the way to the Aqueduct Road. Then, the winds rising, the chill blasts whistling amongst the mountains, the first scattering of snow hurrying betwixt the peaks, the parties had returned. No trail of the prisoner, or others, had been found. It was supposed then that the fugitives, ill-armed and ill-provisioned, perhaps lost and disoriented, had perished in the Voltai.

The night of the freeing of Grendel I had crept back to the vicinity of the great portal, and, in the darkness, waited on what, if one were facing inward to the portal, would be the right-hand side, my back close to the wall.

About the First Ahn I might have fled within the portal, even into the arms of guards, had it not been for the words of Grendel that the matter, my reentry into the Cave, would be arranged by Tiresias. And so I waited for the moment in which such an entry might be "opportune." I think that is why I did not bolt inward when, some twenty yards from me, in the darkness, I sensed the movement of a large, sinuous body. Anything that large, moving in such a way, in this vicinity, could only be a larl. I recalled that such a beast had been in the neighborhood of that long, dangerous, winding passageway traversed by Tiresias when he, carrying me, was hurrying to its end, where it opened onto the broad, rocky slope. The beast had raised its head, and peered at us, over a shelf of rock. Tiresias had been aware of its presence, but had scarcely reacted. The larl had not followed us. I had conjectured that it was not hungry. Later, on the night of my reentry into the Cave, I became aware that some relationship existed between the two, although, at the time, I did not understand its nature. In any event, while I backed against the wall, fearing to move, the beast passed me, moving to my right, where it would, in effect, some yards out, cross the slope before the portal. It was scarcely across from the portal when an alarm rang out, and two Kurii, lifting lanterns, ran to the threshold of the portal. Almost at the same time another pair of Kurii, for the guard is doubled after dark, joined them, these carrying spears. In the light of the lanterns the eyes of the larl, catching the light, the body turned toward the portal in the darkness, blazed like tarn disks of gold. The two Kurii with lanterns began to swing them about, which cast startling, darting, awkward shadows on the slope. The two with spears brandished their weapons and stepped threateningly toward the larl, but did not, I noted, much leave the vicinity of the threshold. All four were shouting Kur at the larl. I heard others approaching, and, too, even the voices of kajirae. As attention was fastened on the larl I slipped about the corner of the portal, unnoticed, into the Cave, and, in an instant, was being embraced by Jane and Eve, and there were other kajirae about, too. One Kur, come to the portal, looked at me, and I was indistinguishable amongst others. Looking out, I saw that the larl, as though displeased, had padded away, into the darkness.

"We were afraid," said Jane.

"You are trembling," said Eve. "You are cold."

"It is past locking time," I said, apprehensively.

"Do not be concerned," said Jane. "We have enlisted Chloe. See our thighs."

"You have been claimed for the night?" I said.

"So it would seem," said Eve.

"My thigh," said Jane, "claims that I have been reserved this evening for Astrinax."

"And mine that I have been spoken for by Lykos," said Eve.

"Chloe!" whispered Jane, and Chloe approached.

"I will mark your thigh, barbarian," said Chloe. "Whom shall I say has reserved you for the evening?"

"Desmond of Harfax," I said.

* * * *

Following the revolt of Lucius, as I have mentioned, certain changes were effected in the routine of the Cave. Three of these were most noticeable to humans. First, there was a significant reduction in the displays, usually ceremonial, of the mysterious container which was commonly believed to contain a treasure, most likely of diamonds, but which was understood by some of us to be somehow relevant to the person of Agamemnon himself. Second, there was the disarming of the Cave's humans, which muchly uneased the men. One wields a weapon or is subject to the weapons of another. Tyrants prefer disarmed subjects. It is a sensible first step in civil conquest. It is easier to rule verr than larls. Kajirae, of course, are not subject to weapons. They are subject to the whip. Third, security had been increased in the Cave, Kurii now guarding the great portal and patrolling the halls. The second and third of these alterations were oppressive enough, but, following the escape of Grendel, matters worsened. The movements of free humans and many Kurii were now as subject to scrutiny and supervision as those of slave girls. In many cases records were kept, permissions required, and reporting times noted. It was difficult to tell whether these impositions and restrictions were rationally justified in terms of intelligence available to Agamemnon and his inner circle or were the fruit of unproductive suspicions carried to the pitch of self-destructive madness. I supposed much had to do with the recollection of the revolt of Lucius, which had apparently been as unexpected by Agamemnon and his adherents as by the humans in the Cave. It was my speculation that Agamemnon, helpless and dependent in his metal housing, without a mobile, utilizable body, did not know whom he might trust, and to what extent. Lucius had been trusted, even taken by many to be first in the Cave. Who else might prove unfaithful? Who else in a secret heart might harbor treachery? His plans, as well, had been, if not seriously damaged, certainly delayed by what he presumably took as the defection of Grendel. Too, it was not known for certain that Grendel had perished in the Voltai. I supposed that a mind as mighty and ambitious as that of Agamemnon, filled with the visions of grandiose ventures, frustrated by its dependence and limitations, encountering reverses, balked in its projects, might incline to irrationality, might slip into madness.

In any event, it seemed clear that Desmond of Harfax's small assemblage of determined men was at great risk. Any man who had been in that room for that meeting now stood in extreme peril. Too, how, under the obtaining conditions, could one proceed, how meet and plan? How could one contact others? Might not even something as seemingly innocent as a pack of cards be suspect? How could one recruit? Who, under these conditions, would join such a perilous enterprise? Two men, in earnest conversation, now attracted attention. Three might require an explanation. Unoccupied rooms were locked. What of records, accountings, and reporting times? How, thus, at present, could one gather and store clothing and supplies? How, thus, at present, could one organize an escape? But Pausanias had left several days before. And Gor must be warned. And the snows were imminent; soon looming winter would close the passes, the roads and gates, of the Voltai.

During the day we kajirae were worked; at night we were caged. No longer might our thighs be marked. Even I was uncomfortable, though my slave fires had not yet begun to rage in the manner of several of my chain sisters. From my own sensations, however, I could begin to suspect what men had done to them. Some began to moan in their cages at night. I knew from the house of Tenalion that it was common to deny sex to a slave girl for four or five days prior to her sale, that she might be presented to buyers in a more needful state. I had heard that some vended kajirae writhed on the block, begging to be purchased. Others needed be restrained by chain leashes, lest they leave the block, rushing to prostrate themselves before one fellow or another to be purchased, their lips pressed to his sandals or boots. Sometimes a proud girl would pretend to disdain, to aloofness, or frigidity, but the auctioneer, after permitting her to maintain for a time her posturing sham, puts his hands on her and she shortly thereafter, even protesting, squirming, and crying out, is revealed to the buyers, and to herself, as what she is, a female. Lying at the auctioneer's feet, she listens to the bids on her. She now understands she is not the woman she took herself to be. She now understands that she is the sort of woman who belongs at a slave ring.

The men, too, of course, muchly resented this deprivation. In time I had little doubt that many would prove to be dangerously frustrated. Gorean men tended to be strong, energetic, ambitious, possessive, impatient, and sexually aggressive. Often little more than honor stood between a Gorean free woman and a chain. The needs of such males, of course, often ignored by, and perhaps not even understood by, Gorean free women, at least in their intensity, were muchly assuaged by the presence of kajirae in their midst, available in the markets, the slave houses, the taverns, and so on. The man whose sexual needs are well satisfied tends to be content, and he who is content is commonly happy, and he who is happy has no need to disrupt his society, hurt others, or prey on his fellows. I have no doubt that the presence of kajirae in Gorean society has much to do not only with its naturalness, for men desire slaves and slaves long for masters, but also with its general harmony, security, and stability.

Too, I have little doubt that the kajira, like the colorful buildings and soaring bridges, the spacious parks and wide boulevards, adds to the charm of Gor. See her, lovely, collared, half-clad, and graceful, bearing her burdens, shopping, hurrying home to her master! She is radiant. She is owned. It is little wonder that many cities, as they might boast of the might of their draft tharlarion, the stamina of their saddle tharlarion, the swiftness of their kaiila, the tenacity and prowess of their hunting sleen, boast of the beauty of their slaves. When foreign ambassadors are in a city masters are particularly encouraged to parade their slaves. When embassies are exchanged with enemy municipalities the banquets are almost always served by naked slaves. For example, if those of Ar visit Treve, the banquet will almost certainly be served by stripped women once of Ar, now in the collar of Trevan masters, which courtesy is returned, of course, should those of Treve visit Ar, where the free men of Treve will be served by stripped women once of Treve, now in the collars of their masters, men of Ar. This is not as insulting as it might be thought, as Gorean men are generally agreed that women are women, and slaves are slaves. What does it matter in what city a woman wears her collar? She is a slave.

As one from a different world, a grayer, more dismal, more crowded, more polluted world, a mass world of homogenized humanity, a world in which excellence is suspect, and must be concealed, a world of cunning and greed, of envy and duplicity, of hatred and fanaticism, a world alien to honor, a world without Home Stones, I have been much impressed by the Gorean pride in person and achievement. Here human magnificence is prized, provided it be well used and honestly earned. Goreans are wary of the Priest-Kings, but, on the whole, leave them to their devices in the Sardar. Let the gods live their lives; let men live theirs.

I was sure that the Kurii did not realize the possible consequences which might attend denying kajirae to Gorean males, men accustomed, almost from the ceremony of citizenship, when they are allowed to hold and kiss the Home Stone, to having such conveniences inexpensively at hand.

Late one night four fellows, with a lamp, broke into the slave quarters. They shook the cages, dragged them about, rattled the bars, but, lacking tools, they could not open them. Some of the girls thrust their arms through the bars, to have them covered with kisses, or pressed their face to the bars, and gripped the bars, that the force of the kisses received might not force them back into the cage. I tried to make myself small in the cage, and shrank back, as men reached through the bars. I had marks on my ankle and one wrist, where they had been grasped. I had a bruise on my left cheek when it had been pulled forward against the bars, by the hair. Then Kurii rushed into the area and the men fled. Two were captured, and put under the snake. Neither died.

"Kajirae," said Nora, "gather about."

We hurried to kneel in her presence, in the slave quarters. She had just returned from the halls.

"Matters outside grow ugly," said Nora. "I fear we are safe, if at all, only in our cages. Altercations take place betwixt men and the beasts. No killing is done yet, for the men lack weapons. They insult the beasts. Happily, few of the beasts understand little other than impatience and disgruntlement. Otherwise heads might be torn away. As it is, several arms and legs have been broken, and men have been swept aside, dashed into walls. There is grumbling. I think the beasts do not understand what is wrong. The men hunger, but not for food, for slaves. They are starving men of slaves, and slaves of masters. It is a punitive thing emanating somehow from the high Kurii, those of golden chains. It affects the beasts, as well, restrictions and refusals. This began, I fear, with the high Kur, Lucius, and now, it seems, a prisoner who was to have been executed escaped, and two Kurii were killed outside the Cave. It is suspected collusion took place. Was the escape abetted? Are there traitors in the Cave? It seems all must suffer. Ela, much of this you know, but I now bring you more dreadful news."

"Mistress?" said Chloe.

Nora seemed unable to continue. She looked about herself, as though fearful that the walls might hear, and speak what heard.

"Please, Mistress," said Jane.

"It is said," said Nora, "that there is a conspiracy of men within the Cave to thwart the projects of the hirsute masters."

I suddenly became very frightened.

"It has been long suspected by the high Kurii," she said. "Random executions have been contemplated."

"May I speak, Mistress?" I said.

"All of you, while we are alone," she said, "have such a permission." I recalled Nora had not been so generous, before she had found herself at the slave ring of Kleomenes. On a chain many a woman has been softened, and improved. It is hard to be an imitation man on a chain.

"What is different now?" I asked. "Why is it now said that such a conspiracy exists?"

"There is an informer," she said.

A gasp escaped us.

"It seems pressures were great," said Nora. "Scrutiny becomes intense. What move could be made? What could be done? The least movement, the least breath of air, might not escape vigilance. How much was already known to the golden chains? Perhaps the net was already flung. Perhaps the cords were inexorably being drawn tight. It must have seemed only a matter of time, and perhaps a very little time, before the plot and its participants would be exposed. Who would be the first to save himself at the expense of others?"

"Who was the informer?" asked Jane.

"Desmond, Desmond of Harfax," said Nora.

"No!" I cried.

"It seems so," said Nora.

"It cannot be!" I said.

"It is his name which is spoken," said Nora.

I recalled that Desmond of Harfax had once said to me, "It is clear how at least one might survive."

"How?" I had asked.

"By betraying the rest," he had said.

Chapter Forty-Seven

A double guard, though it was daylight, had been placed at the mouth of the Cave. It was thus, in effect, sealed.

It had been announced, yesterday, that all conspirators had twenty Ahn in which to surrender themselves, before their names would be revealed to the high Kurii by Desmond of Harfax, who, in full nobility, had come forward voluntarily to perform his bounden duty to his superiors.

He had apparently made the stipulation that he would reveal the names of the conspirators only to Agamemnon himself, thus assuring himself that all would be done fully and properly, without any confusion or mistake, and, also, naturally, one supposes, that he, Desmond of Harfax, would then be recognized personally by a grateful Agamemnon as the informant, and would, thus, be certain to receive his proper reward.

The twenty allotted Ahn, of course, had now passed without incident. Certainly no one had come forward, surrendering himself to the golden chains.

"Free person!" cried Nora.

The kajirae in the slave quarters went immediately to first obeisance position. I did not even know who had entered.

"Allison," said a woman's voice, one I well recognized, but had not heard for months.

"Mistress," I said, looking up, seeing the Lady Bina. It was clear she was free, but she was not well robed. It was different from Ar, and even from the more casual robing of the trail. The robe, I suspected, was of a single layer. It was brown, soiled, and ragged at the hem. It suggested the garment of a Peasant woman, who might work in the fields. Normally the Lady Bina was fastidious with respect to her garmenture. It came midway on her calves. She had fashioned for herself, from similar material, a hood, and veil. The veil was loose about her lower face, more a token of veiling than anything else. The Lady Bina, I supposed as much from vanity as impatience with some of the cultural niceties expected of the Gorean free woman, had always been lax in veiling. I again realized how exquisitely beautiful she was. I thought she might be in jeopardy, particularly now, if she were to traverse the halls alone. But she was not alone. A Kur was behind her. I realized with a start, though I should have expected it, that the Lady Bina was a prisoner.

"You are to come with me, Allison," she said. "We are to witness the deposition of Desmond of Harfax."

"I do not wish to do so," I said.

"I am sorry," she said.

"Why are we to do so?" I asked.

"They want witnesses who are not free men," she said. "One of them might be implicated. We are chosen, I suppose, because he was in the employ of myself and Grendel, and you were in his keeping."

The Lady Bina turned to the other kajirae in the room. "You may rise," she said.

The beast with her turned toward the door.

"We are to go outside, Allison," she said. "Desmond of Harfax is to be led down the hall shortly, to the Audience Chamber of Agamemnon. We are to follow."

She preceded the Kur from the room, and I followed her, a bit behind, on the left, as befitted a slave. She was free. I would heel her.

Outside the door to the slave quarters the Kur stopped, and we, with him, stopped, and waited there. I knelt, and the Lady Bina stood. There were several men in the corridor, mostly along the sides. There were a few Kurii, too.

I saw the Lady Bina looked upon.

Surely it would have been better had she been clad in the Robes of Concealment. Many of the men, as far as I know, had never seen her before. I am sure many did not know what to make of her. Should there not be a collar on her neck? If there was, it would be concealed by the casual veiling she had arranged. But she was not camisked. Could she be free? It would seem so, for the comparative amplitude of her garmenture, but, too, it did not seem all that much, and it was fairly obvious that her robe was thin, and of but a single layer. Too, she was beautiful, surely slave beautiful, that beautiful. When men look upon such beauty it is natural for them to think, as well, of chains and the block.

I kept my head muchly down, and my knees closely together. Even so, I did not doubt but what, collared and camisked, and despite the proximity of the Lady Bina, I did not escape my share of attention.

The way the men were about, and near the sides of the hall, looking back down the hall, toward the direction from which Desmond of Harfax might approach, I was uneasy. It was too much like a gantlet. Almost none of those men, of course, had been at that perilous meeting called so long ago by Desmond of Harfax, at which, I, too, had been in attendance. I was sure they were no part of Master Desmond's party. Yet, too, I sensed hostility amongst them. Goreans do not look lightly upon treachery. Too, even if they were not of Master Desmond's party, most might have been sympathetic to any band of men who, in the face of the Kurii, might have dared to secretly enleague themselves. Certainly there was much disgruntlement in the Cave amongst the humans, and, as nearly as I could determine, amongst several of the Kurii as well. The new regulations chafed all.

Amongst the men I did see two who had been at the meeting, Trachinos and Akesinos.

I found it hard to believe that Desmond of Harfax would have betrayed his fellows. He had seemed to suspect that someone might do so. If this were inevitable, I supposed he thought the survivor might as well be he. How then could one blame him in such circumstances? Would not the rational agent seize such an opportunity before it was seized by another? Should he not be praised for his initiative, and astuteness? Yet I was muchly discountenanced by his decision. It did not seem like the Master Desmond I had thought I had known. I saw him now as tarnished. I had feared I was unworthy to be the slave of so fine a master. Now I did not even wish to belong to him. Had he not behaved as I might have expected a man not of Gor, but of Earth, cunning, self-seeking, and devoid of honor, to behave? Of Gor, was he not more of Earth than Gor?

I looked up, as I heard a ripple of awareness about me. Leaning forward I saw, approaching, Desmond of Harfax, followed by two Kurii, who occasionally bared their fangs threateningly, and growled, as men started to surge closer to their charge. Desmond was smiling, which seemed the more to anger the men about. He did not seem to notice frowns, and raised fists, nor did he see fit to respond to hissed insults, as he passed.

When he came to our place he paused and saluted the Lady Bina, who did not, as far as I know, return his salutation. I put my head down, as I did not want to look upon him. I felt my world had collapsed. What, now, could be believed? What, now, could remain in its place?

"Traitor!" I heard, and I looked up to see a shape from the side, Akesinos, hurling himself upon Desmond of Harfax, his hands clutching for his throat. In a moment, scuffling, they were rolling in the hall. "Stop, you fool!" said Desmond of Harfax. "Let me alone! You will spoil all!" I do not think this was picked up by the translators. Trachinos pulled Akesinos bodily from Desmond of Harfax. "Run," said Desmond of Harfax to Akesinos. "Mix with the others!" Akesinos sprang to his feet, eluded the grasp of the nearest Kur, and fled down the hall. One of Desmond's Kur guards started after him, but men crowded together, as though preparing to follow Desmond and his guards, and the Kur must thrust them from his path, following which he stopped and wildly looked about, nostrils flaring. Then he returned to his post, with his fellow, by Desmond of Harfax.

The Kur who had remained with Desmond of Harfax turned on his translator.

"To the Audience Chamber of Agamemnon," he said, "Theocrat of the World, Eleventh Face of the Nameless One."

Desmond of Harfax, shaken, his tunic torn, bruised, then continued on his way, followed by the two guards.

No longer did he seem so insouciant and jaunty.

Had the hands of Akesinos found their mark would he not have perished within the Ehn?

The Kur who had the Lady Bina under his supervision indicated that we should follow the two guards and Desmond of Harfax, which we did, he following. Master Desmond was subjected to no further attacks before we reached the double doors, large, suitable for the passage of Kurii, which led into the audience chamber.

By the time we reached the entrance, I was very much afraid, and not, as before, for those whom a miscreant might betray, but for another, one who had in mind the assassination of Agamemnon, said to be Theocrat of the World, and the Eleventh Face of the Nameless One.

In the scuffle with Akesinos the sound had been slight, but unmistakable, and, within a rent tunic, hastily clutched closed, I had caught a glimpse of gray steel.

Desmond of Harfax was carrying a weapon into the audience chamber.

Chapter Forty-Eight

It was a distraught Desmond of Harfax who was led before the dais, for on the dais, on three tables, were three containers.

Timarchos and Lysymachos stood beside the central container.

"Tal, noble Desmond," came a voice from the central container.

"Tal, noble Desmond," came a voice from the container to the left.

"Tal, noble Desmond," came a voice from the container on the right.

In my account of what followed, it should be understood that the words attributed to Agamemnon might come, and did come, variously, from one or another of the three containers. Sometimes the left-hand container seemed to speak, sometimes that in the center, and sometimes that on the right.

It seemed reasonably clear that there could be but one Agamemnon, and so but one housing for that dangerous and mighty mind, but it was not clear in which housing, if any, that mind reposed.

One would suppose it would be in the central container, not so much for its location, as for the fact that Timarchos and Lysymachos were in attendance on that container. To be sure, their positioning might be intended to divert attention from another container, that truly housing Agamemnon, but, if so, which one might it be? Too, might one not think that a more subtle ruse might be projected? If A seemed most likely, and then one might be led to suppose B or C crucial, but which, but then, if either B or C might seem crucial, might that not be a way of diverting attention from A, which, after all, might be the crucial container, and so on. Might there not be indefinite subtleties, one lurking behind the other, in this kaissa of choice?

"Tal, Noble Agamemnon, Theocrat of the World, Eleventh Face of the Nameless One," said Desmond of Harfax.

"It is our understanding," said Agamemnon, "that you have discovered, and have come forward to reveal, a most heinous plot, disrespectful of our majesty, threatening to our person, and inimical to the welfare of worlds."

"Yes," said Desmond of Harfax.

"Our penchant for mercy is well known on more than one world," said Agamemnon. "Did we not allow all conspirators twenty Ahn in which to surrender themselves?"

"The generosity of your offer was beyond question, Lord Agamemnon," said Desmond of Harfax.

"But, unfortunately," said Agamemnon, "none availed themselves of our gracious offer."

"It seems so," said Desmond of Harfax.

"And thus is demonstrated their guilt, the villainy of their ways, and the depth of their depravity."

"True," said Desmond of Harfax.

"And thus, by their own fault, they have placed themselves beyond the pale of my mercy."

"It is tragic," said Desmond of Harfax.

"One sorrows," said Agamemnon.

"How can it be helped?" asked Desmond of Harfax.

"True," said Agamemnon. "But now, reveal, clearly, and without exception, the names of all traitors, whether human or Kur."

Several of the Kurii in the room stirred, uneasily. It had not occurred to them that Kurii might be enumerated. In such denunciations, of course, it is recognized that some temptation might exist to enlarge a list somewhat, particularly by happening to include in it personal enemies, individuals of whom one disapproves, individuals whom it is recognized that certain important individuals might like to have denounced, and so on.

"But first, great lord," said Desmond of Harfax, "may I approach you more closely?"

"No," said Agamemnon.

"I would like to speak more intimately," said Desmond of Harfax.

"Remain where you are," said Agamemnon.

The bodies of both Timarchos and Lysymachos tensed.

"Certainly," said Desmond of Harfax. "It is only that I thought we might speak of something more privately."

"Of what?" asked Agamemnon.

"It is clearly understood, of course," said Desmond of Harfax, "that I bring the matter of egregious treachery to your attention simply, and only, to frustrate treason, and protect the person and plans of your lordship."

"Of course," said Agamemnon.

"Such is my duty, and privilege," said Desmond of Harfax.

"Agreed," said Agamemnon.

"But, too," said Desmond of Harfax, "might one not expect some token of gratitude from your lordship, however negligible, no matter how undeserved it might be?"

"The generosity of the Theocrat of the World, the Eleventh Face of the Nameless One," said Agamemnon, "may be depended upon, and is well known."

"Would a thousand pieces of gold, tarn disks of double weight, be appropriate?" asked Desmond of Harfax.

"Would your life be appropriate?" asked Agamemnon.

"What of yours?" cried Desmond of Harfax leaping to the dais, thrusting the central container to the floor, and falling upon it with his knife. He struck it twice before Timarchos seized him, lifted him, and threw him, knife in hand, a dozen feet from the dais. Immediately Desmond of Harfax was disarmed and seized by Kurii. The container he had attacked lay open, on its side, on the dais, its lid on the floor beside it. The container was empty except for some wires, what appeared to be small boxes, and a small disk-like object with screening upon it.

Desmond of Harfax had chosen incorrectly.

He had gambled and lost.

"Do not kill him!" came from one of the two remaining containers, that on the left.

I was afraid Desmond of Harfax might have had his arms torn from his body. Such might be done by an enraged Kur.

"Let him rather contemplate what might be done to him," came from the container on the right. "He will be supplied with several possibilities, and assured that his fate will exceed them all."

"Perhaps it will take him a year to die," said the container on the left.

"Excellent," came from the container on the right.

How brave, and foolish, Desmond of Harfax had been! Did he think that so mighty a foe, so jealously guarded, might be so easily disposed of? I recalled that he whom he had spoken of as his principal, who had been, as it had turned out, Grendel, had said nothing of the assassination of Agamemnon. He had been silent with respect to that matter. This silence, I suspected, had puzzled, or displeased, Desmond of Harfax. Striking a blow at the heart of the conspiracy, by doing away with Agamemnon, had seemed to him a consideration of paramount importance. Be that as it may, it clearly was not an easy blow to strike.

Desmond of Harfax struggled futilely in the grip of two Kurii.

I wondered if Agamemnon was even ensconced in one of the three containers on the dais. Then I realized that in all likelihood he would be. Presumably, given the unrest in the Cave, the abortive revolt of Lucius, who had presumably been as trusted, or more trusted, than any, and the possible existence of dissidents amongst the Kurii, perhaps even some lingering followers of Lucius, I did not think he would dare to be far from Timarchos and Lysymachos.

There had been nothing secret about this meeting in the audience chamber of Agamemnon. Indeed, it had, in effect, been publicized. One of its purposes was to inspire terror in the hearts of the disaffected. It may also be remembered that the leader of the revolt, Lucius, and certain followers, had remained at large in the labyrinthine recesses of the Cave. This was due, in particular, not simply to the extent of the Cave and its passages, many of which were remote and unfamiliar, even natural, but because of a number of constructed private or secret passages. These were known to few but high Kurii, such as Lucius. With primitive weapons, of course, such as existed in the Cave, it would be extremely dangerous to pursue the dissidents into such places. Too, some had been clearly barricaded. The thought of Agamemnon and his adherents appears to have been that the putatively small number of remaining dissidents who might conceal themselves in such passages would perish for lack of water, or be starved out. Should they emerge into the larger halls they could presumably be easily met and dealt with. What was not understood was that Lucius and his cohorts had supplied several of these passages with reservoirs of water and stores of food, in case a retreat to them became necessary. The maps of the secret passageways had been taken by Lucius, and the adherents of Agamemnon knew little of their nature or whereabouts.

What is most relevant to this account is the fact that by means of one of these secret passageways, as to many other important locations in the Cave, one might obtain access to the audience chamber of Agamemnon.

"Take him away, to the place of cells," came from one of the containers, that on the left.

"No!" cried a Kur. "Kill him now! Be swift! Be done with it!"

"He is a man," said another Kur. "Men may side with him."

"Men are dangerous!" said another.

"Men are not to be trusted!" said another.

"Very well," came from the container on the right, "kill him now."

"No!" I screamed.

A Kur paw struck me from my knees, feet away, to the floor of the chamber.

"Let all the men be killed," called another Kur.

"We can hire others," said another Kur.

"Hundreds will rush to serve," said another.

"Such need only the smell of gold," said another.

"Speak your last, Desmond of Harfax," came from the container on the left.

"Gladly," cried Desmond of Harfax. "Down with the tyrant! Down with Agamemnon!"

One of the Kurii near Master Desmond raised a massive paw. One blow from such a paw could break a neck or back.

"I will speak!" cried out a voice, a woman's voice.

On more than one translator, as Kurii turned about, I heard, "She is free."

"Noble beasts!" cried out the Lady Bina. "Repudiate Agamemnon! How can he be Kur? He has no body! I know his world! It rejected him! He is no Kur! He is only the brain that once inhabited a Kur body! Now he is an artificial thing, a brain armed with a hundred artificialities, an artifact of your wondrous science. Do not listen to such an object! Do not serve so monstrous a contrivance!"

"Kill her!" came from the container on the right.

It was not clear for a moment what then occurred, but a concealed portal, at the rear of the audience chamber had opened, and some fourteen armed Kurii, led by Lucius, thrust their way into the room. Several had axes, and two carried the massive crossbow with tiered quarrels, of the sort I had first seen in the place of cells.

"Die, Agamemnon!" cried Lucius, and from diverse translators in the chamber, those activated, perhaps more than a dozen, there broke forth a startled medley of Kur and Gorean, producing a confused storm of sound.

As weapons were not permitted in the audience chamber, only the newcomers, Lucius, and his cohorts, were armed. Two Kurii rushed to the doors to exit, but were felled by quarrels, and one died clawing at the wood. I supposed the noise in the audience chamber might carry to the hall outside. On the other hand, the Kurii in the nearby halls would not be armed, either. The armed Kurii were mostly posted in the far halls, where it was thought that Lucius and his followers might emerge, presumably in an attempt to escape the Cave. The nearest armed Kurii would be at the great portal, and they would doubtless be summoned. Others would hurry to secure weapons. Presumably, under the circumstances, these would be supplied. This would mean that whatever Lucius and his cohorts would do must be expeditiously accomplished. It seemed likely they hoped, in this projected coup, to dispose of Agamemnon quickly and then present themselves to a confused, leaderless community as bold, patriotic liberators. In any event, several Kurii hurried to interpose themselves between the newcomers and the dais. Snarling, unarmed, they confronted the newcomers. Their own bodies would be the shield of Agamemnon. The common Kur is fanatically loyal to his lord, unless his lord is thought to have failed him, in which case the bond of allegiance is regarded as dissolved. This behavior, the loyalty to a chieftain, so to speak, had doubtless been selected for in millennia of Kur warfare, even prior to the development of sophisticated weaponry, which, as I understand it, exists on the steel worlds. In seeing these Kurii, unarmed, interposing their own bodies between weapon assailants and a leader, I learned more of what a Kur might be, and often was. I heard the snapping vibration of the cables of the crossbows, again and again. Kurii fell. Some of the newcomers rushed upon the defenders with axes, and limbs and heads were smote away, but Kurii loyal to Agamemnon threw themselves on the assailants, seized axes, and there were terrible struggles for the weapons. A throat was bitten through, and I did not even know if the victim was of the newcomers or not. Back in the room, closer to the portal through which the newcomers had emerged, Kur struggled with Kur. I was then on all fours, looking wildly about. I did not see the Lady Bina. I did see that Desmond of Harfax was free, one of his captors, headless, beside him. Desmond of Harfax was on all fours, looking about. He crawled amongst the struggling bodies. I think he was searching for his knife. The Kurii took no note of him. The crossbow cables were sprung again and again. Then one of the crossbows was wrenched from a newcomer, but the quarrels were lost from the guide. One was hurled like a small javelin and a Kur fell. Again I did not know one combatant from another. The doors to the audience chamber were pulled open from the outside and four armed Kurii, the guard from the great portal, entered the room. They were momentarily confused at the melee. One of the crossbowmen, back by the wall, must have been waiting for them. Three were felled by the tiered quarrels, and the fourth was cut open from behind, down the back of his spine, by an ax. I supposed then the great portal must be unguarded. No other Kurii entered. I did not know if arms had been issued, or not. I did know there was much dissatisfaction in the Cave. No men entered. I supposed mercenaries, even if armed, if they knew at all of this small war, would not regard it as their affair. It would be a matter, rather, betwixt possible paymasters. The exit was partially blocked by bodies but before it, too, now stood two of the Kurii of Lucius, with axes. Much carnage had ensued within the chamber. Bodies, some alive, and parts of bodies, were strewn about. In the end, weapons had had their way. The dais was now undefended. At one side, the left, as one faced the dais, lay Timarchos and Lysymachos. Timarchos, as it turned out, could not rise, so beaten he had been by the haft of an ax, and Lysymachos was lying against the wall, bleeding. Lucius had commanded that they not be slain. The reason for this shortly became clear. He knew more of the dangers posed by Agamemnon than his followers.

The quarrels had been expended.

"Bar the door," said Lucius.

This was done by the Kurii who had guarded it. They then came to stand with Lucius, before the dais, with two others of his cohorts. Only these five, now, had axes. Of the party of Lucius, then, including Lucius, there were only these five. Of the party of Agamemnon only six were left. These were away from the dais. All save one, a silver-chain Kur, seemed weak, scarcely able to move. Each, save the silver-chain Kur, was bleeding. Two slumped against the wall. The silver-chain Kur, back amongst them, crouched down, warily, looking toward the dais. Back with these Kurii, to the side, was Desmond of Harfax, his knife now in hand, and, on the other side, the Lady Bina and myself.

Lucius turned about, to face the dais. "Ho, Agamemnon," he called out. "You have lost!"

The two containers, one on the left, the other on the right, as one would face the dais, had been damaged. I did not know the extent of the damage.

"I announce the new order," said Lucius. "The new day is upon us! Tyranny is done. Freedom is victorious! Justice triumphs! Let all rejoice! I, Lucius, am now Theocrat of the World, the new Face of the Nameless One!"

"What is going on?" came from one of the containers.

"Can you hear me?" asked Lucius.

"Yes," came from one of the containers.

"You are our prisoner," said Lucius.

"What will you do with me?" came from the container on the left.

To this question Lucius did not choose to respond.

"I know secrets of great power, and the location of great wealth," came from the container on the left.

"I am sure you will share such things with us," said Lucius.

"Where are my armies, where are my fleets?" asked the container on the left.

"You are not on your world," said Lucius. "You left your world."

"I am on Gor?" asked the container on the left.

"Yes," said Lucius.

I suspected that Agamemnon, whom I took to be deep, was not as confused or disoriented as his responses might suggest. On the other hand, I did not know. It seemed clear that both containers had been damaged, and it was surely possible that this damage might have had its effect on whatever it might be which was contained in them.

"Where are my followers?" asked the container on the left.

Lucius, I noted, now, in his responses, addressed the container on the left. The other, on the right, had not spoken.

"They have abandoned you," said Lucius.

"Did none defend me? Did none fight for me?" asked the container.

"None," said Lucius.

"What of Timarchos and Lysymachos?" asked the container.

"They were the first to desert you," said Lucius. "Only I was loyal to you."

"Noble Lucius," came from the container.

"But you failed me," said Lucius.

"Forgive me," said the container.

"Amends may be made," said Lucius. "You may reveal to me secrets of power, the location of great wealth."

"You will then let me live?" asked the container.

"Of course," said Lucius.

"Be careful in lifting my container," came from the container. "It is delicate, and heavy."

"Unbar the door," said Lucius to two of his cohorts. "We will carry the container into the hall. Agamemnon is helpless, and our prisoner. This will impress all, Kurii and humans. It will manifest the success of our cause, the absoluteness of our victory. It will be uncontestable. All will then acknowledge us, all will grant that the day is ours, that the new order is upon us."

The large double door to the chamber, leading out to the hall, was unbarred, and swung open.

"I have waited long for this day," said Lucius, "years of secret thoughts, of hypocrisy, and deception, months of planning, days of strife, weeks of withdrawal, of hiding in tunnels, and waiting, and then, by means of an unexpected, bold, and glorious stroke, victory!" He then signaled to his two cohorts who were at the dais. "Put aside your axes," he said. "It will show we are now at peace. Do not fear. None in the halls are armed. Good. Now, seize up Agamemnon, and carry him, bodiless and helpless, into the hall, in triumph."

"All hail Lucius," called a Kur, from amongst those back by the wall. It was the silver-chain Kur. He hobbled, as though he might have been injured, toward the center of the room. His fur was drenched with blood, but it was not his own. He had fought little, if any. Rather he had abided the outcome of the battle. "Hail Lucius!" he said. "Hail Lucius."

I then recognized him, as I had not before. It was the Kur who, when an iron-chain Kur, had stood before Agamemnon with another Kur in the audience chamber, a silver-chain Kur. There had been mutual protestations of some sort, in which perhaps the iron-chain Kur might have been denouncing the one with the silver chain, and the one with the silver chain might have been defending himself. It was hard to say, as this took place in Kur, and there were no activated translators in the room. The silver-chain Kur had then been slain, most unpleasantly, by Agamemnon, then housed in the large, crab-like metal body, and the silver chain, with garlands, had been awarded to former iron-chain Kur.

Lucius turned away, disdaining to acknowledge the celebratory acclaim of the silver-chain Kur. He turned back to the container on the left, which had been the only one from which a voice had emanated of late.

"Be careful," he said to his fellows at the dais. "Do not drop it. It is heavy."

The two Kur cohorts of Lucius reached to the container, that on the left. They lifted it, and seemed surprised. "It is not heavy," said one of them.

There was a sudden fierce, almost deafening, crackling sound, and a great blast of light, and the Kurii who held the container reeled away from it, and the Lady Bina and I screamed. When we could see again, we could see skulls, and blackened bones, and flesh, like soiled, burned rags strewn about the dais and the adjacent flooring. Smoke came from the remains. The stink was wrenching.

"You did not warn us!" screamed Lucius to Timarchos and Lysymachos.

"Kill us," said Timarchos.

The container had been blasted open, and it lay on the floor of the dais. Within it was a miscellany of debris, much of it melted. The interior of the container itself was bent, and charred, as though it had been exposed to great heat.

Lucius turned angrily to the last container, that on the right, as one would face the dais. "So, noble Agamemnon," he cried. "We have found you at last!"

"Do not hurt him," begged Timarchos.

"Hail Lucius!" cried the silver-chain Kur who had been ignored. He cried this more desperately, his right paw raised in salutation.

Lucius turned about, annoyed.

"I was in the chamber," said Lucius, "when you falsely informed on your superior, and won thereby a silver chain. Agamemnon knew the fraudulence of your charges but saw fit to reward you, that more honest informers might not fear to come forth, with more reliable intelligence."

"No!" cried the silver-chain Kur. "It was true, all true!"

"Now," said Lucius, "you would betray Agamemnon, from whom you received the silver chain."

"His day is ended, he is done!" said the Kur.

"Where are your wounds, where is the blood you shed on his behalf?" asked Lucius.

"Hail Lucius!" said the Kur.

"One who would betray him would as soon betray another," said Lucius.

"No!" cried the Kur.

"Kill him," said Lucius.

"No!" cried the Kur, and perished beneath two axes, those of the Kurii who had hitherto guarded the door to the audience chamber, who had then joined Lucius at the dais. Lucius then turned back to the dais and pointed to the last container, that on the table to the right, as one would look to the dais.

"Put aside your axes," said Lucius, "and pick it up."

But neither Kur had put aside his ax.

"Now!" said Lucius.

Each retained his weapon. They looked at the blasted remains of their fellows.

"Yes," said Lysymachos. "Pick it up!"

"Do not be afraid," said Lucius. "It could not be as before, or it would destroy the contents of the box."

"Do not be afraid," said Timarchos, obviously in pain, but yet seemingly alert, leaning forward, his eyes glistening. "It is harmless," he said. "It cannot hurt you now."

Clearly these protestations by Timarchos and Lysymachos, so readily offered, even eagerly offered, encouraging contact with the container, did little to assuage any apprehension on the part of the two Kurii.

"Pick it up!" said Lucius. Clearly, in Kur, this was said with impatience and force. The translator, of course, clicked out the words with no hint of the passion with which they had been uttered.

"Show us," said one of the two.

"You are leader," said the other. "Lead."

"Yes," said Lysymachos. "Fetch the container yourself, noble Lucius."

"It is harmless," Timarchos assured him.

"Touch it, noble Lucius," said one of the two Kurii.

"Grasp it boldly," said the other.

"We will follow," said the first Kur.

"Do not fail us, noble Lucius," said the other.

"It is harmless," said Lucius. "But it is not needed. I will destroy it." Lucius grasped his ax with both hands, near the bottom of the haft. He raised the ax.

"Do not strike," said a voice in clear, even, calm Kur. This sound came from the back of the room, from the very portal through which Lucius and his minions had entered.

There, tall, and mighty, in full harness, stood Grendel. Behind him was the eyeless Tiresias.

"You perished in the Voltai!" cried Timarchos.

"How is the wretched, blind exile alive?" asked a Kur. "He was put out for larls and sleen months ago."

"How dare you present yourself here," cried Lucius, "amongst true Kurii, you, a monster, an enemy to all, badly spoken and deformed. See his eyes, see his hands!"

A murmur of revulsion passed amongst the Kurii in the room.

Some looked away.

"I remember him," said a Kur. "I remember him from the world, from the arena."

I understood little of this.

"He survived the arena," said another Kur.

"Before thousands," cried the Lady Bina, "he bespoke himself my champion."

"Many died," said another.

"He fought well," said another.

"He survived," said another.

"Rings were his," said another.

"You are not now in the arena," snarled Lucius, and readied his ax.

"Give him an ax," cried a Kur. "He is not armed."

It was true that he carried no ax. He did have the side knife in its sheath, part of the harnessing, but he made no attempt to draw that blade.

"You live, glorious Grendel!" cried Desmond of Harfax.

"Arm yourself, or flee, dear guard, sweet monster," implored the Lady Bina. "His eyes mean death."

Grendel stepped forward, to the center of the room, and Lucius, with a cry of rage, unintelligible in the translator, rushed forward and his ax, bright and double edged, described its swift, terrible arc, and in a moment might have cut away a head and part of a shoulder, but it was suddenly arrested in its flight, shaken, trembling in the impact, its haft beneath the blade grasped in a mighty hand, one which had scarcely moved. In the chamber there were cries of astonishment.

Then Grendel wrenched the ax from the hands of Lucius. And Lucius backed away, and Grendel observed him, the ax in his right hand.

Lucius turned to his two cohorts. He pointed to Grendel. "Kill him!" he said.

"No," said one of Lucius' Kurii.

"Obey!" cried Lucius.

"You have lost," said the Kur.

"Stand and be slain," said the other.

"No," said Lucius. "No!"

He moved rapidly, unopposed, to the large double door of the audience chamber.

"Do not flee the Cave!" called Grendel.

"A guard has been set, a guard has been set!" called Tiresias.

But Lucius had departed.

Grendel dropped his ax, and the two Kurii who had served Lucius dropped theirs as well.

"What men will," cried Desmond of Harfax, "may now escape the Cave. There is work to be done. We must forestall treason! We must warn a world. We must make our way to the cities. We must transmit tidings of subversion. What has been set afoot here is now abroad. We must move before the snows!"

"The snows have begun," said Timarchos.

"Last night," said Lysymachos.

"There is no time to lose," said Desmond of Harfax. "We will fight our way through them!"

"The passes will be closed," said a wounded Kur.

"We shall leave as soon as possible," said Desmond of Harfax. "Only one last thing remains to be done."

He then ran to the dais and leaped upon it, his knife raised.

"Stop!" cried Timarchos.

"Do not!" cried Lysymachos.

Before the knife of Desmond of Harfax could fall Lord Grendel darted forward with the speed of a charging sleen, and caught Desmond of Harfax about the waist, lifted him, and spun about, hurling him several feet away, back, to the center of the room.

I ran to Desmond of Harfax, and knelt beside him. "Master!" I wept. He was confused, and stunned. I feared an arm might be broken.

On the dais Lord Grendel had approached the table on which reposed the last container, that which had been on the right side of the dais, as one would face the dais.

"Is it Grendel?" came from the container.

"It is Grendel," said Lord Grendel.

"Kill it!" cried Desmond of Harfax, from the center of the room, now on his feet, unsteadily, grasping his arm.

"Forgive me, dear Desmond," said Grendel.

"Kill it, kill it!" cried Desmond of Harfax.

"No," said Lord Grendel.

Timarchos, with great pain, struggled to his feet, and Lysymachos, weak and bloody, stood, as well.

"My son," came from the container.

"Father," said Grendel.

He then placed the damaged container tenderly into the arms of Timarchos.

Chapter Forty-Nine

"Do you not think, dear Grendel," asked the Lady Bina, "that I should be a Ubara, somewhere, somehow?"

"I am only a beast," he said.

Tor-tu-Gor was bright outside.

A few days ago had been the vernal equinox, with which you begin your year, as Nature does. We were now again in the House of Epicrates, in Ar.

If I had been unclear in the Cave of Agamemnon as to whom I belonged, there was no longer any doubt about that. The collar of the Lady Bina was again on my neck.

To me this was a source of great sorrow, but I was a slave, and the slave has no control over whose collar she wears. To be sure, the Lady Bina, though strict, following the counsel of the Lady Delia, who had clear ideas as to how a slave girl should be owned, managed, and worked, was a good Mistress. As long as I was fully pleasing, I had little to fear. But I had hoped to belong to another. I could think of one to whom I would have been happy to have been sold for a copper tarsk-bit, whereas there were others from whom I would have hoped that the Lady Bina would have resisted offers of tarn disks of gold.

I will speak of several things.

It may be recalled that in my first visit to the audience chamber of Agamemnon with Grendel, that in which Grendel had been addressed by Agamemnon, and later awarded a golden chain, at one point Grendel, in being addressed by Agamemnon, had seemed muchly taken aback, had seemed very much startled and shocked. I followed nothing of that at the time, of course, as that meeting was conducted entirely in Kur, but, as I later learned, that was the point at which Agamemnon had told Grendel of his alleged share in his parentage. As it is explained to me, Grendel was the result of an experiment. The genetic materials of several male Kurii were blended in some manner and then fused with the egg of a human mother. In this way he had several fathers and a human mother. Apparently his mother did not long survive his birth. Agamemnon claimed to be one of these fathers. I do not know if that claim was true or not, but it could have been true, given the science at the disposal of the Kurii on the steel world. Indeed, Agamemnon might have lost his Kur body generations before Grendel was born, but it would have been easily possible for portions of his genetic material, his seed, samples of his hereditary coils, and such, to have been maintained in a viable state, and later utilized in the experiment in question. As stated, I do not know if Agamemnon's claim was true or not. It might have been a judicious fabrication, intended to better secure Grendel's allegiance to his cause. One does not know. It could, of course, be true. Indeed, it is quite possible, given the importance of the experiment, and its projected political aim, that of securing alliances with Gorean humans, that Agamemnon would have wished something of himself, his intelligence, vision, cunning, might, and power, to be incorporated in Grendel. The truth of the matter doubtless lies on a distant steel world, in some archive of experiments. The experiment, as noted, had a political end in view, that of producing a Kur-like thing, with Kur allegiances, with enough human characteristics to interact profitably with Gorean humans, garnering alliances, and such. The experiment failed, however, as the humans tended to not only not identify with Grendel, but, for the most part, to loathe him, and recoil from him. His reception amongst Kurii was similar. He found himself understood as little more, if anything, than a hybrid monster.

It may be remembered that when Lucius had failed to dispatch Grendel, and had lost the respect and allegiance of the only two Kurii who remained of his followers, he had departed from the audience chamber. It had been supposed and it had, indeed, been the case, that he would try to escape the Cave, in which he would now be viewed as little more than a fallen, treasonous fugitive. Grendel had called to him not to leave the Cave, and Tiresias had warned him that a guard had been set.

The guard was the larl with which Tiresias, in his exile, had formed a symbiotic relationship. Grendel's many trips from the Cave, which had been hitherto noted, were mostly concerned to bring food to Tiresias. Tiresias shared this food with the larl in question. In this fashion, the larl received food and it, in its turn, not only refrained from attacking Tiresias, the source of the food, but guarded him against the inroads of other predators. Tiresias had managed to get the larl to cross the entryway of the great portal on the night of my return to the Cave simply enough, by luring it with food from the opposite side. The larl had been stationed near the exit of the Cave by the food signal, which it had come to recognize. This was a portion of the plan of Grendel and Tiresias, to prevent the escape from the Cave of enemies. If none had attempted escape, Grendel would have seen to it that food, in the usual manner, would have been delivered to the larl. A strange Kur, Lucius, whose scent was unfamiliar to the larl, was taken for food, and attacked. Had Lucius realized what was involved he would have taken food with him, to cast to the larl, but he knew nothing of this. From the larl's point of view, which had been given the food signal, it seemed that that which emerged from the Cave must either bring food or be food. Apparently Lucius had been attacked within a hundred paces of the Cave. The last seen of Lucius had been a limp body being dragged away, over the rocky slope toward the maze of passageways which led back into the mountains. Some days later, no longer fed, the larl had drifted away. One supposes it may have been the same larl which, in the chaos of the revolt, when the great portal was temporarily unguarded, had wandered into the Cave. That, of course, is not known.

It may be recalled, as well, that Agamemnon had desired Grendel, a former hero of the very revolution on the steel world which had dethroned Agamemnon, to return to the steel world and use his station and prestige to influence its support of his schemes on Gor. As I understand it, this was not as impractical as it might seem as, first, Grendel's word would be taken seriously, and might be persuasive; second, the current establishment on the steel world would be in no way threatened; and, third, and perhaps most importantly, those of the steel worlds had long coveted a natural world, after, it seems, they had destroyed their own long ago. Presumably any plausible opportunity to obtain a natural world might be welcomed, and seized. For Grendel to undertake this dark embassy it was necessary, naturally, that a means of transportation be provided. In his explorations outside the Cave, Grendel had located the ship in its concealed housing within the Crag of Kleinias. This ship was unmanned, but prepared in such a way that, activated, it would reach the intended steel world. Consider a crossbow set in place, with its quarrel in the guide, a crossbow trained on a distant target. It might remain quiescent, indefinitely, until the trigger was pulled, and then the quarrel would move to the target. So, too, the ship, a ship without sails, a ship which might scorn both water and air, a ship which might by itself seek its far port. It was on this ship that not Grendel but Tiresias would seek the steel world. The point of this was to make available to him the biological science of the steel-world that, by its knowledge of, and manipulation of, the hereditary coils, tissue might be regenerated. I am told that burned, ruined flesh might be restored, that limbs might be regrown, that eyes, from one's own hereditary coils, might be formed anew. Thus, if all went well, Tiresias might again see, as well or better than before. Apparently, long ago, in the time of the revolution on the steel world, the Lady Bina herself had undergone terrifying injuries, having been the object of some sort of attack. She had been muchly lacerated, torn, broken, and disfigured. But, it seems, by means of her own hereditary coils, her health, vitality, and beauty had been restored, if not enhanced. In any event, one snowy morning, several of us watched the departure of the small, remarkable ship, emerging from its housing, rising through the falling snow, then fading from sight, a ship with no crew, and with but one passenger, Tiresias, whom we all wished well.

Timarchos and Lysymachos, with supplies, bearing the container housing Agamemnon, had soon left the Cave. This was thought judicious as the always fragile trust and relationships on which a civilization implicitly relies had been muchly disrupted. Lucius had not managed to secure the governance of the Cave and Agamemnon was deemed to have lost it, for, given the decimation of his chief supporters, he no longer had the power to impose discipline and order. Further, his downfall was not received unwillingly by either men or Kurii, given the rampant dissatisfaction which had preceded it in the Cave. Grendel, and his party, might have provided a rallying point for those who recognized the dangers of lawlessness and anarchy, but his concern was elsewhere, and he would leave the Cave, accompanied by the Lady Bina, Desmond of Harfax, Desmond's cohorts, and several of the men from the Cave, willing to essay a return to civilization, even in the season. He would take some animals with him, the sort spoken of as kajirae. Most of the men and, one supposes, most, or all, of the surviving Kurii remained in the Cave. Certainly no Kurii accompanied us. One supposed some of the men at least, and perhaps all, would attempt to return to civilization in the spring, when the passes would be open. It seemed unlikely that the Cave, in any case, even if inhabited by several Kurii, would remain the center of future conspiracies. The fate of Timarchos, Lysymachos, and Agamemnon is not known. It is possible they managed to make their way to some sort of safety. There are, apparently, various enclaves of Kurii, usually small groups in remote areas, where interaction would be unlikely between them and native Goreans. Perhaps they managed to reach one of these enclaves. Perhaps not. They may have perished in the Voltai, from starvation, from animals, or hostile men or Kurii. But perhaps, too, they managed, somehow, to return to a steel world, not their original world, on which they would be unwelcome, but another. There is much here which is not known.

As mentioned earlier the containers, one of which housed Agamemnon, had been damaged in the audience chamber. The major effect which this damage seems to have had on Agamemnon was the damage to that portion of the device by means of which the ensconced brain was enabled to generate a visual consciousness. In this way, Agamemnon's awareness of who, or what, was in his vicinity had been impaired. Because of the trust accorded by both Timarchos and Lysymachos to Grendel, and because of him, to Tiresias, Agamemnon was occasionally left in the keeping of either Grendel or Tiresias, or both. Timarchos and Lysymachos were well aware that Agamemnon was not without enemies in the Cave.

One day, as I often was, I was in attendance on Tiresias, that I might fetch for him, or help him about, as he might wish. On that day, Tiresias was with Agamemnon.

"Bring me eyes," had said Agamemnon.

"I have no eyes to bring," had said Tiresias.

"Who is there?" had asked Agamemnon.

Tiresias had made his presence known.

"It was I who had you put out, into the mountains," said Agamemnon.

"Yes," said Tiresias.

"It is the Kur way," said Agamemnon.

"That is my understanding," said Tiresias.

"Are you going to kill me?" asked Agamemnon.

"No," said Tiresias.

"It is the Kur way," said Agamemnon.

"I am Kur," had said Tiresias. "And it is not my way."

The next day, their preparations complete, Timarchos, Lysymachos, and Agamemnon had left the Cave.

When Grendel had been saved from his projected executioners I had urged him to flee, but he had refused to do so. Rather, he and Tiresias would hide, and where, it seemed, they would not be sought. He would remain. He had, it seemed, "work to do." Where he would not be sought turned out to be the Cave itself. In his explorations outside the Cave, as noted, he had located and investigated the waiting ship, inert, waiting for its activation. He had forced his way into its housing, and, from within the housing, had obtained access to the interior of the Cave. Thus, while search party after search party left the Cave and scoured the icy, cruel terrain of the Voltai, he and Tiresias enjoyed the comforts of shelter. Snow provided drink, and an occasional mountain verr was secured for food. Grendel was well aware that Lucius and some cohorts remained at large and this suggested either, or both, of two possibilities, one, their retreat to remote portions of the Cave or, two, their access to concealed passages. Presumably the possibility likely to be of greatest interest to the fugitives would be that of concealed passages, by means of which important areas of the Cave, central halls, major chambers, and such, might be conveniently at hand. With this in mind, and the conviction that a private access, which might be utilized under certain conditions, as well as a public access, generally available, to the housing of the ship would be likely, Grendel addressed himself, over several Ahn, to the walls and flooring of the ship's housing. As a result of this investigation, he had eventually discovered a trap, which led by a flight of stairs, to a private passageway which, in turn, connected with a network of such passages. As a result, Grendel soon had at his disposal the same roads, and tunnels, so to speak, which were serving Lucius and his cohorts. Moreover, he had the advantage that Lucius and his cohorts were not aware of this intrusion into what they took to be their private domain. Accordingly, from time to time, he was able to follow their movements, and, occasionally, overhear their conversation.

Unfortunately it took eleven days after the incident in the audience chamber before our party could depart the Cave. The time lost was regretted, but the rigors and dangers of the Voltai are not to be taken lightly, even in the summer. In the winter her passes are treacherous, and sometimes closed. We laid in abundant supplies of various sorts, food, clothing, blankets, shelter gear, tools, ropes and other climbing tackle, and weapons. Sledges must also be built. These preparations, too, might have proceeded more apace had conditions in the Cave been more settled. Gangs had been formed both for predation and for self protection. Small wars might take place in the halls, as borders were crossed and claimed territories encroached upon. Riches were acquired, hoarded, and then defended. Many men expected to leave the Cave in the spring, rich. Kurii, too, who kept much to themselves, might also kill for food, men or one another. Our own gang must be formed to defend our supplies and other goods. Grendel accepted some to share our trials and rejected others. His criteria were less strength and prowess than reliability and honor. One would not wish to find a knife at one's throat when the Aqueduct Road was nigh. Most of the kajirae would remain in the Cave, presumably to be fought over as work and pleasure objects by the gangs. There were twenty-two men in our group, and one free woman, the Lady Bina. Our leader was Grendel. Our familiar fellows were with us, Astrinax, Lykos, Desmond of Harfax, Trachinos, and Akesinos. Kleomenes, who had been the leader of the tarsk hunters, was with us, but not his hunters, who had chosen to remain in the Cave until spring. Kleomenes brought a slave with him. Her name was Nora. At night he kept her chained by the neck to his right foot. Shortening the chain she was slept at his feet, lengthening the chain he could draw her to him, for his pleasure. I did not think she needed be chained. I do not think she would have left him for anything. She was his slave. He was her master. Lady Bina took her three slaves with her, Allison, Jane, and Eve. Trachinos had with him a slave, as well, Mina, who had once been the Lady Persinna of Ar. She was now his love beast. One last slave was with us, Chloe, who had been brought along by one of those fellows who had petitioned to accompany us, and had been accepted. He claimed he wanted her to keep him warm at night, and that he would sell her in Venna. I was not sure that we would reach Venna. Mina and Chloe could read. We other kajirae could not. Pausanias and his wagons were months ahead of us.

As witnessed by this narrative, we survived the Voltai. I think this would not have been possible without the determination and courage, the strength and power, the leadership, of Lord Grendel. I have wondered if, sometimes, there might not be something in that mighty body of the will and power, the energy and resourcefulness, the astonishing capacity, of he alleged, long ago, to have been as Kur amongst Kurii, dreaded and dangerous Agamemnon, known as Theocrat of the World, the Eleventh Face of the Nameless One.

It might also be noted in passing, that considerable wealth had been amassed by Kurii and their agents in the Cave, by means of which mercenaries were to be paid and subversion purchased in various cities. Much of this had been transported from the Voltai by Pausanias, to abet the work of the conspiracy, but much had remained, as well. Indeed we have mentioned how those of the gangs which had formed in the Cave after the onset of anarchy had made it a point to acquire and defend portions of this wealth, each gang as much as possible. In any event, Grendel had made it a point to appropriate for himself and his followers what gold and silver might be brought to hand without jeopardizing the return to civilization. As a result of this the gold and silver amassed was divided amongst himself, the Lady Bina and the free men. This was divided and placed in sealed packages, each properly inscribed with the name of the free person to whom it was to belong. The Lady Bina, as she was a free woman, was given five portions. It is not unusual that the Gorean free woman, in virtue of her freedom, is prominently advantaged. If anything, Grendel had given her less than many men would think her due. The free woman on Gor has a status and power which would astonish most of the putatively free women of my former world, but then the Gorean commonly thinks of the women of my former world not as free women, at least as he understands that, but rather as slave stock. In any event, the Gorean free woman, even of the lower castes, is accorded considerable respect. Her entitlements and privileges are seldom challenged. Most men will yield place to her. To be sure, should she be stripped, and collared, and flung to the feet of a man this all changes. Grendel placed this wealth, in its several sealed sacks, in the sledge in the keeping of Trachinos and Akesinos. At the end of the journey, each sack was present and sealed, as before. Grendel had chosen well.

"Allison," said the Lady Bina, "I have an errand for you to run."

"Yes, Mistress," I said.

"Tidy yourself," she said. "Remember that you are a reflection on me."

"Yes, Mistress," I said.

The fate of Agamemnon's conspiracy was not clear. Given his downfall in the Voltai it would, at least for a time, lack central direction. On the other hand, in its way, it was still afoot. Pausanias had left the Cave long before our departure. One supposes then that he by now, ignorant of developments in the Voltai, and following his instructions, would, by means of various well-placed agents, be carrying Agamemnon's plans forward. He would doubtless be unaware of the downfall of Agamemnon until at least the spring. To be sure, it was clear that Agamemnon's plan might be implemented in the absence of its prime architect. Agamemnon's conspiracy then, even without Agamemnon, might still be afoot. Another possibility would be that the active, seething brain that was now Agamemnon might reassert itself, might acquire new housings, even new bodies. One did not know how much of Kur science might be available on this world. Too, might not another steel world bring Agamemnon to one of its own laboratories and there restore and rearm him, that he might further pursue, perhaps now to their own advantage, planetary imperialisms?

Desmond of Harfax had wanted to kill Agamemnon. Grendel had been unwilling to do so.

In any event, it was now clear to many, if not enough, that Kurii were active on Gor, and had designs on the world. If nothing else, perhaps one might now look more carefully at the civil conflicts that so often erupt in Gorean cities.

"Are you ready, Allison?" inquired the Lady Bina.

"Yes, Mistress," I said.

We had arrived in Ar some weeks ago. The Lady Bina had given Jane to Astrinax, and Eve to Lykos. They were not even sold. They were given outright. I rejoiced for them. I, however, to my dismay, had been retained. "Am I not, too, to be given to someone?" I had asked, looking up, excited, hopeful, trembling, to see what would be done with me, appropriately kneeling. Then she looked at me. I did not understand her expression. Then she said, "A lady needs a slave. You may now kiss my sandals, and thank me for deigning to keep you, despite your many faults." As I kissed her sandals, tears ran from my eyes. I could hardly speak. "Thank you, Mistress," I whispered, "for deigning to keep me." "Despite your many faults," she reminded me. "Despite my many faults," I said, and collapsed, weeping.

"Prepare supper," she had then said.

"Yes, Mistress," I had said.

I did not know where Kleomenes had gone, as he left us in Venna. The last I had seen of him he had purchased a saddle tharlarion, a hunter, and was departing, westward, Nora on foot, chained by the neck to his stirrup. The fellow who had decided to sell Chloe in Venna had apparently changed his mind. I last saw him on foot, Chloe behind him, heeling him, carrying his pack. She was humming, and he did not turn and cuff her. They were bound somewhere north, perhaps Torcadino or even Brundisium, on the coast. Trachinos, who had originally claimed to be from Turia, was apparently curious to see what

Turia might be like. In any event, he had purchased a wagon and tharlarion, and was allegedly returning to Turia. The last I had seen of him was his wagon, ·disappearing down the road. His slave Mina followed on foot, chained by her wrists to the back of the wagon. I thought that, soon enough, she would be beside him on the wagon box, though perhaps braceleted or shackled. Astrinax had returned to Ar, to his jobbing, and Lykos, too, was now in Ar. He had opened a day stall on the Street of Coins. It was not easy to think of him with scales and an abacus. It was easier to remember him on his rope, ahead of the wagons, plunging his great staff through the snow, wary of concealed crevices. Grendel had followed him, with his hands on the rope, the other end about his own waist, to draw him to safety if the snow gave way. It had, several times. Akesinos had remained in Venna, to hire himself out as a wagon guard, an honest guard, I hoped. He had also invested some of his resources to obtain a share in a small tavern in Venna. He had offered half a silver tarsk to the Lady Bina for me, but his offer had been declined. Thus I escaped becoming a paga girl. I did not know the whereabouts of Desmond of Harfax. Nor was I now interested in knowing his whereabouts. He had not approached the Lady Bina on my behalf, he had made no offer to buy me. I now realized how little I meant to him. How right I was to have hated him. And how right I was to hate him now.

"Turn about, Allison," said the Lady Bina, "and place your hands behind your back."

"Mistress?" I said.

"Now," she said.

To my surprise, and lack of ease, I felt slave bracelets snapped on my wrists.

I pulled a bit, at the pinioning.

"There is no point in struggling, Allison," said the Lady Bina. "You are secured, perfectly."

"Yes, Mistress," I said. "May I ask why?"

"There are several reasons for back-braceleting a slave girl," said the Lady Bina. "It makes her helpless, it increases her sense of vulnerability, it is sexually stimulating, it reminds her that she is a slave, it considerably reduces her juicing time, it nicely accentuates her figure, and such."

"Surely," I said, "there is little doubt about a girl's figure if she is in a slave tunic."

"And doubtless less, if she is camisked," she said.

"Doubtless," I said.

"You were camisked in the Cave," she said.

"Yes, Mistress," I said.

"Would you prefer a camisk?" she asked.

"No," I said. "Not in the public streets."

"Perhaps you would prefer such in the privacy of a domicile," she said, "that you might thereby excite yourself and a master."

"Perhaps," I said. To be sure, slave girls were not unoften kept naked indoors, save for their collar.

"It is not wise to excite strangers," she said. "Some are brutes and ruffians."

"Yes, Mistress," I said.

"To be sure," she said, "slave tunics are not much better."

"They are designed to be provocative, and revealing," I said.

"They are designed to divert attention from free women," she said, "and thus they increase the security of the free woman."

"I do not think that is the main reason," I said.

"Oh?" she said.

"Men like to see slaves thusly," I said.

"Perhaps," she said.

I jerked a little at the bracelets.

"Usually you do not bracelet me so," I said.

"No," she said. "But on this errand I do not want your little hands to be busy."

"My hands," I said, "are no larger or smaller than those of Mistress."

"But," she said, "they are the hands of a slave."

"Yes, Mistress," I said.

"I have here," she said, "a small sack, on its cord, which I will hang about your neck. I have tied it shut, with my signature knot. It contains a message which you, as you are illiterate, cannot read, even if you could reach the sack. You will seek the shop of Amyntas, the wine merchant. It is on Teiban, near Clive. Present yourself, on behalf of your Mistress, Bina of Ar. The message will be read, and a small package will be placed in the sack, which will be knotted closed. Presumably that will be done with the signature knot of Amyntas. You will have been expected. This has been arranged. Return then."

"Yes, Mistress," I said. "Must I truly go braceleted?"

"Surely you have seen braceleted slaves in the streets," she said, "front-braceleted, and back-braceleted."

"Yes, Mistress," I said.

"Would you prefer to go back-braceleted, and nude?" she asked.

"No, Mistress," I said

"Be careful on the stairs," she said.

"Yes, Mistress," I said.

"And do not dally," she said.

"No, Mistress," I said.

I then exited the domicile. I wondered how many kisses, and embraces, I might be forced to endure, back-braceleted. That might have much to do with whether or not free women were in the vicinity. Once, though I had not been back-braceleted, I had been seized and lip raped by a strong, handsome Tarnster. A frowning free woman had rushed over and berated the fellow, roundly. Even though I was frightened, and squirmed, he had not discontinued his attentions. I was helpless in his arms. I could not help myself. I must have moved as a slave. How can one help being a slave, if one is a slave? When satisfied, he laughed, and thrust me down, to my belly, a well-kissed slave, and faced the free woman. "Perhaps you would like to be in a collar," he snarled. The free woman had then turned about, and fled. I had thought the matter done, but the free woman had turned about afterwards, and followed me. She accosted me, and, when I knelt before her, as I must, she struck me and kicked me, several times. "Slut," she cried. "Slut! Seductive slut!" "I was seized, Mistress!" I protested. "I saw you!" she cried. "They like your sort in the paga taverns! Run to a paga tavern, grovel, and beg to be caressed!" "Please do not hurt me!" I begged. "Would that I owned you!" she said. "If you so much as raised your head in the streets, you would be lashed!" I recoiled under her blows. "Slave," she said. "Slave, slave, slave!" "Yes, Mistress," I said. "I am a slave." She struck me twice more. She then turned about, and left. "Yes," I thought, "she would like to be in a collar."

* * * *

I hurried up the stairs to the second floor of the house of
Epicrates, where we maintained our domicile.

I was dirty, weeping, and bruised. My tunic was torn. Shortly
after having received the package, I had been set upon by two
men, who had been hooded. A wad of cloth had been thrust into
my mouth and tied there, with another band of cloth, knotted
behind the back of my neck. I had then been drawn into an
alley, flung to the gutter, in the alley's center, and the sack I had
worn about my neck had been cut away. The two men had then
tied my ankles together and fled away. They had not made use
of me. I was muchly helpless, and in consternation. Perhaps, if
my wrists had not been pinioned behind my back, I might have
offered the assailants some resistance, or, at least, delayed their
depredation long enough to attract the attention of passers-
by. I must now try, painfully, miserably, bit by bit, to edge my
way to the mouth of the alley. But, a moment later, a Leather
Worker, passing by in the street outside, was in the mouth of
the alley. He, apparently curious, was looking after the two
running fellows. He then looked into the alley, saw me, and, a
little later, my ankles had been freed. I looked at him, wildly,
piteously, over the gag. I made muffled noises, begging that the
gag be removed. But he left it in place. "I wonder why they ran,"
he said. Then he said, "You are pretty." His hands were on my
ankles. I shook my head, wildly, negatively. And then he made
use of me. For a time I squirmed, in protest, but then, after a bit,
a slave, overcome, mastered, submitted, I threw back my head,
helpless and lost, in a grateful bliss I was unable to resist, a bliss
I only hoped would be prolonged. When he was finished with
me he removed my gag but placed his finger across my lips, that
I would not speak. He then drew a copper tarsk-bit from his
pouch and placed it in my mouth. I could not then well speak,
for the coin in my mouth. "That is for your master," he said.
He then stood up. "I wager those two," he said, looking down
the alley, "did not even pay." I made clear to him, with small
sounds, kneeling before him, that I wished to speak. He put out
his hand and I dropped the coin from my mouth into his palm,

"They did not make use of me," I said. "I was robbed." "No wonder they ran," he said. "But do not concern yourself. No one would entrust anything of value to a slave." "May I go, Master?" I asked. "You are a hot little pudding," he said. "I cannot help myself," I said. "I could not resist." "A barbarian, too," he said. "I heard that they were all inert." "Inertness is not permitted to us," I said. "We are in collars." "I have heard, too," he said, "that they are disgusting creatures, helpless, marvelous slaves, who will pant, beg, and crawl for it." "We are women," I said. "Slaves," he said. "Yes, Master," I said, "slaves." "What do you cost?" he asked. "Apparently only a tarsk-bit," I said. "Do not be bitter," he said. "May I go?" I asked. "The ruffians bruised you," he said. "You must be in pain." "May I go?" I asked. "Please, Master." "Open your mouth," he said. He then replaced the coin in my mouth. "Remember," he said. "That is for your master." I made a single small noise. If gagged, one such noise signifies "Yes," and two, "No." It is not unusual for a slave to carry a coin or coins in her mouth. She is not permitted a pouch, and slave garments, like most Gorean garments, save those of artisans, and such, do not contain pockets. I then sprang up and hurried from the alley.

In the domicile, I knelt before my Mistress, the Lady Bina, and dropped the coin at her feet. Lord Grendel was also present. I then, shaken that I had been robbed, miserable in the pain of my bruising, distraught that I had failed to return home with the package, frightened that I would be punished, poured out, in a torrent of tears what had occurred. I did not neglect to explain the origin of the coin. I may have omitted some of the details pertaining to the later phases of my usage. To be sure, such might have been conjectured, as I had been paid, or, rather, as my master or mistress, as the case might be, had been paid.

"I have failed you!" I wept.

"Not at all," said Lord Grendel. "You have done splendidly."

"Master?" I said.

"It was intended," he said, "that the package be stolen. We have let the importance of the wine shop of Amyntas be known in certain quarters. Certain individuals have even permitted themselves to be bribed, to let a certain code sheet fall into certain hands. Indeed, this domicile is doubtless under surveillance, now that spring has come. The package stolen from you contained a code deck, whose message would be revealed by the purchased code sheet. The message, intended to fall into certain hands, specifies a supposed meeting of more than a hundred operatives opposed to the plans of Agamemnon. The enemy will doubtless wish to eliminate these operatives. When they attack the meeting site they will find it empty, but they, themselves, will be surrounded and attacked. In this way we hope to obtain a number of prisoners, who, if not of the importance of Pausanias, and such, might be important, and, properly persuaded, might lead us to the higher, even the highest, conspirators. If this plan proceeds to fruition we will not have ended the conspiracy, of course, which is far reaching, and may have support from various steel worlds, but it should deal it a serious blow."

"Should I not have been told?" I said.

"Certainly not," said Lord Grendel. "You must play your part in total ignorance. An inadvertent look, a mere expression, a lapsed word, a too-ready acquiescence, might have brought about the ruin of the entire plan."

"Might I not have been killed?" I said.

"No," said Lord Grendel. "No more than a kaiila or tarsk."

"The men were hooded," I said.

"Certainly that, or masked, or veiled," said Lord Grendel, "that you would be unable to recognize them."

"I was back-braceleted," I said.

"To further protect your life," said Lord Grendel. "Had you been able to offer the least resistance, and had you been so foolish as to have done so, which we feared you might, delaying the theft, or jeopardizing it in any way, you might have been summarily slain. It is possible you owe your life to something as simple as a pair of slave bracelets."

"Might they now be removed?" I asked.

"Certainly," he said.

"Thank you," I said.

"I wager," said the Lady Bina, "there is someone whose bracelets you would like to wear, and perhaps his shackles, as well."

"Mistress?" I said.

"Someone by whose coin you would like to have been taken off the slave block," she said.

"I will have to sew my garment," I said. "It is torn."

The Lady Bina fingered the tarsk-bit. "When I bought you," she said, "I thought you might be of interest to men."

"Yes, Mistress," I said.

"Is this," she asked, looking at the coin, "all your use was worth?"

"I had nothing to say about it," I said. "It was what he gave me."

"I would have supposed you should have brought twice that," she said, "two tarsk-bits."

"Ela," I said, "Mistress was not there to negotiate."

"Many men," said Lord Grendel, "coming upon a luscious kajira, gagged, and secured, helpless, totally at their mercy, in a secluded place, would not pay at all."

"Would it not be the same with a free woman?" I asked.

"Certainly not," he said. "The free woman would be instantly freed, succored, and restored to dignity. And if not, if one were so boorish, or foolish, as to risk torture and impalement, one would not pay, anyway, as the free woman is priceless. To give her a coin would be a great insult."

"And we are quite different?" I said.

"Quite," said Lord Grendel. "You are not priceless. You are worth what men will pay for you."

"At least," I said, "we have some sense then of what we are worth."

"Of course," said Lord Grendel.

"But he did pay," said the Lady Bina.

"That suggests," said Lord Grendel, "he was well satisfied."

"Was he well satisfied, Allison?" inquired the Lady Bina.

"I think he was pleased with a slave," I said.

"And you, Allison," said the Lady Bina. "Were you well pleased?"

"Please do not make me speak, Mistress," I said, my head down.

"Speak," she said.

I looked up at her, tears in my eyes. "I am a slave, Mistress!" I said.

"I understand," she said. "Excellent."

"As I understand it," said Lord Grendel, "a copper tarsk-bit is the usual price for a use, for example, to be placed in the pan beside a secured camp girl, to be put in the chained neck box of a coin girl, and such."

"Good," said the Lady Bina. "Then a single copper tarsk-bit is not a negative reflection on the quality of the slave."

"Not at all," said Lord Grendel.

"Excellent," she said.

"And in the taverns," said Lord Grendel, "a tarsk-bit will usually purchase a goblet of paga, and, if the customer wishes, the use of a paga girl. Sometimes dancers are extra."

"I am very pleased," said the Lady Bina, smiling upon me.

"Am I not to be despised?" I asked.

"No," said the Lady Bina.

"I cannot help myself," I said.

"Nor should you," said Lord Grendel. "Rather, you should desire it, with all your heart, to be so alive, and female."

"But you do not understand," I said, "how helpless one is!"

"You do not yet know how helpless a slave girl can be," said Lord Grendel. "When your slave fires are better kindled, you will begin to understand."

"You may begin to repair your garment," said the Lady Bina. "After that, you may prepare supper."

"Yes, Mistress," I said.

"And thus," she said, "you see the difference between a mistress and a master."

"Mistress?" I said.

"A master," she said, "would doubtless have you prepare supper before repairing the garment, that he might see you serving in a torn tunic."

"Yes, Mistress," I said.

"Or less," she said.

"Yes, Mistress," I said.

Chapter Fifty

"Scribe's Urt," had said the Lady Bina, and I located the card, and placed it on the pile.

Only one other card was left, and so she needed not read it. It was Warrior's Sleen. I placed the last card on the pile. As I suppose is clear, when one wishes to transmit the message, one takes a deck, rearranges the cards, inscribes the message on the edges of the deck, and then replaces the cards in the usual order. The recipient, then, who has the card sheet used for the particular message, places the cards in the order prescribed by the sheet, and, once again, the message is visible. In the Cave, the visible message was in substitutions, a Tau for an Al-Ka, or such, but often enough, now, it was in clear Gorean. Substitutions were still used if the matter was sensitive, but, now, often enough, this layer of security was omitted. All that was sought, frequently enough, now, was a certain level of privacy. To be sure, the message could be in clear Gorean, inscribed openly on a sheet of paper, and it would have remained opaque to me. The Lady Bina would not even tell me the names of the letters, or their values. "You do not need to read, Allison," she informed me. "I have little doubt, Mistress," I said, "that you are far more intelligent than I, but I am sure that I, just as you have, might learn to read." "I am still learning," she said. "Cursive script is a bother." "Even so," I said, "is there that much difference between us?" "There is a considerable difference between us," she said. "And what is that?" I asked. "Your neck is in a collar," she said.

When the Lady Bina or Lord Grendel received, or sent, a card message, I was often used. In preparing a message, I would rearrange the cards, randomly, following which the message would be placed on the edges of the deck. After that, I would read the order of the cards that the card sheet might be prepared. After that, I would place the cards again in the normal order, in which case the message disappeared. In receiving a message, which would have the cards in the normal order, as in the current case, the Lady Bina or Lord Grendel would read from the appropriate card sheet, and I would place the cards in the order prescribed by the card sheet, after which they would have the message, either in clear Gorean or in a substitution related to clear Gorean. I was also used to carry these messages back and forth. The wine shop of Amyntas remained a station in this exchange, but only one, to which I would deliver a message or from which I would receive a message, to be returned to the Lady Bina or Lord Grendel, almost always Lord Grendel. Sometimes Lord Grendel would deliver a message somewhere in person, and, sometimes, retrieve a message from some unknown source. This was almost always done at night.

To my apprehension, particularly at first, I would deliver and receive these messages as I had at first, when I had been robbed on my way to the wine shop of Amyntas, that robbery which had placed false information in the hands of the conspirators, namely, with the sack tied about my neck, closed with a signature knot, and my wrists braceleted behind me. You may well imagine my fear, at first, in this sort of coming and going. Anytime anyone came close to me, I would tense, and almost cry out. I would start when a shadow fell across my body, or on the street before me. A word, casually spoken, in a crowd, might make me half faint in fear. I half expected, particularly at first, to be seized, gagged, and thrust into an alley or doorway. The first time I had scarcely been uneasy, fearing little more disruption in my service than an occasional stolen kiss. Certainly I had not expected to be seized, rudely dealt with, and robbed. Now, when there was little, or nothing, to fear, I was as skittish as a tabuk doe who has caught the scent of a sleen. Lord Grendel had been very wise not to inform me of the nature of his plans, and his expectations, when I had carried that first message.

"Very interesting," said the Lady Bina, considering the

deck of cards, and turning it about a bit. "Yes," she said, "very interesting."

"Mistress?" I said.

"Curiosity is not becoming in a kajira," she said.

"Please teach me to read, Mistress," I said.

"Do not forget, Allison," she said, "that you are in a collar."

"Yes, Mistress," I said. "Forgive me, Mistress."

"My offer," she said, looking at the cards, "was refused, again refused."

"What offer?" I asked.

"This is a matter between free persons," she said.

"Yes, Mistress," I said. "Forgive me, Mistress."

"Well," she said, "I shall respond."

"Mistress?" I said.

"I shall wipe the edges of this deck clean," she said. "I will then mix the cards, and inscribe a new message. You will then put the deck in its normal order and deliver it to the wine shop of Amyntas."

"Must I be back-braceleted?" I asked.

"Of course," she said.

"I will be helpless," I said.

"Of course," she said.

It was now a month and a passage hand after I had been robbed on the way to the shop of Amyntas. I had gathered, though I had not been explicitly told, that the ruse of Lord Grendel and his associates had been successful. A number of men, apparently several, masked and armed, perhaps two hundred, had converged on a given barn outside the city, had broken into it, and found it empty. Attempting to withdraw, they found the building surrounded by a large number of armed men, many armed with crossbows, and some, Peasants, armed with the great bow, the Peasant bow. A torrent of quarrels and arrows apparently made departure unwise. Fires were set about the building to further discourage any projected withdrawal. As negotiations apparently proved inconclusive, the barn was set afire, following which the occupants must weigh a number of options, none welcome, dying in the fire, dying of missile fire, or surrender. The rumors of this I heard in the city universally understood the event as the cornering of a large number of bandits by vengeful Peasants. As Lord Grendel had left the domicile the afternoon of the event with his ax, and returned in the late morning, in high spirits, I am supposing that the affair may have had less to do with bandits and more to do with the hirelings of Kurii and their allies. As far as I know, no Kur was personally involved in the business. Shortly thereafter, as I understand it, the market for male work slaves in Ar was considerably depressed, with the result that several, stripped and coffled, were herded to Torcadino.

Late that afternoon I arrived at the shop of Amyntas, entered, knelt, put my head to the floor, then knelt up, and, at his gesture, rose to my feet. He then checked the signature knot on the small sack tied about my neck, the signature knot of the Lady Bina. On my former world, which may be called Terra, or Earth, we do not use signature knots, or, perhaps better, have not done so for a long time. You secure packages with such knots, boxes, even doors. Satisfied with the knot, he undid it. He would, of course, when he later closed the sack, do so with his own signature knot. He placed the deck of cards on the counter behind him, took me by the hair, and pulled my head down, to a ring set in the floor. He had never done this before. Usually I was tethered, kneeling, by a loop of chain slung about the ring and the linkage of my slave bracelets. But now I was fastened by the neck closely to the floor ring. "You may lie down, if you wish," he said. "Thank you, Master," I said. I did not ask the meaning of this departure from his normal procedure. It is done with us as masters please. We are slaves.

Amyntas then summoned an assistant to mind the shop, while he took, I suppose, the cards into the back, to work out the message. Doubtless he had a pertinent card sheet. I lay there for a time. Customers came and went. A chained slave is a common sight on Gor. There are many slave rings in public places, to which a slave might be fastened. This is a convenience to masters. Some of these places are in the shade, and furnished with a pan of water. My head was held close to the floor. I sensed that more than one fellow regarded me. One fellow brushed me twice on the left thigh with the side of his foot. "Not bad," he said. I pulled a little at the bracelets. I heard two men laugh. One approached me, and put one hand on my right ankle and his other hand on my left leg, just below the knee. I made a tiny, inadvertent noise. "Good," he said. I was afraid then that he had learned something about me, something of which I might even be unaware. After a few Ehn I was released from the ring, and stood. The sack was then, with its new signature knot, tied about my neck. "You are Allison, are you not?" he asked. "Yes, if it pleases Master," I said. This was the first time he had asked my name. "You are pretty," he said. "Thank you, Master," I said. I had the sense I was being appraised. "You are a barbarian, are you not?" he asked. "Yes, Master," I said. I had hardly spoken to him before. "Interesting," he said. "Master?" I asked. "Hurry home, Allison," he said. "Yes, Master," I said. He then gave me a sharp, stinging slap below the small of the back, and I cried out, and stumbled away, before I caught my step. Slaves may be so treated. We are not free women. Men enjoy treating us as they wish. They are men, and our masters. We have nothing to say about such things. I suppose that one might find them humiliating, but we do not do so. We do not object. It reminds us that we are slaves, and, of course, of sexual interest. I did not look back. I hurried away. Several things had been different this time. I did not understand why this might be. Perhaps there was no reason. Too, what kajira is foolish enough to question a master?

Chapter Fifty-One

Fruits and sauces in hand I was ascending the stairs to the domicile.

"Jane! Eve!" I had cried, delighted, for both were at the top of the stairs. Soon, how joyfully, embracing and kissing, did we greet one another!

I now understood the extensive preparations, the mysterious recent behavior of Lord Grendel, the excitement of the Lady Bina, the ka-la-na purchased, the flavorsome herbs, the bosk and tarsk, the early cooking. Entertainment this night was in the domicile. The Lady Delia, companion of Epicrates, had even assisted the Lady Bina with the menu, and the decorations. I had hoped that our guests would be who they were, as I knew both Astrinax and Lykos were in Ar, and, presumably, with them, two slaves.

Jane, Eve, and I busied ourselves with the final cooking, the readying of vegetables and salads, the arrangements of vessels and dishes, the setting of places. Never had I known them so happy, so radiant. As slaves, owned women, belongings, mere properties, it was theirs, choicelessly, to obey and submit, to strive to be pleasing to masters. In this, women, they found their happiness and fulfillment. They were not men. They were preciously, essentially, and perfectly female. How solicitous they were of their masters. How deferent they were, how graceful, how softly spoken, how eager, how warm, how feminine, how pleased to be owned, to belong, to be collared. And, as slaves, they knew themselves to be not only perfectly and helplessly owned, but to be desired as only a female slave can be desired,

desired with all the robust, possessive lust of a master, desired categorically, desired without concession, without quarter, without compromise.

"Would," said Astrinax, lifting his goblet, "that one other were here, one we know well, one with whom we shared many perils and hardships, the noble Desmond of Harfax!"

"Yes," said Lykos.

"Yes," said Lord Grendel.

"Yes!" said the Lady Bina.

A round of ka-la-na had been first served, with a wrapper of nuts.

Jane, Eve, and I were kneeling a bit behind and to the side the diners, Jane near Astrinax, Eve near Lykos, and I near the Lady Bina. The men sat cross-legged, before the small table, as is typical, while the Lady Bina knelt demurely, as is common with free women. In larger, richer domiciles, with more sumptuous appointments, there are sometimes supper couches, and the diners eat while reclining.

"May I take this opportunity," said Astrinax, "to render thanks to the noble Lady Bina for the gift of a lovely slave girl."

"And I," said Lykos, "for the gift of another."

Jane and Eve, though in collars, put down their heads and blushed with pleasure.

"It is nothing," said the Lady Bina. "We all owe one another much, and what is a mere collar girl?"

"Nonetheless," said Astrinax, "they are pleasant to have on one's chain."

"Quite," said Lykos.

"It might interest you to know," said the Lady Bina, "that I made a similar offer to Desmond of Harfax, twice."

"I did not know that," said Astrinax.

"Yes," said the Lady Bina, "I offered our pretty Allison twice to Desmond of Harfax, but he would not accept her."

"Interesting," said Astrinax.

"What is wrong with her?" asked Lykos.

"I do not know," said the Lady Bina.

"Perhaps she should have more meat on her," said Lykos.

"Perhaps her character left something to be desired," said Astrinax. "Long ago, she confessed to me, and to her then master, Menon, he with the restaurant, that she would steal a candy from another slave, if it might be done with impunity."

"I would not do so now, Master!" I said.

"Why not?" asked Astrinax.

"I have changed," I said. "I have been longer in the collar. I have learned much in the collar. A woman learns much in the collar. I am different now."

"I am sure you are," said the Lady Bina.

"What, then, is the difficulty," asked Lykos, "not enough meat?"

"I do not think so," said the Lady Bina. "I have seen enough fellows turn their head to look upon her."

I do not think I was all that aware of this, at least at the time, but I was pleased to hear it. I felt warm. A slave likes to know that men look upon her with pleasure. She is, after all, a slave.

"It seems," said the Lady Bina, "that he simply did not want her."

Tears sprang to my eyes.

"It is my understanding," said the Lady Bina, "that she is a likely collar slut."

"Mistress!" I protested.

"Is it not true?" asked the Lady Bina.

"I cannot help what I have become," I said. "I am collared!"

"You were always a collar slut, Allison," said Astrinax. "It is merely that you were not always in a collar."

"I do not understand why he would not accept her," said the Lady Bina.

"She is not hard on the eyes," said Lykos, regarding me. "She has nice legs, and ankles."

"Perhaps her hair," said the Lady Bina.

"It is muchly grown out now," said Lykos, "and there are many slaves whose hair is no longer."

"And it will grow, of course," said Astrinax.

"Stripped and shackled she would be block ready," said Lykos.

"What, then?" asked the Lady Bina.

"Let us hear from Allison," said Astrinax.

"I may speak?" I asked. I did have a general permission to speak in the domicile, but, under the circumstances, I thought it well to inquire.

"Do so," said the Lady Bina. "You must have views on the matter."

"I certainly do!" I cried.

"Speak," said the Lady Bina.

"Noble Desmond of Harfax" I said, "has never had the least interest in the slave, Allison. His supposed interest in her was feigned, in order to better spy on Lord Grendel, whom he suspected of subversive designs. The slave, Allison, was no more than a means to an end, a possible source of information, a pretext by means of which he might obtain a proximity to Lord Grendel, to which end he joined Lord Grendel's expedition to the Voltai. It is thus not surprising, given the denouement of the expedition, that he should cease to maintain the deceit of interest in a slave. She was no longer of value to him."

"You see him, then, as a liar, a fraud, a hypocrite?" asked Astrinax.

"Certainly, Master," I said. "And what may be less clear is that the slave, Allison, had been long aware of his transparent machinations. He fooled her not at all. She easily saw through his childish programs, and secretly despised him all the while. It thus came as no surprise to her that he would not contact the Lady Bina with respect to the slave, Allison, to bid for her, to accept her even as a gift, even to inquire after her. This is precisely what the slave anticipated."

"I see," said Lykos.

"Moreover," I said, "Desmond of Harfax is despicable, so shameless that he has not even acknowledged his duplicity to his fellows. He is a petty, sly, crass fellow who, without leave, without gratitude, has slipped away somewhere, with no word of thanks, no token of the least gratitude, to those with whom he shared miseries and perils, those without whom he may well have perished unnoted in the Voltai. He has not even had the dignity, and kindness, the courtesy and thoughtfulness, to attend this dinner. I assure you, it is a great joy to me that he would not accept me, even as a gift. Muchly do I rejoice in my good fortune. Let it be known to all that that pleases me. It is my greatest fear that I might be owned by him. I would strive to be the worst possible slave to him! I despise the shameless, ungrateful, hypocrite, and fraud, Desmond of Harfax! I loathe him, I hate him! He is thief of trust, a promoter of pretense. He is conniving, base, and worthless! He is a monster! He is ignoble, and without honor."

"Thank you, Allison," said the Lady Bina, glancing briefly toward the door to her sleeping chamber.

"I did not think him such a scoundrel," said Astrinax.

"Nor I," said Lykos.

I shrugged, and looked down.

"Let us address ourselves to our feast," said Astrinax.

Jane and Eve made to rise to their feet, to serve.

"Hold," said the Lady Bina, smiling. "Allison has recently brought a package from the shop of Amyntas. Let us see what it contains."

Lord Grendel produced the small sack from a pouch at his harnessing, and the Lady Bina undid the knot. "It is the signature knot of Amyntas," she said. "Yes," she said, "it is a deck of cards, all doubtless in proper order." She placed the sack on the table, beside her plate. Lord Grendel then, also from his pouch, handed her a folded sheet of paper, which the Lady Bina opened. "Allison will help us," she said. "She is illiterate, of course, but she recognizes cards by the designs, and she is quite adept at arranging them."

"Should we not eat?" I said.

"Let us first see what we have here," said the Lady Bina.

She then began to read the list of cards from the card sheet, and, as the deck was in order, the cards easily located, I quickly put the cards in the order called for by the card sheet.

"Good," said the Lady Bina. "Here is the message."

Astrinax and Lykos were smiling, which did not make me easy.

Moreover, I remembered the differences attendant on my last visit to the shop of Amyntas, at which visit I had received the sack just opened.

This recollection did little to assuage my lack of ease.

"Oh, look!" said the Lady Bina, brightly. "There is something additional in the sack." She drew forth from the sack two coins. They were clearly not copper, but silver.

"Two," said Astrinax.

Lykos looked at me. "That seems about right," he said.

"Here is the message, Allison," said the Lady Bina, holding one side of the deck toward me. "It is simple, it is short, it is in clear Gorean. Would you like to try to read it?"

"I cannot read, Mistress," I said.

"It has to do with you," she said.

"I cannot read, Mistress," I said.

"Astrinax?" said the Lady Bina, handing the deck to him.

"'As agreed,'" read Astrinax, "'here are two silver tarsks, for full and clear title to the barbarian slave currently known as Allison, the property of the Lady Bina of Ar, resident in the house of Epicrates, pottery merchant, of Ar.'"

"Mistress?" I said.

"You have been sold, Allison," said the Lady Bina.

"To Amyntas, of Ar?" I said.

"Not at all," she said.

"To whom then, Mistress?" I said.

"It is written there, clearly," said the Lady Bina.

"To whom, Mistress?" I begged.

The Lady Bina looked to Astrinax.

"To Desmond of Harfax," he said.

I looked about, wildly, from face to face.

"Sold?" I said.

"He did not want you as a gift," said the Lady Bina. "He wanted you to know that you were bought and paid for as the animal, the property, you are. He thought that would help you to better understand that you are a slave, that you not only could be bought and paid for, but that you were bought and paid for. Coins have changed hands and now you are his."

"He has bought me?" I said.

"Yes," she said.

"I have been purchased?" I said.

"As might be a tarsk," she said, "or any other form of animal."

"He now owns me?"

"Yes," she said.

"Oh, Mistress!" I cried, elated.

"Surely you are plunged into despair," said Astrinax.

"Oh, please, please, dear Lady, and dear Masters," I said, suddenly, frightened, plaintively, "do not tell my master how I spoke this evening, do not tell him what I said!"

"We will not say a word to him," said the Lady Bina.

"Not a word," said Astrinax.

"Not a word," said Lykos.

"Thank you, Lady," I breathed, "thank you, Masters!"

"It will not be necessary," said the Lady Bina. "He has heard every word."

I looked toward the door of her sleeping chamber. In the threshold stood Desmond of Harfax.

"Master!" I cried, and threw myself to my belly before him, crying out in joy. I tried to press my lips, fervently, again and again, those of a slave, his slave, to his boot-like sandals, but I could not do so. He drew back. "Strip," he said. I knelt up and slipped the tunic over my head, putting it to the side. "Master!" I said. But then he turned me about, and thrust me down, to my belly. My wrists were jerked behind my back, and bound together. In a moment my ankles had been crossed, and lashed, the one to the other, closely. "Please, Master!" I said. "Forgive me! I did not mean what I said! I love you, my Master! In my heart, though muchly resisting, I knew myself your slave, even from the Sul Market, long ago! And did you not look down upon me, kneeling at your feet, and know that I was your slave?"

But then I could speak no more, for the large leather ball, with its inserted, buckled strap, which had been forced into my mouth. Then it was secured in place, the strap pulled back, and buckled shut, tightly, behind the back of my neck. No longer might I utter intelligible sounds. Such were not now permitted to me. I whimpered, but his hand was placed in my hair, and twisted, and I winced, and knew I was to be silent.

He then knelt across my body. I was conscious of a flash of metal before my eyes, and then I felt the placement of a collar about my neck. It fit, closely. There was a clear, decisive snap, and it had been locked on me. I still wore the collar, as well, of the Lady Bina. "Key," said Desmond of Harfax, extending his hand to the side. The Lady Bina placed the key of her collar into the palm of his hand. In a moment that collar, which remained her property, as I had been, had been removed. Desmond of Harfax then adjusted the new collar, his collar, on the neck of his newly purchased slave, Allison, a barbarian. At no time had she been without a collar, even in the brief moment of a transition between collars.

"What are you going to do with her?" asked Astrinax.

"What I please," said Desmond of Harfax.

"You heard what she said?" asked Lykos.

"Every word," said Desmond of Harfax.

"You were badly bespoken," said Astrinax.

"Had a free man spoken so," said Lykos, "it would doubtless be daggers on the high bridges."

"Axes outside the great gate, swords at dawn, on the Plaza of Tarns," suggested Astrinax.

"A free woman, however," said the Lady Bina, "might utter such calumnies with impunity."

"Yes," said Lykos, "unless she were seized, stripped, and collared."

"But this is a slave," said Astrinax.

"She was insufficiently deferent," said Lykos, "and she spoke ill of a free man."

"Feed her alive to sleen," said Astrinax.

"Too quick," said Lykos.

"Throw her into a pit of osts," suggested Astrinax.

"Too quick," said Lykos.

"A pool of eels?" said Astrinax.

"Better," said Lykos.

"There are many excellent possibilities," said Astrinax. "A dark cell filled with hungry urts, a garden of leech plants, smearing her with honey and staking her out for insects, ants, jards, or such."

I whimpered, on the floor, on my belly, nude, gagged, bound hand and foot. I squirmed, utterly helpless. I had no hope of freeing myself. I had been bound by a Gorean male. My fate was wholly in the hands of others. How could I sue for mercy? How could I perform the desperate placatory behaviors which I had learned in the house of Tenalion, behaviors which might mean the difference of life or death for a slave?

"She cannot plead for mercy, Mistress and Masters," said Jane. "Permit us to plead for her! Show her mercy!"

"I am sure she did not mean what she said," said Eve. "She

spoke in misery and unhappiness. She was distraught. She thought herself rejected, and scorned!"

"She is a slave," said Astrinax. "It is perfectly acceptable for slaves to be rejected and scorned."

"Let them learn that they are slaves," said Lykos.

"Show her mercy!" begged Jane.

"Please, please, Mistress and Masters, be merciful!" said Eve.

"She has not been fully pleasing," said Astrinax sternly.

Jane and Eve regarded him, frightened. Eve regarded Lykos. She touched her collar. Her fingers trembled.

"Now be silent," said Astrinax.

"Yes, Master," said Jane.

"Yes, Master," whispered Eve.

"Now, Jane and Eve," said the Lady Bina, "let us be up, and about, and serve. Fetch fruit and salads. Warm the main dishes. Bring more ka-la-na."

"Yes, Mistress," said Jane and Eve.

"And later," said the Lady Bina, "remove your tunics and serve the ka-la-na to your masters, as befits female slaves. I understand that that is a beautiful ceremony, and afterwards, on mats I will provide, you may serve your masters the ka-la-na of beauty, of which I have heard."

"Here, Mistress?" asked Jane.

"Yes," she said.

"Yes, Mistress," said Jane and Eve.

"Let us feast," said Astrinax.

"By all means," said Lykos.

Desmond of Harfax reached down, took my bound, right ankle, and dragged me into the sleeping chamber of the Lady Bina. There he shackled my left ankle to a floor ring, and returned to the main room to join the feasters. For Ahn, until dawn, I listened to the conversation, the recollections, the pleasantries, the merriment, in the next room. Then it was quiet outside the room, and, after a bit, after struggling a little, futilely, and hearing the light sound of the chain on the floor, which held me to the ring, I fell asleep. I did not know what would be done with me. Knowing that Desmond of Harfax was a decent and honorable man, though he might be a fearsome and demanding master, I was not afraid that I would be fed to sleen, cast to leech plants, or such. I was afraid that I might not be kept, that I might be given away, or sold. I knew I had not been pleasing, and it is a frightening and terrible thing for a slave not to be pleasing to her master. I did not awaken for several Ahn, because it was late morning, or early afternoon, when I stirred, and, as my consciousness and remembrance returned, found myself as I had been before, a bound slave. I think that Astrinax and Lykos, and their slaves, had departed. I sensed that Lord Grendel was outside, on the roof, where he commonly slept. The Lady Bina was in the room, on her couch, asleep.

Turning a little, I saw Master Desmond in the threshold.

I struggled to a kneeling position, and put my head down to the floor.

He pulled my head up, by the hair, not hurting me, but as a master might do such a thing. He then unbuckled the gag, and pulled the leather ball from my mouth. I was afraid to speak, and so remained silent. He unbound my ankles, and thrust a wastes bucket to me, and then exited the room. Gratefully I relieved myself. I then edged the bucket away, and remained kneeling, but up, as he had left me, my hands tied behind my back, my left ankle chained to the ring. I kept my knees closely together. When he reentered, I lowered my head. He was bearing a goblet of water, and he helped me drink from it. He then left the room again and, when he returned, he had some meat and bread, which he fed to me by hand. I looked up at him, grateful for his kindness. I wondered if he could read the gratitude, the hope, and tenderness, and the fear, in the eyes of a slave. I still did not dare to speak.

"Stand," he said, coldly.

Frightened, I stood. He then put my wrists in slave bracelets, and then untied the binding fiber with which I had been hitherto secured. I gathered we were going into the streets. Binding fiber can be cut with a knife. It, and that which had bound my ankles, he returned to his pouch. Then, from the pouch he produced a leash and collar. I would then be leashed and collared in the streets. I saw nothing of a tunic or camisk, or ta-teera, or slave strip, and so I understood I was to be marched naked through the streets on a leash, as a low slave or punished slave. How amused would be other slaves, to see me so. To be sure, I was a barbarian.

Lastly, as I was now braceleted and leashed, he freed me of the shackle on my left ankle.

"Precede me," he said.

"Yes, Master," I said.

Chapter Fifty-Two

I cried out, in misery.

I was tied on my knees, my hands before me, fastened to the ring, in the small, bright courtyard, behind a house on Clive, that in which Desmond of Harfax had rented a room.

The lash fell again.

"Know that you are a slave," said Desmond of Harfax.

Again the lash fell.

"Yes, Master," I wept, "I know I am a slave! I am whipped! I am whipped! I am whipped as the slave I am! I am a slave, a slave!"

"And who whips you?" he asked.

"He who owns me!" I cried. "Desmond of Harfax!"

He then gave me another stroke.

"Yes, Master!" I wept. How deeply, and well, I then understood the word 'Master'!

I was a slave, and he was my master.

He then left me with my thoughts, and the pain.

* * * *

"Please whip me, Master," I had said.

"Why?" he had asked.

"That I may know myself a slave," I said, "and yours."

"The whip hurts," he said.

"No one is more aware of that than I," I said.

"Why then would you be whipped?" he asked.

"That I may know myself a slave," I had said, "and yours."

"You will have no doubt about that," he said.

"Yes, Master," I had said.

* * * *

After some Ehn he returned.

"Please do not whip me any more!" I said.

"You are content?" he said.

"Yes, yes!" I said.

"You do not wish to be whipped further?" he said.

"No, no, Master!" I wept.

"I see," he said.

"Please do not whip me any more!" I begged.

"It hurts does it not?" he said.

"Yes, Master!" I said.

"But you are now," he said, "well aware that you are a slave, and my slave."

"Yes, Master!" I said. "It is done. No more, please! Do not whip me further! I beg it!"

"This is the whip," he said, holding it before me.

I shuddered in the bonds. "I fear it," I said, "the very sight of it."

"You may kiss it," he said.

I kissed the whip, fervently.

"Perhaps," he said, "you will try to be a good slave."

"I will strive to be a good slave," I said.

"You have been whipped," he said.

"Yes, Master," I wept.

"You must expect such things if you are not fully pleasing," he said.

"I will strive to be fully pleasing!"

"Who will strive to be fully pleasing?" he asked.

"Allison will strive to be fully pleasing," I said.

"Do you think you have been fully pleasing?" he asked.

"I fear not," I said.

"As I recall," he said, "you were long aware of my transparent machinations, my childish programs, and such?"

"Please forgive the foolish words of a foolish slave," I said.

"And you secretly despised me all the while?" he said.

He then again put the whip to my lips, again I kissed it, fervently. "No, Master!" I said.

"More lingeringly," he said. "And lick it, devotedly, as the pretty little slut and slave beast you are."

"Yes, Master," I said.

"And if you came into my power," he said, "you would strive to be the worst possible slave to me?"

"No, Master," I said. "I would strive to be the best possible slave to you, a slave of slaves to you!"

"And there was much else," he said. "Was I not to be petty, sly, crass, duplicitous, dishonorable, ignoble, a hypocrite, a fraud, a monster, and such?"

"I did not speak, Master," I said. "It was my rage, my disappointment, my loneliness, my sense of loss, my thought of being unwanted, of being ignored and abandoned, such things which spoke."

"Perhaps," he said, "you should be again whipped, and richly whipped."

"Please no, Master," I said.

"You are afraid, are you not?" he asked.

"Yes, Master," I said.

"Why?" he asked.

"Because I am a slave," I said. "I have felt the whip. I know what it is like. I shall do my best to be pleasing to my master."

He then undid the flat, narrow leather straps which had bound my wrists to the ring.

I then turned about, gratefully, to kneel before him. It was my hope he might later permit me clothing. I would do my best to be worthy of a garment, be it only a slave strip.

He was looking upon me.

"Master?" I said.

"I find you of slave interest," he said.

"A slave is pleased," I said.

There were trees, and grass, in the small courtyard, and flowers, mostly talenders, and dinas, some veminium. A tiled walk wound its way through the vegetation. Flowering shrubbery was about. Here and there, there were small, concealed nooks in the garden. In one corner, there was a small reservoir, with a slatted wooden lid. The day was warm. A light wind rustled through the leaves overhead. The courtyard, like most Gorean courtyards, was rather small. It backed the domicile, which had four floors. At the rear of the courtyard was a small, opaque, wooden gate. Two of its walls were common walls with adjoining domiciles. The back wall was adjacent to an alley, access to which was provided by the rear gate.

I sensed I was being looked upon as one looks upon what I was, a slave. I did not object. We are not free women.

How warm, and pleasurable, it is to be looked upon as an object, one which is owned by a master.

We are not free women.

"May I speak?" I asked.

"Yes," he said.

"Where has Master been, for so many weeks?" I asked.

"About," he said, "even to Port Kar."

"But Master did not forget a slave," I said.

"Some slaves," he said, "are hard to forget."

"A slave is pleased," I said.

"I should get rid of her," he said. "I should sell her."

"Please do not do so," I said.

"There is something about you," he said, "which is of interest to me."

"Of slave interest," I said.

"Of course," he said.

"Doubtless a slave's body," I said. On Gor my body had been freshened, trimmed, toned, vitalized, and turned into an instrument for a man's pleasure.

"It is more than that," he said. "Such things may be purchased off any block."

"What then?" I asked.

"I do not know," he said.

"Whatever it is," I said, "it is now in Master's collar." I was well aware that it is the whole slave which is owned, every strand of hair, every drop of blood, every fear, every hope, every tremor, every feeling, every thought.

"You are, of course, a barbarian," he said.

"And I cannot even read," I said.

"And you will be kept that way," he said.

"As Master pleases," I said.

I kept my knees closely together. It was in this fashion that I had been accustomed, over the past months, to kneel.

"Master did not forget me," I said.

"No," he said.

I was pleased to see that he was folding the five blades of the slave whip about the staff, which might easily accommodate a two-handed grip.

"I think Master cares for me," I said.

"Do not be foolish," he said.

"I understand that Master finds me of interest," I said.

"Of slave interest," he said.

"Perhaps a slave might be freed," I suggested.

"I am not a fool," he said.

There is a saying, of course, that only a fool frees a slave girl. I wonder if it is not true. What man truly, honestly, does not want a slave?

"Perhaps Master finds me of companion interest," I said.

"You are a barbarian," he said.

"Even so," I said.

He walked about me, a bit, and then, again, stood before me.

"You are nicely marked, and collared," he said.

"Will you not free me?" I asked.

"No," he said.

I uneasily noted that he was slowly, thoughtfully, unwrapping the blades of the slave whip.

"Master?" I said.

I saw him shake loose the blades of the whip, and they dangled. I could see the shadow of the blades on the ground.

"But I may sell you," he said.

"Please do not," I said.

"Do you wish to be freed?" he asked.

"I have learned on Gor what I suspected on Earth," I said. "I am a slave. I need a master."

"Any man will do," he said.

"Yes," I said. "Any man will do. I am such as can be owned, and mastered. But every slave hopes for the master of her secret dreams, the master of her heart, he for whose collar her throat was bred for millennia."

"And every master," he said, "for she who was born to wear his collar."

"A slave," I said, "wants to be owned, to belong, to love, to serve, to be helpless, to be mastered, to be subject to discipline, to be dominated without qualification, concession, or compromise, to be treated as the female she is, to be overwhelmed, taught, controlled, and commanded. What woman wants to relate to a man by whom she is not so wanted, wanted with such force and power, with such demand and uncompromising will, with such desire, with such lust, that nothing less than her absolute possession will satisfy him? The master will be satisfied with nothing less than his slave, and the slave with nothing less than her master."

"Do you expect me to be easy with you?" he asked.

"No, Master," I said.

"You understand clearly, do you not," he asked, "that you have been bought, that you have been purchased?"

"Yes, Master," I said.

"And for a normal price," he said, "one which might typically take one such as you off the block?"

"Yes, Master," I said.

"Do you realize how you have tortured me these many months?" he asked.

"Perhaps I have been tortured, as well," I said.

"Even before the Sul Market," he said, "I saw you, and watched you, conjectured your lineaments beneath your tunic, considered the motion of your body as you walked, observed the carriage of your body, the attitude of your head, those of a trained slave, the nice encirclement of a band of metal on your neck."

I was silent.

"I wanted you," he said. "How could I sleep, how could I eat? But, oh yes, too, I knew of the monster. And I knew there were other such things. I had heard of sky vessels, not those of Priest-Kings. Masses of half-melted, disrupted metal had been found, though sometimes quickly buried or borne away. In the air, occasionally, were the hints of rumors. I learned of others, others also suspecting dangers, dangers undreamt of by most. Contacts were made. Should investigations not be initiated? Should some surveillance, of a type, where possible, not be attempted? Were such suspicions foolish? One does not suspect sleen and larls of intrigue and infamy. Was there peril here, at all? And, if so, of what dimension? And how might it be countered, if at all? So, discovering the strange pet, or guard, of the Lady Bina, a beast whose presence had been noted by several, one actually about in the streets of Ar, I sought to learn its nature, its plans and projects, if any, its relation to others, and such. I soon learned that it was rational, and could communicate in Gorean, by means of a translator. And later I learned it might, when it wished, dispense with the translator. Soon I discovered that the Lady Bina, who seemed somehow associated with the beast, owned a barbarian slave, the very one whose flanks and carriage had tormented me. I confronted them in the Sul Market, and knelt the slave, she then half-naked. I looked down upon her and knew that I must have her in my collar. I must make her mine! I must own her! But what was her relationship to the Lady Bina and the monster? Surely she was a shapely thrall, but what else? I feared she might be in some terrible danger."

"Master was solicitous for the welfare of a slave?" I asked.

"Merely for the integrity and welfare of a pleasant set of curves," he said.

"I see," I said.

"Such have value," he said.

"I see," I said.

"They sell well," he said.

"Of course," I said.

"But I thought it possible, as well," he said, "that the shapely slut might be less innocent, not only that she might be implicated, but that she might be a cognizant villainess, a knowing part of some nefarious scheme. And for such things there are serious consequences, even for a slave."

"Lord Grendel," I said, "meant no harm to men, or the world."

"I did not know that," he said. "And I learned that he contemplated a mysterious trip to the Voltai."

"On behalf of a blinded beast," I said, "that he might succor him, and return him to his fellows."

"More was involved in the Voltai," said Desmond of Harfax.

"The blinded Kur knew that," I said. "Lord Grendel, and the others, did not."

"It was my intention," he said, "to join, or somehow follow, this expedition, that I might keep it under surveillance. Accordingly, learning that it was being outfitted and organized by Astrinax, I petitioned service, as a Teamster."

"You were accepted," I said.

"It was not difficult," he said. "Few in Ar were interested in hazarding the perils of the Voltai, particularly in the late summer or fall, and fewer yet when the nature of the expedition, its purpose, its destination, its length, and its time of return, seemed not only obscure, but secret. You may remember that the expedition was still short of guardsmen when it reached Venna."

"Trachinos and Akesinos were placed in fee," I said.

"Bandits," he said, "whose intention was despoliation."

"You were Teamster for the slave wagon," I said.

"I permitted Astrinax to know that the curves of a slave were of interest to me," he said. "He was accommodating."

"I see," I said.

"Your ankles," he said, "which are attractively slender, looked well shackled to the central bar."

"I was given into your charge by the Lady Bina," I said.

"That was natural," he said, "as I was driving the slave wagon."

"It seems things worked out rather well for you," I said.

"Quite," he said. "I was well placed to monitor the expedition and, at the same time, to find myself in the vicinity of a particular slave."

"Who was placed in your keeping," I said.

"Yes," he said.

"But you never put her to your pleasure," I said.

"No," he said.

"Honor?" I said.

"Certainly," he said, "I did not own her. Her keeping was mine, not her use."

"But you came to understand, I trust," I said, "that she was not some sort of traitress to a species or world, a cognizant conspirator, a cooperating, malevolent, unscrupulous villainess?"

"That sort of thing would have serious consequences," he

said, "for a free woman, one supposes impalement, and, for a
slave, as she is a beast, presumably something like heavy chains
and drawing ore carts in the mines."

"I am pleased that you then understood her to be innocent,"
I said.

"In any event," he said, "I no longer feared that she might be
knowingly implicated in some planetary felony, some broadcast
treason, some subversive, global malefaction."

"Good," I said.

"I found her too simple, too petty, too shallow, too trivial, for
such things," he said. "She would lack the depth, the force, the
power, for such calculations, such intrigues, and risks."

"I see," I said.

"She was only a meaningless, worthless little barbarian collar
slut," he said. "What conspirators would entrust matters of
import to one such as she?"

"Indeed," I said, annoyed.

"Only a self-centered, simple, shallow, naive little brute," he
said, "a trivial, selfish little beast, of inferior character, who
would steal a candy from a sister slave, if it might be done with
impunity."

"You listened to Astrinax," I said.

"He made clear to me what you were, in that pretty collar,"
he said.

"I am different now," I said.

"How I wanted to take you in my arms," he said, "and teach
you what it was to be a slave!"

"But you did not do so!" I said.

"Can you imagine the torture," he said, "what it was to be
with you, each day, day in and day out, Ahn by Ahn, so close,
wanting to get my hands on you, wanting to seize you, and
ravish you, again and again, to take your meaningless pettiness
in hand, and make it cry out, and moan, and leap spasmodically,
helplessly, in my arms, gasping, and begging for more, fearing
only that I might, for my amusement, too soon desist in the
depredations to which your body was subjected."

"It was not only you who were tortured," I said. "You speak of
torment! What do you know of torment? What do you know of
a woman's slave fires, once men have kindled them, and forced

them to burn? Can you imagine what it is to feel such things, not just in one's belly, but throughout one's helpless slave's body? We cannot seize and command a master! We cannot exceed the length of our chains! We can only beg! And will men be kind to us, or not? It is up to them and not us, for we are slaves! Can you imagine what it was to be naked in a slave wagon, shackled within reach of you? Can you understand what it is to serve a master, to cook for him, to serve him food, to fetch and carry for him, and not be touched? Can you understand what it is for a woman to wear a man's bonds, and not be exploited at his whim? Can you imagine what it is to be half stripped, and collared, only a slave, readied by an entire society for service and sex, and be ignored? Can you imagine what it is to be clad only in a tunic, or a camisk, as in the Cave, near one to whom you would beg to belong, and not be so much as touched?"

"It seems," said he, "that we have tortured one another."

"Yes, Master," I said.

"If you are telling the truth," he said.

"Master?" I said.

"You do not think I trust you, do you?" he asked.

"It would be my hope that a Master might trust his slave," I said. "Surely she would be punished, if found untrustworthy."

"And severely," he said.

"Yes, Master," I said.

He looked away, angrily. I could not see his face.

"Slaves are not free women," he said. "Slaves are meaningless. Why should one care for them?"

"Men are sometimes fond of their possessions," I said.

I knew that some men, while professing to despise their slaves, scoffing at the very thought that they might find them of interest, would risk their lives for them, even die for them. How precious then must be a mere collar slut, marketable goods, to some men! Who then is slave and who is master? It becomes clear, of course, when the whip is removed from its peg.

One might risk one's life or die for a free woman because she is free, or because a Home Stone is shared, or because it is expected, or because it is thought to be a duty, or a matter of honor, but why might one risk one's life for, or die for, a slave?

What could be the reason?

She is no more than her master's beast. She strives selflessly to serve her master. She is submitted. She is worked. She is owned. She is under discipline. She is dominated, and as a slave is dominated. She strives to be found pleasing. She is needful. Well she knows the restlessness and agony of slave fires, imposed on her by men. She is ready on her chain. She knows herself no more than his meaningless, begging pleasure object. She is an eager and subservient passion beast.

How utterly different is the exalted, noble, proud free woman, suspicious and demanding, bargaining and calculating, insisting on her hundred rights, jealous of a thousand prerogatives!

How strange then that men would be willing to risk their lives, even die, for the slave, no more than a collared chattel.

"Why should a man care for you, not that one does?" he asked.

"I do not know," I said.

He turned about, and I lowered my head, unwilling to meet his eyes.

"Perhaps as an investment," he said. "One might improve you, with chain training, whip training, slave dance, and such, and then sell you for a profit."

"Perhaps, Master," I said.

"You are poor stuff," he said.

I looked up.

"Might I not now bring a good price on the block?" I asked.

"That would be easy enough to see," he said.

"Please do not do so," I said.

"Poor meaningless stuff," he said, looking down upon me.

"You bought me," I said.

"Yes," he said, "I bought you."

"I know you had the means to buy others, Master," I said. "Why then did you not buy them?"

"Do you wish to be beaten?" he asked.

"No, Master," I said.

"I do not know why," he said. "The pens are filled with slaves, well worth collaring, and training to one's taste."

"Yet Master did not forget me," I said.

"You are shoddy, inferior, meaningless merchandise."

"Perhaps less so now than before," I said.

"Speak," he said.

"I remain unimportant, and meaningless, of course, as I am a slave, Master," I said, "but I think I am different now from what I was, perhaps a little better, perhaps a bit more worth owning. Perhaps I am not now so shallow, so sly, so cunning, so petty, so selfish, so trivial, so worthless, as I once was. I have learned much in the collar. In the collar a slave is well taught. I want now to be worthy of my collar. It is a gift bestowed upon me by a man. I want now to be pleasing to my Master. I would hope to be worthy of wearing his collar, not only in service, devotion, and helpless passion, but in character. I desperately want him to approve of me. I will try to be a slave who is worthy of his ownership!"

"How clever you are," he said.

"Master?" I said.

"Do you think I do not know you?" he asked. "From Ar, from the wagons, from the Voltai, from the small feast in the domicile of Epicrates?"

"I do not understand," I said.

"You are a lying little slut," he said.

"No, Master!" I said.

I wondered how much this had to do with me, and how much it had to do with him. Was he fighting his own feelings? Might that be? Was he afraid of himself, and his feelings, standing before one who was no more than a kneeling, helpless, collared, branded animal? Did he now fear that he might care for a mere slave?

How absurd!

What had he to fear? The collar was on my neck, and his was the whip.

"I have waited a long time to own you," he said.

"And have I not waited a long time to be owned?" I said.

I looked up at him, and was suddenly afraid.

How bright his eyes were, how tense his body!

Might not a starving larl so gaze upon a tethered tabuk doe, a hungry sleen upon a penned verr?

In the streets of Ar I had once seen a leashed slave being dragged running and stumbling, weeping, toward a domicile, but the master found himself unable to wait, and she was thrown to the paving stones of the street, there to be publicly and rudely ravished. I had turned aside, and hurried away, but had been stirred.

I had heard, too, of purchases made off the block which were unable even to reach the holding rings or slave cages, but were enjoyed in the very aisles of the market.

I was afraid but stirred, too, as only a slave can be stirred, for she knows herself helpless and choiceless, that it will be done with her as masters will. She is without recourse.

Gorean men, I knew, had not been culturally reduced, societally diminished, confused, crippled, taught to mistrust themselves, to doubt themselves, to castigate themselves for the simplest and most natural feelings and desires, to misinterpret and fear them, not taught to betray themselves and their manhood. As well, for the purposes of the deficient, insane, or eccentric, might one be taught the wrongness of breathing, of eyesight, of the circulating of blood, the pumping of a living heart?

It had not occurred to Gorean men, I knew, to denounce manhood, no more than to proclaim it. They just lived it, as they were men. And without men, how could there be women?

How frightening it can be to be a slave, but, too, how can one feel more female?

I looked up at him, and was frightened.

How I sensed that I was seen!

"Master?" I said.

How he was looking upon me!

He did think me unworthy, still, I realized, a liar, a would-be thief, a deceitful, self-centered, manipulative, worthless, little hypocrite.

That was how he saw me!

Perhaps I had been such, more so on Earth than here, but I did not think I was such now.

"No, Master," I whispered, shaking my head. "No, Master."

Of course, he was looking upon me as a purchasable chattel, for that is what I was, but, too, he seemed to see me now not as a mere chattel, but as a particularly worthless one, one suitably despised, yet one that he found, despite himself, and perhaps against his best judgment, one of interest, of slave interest, of keen slave interest.

I sensed he was angry with himself.

He was perhaps furious with himself, to find himself attracted to me. Did he despise himself for this? Could he not help himself? Was I, I wondered, as irresistible to him, as he was to me?

Could that be?

I was beneath his gaze.

I was naked before him, and kneeling.

I fear I trembled.

I knew myself desired, and not as a free woman might be desired, in all her lofty, precious, august dignity, encircled with customs, codes, traditions, conventions, proprieties, and rights, but as a slave is desired, with all the raw, uncompromising, unmitigated lust with which a slave is desired, a rightless animal whose obedience is to be instantaneous and unquestioning, who hopes to be pleasing, who hopes to serve the master, whose passion is to be unqualified and unrestrained, who exists, as a belonging, an owned female, to give him inordinate pleasures.

"You are a despicable, vain, pretentious, tormenting little she-sleen," he said, "but, little she-sleen, your time of tormenting is now over."

"I do not understand," I said.

"You have played your games enough," he said.

"I do not understand," I said.

"Get your knees apart," he snarled.

"Master?" I said.

"Now," he said.

"Yes, Master," I said.

"Now," he said, "that is the way you should be."

Yes, I thought to myself, this is how I should be, and how I want to be. On Earth I had been a slave, not collared. I had been exploitative, selfish, shallow, petty, and nasty. Then, suitably enough, appropriately enough, I was brought to Gor and must wear the collar for which I was born.

"I am in the position of a slave, a pleasure slave," I said, "before my Master."

"You were trained as a pleasure slave, were you not?" he asked.

"Yes, Master," I said, "in the house of Tenalion, in Ar."

"Stand," he said, "face away from me, put your hands behind your back."

I did so, and was braceleted.

He then took me by the hair, forced my head down to his hip and then, I in leading position, he drew me beside him deeper into the courtyard, and then, in a concealed place, on the thick, soft, flowing grass, so rich and deep, so living, threw me to his feet.

I looked up at him.

I jerked a little at the bracelets.

"Here, Master?" I said.

"I am tired of being tortured," he said. "You may be worthless, but you are an interesting piece of meat, on which I intend to feast."

Then he took me in his arms, and I felt ecstasy.

* * * *

"Yes, yes, Master!" I cried out, a third time.

"Please free my hands!" I begged.

"No," he said.

* * * *

Later, my hands freed, I clung to him, under the moons of Gor. Later he let me creep to his thigh. Still later, he lifted me in his arms, almost as though I might be free, and he carried me into the domicile, and up to his room. There he lit a lamp, and chained me by an ankle, to the ring at the foot of his couch. I gathered I would be slept there, chained at his feet.

"Thank you, Master," I wept.

In the collar I had found my fulfillment, my joy, and my redemption.

"Oh, please, Master, again," I begged.

He then drew me to him, again.

* * * *

"Surely I am not to be back-braceleted again?" I said.

Then my wrists were again braceleted behind my back.

"On the furs," he said. "Kneel, get your head down!"

"Yes, Master," I said.

His hands were then on me.

I jerked at the bracelets, but was helpless within them.

"Ohh," I cried, softly. "Oh! Oh! Yes, Master, yes!"

* * * *

"Master will not sell me, will he?" I said, frightened.

"How good are you?" he asked.

"Surely Master has formed some sense of my possible value," I said.

"We shall see," he said.

"Oh!" I cried.

* * * *

"Are you suitably humbled?" he asked.

"I have been long humbled," I said. "I was humbled as soon as I was collared. A slave is not permitted pride."

"Still," he said, "I occasionally felt you were a bit pretentious."

"It is hard to be pretentious," I said, "when one is muchly bared, in a slave tunic."

"I occasionally thought you an arrogant little slut," he said, "when you were in my keeping, you knowing that you would not be touched."

"I was angry," I said.

"You wanted to be touched," he said.

"Of course," I said.

"You were a tempting little tasta," he said.

"Perhaps I taunted you a little, a subtle movement, a way of turning, a glance over my shoulder, a smile."

"I was well aware of such things," he said.

"I hoped you would be," I said.

"It is one thing for a free woman to do such things," he said. "It is quite another for a slave."

"I do not think so," I said.

"A slave might be simply taken in hand," he said.

"Of course," I said.

"You are seductive little brutes," he said.

"We are slaves," I said.

"Slaves want to be touched," he said.

"Of course," I said. "Oh!" I said, for I was touched, and as a slave might be touched.

How helpless we are!

"It is pleasant to touch you," he said.

"I assure you," I said, "I am now well touched."

"It is a beginning," he said.

"You will not sell me, will you?"

"Now that you have been reduced, shattered, and well used, again and again, and have cried out, piteously, for more, and more, again, and again," he said, "it would be amusing to take you to the market, and rid myself of you."

"It may be done with me," I said, "as Master pleases, for I am a slave."

"What would you like?" he asked.

"Keep me in your collar," I begged. "I have been yours, even from the Sul Market!"

"Do you think you might be a good slave?" he asked.

"I will try my best, Master!" I said.

"Very well," he said. "Please me, and as the slave you are."

"Yes, Master," I said, gratefully.

* * * *

"On your world," he said, "I would suppose you were literate."

"Yes, Master," I said.

"And you had station and resources, were refined, and educated, might come and go as you pleased, muchly had your way, were elegantly clothed and shod, and such?" he said.

"Yes, Master," I said.

"And here you are a naked slave," he said.

"It is my hope," I said, "that my Master, if I prove sufficiently pleasing, may grant me a garment."

"A rag, or such," he said, "provided, of course, that you are fully pleasing."

"Yes, Master," I said.

I had sensed, on Earth, that I should be the slave of men such as those of Gor, but I had not anticipated my transposition to Gor, and my marketing.

"Here," he said, "you are illiterate."

"I cannot even read my collar," I said.

"You do not need to read it," he said, "as long as you know what it says."

"May I ask what it says?" I asked.

"It says," he said, "'I belong to Desmond of Harfax.'"

"I hope to please him," I said.

It is a common way, amongst slave girls, when inquiring another girl's master, to ask, "Who whips you?" I would then answer, "Desmond of Harfax," or "My master is Desmond of Harfax." To be sure, the girl may never have felt the whip, at all. If a girl is pleasing she would be seldom, if ever, whipped. And, naturally, we try our best to be pleasing and hope to be found pleasing. It is in our best interest to be found pleasing. We are not free women. We are slaves. To be sure, whereas one may surely hope to be found pleasing because one fears the whip, I think it is common, particularly after one has been in a master's collar for a time, to hope to be found pleasing because one wishes to be found pleasing, and not for fear of the whip, but for another reason, one perhaps best concealed from the master.

"We are soon to Harfax," he said.

"I do not even know the caste of my Master," I said.

"It is what I wish it to be," he said, "a Metal Worker, a Forester, a Poet, or Singer, a Cloth Worker, a Peasant, a Scribe, such things."

"I do not understand," I said.

"It is sometimes convenient to be of one caste, sometimes of another."

"It is a disguise," I said.

"Of course," he said. "In some ventures, in some pursuits, it is well to blend in, to attract less attention."

"But Master must have a caste," I said.

"My robes," he said, "were I to wear them, would be white and gold."

"They would indeed stand out," I said.

"As you might suppose," he said, "in Merchantry, particularly in high Merchantry, one may become aware of many things. One becomes familiar with routes and cities, with goods and markets, with customs and politics, with fears and rumors. One hears much, one sees much, one learns much. I have dealt with men from Torvaldsland, from Bazi, Schendi, and Turia. It became reasonably clear, in Merchant councils, met at the fairs, that scattered, unusual purchases were being made, and that caravans were occasionally being embarked for obscure destinations, which would seem outside familiar markets. Some feared the prerogatives of our caste were being eroded, others that sources of gain were being ignored, or concealed from the caste, others that mysterious doings were afoot which might warrant some investigation. I had learned of mysterious ships, and had come to know of the existence of a Kur presence on our world. Uneasy, I feared subversion, and alien intrigue. I ventured to Ar, which I thought likely to be the center of such things, if they existed. In Ar, rather inadvertently, in a tavern, from a man named Petranos, I learned of the Lady Bina and Grendel."

"Master frequents taverns?" I said.

"Perhaps I will sell you to one," he said.

"Please do not do so," I said.

"I thought it advisable to look into the matter," he said. "Meanwhile I had discerned a troublesomely attractive slave girl, who, absurdly enough, was a woman's slave. Clearly she should have been a man's slave."

"Yes, Master," I said, snuggling closer to him.

"Much of the rest," he said, "you know."

"Master has made contacts," I said. "Master has been as far as Port Kar. A slave conjectures that what was learned in the Voltai has been communicated to others and may be acted upon by many who are concerned with such things."

"That is my understanding," he said.

"The matters of kaissa sheets, of plans, of subversion, have been made known," I said.

"I, and others, have done what we can," he said. "I think that, by now, the councils of a hundred cities have at least been contacted. To be sure, I suspect that the faction-ridden councils of most will ignore the matter, regarding it as ludicrous, dismissing it as the unimportant, irrelevant product of farce, hoax, or hysteria, perhaps, at best, as unwarranted alarms broadcast by madmen."

"Master has done what he can," I said.

"As of now," he said. "Meanwhile, my affairs have been long neglected."

"Master will to Harfax?" I said.

"Yes," he said. "In the guise of a wainwright."

"That is one who builds wagons, or tends to them," I said.

"Yes," he said.

"Few then will suspect that he carries riches with him from the Voltai."

"I will buy a wagon, a tharlarion, and join a caravan," he said.

"Is Harfax beautiful?" I asked.

"I find it so," he said.

"I shall look forward to seeing it," I said.

"You will first see it," he said, "afoot, chained to the back of my wagon."

"I am to be chained to the back of a wagon?" I said.

"Do you object?" he said.

"No, Master," I said. I had no wish to be beaten.

"Harfax is beautiful?" I said.

"I think so," he said.

"I suppose there are slaves there," I said.

"Of course," he said. "Harfax is noted for the beauty of its slaves."

"I am jealous," I said.

"There will be many beautiful slaves," he said. "Many will be for sale."

"Keep me, Master," I begged.

"See that you are worth keeping," he said.

"I will do my best," I said.

"Before we leave," he said, "we will visit Grendel and the Lady Bina, and Astrinax, and Lykos, and perhaps some slaves."

"I would very much hope to do so," I said.

"A small feast, or two," he said, "would be in order."

"There is a private dining room in the restaurant of Menon," I said.

"Excellent," he said, "but I am thinking, too, of the garden behind the house."

"Master has pleasant memories of the garden?" I said.

"Yes," he said.

"A slave is pleased," I said.

My master had taken much pleasure from his slave in the garden. Her feelings were unimportant, but how could she forget the grass, the smell of flowers, the wind in the leaves overhead, the strength of his arms, her helplessness, his hands, his touch, his lips, his caresses, his tongue, forcing her to endure a hundred intimacies, some anticipated, some unexpected, some imperious, some beautifully subtle. Often must her mouth be covered lest her cries, those of an uncompromisingly ravished, exploited chattel, annoy the neighborhood.

"We might set up a table, and sit on mats," he said.

"But not in a certain place," I said.

"No," he smiled, "not in a certain place."

That place, I gathered, quiet and secluded, with its soft grass and flowers, might be a private place, a very private place, one reserved for a master's different feasting.

"The Lady Bina may wish to entertain again," I said.

"I suspect so," he said. "But eventually we must to Harfax."

"When?" I asked.

"In a few days," he said.

"I am naked and shackled," I said. "I am at Master's mercy."

"So?" he said.

"Is it not time for shackle check?" I asked.

"She-sleen," he smiled.

"Master?" I said.

He knelt beside me, and put his hand about my left ankle, and examined the enclosing shackle. My ankle was well grasped. I moved a little. I trembled, a little, from the closeness of my master. He then jerked the chain against the shackle ring, and then against the slave ring, set in the couch.

He then stood up, and I put out my hand to him.

"The slave is secured," he said.

"Master!" I said.

"What?" he asked.

I put my head down. "Nothing," I said.

He turned away.

"Master," I said, frightened.

"What is wrong?" he asked.

I looked up.

"What is it?" he asked.

"I begin to sense," I said, "what it might be, to be denied."

"Just now?" he asked.

"Earlier, too, sometimes," I said, "amongst the wagons, in camps, in the Voltai, in the Cave."

"More so, now?" he asked.

"Yes," I said.

"You had subsided," he said. "Now things are beginning, again."

"Did you do this to me?" I asked.

"Not I alone," he said. "You have felt such things before."

"Yes," I said, uncertainly.

"It is common," he said. "Sometimes it begins as early as the block, your bare feet in the sawdust, the men bidding on you, you knowing that you are being sold, sometimes from as early as your first enclosure in a slave cage, you kneeling there, looking out, grasping the bars, sometimes with your stripping and the locking of the collar on your neck. Even on your old world you must have felt such things."

"Restlessness, desire, curiosity, a helplessness one attempted to dismiss," I said.

"But here it is different," he said.

"Here I am a slave," I whispered.

"You are aware of your vulnerability, of what is expected of you, of how you may now be, and must now be, what you have always wanted to be," he said.

"I am afraid," I said.

"Surely you have felt the restlessness, the agitation, the discomfort, the uneasiness of a female slave before," he said.

"It makes me helpless," I said.

"I expect your slave fires began to burn as long ago as the house of Tenalion," he said.

"One cannot help such things," I said.

"Nor should you," he said.

"One must try to suppress them, to deny and crush them," I said.

"You are no longer on Earth," he said.

"One must try!" I wept.

"You are on Gor," he said. "It is not permitted."

"One must try!" I said.

"Why?" he asked.

"I must crush them!"

"You will not be able to do so."

"Surely you will be understanding with me, and kind to me," I said.

"No," he said, "and neither will any other master."

How pleased I was to hear this, that I would have no choice but to be, and choicelessly so, as I wanted to be, a vulnerable slave, at my master's mercy.

"I think what you may not fully understand," he said, "is, as I suggested earlier, that more is involved here than permissions, commands, and such. Once things have begun, as I think they have with you, they will take their course, as much as hunger or thirst."

"One cannot die of such deprivation," I said.

"Happily not," he said, "or, as I gather, the population of females on your former world would be considerably diminished."

I did not respond to this. I did know that many, if not most, women of my former world lived in a sexual desert. How astonished then were some for the discovery, on Gor, of true men, at whose feet, stripped and collared, they might gratefully kneel.

"They can, of course," he said, "be miserable, know agony, suffer recurrent, excruciating discomfort."

"Yes, Master," I said. Often enough I had heard of deprived slaves, being readied for sale, moaning, and scratching at the walls of their kennels. I had heard, often enough, too, of beautiful slaves crawling to the feet of hated masters, begging piteously for the relief of a caress.

"Sooner or later," he said, "slave fires begin to burn in the bellies of slaves. Then, over time, they become more frequent, and more intense. They will rage within you, and enwrap you, belly and body, in their enveloping, insistent flames."

"Men are cruel," I said.

"They are men," he said.

"Masters!" I said.

"And women?" he asked.

"Slaves!" I said, angrily.

"I doubt that you are, at present, aware of this," he said, "but the strongest bond on a female slave is not fiber, leather, cord, or iron. It is her slave needs."

"Men have made her so!" I said.

"Yes," he said.

"But I would not," I whispered, "have it otherwise."

"It will not be otherwise," he said.

"No wonder free women hate us so!" I said.

"They know women belong to men," he said, "and in the slave it is manifest, for there before them is a woman who belongs to men."

"Yes, Master," I said.

"Too," he said, "they are furious that the slave's beauty is public, as they secretly wish was theirs, and that men, when they want pleasure, rather than station, opportunity, advancement, position, prestige, and such, seek out not them, but the slave. They resent it, too, that the slave's sexual needs are deep, profound, and blatant, and that she satisfies them. Too, they suspect the slave's erotic ecstasies, afflicting her entire mind and body, the glow imbuing her entire yielded, subdued existence, the profundity of the submitted female's succession of uncontrollable orgasms, the raptures of a begging, thrashing chattel's responses, the daily joy, in large things and small, she knows in a master's collar."

"Master," I whispered.

"Yes?" he said.

"Take me," I begged.

"Your slave fires have begun to burn, have they not?" he asked.

"Yes!" I said.

"You have begun to sense what might be done with you, what you might become?" he said.

"Yes!" I said.

"Perhaps I should deny you," he said.

"Please do not deny me, Master," I said. "Be merciful, Master!"

"Do you, a former woman of Earth," he said, "beg for sex?"

"Yes, Master," I said. "I beg for sex. I beg for sex!"
"As a slave begs for sex?" he asked.
"Yes, Master," I said. "I beg for sex. I beg for sex, as a slave begs for sex!"
"Very well," he said.
"Master, Master!" I sobbed, joyfully, gratefully.

Chapter Fifty-Three

Harfax is indeed beautiful.

This writing, as it should be, and, as I suppose is clear, is addressed primarily to Goreans.

I have written it in my native language, surely unknown to most of you, which is called "English." My master, Desmond of Harfax, of the house of Desmond in Harfax, in the high Merchantry of Harfax, has arranged, as I understand it, to have it translated into Gorean. Thus, it is intended, at least in part, to come to the attention of at least some Gorean speakers. At least several copies will be transcribed and distributed. It is my conjecture that it is as unlikely to be taken any more seriously by them than, as I gather, the numerous warnings issued privately to various city councils on known Gor. Most, as I understand it, were dismissed as charlatanry. But perhaps some of those who so dismissed them had already been contacted by agents of Kurii. The wagons of Pausanias left the Voltai long before Lord Grendel and his party could reach civilization.

I must apologize to Masters and Mistresses, free Goreans, who might read this narrative. In some respects I have doubtless told what you already know. My excuse, I suppose, is my background, which is quite other than yours. Accordingly, I have remarked often, I fear, on matters familiar to you, but which I found striking, or of interest. But, too, I have been told, it might be read, in its original language, by some of my former world, as well. In a sense then, it is written for two worlds. The primary motivation of the writing, I suppose, is to carry forward, particularly for Goreans, the project of apprising citizenries of fearsome, largely unrecognized dangers. To be sure, as I understand it, my former world, Earth, despite its poisons and pollutions, its depleted resources and ecological injuries, its filths and crowdings, is not outside the purview of Kur attention. Apparently, both Earth and Gor, at least for the time, owe their precarious security to the informed self-interest of Priest-Kings, who prefer for Kurii, on the whole at least, to be restricted to distant, relatively innocuous habitats, concealed amongst the remote "river of stones." Whereas Kurii are primarily interested in Gor, as a fresh, unspoiled world, the resources of Earth, and its relative proximity to the orbit of Gor, would make it a dangerous staging area for attacks on Gor. A great deal in this writing, of course, is very personal. My master, Desmond of Harfax, has been very indulgent in this regard. He has recognized that this writing might be of possible service not only for its monitory aspects, political and military, particularly for Gor, but for its value to a slave, permitting her to tell her story. It has done her a great deal of good to have been "permitted to speak" in such a way. How much happier we are when we are permitted to express ourselves! Sometimes my master, when it pleases him, loosens the disrobing loop on my tunic, allowing it to fall to my ankles, ties my hands behind my back, and kneels me before him, while he reclines in a curule chair, allowing me to speak. Whereas I have a general permission to speak, I love such times, for it reminds me that I am a slave before her master, and that I require permission to speak. Indeed, it was at such a time that I first asked for permission to write my story. To my delight I learned that he had already contemplated commanding me to such a writing, for three reasons, a monitory reason, contributing to informing Goreans, and others, of danger; a personal reason for me, that I might be able to profit from the ventilative salubrity of self-expression, of narration, reflection, contemplation, and confession; and, lastly, that he might know more of his slave, her innermost feelings, thoughts, and emotions. Nothing in a slave may be hidden from the master. This is not unusual, as men are often closely concerned with their possessions. Many masters, for example, are very well aware of their slave's body, every part of it, every mark, every fault and blemish. I do not know, but I suspect very few female free companions are studied, and examined, with the same interest and thoroughness. Indeed, perhaps it would be improper. And just as, of course, a master might well know the lovely, vulnerable map of his slave's body, he is, too, interested in the map of her history, her background, her feelings, her thoughts, and such. I have been told that even a master with a large pleasure garden, well stocked with kajirae, may force the poor slave to speak at length of herself, either before or after she is put to use. To be sure, there are also masters, as I understand it, to whom the slave is no more than a frightened, impersonal object, of less concern than a pet sleen or kaiila. Indeed, I fear many slaves start out that way. They need not, one hopes, end up that way.

I think I have made clear, however, that many masters are reluctant to admit that they might care for a slave. Who, for example, would be inclined to admit that he might care for a mere slave?

They are nothing. Buy them in any girl market. Buy them and sell them. They are cheap.

It is time to close this story.

Please forgive me, Masters and Mistresses, for my weaknesses, my failures, my foolishness, my many faults.

You expect them, of course, in a slave.

Dear Masters, remain true to the mastery.

Dear Mistresses, remember that we are not so different from you, and that you, too, one day, might be collared.

I wish you all well.

Allison, if her Master pleases.

Appendix

The text, as I have it, contains no detailed exposition of the nature of the "deck" which seems to be in question here. To those readers accustomed to the uniformities and standardizations of a modern industrial and technological society, where diversity has come to mean thinking alike and agreeing on everything, the genuine liberties and remarkable differences of a plurality of, say, municipal cultures is likely to be troubling. If one expects everything to be the same, it is easy to object when something is found not to be the same. On the other hand, if one does not expect everything to be the same, one is less likely to be troubled. To take a simple example, consider the Gorean alphabet, or alphabets. From the above text it would seem that one Gorean alphabet might contain, say, twenty-eight letters, and another perhaps more or less. That the modern English alphabet contains twenty-six letters is obviously arbitrary, and requires that several different sounds, in some cases, be represented by the same letter, say, 'a'. One might have a different letter for these sounds. An alphabet presumably represents a pragmatic compromise between enough letters to be useful, and few enough to be manageable. In one Earth language, English, its entire vocabulary is specifiable in terms of some fifty phonemes, or sounds, out of a theoretically infinite number of sounds which a human being might make. Here, too, we see something of a pragmatic compromise between elegance and utility. Another example of Gorean difference, which some may find troubling, is that in some versions of kaissa the piece called the Home Stone is permitted to capture, and in other versions it lacks this capacity. Goreans do not object to this. They merely wish to know which version will be played. Returning to the question of cards, I will supply an account, however inadequate, of the nature of a Gorean "deck." It is based on the only account I have been able to find in what one might refer to as the Gorean Miscellany," a plethora of materials often accompanying, but independent of, various narrative manuscripts. Almost all of the "Miscellany" has accompanied the Cabot manuscripts, and this material, much of it unorganized, and sometimes tantalizingly incomplete, seems to have little in common other than the fact that Mr. Cabot may have found it of interest.

In any event, at least one Gorean deck of cards, presumably one commonly found, as it appears in the "Miscellany," contains sixty cards, divided into five suits. It will be helpful, I think, if we devote some attention to the number "60," as it is a most interesting number. It is the smallest number which contains the largest number of factors. It contains twelve factors, which is germane to the twelve cards in each of the five suits. The twelve factors of 60 are, 60, 30, 20, 15, 12, 10, 6, 5, 4, 3, 2, and 1. The number 60 is sometimes referred to as "The Great Number," "The Ubar's Number," "The Sacred Number," "The Priest-Kings' Number," and so on. The five suits are named for the five high castes of Gor, namely, the Initiates, whose color is white; the Builders, whose color is yellow; the Scribes, whose color is blue; the Physicians, whose color is green; and the Warriors, whose color is red. Each of these suits consists of twelve cards, respectively the Tarn, the Larl, the Sleen, the Panther, the Tarsk, the Tharlarion, the Urt, the Verr, the Vulo, the Jard, the Vart, and the Ost. The Initiate's Tarn would be white, the Builder's Tarn yellow, and so on. The values follow the factors of 60. A Tarn counts 60, the Larl 30, the Sleen 20, and so on, until one reaches the Ost which has a value of 1. Thus, a Larl at 30 would take precedence over a Sleen at 20, but two Sleen, giving us 40, would take precedence over a Larl, which is valued at 30. There is nothing in the Miscellany, to the best of my knowledge, which, at least to date, gives us the rules for any particular game. One supposes, naturally, as with most decks of cards, any given deck might sustain an indefinite number of games.

—J. N.

CPSIA information can be obtained at www.ICGtesting.com
Printed in the USA
LVOW042020090113

315060LV00001B/37/P